THE WILL TO REMEMBER

ROGER D. EVANS

ISBN: 979-8-218-79774-4 *(Paperback)*
     979-8-218-81216-4 *(eBook)*

Printed in the United States of America
Edition 1.3 Revised June 2026

PREFACE

May this story serve as a testament to the enduring human spirit and a solemn reminder to never forget the atrocities of the Holocaust. This work is dedicated to those whose lives were tragically cut short. May their memory be a perpetual light, reminding us of the dangers of hatred and the importance of remembrance for the six million Jews and countless others whose lives were stolen. May their memory continue to inspire us to build a future free from prejudice and violence.

Contents

PART I

CHAPTER ONE

"For Your sake we are being put to death all day long;
We were considered as sheep to be slaughtered.[1]"

~Romans 8:36

Jozefow, Poland
June 17ᵗʰ, 1932, 6:44 a.m.

A breath of cool air, still holding the scent of last night's rain, drifted through the half-opened bedroom window and brushed across eight-year-old Icek's face. The sky outside was just beginning to blush with the promise of sunrise. He'd only meant to glance at the brightening June horizon, but a sharp, piercing scream shattered the pre-dawn quiet. It was his mother, her belly swollen after nine months of pregnancy.

"I can't stand it!" Her voice cracked, raw with a terror that chilled Icek to the bone. "No, no, no, this can't be happening!"

Icek froze—every muscle tensed. His father shot past him, a blur of legs disappearing down the narrow hallway. Icek had never seen his father move so fast. He clamped a hand over his mouth, stifling a whimper, and scrambled for yesterday's clothes, pulling on his trousers as he stumbled down the hall, his heart hammering against his ribs. He didn't wait for permission, pushing open the door to his parents' bedroom and rushing to his mother's bedside.

He heard his father's low, urgent voice. "Henna, darling, please take my hand. Let me help you through this."

Icek bit his lip, tears stinging his eyes. He fixed his gaze on his mother's face, contorted in pain. *Is this what it's like when a baby comes?* He tried to shrink back, to become invisible so as not to interfere with his father's frantic efforts. His tiny fists clenched, a silent, desperate prayer rising within him—a plea for something, anything, to ease her suffering. He couldn't bear to watch, yet he couldn't tear his eyes away.

His mother gasped, air whistling between clenched teeth. "Abram, it's horrid," she panted, the words ragged. "Like a dagger in my side." Her hands, white-knuckled, suddenly splayed open, fingers fluttering like a bird about to take flight. "I'm so worried. It wasn't like this when Icek came into the world. Something's wrong. Something's terribly wrong!"

His father crouched beside her, his large hand gently covering her clenched fists. "Don't think like that, dear."

He stood and motioned Ryfka to come by his side. She approached with concern on her face, and in a whispered tone, he said, "I didn't tell you earlier because I thought it would upset you. Last night, when going to fetch the midwife, Serena's husband revealed she was dealing with the pregnancy of her niece in Warsaw. Serena is not expected to return for two more days. Ryfka, we have no other midwives for miles." Abram asked, "Do you know anyone in town who could help Henna… perhaps a person who knows more than you about delivering babies?"

Ryfka tilted her head toward the floor and said, "Oh my. Your news is dire. If this were a routine delivery without the pain and the bleeding, there might be someone in town who may be able to aid." Suddenly, Icek's father turned, walking about the room, his face displaying a blank stare as he turned back again and peered into Ryfka's eyes.

Icek watched, mesmerized, as suddenly his father threw his head back, a raw, animal howl erupting from his throat, directed at the darkened ceiling. "Why, dear Lord, are you putting my Henna through this nightmare? Why, God?"

Icek wrapped his arms tightly around himself, rocking back and forth as his world tilted on its axis, a small, silent vessel of grief. His body swayed in a rhythmic counterpoint to his parents' desperate prayers, each movement accompanied by a silent tear tracking down his cheeks.

"I'm here, darling," his father said, visibly calming himself, his voice thick with unshed tears. "We'll get through this. It will be alright."

He stroked her hand, a feather-light touch. Each time a moan escaped her lips, a fresh wave of pain etched itself deeper into his father's brow.

Father and son locked eyes, a shared look of helplessness passing between them. His father's frown, a landscape of worry, couldn't meet Icek's gaze, shielding him from the full force of his despair. They listened, their breaths held captive, to Henna's ragged breathing—a rasping intake, a long, shuddering exhale. Abram's fingers pressed against her wrist, a silent measure of her life force. Icek watched, his mind cataloging this image, branding it into a hidden corner of his memory, a place he would never willingly revisit. They waited, braced for the next onslaught.

Forty minutes passed—an eternity measured in shallow breaths. Henna's breathing finally eased, slowing to a fragile rhythm, then her body went limp, sinking into the mattress as if surrendering to an uneasy slumber.

"Father," Icek whispered, his voice choked with emotion, "were you with Mother all night?"

"Gramma Ryfka and I took turns. Thank God she lives with us! She has a wisdom about these things, a way of comforting Henna that I don't possess."

"Thank God," Icek echoed, reaching out to pat his mother's forearm, a small gesture of comfort.

"The pain seemed to lessen just before I relieved Ryfka. She fell asleep soon after I settled into the chair." He glanced at the worn chair at the foot of the bed as if to confirm its existence. "I dozed off, my body draped across the foot of the bed. A couple of hours later, she woke up screaming. I felt useless. Seeing your mother in such agony— it's uncharted territory for me. Nothing like this has happened in our ten years."

Icek pictured the night as a storm: his mother's anguished cries, the metallic clang of cookware as Ryfka moved between the kitchen and the bedside, and now, this unsettling quiet. It had been a rough night, his mother fighting unseen demons.

His father stood, stretching his stiff limbs, his head rolling from side to side as if trying to work out the kinks of his awkward sleeping position. "I know. You do everything I ask and more. You're a rock, Icek." He sighed, his gaze earnest. "I haven't told you enough, son.

You're a Godsend to this family. A little brother or sister would be blessed, indeed."

Icek's chest swelled with a fragile pride. He followed his father as he went to the window and pushed it open wider. A rush of cool, damp, earth-scented air filled the room. The sun had climbed higher, shafts of bright light piercing through the cotton-ball clouds, casting a warm glow across the horizon. The diffused light illuminated his mother's reddish-brown hair, bathing her face in a soft radiance, her pale complexion reminding Icek of a delicate porcelain doll.

His father returned to the bedside, his eyes fixed on his mother's chest, watching the slow rise and fall. The pause between breaths seemed to stretch, an unnerving silence. He gently placed his hand in hers, and the contrast struck Icek with a sudden force. His father's hands, stained with grease and calloused, the nails bent and chipped from years of handling heavy tools at the mill, were a stark contrast to her delicate, smooth, almost silken skin.

Icek held his breath, biting his lip, as his father squeezed his mother's hand. His rough knuckles whitened with the pressure, but her hand remained limp, unresponsive. She remained in a deep, unsettling sleep, while the lines beneath his father's eyes were darker, his usually vibrant features drawn and hollow.

His father sighed deeply, turning to face Icek. "Son," he said, his gaze locking with Icek's, "Your mother, she's losing a little blood. Not much, they say it is common. Women, they call it 'spotting.' A little here, a little there. It started a few days ago, and it hasn't changed. We need a doctor, but there are none nearby. I've searched for the midwife. I just found out a couple of hours ago from the rabbi that the midwife, Serena, the same one who delivered you, is tending to a pregnant niece in Warsaw. Rabbi had talked to a member of the synagogue earlier today who knew her whereabouts. Until Serena gets back in town, we must rely on anyone experienced with childbirth that the rabbi may find, but it the meantime, it will be you, me, and Ryfka. Don't worry, son, Ryfka has been around plenty of deliveries in her time. The rabbi promised me he would bring Serena here the minute she arrives back in Jozefow."

"Father, what is a midwife?"

"Of course. You wouldn't know." He let out a deep sigh and lowered himself into the chair beside the bed. "A midwife is a woman who helps mothers bring babies into the world. Most midwives have seen more births than many doctors. We only have one in town, and, well, babies come when they're ready, midwife or not."

Icek's brow furrowed. "But what if the midwife doesn't come in time? Does Mother have to do it alone?"

His father pressed his hands together, a silent prayer, lifting his eyes heavenward. Icek wondered if it was the same prayer he had whispered through the night.

"Yes." He nodded. "Mother needs a midwife. In the meantime, we'll do everything we can do until she shows up." He moved to the window again, his hands clasped as he stared out at the awakening world. "We're at the mercy of nature, son," he whispered. "For other mothers, their bodies tell them it's time. That's how it works. A woman can only guess when the time will come."

"Father," Icek said, a puzzled expression on his face, "what is 'going into labor'?"

His father turned, his tired eyes studying Icek, before he nodded and answered, "It's when a mother, well, it's when the baby decides it's time. Like the baby is saying, 'I'm coming!' And the mother—she can't stop it. The baby is on its way. And… it's usually quite loud."

"Father, the midwife will make it in time, right?"

Abram's gaze shifted, avoiding Icek's direct gaze. A grimace flickered across his face. "Yes, son. The rabbi will see to it." He added, almost to himself, "And Ryfka needs her rest. She was up most of the night, helping me. She deserves to sleep."

Tears welled in Icek's eyes, a reflection of his mounting fear. His father gestured for him to follow. "Come, Icek. We both need a break. And I want to show you something."

Abram led him into the front room of their small, humble home, where he now paced restlessly. "Icek, last night, I looked at this room through your mother's eyes. I saw the furniture, the little rug, the framed picture of your mother and me on our wedding day, on the dresser."

He picked up the sepia-toned photograph, his fingers tracing the edges lovingly. "Your mother wore Ryfka's wedding dress. I borrowed a suit. We couldn't afford much, but our love, it wouldn't wait."

Icek took the picture, studying his mother's image—the thick, shoulder-length hair, the radiant smile, the mischievous glint in her eyes.

"Looking at this last night, it reminded me how lucky I am," his father said, a sad smile playing on his lips. "Look at me, son. A hooked nose, ears like a chimpanzee, skinny like a scarecrow, and cheekbones that almost touch my nose. I wear a beard and this thick mustache to hide most of the ugly."

Despite his worry, Icek snorted, then giggled.

"I'm not what most women would call handsome," he continued. "Yet, somehow, I won your beautiful mother."

"God made you for Mother," Icek said, his voice firm. "And Mother for you. He brought you together."

Abram's eyes twinkled. "That's a fine answer. Henna didn't fall in love with my looks."

"Father, you are handsome!"

"Thank you, Icek, but when I'm with your mother, I don't feel it."

Icek gazed at the photograph, wishing he could conjure that smile on his mother's face again. "Mother showed me this picture—I never knew the story." He looked around the room. "We were poor then, weren't we, Father?"

His father gestured around the room. "Every item you see, we bought used—secondhand shops or private sellers. Your mother had a gift for finding bargains, mostly from the Catholic families in Jozefow. Each piece has a story, a memory of how it came to us, how it fits your mother's taste." He smiled, a wistful expression softening his features. "I had little say. 'Well, Abram, what do you think?' she'd ask. 'Should we buy this?' And I always said yes. Every object is connected to your mother." He paused, picking up his coat, a dark, worn, military garment with a missing button. "Look, son, look here, your mother, her love, made a piece of trash my favorite coat.

"Yes, we were poor, Icek, but compared to those days, we are wealthy, indeed."

Without warning, his father sank into the plush armchair, the dam finally breaking as tears streamed down his face. The only sound in the room was the steady tick-tock of the clock.

Icek watched, frozen, unsure how to respond to his father's uncharacteristic display of grief.

"Watching the one you love suffer is hard," his father admitted, his voice thick with emotion. "I hope you never have to see someone you love in such pain."

Jozefow
June 18ᵗʰ, 1932, 8:46 a.m.

Icek shadowed his father's every move, watching as he grabbed a small cloth, dampened it from the water pitcher on the chest of drawers, wrung out the excess, and gently cleansed his mother's face.

The coolness caused her eyelids to flutter open. "So, we haven't brought our little one into the world yet," she said, her voice weak and strained.

"Hello, darling," his father said, dabbing at the droplets of water on her forehead. "How do you feel?"

"Weak. Thirsty. Can I have some water?" She angled her face toward him.

He turned to Icek. "Icek will get it. Water will be fine."

Eager to help, Icek jumped up and hurried to the kitchen. He grabbed the metal pitcher, and the back screen door slammed shut with a muffled smack as he headed outside to the well, the dampness from the overnight rain seeping through the worn soles of his shoes. Beads of water clung to everything, and he tilted his head as a lone robin's song pierced the morning quiet.

He reached the well, the pump handle screeching with each laborious stroke. Frigid water gushed from the spout, splashing his legs and soaking his trousers to his shins. Even in June, the deep Polish frostline kept the water icy cold.

He hurried back, the overflowing pitcher sloshing, the cold water stinging his skin. He hoped the chill would offer his mother some slight relief.

"Here, Father," he said, handing him the pitcher.

His father filled a glass from the bedside table and propped up Henna's head, helping her take small, careful sips. "Tiny sips, darling," he murmured.

"Thank you, dear Icek," she said, her voice a whisper. "I hate that you have to see me like this."

"It's alright, Mother. Having a baby is hard work," Icek replied, repeating what he'd learned.

His mother drank. "This feels so good. Why am I not better?"

"Close your eyes and rest," Abram said, his voice soothing. "You need to conserve your strength."

"Alright, doctor. I'll be a good patient."

Henna closed her eyes as Icek, and his father quietly left the room.

Out of earshot, his father muttered, "She's so pale."

Fear creeping into his voice, Icek asked, "Father, what does pale mean?"

"Icek. She lost blood last night. Pale—it means the color is gone from her face. This is a difficult pregnancy."

"But how…" Icek asked.

"All I know," his father interrupted, his voice rising slightly, "is that we didn't have any of this with you. She's eight years older, yes, but why is this happening?" Will a midwife or a doctor even be able to help? He finally turned to face Icek, his gaze searching. She's so weak. Where are the rabbi and Serena? "We need help, and quickly."

CHAPTER TWO

Jozefow, Poland
June 19th, 1932, 8:09 a.m.

When Icek awoke, stiff from sitting in the chair beside his mother's bed, he saw that Grandma Ryfka resembled a curled-up cat on the floor, nestled in a mound of quilts and feather-stuffed pillows. A duet of snores, one deep and rumbling, the other a whistling sigh, filled the room. His mother lay on her side, a sliver of her pale cheek visible above the blankets.

He crept closer, peering at her. Were her eyelids fluttering? Was the tense line of her mouth relaxed, or was that just wishful thinking? The only other sound was a cheerful bird song. Two common chaffinches perched on a branch outside the window, their tiny bodies vibrating with song. As they chirped, the wind ruffled their feathers, making the branch bob. Icek remembered his father pointing out the difference—the male with his weathered grey cap, the female a symphony of soft browns. This pair, clearly courting, filled the air with their melody.

"The locals call a group of chaffinches a 'charm,'" his father had said, his eyes crinkling at the corners. "Because their song is so pleasing." Now, the birds' music soothed Icek, easing the frantic worry about his mother.

He tiptoed back to the bedroom and stared, then slid into the chair, the wood scraping harshly against the floor. His mother's eyes fluttered open, and a faint smile touched her lips as she focused on him.

"Do I look as weak as I feel?" she whispered.

He hesitated, searching for the right words. "No, Mother," he said, then quickly looked away, unable to meet her gaze. He hated lying. "You look fine."

She sighed, a breath that seemed to catch in her throat.

"Can I get you anything?" he asked, desperate to change the subject. "Shall I read to you?"

He had devoured every book in the house, his reading skills far beyond his eight years. He knew the Hebrew alphabet and had committed the prayers to memory. Yiddish was fast becoming a second tongue, a bridge between his parents' world and his own.

"Later, maybe. Your father says I need to rest. Just sit with me. Until I sleep."

A strange sense of pride swelled in Icek's chest. To be with his mother after days of hushed whispers and anxious glances felt like a privilege. But the peace shattered when a sharp cry, a gasp of pain, tore from his mother's throat.

Ryfka jolted awake, her voice sharp with alarm. "Go to the kitchen, child," she ordered firmly. "Seeing you upset will only add to her distress."

He retreated, his ears straining to filter out the sounds from the bedroom. Each whimper sent a fresh wave of fear through him. It felt like an eternity before Gramma Ryfka finally appeared, her movements slow and deliberate. Her dress was rumpled, and her usually neat grey hair was a tangled mess pulled back with a faded scarf. Her face was drawn, etched with exhaustion. Icek knew that look. He'd seen the fleeting sadness that would cloud her eyes when she thought no one was watching, the way her shoulders would slump when she was alone.

He'd been too young to understand until the night his father had told him about Gramma's husband, Johanne Andrej Mikolaj, lost in 1910. Twenty-two years, and still, a stray scent or a familiar phrase could send her spiraling back. Yet she never failed to remind them how grateful she was to be part of their family, a lifeline in her sea of grief.

Icek cleared his throat, his gaze fixed on the floor. "Gramma," he began, his voice barely a whisper, "can I ask you something?"

Ryfka's eyes, usually bright with a fierce love, were dull. "I know what you're going to ask," she said, her voice heavy. "And the answer is—only God knows what will happen. To any of us."

He looked up, tears welling. "But Mother will be alright, won't she?"

Ryfka wiped her face with her apron, avoiding his gaze. "She's resting now. Thank God. But we must be prepared. The pain will likely return."

He straightened slightly, a flicker of determination in his eyes. "I'll check on Mother. Every five minutes."

She bent down, her wrinkled cheek brushing against his. "You're hungry, child," she said, her voice softening.

Icek watched her move about the kitchen. Sunlight streamed through the two windows, illuminating the dust motes dancing in the air. The room smelled of woodsmoke and something indefinably comforting—Gramma's presence. He watched her build a fire in the cast-iron stove, her movements practiced and precise. Crumpled newspaper, a shower of kindling, the scratch of a match, and the dry wood crackled and popped, sending fragrant smoke up the chimney. "Gramma," Icek said, his stomach rumbling, "why does the smell of the stove always make me hungrier?"

She smiled, a network of lines crinkling around her eyes. "Simple, Icek. You smell the smoke, and you know food is coming." He nodded, looking out the window at the outbuilding where his father had gone.

"You've always been here," he murmured.

Gramma Ryfka's eyes held him. "God brought you into this world, Icek. You've brought so much joy—and this new baby will bring more." She stepped closer, hugging him tightly.

He breathed in her scent, a mixture of lavender and woodsmoke.

"Henna, she's a good mother. Look at you," Gramma said, her voice thick with emotion. "And now you'll be a good big brother. A good son."

He lifted his chin, a small, proud smile on his lips. "Gramma, how do I learn to be a good big brother?"

Her smile deepened. "It will come naturally. Be the good son you are, and the rest will follow. But if you need a lesson, help your mother with the baby. The more you help, the better it will be."

He grinned. "I hope it's a boy."

Gramma Ryfka turned back to her preparations. "I thought you might want a brother."

He watched her, every action a testament to her strength. "Gramma," he said, "you said God sent you to us. But who told God we needed you?"

She chuckled, a low, rumbling sound. "No one had to tell Him, Icek. He answered my prayers."

Icek's brow furrowed. "Your prayers?"

Her smile widened. "I pray for you all. Every day."

He stared at her, his eyes wide with wonder. "God must like you for Him to answer them. Did He talk to you? Can I learn to talk to God, Gramma?"

"God loves us all, Icek. He listens. You can talk to Him anytime. And when He answers, it won't be a voice. You'll feel it. Inside."

Icek frowned, trying to grasp the concept. "So, I talk, but He doesn't talk back. I can't see Him, but I'll feel it?" He mulled on that for a minute, then conceded, "Maybe I'll understand when I'm older?"

Ryfka's smile was a mixture of amusement and deep faith. "That, Icek," she said softly, "is what we call faith. It isn't easy. But you'll understand. One day."

Before Icek could ponder this further, Gramma Ryfka disappeared, returning moments later with a handful of eggs and a bucket of water. He watched her, his stomach anticipating his favorite breakfast—eggs fried sunny-side up. She was standing in the doorway when a scream, sharp and terrifying, ripped through the house.

From the kitchen, Icek heard his mother's strained voice, followed by Ryfka's urgent tones. He couldn't make out the words, but the panic in them was clear. Then, another sound—his own cry of alarm as he saw a wagon rattling up the lane. It was the rabbi, and sitting next to him was an older woman, her thin frame hunched against the jolting ride. It had to be the midwife.

His father rushed out of the outbuilding to greet them. Icek followed, his bare feet padding on the dew-kissed grass, reaching the wagon just as his father spoke.

"Good morning!" he said. "Praise God you made it."

"It's all about having faith," the rabbi said with a deep grin, glancing up to the heavens. "God delivers." He stepped down from the wagon and took the midwife's hand. "Serena, you must remember Abram. You delivered his son, Icek, in this very house about eight years ago, if my math is correct."

Minutes later, they were all in the bedroom, the rabbi having left, and Ryfka sent Icek back to the kitchen. This was no place for the boy. The midwife, Serena, her face a mask of professional concern, stood beside Abram. She seemed frail next to his towering frame while Abram made the introductions, his voice strained. Serena's smile, revealing gaps where teeth should have been, was polite but distant. Eight years had aged her; her hair was now a brittle gray, and the lines on her face were deeper. Ryfka and Serena exchanged strained pleasantries while Abram moved to Henna's side.

"Darling," he said, his voice soft, "you remember Serena. She's here to help."

Ryfka prayed the midwife had answers.

"Hello, Serena," Henna whispered. "Do you remember Icek?"

"The house, the delivery, yes," Serena said, her voice surprisingly warm. "But Icek has grown so." Her worn clothes and battered leather bag spoke of countless journeys and births, and Ryfka watched as she took a stethoscope from the bag, its metal shining against Henna's skin. Her expression was unreadable as she asked questions, her voice calm and methodical. She felt Henna's forehead, searching for a fever. "How do you feel now?" Serena asked.

"Closer," Henna gasped, her face contorted. "Worse than with Icek."

Ryfka, glancing toward the kitchen to ensure Icek was out of earshot, cleared her throat. "And the bleeding," she said quietly. "Much more than with Icek."

Serena nodded, her gaze steady. "Let's see." As Serena lifted the blankets, Ryfka saw a flicker of something in her eyes, a momentary hesitation that sent a jolt of fear through her. *Is it defeat?* she wondered. *Is this what losing looks like?*

The midwife's face tightened as she examined Henna, pressing and prodding her swollen abdomen, listening with her stethoscope. Then

Serena pulled the blanket back down, her hands trembling slightly. She struggled to fill a basin with water before finally washing her hands. She turned away, her back stiff.

"Say something," Abram pleaded, his voice raw. Ryfka's heart clenched at the sight of the midwife's slumped shoulders.

She turned, her face a mixture of puzzlement and concern. "It may surprise you," she said slowly. "Not one, but two. Twins."

"Twins!" Henna gasped, her eyes wide with disbelief. "Are you sure?"

Serena stood firm, her hands on her hips. "I have years and hundreds of births behind me. Child, you have two babies. I am sure."

Henna stared at her. "My sister, Asia, is my identical twin— married to a Polish concert pianist in America. I didn't think twins could have twin offspring."

Serena shrugged. "The chances, I don't know. But two babies, yes." She turned toward the door, beckoning Ryfka and Abram to follow her. "Let's have a private talk."

"We'll be back," Ryfka said to Henna, her voice trembling. Henna's eyes, huge and frightened, searched for answers.

Abram leaned down, kissing her forehead. "Two gifts," he murmured, loud enough for Ryfka to hear.

"Maybe a girl," Henna whispered, a faint, hopeful smile touching her lips. "The girl you wanted."

"Abram?" Ryfka's voice was sharp with urgency as she led him into the kitchen. "Help me here."

Abram gently touched Henna's face. "Back soon, darling. Relax. Not long now."

CHAPTER THREE

Jozefow, Poland
June 19th, 1932, 6:13 p.m.

Abram burst into the kitchen, his brow a knot of worry. He yanked out a chair, its legs scraping against the floor, and sat beside Ryfka. "What? What has happened?"

Icek stood at Ryfka's side, tears pooling, his arm laying protectively around her shoulder as she slumped at the kitchen table, her face buried in her hands. Sobs wracked her body as a storm of grief unleashed.

Icek swiped at his wet cheeks. "I don't know, Father. Ms. Serena whispered something to Gramma, and then…" He gestured helplessly at his grandmother's shaking form.

Abram was out of the room in an instant, his long strides eating up the distance to Serena. He seized her arm and hauled her down the hall, away from the sounds of Ryfka's despair.

"Serena," he said, his voice low and urgent, "I know you've seen a lifetime of this. But are you certain? Should I ride for the doctor?"

Serena struggled to meet his gaze. Her words tumbled out, hesitant and fractured. "Abram, do you remember Sonja Adamowicz?"

"Sonja, yes." Abram's heart tightened. "Last winter, the bleeding, and she nearly died." He trailed off, remembering the terror of that night. "You saved her."

"She was the only one, Abram. Out of all the difficult births, Sonja was the only one who lived." Serena's voice was barely a whisper. "It was a miracle, Abram. We still don't know how her bleeding stopped."

She stood in the shadows, her hands twisting in front of her. She looked everywhere but at Abram. "I wish there were something else I could tell you." Her voice was thick, her throat constricted. The words seemed to claw their way out. She forced herself to meet his eyes, her eyebrows pinched together in a mask of pain. "Abram, your wife is in a bad way. First, she has been suffering what we call pre-labor—the onset of contractions before the babies are full term. My hands are tied, as

"

there are no treatments for pre-labor other than keeping the patient as comfortable as possible. Once she goes beyond the pre-labor, we will be at the first stage where the cervix dilates. She could be in this stage for hours and hours. I've seen this before, but the bleeding is the worst sign. Her placenta has slipped. Therefore, it is dangerously out of position. That's what's causing the blood."

Abram stared up at the ceiling, a silent plea escaping his lips. Then, his head dropped, his shoulders slumping. "Oh God, no," he whispered, the words choked with despair. "What have we done against you, dear God, to deserve these problems?" His eyes snapped to her again. "Are the babies at risk? How can you know all this just from looking at her?"

Serena moved away, her gaze fixed on her worn boots.

Her voice was thin, cracking under the weight of what she had to say. "Experience, Abram. Hundreds of births. Thirty-five years of experience. Plus, I've worked with doctors and learned from them. I've seen this."

Abram reached for her, his hands gripping her shoulders. He looked into her eyes, a desperate plea in his own. "I'm sorry, Serena, for doubting you." His voice was rough with shame. "Please. Tell me, what does it mean?"

She flinched from his gaze, her voice flat, devoid of hope. "The babies are not the immediate problem. It's Henna. Each child has its own placenta. With the placenta where it is, when the child comes, the placenta is subjected to pressure. It could tear, Abram. A river of blood. And we won't be able to stop it."

Abram's face went blank, his eyes staring vacantly into the middle distance. He looked lost, like a child caught in a transgression he didn't understand. He tightened his grip on Serena's shoulders, his gaze searching her face. He thought, *Is the answer to an impossible question hidden in there?* His voice was soft at first, then exploded. "Are you saying that my Henna might die giving birth?"

Serena stepped back, out of his reach. She met his gaze, her own filled with a sorrow that mirrored his. "Yes, Abram," she whispered. "That's what I'm saying. Blood loss causes most deaths during childbirth. If we could get her to a hospital, maybe we could save her, but it's three hours. We don't have time. Soon, she will be out of pre-labor and into actual labor. Since she is not a first-time mother, she shouldn't suffer through the average of twelve to thirteen hours of labor—her time will be much less, perhaps taking two to three hours."

Abram grabbed her shoulders again, his voice rising to a shout that startled her. "What am I supposed to do? Just stand here and watch my wife, my darling wife, slip away? There has to be something!" Tears streamed down his face now, wetting the thicket of his beard. "The doctor! Can't a doctor help?"

"Abram," Serena said, her voice firm despite the tremor in her hands, "Henna doesn't need a doctor. She needs a miracle."

Abram stood there, frozen, his arms now crossed tightly over his chest. Then he reached up to stroke his mustache as his mind raced, the trembling of his hand betraying the turmoil within. He covered his eyes with his hand, his muscles drawn tight. Shrugging and fighting a slight, defeated movement, he pressed his fist to his lips, his eyes squeezed shut, feeling hopelessly lost.

Serena reached out, embracing him, her arms wrapping around his shaking frame. "Abram, you'll get through this. I know how you must feel."

He pushed her away, a raw animal sound escaping his throat. "No! You don't know! You have no idea what we have! She's a part of me. I can't live without her!"

Just then, Ryfka burst down the hall, her face streaked with tears, her voice a terrified cry. "Please! Come! Henna—she's calling for help!"

The world seemed to tilt as Abram's wild grief fractured, replaced by a sharp terror. He stared at Serena, his own eyes red-rimmed and glistening, the unspoken apology hanging heavy between them.

Serena met his gaze, her expression softening for a breath. "Later, Abram," she said, her voice firm but not unkind. "Right now, Henna needs us. Let's go." She was already moving toward the room. "We'll do everything we can to bring these babies into the world and try to save their mother."

Abram nodded, a choked sound in his throat, and followed.

June 19ᵗʰ, 1932, 8:17 p.m.

The sun was sinking lower, casting long, purple shadows across the yard. Ryfka glanced through the window and saw Abram and Icek at the table in the yard, their figures etched against the fading light. Abram's arm was around Icek, his head bent close as if explaining something of the utmost importance, a brief, stolen moment of calm before the storm was to break.

Ryfka hurried to the back door, her voice tight with urgency. "Abram! Hot water! Towels! As fast as you can! Hurry! Serena says we can't waste any time!"

Icek looked up from where Abram had just been murmuring to him, his face a question. "Is everything alright?"

"Don't ask questions, son," Abram said, his voice strained, already pushing himself up. "Just help me. Get the water boiling. Find the towels. Do as I say."

"Okay, Father," Icek said, his voice small. "Whatever you need."

Ryka fled back inside, to the room, where Serena pulled the blanket back from Henna's pale, sweat-slicked skin. She instructed Henna to draw her knees up and brace her heels against the edge of the bed. "Be ready," she said, her voice low and steady. "When I tell you, push."

She motioned to Ryfka. "My bag. There are instruments—they look like large, curved spoons. Stainless steel. Bring them."

Abram, his face ashen, entered, carrying a steaming pan of water, while Icek followed, clutching a stack of clean towels. Serena met them at the doorway, her voice firm but gentle. "Set them down here. Stay out now. Please. Ryfka will get what we need. Go and wait. Let us do what we can."

CHAPTER FOUR

Jozefow, Poland
June 19th, 1932, 8:32 p.m.

Serena's voice was calm, a practiced contrast to the urgency in her eyes. "Henna, you're ready to deliver. But we have a slight complication. A portion of the placenta is present. We need to move it to ensure a clear passage for the baby."

Henna gripped the bed sheets, her knuckles white. "The babies, are they alright?" Her voice was a thread of sound, stretched taut with fear.

"They will be, as long as we address this quickly." Serena's tone was firm and reassuring, but her hands moved steadily, betraying the underlying tension.

Serena worked swiftly, explaining each step in a low murmur— her words meant to soothe as much as inform. Cold and sterile metal instruments glinted in the lamplight, and within moments, Ryfka watched as she gently repositioned the placenta, clearing the birth canal.

"Alright, Henna. We need your help now. Your baby's head is crowning. When you feel the next contraction, I want you to push."

Henna's face was pale, streaked with sweat and the earlier blood loss. Her breath came in ragged gasps, but she nodded, summoning a strength that seemed to come from somewhere beyond her depleted body. With the next contraction, she bore down, her body trembling with the effort. The baby's head emerged, a dark, wet crown.

Serena cupped the tiny head, guiding it with a gentle tug and a practiced rotation. With a final, slippery rush, the baby was free, its body still glistening.

Wiping a sheen of sweat from her brow, Serena let out a breath. "Henna, it's a girl. Your first daughter."

A thin, wailing cry filled the room, a sound of new life, fragile yet insistent.

Before Henna could even fully process the news, Icek and Abram burst through the doorway, their faces etched with worry. Ryfka, ever practical, held out the tiny, squirming bundle.

"You're just in time," Serena announced, her voice still carrying a note of relief. "A healthy baby girl—Henna is stable, for now. Take your daughter, clean her up. With any luck, there'll be another one joining her soon."

Abram took the baby, his gaze fixed on the tiny, wrinkled face, oblivious to the newborn's cries. He handed the swaddled infant to Icek. "Look, son. Your new sister." He started down the hallway, his steps measured, as if trying to contain the whirlwind of emotions within him.

Serena turned back to Henna, her expression shifting, the momentary relief replaced by a furrowed brow. "Ryfka, I need you. The second baby is close, very close."

A scream tore through the air, a raw, primal sound that ripped through the fragile calm. "The cramping is unbearable! I can't." Henna's voice was choked with pain.

Icek, cradling his newborn sister, froze in the hallway, his eyes wide with a mixture of wonder and terror. He glanced at his father, seeking reassurance. "Father, is Mother…?"

His father turned, his face calm, though Icek was certain he didn't feel calm. "Icek, this is how babies are born. The pain your mother is feeling is no different from what she endured when you were born." He tried to sound steady, but his voice wavered slightly.

His mother screamed again, an anguished sound.

"We must hold fast to our prayers—may God see us through. Be patient, Icek," his father said in a whisper, though his face had lost its color.

Icek tended to his newborn sister in a room down the hall with his father at his side. The terrifyingly loud sounds of pain from his dear mother joined the crying of his new sister, and his emotions took over. Before long, he, too, was in tears.

Serena looked to see if the baby's head had made its way to the birth canal. A glance resulted in a sudden distressed expression filling her face. She looked into Ryfka's eyes, and Ryfka knew from the dire expression that something wasn't right.

In a voice a bit above a whisper, Serena began speaking. "A large portion of the placenta is exposed. I don't know if I can push the tissue to the side far enough. I have never seen this before. I must get the tissue out of the way before the pressure builds too high from the force of the baby on the placenta wall," Serena explained in a trembling voice. The heat and the stress of the moment had soaked her gray hair, and she grabbed a towel to wipe away the moisture from her face. Avoiding any eye contact with Henna, Serena spoke in a subdued tone outside Henna's hearing as she talked Ryfka through options to try and suppress the chance of a tear in the placenta.

Ryfka then said, "And if we are unable to prevent a tear in the placenta, what will happen to Henna?"

Sarena looked at Ryfka, bit down on her bottom lip, and began shaking her head to signify that they could lose Henna if this were to happen.

Seconds later, Ryfka began shedding tears and from that point on avoided any eye contact with Henna.

Serena began speaking in a voice barely above a whisper with deep concern on her face. "Ryfka, please hold Henna's hand and try to calm her down."

With a slight frown, Ryfka grabbed a washcloth, dampened it, and rubbed Henna's face while Serena continued her thorough exploration of Henna's abdomen, shaking her head slightly. Ryfka murmured, "Please. Please, Henna. Try and relax. Let Serena do her work." She glanced at the door to see if there were any sign of Abram and Icek. *Are they listening to this horrid commotion?*

By this time, Henna was screaming at the top of her lungs, "The pain, the pain, I can't stand the pain. Please help me, dear Lord. Please, somebody help me."

Abram's heavy steps hurried down the hall and entered the room. "Please, Ryfka, go to Icek. I will stay with Henna."

Ryfka, with reluctance, responded, "Very well, Abram. I know Icek has never tended to a newborn." She then looked into Henna's eyes and said, "Darling, it won't be long now," before she left the room.

Serena, concerned, looked at Abram and said, "I think I have the placenta in a safe position. Be ready to push, Henna."

Abram looked at his wife, then stared into Serena's eyes and said, "I'm putting all my trust in you."

"I'm ready," Henna said.

Henna looked at Abram while he wiped the sweat from her brow. He tried to hide from her that he had no confidence in a good outcome.

Serena glanced up at Henna, then looked at Abram with a true sense of regret. He saw it there in her eyes. This would not be another Sonja Adamowicz, as there was no sign of a second miracle. He felt ill as he realized he had lost all confidence in her ability to save Henna.

"The head is here, Henna. Push! Push hard!" Serena cried.

Abram wiped Henna's face, kissed her forehead, and whispered, "Our second baby is moments away. You are doing great."

Serena looked up to the heavens and said, "Dear Lord, please, Dear Lord."

Abram assured her, "You're doing wonderfully. The head is out. The head is out."

Serena said in a quiet, confident voice, "Henna, just like last time, you're going to feel a slight tug."

"You're doing great," Abram said again.

Serena's eyes suddenly widened to twice their size. "Oh my God, it's happening. The baby is almost out. The baby's out. Oh no. She's hemorrhaging," she yelled, "Hurry, Abram. Take the child from me while I try to control the bleeding."

Abram reached for the newborn and placed her in a fresh towel. With tears in his eyes, he began wiping the baby clean, and within moments, the tiny little girl signaled to the world that she had arrived.

Abram's face was soaked with tears. The joy of a precious new baby girl and Henna's ferocious bleeding created a swing of emotions he had never experienced.

In a trembling voice, Abram said, "I'll get this little one to Ryfka and return as fast as possible."

"Please do hurry," Serena said as he left the room.

Serena tried everything—nevertheless, the bleeding continued.

"I'm so cold," Henna whispered in an unsteady voice. "I'm so cold."

"Try to remain still and calm, Henna," Serena said as she worked to contain the bleeding.

Abram returned, and in an instant, he could tell from the expression on Serena's face that the situation had become dire.

"Please, Abram, try to comfort Henna. I'm trying my best. With any luck, we will have this situation under control soon."

I can't believe what I'm seeing. Moments ago, Henna's face was beaming with life. Why is she so pale? Why does she look different by the minute?

A massive lump had formed in his throat, as in that moment, he imagined his life without Henna. The beautiful pinks and peaches of a perfect face from only days ago had disappeared, and now, the blues of death approached. Even her lips were nearing a shade of blue. Her skin had become cool to the touch.

"Hello, darling. I understand we have two more girls in the house," Henna whispered.

"Yes. That's right, two beautiful girls at that. Unlike you and Asia, the twins are not identical. They both have unique features. Icek is already proving himself a responsible big brother," Abram said.

"We both appreciated that Icek would cherish a little brother or sister," Henna muttered in a weak voice as she reached to adjust the covers.

Abram glanced over at Serena, looking for any positive expression on her face that would lead him to believe the situation had improved. Instead, Serena's solemn expression caused the near-suffocating knot to reappear in his throat.

"Please, Henna, please try to relax," Abram said as tears flowed freely from his eyes.

Catching his attention, Serena motioned for Abram to step away.

"Henna, I must check the babies for a minute," Abram said as he stepped out of the room. Serena followed him.

Down the hall, the two stopped and faced one another.

"Abram, she hasn't much time left. I have not been able to stop the bleeding. You must decide. It would be best to consider allowing your son to say goodbye to his mother. He may not be old enough to understand but leaving him out of the entire process may have a disastrous impact on his life. If he were my son, I would want him with me so we could all say goodbye together. What are your thoughts?"

Abram stood speechless. His face filled with realization. He buried his face in his hands to hide his emotion. He began sobbing, as he could not control his feelings for the first time in his life. Nothing in Abram's life thus far had ever created the level of emotion he now experienced.

With his face engulfed in tears, Abram began speaking. "Serena, how much time does Henna have?"

"I estimate she will leave us within twenty minutes or less."

Abram's current role was to be strong, keep his composure, and lead the way for his family. He collected his thoughts and tried to prepare his son and mother-in-law for their life without Henna.

"I want the two new family members to see their mother. I will get Ryfka and Icek to bring the twins in here," Abram said out of earshot from Henna.

"Good idea," Serena said.

Henna tried to enjoy the moment with a newborn under each arm, but her precarious condition would not allow the celebration, as she grew weaker by the moment.

"They are beautiful, so beautiful," Henna uttered.

Henna's voice now was almost inaudible, and she struggled to keep her eyes open.

"Henna, we are going to take our new arrivals back to their bed," Abram said as he motioned for Serena and Ryfka to take a baby.

"Please let me kiss each of the children before you take them away," Henna whispered.

The babies, each bundled in their towel, were placed within reach of their mother's lips. Henna's lips gently caressed the tiny cheeks of the newborn infants. She held each petite face close. The smell of a newborn caused her to flash back to those initial minutes she had spent with Icek: a fragrance she had never forgotten.

How could anyone be so blissful and sad in the same instant? *Have I done something so cruel to deserve this?* She recognized that in a brief time, she would leave the world. Even in her weakened state, she conceded the full depth of her life's demise. Soon, her flesh and blood would be left behind, though the confidence that all her family would one day be together again warmed her heart.

In an instant, no one in the room had dry eyes.

Henna motioned for Icek to come to her, and wiping his eyes clear of the tears, he made his way to her side.

With a voice barely above a whisper, Henna said, "Icek, your mother will leave this world soon. God doesn't always let things happen the way we want them to. Sometimes, we must let our fate take over. I know very soon I will be in the arms of my Maker. I must tell you a few things," Henna whispered.

"No, Mother, you are not leaving us. Please, Father, tell Mother she will live—tell her she isn't going to die. Please, Father, you must tell her," Icek cried.

Henna saw that Abram couldn't speak. His throat worked, and he swallowed and opened his mouth, but the words would not come. He stared into Icek's eyes. Perhaps feeling if his voice couldn't tell the truth, his eyes would.

With his crying out of control, Icek finally seemed to sense that his mother would soon be gone.

"Mother, please don't go. Please, Mother. Please don't leave," Icek cried.

Serena and Ryfka left the room while Abram and Icek stood at Henna's side. Abram remained speechless.

Henna, her whisper barely heard, said, "Icek, you must promise to always care for your sisters, Gramma, and Father. Please, son, promise me."

"I promise that I will. I promise," Icek said in a voice filled with tears.

Abram said, trembling. "We will be sure that you are always in our thoughts. We will do everything we can to ensure the girls understand how wonderful a mother they had."

Abram and Icek both wrapped their arms around her. Icek sobbed while Abram tried his best to console them both. "Oh, my darling wife, I love you so." Then he looked up at the ceiling. "God, tell me why," he screamed.

The outburst startled Icek, resulting in a face engulfed in tears and anguish.

"Mother, please don't go. Please, God, don't take my mother."

In a faint whisper, Henna muttered, "I love you." A slight smile formed on her face… then she released a soft gasp of air. The clock's tick, tick, tick remained the sole sound in the room.

Their world went silent. They knew that without seeing it, their lives had changed, and a new chapter would begin.

In a way, the entire house and all its members died along with Henna that day.

CHAPTER FIVE

New York City, New York
June 20ᵗʰ, 1932, 8:35 AM

Asia sat at her desk and felt her pulse throbbing in her head. It was late, and she was behind schedule. Tonight, was different, as Asia's concert pianist husband, Jakub Markowicz, was performing at New York's Philharmonic Hall[1] with the esteemed New York Symphony. In the back of her head, she heard his words as she left her home for work this morning. *You can't be late this evening, as this is the most important day of our lives.*

She yanked open the desk drawer, draped her arms about the pile of paper on her desk, and, in an instant, raked the contents into the drawer. She then slammed the drawer closed and locked it. With her sweater and purse in hand, she rushed down the hall toward her boss, the office of Mr. Chatsworth Williams. His friends and acquaintances referred to him as simply Chats. However, in the presence of clients and visitors, he preferred Mr. Williams.

Passing a mirror on the way to his office, she paused, grabbed her hairbrush from her purse, and applied several brush strokes to her reddish-brown, shoulder-length hair. In her native Polish, she said, "Good enough."

Tapping on the door, she received permission to enter, and spoke. "Hello. Please excuse my interruption. My apologies, as I was unaware you had a guest."

She glanced at the well-dressed, perfect specimen of a gentleman sitting in one of the two wingback chairs across from Mr. Williams's desk. Instantly, his eyes caught her attention.

Embarrassed, she quickly looked away and said, "You were having a conversation, and I interrupted both of you." Focusing her attention away from his eyes to Mr. Williams's tie, she said, "I will be leaving for the day. I must get a head start. As you know, tonight is Jakub's first time in New York's Symphony Hall as master of ceremonies. Plus, we will be at the dinner party that follows the concert. Are there any last-minute things you need from me before I leave?" Asia asked, stepping into the room and standing next to the vacant wingback chair.

Her boss, Chatsworth Williams, the firm's president and a well-dressed, handsome-looking fifty-four-year-old Ivy Leaguer with prematurely gray hair, responded, "By all means, please, leave soon so you're not late. I thought you had left an hour ago! Why were you delayed?" he asked.

Asia replied, "I became embedded in the quarterly reports and lost track of time."

"That will do it. Oh, before you leave, I never had the chance to introduce the two of you. Jack, meet Mrs. Asia Markowicz, my assistant and the glue of the office, she's the wife of the prominent Polish concert pianist Jakub Markowicz. Asia, meet Mr. Jack Reynolds. Jack and I go back about five years, as he worked for our primary underwriter."

Jack immediately stood, walked toward Asia, and smiled.

Chats reached into his suit coat pocket and retrieved a slender, gold cigarette case. Opening it, he said, "Asia, no problem whatsoever. You go ahead. We will get the remainder of the corporate reports out on Monday."

Jack looked into Asia's eyes with an intense, near-sensual stare. He thought. *What is that fragrance she is wearing? Asia is likely the most beautiful woman I have ever seen.* After about four seconds of his stare, Asia quickly focused her look at the floor.

His enormous hands clasped her tiny one like a flower placed between his palms for safekeeping. He said, "I thought I recognized that accent. You are a native-born Pole, aren't you?" Jack asked.

Asia thought for a moment. *I appreciate that it would be impolite to cut the conversation short—I don't want Jack to consider me rude at our first time meeting one another while in the presence of Chats.* She closed her eyes and tilted her head, then broke his hold from a handshake that lasted well beyond the typical business greeting. Asia returned a slight smile and then took a couple steps back. *I am happily married to a wonderful person. That said, I know when my heart is fluttering out of control as a result of staring into the eyes of a charming, handsome man. But I'm happily married—how has this happened?*

Chats observed Asia, who, for the first time, appeared uneasy. *What's different? What about Jack might be making her uncomfortable?* She started pulling her fingers through her hair, something he had yet to witness from Asia. He could tell that Jack found her attractive.

Crossing and uncrossing her arms, minus any eye contact and continuing to fidget with her hair, she replied, "Yes, I have been in this country for almost five years. I have tried to learn to speak with an American accent but have given up. So many people here speak with an accent, the melting pot and all," Asia said as she ventured to the door.

Chats followed her, gave her a warm hug, and said, "The wife and I are looking forward to this evening's concert. By the way, will Jakub be performing a Dvorák piece?"

"Yes, but please don't ask me about the specific work. Jakub has been practicing this piece for the past nine weeks. Expert conductors worldwide have recognized the Dvorák movement as a rare piece for a concert performance on piano. We shall see. Jakub is quite confident in his abilities. I will never give it a second thought," Asia explained.

Approaching Asia once again, Jack asked, "Asia, does your name have an English translation? What a unique name, certainly not common."

This gentleman is natural at conversation, or he's taking this opportunity to practice his flirting skills. Her heart convinced her that the latter best fit the situation.

"Yes, I get that question all the time. I believe Joan is the closest American name to my translation of Asia. You know, like Joan of Arc."

Jack, watching her every move, tilted his head and, with squinting eyes, said, "Really? That's interesting."

Asia walked toward the door, turned her head, and said, "Jack, it was very nice to meet you." He again approached her and grabbed her hand. This time, he placed her hand between his.

"Yes, nice to meet you as well, Asia," Jack said as he gazed again into her eyes.

Asia responded by focusing her attention on his tie. Facing the two gentlemen and back-stepping toward the door with little eye contact, she said, "I shall see you on Monday, Chats. I hope you enjoy the concert this evening."

"You tell Jakub I wish him the best for the evening gala."

Asia left the room and walked toward the elevators. *What a handsome man, with stunning blue eyes and a face that could easily be on the Hollywood big screen. I couldn't let him know for an instant that he's more attractive than most leading men in movies. How often have I heard that handsome men are a dime a dozen in America?*

He may have above-average looks, but not compared to my soulmate, who is an outstanding concert pianist with a heartfelt personality. My Jakub loves me more than anything and is also very handsome, a dignified, classically trained pianist. Jack is nothing but another pretty American male face—he may try to sweep me off my feet, but he won't get anywhere!

Chats, sitting at his desk, gathered documents strewn across his desk, stacked them in a neat pile, placed them in the top drawer of his credenza, and said, "Look at the time. I too must be leaving in twenty minutes to make it to the concert on time." He then took one last drag from his cigarette, blew the smoke toward the ceiling, and remarked, "Pity you're not attending. My wife Claire and I are both looking forward to this evening. She can't wait to brag to her friends of prominence that she's a friend of the performer."

He stepped over to where Jack was sitting and offered him a cigarette, who politely declined. Chats grabbed one for himself and began compacting the tobacco by slamming the end of the white stick into the surface of the gold case. Between sips of coffee, he lit the end of the new smoke with the one he had yet to finish.

He took a long drag from the fresh cigarette, exhausted the smoke toward the ceiling, and said, "Asia's husband chose a wonderful artist for his performance. It's unfortunate how Dvořák came from humble beginnings of working in the family butcher shop, became world-renowned, and, at the time of his passing, left behind a mere pittance. Antonio Dvořák was born in 1841 and died in 1904. He taught here in New York at the New York Conservatory of Music and wrote nine symphonies—the ninth was his best, 'e Minor, Op. 95-From the New

World,' which I believe Jakub is performing this evening. Indeed, it is sad to think of Dvořák as almost broke at the time of his death."

Jack shrugged and looked at Chats in disbelief, "Please tell me, how do you remember all those details?"

He took another drag from his cigarette and smiled. "Oh, it's nothing. I don't do it intentionally, as my mind refuses to forget the factual information I pick up along the way. My parents sought to understand whether or not my unusual talent for memory was for better or worse. Did I have a superpower or a defect? The doctor quizzed me a bit and said he thought I had hyperthymesia. My parents looked at each other in a state of shock and asked in unison, 'What is hyperthymesia?'

"To be sure of the diagnosis, he recommended my parents speak with a neurologist, as they specialize in the field of memory. So, there I was, a few days later, in the office of one of New York's finest specialists. Within ten minutes of a one-on-one with the brain doctor, he diagnosed me as having hyperthymesia. In other words, there is very little of what I have seen, heard, or read that is not retained."

Jack stood and turned slowly, staring at Chats as though he had seen a ghost. "That's pretty funny—you're joking. Oh my God, you're serious. I must sit for this explanation. Wait a minute," he said as he scratched at the half-day hair growth on his chin and sat in the wingback chair. "You mean to tell me you remember everything?"

"I can tell you about our first phone call when we hired your former firm to represent us in that insurance fraud investigation for the office furniture manufacturer. You took a train from their Connecticut office to meet for our first time—and that was five years ago. I can tell you the details of my seventh birthday—what my parents were wearing, the weather, and where we had lunch." With a huge grin, Chats continued, "First, the condition is so rare, literally, no one has heard of it. Second, when I heard the doctor explain the condition to my parents, they refused to believe that such a memory in a human could exist. The doctor then asked my parents to quiz me on my last five birthdays. In amazement, they became dumbfounded that I could recite each birthday to an infinite level of detail."

"Chats, I'm not doubting what you say, I simply heretofore have never heard of such a talent."

Chats stood, walked about the room, and said, "Now, I ask you, have you figured out the reason I dealt with only you during your five years at the underwriting firm? And why we got along so well during those five years? I told the president of your firm I wanted you exclusively for all my underwriting needs."

"Based on your sensational memory, you tested me on several occasions to be sure I wasn't the storyteller or the bull-crap type."

"Splendid. Your ability to comprehend the situation is excellent. Now you know my motivations for bringing you into the firm."

"My Pops' guidance about lying was pretty good after all. He told me time and time again, 'If you don't lie, you won't have to remember what you lied about.'"

"Great advice!"

"Father also explained that all that a man has is his character, and once his character is compromised, you are damaged for life, as there are no second chances at a first impression. And, unlike others in life, many don't mind a white lie here or there. But for you, Chats, any mistruth is a deal breaker."

Chats remarked. "And why, perhaps, did I choose today to give up my secret? Can you guess?"

"Is it because you learned that I, too, always tell the truth?"

"Exactly," Chats replied.

Chats took another drag from his cigarette, exhaled, and said, "Let me put it this way: Those willing to speak the truth in society are not only rare but also nearly impossible to find. And lucky for me, I will soon have two people working for me who share this trait—you and Asia."

"So, Chats, your method is simple, correct? You determine this trait of a person to never lie by asking questions that you already know the answers to—correct? This way, you can confirm whether the person is telling the truth or lying."

"Exactly! You and Asia are both on the same level of respect in my book, and by the way, there are no other business associates to whom I can say the same. I told you about my gift in total confidence, and I trust that you will never let the hyperthymesia cat out of the bag, as in this business, truthfulness is priceless."

"I trust you tested the other employees as well."

"Did I test each employee to determine if they spoke the truth? The answer to that question is no. You learn through everyday conversation that it is human nature to stretch the truth—during the five years of your underwriting position, you proved yourself to me. For Asia, I must say, stretching the truth is not part of her make-up. Honor, truthfulness, and integrity are why I will forever value your role as an employee. In my business, I need these traits, and if you had been dishonest, I would have discovered this. Asia, by the way, has never been told, and I plan never to reveal my hyperthymesia secret to her."

"Chats, I guess I owe you a gracious thank you for the trust you have in me."

Chats took another drag on his cigarette, exhaled the smoke to the ceiling, and said, "Earned trust is the best kind. Since we will be working together, my gift, as my wife calls it, will come in quite handy as time goes on with your assignments in our company."

Jack scratched his head and rubbed his neck. He did a left-to-right and then up and down with his head and said, "Understood, sir. I have already forgotten the name of your condition. I must say that since I know about your gift, how have you escaped the military intelligence people, or the FBI, the Secret Service, etcetera?"

Chats walked toward the large wall of glass in his office, took a deep drag from his cigarette, exhaled it to the ceiling, and said, "Excellent observation, Jack. For the love of their child, an offer of an immeasurable amount of money caused the medical report to disappear. For money, one can hide anything. The doctor who diagnosed my condition immediately wanted to notify the government that he had diagnosed a healthy young man with the condition. The government has had a few employees brought into the government against their wishes, and they eventually take advantage of those with such a gift. The other problem about a person with my condition is that other governments would love to get their hands on me, and they still would if they knew.

As of today, two people on this earth know of my gift—you and my wife. We will keep it that way. Understood?"

"Yes, sir, understood," Jack replied in a confident yet subdued, voice.

"I want to drop this topic and never hear you speak of it again. Now, let's change the subject."

"Yes, sir. I will never bring up the subject. Although, I do have one last question."

"Yes, go ahead."

"Your education at Dartmouth must have been a cakewalk— Dean's list each semester without much of an effort on your part?"

"No. I decided to refrain from being a total smart-ass. Yes, college was easy; in fact, life has been a breeze. However, I am not one to 'raise a flag,' as I had no intention of being even remotely at the top of my class, and, by the way, a great memory does not guarantee high intelligence. It just helps. I have always been leery of attracting attention by being accused of being the smartest person in the room. I learned early that, as college teaches you, beyond a decent memory, one must know how to apply knowledge accordingly. I have never felt that I was the smartest. That said, I will be the disguised person with the best memory. I managed to be in the top ten percentile of my graduating class and was content with the recognition that came with the accomplishment."

Jack, looking out the large window, said, "Being too smart does appear to be a nice hindrance."

"Never quite thought of it that way. Your observation is quite interesting. How about we change the subject? What do you think of my office?"

Jack looked around before he responded. The solid mahogany desk, about three times the size of a typical office desk, was positioned adjacent to a wall of glass that overlooked Central Park,. Two full-size leather wingback chairs faced the desk, and the artwork obtained from travel to virtually every continent in the world adorned the twelve-foot-tall walls. The stuffed Impala head on the judges' paneled wall adjacent to Chats' desk became the focal point for those visiting the space.

"I have never been in an office of this caliber."

Chats surveyed the room with him and said, "Unfortunately, I can't take credit. My father, God rest his soul, hired New York's finest decorators for this office, his Westchester estate, and the Manhattan apartment I inherited."

Standing before a full-length mirror, he continued, "My only credit is maintaining his exquisite dress style. We competed over custom-tailored suits, ties, and shirts. Many of my ties were his. You're a respectable dresser too," he added, approaching Jack. "Nice tie," he smirked.

"I've used a Jewish tailor since moving to New York—he is from the old country, from a long line of tailors," Jack replied.

"Asia is Jewish," Chats announced.

Jack, in an instant, sat and rubbed his forehead, shook his head, and said, "Asia, the beautiful female specimen that I just met, is Jewish? She is among the most attractive females I have ever met. With her hair color, complexion, and green eyes, I would have guessed anything but Jewish. Unfortunately, most of my life, my family ingrained a certain level of prejudice, in particular, the antisemitic comments that center around the Jewish nose and their unique hairstyles, plus the skin tone of the typical Jewish person."

Chats replied, continuing to puff on his cigarette, "I could tell you thought she was up there with the Hollywood actresses."

"I apologize. Was it that obvious?"

"I have to say, Asia had a contentious reaction when she saw you. I have never seen her react in such a way. Maybe intimidated by your presence?"

Jack stood, adjusted his tie in an almost nervous fashion, and said, "My explanation is easy. I have never been in the same room with a person so beautiful."

Chats stepped toward a cabinet along the side wall of his office, opened the door, and retrieved drink glasses, a bottle of Irish gin, and a bottle of tonic. Next, with ice tongs in his hand, he opened a drawer and retrieved ice. "Let's have a toast to your future. Does gin and tonic suit you?"

"One of my favorite mixed drinks. Wow, I am impressed with your liquor cabinet and ice. Nice touch. I never knew such things existed."

"My father had this installed right before he died. At the time, I thought he was losing his mind. Now, I make use of my little bar on special occasions, like this evening. But no one knows it's even here, and I prefer to keep it that way."

"Got it. I have sealed my lips."

They stepped toward one another and touched their glasses together. Looking at one another, Chats said, "Here's to the Jews of the world and Asia, and last but not least, welcome to the firm."

Jack replied, "Cheers!"

Chats sipped his drink, looked at Jack, and said, "Face it, a rare sight is a light-brown-haired, green-eyed, Jewish female. Asia mixes it up to an extreme. I'm not sure of the percentage, but a high percentage of Jewish women have dark brown or black hair. Asia's light brown hair and green eyes are the exception."

"I would have never imagined her to be Jewish, ever," Jack said as he took another gulp of his drink.

"I asked Asia one day about the Jewish custom related to the covering of hair for a married woman. Asia told me that she only followed that custom when going to the synagogue, where she dons a wig or sheitel. She tries her best to follow Jewish customs when she can. However, she has remarked that some of the customs are losing their significance, as many Jews, especially younger married Jewish women, are becoming Americanized."

"You're right. I have never seen that hair and eye color combination for Jews of either sex," Jack reiterated.

Chats said, "I had similar experiences with my upbringing, too. Asia and my Jewish roommate in college changed my opinion of the Jewish faith," he said as he took another drag from his cigarette and another swig of his drink.

Jack walked over to the large, floor-to-ceiling wall of glass, peering out to watch the Central Park activity, and said, "In your opinion, is she better off here than she would be back in Poland?"

Chats, watching Central Park visitors mill about, said, "She is better off here for sure, as you will find out after you reach your new assignment. We are lucky in this country, as most keep their opinions to themselves. Our marine insurance division manager, Trevor Whatley, has spoken countless times about what's happening in Germany. By the way, you will soon meet Trevor when you arrive in England. He, too, a military veteran, was in the thick of things in World War I as a member of the British Army infantry. He experienced more action than he cared to talk about. Your US Marine Corps experience and his World War I doughboy experience will blend well together. I have a ton of respect for Trevor."

"I look forward to meeting Mr. Whatley," Jack said.

"Trevor has recently traveled throughout Germany and, in fact, most of Europe, inspecting our client sites for risk. He was close to tears on the phone while telling me the antisemitic foolishness that he had observed. I respect his great insight. He is concerned there will be another war. By the way, we must prepare our clients for exclusion from our coverage, as we do not insure them for damages that result from an act of war. Trevor has been quite vocal about the latest German laws that focus on limiting the rights of the Jewish population in Germany. Antisemitism is prolific. Frankly, I don't know where things will lead. The treatment toward the Jews has been horrific."

Jack stepped away from the window and approached a large map of the world that was adjacent to the window. He looked at the countries he knew to be in the news as of late, such as Germany, Poland, France, and Czechoslovakia. "There are plenty of locations where the politics can get pretty hot." He moved toward the glass wall, paused momentarily, and said, "I know little about the Jewish religion. I know Jews are prominent in finance, banking, and general commerce. I know Jesus as a Jewish carpenter, but my prejudice is baseless. Can European prejudices against the Jewish population lead to war?"

Chats extinguished his cigarette into an ashtray on the edge of his credenza, an unusual dish in brass with images of strange animals, some perhaps, mythological, as the item seemed an antique from a distant land. The container, an obvious relic from some faraway land, contained a pile of spent butts: the day's supply of expended cigarettes.

"My Jewish roommate at Dartmouth, Itzhak Blumenthal, became my best friend through our years in school together. It started when a Jew befriended a Methodist—the rest is history, as we both learned respect for those with values. When you live with someone for four years, you get to know one another. After a while, I gained more and more confidence to discuss my Methodist religion vs. his Judaism candidly."

"Tell me, what did you learn from the experience?"

"For one, I learned that when a beautiful and talented young lady walks into your office for an interview, and within minutes you find out she is Jewish, you realize that religion doesn't change anything. Others in this building, I will not repeat their names, told me that I suffered an oversight in good judgment when I hired a Jew."

"I think you made a great decision."

"Well, Jack, thanks for the compliment related to my Asia decision. If you get me started on Jews, I tend to ramble on. It was great to have this conversation, but I must get going. I have a cab for the trip home due downstairs in exactly eleven minutes."

"I understand. I will be on my way. I must continue to familiarize myself with our product offerings, policies, procedures, and details. Enjoy the evening concert, sir."

"Have a good evening, Jack."

CHAPTER SIX

New York City, New York
June 20th, 1932, 7:50 p.m.

A sia entered the ballroom—her gloved hand tucked into the crook of Jakub's arm. He adjusted his top hat with a subtle flick of the wrist, the tails of his tuxedo swaying as they moved into the throng. His step was light and confident, the intricate piano solo of Dvořák[2] still echoing in her mind, a testament to his flawless performance. Asia's mint gown shimmered as she turned, absorbing the scene: a kaleidoscope of dark suits and vibrant dresses, the light fractured a thousand times by the crystal chandeliers overhead. "Jakub," she breathed, her voice barely audible above the murmur of the crowd, "look."

Jakub followed her gaze, a slight smile playing on his lips. He touched the spot on his arm where she'd playfully pinched him earlier. "I still might wake up," he murmured, then his eyes widened, taking in the scale of the room. "Asia, they told me they reserved the entire place, but I didn't truly believe it." He paused, a flicker of wistfulness crossing his face. "If only our families could see this. To think, Henna's never even been inside a hotel."

The subdued clinking of china, crystal, and silver cutlery formed a low, constant hum beneath the buzz of nearly three hundred conversations—the sounds, animate and inanimate, blended into an almost palpable wave. White-gloved hands appeared, as if by magic, bearing silver trays laden with refreshments. Servers, a blur of white shirts, black trousers, and silk bowties or scarves—each topped with a jaunty black cap trimmed in white silk—navigated the crowded tables. They were everywhere and nowhere at once, their numbers impossible to discern, topping off coffee, refilling water glasses, and replenishing breadbaskets with an almost invisible efficiency.

Asia tilted her head back, tracing the frozen cascades of the chandeliers. "Jakub," she whispered, "look at those." He followed her gaze upward, where layers of cigarette smoke softened the edges of the ornate ceiling. A distant melody, faint as a half-remembered dream, drifted toward them. "Beethoven," he recognized, his voice low. "At the far end." The beauty of the string quartet's performance was sadly diminished, almost lost in the ambient roar.

After a seventeen-minute wait—each tick of the clock amplifying their anticipation—they were finally seated at the head table. Flowers and congratulatory cards, a testament to Jakub's triumphant performance, soon covered its surface. The concert, ending in a series of standing ovations, had been everything they'd hoped for.

A steady stream of well-wishers flowed toward them. Some held out programs for a signature, and others wanted to shake the hand of the maestro.

Chats Williams and his wife Claire rose from their seats as if propelled by springs, beaming with parental pride. Claire's bright yellow gown, its neckline plunging daringly low, drew eyes from across the room. The delicate lace that clung to her chest accentuated her curves. She dabbed at her eyes with a handkerchief pulled from her purse.

Chats, embracing her, spoke in a voice thick with emotion, "Are you as proud of these two as I am?"

"Indeed," she whispered, her voice catching.

A random couple, seated about twenty feet away, began tapping their silverware against their crystal glasses. The sound, picked up by other guests, quickly escalated into a rhythmic clamor that drowned out all the other noise.

Claire, her voice rising above the din, called out, "Toast! Toast! Toast!" The audience joined in, echoing around the room: "Toast! Toast! Toast!"

Chats stood, raising his hands in a calming gesture. Slowly, the room quieted, leaving only the distant, elegant strains of Bach played by the string quartet. "Please, Jakub," Chats said, his voice resonating in the sudden silence, "would you stand?"

Asia gave Jakub a gentle nudge, her eyes shining. "This is your moment, darling," she whispered.

Jakub rose, a blush creeping up his neck. He shifted his weight, his hands moving restlessly from his pockets to his sides, then rubbed his beard in a nervous gesture. His eyes darted around the room, unable to settle on any one point.

Chats continued, his voice filled with warmth. "To quote Dante, 'Art, as far as it is able, follows nature, as a pupil imitates his master; thus, your art must be, as it were, God's grandchild.[3] ' Jakub, you are that grandchild of God of whom Dante spoke."

Jakub's blush deepened his body language, a mixture of surprise and humility. *Such kind words in front of so many are a first for him*, Asia thought, watching as a wave of embarrassment washed over him.

Asia's chest rose and fell rapidly, her lower lip trembling as tears threatening to spill as she fought to contain her overwhelming pride. Finally, she surrendered, a single tear tracing a path down her cheek.

The crowd erupted again, chanting, "Speech! Speech! Speech!"

Jakub stood, gazing out at the now standing-room-only crowd. He cleared his throat, raising his hands in an attempt to quiet the enthusiastic applause. The room fell silent, and he glanced at Asia, her heart filled with encouragement, and a small, proud smile broke across his face.

"To be frank, ladies and gentlemen," he began, his voice slightly shaky, "I am more terrified of giving this speech than I was of performing that complex Dvorak piece earlier this evening. At the University in Warsaw, they taught me how to perform," he gestured broadly, a hint of self-deprecating humor in his tone, "but, alas, they neglected to instruct us on speaking to an audience of this magnitude."

Laughter and cheers rippled through the room. Asia, reaching beneath the table, tugged gently on his trousers, then looked up at him, her smile wide, and mouthed, "You're doing great, dear."

He returned the smile, silently mouthing the Polish phrase, "I love you, darling."

"A classical musician dreams of nights like tonight," he continued, his voice gaining strength. "We spend countless hours honing our craft, often wondering if we will ever be good enough to perform in a world-renowned venue with an orchestra as prestigious as the New York Symphony."

Another wave of applause, louder this time, washed over him.

"Thank you! Thank you!" he said, his voice filled with genuine gratitude. "Fifteen years ago, my dream was to perform at small village venues in Poland. Perhaps I dared to imagine a concert in Prague, Lodz, or Krakow, but New York City? Never in my wildest dreams. And yet, today, I am living that dream."

He paused, pulling out a handkerchief to dab at his eyes.

The crowd responded with a standing ovation.

"Please, please, be seated," he said, his voice thick with emotion. "I sincerely hope you enjoyed listening to the concert as much as I enjoyed performing. The pleasure of entertaining you tonight has been overwhelming, and I cannot fully express my gratitude for your presence." He looked at Asia, bending slightly to whisper, "Please stand with me."

Asia rose, her hand finding his. They raised their joined hands, a symbol of their shared journey. She blushed as she leaned in, kissing him softly on the cheek, then giving him a warm hug.

Jakub, gazing into her eyes, said, "I want to thank my beautiful wife Asia for her unwavering support throughout my career, and most importantly," he added with a twinkle in his eye, "for her sacrifice of sleep while I practiced—when I should have been sleeping in bed beside my darling wife." He looked at her, his voice softening, "Thank you for putting up with me and my profession." Asia hugged him again, another quick kiss on the cheek, and then sat down.

Another roar of appreciation—whistles, clapping, cheers—filled the room.

"I would also like to thank the staff and musicians of the New York Philharmonic Symphony and everyone else who made this evening possible. Please, a round of applause for the orchestra!"

The audience was on their feet, and there was another standing ovation, even more enthusiastic than the last.

Jakub, waving to the crowd in a sweeping gesture, bowed repeatedly, murmuring, "Thank you, thank you," turning to face as many people as possible.

"Thank you for that incredibly generous gesture of appreciation. And I must also thank the Czech composer, Mr. Antonín Dvořák, wherever he may be, for writing such an extraordinary and dynamic piece of music—'Symphony No. 9 'From the New World,' the 4th movement piano solo arrangement. Mr. Dvořák, a fellow Eastern European, was born the first of nine children and raised in Nelahozeves, a village on the Vltava River north of Prague."

The crowd responded with cheers and thunderous applause. Jakub continued, raising his voice slightly to be heard above the din, "Again, to all the guests here this evening, please enjoy yourselves, and thank you, from the bottom of our hearts, for being here. And finally, my deepest gratitude to Mr. Chatsworth Williams for his incredibly kind words. To be mentioned in the same sentence as the great Italian poet Dante is one of the highest compliments of my career. Mr. Williams, I owe you a gracious thank you."

The applause was deafening, punctuated by whistles and cheers.

"Please, please, be seated and enjoy yourselves," Jakub said, finally taking his seat.

Chats and Claire, navigating the throng of people, slowly made their way to Jakub and Asia's table.

Jakub and Asia stood to greet them, and Chats took Asia's hand, kissing it gallantly. "Asia, you look absolutely exquisite. I don't believe I've ever seen you look so radiant." He then extended his hand to Jakub, clapping him on the back. "Wonderful speech, Jakub! You truly hit that one out of the park."

Asia, still blushing from the compliment, gave Claire a brief hug. "Thank you, Chats. That's one of the kindest things you've ever said to me."

Jakub said, "What a magnificent toast, Chats. I never realized that the quotation originated from Dante. It came up several times during my studies in Warsaw, but I haven't encountered it since coming to America."

Chats chuckled. "I seem to retain more insignificant, yet to me fascinating, information than most. Perhaps that toast is another of those little tidbits."

"On the contrary, you're a true gentleman. Those who don't appreciate your knowledge are simply envious," Jakub replied.

"You're too kind," Chats said, taking a sip of his martini.

Claire, rummaging in her purse, finally retrieved her compact. She opened it, checking her reflection. "Asia, how about we powder our noses?" She took Asia's hand, leading her away from the table. "Perhaps these gentlemen can share some trivia while we freshen up."

Chats took a long drag from his cigarette, then another sip of his martini, addressing Claire and Asia, "You two go and do whatever it is ladies do in pairs in powder rooms. When you return, perhaps we'll have solved half the world's problems."

Jakub smoothed the front of his shirt, a nervous tic, and tugged at his sleeves as he scanned the glittering room. "Chats, it's… remarkable. So many faces I recognize from newspapers and magazines. Everyone is impeccable—tuxedos, shimmering evening gowns. True high society." He let out a slow breath. "I believe I even spotted a few film stars, the governor, and other prominent politicians."

"Indeed," Chats confirmed, a hint of pride in his voice. "At least a dozen from the silver screen, several key political figures, renowned authors, and a few celebrated musicians. You performed with the New York Philharmonic, one of the world's most esteemed orchestras, in a city of this magnitude. This kind of audience is only natural."

"You know, Chats," Jakub said, his voice lowering, a new gravity settling in, "I hadn't allowed myself to consider who was out there. Our professors trained us always to block out the crowd, to focus solely on the performance. But now… reflecting on the sheer influence gathered in that audience… it's rather intimidating, looking back."

Chats broke in, "That profound statement is indeed worthy of a toast. Cheers to a maestro who understands nerves of steel are the most important part of the tool bag of a performer."

Jakub lifted his glass. "To us, Chats!" They clinked, and he drank, but the celebratory mood seemed to drain from him as he lowered the crystal. "Speaking of this city's 'magnitude'… It's a strange thing. On the drive over, Asia and I passed queue after queue. People of all ages, threadbare and worn, were waiting for a bowl of soup. It stretched for blocks in multiple places." His voice was low, troubled. "To see such desperation amidst so much… well, this," he gestured vaguely at the opulent surroundings, "it's a bitter pill. Is this what the Depression has left us with? Such widespread hunger?" He looked at Chats directly. "It's not like this in Park Slope. Not to this extent."

Chats met his gaze, his expression somber. "Four years since the Crash, Jakub. The wounds are deep and healing is slow." He let out a breath. "And now, the drums of war beat louder. Some whisper it'll be an economic cure. Perhaps." A muscle twitched in his jaw. "But I'd take a thousand breadlines over a single battlefield any day." He sighed, then asked, "Can I get you another drink, Jakub?"

"Yes, please. A vodka, straight up. And for Asia a Chablis, if you don't mind."

"Certainly. I'll be right back."

As he made his way through the crowd, snippets of conversations reached his ears. Friends he hadn't seen in ages stopped him, eager for a brief chat. He exchanged pleasantries with a few politicians and a couple of Broadway actors.

Approaching the bar, he overheard a German conversation between two young bartenders. German, one of his five languages, allowed him to follow their words easily. One of the bartenders, sporting a mustache reminiscent of Adolf Hitler, did most of the talking, while the other, a blond man with a chiseled jaw and strikingly fair features, restocked the bottled beer. Both men, seemingly in their twenties and possibly recent arrivals in New York, spoke a mixture of German and heavily accented English. The blond man's muscular build hinted at a capacity for physical strength. Chats, glancing dismissively at the Hitler-Esque mustache, instantly categorized him as a lowlife.

"Excuse me," he said, his voice laced with sarcasm, "Have you two numbskulls considered the possibility that there might be other German-speaking people in this venue? Tell me, did you learn your prejudice or inherit it?"

"We apologize, sir," the blond man with the chiseled jaw said, his voice surprisingly calm. "We were simply discussing the possibility of having to work overtime tonight. We weren't speaking about anyone in particular."

"Did you honestly believe no one would understand you?" Chats retorted, his voice rising. "I can tell one of you is from northern Germany and the other is a Berliner. So, cut the small talk. You were discussing how unbelievable it is that this entire evening is to honor a Jew. A filthy Jew, at that."

"So, what if we were? What are you, a Jew or a Jew lover?"

Chats reached across the bar, his hand closing around the blond man's throat.

"Listen here, you despicable excuse for a human being," he growled. "This wretched economy has forced countless homeless men into soup lines, forcing them to sleep on the streets, some near starvation. Any one of them would gladly trade places with you. Many of them don't speak with an accent; they were born here. That statue out in the harbor stands for the 'Land of the Free,' and you, with your thick German accent, have the right to your own opinion about Jews. Our society tolerates that. We have free speech. But that doesn't mean I have to listen to it."

He released his grip, shoving the young man backward into the back counter. Liquor bottles and glassware crashed to the floor, the shattering sound silencing conversations nearby. A small crowd began to gather.

The young man, regaining his composure, recognized the precariousness of his situation. He couldn't afford to lose his job.

"This is all a big misunderstanding," he said, his voice carefully neutral. "This gentleman misinterpreted something we said. I apologize if anyone was offended."

"Here you go, Jakub. I had them make it a double," Chats said, handing him the drink.

"What was all the commotion at the bar?"

"Something about freedom of speech, I believe. It's all under control now."

Jakub placed his drink on the table, his eyes scanning the crowded room. People continued to approach, holding out programs and pens, seeking autographs. He searched for Claire and Asia, and after ten minutes of scanning the dense crowd, the two of them appeared deep in the throng conversing with none other than the Mayor of New York and his wife. Claire looked perfectly at ease mingling with the city's elite. He was thrilled that Claire introduced Asia to James J. Walker, the mayor, and his new wife, the English actress Betty Compton.[4] Ms. Compton, a former member of the Ziegfeld Follies, had even shared the stage with Fred Astaire in "Funny Face." Claire was clearly in her element.

Taking another sip of his double vodka, Jakub said, "Chats, why don't we 'mosey on over,' as the American cowboys say on the radio, to where the mayor and his wife are? You could introduce me while our wives are with them."

"Excellent idea, Jakub. Let's 'mosey' as you say. Did you know the mayor and I are golfing buddies?"

"I had no idea."

Chats, unsure if the mayor would recognize Claire as his wife, decided he would make that connection as well.

Chats shook the mayor's hand vigorously, then took the hand of the mayor's beautiful wife, kissing it with a flourish.

"It's wonderful to see you both again. I trust you enjoyed the concert this evening. I see my wife Claire has introduced you to the wife of the man of the hour. Please allow me to present Mr. Jakub Markowicz, the maestro himself."

"Yes, it's a pleasure to meet both the spouse of such an extraordinary artist and the maestro," the mayor's wife replied, her voice warm and gracious.

"Hello, sir. It's an honor to meet you and your wife. I hope you enjoyed the concert," Jakub said, extending his hand.

"The pleasure is all ours, Jakub," the mayor said, shaking his hand firmly. "I'd like to discuss the possibility of you being a guest musical entertainer at an upcoming event at the Maidstone Club in the Hamptons, as our guest, of course. And my wife and I would be delighted to have you and your wife over for dinner sometime. I'll have my secretary contact you. By the way, we thoroughly enjoyed your remarks this evening."

Asia and Jakub strolled through the venue, Jakub pausing frequently to greet newfound admirers and sign programs and napkins. They were both touched by the genuine kindness extended by the audience. Asia couldn't help but dream of a repeat performance.

She stopped, looking into Jakub's eyes. "Does the evening have to end?"

He took her hand, his gaze meeting hers. "In a few hours, we'll be back in our Park Slope[5] apartment, ordinary Brooklyn residents once more. But we've made memories tonight that will last a lifetime." He looked upward, a silent prayer forming on his lips. "Thank you, dear Lord. If you were to take me home tomorrow, I could say I've experienced at least one day of paradise on this earth."

Asia chuckled softly, a wide grin on her face. "And here I thought I was your one day of paradise." She playfully squeezed his hand. "Be careful what you wish for—answered prayers can be dangerous, you know." They linked arms, heading toward the exit.

"The highlight of my evening was that personal invitation to the mayor's residence," Jakub said. "And yours, dear?"

"Mine was the realization that you are my husband," she said, her voice filled with emotion. "I take so many things for granted, even you sometimes." She leaned in, pressing a lingering kiss on his lips. "I love you so much, Jakub, and you know—I don't say it nearly enough. You are my life!"

"That's so sweet of you to say, Asia," he replied as a small crowd began to gather around them.

"More autographs," he said, a hint of amusement in his voice. "I'm discovering that signing autographs is something I could easily get used to." He pulled her close, whispering, "I love you, darling!" Then, his voice returning to a normal volume, he asked, "Do you really think the mayor's invitation is genuine or just a polite gesture? Will we actually dine at his residence one day?"

After fifteen more minutes of signing autographs, Jakub and Asia finally managed to escape the admiring crowd. They strolled through the smoke-filled restaurant, greeting as many guests as possible and expressing their gratitude one last time before preparing to leave. Still, more guests requested autographs, signing everything imaginable. They both wished they'd kept track of the number of signatures and handshakes.

"Perhaps we should have mingled earlier," Jakub said, stopping to chat with a group of Polish-speaking guests who were curious about their hometowns in Poland. "I had no idea it would take so long to greet everyone."

"I didn't realize my birthplace, Jozefow, was such a mystery to other Poles," Asia added.

The crowds gradually thinned as Jakub and Asia approached the concierge desk at the front of the venue and entered the queue for public transportation. They gazed out the doorway at the calm summer night, a steady stream of traffic flowing past, watching as guests lined up at street level, waiting for transportation. Turning to Asia, Jakub said, "It looks like it might be a while before we get a taxi. Why don't you have a seat?"

She looked into his eyes, a smile on her lips. "I'm fine. It shouldn't be too long."

They stepped into the high-ceilinged lobby, where a small bar featuring ten or so barstools and a thick, polished, mahogany countertop stood to one side. Behind the bar, rows of framed, autographed photos of performers adorned the wall. The double doors to the street propped open allowed the faint scent of vehicle exhaust to mingle with the air inside. The exhaust drifted through the space as a long line of vehicles queued to load guests into waiting taxis. Jakub and Asia approached the concierge desk, where a short, stocky, red-haired concierge greeted him with a broad smile and a thick Irish accent. "Hello, Mr. Markowicz. I hope you enjoyed your evening. How may I be of assistance?"

Jakub raised his eyebrows, surprised. "Interesting. You know who I am?"

"Indeed, sir. I watched you thanking everyone for the festivities tonight. That was quite an impressive speech, if I may say so. My wife and her mother were in attendance; they adore classical music."

"Thank you. I do hope your wife and mother-in-law enjoyed the performance. Could you arrange a taxi for us, please?"

"Certainly, Mr. Markowicz. I'll have one here shortly. By the way, my wife's a big fan, and, well, do you think you could sign my program, the one I kind of, uh, 'snatched' earlier this evening?"

"Of course. What's your wife's name? I'll address it to her."

The concierge, his grin widening, handed over the program. "My wife's name is Maggie."

Jakub, as he wrote, said, "To Maggie—All the best! Hope you enjoyed the performance." He signed his name and then asked, "Do you think the cab will be long?"

"It's almost three o'clock in the morning. It could be fifteen minutes or so."

"Alright. We'll wait over in the bar area."

"I'll come and get you, sir."

They sat, resting their weary bodies. Still, autograph seekers appeared, requesting signatures on a variety of items. Jakub signed a purse, the sleeve of a jacket, the inside band of a woman's hat, and countless programs. After about ten minutes, the requests finally subsided.

"Sir, Mr. Markowicz, sir! Your taxi is here," the bellman announced, his voice slightly breathless. "The driver is approaching as we speak."

"Oh, thank you," Jakub replied, handing the concierge a generous tip. "Have a good evening, sir, and please tell your wife and mother-in-law that I hope they enjoyed the performance."

They walked toward the waiting taxi. The driver, almost as wide as he was tall, was a massive man with bushy, white-blond hair and a beard that hadn't seen a trim in months. He reeked of cigar smoke and chewed on the stub of a cigar, speaking out of the side of his mouth in a thick Cockney accent. "Just you and the ball and chain, mate?"

"Excuse me?" Jakub said, staring at him.

"Ya know, mate, the ball and chain—the wife. The two of you, you and your wife, mate?"

"Oh, yes, I understand. British slang for wife. Quite amusing. Yes, just my wife and I, kind sir."

The driver had, at best, three teeth remaining on his upper jaw and perhaps five in total on his lower jaw. *How odd*, Asia thought. *The poor man has lost most of his teeth—patches of scar tissue where his beard won't grow. Did he perhaps run into a wall while driving his cab? How sad.*

"Where to, then? Where do the missus and you need to go?"

"Brooklyn, Park Slope, 1 Prospect Park SW."

In a thick, almost unintelligible Cockney accent, he replied, "Gotcha. She's a gem of a building, six stories, built in 1921. Me uncle from Ireland was a mason on that one. Know where it is. You got it. By the way, are you a famous bloke or something?"

"Yes, he is famous," Asia interjected with a proud smirk forming on her face. "He's the renowned pianist, Mr. Jakub Markowicz. You can tell your friends you had the pleasure of driving a famous musician."

"A celebrity? Bloody hell! I can't wait to tell me wife I drove a flipping concert pianist and his lovely wife home. Could you sign me racing form? I like to collect autographs of me famous patrons."

"Certainly. To whom shall I address it?"

"Me ball and chain—her name is Dorthy."

He signed the racing form, "To Dorthy, Jakub Markowicz, Concert Pianist, New York Philharmonic Symphony." Jakub passed the signed form forward and handed it to the driver.

"Thanks, mate! Bloody hell, where's that accent of yours from, mate?"

Asia answered, "We're both from Poland."

"Bloody Poland? I was in the Great War, spent most of me time at the Battle of Somme,[6] in France—'tis where I lost me teeth. A Kraut mortar shell landed about a meter away. The bloody round killed three of me mates and blew out me guts, plus a mouthful of shrapnel that took out most of me teeth. I weighed ten stone at the time. Something down there doesn't work like it used to, as today I weigh in at more than twenty stone. It has something to do with me intestines, how the docs wired me intestines. Me wife didn't recognize me when I got off the transport ship. She loves me just the same, though. It wasn't good—horrific, actually. All of us saw too much. Bloody hell, nearly twenty thousand of me mates didn't make it home."

Asia said, "Oh, I'm so terribly sorry. It sounds absolutely dreadful, unimaginable for any human to endure."

"Many thanks, madame. It was a long time ago. Me problem is the bloody mirror and photographs. I feel like the same bloke who went to war—but the bloody mirrors and photos tell a different story. The wife is French, and she hears from her family quite often. Another war might be in the bloody works. I pray not."

That is one of the most harrowing war stories I've ever heard, Asia thought.

"Driver, you can stop in the middle of the next block. Finally, here!" Jakub announced.

"Okay, Maestro."

Jakub paid for the cabbie, offering a generous tip and heartfelt words. "I sincerely hope, for all our sakes, that there isn't another war. You know, we might not have won that war if it hadn't been for the sacrifices of people like you."

"Thanks, Mate!"

The cabbie drove off into the night.

"That poor, poor man," Asia said, her voice filled with compassion. "His story brought tears to my eyes. It's such a tragic tale. Where was God the day he was injured?"

"Dear, there's a reason that poor man survived that experience while his comrades perished. We'll never fully understand God's plan. I'll collect the mail while you run upstairs and start that bath you've been longing for."

"What a truly unforgettable evening, darling," she said, unlocking the door to their apartment. "I never imagined an evening would be so wonderful."

"I will be right with you. I wish to collect our mail and the newspaper as well."

Jakub entered the apartment, his arms laden with the newspaper, letters, bills, and a stack of a dozen or so telegrams. *Presumably, well-wishers who couldn't attend the concert,* he thought. He scanned the return addresses.

"It seems news travels quickly, even across the Atlantic. We have a telegram from Poland. You must have told your friends in Poland about our big event. I suspect it's one of my music colleagues from the university."

"No! Not from me. No one over there knows anything about the concert," Asia insisted.

"Perhaps one of my colleagues happened to hear about it and wants to offer congratulations. I'll open it, and we'll know for sure."

Who from Poland would be sending a congratulatory telegram? He couldn't focus, his mind racing, unable to even guess who the sender might be.

He stopped in the hallway, out of Asia's sight, and tore open the telegram.

June 20, 1932, 16:26:00 hours stop
Henna died during childbirth stop
Excessive Bleeding stop
Twin girls are fine stop
Details to follow stop
Abram stop

The words swam before his eyes, refusing to register. His arms went limp, the telegram fluttering to the floor. A massive lump formed in his throat, choking him.

Asia called out, "Bring the telegrams in here! You can read them to me while I relax in this glorious, heavenly bubble bath."

Jakub, the telegrams clutched in his trembling hand, stepped into the bathroom doorway. Asia, standing in her housecoat, turned off the bathwater as she saw his face. A grimace suddenly contorted her features—every line etched with worry. She stared into his eyes, her voice a terrified whisper, "You're scaring me. You look as if you've seen a ghost."

He stared down at the floor, his voice barely audible, "Let's go into the living room—you can bathe later." He turned, his gaze unfocused, and walked out of the room.

"What is it? What's in the telegram?" she cried, her voice rising in panic.

He took her hand, gently guiding her to the couch. They sat in silence, his hand gripping hers tightly. He cleared his throat several times, attempting to speak, but the words caught in his throat.

After a long, agonizing pause, he finally managed to say, "Asia, something terrible has happened."

"Jakub, please, tell me what's going on! You read the telegrams, and then you tell me I need to sit down. I'm terrified. Please, Jakub, explain. Oh no!" she cried, her voice cracking. "Something's happened to Ryfka. Oh my God, Mother has died?"

"Asia, it's not your mother."

"Oh my God, it's Icek."

"Asia, it's not Icek or your mother. It's Henna."

She covered her face with her hands, a strangled cry escaping her lips. "No! No! It can't be Henna!"

He reached for her hands, his fingers intertwining with hers. "Oh, my Asia, please let me hold you."

Asia pulled away, her body rigid with disbelief. She stood, pacing across the room, then stopped, turning away from him. "Did she have an accident? What do you mean it's Henna? Henna's fine. I received a letter from her just last week. She said she was experiencing a bit more cramping than with Icek, but she was thrilled. She was so excited about having a baby girl, and I could feel her joy even through the letter. Abram wanted a girl so badly."

Jakub stood, wrapping his arms around her. "Oh, Asia. How can I possibly tell you this? Please, God, give me strength. Asia, Henna is gone. She died giving birth to twins."

She broke free from his embrace, her movements jerky and uncontrolled. She walked down the hall, removing a framed photograph of her and Henna from their high school graduation from the wall. Clutching the picture to her chest, she sat at the kitchen table, her body shaking. "There must be a mistake. Henna can't be dead. No. No. I refuse to believe it. There must be a mistake. Please, God, tell me this isn't true. She's my identical twin. We came into this world together. She's not supposed to die. Oh my God, Icek no longer has a mother!"

Jakub sat beside her, watching helplessly as her tears flowed, a torrent of grief unleashed.

She's speaking in a jumble of Polish and English non-stop, he thought, his concern growing. *Are these signs of shock? Is losing an identical twin sister so profoundly different, so much more devastating, than losing another sibling? What am I supposed to do? Is her grief clouding her judgment? Has she lost control of her emotions?* Words he'd never imagined hearing from her poured out in a chaotic stream.

Asia stood abruptly, turning to face the empty room, suddenly going silent. Her arms crossed tightly over her chest, her shoulders slumped, and she wept quietly. She began to pace again, her hands and arms moving in frantic, uncontrolled gestures.

He moved to comfort her, his arms reaching out.

They embraced, his hand stroking her back, his fingers gently running through her hair. "We'll get through this together," he whispered, his voice filled with love and reassurance. "I'll help you in any way I can, darling."

Asia screamed, a raw, primal sound, "No, dear God, please God, not Henna!"

CHAPTER SEVEN

Hamburg, Germany
June 20th, 1932, 3:15 p.m.

Helmut, driving his Hamburg Police vehicle, pulled into the Hamburg Police headquarters. His shift had ended. He and his nine-man patrol had been keeping watch over the Jewish section of Hamburg, where, in recent weeks, petty crime had skyrocketed. As a lieutenant, he supervised the patrol unit overseeing the Jewish quarter.

Helmut flipped through the reports, his brow furrowed. The list of petty thefts had become a grim catalog of violence, each line a reminder of the escalating brutality. He pushed the papers away, a sudden craving for the comfort of his home and a glass of whiskey flooding him. He prepared his reports, signed them, and submitted them to the station chief, then he grabbed his bicycle and began pedaling the two kilometers to his home. Unfortunately, police department management had him and his men working double shifts. He had enough time to grab a meal, lie down for a ninety-minute rest, and get back out and continue his assignment to protect the Jews.

Helmut pulled up in one of Hamburg's oldest neighborhoods in front of his home. His father had passed years ago and willed the property twenty-five years earlier. The two-story house looked like it came out of a storybook, with a white picket fence and a thatched roof. Olga and his two children, Heidi and Helmut Junior, were out front awaiting his arrival. Olga swept the front porch as her two little ones played in the front yard. She went about the house in a marvelous mood of cheer, a stark contrast to the grim realities he faced in his professional life.

He parked his bike while his wife and children ran to greet him. The children's faces lit up with joy as they saw their father, their excitement palpable in the air.

Entering their home, a child joyfully clamped to each leg, with Olga's arm draped warmly around his shoulder, the four of them moved as a happy tangle.

With a laugh, he scooped Heidi into his arms, her giggles mixing with the familiar scent of bay rum and pipe tobacco that clung to his uniform. Little Helmut, his father's miniature echo, stubbornly maintained his grip on one trouser leg.

"Well, now," his voice rumbled, warm with surprise. "What's all this fuss? Olga, you're a vision! And the children—scrubbed and shining like new pfennigs." His nose twitched. "And is that Sauerbraten I smell?" He inhaled deeply, eyes widening in delight.

Olga, her figure accentuated by a snug black sweater and camel-colored slacks, had thrown on a vibrant floral apron, a stark contrast to her usual elegant attire. Her blonde hair was always immaculately styled, and her light blue eyes sparkled with a hint of mischief. She leaned in, pressing a light kiss to his cheek. "No special occasion, my love. Just us. A family showing its hard-working man a little appreciation." Her words carried a deep sense of gratitude and love, making Helmut feel genuinely valued.

He held her gaze, a playful suspicion flickering in his eyes. "Nearly perfect makeup, an outfit that could stop traffic, a feast simmering on the stove, and two angels behaving themselves. This nearly perfect evening isn't some elaborate apology. You didn't finally succumb to that evening gown that spoke to you, did you?"

A delicate blush, almost imperceptible beneath her carefully applied rouge, crept up Olga's neck. "Trust me, darling," she murmured, her voice confident. "Your family adores you. Never doubt that."

He continued to appraise her, a warmth spreading through his chest despite a lingering, almost humorous self-criticism. *She looks at me like I'm—like I'm someone worth looking at. He ran a hand through his thinning hair. Clark Gable, I'm not.* But the way her eyes lingered, the way her smile held a secret only they shared, made him feel almost handsome.

Olga's meticulous attention to her appearance was not a mere vanity but a form of armor. Helmut knew this. He'd seen the way heads turned when she visited him at the precinct, the way eyes, both male and female, lingered a beat too long. The attention, he knew, was often unwelcome, but her carefully constructed façade—the impeccable style, the confident smile—was her shield. It gave her strength and a presence that inspired him and helped her navigate a world in which the public judged by appearance alone.

The look on her face reminded Helmut of the power she held, the confidence that radiated her being.

Helmut could not take his eyes off Olga as she moved about the kitchen with a large spoon in one hand and a fork in the other. Bread in the oven, potatoes on the stove coming to a boil, and two rambunctious children playing and making a commotion made the moment. Wagner's grand, soaring melody filled the kitchen, setting a dramatic backdrop for the family's evening. The routine of preparing dinner, the music, and the children's playful antics all contributed to the warm and comforting atmosphere of their home.

"Helmut dear, it is all about making sure I do my best you have a nutritious meal before going out for your second shift of work for the day." Before she completed the sentence, Helmut, exhausted from the long hours of the week, lay fast asleep on the ottoman.

"Mother, what's for dinner?" Helmut's little voice asked, with his head pointing to the ceiling. He tugged at her apron as she stood next to the stove.

She wiped the sweat from her forehead and said, "Please hand me that dish towel," as she looked down at the pale-blonde head of hair, a freckled face, bare feet, and classic five-year-old attire of green leather pants with a white, short-sleeved shirt. "You have sampled each dish here. Are you sure you need me to tell you what is for dinner?"

Sitting on the floor of the kitchen and licking cake frosting from his fingers, he replied, "Mommy, I like sauerbraten."

"Son," she declared, "there is very little in the world of food you do not like. You are very much like your father." She stepped toward the dining room, opened the cabinet, and said, "We will have a special meal this evening, so please help me set the table with the good dishes."

Barely tall enough to reach the dishes, he went to the buffet and removed the heavy, navy-blue, flower-patterned plates, cups, and saucers.

With a puzzled look on his face, he asked, "Are our gramma and grampa coming to eat or something?"

"Like I said, son, your father has been working so many hours. No, son, it will be the four of us."

Heidi, a freckle-faced, curly-haired, pale-blonde-headed, blue-eyed little angel dressed in a bright yellow sun dress and walking in her mother's high heels, entered the room and began helping her brother with the table setting.

Olga, with her hands resting on her hips, looked into little Heidi's eyes and said, "Heidi, please, dear. We have told you many times that you must be five years old to set the table. You have a couple of years yet. Trust me, sweetheart, you will be five soon."

"I help, Mommy!" Slighted, Heidi shoved her hands into the pockets of her dress and left the room, her bottom lip protruding and her head tilted toward the floor.

"Heidi, you can do one thing for me, dear."

"What, Mommy?"

"You can be a big girl and wake your father."

Helmut jumped from his lying position to a standing position and said, "Sleep? Sleep in this house. Not a chance." He scratched his head.

Olga stepped over, put her arms around her husband, and said, "I really tried today to have something special for you. You work so hard for this family. Did you at least have a good nap, dear?" she asked as she took her husband into her arms.

With clenched fists, he ground each eye simultaneously in a circular motion, walked into the kitchen, and said, "I don't know if the noise or the smell of sauerbraten cooking woke me up. This time, I will go with the cooking slant."

Helmut walked into the living room where his little Heidi had continued pouting. He picked up his darling little angel and said, "How's my little

Heidi today? You look so pretty in your sundress. I love your mother's shoes on you. Are things going your way?"

"Couldn't set the table. Mommy won't let me. Mommy mad at me!" she said as she tugged at her blonde curls.

"That is horrible! I shall have to speak with her. Anything else bothering you today?"

Folding her arms and holding them against her chest as she frowned, she exclaimed, "Mommy say, me can't play with Annie. No play, she says. Annie likes me. Annie, my friend. Why can't we play?"

Pretending to be devastated, Helmut placed his head in his hands and said, "Oh no!" as he pretended to stomp his foot. Helmut was relieved that Olga had made it happen. After being prodded for days by Helmut, Olga had discussed excluding Jewish playmates with Heidi. He hoped Olga had discussed excluding Helmut Junior's Jewish playmates as well. He thought, *I hope the kids understand that soon, no one will play with the Jewish children. I am so glad it was not I who broke her tiny heart and fractured a three-year-old's precious feelings. Today's actions must have broken more hearts than the hearts of two small children.*

Helmut carried his little parcel into the kitchen, looked into Olga's eyes, and said, "Hello, dear. Heidi tells me we have to talk."

Olga, with a stare at Helmut, winked and said, "Heidi, Father and I will talk after dinner. Are you ready to eat, Dad?"

He stepped toward his wife and whispered, "I understand you spoke with a certain child today. You will have to tell me how that discussion went." Helmut headed for the bathroom.

They finished their meal, and with the dishes done, the children were in bed and hopefully asleep. Helmut said, "What a beautiful dinner!" holding her hand in his as they walked into their bedroom.

"Supper was nice—even the children enjoyed it as well. However, I didn't think we would ever get them to sleep this evening," Olga said as she drew her bath water.

"Let's see, we met in 1920, and this is 1932. You know me well after twelve years, don't you?" he said as he massaged her hand.

Olga looked into his eyes and said, "I know how difficult the last week has been for you. I wanted to show you how much I appreciate how hard you work for this family." Then they embraced one another and kissed.

"I am in the mood to spend this beautiful evening with my overly attractive wife—but, then again, duty calls," he said as he pressed his fingers to her lips.

"You are talking to my heart," she said as she clasped her hands behind her back. "How about I pretend I'm not feeling well, and one of the children is ill? I can call the watch commander. What do you think?"

"I think that sounds wonderful, but not tonight. My men know the beauty of my wife—so they would understand," he said as he raked his hand through her hair, "But tonight, I can't leave my men shorthanded."

"Okay. Your loss, Mister Dedicated Commanding Officer," she said as she disrobed and stepped into her bath.

"Darling, keep that thought, as we may be able to carry out that ploy later in the week."

"Promises, promises," she said as she lay in the tub.

He stood in front of the mirror, and within an instant, he gasped. He didn't like the image reflected. *Am I this fat and this old?* He stared at a forty-three-year-old police officer with twenty years in the Hamburg Police Force. He had hoped for a career in engineering, but that career did not materialize. There were many reasons he had become a police officer. Number one, policing didn't require a formal education, and he often wondered if he even had the intellect to become an engineer. He would never know the answer to that question.

He would often compare his job in law enforcement to what his life may have been like as an engineer, his dream vocation. He entered this mood whenever he sensed the department taking advantage of him. His jealousy of other occupations outside of police work often haunted him. Society protected engineers from the seedy side of life. They never had to deal with the lowest class of humans walking Hamburg streets.

"I'm so tired of dealing with Jew-haters, thieves, thugs, prostitutes, drugs, drunk people, violence, and all the other seedy situations I see each day. Every day, there is no escaping the world of thugs," he said aloud as he looked into the bathroom mirror. *Forty-three-year-old? I look more like I'm fifty-three.* He had learned engineers dealt with mechanical or structural problems, not problems created by the scum of the earth types. He grew tired of dealing with the dishonest people of the world.

Like engineers, police officers solved problems and were drastically impacted by immovable, rigid, and non-retractable social issues—*three sixteen-hour days to combat the hate for the Jews in Hamburg.* The hatred for anything Jewish raged throughout all of Germany.

The summer wind broke across their faces as the curtains barely swayed in the warm, summer night breeze. The two snuggled on their couch as they both sipped on an after-dinner tea.

"Olga, it was so nice to tuck them in this evening. I don't always get the opportunity to give them that kiss on the cheek. It makes going out for a double shift that much easier."

Olga stood and stepped to the ironing board and finished pressing Helmut's police uniform. "I know you will be patrolling the streets of Hamburg again. Will you be looking out for the safety of Hamburg's Jewish population?"

He rose and sat at the dining room table. She joined him, and Helmut reached across, took her hand, and said, "Things are getting out of hand, Olga. I have no idea what may become of all this anti-Semitic nonsense." Tears welled in his eyes as he continued, "Last week, hoodlums desecrated a Jewish cemetery, and this week, we must tell our children they can no longer associate with their Jewish friends. In a few hours, I'll be protecting Jews as they leave their place of worship," he said, his voice laced with disgust. "Some of those causing the harm are off-duty policemen from our department." He slammed his fist on the table. "I don't know how long I can pretend. I am not like the others. Jews are human beings, too. They are not the rabid animal species that non-Jewish Germans make them out to be."

Olga stood and walked out of the room, a scared look on her face. She turned back to face Helmut, stared into his eyes, and twisted her wedding ring, her voice tight. "Helmut, you understand we had no other choice, not with the way things are going. Helmut Junior and Heidi could be hurt; mistaken for something they are not."

"Olga, please. I agree with you. I'm frustrated that the politics of our time have come to this. For Christ's sake, my brother is married to a Jewish woman—one we've come to love like a sister."

Helmut sat on the edge of their bed. "Tonight, I will go to work and watch my peers enjoy the brutality as party thugs inflict pain and misery on fellow humans as they leave their place of worship. Olga, we all worship the same God. Things aren't going to get any better as time goes on. Worst of all, I'm a lieutenant. Management expects me to lead. I'm their mentor. If I don't pretend to hate Jews, what will happen to my career? I must pretend I hate everything Jewish, that everything happening to anyone Jewish is justified. A person of authority is supposed to draw the line somewhere. Olga, I don't know if I can continue."

"Maybe this… this Jewish situation will fizzle out over time, dear," Olga said, her voice hopeful. "Perhaps we're seeing the worst of it right now."

"Not a chance." Helmut shook his head. "I've watched this degrade for more than ten years. It's worsening with the government's devaluation of the mark, unemployment at thirty percent, and weak political parties. We're fortunate I've even had a paycheck this long." He shrugged, jamming his hands into his pockets.

Olga stepped to Helmut's side, placed her arm around him, and said, "The newspapers say we are in for sweeping changes with the new party and its leader, Adolph Hitler. Maybe we are destined for good change?"

Olga handed him the pressed uniform as she tucked her freshly washed hair behind one ear at a time.

He stood and buffed his boots while Olga retrieved fresh socks and underwear from the bureau. She watched as he struggled to snap the top button on his trousers and said, "Trousers getting a little snug?"

He took a deep breath, held it, snapped the button, and said, "Too much sauerbraten?" He then raked his hands through what little hair remained on his balding scalp.

"Too much beer in the beer hall," Olga said with a slight smile.

"That too," he replied as he worked to wedge his hands in the pockets of his trousers.

They both left their bedroom, headed downstairs, and sat at the kitchen table.

"What is to become of your brother and his Jewish wife with all these Jewish problems we are seeing?" she said with deep concern written all over her face.

"You know yourself how we both tried to convince him that marrying a Jew would be a mistake. Love is blind! I tried my best for days to convince Hans that marrying Fraida would result in a life filled with prejudice. Hans does not see the world through the same lens I do. His world is the innocent world of processing a ship's cargo. He doesn't see the thugs of the world, the homeless German clubbing an innocent Jew on the street to steal a small sack of groceries. He doesn't see what happens when the Jew calls us for help. Even if we were to catch the thief, we would do nothing. It is a poor, homeless German against a Jew. I have seen my men expressing complete sympathy for the perpetrator who commits a crime against a Jew when the thief is doing nothing but trying to feed himself or his family. My men couldn't care less for the Jew. No one in the department at any level will do anything to help them," he said as he wiped the sweat from his forehead.

"So many people know that your brother married a Jew. The prejudice may come down to our level before this situation ends," she said as she put her head in her hands while trying her best to grasp the future.

Helmut stood, walked about the room, put his hands on his hips, and said, "You're right, Olga. I haven't thought much about that side. It has been seven months since their marriage. Perhaps people will forget that we have a Jew by marriage in our family."

The unknown future with a Jew in the immediate family caused Helmut to think horrible thoughts. He sat at the table, placed his head in his hands, and looked at Olga with a stern grin.

"For Fraida, we both need to work on an essential aspect of her life."

"What part of her life is that?"

"She needs to dissolve her present religion of Judaism and become a Lutheran like the rest of us. If she continues to attend the local synagogue, she will do nothing but compromise our entire family."

"We have a major factor in our favor," Olga said.

"And what is the factor?"

"At least she doesn't look like a Jew. She can pass for purebred Aryan."

"I agree. The government is issuing policies in the coming months that will impact the livelihood of each Jew in all of Germany. Should Hitler get elected this November, the rumors of the policies coming to Germany concern limiting the role of Jews in everyday life will restrict the rights of anyone Jewish in all of Germany. There are even rumors that the Jews will disappear from the face of the earth."

"Oh, please, Helmut, how could all the Jews of the earth disappear? Where in the world did you hear such talk?"

"Trust me, Olga, I hope for the sake of the millions of Jews that these are all rumors."

"Dear, please never share that thought with anyone else—they will think you have lost your mind."

Helmet checked his pocket watch. "Time to go, my love. I must leave now, or I will be late. One must not be late in protecting Jewish citizens. Thank you for such a fine dinner, darling."

They embraced one another.

"Don't look now, but we have two sets of eyes staring at us at the top of the stairs. They never fell asleep."

"That's okay. I will go up and hug the children one last time," he said with a happy grin.

Helmut, at the top of the stairs, said, "You two were supposed to be asleep hours ago. One last hug." He picked up Helmut Junior and little Heidi and kissed them both. "Off to bed for sure this time. Daddy must leave for work. Helmut, you must do everything Mother asks of you. As you know, in my absence, you are the man of the house."

Heidi grabbed her father's leg and gave it a big hug.

As he approached the door, he blew kisses and again said, "Love you all!"

He left, headed for his bicycle for the ride back to police headquarters. He thought, *what is the world coming to when a mother has to tell her three-year-old daughter, 'Sorry, little one, you must no longer play with your Jewish best friend, Annie.' Where and when will this ever end?*

PART II

CHAPTER EIGHT

Jozefow, Poland
June 21ˢᵗ, 1932, 6:11 a.m.

Abram pushed open the screen door, the rusty hinges groaning in protest. The dawn painted the horizon with streaks of pale pink and orange, another sunrise without Henna. His eyes burned, gritty from a night of restless tossing. Three hours, maybe less. Another day. Henna's Funeral. He swallowed the lump in his throat with a physical ache.

He squared his shoulders, drawing a shaky breath that did little to calm the tremor in his hands. *Be strong. For Icek. For the girls.* He hardened his gaze, a mask of composure settling over his face. But inside, the words tumbled like stones. *Unprepared. I should be the one in the ground. Henna should be mourning me, not the other way around.* A quick swipe of his shirtsleeves across his eyes, a futile attempt to hide the dampness. He turned, the silence of the house pressing down on him. The struggle to maintain his composure was a constant battle, a testament to the depth of his grief.

He had forbidden anyone to enter their bedroom, the room where Henna had died. He pushed the door open, the scent of stale air and something metallic, coppery, hitting him like a physical blow. The room was as it had been when the rabbi and the two women from the congregation had taken Henna's body away—a scene frozen in time, a monument to his loss. Her nightgown, stained and rumpled, lay discarded at the foot of the bed. The mattress, stripped bare, revealed the dark, horrifying dried blood, a map of her final agony. The air hung heavy, thick with the echoes of screams, moans, and the suffocating weight of that day.

Why, God? The silent scream ripped through him. *We were good! Faithful! Why her?* He ran a hand over the smooth wood of the bedpost, remembering the feel of her hand in his, her last whisper—'I love you,' the faint smile that had flickered across her lips as she slipped away. It was happening all over again. The raw wound ripped open. He yanked the curtains closed, plunging the room into a merciful darkness. He locked the door, the click echoing in the sudden silence, and fled.

He crept down the hallway, his steps silent on the worn, wooden floor. Pausing at Icek's door, he peered through the crack. His son lay curled on his side, clutching the wedding photo. His shoulders shook with silent sobs, his small hand wiping at the tears that streamed down his face, tracing the outline of Henna's smiling image.

A wave of empathy, sharp and painful, washed over Abram. *He's drowning in it, just like me.* He knew that grief. He'd felt it himself, the gut-wrenching loss of his parents. But this, this was different. What they experienced was the loss of a mother, a wound that would scar him, a void that would never truly be filled.

He'll make it. We all will. For Henna. For her memory. The shared grief between father and son, a bond that nothing in life could break, was a testament to their strength.

He moved to the kitchen, the familiar ritual a small comfort. He fed the newspaper into the stove. The crinkle made a sharp sound in the stillness—the kindling caught quickly, the flames licking at the wood, a tiny spark of warmth in the cold house. The small teapot sat waiting, a silent sentinel. Minutes later, the first tendrils of heat began to radiate outward. Abram thought *I could always rely on the routine of making tea, which is a small solace, a way to distract me from the overwhelming troubles of life. With assistance from the Almighty, Gramma Ryfka and Icek can eventually work through their grief.*

The teapot began its familiar, high-pitched whistle, a jarring sound that sliced through the quiet. Abram flinched. He glanced at the empty chair by the window—the one Henna always claimed at sunrise. He could almost see her there, her face turned toward the light, her voice whispering, '*Our gift.*' Those were her words for the sunrise, a daily miracle she never took for granted. '*We must be doing something right,*' she'd say, her eyes locking with his, '*He's given us another day.*' The warmth of the sunrise, a symbol of hope and new beginnings, was a comfort in the midst of their grief.

The tears welled again, blurring his vision. *Is this my fault? Did I displease Him?* He turned away, the weight of the question unbearable. Back down the hall, back to the porch. *Henna is gone. Gone.* The words echoed in the hollow space where his heart used to be. *How will I live without her?*

A yawn stretched Icek's small frame as he padded down the hallway, arms reaching for the ceiling. He paused at the end of the hall, peering toward the open door. His father sat silhouetted against the burgeoning sunrise, a fiery ball of orange and yellow just cresting the horizon.

"Morning, Father," Icek said softly, stepping onto the porch. Abram didn't respond, his gaze fixed on the distance.

Icek sat beside him, his arm circling his father's shoulders. He felt the tremor in his father's frame and saw the quick, cautious wipe of his eyes. *He's crying, too.* The realization was a small crack in his own carefully constructed wall of composure. "I'll wake Gramma, get her tea, and empty her bedpan." His voice trailed off.

"That sounds fine, son." His father's voice was thick. "Were you able to sleep?"

Icek shook his head, the lie catching in his throat. "Nightmares, Father. I woke up a few times."

They stood, embracing a clumsy, desperate hug. His father's gaze remained fixed on the sunrise. "Me too, son. It's the first night without her. We'll get used to it."

He turned away, staring out at the fields. Icek said, "Father, I will see Mother again, right?" His voice was a choked whisper.

The words sounded hollow, even to his ears. Icek felt the tears welling again. "I kept hearing her voice. I even went to check on her." He choked on the words. "Father, how do we do this? Live without her?"

His father's hand tightened on Icek's shoulder. "It won't be easy. But we have each other. The girls will remind us of her. Every day, we'll see a little bit of your mother in them. Our unity as a family and our shared memories of Henna will be our strength in the days to come."

Icek sniffed, wiping his eyes. "I'll get Gramma's tea ready," he mumbled, turning toward the door.

"I love you, son," his father said, his voice raw. "We'll get through this. Together. I promise."

Ten minutes later, Ryfka shuffled onto the porch, a steaming cup clutched in her distorted hands. She stared down into the swirling tea, her face etched with a weariness that went beyond mere lack of sleep. "Good morning, Abram. I sent Icek to the henhouse. Eggs, water, maybe some melons if they're ripe. He needs something to do. He's taking it hard."

Abram stood, stepping toward her. They looked at each other, a silent acknowledgment passing between them. *This life without Henna is our life now.* The forced smiles they exchanged were fragile, brittle things.

He rested his head in his hands, his voice a muffled groan. "Good. He needs to be occupied. Busy—it's the best way."

Ryfka followed him to the kitchen table, her movements slow and deliberate. They sat, the silence stretching between them, punctuated only by the gentle clinking of her cup.

"I agree. We need to keep going with our chores." Ryfka paused, her gaze distant. "Does he understand what today will bring? I know it's not my place, but have you spoken to Icek about it today? About the funeral? I thought about explaining Jewish customs, but it should come from you. A father should explain these things to his son. I wouldn't do it justice. It's not my say," Ryfka explained. She turned toward the stove, the pretense of heating water a way to avoid his gaze.

Abram rose, walking to the window. He watched Icek making his way back from the chicken coop, his slight figure dwarfed by the vastness of the fields.

He turned away, staring out at the fields, his voice a choked whisper. "Last night, I explained the wooden coffin. No metal. An aron, as we call it. And the Chevra Kaddish."

Ryfka folded her arms, her brow furrowed. "Had he heard of these customs before? What did he say about the Chevra Kaddish? About how only women prepare the body?"

Abram's hand went to his pocket, the other scratching absently at his beard. A look of frustration crossed his face. "No. He knew nothing. I told him about the women-only custom and the linen shroud. But I confused him. I didn't mean to." His voice cracked, "He didn't understand that he wouldn't see his mother again. That last time before the Chevra Kiddish, that was it. Since our faith dictates that we don't view the body after the coffin is closed—he reluctantly understood—this, I know, broke his heart."

"Oh my," Ryfka said.

"I also told him there was no need for him to worry about his new baby sisters. He knows that the rabbi arranged for wet nursing. He can be confident the twins are being well cared for. When the rabbi arrived to pick up the twins, he had two baby bottles filled with homemade baby formula. He mentioned the ingredients—cow's milk, water, and cream, in specific ratios. This was something new to me as I never knew anything about a mother's milk substitute."

Ryfka remarked, "Thank the lord above for the rabbi. The rabbi was sent from heaven above. Maybe after the burial we can go by and visit the wet nurse and let Icek hold his sisters?"

"That is a great idea. He will need something to lift his spirits after the burial of our dear Henna."

"Abram," Ryfka whispered, her own eyes filling with tears, "Why did the Almighty take our dearest Henna? Why?" She wiped the tears with her apron.

Icek returned, his basket laden with eggs. He paused on the steps— his gaze fixed on the sky.

Ryfka had noticed him pausing to look heavenward. She followed his gaze and said, "Icek, what are you looking at?"

Icek sat heavily on the steps. "I keep thinking I'll see the angels coming to take Mother to heaven."

Abram knelt beside him, grasping his hand. "Son, the angels, they've already come. Your mother, she's been in heaven since the moment she left us."

Icek stared at him, his eyes wide with confusion. "So quick? Doesn't God—I mean, doesn't He have to ask questions before He lets you in?"

Abram managed to make a weak smile, pulling Icek close. "No, son. God knew Mother. From the beginning to the end. He knew she was His child."

Ryfka wiped her eyes with the corner of her apron again. She reached out, her hand resting on Icek's shoulder. "Icek, we may not have her here with us. But Henna, she's in our hearts. Forever. The memories we'll have until our own time comes."

CHAPTER NINE

Jozefow, Poland
June 21ˢᵗ, 1932, 5:40 p.m.

Abram's gaze climbed from the rutted road to the sky, where moments ago, it was the palest of blue, now it deepened to an indigo that threatened a storm. *Please, let it stay clear,* he thought, his hands tightening on the wagon's reins.

Beside him, Ryfka, out of earshot of Icek, who lay nestled amongst burlap sacks in the wagon bed, mirrored his action. Her brow furrowed—a landscape of worry etched onto her face. 'Not today,' she murmured, a breathy prayer lost to the wind. 'Not on this day.'

Abram steered the wagon along the track, two ribbons of bare earth cutting through the undulating green of the countryside. The synagogue, their destination, was a distant silhouette, still three hundred meters away. Icek hadn't spoken a word since they'd left home. *Unnatural quiet,* Abram thought. But then, this was Icek's first real brush with death, the first time he was old enough to grasp the finality of it.

The sky continued to darken, mimicking the premature twilight of their grief, even though sunset was hours away. Ahead, the synagogue came into clearer view. A collection of vehicles—horse-drawn wagons, a few battered trucks that coughed rust and age, saddled horses, and buggies—clustered beneath the shade of ancient elms. A throng of mourners gathered before the building, a somber tapestry of dark clothing. The sight of the community standing in solidarity was a testament to the strength of their bond.

Abram's chest constricted. His throat felt like sandpaper. He gripped the reins, his knuckles bone white. A ragged breath caught in his lungs. He thought, *I don't know if I can do this.* The weight of his grief and the responsibility of guiding his son through this difficult time were almost too much to bear.

Ryfka's voice, though soft, held a core of steel. "These are the people who loved Henna, Abram. Remember her warmth, her laughter at the synagogue? She made no enemies, only friends."

They found a vacant space in the shade of an enormous oak tree. They secured the wagon and made sure their cherished horse, Boris, was in the shade. The three of them descended, becoming part of the grieving crowd. A sudden, fierce gust of wind whipped through the gathering, making the tree leaves shiver and reveal their pale undersides. Miniature dust devils danced across the dry ground. Icek, clutching Abram's hand, stared skyward, searching, perhaps, for a sign, a glimpse of his mother in the turbulent clouds. He scanned the faces of the mourners, his young eyes wide and solemn, as if committing each detail to an internal, everlasting record.

A horse-drawn wagon bearing Henna's coffin stood before the synagogue. Mourners, twenty-five strong, formed two somber lines behind it, ready for the procession to the graveyard.

Rabbi Andrjez Lamm, a small man dwarfed by his voluminous black robe and a towering, cylindrical hat, stepped forward. His full gray beard, reaching his mid-chest, swayed as he cleared his throat. His voice, surprisingly deep and resonant, filled the sudden hush.

"Welcome, family, friends," he began. "We gather in sorrow but also gratitude for the life of Henna Cweta Kelner. Born on June 15th, 1900, this world departed on June 20th, 1932. The wife of Abram Irving Kelner, mother of eight-year-old Icek and two precious daughters, Matya Asia, and Edna Henna, were brought into this world just yesterday by the grace of God. Let us pray."

He began to recite Psalms 23, his voice a low, steady drone joined by the murmured responses of the mourners:

"A song of David. The Lord is my shepherd; I shall not want."

Icek stood rigidly, a small, unmoving figure amidst the swaying bodies. Abram placed a hand on his son's shoulder, feeling the boy's slight tremor. Tears tracked silently down both their faces. The weight of his grief and the responsibility of guiding his son through this difficult time were almost too much to bear.

"May only goodness and kindness pursue me all the days of my life, and I will dwell in the house of the Lord for length of days."

The rabbi concluded with a resounding "Amen!" his arms lifted toward the darkening sky, a gesture of both prayer and farewell.

He turned to Abram and Icek, then addressed the gathering. "We cannot fathom the mysteries of the Almighty's will. We question, 'Why—why take a mother from newborn daughters?' We will not know, not in this life. But we do know that we were blessed with Henna's presence for thirty-two years—a gift. And she leaves behind echoes of herself, fragments of her spirit: endless love and countless memories for her husband. And look at young Icek." He said, his gaze softening as it rested on the boy. "He has her eyes, her complexion, her gentle spirit— a living testament. And there is Asia, her twin sister, living in America. Henna's light shines on, even in her absence." He paused—his voice thick with emotion. "We must trust that one day, the answers will be revealed. Until then, we hold onto the memories, the love, the precious gifts. May God bless and welcome Henna into eternity and watch over Abram and his family. Thank you for being here."

The rabbi moved through the crowd, offering a hand and a murmured blessing to each person. He then positioned Abram, Ryfka, and Icek at the rear of the wagon. The procession began, a slow, silent march toward the cemetery. As the wagon moved, the wind died down, and the clouds parted, revealing a sliver of blue. Ironically, the promise of a beautiful summer day hung heavily in the air.

Ten minutes later, they reached the graveyard. Henna's grave, nestled beneath the spreading branches of a great oak, had been prepared by Abram's friends from the mill.

Abram watched Icek. The boy stared at the coffin, his face unreadable. Six pallbearers, their movements slow and deliberate, lifted Henna's coffin from the wagon and placed it beside the open grave. Mourners followed behind.

The rabbi read Psalms 91, nineteen verses of comfort and hope, his voice echoing across the quiet expanse. The mourners listened with their heads bowed.

When he finished, the pallbearers lowered the coffin into the earth. They then retreated, along with the rabbi and the other visitors, to wait by the wagon. Ryfka, Abram, and Icek each knelt, took a handful of the rich, dark soil, and let it fall onto the wooden lid of the coffin—a final, tangible farewell.

Ryfka and Abram stepped back, but Icek remained, rooted to the spot. Ryfka, her voice laced with concern, asked, "Abram, what is he doing?"

Abram watched his son, his gaze steady. "He's imprinting this moment, Ryfka, and burning it into his memory. He won't forget this. I did the same when we buried my father."

Icek stood perfectly still, a small, solitary figure against the backdrop of the grave. He was murmuring, but his words were indistinct, lost to the gentle breeze. There were no tears, only a profound stillness. He scanned the scene one last time, a slow, deliberate sweep of his gaze, before turning toward the wagon, his face a mask of stoic grief.

"Who is he talking to?" Ryfka whispered.

"He's saying goodbye to Henna," Abram replied, his voice barely audible. "He knows her spirit is here. He feels it."

The rabbi approached, his hand resting briefly on Icek's shoulder. "Icek, my son, bless you. Your mother is in God's hands now. She is at peace. Go in peace, yourself." He continued on, away from the grave, embraced Ryfka, shook Abram's hand, and then led the mourners back toward the synagogue.

Ryfka and Abram waited. After several long minutes, Icek turned from the gravesite and walked toward them. The three of them embraced, a silent huddle of shared grief.

Ryfka dabbed at her eyes with a flower-patterned handkerchief. "I'm sorry," she said, her voice choked with tears. "I can't seem to stop crying."

Icek looked up at her, a faint smile touching his lips. "It's okay, Gramma. Father says it's good to cry. Isn't that right, Father?"

"Yes, son. Crying is a release. It's a way of honoring the one we've lost."

Icek's gaze met his. "Father, can we bring the twins here when they're old enough to understand?"

"We can come here as often as you like, Icek. I still visit my parents' graves, even after all these years. It's a way of keeping them close. I intend to come here often."

Ryfka nodded. "Your father is right. I've visited my dear Johanne Andrej Mikolaj's grave countless times. It's a comfort, a connection."

After exchanging hugs and handshakes with the remaining mourners, they climbed into the wagon and began the journey back to town.

The plan was for Ryfka to stay in town, away from the house that held so many fresh, painful memories. Rabbi Lamm arranged wet nursing for the Kelner twins, and both girls are thriving and well cared for.

Abram needed time alone with Icek.

Ryfka sat between Icek, who surprisingly took the reins, and Abram, now riding shotgun. They headed toward the home of Sylvia Banik, one of Ryfka's closest friends.

Icek guided Boris with an unexpected competence. "You're a natural," Abram said, a flicker of pride in his voice. "Are you sure you've never done this before?"

"No, sir. You never let me."

"Your mother would be proud, son."

"Do you think she's watching from heaven?"

Ryfka's voice was firm, unwavering. "I do, Icek. And she sees her son growing up, taking on responsibilities. You'll have your own family someday, Icek."

"I don't know, Gramma. I'm not sure I ever want to get married."

Abram chuckled softly. "We all say that son. But it's in God's plan. You'll marry—you'll have children. It's the way of things."

"If you say so, Father."

"I do. And so does the Almighty," Abram added, glancing at Ryfka.

"Indeed," Ryfka confirmed. "The Tanakh says, 'Be fruitful and multiply; swarm upon the earth and multiply thereon.'"

"That's right, son. You must not forget it."

They arrived at Sylvia's house, and Icek brought the wagon to a smooth stop. Moments later, the rabbi arrived on horseback, dismounting and tying his horse to the wagon.

Sylvia emerged from the house and settled into a rocking chair on the porch. Abram helped Ryfka down and escorted her to the porch. The rabbi approached and whispered to Abram, "Ryfka will be safe here tonight. I'll stay until they tire of me. You go with Icek. Show him that life, even without his mother, will go on."

"Thank you, rabbi. Your words are a soothing ointment to my soul." He climbed back into the wagon, letting Icek keep the reins. Abram thought, *How do I convince myself? How do I navigate this new world without Henna? How do I raise motherless children?*

Twenty minutes later, nearing home, Abram watched Icek. The boy hadn't spoken for the last kilometer—his gaze fixed on the horizon. Tears had flowed silently, intermittently, since they'd left Sylvia's. The uneven road rocked the wagon, a physical manifestation of the emotional upheaval they were experiencing. The silence between them was heavy, palpable, filled with unspoken grief and uncertainty. Only the rhythmic rumble of the wagon wheels and Boris's steady breathing broke the stillness.

Abram decided to break the silence. "I never realized how many friends your mother had," he said, his voice rough. "I didn't recognize some of the people who came to pay their respects. It shows how much she was loved. And you, Icek, were her world. Her pride. And she reminded you of your promise, didn't she? To take care of me, the twins, and Ryfka."

Icek nodded, his young face resolute, though his voice trembled slightly. "I promised. I promised her."

The sun dipped lower, casting long shadows. Abram decided a change of subject was needed. A shift toward the future, however daunting. "We're both going to be tested, Icek. You've never been around infants, let alone two. It's going to be different. Babies need their mother's milk to thrive. Without your mother, we have to find another way. And babies, they eat, they pee, they poop. Constantly. And they cry. Our lives are going to change. I can't stop working. If I don't work, we don't eat. You and Ryfka, you'll have little time to yourselves until the twins are older. Much older."

The only sounds were the wagon rumble, the chirping of insects, and Boris's heavy breaths. The silence had taken on a new dimension, a shared understanding of the challenges ahead.

Icek unhitched Boris, lit a lantern, and led the horse to his stall, providing fresh water and food. He brushed Boris's coat with slow, deliberate strokes, the same way he'd done countless times before. But this time was different. He thought, *last time, Mother was waiting for me*, her warm and welcoming smile, her belly swollen with the promise of new life.

He glanced at the setting sun, a fiery spectacle of color, and the reality crashed down on him. *I will never see that smile again.* Tears welled up, blurring his vision.

With the barn secured, they walked toward the house. About twenty-five meters from the entrance, Icek stopped. "Father," he said, his voice barely whispering, "can we not go inside yet?"

"Of course, son." Abram's voice was gentle. "Let's get some chairs, some firewood. We can build a fire and sit outside for a while." He placed a hand on Icek's shoulder, feeling the boy's slight tremor. "I need you, Icek. Just as much as you need me. It'll be hard walking into that house without her. Take your time. We'll sit, we'll think, and we'll be together."

Icek helped gather kindling and newspaper, his movements practiced and efficient. "Father," he said, his voice stronger now, "I've accepted that Mother is in a better place. No more pain, no more sadness. Like the rabbi said, 'God is taking care of her now.' I'll talk to her every day. I know she won't answer, but I think she'll be listening."

Abram knelt by the fledgling fire, adding more kindling. "You do that, son. And she will hear you. And sometimes, you'll feel her answer deep inside."

They stood, embracing. Abram said, his voice thick with emotion, "Thank God we have each other."

"Father, what will we do about Mother's things?"

"The rabbi will be by tomorrow with a wagon. He'll take her belongings to the synagogue to be distributed to those in need. He asked for my permission at the funeral. What's left that can't be used, we'll burn it. It's not disrespectful, son. It's a way of letting go."

Icek nodded, his eyes clear and unwavering. "I understand. We'll have the photos, the family Bible, and her favorite chair on the back porch. And I feel her, Father. Right now. I feel her near us."

Abram looked up at the sky, the last sliver of the sun disappearing below the horizon. "I feel her, too, Icek. It's a good feeling. A comforting feeling." He placed his hand on Icek's shoulder, a silent acknowledgment of the boy's strength, a strength that surprised even Abram himself.

"Father, what will be my job with the twins?"

"Your job will be whatever Ryfka or I or anyone who comes to help asks of you. It's going to be a rough road, son. But God will provide. He's already working on it; new mothers, wet nurses, to provide milk for the girls."

Icek looked skyward. "The help will come from heaven, right, Father?"

"Yes, son. He's finding the women who can help. Women who have recently given birth have enough milk to share. It sounds strange, I know, but it's nature's way. It's God's plan."

"God is pretty smart, isn't he, Father? I... wish He could have saved Mother."

"We'll never know why, Icek. But there was a reason. And one day, when we're all reunited, we'll understand. We'll have the answers."

"How often do babies eat?"

"At the beginning of a newborn's life, they seem to be hungry at all times of the day. And they poop even more than they eat. And their poop has a smell unlike anything you've ever encountered. And sleep? Your sleep and my sleep—they become a precious commodity."

Icek grimaced. "I'm really not sure I ever want to get married and have kids."

Abram chuckled softly. "We'll find help, Icek. We'll get through this. The first twelve months, they're the hardest." He paused, his gaze drawn to the horizon. "Icek," he murmured, "look at that sunset. It's magnificent."

Icek followed his gaze. "Do you think Mother had something to do with it?"

"We can't know for sure. But we can't rule it out, either. We must never underestimate the power of the unseen."

An hour later, they continued to sit by the fire, the flames casting flickering shadows. Abram spoke, his voice softer and more reflective now. "Do you know how I met your mother?"

"She started to tell me once, but she never finished the story."

"I thought you knew."

"You're going to tell me, Father?"

"Yes, son. It's a story that warms my heart, even now."

"Mother's spirit is alive in your heart, right, Father?"

"Yes, Icek. The heart holds onto the things that matter most. And no mortal man has ever figured out how to empty it. Thank God for that."

"And how did you two meet?"

"It was at the Jozefow synagogue, an outdoor concert, a beautiful spring day in 1918. She was eighteen. She and her sister, Asia, were sitting on a blanket in the back of their wagon, a picnic basket between them. I'd never seen identical twins before. They were radiant. Beautiful, funny, full of life. And they could sing. Harmonies that sounded like angels."

"Did you know her before that day?"

"No. I was handing out programs, small sheets of paper listing the songs the musicians were to perform, plus a small paragraph about the college they were from. And Henna approached me. 'May I have a program?' Our eyes met, and everything changed. My heart melted. We just stared at each other, speechless. Asia came over and broke the spell, asking, 'Are you two alright? You look like you're in a trance.'" He chuckled at the memory. "It was a miracle, really. Seeing two identical girls is so beautiful, so captivating. And Asia, she was drawn to Jakub, the pianist, her future husband. He was playing in a quartet that day, classical music, something I'd never heard before—a giant piano, a cello, a viola, a violin. They played for two hours, and I sat between your mother and Asia. Asia loved the music—she loved Jakub. And I fell in love with your mother."

"You and Uncle Jakub both fell in love at the same time?"

"Yes, son. On the same day, at the same moment. You'll know it when it happens, Icek. You'll feel it. It hits you like a thunderbolt."

"You don't know it? You feel it?" Icek pondered.

"Exactly. No one has ever been able to explain love. It's a mystery."

"It sounds like one."

"It is son. It is."

"Who got married first?"

"Your mother and I. September 7th, 1920, right here in Jozefow. Asia went on to study music at the same school as Jakub."

A long silence followed. Abram's head fell into his hands, and he wiped his eyes with the red handkerchief he always carried.

"I'm sorry, Father. I didn't mean to make you cry."

"No, Icek. It's the dream. To grow old together. We talked about it so much, your mother and me. For twelve years, I was blessed. Truly blessed."

Icek stood and added more logs to the fire, his movements deliberate and careful. "Do you think Mother is happy in heaven?"

"I do. I think Mother is watching us right now. I feel her spirit."

"Maybe someday, maybe I'll learn to feel it too?"

"You will, son. And it will warm your heart. Ryfka feels her husband's spirit, even though he's been gone for years. You can see it when she prays. She talks to him—she feels his presence. She's told your mother and me about it many times."

"What happened to Gramma's husband? I know she misses him. I've seen his picture, but I never asked. I was afraid it would upset her."

"It's painful for her to revisit those memories. She was Ryfka Amelia Dmowski before she married Johanne Mikolaj. He died in 1910, at forty-seven, in a barn fire. He tried to save the workhorses. The roof collapsed. He didn't make it. Ryfka's never been the same. I tried to encourage her to see other men, but she said it would be disrespectful to Johanne."

"Our family, we've had our share of sadness."

"Every family does, Icek. Things happen that we don't plan for, things that shouldn't happen, but they do. We never dreamed your mother would have trouble with the twins. But we knew the risks. So many women don't survive childbirth. We just refused to talk about it. And now, she's gone. And you, Icek, you'll remember every detail of these past few days. Every moment, just like I remember my father's death, Ernst Marek Kelner, born February 17th, 1869, died at fifty-two in 1921. It's the clearest memory I have. And my mother, Agata Krystyna, born in 1877, died in 1908 of typhoid fever. I remember her love for my father, her cooking, and their singing together. I wish I had more memories, but I was only nine. When Father died, it was a storm, a lightning strike. He was harvesting hay. The power of it burned his clothes and his body. Seeing his body lying in the back of a wagon, covered with a tarp, it's an image I'll never forget. The rabbi thought it was important for a son to see his father. But I couldn't recognize him. And I wished, later, that I hadn't seen him like that. I still see it, Icek, as clear as day."

"That's, that's an awful way to die."

"I thought so, too, for years. But maybe it's quick. Maybe there's no suffering. We can't know. You would have loved your grandfather, Ernst. He told stories, he played the guitar, and he sang Polish folk songs. He's always in my thoughts."

"A lightning strike is something you can't plan for."

"Exactly, Icek. It's one of those things I was talking about. The bad things that happen that we can't prevent. We have to accept that."

"I'll be nicer to Gramma. Maybe it will help her be less sad."

"Ryfka adores you, Icek. She thinks you're the finest young man in Jozefow."

"When we get back to the house, I'm going to write all this down. So, I can tell the twins and my children someday."

"You can, Icek. But most of it's in the Tanakh,[8] the Hebrew Bible. Adding your details wouldn't hurt."

CHAPTER TEN

Jozefow, Poland
June 22nd, 1932, 7:35 a.m.

The sun, already well above the horizon, cast long shadows across the yard. Abram, stiff from a night spent dozing in a lawn chair not meant for sleeping, pushed himself up. A stretch cracked his back, and a yawn escaped him. "Icek? You up?"

"Father?" Icek's voice was thick with sleep. "What time is it? This chair wasn't easy to sleep in."

"Son, I woke up in the middle of the night and thought I heard the twins crying. I know this is impossible, as the twins are miles away, safe at the home of a wet nurse."

"Father, do you think the twins are doing okay? What if they don't like their food?"

"No worry there, as babies come into the world pretty darn hungry. We will see them soon. It's time we moved from the backyard to the house. We have plenty to do today. We need to get moving, son." Abram's voice was firm, but a tremor ran beneath it. "We need to get the wagon and Boris and load Mother's bedding for the burn pile by the barn." He paused, his gaze meeting Icek's. "This won't be easy, son. Not for either of us." He placed a hand on Icek's shoulder, its weight conveying more than words. "We have to help each other. We've lost your mother. A piece of our souls went with her." He drew a shaky breath. "We'll go into the house, and Henna won't be there. She'll never be there again." He squeezed Icek's shoulder.

"Will we ever be used to Mother not being here?"

He shook his head, unable to finish the thought. "We'll put the loss of your mother behind us in time. But get over it? Never." His voice cracked. "God should have taken me. I should have gone before her." Its unfairness hung heavily in the air.

They walked toward the barn, the silence punctuated only by the crunch of their boots on the path.

"It's the forever part, Father," Icek said, his voice small. "That's what I can't figure out." He blinked rapidly. "I keep seeing her lying in bed, a baby in each arm. That smile, even if it was just for a minute, she was so happy to be a mother."

"I know, son." Abram pulled Icek into a rough embrace, a rare display of open affection. For a long moment, they clung to each other, and Icek felt the dampness of his father's tears on his neck.

"Why, God?" Abram's voice was a raw whisper directed at the empty sky. "Why Henna? My beautiful wife, why?"

They continued up the path, the barn doors looming ahead. Icek heaved them open, the familiar creak echoing in the sudden stillness. Boris shifted in his stall, snorting and stamping his hooves, the same excited greeting he gave to anyone who entered.

With the wagon and Boris positioned outside their home, Icek and Abram exchanged a look, a silent acknowledgment of the task ahead. They paused, bracing themselves, then stepped inside.

Icek went into the kitchen, the familiar scent of woodsmoke and something indefinably his mother catching in his throat. He reached to pull out a chair at the table, but his hand froze. An envelope lay on the worn wood, addressed to the Kelners in a neat, precise hand.

"Father, look." He held it out. "It's from Bernard Goldstein, the rabbi's assistant. He must have been here earlier."

Abram took the letter, his fingers tracing the familiar script. He unfolded it and began to read, his brow furrowing with each line.

June 21, 1932

Abram,

May our Heavenly Father be with you as you and your family journey down this new path. May God bless all. The twins are well cared for. They are being wet nursed by Anita Swartz. Her son was born last week, and she has plenty of milk to breastfeed the twins and her son. Ryfka is with her as well. While a wet nurse feeds one baby, another set of hands will care for the other child.

By the way, Ryfka was not feeling well, which is indeed understandable, considering what she had been through the previous few days. She said she thought she overdid things. She was looking forward to catching up on her sleep. There were eight births in the previous month in our village, and another four will occur in the next week or so. We will solicit candidates for others to act as wet nurses in the coming days. We are confident we will have this covered. Our members are working together to keep the twins supplied with clean diapers. A few congregation members and I will stop by in the morning to help you navigate the next few days. We will bring you meals and assistance in keeping your home clean. A new feather bed is being donated, complete with fresh linen. I suggest that you collect Henna's bedding and mattress and burn them.

We had members there today sorting through Henna's clothing. We hope you agree that removing her clothing will benefit you and the family. Henna's attire will be welcomed by those less fortunate members of our synagogue, as plenty in our congregation are needy. Also, we straightened up the entire home, cleaned all dishes, and washed the linen and any dirty clothes that our parishioners found. It will be best to allow the twins to stay with Anita, as with breast milk each day, they will be more muscular and have a lower likelihood of developing an illness.

With the breastfeeding of her son and the twins, Anita's milk will soon deplete. That is why we have already notified the other young mothers in the area. We hope that several local mothers will share wet nursing for the twins. We must not compromise the quantity of breast milk available for newborns in our village.

More than anything else, please go to work and return to your old routine. We will cover for you each day while you work. Your family deserves a sense of normalcy in your life as fast as we can deliver it, particularly for Icek. We will have a couple of women from the synagogue at your home before you leave each day. Remember, God will care for you and your loved ones as you suffer this loss.

God Bless,

Bernard Goldstein

His father lowered the letter, his gaze distant. "Icek," he said, his voice heavy with gratitude, "fold this, put this letter in the Tanakh. Years from now, this will be a record of the kindness of our village and of the people who stepped in when we needed them most." He shook his head slowly. "We're so fortunate, so fortunate to have this help." He gestured toward the bedroom. "Let's get the mattress and bedding. Add it to the fire I've already started."

They worked in silence, the task grim and heavy. The mattress, stained with the evidence of Henna's final struggle, was awkward and bulky. They wrestled it, along with the bloodied clothes and blankets, folding the feather mattress with difficulty but getting it through the doorway. They heaved the items onto the wagon, their weight settling like a stone in Abram's chest.

"Icek, grab the small bench from the porch," his father said, his voice rough. "We'll need a place to sit while the fire burns."

"Good idea, Father."

They headed toward the barn, Icek leading Boris, the wagon piled high with the remnants of Henna's life. Abram grabbed the lantern from its hook in the barn, the metal cold against his palm. He poured fuel onto the pyre, the acrid smell stinging his nostrils, then they positioned the bench a safe distance away and sat, staring into the growing flames.

As the first lick of fire caught the edge of the mattress, a plume of smoke rose, twisting toward the sky. His father watched it, his jaw tight. He reached for Icek's hand, gripping it tightly. "The sun has risen only once since we buried Henna," he began, his voice low and raw with grief. "We've burned her bed, her clothes will go to the needy, but the memories, son, they stay. They're woven into the very fabric of this house. Everywhere we look, there's proof that Henna lived, that she was here."

Icek gazed up at the vast, cloudless expanse of blue. The sheer, indifferent beauty of the day struck him with a fresh wave of sorrow.

"It's too pretty a day for this, son," his father murmured. "Too pretty to be burning your mother's things."

"Maybe, maybe Mother planned it this way, Father," Icek said softly. "She's up there, somewhere, isn't she?"

His father followed his gaze, his heart clearly aching. "Yes, son," he whispered. "She is. She's watching over us right now."

CHAPTER ELEVEN

Park Slope, Brooklyn, New York
July 1ˢᵗ, 1932, 7:35 a.m.

Jakub, toothpaste foam clinging to the corners of his mouth, leaned into the bathroom doorway. "Asia?" he called, his voice muffled by the minty froth. "The rabbi, isn't it today?" Glancing at the clock on the wall, its hands pointed firmly at half-past nine.

Asia, perched at her vanity, carefully applied a stroke of rouge to her cheek. "Ten-thirty, Jakub," she replied, her voice calm, almost measured. She picked up a silver-backed hairbrush, her gaze fixed on her reflection. "Has it really been twelve days?"

Jakub crossed the bedroom, the floorboards creaking softly beneath his stockinged feet. He reached out, his hand hovering over Asia's shoulder for a moment before resting lightly on her cheek. His mind was a whirlwind of guilt and regret.

"Good morning." The scent of her perfume was a familiar, comforting jasmine, filling his senses.

Asia looked down at the small calendar on her dresser, a tiny 'x' marking each passing day. "Yes. Twelve."

She placed the brush down with a delicate clink and turned her head slightly, her eyes still shadowed with a lingering sadness, meeting his. "Thank you," she said, her voice barely above a whisper, "for arranging this. I needed to be out of these walls." Her fingers traced a pattern on the embroidered runner of the dresser, a nervous, repetitive motion. A stray strand of light-brown hair escaped her carefully coiffed style—she absently tucked it behind her ear. She started again on the task of pulling a brush through her hair, "And, Jakub, I keep thinking about the trips, the ones we didn't take."

She stood, turning to face him fully. The embrace was automatic, instinctive. He held her close, inhaling the jasmine again, trying to offer a silent reassurance he wasn't sure he felt himself. "Hindsight," he whispered into her hair, his voice tight with shared grief, "it's a cruel teacher. We couldn't have known." He pulled back slightly, cupping her face in his hands. "We should have gone—both of us. Icek, he's almost nine. Nine years, and all he knows of us are letters, and…" He trailed off, his thumbs tracing the delicate bones of her cheeks, a silent acknowledgment of their shared pain.

Asia's gaze was steady. "Photographs. Thank God for those, at least. But they don't even have a camera, Jakub." She shook her head, a small, frustrated gesture. "We could have sent them a camera, plus film—we could have had real pictures." Her words carried the weight of their regret, a longing for a past that neither of them could change.

Jakub squeezed her shoulders gently. "We can dwell on 'should haves' all day, Asia. It won't change anything. It won't bring her back." He felt a familiar ache in his chest, a dull, persistent throb. "We're not perfect. We never are. We just ran out of time."

Asia's lower lip trembled after looking at her reflection. With an unsteady hand, she blotted a tear. A fresh wave of tears arrived, threatening to spill over. "She was me, Jakub. My other half. I look in the mirror, and I see her, but it's not her."

Jakub reached into his pocket, pulling out a neatly folded handkerchief. He gently dabbed at the tears that traced paths through her carefully applied makeup. "I know," he said softly, his voice rough with emotion. "No one else can understand that. No one. I can't fix it." He watched her, his heart heavy. She was dressed impeccably elegant as always, but the light in her eyes had dimmed. "Look," he said, forcing a lighter tone, "I feel like a walk. You take a cab. I'll meet you at the synagogue after your appointment."

"I love you, Jakub," she said, the words a lifeline. Another embrace, a quick kiss, and then the practicalities.

"You'll be late," he said, gently nudging her toward the door.

She left, and the apartment immediately felt vast and empty without her. Jakub wandered, his hands clasped behind his back. He stopped at the window leading to the fire escape, the metal cool beneath his touch. He unlatched it, the hinges groaning in protest, and crawled out, settling onto one of the worn folding chairs. The city noise rose to meet him—

a cacophony of honking horns, the shouts of vendors, the rumble of distant traffic.

He closed his eyes, trying to focus on the sounds to distract himself from the gnawing emptiness. *How many others out there are carrying this weight today?* he thought. We can't be alone in this. He pictured Asia, her face drawn and pale. *I have to find a way to do something. Maybe the rabbi can reach her where I can't.* He thought of the doctor's visit, the clinical words— *complicated grief, lifelong impact.* They didn't help.

Back inside, he sat at the piano, his fingers automatically finding the familiar keys of a Beethoven sonata. But the notes felt hollow, his concentration fractured. He stopped abruptly, the silence of the apartment pressing in on him. *I'm just making mistakes,* he thought, frustration simmering beneath his sadness.

He glanced at the clock. Forty minutes. He couldn't stay here, trapped in this suffocating stillness. He rose, a sudden decision forming. He'd go to the synagogue. Maybe he could take his sweet wife to lunch—a small hope, fragile but persistent.

The warmth of the summer day enveloped him as he stepped onto the street. The cloudless sky, usually a source of joy, felt indifferent to his turmoil. He pictured other days, brighter days—strolling with Asia in Prospect Park, the salty spray of the Staten Island Ferry on their faces, the hushed reverence of the art museum. *Not today,* he thought. *Not yet.*

The synagogue came into view, its familiar stone facade a comforting sight. Jakub's gaze fixed on the entrance. *Please, let it have helped,* he thought, a silent prayer. *Let my Asia be a little bit better.*

Restless, Jakub walked to the nearby newsstand. The vendor, a stout man with a bushy grey beard that obscured most of his chest and a gap-toothed smile revealing teeth the color of a faded pumpkin, greeted him with a thick German accent. "Morning, fine, sir. Is there something I can get for you?"

"A *Daily*," Jakub replied, handing over the coins. He scanned the headlines, his eyes searching for any mention of Europe, of Poland. The front page was dominated by Amelia Earhart's daring flight and Roosevelt's presidential campaign. He breathed a small sigh of relief. *No news is good news,* he thought.

A small voice broke through his preoccupation. "Hey, mister! Shine? Your shoes could use some love, sir. I'll sparkle 'em! Whaddya say?"

Jakub looked down. A boy, no older than seven, with a shock of fiery red hair, a constellation of freckles, and an eager grin that revealed a prominent overbite, was perched on a battered shoeshine box. His clothes were worn and patched, his baseball cap frayed and faded.

Jakub tucked the newspaper under his arm. "How much?" he asked, a flicker of amusement warming his somber mood.

"One shiny dime, sir!"

"You've got a deal," Jakub said, placing his foot on the box.

The boy worked with a focused intensity, spitting and buffing, his tiny hands moving with surprising dexterity. Jakub alternated between glancing at the synagogue door, reading snippets of the newspaper, and watching the boy.

"You got a funny accent, mister," the boy said, his voice muffled by his efforts. "Like my neighbor, Vladimir. He's from Russia."

Jakub lowered the newspaper slightly. "Poland," he corrected gently. "Warsaw. A long way from Russia."

He checked his pocket watch. Eleven minutes.

"Finished!" the boy announced, beaming with pride. "How's that?"

Jakub examined his shoes, the leather gleaming. "Excellent work," he said, genuinely impressed. He handed over a dime and an extra nickel. "And tell me your name, young man."

"Mikey McCreary, sir!"

Jakub shook the boy's hand, the small grip surprisingly firm. "Pleasure to meet you, Mikey McCreary. I'll be back."

"Thanks, mister! Tell your friends! I'm here every day!"

"And I'm Jakub," he said as he walked toward the synagogue.

Mikey, a bright face with unexpected joy, chirped, "Swell, Mr. Jakub! See ya soon!"

Jakub spotted her half a block away, walking toward him. Asia's beige skirt and white lace blouse, even from a distance—*it's easy to see the beautiful Asia heading his way.* Her light-brown hair, how it caught the sunlight, and her breathtaking looks—*I am one lucky guy.* But there was something new, something he hadn't seen in days: Asia wearing sunglasses. He thought *she's hiding her crying eyes.*

He thought about Asia having to, yet again, tell the story of how much she missed her sister, losing her twin sister, and her guilt for not having traveled back to Jozefow to visit her family. *I must do my best to listen and do everything possible to cheer her up.* He waved both arms in the air to attract Asia's attention, trying to catch her eye.

They met halfway. The embrace was familiar and comforting. The scent of Asia's jasmine perfume was a brief moment of normalcy in a world that had turned upside down.

"Hello, darling," he said, his voice carefully neutral. "There's a café around the corner. Tea? Coffee? Or maybe a glass of wine?"

"Wine," she said, the word is a small concession. "That sounds nice."

The waitress greeted them with a polite, "Table for two?"

"Outside, please," Jakub replied, gesturing toward the sun-drenched sidewalk. "It's a beautiful day."

They settled into a quiet corner table, the waitress placing menus before them and leaving with a practiced smile.

"This was a good idea," Asia said, taking a sip of the ice water the waitress had left. The clinking of the ice against the glass was a slight, sharp sound in the relative quiet. "Wine, fresh bread, a salad. It all sounds lovely."

The waitress returned with an order pad in hand. "Have you decided?"

"Yes," Jakub said. "My wife will have a glass of Pinot Grigio, and the house is fine. I'll have the Chablis. And we'll both take the garden salad and fresh bread."

The waitress paused, her pen hovering over the pad. "Excuse me, sir," she said, a hesitant smile on her face, "but are you Jakub Markowicz, the pianist?"

Jakub felt a flush of warmth. "I am," he admitted. "Were you at the symphony?"

"Yes! I'm a student at the Manhattan School of Music, cello. A few of us went. And I'm sorry, but I recognized you because of your wife."

She gestured toward Asia, her eyes widening slightly. "We were quite a way back, but after that speech about Dante, well, she's just so beautiful."

Jakub turned to Asia, a genuine smile spreading across his face. "See? I'm not the only one who thinks so."

Asia, her cheeks tinged with a faint blush, joined in. "Thank you," she said to the waitress, her voice regaining some of its former warmth. "That's very kind. Would you like an autograph?"

The waitress's eyes widened. "Oh, I don't want to be a bother. I've never..."

"It's no bother at all," Jakub assured her, gently touching her hand. "Thank you for coming to the concert. And good luck with your cello."

"I'll get your order in right away," she said, her voice a little breathless. "Thank you. I won't forget this."

Asia watched her go, a faint smile playing on her lips. "Well," she said, "that was unexpected. You have fans everywhere." She paused, taking another sip of water. "And, apparently, so do I. But Jakub, about the rabbi?" She hesitated, her fingers tracing the rim of her water glass. "The rabbi said it might help if I went to Jozefow. To see Abram and the twins."

Jakub's fork, halfway to his mouth, froze. "Jozefow?" he repeated, the word a question. "What would be the purpose?"

Her face lit up, a spark of genuine animation returning to her eyes. The grip she had on Jakub's hand intensified. She leaned forward, her voice dropping to a conspiratorial whisper. She held his hand tightly. "Jakub, imagine if they were here—Abram, Ryfka, Icek, the twins. We could get a bigger place. I could help raise Henna's children. It would be therapeutic, the rabbi said. Chats could handle the details. What do you think about immigration?" Her voice rose with a desperate plea. "Darling, please say something!"

He stared at her, his mind reeling. He set down his fork, the clatter loud in the sudden silence. "Asia," he said slowly, carefully, "I don't know what to say. It's a lot to consider. Bringing them all here, Abram, leaving Poland? And Ryfka? And the twins, so young, on that journey."

He shook his head, trying to process its enormity. "It's not impossible, but…"

She squeezed his hands, her eyes shining with desperate hope. "But it would be everything, Jakub. For me. For them. Being able to care for Henna's children would be the greatest gift."

Lunch proceeded, the conversation swirling around the impossible yet suddenly tantalizing prospect of bringing the family to America.

Jakub provided the autograph—a carefully penned message of encouragement to a budding musician, and Asia, at Jakub's insistence, added her signature. This small act seemed to lift her spirits further.

As they left the café, they passed the newsstand, and Jakub spotted Mikey McCreary, his shoeshine box gleaming in the sun.

"Asia," he said, "there's someone I want you to meet."

Mikey, spotting them, jumped up, his face breaking into a wide grin.

"Asia, this is Mikey McCreary, the best shoeshine artist in New York. Mikey, this is my wife, Asia."

"Pleased to meet you, ma'am," Mikey said, his voice brimming with enthusiasm. "Your husband's a great customer! Promised to come back and spread the word!"

Asia smiled a genuine, warm smile that reached her eyes. "Mikey, it's lovely to meet you. I have a nephew who is about your age. He might be coming to America soon."

Mikey's eyes widened. "Really? Swell! I can show him around!"

"We have to go now, Mikey," Jakub said, "but I'll see you soon."

"That'd be swell, Mr. Jakub!"

Back in the apartment, the silence felt different now, less oppressive. Jakub sat at the piano, his fingers moving over the keys, playing a Mozart piece, a melody that Asia loved. He glanced up at her, her face softer, less strained.

"Darling," he said, his voice gentle, "I'm so glad you saw the rabbi. You seem better."

She met his gaze, a faint smile playing on her lips. "Better?" she echoed. "Is it that obvious?"

"Yes," he said, "very."

She sighed, a long, slow exhale. "The darkness lightens a little because the rabbi, Jakub, offered help. He told me that even though Henna is gone, she remains." She touched her chest, her hand over her heart. "In here. Nobody can take away the memories. Ever."

Jakub rose from the piano stool and went to her, taking her hand. He pulled her close, the familiar comfort of her presence a balm to his own aching heart.

Maybe, he thought, *just perhaps, she's coming back to me*. The question of Poland, of the twins, hung in the air, unspoken but ever-present. He knew it wouldn't go away. He thought of Chats, the practicalities, the possibilities. *A business trip? Could it be done?* He looked at Asia, her face still etched with a lingering sadness but with a flicker of hope rekindled. *For her*, he thought, *I'll do whatever it takes.*

CHAPTER TWELVE

Park Slope, Brooklyn, New York
July 2ⁿᵈ, 1932, 9:30 a.m.

Jakub sat at his piano on Friday morning, fingers hovering over the keys. He launched into Beethoven's *Moonlight Sonata No. 14, Op 27, No. 2, I.* The familiar notes, usually a comfort, felt clumsy and disjointed. He stumbled—a sharp discord jarring the quiet apartment.

"Damn it!" The words escaped in a frustrated hiss. He slammed his hands into his lap. His reflection, pale and strained, stared back from the polished wood. The Warsaw Music School loomed in his memory, the sonata a symbol of his past mastery, a skill that now felt agonizingly out of reach. *Will I ever be able to master a complicated piece again?* he pleaded, not bothering to voice the words. *Please, dear God, grant me the skill I once had.*

He loved the work—it ranked as one of Beethoven's most famous pieces, performed by some of the best symphonies in the world. He glanced at his watch. Ten-fifteen. Mr. Williams expected him for lunch at eleven thirty. The sonata, a sixteen-minute endeavor, would have to wait. *I mustn't be late.*

A wave of guilt washed over him. He should be practicing and pushing himself, but his mind was a whirlwind of worries, all revolving around Asia. Claire Williams's call, just days after Henna's death, echoed in his ears. The offer of help, the unspoken understanding of Asia's fragility, was a lifeline, and he'd grasped it.

He rose, the unfinished sonata a silent reproach. A quick scan of the apartment revealed the aftermath of grief, a lingering disarray that mirrored the chaos in their lives. *I'd better get this place in order.* Dishes were piled in the sink, a rumpled bed, with clothes scattered about. He moved through the rooms, a whirlwind of tidying, each action a small attempt to impose order on the disorder. The laundry basket, overflowing, was the final task.

He rechecked his watch. *Time is on my side.* A quick trip to the florist and the wine shop, and he'd be ready.

The scent of lilies and roses enveloped him as he stepped into the flower shop, a familiar haven just two doors down. Sheila McAllister, the owner, her voice a warm Scottish burr, greeted him. "Hello, Jakub. Any news on Asia? Those in the neighborhood have been wondering. None of us can even begin to understand." Her voice trailed off, sympathy etched on her face.

"Difficult, as you can imagine," Jakub said, the words heavy with understatement. "Asia's psychiatrist says it will take time. A slow process, but she is making progress." He forced a hopeful tone, needing to believe it himself.

"So glad to hear this."

"Today, I need bright, cheery," he gestured vaguely, "something to lift the spirits." He'd cleaned and prepared, but the apartment still felt hollow. "Flowers, a splash of color, might help."

"You came to the right place. I will fix you up free of charge. I miss seeing Asia. You're a favorite customer."

"Thank you," Jakub said, gratitude warming him. "I'll be back shortly. I must pick up wine for dinner."

Back in the apartment, the vibrant bouquet, a riot of color, sat on the dining room table next to the bottle of wine: a small victory, a fragile attempt at normalcy. Jakub rushed downstairs, hailing a taxi with a wave, determined to keep moving forward despite the weight of his decisions.

The chill of the morning air did little to cool the heat coiling in his gut. He'd been pacing the corner, the imagined conversation with Chats replaying on a frantic loop, each word rehearsed, dismissed, then rehearsed again. When the yellow cab finally rumbled to the curb, its arrival felt less like a rescue and more like a summons.

He hadn't told Asia. The words lodged in his throat every time he'd tried, the secrecy a raw, chafing thing against his conscience. Betrayal, he knew, even as he clung to the necessity of it. Chats needed to understand what Asia was contemplating: a perilous journey back to Poland—a desperate, complex scheme to bring family members to New York. Could the decision shatter the delicate balance of their operation?

Jakub thought, *could there be an option to have Chats dispense of Asia, his right-hand person, for an extended period? Surely, Chats, with his pragmatic mind and extensive resources, could devise a better way,* he reasoned, the thought a desperate anchor. *He'll see angles we haven't and maybe find a path that serves them both with the least fallout.* This mantra battled the sick certainty that Asia would see his actions as a profound breach of trust. *But Poland... for a Jew, in these times?* The very idea was a cold dread seeping into his bones. *I wouldn't be able to live with myself if something happened to her because I stayed silent.* Going behind her back felt like severing a limb, but this, he convinced himself as he reached for the cab door, was a terrible, unavoidable necessity.

"Where to?" the driver asked, his voice a gravelly New York drawl.

Jakub gave the address of the Williams Insurance Agency, adding, "And then, driver, I am picking up a friend and heading directly to the Central Park Boathouse."

"Got it," the driver replied, his voice still a gravelly New York drawl. "Good choice, the Boathouse. You are in for a treat. Ever been there?" Jakub was intrigued by the driver's knowledge. It was as if he was about to embark on a journey not just to a physical location but also through time and history.

"First time," Jakub replied.

"The Central Park Boathouse dates back to 1869 and is still going strong."

"Wow! A success story." Jakub replied.

The sky, a bruised gray, threatened rain. *Could Asia ever convince her relatives in Poland to live in New York?* The question, unanswered, hung in the air. He shifted restlessly, the taxi inching through Friday traffic. The air, thick and humid, pressed down on him, a stifling reminder of the New York summers he and Asia still struggled to endure. He'd often remarked to Asia that it wasn't the excess humidity but the lack of significant air movement that made New York summers so uncomfortable, a small, shared joke in their ongoing battle with the city's climate.

The American Independence Day weekend loomed, adding to the usual Friday frenzy. Cars crawled bumper-to-bumper, horns blaring a discordant symphony. He'd planned for the delay, but the minutes still ticked by with agonizing slowness. Finally, through a gap in the buildings, he saw Central Park, a glimpse of green amidst the concrete.

As he stepped out, Chats, umbrella already open against the now-falling drizzle, stood waiting, a beacon of calm in the urban chaos.

"Hello, Chats!" Jakub said, extending his hand as Chats ducked into the waiting cab.

They shook hands, a brief, firm clasp.

"Great to see you again, Maestro! Nothing like a July rain."

"I have to agree; however, I can do without the burst of humidity we get after a summer rain."

"Agreed. I am not a fan of high humidity."

The cab ride to their lunch began. Jakub briefly rolled down the window, letting in the damp city air, a moment of connection with the outside world before the heavy conversation.

"So glad we're having lunch," Chats began. "I'm hoping to get an understanding of Asia from a husband's perspective. I know she has to be going through a lot—the death of an identical twin—I can't imagine. I'm concerned about her. She has crawled into a shell. And who can blame her? How do identical twins deal with the death of their look-alike sibling? I have no words!" He shook his head.

Jakub turned to the window for a moment, feeling the breeze, then rolled it up before saying, "Thank you for your continued concern. Progress is slow, but it's there. Time, they say…" He couldn't bring himself to finish the cliché.

Chats thought carefully before he spoke. "The pain one goes through when losing a sibling must pale in comparison to the loss of an identical twin. Her absence is devastating to those who love her. I am the furthest from a psychologist, but in my humble opinion, the cards were all stacked against Asia. We mustn't blame her. For you or me, there are no comparable life situations—we can't relate. Perhaps losing a wife, son, or daughter may be similar. However, I don't think so. How do you measure the closeness of identical twins?"

Perspective, Jakub thought, feeling the weight of Chats' words.

Chats continued, "By the way, the Greek poet Menander coined the phrase 'time heals all wounds' around 300 BC and said, 'Time is the healer of all necessary evils.' I'm afraid I have to disagree that time heals all wounds. You see, in my opinion, the wounds remain. In time, the mind, protecting its sanity, covers them with scar tissue, and the pain lessens, but it rarely disappears."

Jakub ran a hand through his hair, an unsettling thought. "An interesting perspective, Chats. One I shall not share with Asia, as in our case, I hope time does indeed heal her wounds—your opinion and knowledge are admirable."

"Why, thank you, Jakub. Tell me, have you been to the Central Park Boathouse?"

"No, sir. Today will be my first visit."

"I'm sure you'll bring your darling Asia there many times in the future. It's not really a restaurant, more an assortment of docks with food concessions. I like the atmosphere, especially on the July Fourth weekend, and I love the aroma of Italian sausage on a sourdough bread roll with green peppers and onions. The spices they pack into that sausage are like no other sandwich in the city. I recommend the Italian sausage if you want serious indigestion." He grinned, a mischievous glint in his eye.

The Boathouse was a sensory overload. A vast wooden walkway led to a cacophony of sights and sounds—vendors hawking their wares, music blaring from unseen speakers, waiters shouting, patrons excitedly chattering, and fireworks distantly popping. The air, thick with the aroma of grilling meat and spices, made Jakub's stomach rumble.

Jakub, following Chats' lead, navigated the crowd to a table. Beers were ordered, along with the promised Italian sausage sandwiches. They arrived quickly—mountains of food piled precariously on paper plates.

Jakub stared at the overflowing sandwich—its sheer size almost comical. He shook his head slightly. The sausage, nestled in a sourdough roll with peppers and onions, looked like a miniature country. The pickle spear was a small tree on the plate, and the crisps, thick and golden, resembled a mountain range. He tucked a cloth napkin into his shirt, a futile attempt at elegance amidst the casual chaos. "The pickle alone could be a meal, and these crisps." He nibbled one, a satisfying crunch, and gave a thumbs-up.

Chats, mid-bite of his pickle, nodded. "What do you say we enjoy our food and drink and dive into what you want to discuss after our meal? Will that work for you?"

"That works for me, Chats. We will speak after we finish."

Chats took a long pull from his mug of dark stout, wiping the froth from his lips with the back of his hand. "By the way, compliments on your performance from colleagues and friends—I've lost count. Many from some of New York's most prominent citizens. The mayor himself rang. 'Flawless execution,' he declared, referring to the Dvořák piece you performed. 'The sheer talent,' he gushed, which prompted him to inquire about a private performance at his Hamptons haunt, *The Maidstone Golf Club*." Chats hesitated, a wry smile playing on his lips before continuing, "The irony, naturally, is the club's current stance: 'No Jews Allowed' as members. I trust this comes as no shock?"

Jakub's smile turned into a tight grimace. "Not in the least. As a Jew, you get used to it. The world will change, eventually. In my lifetime? Only God knows."

"Jakub, what are your thoughts on a private Hamptons performance? You have never graced those shores. Be prepared, as men of success and influence abound—connections many would pay dearly to state they were in the same room—could be worth their weight in gold for the future."

Jakub ran a nervous hand through his hair. "Absolutely, Chats! Your insight is, as always, spot on! A smaller venue is intriguing. I anticipate it eagerly. Naturally, I'll need to peruse the particulars of my contract, but a private function shouldn't pose a problem. The question remains, will they endeavor to cloak my Jewish heritage once the ink is dry?"

"Most who watched you perform with the New York Philharmonic Symphony had a hunch you were Jewish," Chats said, unable to suppress a smile. "With a name like Jakub Markowicz, that is not the name of the typical white Anglo-Saxon, you know, like Jim Smith. Plus, you sold out the venue. Unfortunately, in the world of discrimination, allowing Jews to perform is entirely different from granting them lifelong membership. You're only there for several hours."

Jakub offered a sly grin. "One presumes so. I'm not petitioning for a house next door to become their neighbor. We, of the Jewish persuasion, are accustomed to such distinctions. None of us has tasted the nectar of full societal acceptance—and likely never shall."

A frown of disgust formed on Chat's face as he said in a low, angered tone, "I have trouble dealing with such behavior. Prejudice—it is so unacceptable. Thank God our country has a limited number of bigots."

"We have antisemites all over my native Poland, and I know the movement is flourishing, as Adolf Hitler is doing his best to launch a national movement against Jews."

"Yes, I have read quite a bit about the Nazis and Adolf Hitler—the more I read, the more concern I have for humanity. Oh, I almost forgot, the mayor reiterated, don't even think of coming without your adorable wife. So, think about it. No quick answers are required today. Oh, by the way, the club has a 1920s Bösendorfer Concert Grand. I guess that means something to a concert pianist like yourself?"

"Yes indeed. I would pay the mayor to have the opportunity to play a Bösendorfer. I do wonder which model. My Warsaw colleagues will be envious when they find out I played such a rare and expensive instrument." A thrill of anticipation shot through him at the prospect.

The remnants of their lunch sat between them. Chat gestured towards Jakub's plate. "So, the Italian sausage?"

"You were right. I can't wait to bring Asia here. The ambiance is nothing like Poland. Thank you."

"Glad I could introduce you. Now, Asia. You have my sympathies again. I've spoken with her several times. I have no idea what it's like losing an identical twin. It's impossible to put behind you. I feel for her."

"You're right, Chats. Lunch—I talked her into lunch the other day. It's a small thing, but progress. I wanted to give you some insight into what she might ask."

"By all means, please speak candidly."

"Asia wants to bring her family here, to the US. Asia, broken-hearted and desperate, may soon request a leave of absence. More significantly, I have a strong suspicion," Jakub lowered his voice, "that Asia is formulating a plan to travel to Poland. Her objective would be to orchestrate a way to bring not only the newborn twins, Icek, and Abram but potentially other family members out of Poland and into America. She wants to relocate them as immigrants and have them live with us. She may ask you for an extended leave of absence so that she can be the one who rescues her family out of Poland. She has talked about a leave of absence. I know she is your 'right-hand man,' so to speak, in your employ. Regardless of what I say, she remains apt to make an emotional decision. A professor of mine spent an entire class on the hazards of making emotional decisions. I am her husband, but regardless of what I say, she refuses to hear my logic. I'm too close to her for her to respect my opinion at a time when she has convinced herself that personally retrieving her family is the only choice she has. I'm hoping she will listen to you, as she has yet to consider the ramifications of the risk should she travel to Europe. I think she will listen to you." He held his breath, gauging Chats' reaction.

"Before we go any further, would you mind them living with you here in America?"

"Do you mean my in-laws living in the same home as us? There are no issues whatsoever. I'm not sure how I will continue my rigid schedule of piano practice for two hours per weekday night with the newborn twins and young Icek in our home, though." The thought flickered through his mind—a fleeting concern quickly suppressed.

"Forgive me, I occasionally forget—you are not native-born Americans. A typical American family might raise an eyebrow at the, shall we say, communal living arrangement: a mother-in-law, Ryfka, if I recall correctly. And a brother-in-law, Abram. Correct so far? Then, I believe there are twin nieces, Matty and Edna, and a nephew, Icek. Have I grasped the family tree? Thus, the inevitable question arises: Will Asia ask me to lend my assistance? To facilitate the entry of those individuals I just mentioned into the US?"

"My dear Chats, I struggle to keep those names and relationships straight, and I am family. You've truly astounded me. Yes, you assume correctly, Asia requires a strategy. We both witnessed the deluge, the relentless flow of souls arriving at Ellis Island—hundreds daily, so the newspapers proclaim. I'm acutely aware our current residency status is delicate, given, shall we say, the press and their unfavorable printed opinions surrounding immigration. We must embark upon the proper path, the one with the least bureaucratic entanglement, to avoid the dreaded red tape."

"My contacts in Germany tell me there is extreme prejudice against anyone Jewish. The government promotes intolerance—rumors abound. Right-wing zealots are forcing Jews out of positions. Social and political restrictions make it unsafe to be a Jew in Europe. I don't know. We have our prejudice here—the Chinese, the Negro, the Jews. Getting Jews out of Europe is a good thing, in my opinion."

"So, Chats, you think you can assist us?"

"Weaning the babies before a six-to ten-week ocean voyage must be the first consideration. Perhaps I can sponsor an airplane-based business trip? Asia knows the insurance business, and there are always loose ends to address—I can think of certain scopes of work that would suit Asia quite well for our European region. In the meantime, we must first identify potential scopes of work along with the timing of such work. The State Department has accelerated the process to address Polish citizens, like Asia, her family, and you." He nodded decisively and straightened his hat. "I must get back to the office," Chats said. "I will be prepared for Asia's questions, and don't worry. She will never know we had lunch with the intent of talking about her family."

"Mr. Williams, I mean, Chats, thank you. You are a good friend. The Bösendorfer—I look forward to it. Thank you."

"One last thing, Jakub. Asia's considerable progress in stepping away from her depression speaks to her character, as she appears better each day. I am confident she will get there. As always, she will persevere, although not without difficulty. Thanks for having lunch with me today. I enjoyed the time, the ambiance, and the discussion," Chats said as he stepped away.

"My pleasure, sir," Jakub said, snatching the check before Chats could reach it. "My invitation—my treat."

"Well, thank you, Mr. Maestro. Hope to see you soon." Chats waved a farewell and melted back into the crowd. Jakub watched him go, a mixture of gratitude and apprehension swirling within him. He'd taken a step, a gamble, for Asia, for their future.

Now, all he could do was wait.

CHAPTER THIRTEEN

Park Slope, Brooklyn, New York
July 3rd, 1932, 2:30 p.m.

Asia paced the apartment, a flutter of excitement in her chest. *Soon,* she thought, picturing her family stepping off the ship, their faces alight with the promise of a new life. *America. It has to work. It will work.* She moved to the window, the city sprawling beneath her, a grid of hope and uncertainty. But a shadow of doubt crept in. Would they share her optimism? Would they embrace this new, arranged life? The thought snagged, a loose thread threatening to unravel her carefully constructed plans. *What if? No. It's too late for doubts. My family's move to America is happening.*

She stepped onto the fire escape, the humid July air thick with the rumble of holiday traffic. American flags, a riot of red, white, and blue, rippled from flagpoles, fire escapes, and car antennas. The sporadic pop and crackle of fireworks punctuated the city's hum—a premature celebration of independence, a day away. Asia pulled on a wide-brimmed beach hat, shielding her eyes from the afternoon sun. Her mission was clear.

She traced the lines of circled advertisements in the newspaper housing section—a tangible representation of her dream—a home for her family within walking distance. After all these years, she could almost see them here, in this vibrant, chaotic city. *Why do I believe this so strongly?* The question lingered, unanswered, and was replaced by a surge of determination. She would raise the twins and have her family close. Chats, along with his lawyer friend, was working tirelessly. The news could arrive any day. She had a real sense of comfort as she envisioned Jakub walking into a place she had secured. A relief, it was the start of bringing closure to a challenging time.

Satisfied with her selection, Asia folded the paper, a small, triumphant smile playing on her lips. *Reasonable rentals do exist.*

In the kitchen, she poured a glass of lemonade, its tartness a refreshing counterpoint to the summer heat. The mailbox key felt cool in her hand as she headed downstairs.

Back in her apartment, the bundle of mail lay on her lap. With the chilled lemonade, she sank into her favorite armchair, the worn fabric familiar and comforting. *A letter with a Polish stamp, Mother's handwriting instantly recognizable. Her heart skipped a beat.* Since the telegram, that stark announcement of Henna's death delivered on the heels of their celebratory concert, there had been only silence.

Asia's hands trembled as she held the letter, a tangible link to a life that felt both distant and painfully present. Her breath hitched, a wave of moisture clinging to her palms. Then, a surprising calm descended— a quiet certainty that settled deep in her soul. The thought flickered, then vanished. *No. I need to know. Now.* She couldn't bear the suspense any longer. She had to know what her mother had to say, even if it meant facing painful memories.

She carefully slit the envelope, a pause, a held breath. A whisper escaped her lips, "Will this make it worse? What will Mother say? Will she force me to remember what I want to forget?" The paper unfolded, revealing her mother's neat script, and Asia's heart raced as she read, her palms growing clammy with each passing word. The physical manifestation of her anxiety was a testament to the emotional turmoil she was experiencing.

June 22, 1932

> *Dear Asia and Jakub,*
> *I hope this letter finds you both as well as can be expected, given Abram's telegram about Henna.*
> *I wanted you to know that everyone agreed she would have loved the memorial. The rabbi's words were beautiful, Asia—truly flattering to your beloved sister—the service, the heartstrings, the tears that flowed. You would have been proud. Even the rabbi, usually so composed, at times appeared moved. He found those perfect moments to interject humor, and it caused many to laugh. It was Icek's first funeral. Icek had no idea what to expect. We described to him our customs and traditions for a family member's demise. Icek felt discomfort from not being allowed to see her once the staff*

took her from our synagogue. I swear it appeared that every member of the synagogue showed up.

Serena, the midwife who attended both Henna's labor with Icek and Henna's labor with the twins, had warned us. She saw the hemorrhage, the way Henna's life was slipping away. Abram was in complete denial. Helpless, all of us. Henna's fate was already written. Serena, bless her, said the kindest thing: 'Henna feels no pain. She will go with God peacefully.'

I told Icek that God meant for him to be there in that room. I watched her last breath leave her body. It's a scene where I can't escape—Asia, the scene replays day and night. But before that, those precious minutes, she held the girls, her face radiant, a beam of pure joy. And then, that final smile, so warm, so loving, before she whispered, 'I love you.' It was, I can't describe it. It's a pain I can't entirely accept.

The twins are thriving, for now. The rabbi arranged for wet nurses and mothers from the town who had recently had their babies. Icek learned a new phrase: wet nursing.

Henna and Abram had chosen names weeks before: Ernst Marek for a boy, after Abram's father, and Amelia Krystina for a girl, after my mother. But the actual naming didn't happen until after their birth. Abram and I talked. We decided. Matya carries your middle name, Asia, and Edna, Henna's. I told Icek they both have his features, and Abram sees Henna and you in them.

I try to find joy. Remembering that time heals. But Abram, he's taking it the hardest. He finally went back to work after a much too long delay. I tell Icek every day to be patient with his father, that his heart is broken.

The rabbi found a widow from the synagogue. She'll be there when Edna and Matya no longer need the wet nurses. I haven't met her yet.

I must close. I hope you can come to Poland. But don't worry about us. I will endure. We miss you.

Love,

Mother

Asia carefully placed the letter on the edge of the couch. Her gaze drifted across the living room, landing on the large mirror on the far wall. Her reflection stared back, a ghost of a smile playing on her lips. But in her eyes, the news of Henna's death was fresh, raw. Tears welled, and she wiped them away with the back of her hand, a gesture of weary resignation.

Jakub found Asia curled on the couch, a light blanket pulled around her, seemingly asleep. On the coffee table, a letter lay open, and the Polish stamps and postmark were a stark reminder. He picked it up, his own heart heavy.

He read Ryfka's words, and it was like hearing the news all over again. The tears came unsolicited. He saw the dampened handkerchief beside the envelope, a testament to Asia's grief. The postmark revealed the agonizing journey of the letter, arriving days after Henna's death, a delayed echo of tragedy. *If only I had been there, maybe things would have been different.* The thought was a useless, painful refrain. *Ryfka's letter must have devastated her. She's reliving it all again. She probably cried herself to sleep.*

He rushed out, leaving Asia undisturbed, and headed for the nearest payphone. He dialed Mr. Williams's private line, his hand sweating as he waited, his gaze fixed on the hazy summer sky.

"Hello, Chats Williams. How can I help you?"

"Chats," Jakub said, wiping his brow, his voice tight with anxiety. "It's Jakub. I hope you're well despite this heat. We received a letter from Ryfka, Asia's mother. It brought Henna's death back, front and center. When I got home, Asia was asleep, but I could tell she'd been crying. I cried too, Chats, after reading it."

"Take a breath, Jakub," Chats said, his voice calm amidst the clinking of ice and the hiss of a cigarette being lit. "It's perfectly understandable. I'd be worried if you weren't emotional. Letters and telegrams were inevitable. This one just caught you off guard. Asia and I spoke earlier. She's planning to come in tomorrow. Do you think she needs more time?"

"No, the opposite. Work will distract her. But this letter has set her back. The progress she made, with the rabbi's help, focusing on getting her family here, has evaporated. She's feeling it all again like the day we got the news."

"Vulnerability is natural, Jakub. We don't deal with death often enough to master it. But we have more pressing matters. My college roommate, the immigration lawyer, and I are facing a steep climb. I don't have all the details, but there are significant obstacles."

"Chats, thank you. But please, keep those obstacles from Asia for now. She's too fragile."

Chats paused for a moment and said, "Understood. I want to get her back to the Asia we knew prior to Henna's passing," he said, a wistful note in his voice. "We need to let her heart guide us, Jakub. But she should come to work tomorrow. It's not about prioritizing business over her grief. It's about her well-being. I know her. She needs to feel in control. But if she needs weeks off, we'll make it work. However, too much time alone, and she'll sink into depression."

"I agree, Chats. I'll talk to her and guide her."

"Good. Try to have a good evening despite everything."

"Thanks, Chats. Bye."

The call ended.

CHAPTER FOURTEEN

New York City, NY
July 18th, 1932, 9:45 a.m.

Chats sat at his desk, the scent of his freshly lit cigarette mingling with the warm air of a New York summer day. Outside, the skyline stretched, a panorama of steel and glass under a cloudless sky. His mind, however, was far from a clear view, tangled in the complexities of Asia's family plight. The days since Asia lost her twin had rushed by, leaving behind a residue of guilt and a fierce determination to do what was right, regardless of the bureaucratic labyrinth of immigration. The fact that they were Jewish was a significant obstacle, and he felt a surge of indignation. *Hogwash!*

He glanced at his watch, the ticking a reminder of the impending meeting. Today, Matthew Billingsly, an old Dartmouth chum and a seasoned immigration lawyer—two decades in the trenches—was offering a precious hour. A friend in need, and today, that friend was him.

He remembered their last lunch, the easy banter that came with years of shared history. Matthew's firm had just relocated from the Lower East Side to the recently completed 70 Pine Street, the Art Deco tower. Chats couldn't resist the teasing that started when Matthew's firm relocated, as Chats would quip, 'tallest building in Lower Manhattan, and you're stuck on the fifth floor?' Matthew had roared with laughter, the sound echoing in the cavernous lobby.

He pressed the intercom button, his voice calm as he called for Asia.

Moments later, she stepped into the room—a burst of lime green, her dress catching the light as it hugged her form. A matching bow sat neatly in her hair, her presence as radiant as her outfit. "Good morning, Asia," he said, a plume of smoke escaping his lips as he gestured to the dress. "New?"

She paused, lifting her chin slightly, a hint of defiance in her eyes. "Yes. Jakub said I needed a 'picker-upper,' as you Americans say." She sipped her coffee, the steam momentarily obscuring her reading glasses. "He thought I needed some magic."

"And did it work? Did the dress lift your spirits?"

She lowered her coffee, her gaze steady. "As embarrassing as it is to admit," she began, her voice tight, "the down days—the doctor has me on medication. It helps, sometimes. It makes me sleepy. But nothing truly fills the hole left by my sister. Losing an identical twin, it's a loss that stretches a lifetime."

Chats exhaled a long stream of smoke, turning to the window: Central Park sprawled below, a tapestry of green dotted with early morning visitors. "You look stunning, Asia," he said, his voice softening. "And strong. But beyond the outward appearance, how are you, truly?"

"Fine," she said, a little too quickly. "No complaints. Except for the lack of progress. My family, they're still so far away."

"That's precisely why I asked you here." He reached for a box on his desk. "I picked up some pastries from Mamma Mia's—fresh coffee on the bureau. Help yourself. A little Italian indulgence before we dive into the deep end."

"Thank you, sir." She refilled her cup and poured one for him, the aroma filling the office. Taking a bite of a pastry, she sighed. "Delicious. May I take one for Jakub? He's never had anything like this. What did you say the bakery was called?"

"Take the whole box. Mamma Mia's. Sounds Italian enough, right?"

"It's going to cost me, you know."

"Please?"

"Pounds," she declared, pointing a finger at her waist. "This will add pounds."

Chats chuckled. "Too funny. Take those tasty treats home to Jakub. He needs to be fattened up. Now, let's get down to brass tacks."

Asia's eyebrows rose. "Brass tacks? Another new saying?" She gave a small, knowing smile. "And I suppose you know the origin?"

"Of course," he said, enjoying the familiar game. "It comes from the haberdashery trade. Measuring fabric by arm's length was unreliable. True accuracy came from the brass tacks fixed on the shop counter, marking a precise yard."

"So, we will discuss immigration with substantial accuracy?"

He took a sip of his coffee, savoring the pastry. "Yes. With the best accuracy my friend Matthew Billingsly can provide. Dartmouth, the same year as me. He's the sharpest thinker about immigration in the city. If Matthew can't find a solution, well, let's say he's our best hope. I'm meeting him today."

"Oh, Chats, thank you." She began to pace, her dress swirling around her legs. "But is there any hope at this point?"

"I'm as anxious as you to know," he admitted. "I have no frame of reference—little knowledge beyond the obvious obstacles. My phone conversation with Matthew was extensive."

"That sounds promising."

"I want to lay out the facts," he said, his tone serious. "Not to discourage you but to prepare you. Between 1900 and 1915, more than fifteen million immigrants arrived in the United States. The principal source of immigrants was southern and eastern Europe, especially Italy, Poland, and Russia, countries quite different in culture and language from the United States, and many immigrants had difficulty adjusting to life here.[9] Those numbers dwindled between 1915 and 1925, averaging around four hundred thousand immigrants per year to America from all other countries. From 1930 to 1934, the total from all countries that authorities will admit is about two hundred and thirty thousand based on the 1924 Immigration Act. Poland will be allowed to have a little over twelve thousand immigrants in the 1930 to 1934 period. We're talking about twelve thousand for all of Poland. It's a small number, Asia."[10]

Her pacing stopped. She sat down heavily in the side chair, her face pale. "So, I'm doomed? I'll never see my family?"

"I said it was a dilemma," he corrected gently. "Not impossible."

She leaned forward—her hands clasped tightly. "I apologize, Chats. I know you're doing everything you can. All I have are letters, but they give me hope. Mother writes about Abram's concerns. Antisemitism is growing in Poland. He says, 'Why live where you're not wanted?'"

Chats stood and paced about the room. "Matthew says since the 1920s, Adolf Hitler, the charismatic World War I veteran and former corporal in the German Army, has been the leader of the far-right Nationalist Socialist Workers' Party—NSDAP or Nazi Party for short. The political landscape, fractured by economic despair and social chaos, has provided fertile ground for the Nazi Party's poisonous ideology. Behind Hitler—the National Socialists have seen a surge in their electoral fortunes—there is a chance that the Nazi Party becomes the largest party in the Reichstag if the elections go their way later this month. Thus far, news reports say the Nazi Party campaign has been a relentless assault on the senses, with mass rallies, uniformed marches, and a barrage of propaganda that promises a resurgent Germany. Matthew's sources confirm that Hitler's rise involved a combination of political strategy, public speaking, and exploiting economic unrest in Germany during the Weimar Republic. His campaign emphasized nationalism, anti-communism, and promises to restore Germany's former glory. Slogans like 'Germany awaken! Give Adolf Hitler power!' plaster city walls—as if Hitler can use a magic wand and instantly solve the nation's woes.

"For Germany's Jewish population, thus far, this summer has been a summer of escalating fear. The abstract hatred that had long festered in the dark corners of society, where few dared to be outspoken of their dislike of the Jew, is now an everyday act where the dislike of the Jew has spilled onto the streets with alarming frequency. Brown-shirted SA stormtroopers, emboldened by their party's growing influence, engage in unchecked street violence, frequently targeting Jews and their property. Matthew says the seeds of economic persecution are being sown and now they are seeing localized and spontaneous actions against Jewish-owned shops. Hitler is convincing the average German that transfer of Jewish-owned property to non-Jews in Nazi Germany is right around the corner. This aligns with his hatred of Jews as detailed in Hitler's 1925 autobiography, *Mein Kampf.*

"The rhetoric of Nazi propaganda is growing. Even the newspapers are spewing vile caricatures and accusations, blaming Jews for everything from the Great Depression to the supposed decay of German culture. This relentless campaign of dehumanization is having a chilling effect on everyday life. As you can see, Asia, it is not a good time to be in Germany—particularly if you are Jewish."

"From Mother's letters, it is obvious that Abram sees this loss of Jewish property. But what can he do about it?" Asia whispered. "Abram is afraid of where it's all leading."

"I wish I possessed an ounce of your strength," Chats said, shaking his head. "Life has thrown you its share of curveballs."

"Curveballs?" A flicker of confusion crossed her face.

"Never mind," he said, waving it off. "Another silly American expression. We apply this when one deals with a plethora of life's problems."

She nodded slowly, absorbing the information.

He walked to the large world map dominating one wall, tracing his finger across Germany, Poland, and Yugoslavia. "And, Asia, I must strongly advise against any thought of traveling to Europe. Matthew spoke of the dangers for Jews traveling abroad."

Asia gasped, her hand flying to her mouth. "Oh, my God!"

Chat's voice was grim. "The restrictions are spreading, Asia. It will get worse for any Jew."

Asia's breath hitched. She stood abruptly but then froze, her arms wrapped tightly around herself as if to hold herself together. "What have we done?" Her voice was a raw whisper, barely audible. "What have we done to deserve this?"

He met her halfway, taking a half step so that he wouldn't intimidate her. He looked into her eyes, his expression grave, trying to provide a sense of control. "Nothing, Asia. Absolutely nothing. It's irrational, pure hatred. Going back is out of the question. Not now. Not ever, possibly."

She pulled a handkerchief from her pocket, dabbing at the tears that threatened to spill. Slowly, she returned to the wingback chair, sinking into it as if all the strength had drained from her. "Second-class citizens," she murmured, the words heavy with despair. "Where will it end? Will I ever see my family again?" The question hung in the air, unanswered. "So, Jakub and I returning, at present, this is impossible?"

"Yes," he confirmed. "And Matthew explained that should you ever leave America and attempt to reenter—well, reentry cannot be guaranteed. Your current status could jeopardize your ability to re-enter the US—US Customs may not let you and Jakub back in. But let's not jump to conclusions, as Matthew wants to explore all options. Maybe securing a temporary status for your family members that authorities may convert to permanent at a later date. He's going to look into it."

"It sounds incredibly complicated."

"It is," he agreed. "With those numbers, it's an extremely narrow gate." He paused, "More questions?"

"Yes. Jakub's friend, a Canadian citizen, came here with help from his university. He suggested it might be easier for my family to apply to Canada. Is that a possibility?"

"I'm not familiar with Canadian immigration," he admitted. "But it's a good question. I'll ask Matthew."

"I'm anxious to hear what he says. Thank you, Chats. For everything."

"I'll let you know as soon as I have news," he said.

She walked toward him, her eyes brimming with tears, and embraced. "Thank you," she whispered. "I don't know what Jakub and I would do without you and your wife. Your friendship means everything."

CHAPTER FIFTEEN

New York City, New York
July 18th, 1932, 1:00 p.m.

Chats poked his head into Asia's office. "Wish me luck," he said, his voice displaying optimism. "I'm off to see Matthew Billingsly about your family."

Asia rose from her desk, her movements deliberate. She met Chats halfway, her eyebrows lifting, a silent question in her eyes. "Would you mind very much if I hugged you?"

Chat's face softened. "And how long have we known each other? Come here." He opened his arms, and she stepped into them, a quick, tight embrace.

Asia's voice fractured, a hand flying to her chest as if to physically contain the swell of emotion. A single tear, hot and heavy, traced a path down her cheek, splashing onto her tightly clasped hands. "I don't know. I wouldn't have made it," she whispered, the words barely audible, "without you."

Chats, his own eyes suspiciously bright, swiped at them with the back of his hand. His voice was thick with unshed tears. "Now, now, none of that, Asia. You'll have this old fool blubbering, too. But listen to me, child, and listen carefully. You and Jakub, you both must be prepared. Don't be surprised if this rescue doesn't go as planned. Those politicians in Washington are playing their games again." He gestured sharply toward his worn leather briefcase. "Saw something in the Times this morning that chilled me to the bone."

Asia's brow furrowed with concern. "Immigration? They're not—are they making it harder?"

He unfolded the newspaper with a snap, the crisp paper a stark contrast to the grim set of his mouth. "Damn politicians," he muttered, his finger stabbing at a headline detailing Congress's proposed plan to reduce European immigration quotas drastically. "See? They care more about votes than they do about human lives. They're tightening the screws, tighter than ever before."

Asia's forehead creased, her gaze turning distant, unfocused. A wave of weariness seemed to wash over her. "When will it ever end, Chats? This—this constant struggle? This tightening of quotas—it's just another symptom. Another manifestation of the hate and dislike they have for people of the Jewish faith. Why are we so despised throughout the world? It's just another setback, another wall thrown up in our path." The final words were less a question and more a defeated sigh, a lament born of generations of persecution.

"We're going to try. We'll work at every angle with Matthew. He's the best. We'll give it, as they say, the old college try."

A faint forced smile touched her lips. "I promise, whatever happens, I'll accept it. But I won't stop looking for ways to help Henna's twins get out of that mess." Her fingers pressed against her temples, her head shaking slowly, a silent why, why, why directed at the rising antisemitism in Germany. "I have to keep fighting for them. Henna would do the same."

"And I'll be here, whatever happens," he said, meeting her gaze and offering a quick, conspiratorial wink. "Legal or otherwise. Now, I'm off. The meeting's at one-thirty, but I should be back in a few hours."

Asia walked him to the elevator, and a brief, firm handshake was their farewell.

***

The warm, bright city air greeted Chats, and he flagged down a cab. "Seventy Pine, Lower Manhattan," he instructed.

"Thirty, forty minutes, tops," the cabbie replied.

Thirty-five minutes later, Chats stepped out and paid the fare. He was early.

The revolving door spun him into a lobby of polished stone and gleaming metal. Chats paused, hat clutched in his hand, his gaze traveling upward, tracing the intricate geometric patterns that soared toward the distant ceiling. A pang of something like envy twisted in his gut. Seventy Pine—*imagine the rent.* He wandered the main level, pausing repeatedly, taking it all in before approaching one of the grandest entrances in the city.

Stepping into the lobby of Seventy Pine Street was a lesson in architectural audacity. Dark, swirling granite floors, polished to a mirror sheen, reflected the rich earth tones. To his left and right, knots of people stood mesmerized by the elevators—clearly, they were a spectacle. Tourists clustered, admiring the Art Deco interior: deep brown and tan marble floors, granite walls, and soaring white and gray ceilings, all bathed in dramatic lighting. He watched, amused, as they posed for photos in front of New York's most unique feature, its double-decker elevators, the only ones in the city. This 1932 gem, sixty-six stories and 952 feet tall, was already a landmark.

He stepped into an elevator, smiling at the sharply dressed operator. "Five, please."

The ascent was swift, almost startling. "Fifth floor, sir."

He stepped out, facing a pair of ornate double doors—Matthew's law firm. A flicker of self-doubt, a prickle of intimidation, ran through him. He reached for the polished brass handles, substantial and cool beneath his fingers, set into what looked like solid mahogany. *Is my own office even respectable?* The thought was fleeting, quickly suppressed.

He walked down a hallway carpeted so profoundly that his heels sank with each step. He recalled how cold and unforgiving the worn, low-grade carpeting was at his firm. He clenched his jaw.

A plump receptionist, her horn-rimmed glasses perched on her nose, greeted him. "Mr. Williams? Mr. Billingsly's one-thirty. You must be him."

"I am. Pleased to meet you."

"I'll let him know you're here. Please, have a seat."

"Thank you."

Five minutes later, Matthew Billingsly emerged. He was a relatively short man, nearly swallowed by the doorway. The faint glint of a gold watch chain was the only color against the stark black of his suit. He extended a hand, his voice barely audible above the hum of the building. "Chats, good to see you."

He removed his dark-framed, perfectly round eyeglasses, fished a handkerchief from his pocket, and began to polish the lenses. "Come back to the conference room—it's a bit more private."

Chats unbuttoned his jacket and slowly circled the conference room, lightly touching objects as he went.

They settled into oversized, leather-covered, wingback chairs at a conference table that stretched at least twenty-five feet.

"Some of these pieces are collector's items. Worth a fortune."

Chats considered. The conference room door set lock was perfect for the architect's design.

Matthew approached a nearby painting. "I thought they were just reproductions."

"What on earth?" It was like stepping into the King of England's private study.

Matthew returned to his seat. "I know. It's almost obscene. What the board thinks this says about the statement this makes to the public, I have no clue. It is well above my pay grade. I had the same reaction, I assure you. Can I get you anything? A drink?"

Chats chuckled. "Serving a rare French Burgundy, are we? From the finest vineyards?" He winked, a broad grin spreading across his face. "No, Matthew, I'm good."

Matthew opened his briefcase, his smile a fleeting acknowledgment of Chats' humor. His tone shifted, becoming somber. "Let's get down to it. First, let me say how deeply sorry I am for Asia, her husband, and the whole Kelner family. Without that monster Hitler, none of this would be happening. The situation is grim."

Chats met his gaze, a shared understanding of the pain passing between them. "Thank you, Matthew. I'll tell Asia."

Matthew pinched the bridge of his nose, his eyes avoiding direct contact. "It's more than an uphill battle. The 1924 Immigration Act is the first brick wall. Quotas. They set a specific number of visas for each country. They blocked Asians entirely, and then they squeezed Eastern and Southern Europe. It's all based on eugenics—and Chats, this twisted idea of 'desirable' immigrants, favoring Northern and Western Europeans, has no scientific basis whatsoever, in my opinion."

Chats drew in a sharp breath, running a hand through his hair. He pushed himself up from the chair, pacing the room. "It's legislated prejudice! That's what it is!"

Matthew stood, a slight pause before he spoke. "Are you finished? I'm just the messenger, remember?"

Chats stopped pacing, a flush of embarrassment rising on his cheeks. He walked toward the artwork. "Sorry. I, I'm too close to this."

"You have every right to be angry. I'd be devastated if it were my friend. But here's the background. The changes Congress made were all about prejudice. Limiting the 'undesirables,' including Jews from Southern and Eastern Europe. And then Hoover, in 1930, banned anyone likely to become a 'public charge.' Anyone who can't support themselves is a drain on society."

Chats interrupted, "So much for the *Statue of Liberty*, then? What about '*give me your tired, your poor, your huddled masses yearning to breathe free?*'"

"Good point. And did you know, Chats, that a Sephardic Jewish American woman, Emma Lazarus,[11] wrote those words? '*The New Colossus.*' She wrote it to raise money for the pedestal. She called the statue '*Mother of Exiles.*' Do you want me to go on?"

"I'll remember that. Amazing, a Jew wrote that. They don't publicize that, do they? And they should. Yes, please continue. Though I know I won't like it."

"As I was saying, the 1925 Act[12] is the first hurdle. Congress slashed the quota for Polish nationals from thirty-one thousand in 1922 to just under six thousand in 1925. They bumped it a little in 1930 to 6,524. But compare that to the United Kingdom—over sixty-five thousand Brits allowed in that same year."

Chats said, "The Brits are privileged. Never mind, they tried to burn down the White House on August 24, 1814! How did they arrive at those numbers, anyway?"

"Simple. The government used the 1920 census data. The *Bureau of the Census* and the *Department of Commerce* estimated the '*National Origins*' of the white population. They figured out the percentage each nationality represented. Then, they used the '*National Origins Formula*' to calculate the quotas out of a pool of 150,000 annual immigrants. The minimum for any country is a hundred."

Chats stood, crossing the room, his voice tight with anger. "Damn it! The number for all of Poland is minuscule!"

"Exactly. That's the mountain we're facing. The second problem? Asia and Jakub are on a special work permit. It's not immigrant status. They're not on the path to citizenship. It's good they can stay for now. But until they become citizens, they can't sponsor anyone. So, they have zero leverage to bring their family over."

Chats said, "Without a sponsor, her relatives in Poland are just in line. Like anyone else."

"Precisely. Asia's family has no advantage over anyone else trying to get here. Do you see the problem?"

"Yes. I see it. And frankly, it looks hopeless." Chats paced again, his mind racing.

"If one of her relatives married an American citizen, that would work. The American spouse could show the marriage certificate, and they'd be allowed in. But that takes some creative thinking."

Chats said, "We can rule that out, but I'll mention it. Is there any chance the quotas will change soon?"

Matthew stood and began gathering his papers, slipping them back into his briefcase. "It's a political hot potato. The 1929 Crash, the unemployment; Americans want jobs for Americans, not foreigners. Congressmen want to keep their seats, and they listen to the voters. I don't see the quota system budging."

Chats stood, hands shoved deep in his pockets, his face a mask of defeat. "I didn't expect easy answers. But I sought a glimmer of hope."

"I can tell you about some less savory options. But you need to know that if Asia and Jakub are caught, they could be deported."

Chats said, "Matthew, before that, can we talk about European politics?"

"Are you going to ask me if Adolf Hitler is insane? Because the answer is yes. From what I've read, from what people are saying when they come back from Germany, it's a bad time to be Jewish in Europe, Chats. It was a terrible time—Hitler's antisemitism is not just talk. It's dangerous. You need to convince Asia and Jakub to stay away from Germany. And I don't know how fast that poison will spread. Things are unstable over there. And if they were my relatives, I'd do anything to get them here. Anything. Because I think Jews in Europe are in danger as long as Hitler's in charge."

Chats scratched his head. "Look at the papers. He's only been Chancellor since January 30th. Democracy? Gone. Germany's a one-party dictatorship now. Then the Reichstag fire,[13] arson. The very symbol of German democracy burned. And they're blaming three Bulgarians? After the fire, Hindenburg gave Hitler emergency powers. Suspended civil liberties, habeas corpus.[14]"

"They don't even have to tell people why they're arresting them. The SA, the Stormtroopers, Hitler's thugs, he deputized them. They can arrest anyone who opposes him."

Chats asked, "And whom do they arrest?"

"Communists, socialists, state delegates, men, women, even their spouses. In Bavaria, they rounded up ten thousand people. Ten thousand! The prisons are overflowing. They utilize Dachau, outside Munich, to hold the undesirables. And then the *Enabling Act*[15] in March. That gave them the power to change the *Weimar Constitution*. Two-thirds voted, and Hitler got emergency powers for four years."

Chats said, "Understood. And we're on the same page about Hitler. Now, can we talk about those other methods? The ones with the qualifier?"

Matthew smirked slightly. "Right. Rumor is, there's a merchant ship line. For a price, a hefty price, they can get Europeans to Canada's east coast. A handler takes them to a lumber town in Northern Ontario, Sudbury. They stay there, learn some English, and learn the customs. Eight to twelve months later, another handler takes them to Michigan's Upper Peninsula. They walk across the border, where there are no guards."

"There's a large Polish community in Detroit. For a small fee, the handlers make introductions and help them blend in."

"Ballpark figure, per person?"

"Forty-five hundred. No guarantees, of course. But there are hundreds of success stories."

Chats pulled out a small notepad and pen. "Let's see. Abram, Icek, Icek's sisters, the twins Matya and Edna, and Ryfka, the grandmother—five in total, that's $22,500. A small price for freedom. And your role?"

Matthew lowered his voice. "If you decide to proceed, a friend of a friend will contact you."

Chats said, "Understood. If that's the way we go, I'll let you know. Are there other options?"

"There's an Australian route. Handlers are involved again. But it's twice as expensive."

"Thank you. I understand much better now. Matthew, one more thing before I forget. My insurance agents know about Dachau. They say it's a prison that can hold six thousand. Right now, they have homosexuals, gypsies, criminals, and some Jews. The rumor is the Nazis will use it mostly for Jews. The German government is restricting Jewish rights more and more every day. No movies, no government jobs, not even public parks. And this is just the beginning."

"Yes, Chats, that aligns with what I'm hearing. Now, another option. The last one is forged papers. Smuggling them in. The problem isn't getting them out of Poland—it's US immigration. The forgers these days are good. A British passport is a possibility. It is expensive, but again, there is risk. If it's traced back to Asia and Jakub, they could be deported. I wouldn't recommend it unless it's the only way."

"Are those all the options?"

Matthew stood and approached Chats. "Yes, Chats. In this business, there aren't many choices. But I want you to know, my wife and I admire what you're doing for the Kelners. I don't know many people with your compassion. You're a good man, Chats—a truly good man. If they gave medals to civilians, you'd deserve one. I'm proud to call you my friend."

"Damn. I wasn't expecting that. Thank you, Matthew. From one friend to another, thank you."

"You deserve it."

"One last question. What are your thoughts on the Canadian route? It seems the most foolproof. The safest."

"If they were my relatives, that's what I'd do. Ask Asia and Jakub, 'What's twelve or eighteen months compared to freedom? Compared to maybe their lives?'"

"Excellent. I will strongly recommend it, but I am unsure of how much I'll tell Asia at this juncture. I need to process this. But I'd hate to find out later that she lost her family because I hesitated."

Matthew said, "Yes. I understand. Asia and Jakub seem like good people. They don't deserve what's happening—Hitler and all—and what could happen to anyone Jewish in Europe. We'll be in touch."

"Thanks again, Matthew. It's always good to see you. I value your advice. I'll have Elizabeth call Claire. We should get together and have dinner, it's been too long."

"Too long. I'll tell Lizzy. Tell Claire to expect a call. And thanks, Chats."

CHAPTER SIXTEEN

New York City, New York
July 19ᵗʰ, 1932, 9:30 a.m.

Chats looked out his office window, overlooking a fabulous summer morning, Mother Nature doing her job again: flowers, green leaves, and grass a deep green that called to sink bare feet into. Tons of New Yorkers were enjoying a beautiful, clear morning in Central Park. *I adore summer.*

The beauty of the day was interrupted by his thoughts of an endless quest for a solution to Asia's extended family dilemma. He thought, *If only I had better news for her.*

A bitter taste rose in his mouth—*Jewish.* The word seemed to echo in the very halls of Congress, a poison in the ink of new laws. His mind searched, turning to the faces he had recently brushed past. His hands began to sweat. He was at his wits' end. He had learned to respect Jakub and Asia as if they were his offspring. He was disgusted with the human race today.

"Damn it! Asia deserves better news!" he yelled at his empty office.

He would have to confront her with some ideas that would give her a tiny shard of hope. He recalled what his friend Matt Billingsly had told him: *Chats, choosing the legal route is a dead end, as Congress, with their narrow mind, thought it best to keep Jews out of America—they legislated racism!* Chats thought, *Those prejudiced bastards are doing nothing but thinking about being re-elected. The entire lot of Congress is antisemitic.*

"If the legal routes are impossible, what are we left with?" he said out loud.

He thought *illegal methods are risky and require buying silence. Anyone could make a careless accusation, thus compromising Asia and Jakub's current status with the US immigration department. Should I risk introducing Asia to the 'shady' method of bringing in Polish nationals in a less-than-legal manner? Is it worth the risk? If these two were my children, what would my advice be?*

The insurance business had taught him a great lesson—that life was chock-full of dangers, and when the risk was too significant, one must walk away.

He stood up, walked over to the window, and peered into Central Park's activity, *The innocence of Americans in this country.* He thought, *Not a care in the world. Why aren't Asia and her family already here, enjoying our American freedoms? It is best to advise Asia that the stakes are too substantial.* If this were a client requesting a policy when comparable risky circumstances were present, this would be one time when he would say: Sorry, sir, the risks are too high. My company cannot insure you now.

I should frame the discussion as high risk and advise that we take another stab at figuring out how to get her family members later, say, six months. It is unfortunate, as I know a delay has the potential to break her heart. I will ask her to go to the coffee shop to talk there. What are the advantages and disadvantages? Will she be less inclined to cry in a public setting or in a shared environment? Asia won't express her true feelings. I will take my chances.

No matter how they tried, the other ladies in the office could not compete with the Hollywood actress look that Asia sported. Her hair bounced as she made a gesture in conversation and reminded Chats of the starlets he saw in the Hollywood cinema. *The best part of Asia is simple. She didn't come from money, and she appreciates everything in life. More than anything else, family is first. Jakub and she are two of the happiest humans I have ever met.* He was so pleased to have both of them as friends.

He walked down the hall and tapped on the door to her office, peeked in, he asked, "Do you have a few minutes for me? I see you are quite busy." She sat there typing with her glasses on her nose, listening to classical music that played on a local radio station. Her white, lacy dress exemplified the spring season. She had her hair up and wore a pearl necklace with matching earrings.

"Sir, always time for you. You sign my paycheck," she said with a slight chuckle. "Have I ever said that to you before?"

Chats replied, "That is a new one. I have never heard that one before. I shall have to remember it," he said with a big smile on his face. "What do you say we take a walk to the coffee shop? It's a beautiful day, and I need to update you on what I learned in my discussion with Matt Billingsly."

She stopped and, with a look of concern on her face, said, "Jakub and I appreciate what you have done thus far, and we know immigration is a touchy subject. We have resolved ourselves to the fact that the situation is not good. We have prepared ourselves accordingly. Can you give me ten minutes to get this finished and in the mail? I will come down and get you in a bit."

"Works for me. See you in ten or so minutes."

They headed to the elevator, and within minutes, they were walking into the coffee shop.

As they arrived, they heard a newsboy shouting headlines, *"Rising antisemitism in Europe—read all about it!"*

They entered the shop and were immediately overwhelmed by the smell of strong coffee mingling with cigarette smoke, the loud chatter of other patrons, and the sound of cups clinking in the air. They took their seats along the glass front of the store, which provided a clear view of the pedestrian street and vehicle traffic.

A muscle ticked in his jaw as he met Asia's gaze, and he quickly looked away, focusing on the swirling patterns in his coffee. "Let me preface this discussion with the simple truth. My lawyer-friend Matt and I spoke for a while. We explored every possibility that we could conjure up. Nevertheless, it is unfortunate that each option has risks. I hope you know what this statement means."

"Yes, Chats. I do know what this means. There are the legitimate methods and what I would call 'other' methods."

Chat's eyebrows raised, and he said, "You put this to me in an eloquent manner." He nodded. "Yes. We discussed every option known to man. Many of the options are high-risk. So, before we begin, let me qualify what our phrase high-risk stands for. At the recommendation of my friend Matt, before Jakub and you evaluate any option, I will define substantial risk. As you know, you and Jakub are here on a unique work visa that the college sponsored. The best thing is that this permit will get you on your way to US citizenship. For you and Jakub to gain citizenship in the US, you must have a squeaky-clean record, as there is no room for inconsistencies. The slightest infraction with your current status can get you deported. And with the situation in Europe, it is not a suitable time to be Jewish. Face it, Herr Hitler is making life difficult for anyone Jewish. Do you understand this?"

"You are saying something beyond a traffic ticket or jaywalking could get us deported."

"Well stated. You understand the gravity of the situation. Now that you know the consequences of going forward in a less-than-legal manner, may we look at the options for the legal route? Let's discuss the legal route."

"Yes. I am in complete agreement. We must be confident before deciding on a less than legal route, as the consequences are high for all concerned, including Jakub and me," Asia said.

"Matt commented that we have quite a battle to resolve your needs. Bear with me as I explain the background—public opinion has caused most of the issues we will discuss. First, Congress made quite a change for all those wishing to immigrate to this country. The main obstacle is the 1924 Immigration Act. The Act sets quotas, a specific number of visas available annually for each country. The quotas were inspired in part by American proponents of eugenics. Do you understand eugenics?"

"Eugenics? You might want to refresh my vocabulary. I am not even comfortable guessing what it means."

"Not to worry, ninety percent of the population also has no idea. Eugenics, as defined in the dictionary, is beliefs and practices that aim to improve the genetic quality of a human population in the past by excluding people and groups judged to be inferior and promoting those deemed to be superior."

"This sounds a good bit like science fiction," Asia remarked.

"I have to agree, Asia. The US Immigration Service focuses on 'desirable' northern and western European immigrants. They limit immigrants considered less 'racially desirable,' including Southern and Eastern European Jews."

"We are substandard humans in the eyes of the lawmakers. Wow! Not a suitable time to be a Jew!"

"Yes, it is not the best time in the evolution of immigration discussions to be Jewish. These words of law are for a small group of people who want power. It is a terrible way to feel." He thought, *She knows I'm not like this.*

"I know you well enough that you are unlike many other Americans. I have experienced prejudice firsthand many times since I have been in this country. I try to wear my Star of David necklace on rare occasions. I have to tell you, Jakub and I were pretty surprised at the outright prejudice that exists here for anyone who is Negro, or, for that matter, anyone with a different accent other than American."

"I know it didn't take long for you to learn this. Many uneducated citizens live in New York City. You will not find such prejudice in other areas of the country. Remember, my roommate was a Jew, and we are lifelong friends. We spent four years in the same dormitory room at Dartmouth. He was like anyone else—just Jewish. As I have said on many occasions, I despise uneducated, prejudiced humans."

"Chats, you have just reiterated why Jakub and I admire your wife and you."

"Thank you for that comment, Asia."

Asia said, "From what you are saying, Congress has made it almost impossible to immigrate under these new rules. I have never considered myself a second-class citizen of the world until now."

"Asia, the other factor was President Hoover's move in 1930. He banned any immigrant who could become a public charge—those who can't sustain themselves without a handout."

"You mean those who come here and live off of society, as perhaps they are too lazy to work or lack the qualifications to get employment."

"Yes. You are correct. During our discussion, I reminded Matt of the impactful phrase engraved on the *Statue of Liberty*. By the way, a Jewish poet authored it, if you have never heard of it before. I asked Matthew, 'What happened to the *'give me your tired, your poor, your huddled masses yearning to breathe free'* inscribed on the *Statue of Liberty*?' I told him, 'I guess the inscription on the *Statue of Liberty* no longer applies?'"

"So true. You have me now thinking this is propaganda," Asia said.

"The 1925 Act is the first problem. The quota established by the Act for Polish nationals reduced the earlier annual allocation from thirty-one thousand in 1922 to just under six thousand in 1925, and the most recent bump was in 1930 when they raised the quota to 6,524."

"Why such a drastic drop in the numbers?" asked Asia.

"I asked the same question. The government based the quotas on the 1920 census data. The Bureau of the Census and the Department of Commerce estimated the National Origins of the White Population of the United States in 1920 in numbers. They calculated the percentage share each nationality made up. You see, the number is tiny for all of Poland. This small number is the uphill battle you face."

"They have legislated Poles out of the immigrant pool," Asia commented.

"Once you gain American citizenship, the passport and citizenship documents allow you to sponsor your relatives. You can bring your relatives in for sure. However, until you get citizenship, you cannot sponsor other family members. It is hit and miss whether the immigration situation will change anytime soon."

"Chats, thank you so much for what you have done for us thus far. You have enlightened me that the situation is much more ominous than I ever imagined, describing how difficult it is to gain legal entry. You may as well tell me options for a less legal path."

"The immigration topic is a popular topic in an economy where we have high unemployment. Most of us are getting over the 1929 stock market crash. I came close to losing everything. I was lucky."

"I wasn't expecting anything easy to solve this issue. I hoped to see something promising. Anything would be better than nothing," Asia said.

"It is now time to talk about creative methods. Again, with these methods, you and Jakub could risk losing your current work permit status. But, should you get caught, you both risk getting deported. Neither of you may ever be allowed back into the US. First, we could smuggle your relatives aboard a merchant ship. The cost of this choice is high. The fee would be around twenty-five thousand dollars for the family members you mentioned."

"Much too much risk!" Asia said.

"The next option, 'forged papers,' is even more expensive than the last option, as it involves quite a bit of risk for the players and those caught with fake documents."

Asia, with a stern look, stared at the floor and said, "I feel uncomfortable with illegal methods, and Jakub would also have issues with compromising our status here. Add to this, we have the unknowns. If we, as Jews, get sent back to Poland, what will become of us?"

"The immigration authorities would have to have proof that you and Jakub were both part of the scheme." Chats said as he stepped toward Asia and placed his hand on her shoulder. "Unfortunately, you could be implicated. Matthew tells me in the world of immigration law, the defendants are guilty until proven innocent."

Asia, tearing up, and while retrieving a handkerchief from her purse, said, "It is sad. I understand we cannot get my relatives here. The risks are too high. It is not worth the risk. If they were to get caught, the authorities would send them back to Poland. I trust I have now heard all available options?"

He grabbed her hand and said, "Asia, there is no need to discuss this topic further. I acknowledge your perspective on risk, and it aligns with Jakub's opinion. I know many influential people in government; regardless, I will continue my quest to get your family here."

"Sir, you have been too kind. You have made the necessary inquiries. That said, I appreciate your help."

"I wish there were other options. The politics of the world are harsh at this time in history."

"You are so right," she said as tears flowed. "Henna's children, Icek, Abram, Ryfka, what will their destiny be?"

Chats stood, took her hand, helped her up from the table, hugged her, and said, "If I only knew their destiny, unfortunately, I don't have a crystal ball."

They headed back to the office.

CHAPTER SEVENTEEN

Jozefow, Poland
July 18th, 1937, 11:45 a.m.

The wagon wheels crunched to a halt in front of the address shown on the shipping document. Ernst, the driver, spat a stream of tobacco juice onto the dusty road. "My patience is drier than this road—thought we'd never get here." He swiped at the sweat plastering his hair to his forehead, leaving a streak of grime, then jumped from the wagon, the wooden seat groaning in protest, and stomped toward the house. His knuckles cracked against the door. "Hello! Anybody home?" The gruffness of his voice echoed in the stillness of the midday air.

Ryfka, the aroma of simmering cabbage clinging to her clothes, shuffled to the window. She peered through the lace curtain, its pattern blurring with age, and focused on the road. A man stood at her gate, reins in hand, hitched to a horse-drawn wagon. The wagon's bed was burdened by a large, shapeless object hidden beneath a weathered canvas tarp. The man at the door, a looming figure easily dwarfing even Abram, her son-in-law, built like a bear, wore a work shirt stiff with the evidence of hard labor and neglect. Dark crescents of sweat darkened the armpits, and faint, white rings of salt rimmed the collar. His beard, a tangled thicket, pointed in many directions. Ryfka thought, *Are several meals congealed on the front of his shirt?*

The other man, still perched on the wagon seat, was a stark contrast: clean-shaven, dressed in relatively new clothes, and radiating the energy of youth compared to his grizzled companion.

The man on the porch knocked again, his voice a booming challenge this time. "Anybody home?"

Ryfka, her hands still slick from the dishwater, wiped them on her apron, leaving a damp smudge. "Girls," she announced to the twins, her voice a touch louder than usual, "we have guests."

The twins abandoned their lunch, the metallic clang of spoons against ceramic bowls cutting the silence. They pushed their chairs back from the table, their small faces alight with curiosity, and moved toward the doorway.

Ryfka opened the door to the man, her shadow falling across his dusty boots. "May I help you?"

"Yes, madam. I'm Ernst, from the rail station. My helper and I here," he gestured toward the wagon, "have a large crate for Mr. Abram Kelner at this address."

A smile softened Ryfka's features, crinkling the corners of her eyes. "Yes, you have the correct address. Abram is at the mill and won't be back until six. Where's the crate from?"

"From America. A place called… I can't even begin to wrap my tongue around it. Madam, can you read it?" Ernst asked, wiping his brow again.

"Indeed." Ryfka inspected the label with a focused look. "This package is from my daughter and her husband, who reside in Manhattan, New York. We have been anticipating its arrival for quite some time."

"Don't get many packages from America. Where do you want us to put it?"

Ernst and his helper, now on the ground, strained to maneuver the heavy crate from the wagon bed.

"You can put the box in the living room. It will be fine until Abram gets home," Ryfka confirmed.

The twins, their eyes wide with anticipation, scurried into the living room as the two men, grunting with effort, wrestled the crate through the doorway. The scent of sawdust and foreign wood filled the small space.

"Gramma, this is from Aunt Asia in America!" Edna breathed—her voice hushed with wonder.

"Yes, girls, this is the long-awaited shipment," Ryfka confirmed, her hand steady as she signed the delivery slip.

"Gonna need tools to open that. You want my partner and me to do it for you?" Ernst asked.

"That's kind of you to offer, but no. Thank you. My son-in-law will want to do that himself," Ryfka replied.

"Alright then," Ernst declared, turning toward the door. "We'll be on our way."

Ryfka gestured toward the kitchen. "Girls, get the gentlemen some water. By the way," she said, turning back to Ernst, "I know your name, but what is your partner's name?"

"Madam, my name is Boris."

The twins erupted in giggles, their tiny hands flying to cover their mouths. "You must excuse our laughter, sir. Our horse is Boris. Never met a person named Boris, so it's just funny to us."

Ernst threw his head back, a deep, rumbling laugh shaking his frame. "Hey, Boris! What's it like being named after a horse?"

"Matty, Edna, don't be rude. Offer these gentlemen something to drink. They've worked up a sweat."

"Well, thank you, madam. We could both use a glass of water," Ernst replied, wiping his mouth with the back of his hand.

The twins reappeared, each carefully carrying a saucer and a large glass of water. Their tiny faces were serious about the task.

"We have cookies, too," Matty offered shyly, extending a plate piled high with the treats.

"You girls are sure 'grown up' for your age," Boris acknowledged, reaching for a glass and a saucer.

The two men settled onto the floor, their backs against the wall, while the twins perched nearby, peppering them with questions.

Boris cleared his throat, his gaze thoughtful. "Madam, would you mind if I asked you something? How does someone in this little village of Jozefow know someone in America?"

"That's an understandable question," Ryfka said, settling into a chair. "My daughter, Asia, is married to a famous concert pianist, Jakub Markowicz, who teaches at a prestigious music university in New York. They went years ago, invited by the college to perform with a symphony. The university offered him a position, and the rest is history. He still performs, but his primary job is teaching piano to gifted young musicians."

Boris scratched his head, his brow wrinkled. He stepped closer to the crate, his eyes scanning the shipping labels, tracing the crate's journey across continents. "Never met anyone from America. Someday, I'll go there. I want to join the merchant marine when I'm older and sail the seven seas. Have you traveled to America?"

"That's an admirable goal, young man. I hope you achieve it. The furthest I've been from Jozefow is Pulaway, the village of my birth, up the road a piece or two."

"Oh yes, we know that town. We deliver there several times a week."

Boris turned to the twins. "Madam, how old are the twins?"

Ryfka's smile faded, a shadow crossing her face. "The twins turned five last month. Their poor mother, Henna, my daughter, also a twin, died giving birth to them."

Ernst's eyes widened, his expression shifting to one of sympathetic understanding. "Madam, let me get this straight: you birthed twin daughters, and one of those daughters, Henna, whom the good Lord took from you, gave birth to twins?"

"Wonderful. You have it correct. Henna and Asia are my daughters' names. Asia, the surviving twin in America, sent this crate. Well, her husband, Jakub, the musician, and she sent the crate."

Boris blinked—his expression a look of bewilderment. "Twins can have twins?"

"We didn't know twins could give birth to twins, but the rabbi told us, 'We should never underestimate the power of our savior.' I thank God daily for my precious gift of life and the gift of these twins. Edna carries a strong resemblance to her mother, Henna. I can see my daughter when I stare into those green eyes."

He continued to stare at the twins, his expression softening as he watched them dance around the crate. "Must be tough caring for two five-year-olds."

Ryfka wiped her hands on her apron, the coarse fabric leaving red marks on her skin. She wiped the sweat from her face, a faint smile playing on her lips. "I'm lucky there, too. The twins have an older brother, Icek. He's a gift from heaven. Eight years old when his mother died, he saw her take her last breath right here in this room. Before she died, little Icek promised to take care of the twins, and to this day, he keeps that promise. In keeping his promise to his mother, he will hopefully catch our dinner at the lake today."

Ernst, crumbs clinging to his beard after devouring his cookie in two bites, asked, "Madam, do you know what's in the box?"

"You know, it's funny. I haven't the faintest idea." Ryfka chuckled, shaking her head. "You need to know the man who sent the box to understand. My daughter wrote to my son-in-law, telling him she would be sending a crate filled with things we could use. Haven't heard another word since."

Boris, talking with his mouth full of cookies, exclaimed, "You'll have an early Christmas."

"Madam, I apologize for my partner. He is not very worldly, as he doesn't realize that Jews don't celebrate Christmas."

Boris interrupted, "I apologize for that remark, madam. I know you don't celebrate Christmas. I just overlooked that you were Jewish."

"How funny! We all got a good chuckle out of the comment. No harm done," Ryfka said, waving a dismissive hand.

"Thank you for the refreshments," they both said in near unison.

Boris stood, brushing crumbs from his trousers. "Enjoy whatever you received from America. We must get back to the station."

"Thanks again for the hospitality," Ernst echoed his partner's sentiments as they headed toward the door.

The children couldn't believe their eyes. Asia and Jakub had shipped the box from Manhattan two months earlier, and the crate made several stops en route to Jozefow. The crate's travel reflected shipping documents from places in the world's various countries, and they had never seen an American parcel before.

Matty and Edna danced around the large box as it sat prominently in their tiny living room. In an atmosphere of celebration, the two held hands and pranced about in a circular fashion around the mystery.

Ryfka said, "I'm missing out on the fun." She joined the twins' hands and continued their frolicking around the crate, while Ryfka sang a Polish folk song her father taught her as a young girl.

The fun stopped when Ryfka dropped to the floor. She began moaning and talking quite differently from her normal voice, "I don't feel well, I don't feel well." The twins glared fearfully at one another.

"What do we do?" Edna screamed.

Matty said in a terrifying voice—"Edna, quick, see if the two delivery men are still in sight while I stay with Gramma, Edna! Hurry, see if you can catch them!"

Edna ran from the room and headed out the door. The two men were already a couple of hundred meters away. From the top of her voice, Edna screamed, "Please come back, please come back, something is wrong with Gramma Ryfka. Please come back!" With no response, she began running toward the wagon and screaming, "Please help us, please stop! Please help us!"

The younger of the two, Boris, turned, dismounted from the wagon, and ran at full speed toward Edna.

"What's wrong? What's wrong?" Boris shouted as he got closer and closer.

They were now twenty meters apart. "Gramma Ryfka fell. She is on the floor, can't talk right, and her face doesn't look like our Ryfka!"

Boris motioned for Ernst to turn the wagon around and return to the house. In the meantime, he and Edna ran at full speed back toward the house.

They entered the home, and Matty knelt beside Ryfka with her head propped up with a pillow. She rubbed Ryfka's face with a dampened dish towel.

Staring into Ryfka's face, Boris quickly thought. *The left side of her face is sagging. She can't utter a word, and the left arm seems to not move. Her condition is similar to what happened to my grandfather about a year ago. Not the best, as Grandfather passed minutes later.*

Matty said, "Do you know what is wrong? Can you help her?"

Ernst looked on, his hands in his pockets and with tears in his eyes, as Boris gazed up at the twins and, with a voice just above a whisper, said, "This is not good. Your grandmother may have suffered a stroke."

"What's a stroke?" the twins asked quietly at the same time.

He looked at them, trying to be brave. "I'm not a doctor, but I'll tell you what I saw when my grandpa had a stroke. It was like this: imagine your brain is like a garden, and it needs water to stay healthy. A stroke is like when some of the water hoses get blocked, so parts of the garden don't get enough water.

"My grandpa fell in his kitchen. He had some of the same things happening to him that your grandma is having now. He was very weak on one side of his body, like his arm and leg were very sleepy and didn't want to move. It was also hard for him to talk, and he had trouble understanding others. He said the things that he was looking at were fuzzy."

Edna asked, "What should we do? Can we help Grandma?"

"What happened to your grandpa? Did he go to heaven?" Edna asked.

"We have to remember that everyone is different. Just because something happened to my grandpa doesn't mean it will happen to your grandma."

Ernst got closer to the twins and tried to hug them to make them feel better, while Boris helped Ryfka.

"Quick! Let's get her in the wagon. We will all take her to town and see if there may be someone to help her," explained Ernst.

"We can take her to the synagogue if nothing else. The rabbi can get us aid, as he knows everyone in the village," Edna said as she began assembling pillows and blankets in the back of the wagon.

Ernst and Boris surveyed the home for materials to build a stretcher. When the two gentlemen found nothing suitable, they left the house and began a search outside the home.

With two boards and a piece of canvas, they created a military-style body carrier and headed to Ryfka's side.

"Look, Matty, they made a bed to carry Gramma!" Edna proclaimed.

Ernst said, "We must get her on our stretcher and lift her about a meter from the floor to ensure our handywork holds her weight with no issues."

They carefully placed Ryfka on the stretcher to perform a test lift, and it worked. Ernst stared at the twins and then turned to stare at Boris and said, "Are you ready to lift? Let's get her on the wagon."

"I got her. Do you have a good grip on your end? Okay, careful and slow, we don't want to drop her."

"Let's get her in the wagon. Your end first, Ernst," Boris pleaded as the sweat beaded on his forehead.

Ryfka, now lay in the wagon's bed, with Edna on one side and Matty on the other, both held a hand and did what they could to comfort her.

"Okay, girls, are we okay to depart?" asked Boris.

"Yes, we are ready to go," replied Matty.

At the reins, Boris said, "We will not be going fast, as we are afraid we could injure your gramma if we are not careful."

The sun shone high in the cloudless sky, the lone wagon disappearing into the smooth roll of the countryside as they headed for the center of the village.

With a look of dire concern on his face, Ernst said, "Boris, we will head straight for the synagogue."

The five of them soon arrived at the edge of the village. The twins sat on each side of Ryfka, each holding a hand, as the wagon pulled up to the front of the synagogue. The girls comforted Ryfka as best they could. Edna said, "Gramma, we are at the synagogue. The two nice men are looking for the rabbi. Help will be here soon, Gramma."

Ernst, looking like everything would be okay, said, "You two keep her company while we go for help. If anyone appears while we are in the synagogue, come in and let us know."

With a look of concern that lit up his face, Boris looked about the interior of the synagogue, seeking anyone. He quickly got the attention of a passerby. "Hello, madam. We have a grandmother in a wagon out front. We believe she suffered a stroke. Are there any medical personnel around who could examine her?"

A male voice broke into the conversation, "Hello, I am Rabbi Andrej Lamm. How may I help you?"

"Hello, Rabbi Lamm, I am Boris Braunhaufer. My partner and I delivered a crate to the Kelner residence earlier today."

"Ryfka Kelner and the twins?"

"Yes, Ryfka, presently in an immobile state, is in the wagon out front. I am confident a stroke caused her current condition."

"A stroke? Oh, my Heavenly Father, please protect my dear Ryfka. Please, dear Lord! Please take me to her. The dear Lord does indeed work in mysterious ways. A doctor in Jozefow is something we have yet to experience for a year. He sent us Dr. Stein and the nurse, not only for the residents but He sent them for Ryfka—God's Blessings."

As they walked to the wagon, the rabbi asked, "How do you know she may have suffered a stroke?"

Boris said with confidence in his voice, "From experience. We lost my grandfather to a stroke last year, and her symptoms are identical. Ryfka was fortunate, as we lost my grandfather within five minutes of his stroke."

In tears and huddled around Ryfka, the twins recited Jewish prayers while they helped the rabbi into the wagon.

The rabbi, in a kneeling position, thought about how this poor family had suffered in previous years and wondered why God had ravaged this wonderful family with so many unfortunate circumstances. *Why? First Ryfka's husband, then Henna, and now my dear Ryfka? Why?*

"Hello, my dear Edna. Hello, my dear Matty." He grabbed Ryfka's hand and squeezed it. "Hello, my dear Ryfka. We are going to get you some help. You are so fortunate. A doctor and a nurse from Warsaw are in Jozefow today. How are you feeling right this moment?"

Speaking above a whisper, Ryfka murmured in a delicate, subdued mumble of a voice what sounded like, "Where am I? Where am I?"

The rabbi stared at the twins and whispered to them in a voice barely above a whisper, "I regret saying this to both of you. We can only guess what she tried to tell us."

"Shall we move Ryfka into the synagogue?" asked Boris.

Now joined by his assistant, Ms. Klein, the rabbi said, "We will prepare a room for her here. Please, Ms. Klein, get the guest office prepared for her. Have someone help you bring a couple more tables into the office. We will take the blankets we have here, plus others. We must pad the table for Ryfka. In the meantime, we will retrieve the doctor. Let us get moving, we must hurry, as a stroke will not wait on us."

The twins, wiping tears from their eyes, said in unison. "God answered our prayers!"

Ryfka rested in comfort as the synagogue staff arranged a comfortable position on tables pulled together and lined with thick blankets. Regardless, her condition changed little.

Boris and Ernst remained with the twins while staff members rushed to retrieve the doctor and his assistant.

An hour after her stroke, the doctor and his nurse arrived.

The doctor, a bald, frail man with a trimmed gray mustache and beard in a white doctor's gown, exhibited a short stature with glasses on the tip of his nose as he entered the room. "Hello, I am Dr. Stein. I also wish to introduce my nurse, Mary Myers, who will assist."

Nurse Myers approached the twins, embraced them, and said, "We will do our best. The doctor is good at making the sick well again." She then directed them to a small bench to sit while the doctor began his examination.

"Let's see here," he said as he shined a tiny flashlight into her eyes.

He took his stethoscope and placed the pad on areas up and down, and around her neck. He moved the sagging tissue of her left cheek up and down and around. He checked each arm for reflexes. He placed the stethoscope on her chest and, with a small tool, looked into each ear.

"Let's step outside of the room," Dr. Stein said. Boris and Ernst remained with Ryfka. As the doctor left, he said, "We shall return in a few minutes. Please keep Ryfka company—thank you both for your assistance thus far."

The doctor, nurse, twins, and the rabbi met in the rabbi's office.

Upon entering the rabbi's office, the twins asked, in unison, "Is Gramma Ryfka going to be okay?"

"I know the two of you are too young to hear what I have to say today, but based on what Rabbi Mann told me, you two will help in taking care of Gramma Ryfka. So, I will tell you what I know from my brief look at her."

"First, you and your friends saved her life by bringing her to the rabbi today. Your friend, Boris, well, his experience caring for a stroke victim: this experience is why she is alive. We have good news and sad news. First, she suffered a minor stroke. Any stroke causes damage that current medical practices cannot repair. So, the good news is that she experienced a minor stroke. The sad news is she may never walk again. The Almighty may prove me wrong, but I don't think so."

The rabbi said, "Dear God, thank you, and bless Ryfka and these girls." Staring into the heavens and ignoring the structure above them, he said, "We thank you, dear Lord, for placing a doctor from Warsaw here in Jozefow today. We are fortunate that midwives and others were trained by our traveling doctor and nurse in our tiny town today. The gift of having medical help, God blessed us all today."

The twins embraced one another, and both began crying.

"There must be something you can do, please. Can't you fix her so she can walk?" Edna cried.

The nurse, a friendly lady with bright red hair and glasses, smiled kindly. "I'm so sorry, sweethearts. Grandma had something called a 'stroke.' It's like when a little river inside her head got blocked. It happens to lots of grown-ups."

The doctor, now holding their hands, added, "The nurse is right. Grandma is lucky she's still with us. We can help her. A stroke is like when a tiny road inside gets blocked. That road carries blood, like a special juice, to the brain. The brain needs that juice to work, just like you need milk to grow! Without it, it's hard to walk and talk."

"We're going to give Grandma some medicine called 'aspirin.' Have you heard of it?"

Edna said, "Daddy takes aspirin when his head hurts."

"Exactly! It's like a helper for the blood. Grandma needs to take one every morning and one at bedtime. It will make it easier for the special juice to get to her brain."

"Will Grandma get all better?" Matty asked.

The doctor said, "Grandma's body is a little bit hurt inside, and we don't have magic to make it perfect again. But the aspirin will help stop it from getting worse. Sometimes, it even helps people talk a little better after a while."

"She might talk a little funny at first, like she's whispering or mumbling. It might be hard to understand her, but don't worry! It's like learning a secret language. You'll get used to it, and soon, you'll know, without a doubt, exactly what she's saying. You'll become good at understanding her new way of talking."

"How will she pee and poop?" asked Matty.

"Yes, what a great question. First, Ryfka will not be able to walk. She will, one day, gain some use of her arms. We must plan for her to get a wheelchair."

"Wheelchair?" Edna asked. "A chair with wheels on it. Right?"

"You are right—a chair with two wheels smaller than wagon wheels. The chair sports one wheel on each side and two smaller wheels on the back. Ryfka sits in the chair, and one of you pushes or wheels her around your home. Over time, she can move around on her own. We will ensure you have a wheelchair in the coming days."

"I think I saw one of these wheeled chairs on a visit to the train station," Edna said.

"Yes, wheelchairs are popular these days. Over time, your family should get her to the point where she can do things herself. Doing things to make her feel that you two don't do everything for her teaches her to start doing things for herself. We call this self-sufficient. It's a bunch of words for five-year-olds, but these words are good to learn and know. Ryfka's abilities will get better over time. But the changes for the better are taken in baby steps. You see when you were born, it took a long time for you to learn to walk, talk, feed yourself, and go pee and poop. Ryfka can be compared to a small baby right now. The good news—she will get better over time."

Edna and Matty glanced at each other and embraced the doctor and his nurse.

"We must leave in the morning and head back to Warsaw," Dr. Stein said. "We will be back in Jozefow in two months. We will be sure to check on your Gramma Ryfka when we are back here."

The twins hugged both the doctor and his nurse while the synagogue staff said their goodbyes to all. They hugged one another while the doctor extended a special thank you to Boris for his amateur, however correct, diagnosis of Ryfka's condition.

CHAPTER EIGHTEEN

Jozefow, Poland
July 21ˢᵗ, 1937, 8:30 a.m.

Halina and the rabbi stepped down from the buggy and approached the Kelner residence. He tapped a second time. "Anybody home?" The sound echoed faintly, like a whisper in a big, empty room.

Inside, the twins, in aprons covered in messy, colorful paint—red, blue, yellow, all mixed up—looked at each other with big, round eyes. They felt like bouncing balls, full of excited energy. A secret question passed between them without saying a word: Was that the rabbi and Halina?

Pictures they made, all bright and colorful, were spread out on the kitchen table. One had real dried flowers stuck on it, and the other one had painted flowers! They plopped their brushes down, clatter, clatter, on the wooden table. They wiped the paint from their tiny fingers and headed to the front door.

"Oh, it's the rabbi!" Matty yelled, her voice like a little bell. "And Halina is with him."

They ran to the door as fast as their little legs could carry them and peeked through the window. And there it was: the horse and buggy, just like they knew it. They pulled the door open, creaking.

"Hello, Halina. Hello, rabbi." The twins said in near-unison, "We're making pictures, like you showed us."

The rabbi and Halina came inside, Halina going right over to look at the pictures on the table.

"My, you two are such good artists! It will be so much fun putting your paintings up," she said.

The rabbi stepped over to chat with Gramma Ryfka, who was in bed. "How are you, Ryfka? Are you comfy?"

"So nice, nice, nice of you to come, come, come, you came, rabbi. See, see, see, Halina is helping, helping, helping the girls make nice paintings. She's like an angel, rabbi, a real angel!

G-God is v-very, v-very, g-good, g-good. I am a believer that G-God, G-God, G-God s-sent Halina to help us with caring for me and assisting the twins. Halina was s-sent, s-sent, s-sent to help us, for sure."

Matty puffed out her chest, trying to be very grown-up. "Halina said we should say, 'Ryfka is resting... comfy!'"

"I'm so glad Ryfka is resting—comfy! *Comfy*! Now, that's a word so many girls your age have never heard before. My, you two look busy as bees. What did you paint?" the rabbi asked.

Edna pointed to the table, and with a little bit of red paint on her cheek, she said, "We're painting real dried flowers that we pasted with flour and water paste we made. When everything dried, we painted the flowers. Do you like how the painting turned out?"

"Yes, the paintings are very pretty. Perhaps someone at the synagogue will want to buy the paintings from you at the next bake sale?"

"Wow. We never thought of that—selling our paintings?"

"Well, girls, I have a big, big surprise!" He waited a moment, making it more exciting. "I talked to your father, Abram, about the big crate from New York! And guess what? He said he'll open it after supper tonight! I wanted to tell you right away!"

Halina asked. "Girls, what do you say to the rabbi?"

"Thank you, thank you, thank you, rabbi!" the twins shouted like little firecrackers. They jumped and squealed, spinning around like little tops. Their painted aprons flew around them.

From the couch, a voice, slow and bumpy, said, "I am so happy to hear, hear, hear this. You don't know, know, how much we talk, talk, talk about the box from America!"

The rabbi smiled, a kind, warm smile. "While I am here, how is everything going with Halina?"

"She," the voice said slowly, "she is a gift, gift, gift, from up high, Rabbi. We love her, and the girls love her so much!"

The rabbi's eyes got even softer. "She's happy, too. She was all alone after her husband and son were gone. I'm so glad this is good. Halina has been in low spirits for a long time. And Ryfka, you're talking so much better after being so sick—it's amazing! Thank you, God!" He looked up as if talking to someone very special.

"Yes, I am getting better every day."

"It's okay if Halina and the girls help correct how you speak, as it will make you get your voice back."

"Yes, it is helping. Like I say, rabbi, Halina is a gift from God."

"So many people prayed for you, and God heard the prayers."

"People told, told, told me what happened w-when, w-when, w-when I was sick. They said Halina and, and, and, the girls go, go, go for walks, and Halina shows them birds and trees and bugs and ducks! And when they come back, the girls bring me flowers. And they're learning the flower names!" Ryfka said, "I don't know, know, know the names! And seeing the girls so, so, so, so happy. To get flowers, it m-makes, m-makes, m-makes my heart so h-happy. I am so, so, so glad to see the girls learn things."

"That's very good, Ryfka."

The rabbi continued, "Halina will teach the girls to make bread and soap and plant flowers and make butter and other things."

"She was helping the girls talk in Yiddish better, and she even got them to c-clean, c-clean the fish Icek caught! They wouldn't even touch fish before! Halina is a gift, yes, a real gift," Ryfka said.

"I can see the girls love Halina, and Halina loves the girls. Halina feels like she has something important to do for the first time in a long time. God works in funny ways," the rabbi said.

"Thank you so much, Rabbi Lamm, for the happy things you brought to us," Ryfka said.

The rabbi looked up with a big, happy smile and said, "I think the happy things came from God!"

CHAPTER NINETEEN

Jozefow, Poland
July 25ʰ, 1937, 4:50 p.m.

It was a summer evening bathed in a soft, golden light. Not a single cloud dared to interrupt the sky's perfect azure. The arid air carried the faintest whisper of wind.

Ryfka, confined to her wheelchair, was framed by the gnarled branches of the oak. Halina, perched on a stool, oversaw the twins' efforts to liberate corn kernels and snap green beans. Icek, a piece of straw jutting from his teeth, sat with a whetstone singing against steel as he honed the edge of his filleting knife. Seven fish lay glistening on a wooden board: three slender, four that were plump enough to satisfy a hunger. The largest, a speckled beauty, promised a hearty meal for two.

"Tonight, we see what treasures Asia and Jakub sent?" Icek finally asked, spitting the straw. "How did you sweet-talk Father into this? Especially with Gramma unwell, he usually believes such revelries are ill-timed."

Halina's lips curved into a knowing smile. "Divine intervention, my dear Icek."

Icek chuckled. "And what celestial strings did you pull?"

"Rabbi Mann paid Abram a visit. Heaven only knows what passed between them, but the rabbi himself delivered the good news this afternoon."

"We will be pleased with them for sure. Aunt Asia and Uncle Jakub are generous souls. Perhaps there is something for everyone," Icek said.

The distant shriek of the 5:02 train whistle rattled toward Jozefow, signaling Abram's approach.

He guided his wagon toward the house, squinting against the low sun. As he hopped down, his boots crunching on the gravel path, he saw the scene spread out under the old oak tree and stopped.

The twins raced to meet him in a blur of motion, their high-pitched voices a joyful chorus. Abram's face softened as he knelt to receive their embrace. The twins' eagerness was a daily ritual he cherished.

"Are we preparing for a feast?" Abram asked, his gaze sweeping over the kitchen table and chairs now occupying the yard. The tabletop was crowded with place settings, a sweating pitcher, and steaming pots. Had he missed some special occasion?

Icek met him halfway. "Work was okay today?"

"Work was fine, Son. What is all this?" He gestured toward the spectacle.

"We thought we'd enjoy the weather. Halina is showing the girls the art of cleaning fish. She thinks in a couple of years, they'll be doing it on their own."

"I love how Halina thinks years down the road," Abram said, walking over to witness the expert instruction.

Matty, with the unflinching logic of a child, piped up, "Halina said dead fish can't bite! And they are like us. Two eyes, fins are their arms, and they have a butt. Halina said fish breathe water, and we breathe air. We can't hurt them since they're dead."

Abram stroked his beard. "And what inspired this sudden burst of fish-related enthusiasm? Icek, all this time, you needed only to explain that dead fish can't hurt."

Abram stepped toward the table. "Fresh cornbread, potato salad, green beans, corn on the cob, and fresh fish for dinner," he murmured, the aroma making his stomach rumble. He reached across the table to sample a fingertip of potato salad. "Eating outside was a great idea!"

"By the way," he announced, raising his voice for all to hear, "I have a surprise. After dinner, we will open the crate from Asia and Jakub! And remember, since I have no idea what they sent, we must be appreciative regardless, and there must be no complaints."

The twins erupted into a whirlwind of motion, chanting a Polish children's song.

"Thank you so much, Father, thank you!" they sang in unison.

"Father, this is like Hanukkah in July," Matty said, grabbing his hand to escort him back toward the house, her eyes shining.

The last plate was cleared, and the twins scrubbed the dishes with a surprising diligence that Abram noted with a smile. Halina poured tea, accompanying it with tiny, imperfectly shaped sugar cookies. She fidgeted in her chair, running her fingers through her hair.

"I know I am not part of this family," she began, her voice quiet. "However, you must know, I feel like a part of this family after such a short time."

Abram rose, his own voice warm. "Halina, you are part of this family. We took you in as if you were a sister or daughter. We want you to feel the same way. So, yes, welcome to the family."

A ripple of applause startled Halina. Her cheeks flushed as she looked from face to face. "Thank you. I appreciate your kindness," she said, her voice thick with emotion. "Something had been missing from my life for years, and all of you helped me discover what it was. I was lost. I lost my wonderful husband to a horrible sickness, and years later, I lost my only son to typhus in '31. Since losing my son, I lost something dear to me—the will to enjoy life. My purpose. But, in less than a week, you have saved me from me." She dabbed at her eyes with a handkerchief. "Each day, I am allowed to give love, instruction, guidance, and caring—and the gift I receive in return is the love each of you gives me as if we were blood relatives. I can't begin to remember when my mood was this good."

Her words hung in the air, creating a deep sense of connection that Abram felt settle over the small group.

"So, thank you," she finished. "God put me here for a reason. Again, thank you."

Ryfka struggled to form the words, her hand trembling as she reached for Halina's. "You, you, you, are, are, are right. God, God, God, sent, sent, sent you to us. Add to that, He sent, sent, sent, sent you through our rabbi. How much, much, much proof do we need to prove that God played, played, played a role?"

"Amen!" Abram responded.

"Come on," Icek declared, pushing back his chair. "Let's haul that crate into the light. I'll grab the hammer and crowbar from the barn."

Minutes later, the crate sat squarely beneath the oak. Abram watched the twins strain to see as he and Icek pried at the lid. With a groan of splintering wood, it gave way. The twins lunged forward, scattering packing straw.

A peculiar case emerged. Icek hoisted it onto the table. Bold letters spelled out "SINGER."

"Singer? What is a Singer?" Icek wondered aloud.

Abram shrugged. "No idea. Unsnap it, let's see inside."

Icek flipped the clasps, his face a mask of confusion.

Halina gasped. "I know what that is! It's a sewing machine!"

Abram peered over Icek's shoulder. "So, it is. Look at this: sewing patterns for dresses, quilts... ten bolts of material... thread, zippers, buttons... and rolls of cotton." A smile touched his lips. "Someone is going to be busy sewing, but not me. How about you, Icek? Have you ever thought of a career as a tailor?"

"Not so, Father," Icek replied, though his eyes were fixed on the machine's intricate parts. "But I like gadgets, and the Singer contraption looks quite like a gadget."

Halina interjected, "I have experience with sewing machines. I shall show you the ropes; you might have hidden talents."

Abram rummaged deeper into the crate. "Leather work boots! My size, and fine ones at that!" He pulled out a smaller box. "And this is a fishing reel. Son, this is for you!"

He handed the box to Icek. Abram watched his son's eyes widen as he turned the reel over in his hands, admiring its smooth, mechanical movement and the inlaid pearl on its face. Icek's thumb worked the mechanism, and for a moment, a profound stillness came over him. His eyes grew moist.

"Thank you, Uncle Jakub and Aunt Asia," Icek whispered, his voice cracking. Abram saw Icek glance at Ryfka, and she gave a slow, satisfied nod, a silent conversation passing between them.

Icek clawed through the packing material, pulling out boxes of games in English for the twins.

"Asia and Jakub have thought of everything," Icek said. "There are even translated instructions."

"Girls, you are in luck," Halina replied. "I know a good bit of English. I guess you will learn it soon."

Matty asked, "Father, what is English?"

The question sparked gentle laughter around the table.

"That is a good question," Abram said. "I am sure Halina will tell you all about it."

"This one's for Ryfka," Icek announced, handing her a box.

Abram watched his mother's stroke-ridden hands tremble as she fumbled with the wrapping. She pried it open to reveal a black leather purse and, inside it, a small, tan suede-covered box. From it, she pulled a heart-shaped locket. Ryfka's breath hitched. The gift had struck a deep chord.

With a tear-laden voice, Ryfka spoke. "Oh, my, my, my dearest Henna. What, what, what, a wonderful gift. I shall never, never, never take this, this, this locket off. Girls, come, come, come, sit beside me so I can show, show, show you a wonderful picture of your dear mother, Henna."

As the twins crowded around, Abram caught a glimpse of the miniature photograph. His late wife, Henna, smiled out, radiant and young. A familiar ache tightened his own chest. Five years, and the loss of her still felt as heavy as this humid summer air. He saw tears tracking through the dust on his own son's cheeks and knew Icek felt it, too.

Icek, composing himself, delved back into the crate, pulling out American magazines, Shirley Temple dolls for the twins, and a finger-paint set. Then he found two smaller jewelry boxes, one with his name, one with Abram's. Inside each was a wristwatch. Abram turned his over in his hand—a handsome piece with a gold band. He'd never owned a wristwatch, only his father's old pocket watch that had stopped working years ago. He looked at Icek, who was staring at his own watch with an expression of pure disbelief.

"Son, you have no excuses for being late anymore," Abram said, his voice gruff with affection.

Icek looked up, a rare, wide grin spreading across his face. "And Father, does this not hold for you, too?"

"Yes, Son. You can all tell us we have no excuses."

A small box surfaced, containing a broach with multiple-colored stones. "A birthstone for each of us," Ryfka explained, holding it up for the twins to see.

Finally, at the bottom, lay a book: *The Fountain*, by Charles Morgan.

Halina's breath caught. "Oh, my goodness," she murmured, her eyes alight as she clutched it. "I've been wanting to read this for ages." She explained the plot—a love story set during the Great War. "But girls," she added, a shadow crossing her face, "this is very much a book for grown-ups."

Abram, who had been observing the joyous chaos, took a deliberate sip of his tea. His voice rumbled, low and grave. "The Great War. A topic perhaps best left for another time, with the children present."

But he saw a spark ignite in Icek. His son stood, his young face etched with an intense curiosity.

"Father," Icek began, "Was our country part of that War? Did Polish people fight?"

Abram let out a slow breath. He owed his son an honest answer. "Son, it is a confusing chapter. When the Great War began, Poland, as we know it, did not exist. Our lands were divided between the Russian, German, and Austro-Hungarian Empires. Our people were forced into the armies of these powers. Often, a Pole was forced to fight a Pole." His gaze drifted toward the darkening fields, the images of old stories rising in his mind. "Our lands became a terrible battleground. Yet our leaders used the turmoil to reclaim our independence."

Halina moved to Icek's side, resting a hand on his shoulder. "You will learn, Icek. History is a vital teacher."

"How d-did, d-did, d-did, we g-get, g-get, g-get, on this gloomy, gloomy subject of War?" Ryfka asked, her voice pulling them back to the present.

Halina frowned. "She is right. It isn't good for the twins to hear such things. Can we please change the subject?"

Abram stood, making eye contact with each member of his family, their faces illuminated by the lamplight. "On a brighter subject," he said, his voice firm and full of warmth, "let us not forget we must write a thank you letter to Jakub and Asia. They have been much too generous. We are blessed to have them in our lives."

Halina smiled. "What do you say we bring all the gifts inside, put some coffee on, and see if we can figure out one of these American games?"

"Sounds, sounds, sounds, good," Ryfka replied, looking at the twins. "You two can help me get into the house."

The twins sprang to their duty, each taking a side of the wheelchair to guide their grandmother home. Abram watched them go, his heart full. It was a good night.

CHAPTER TWENTY

Jozefow, Poland
July 27th, 1937, 4:35 a.m.

Icek slipped from his bed an hour before sunrise, the chill of the pre-dawn air already seeping into his small room. He hefted his new fishing gear, gifted from Asia and Jakub and wholly set up after a few hours of tinkering—he finally got the settings and the feel just right. He was looking forward to their first use. He tucked the few hard candies Aunt Asia had sent into his pocket, the crinkling paper a faint rustle in the stillness. The lake beckoned, a promise of a fat carp or two for supper.

Each footfall on the path away from home hammered at the edges of his resolve. *Ryfka.* The thought clung to him like the damp morning mist. He pictured her slumped in her chair, the vibrant spark that had always danced in her eyes now dimmed, trapped behind a veil of pain. Her gnarled hands, once so quick and deft at kneading dough and mending clothes, now lay still in her lap. A bitter taste rose in his throat. *Why, Almighty?* he raged silently. *Mother first, stolen by illness, and now Ryfka, robbed of her strength, her independence.*

The first rays of dawn painted the sky with streaks of red and gold, a breathtaking display that should have filled him with hope. Instead, he felt a hollow ache. He tilted his head back, the faint warmth on his face doing little to ease the chill in his heart. *Mother, are you watching? Do you see this?* He imagined her serene face, her gentle smile a distant memory. His brow furrowed as the practical worries of life forced their way forward. The coming months stretched before him, a vast unknown. How long could they rely on Ms. Adamik's help? Would Ryfka's condition worsen, her light fading further? *Seventy-three.* The number echoed in his mind, a knell-tolling of mortality. The thought of the household without Ryfka was a gaping hole he couldn't bear to contemplate.

He clenched his jaw, forcing the unwelcome thoughts away. He couldn't change the future by dwelling on it. Time marched on, relentless, uncaring. He would meet it as it came, one step, one cast of the line at a time. He set his face toward the lake, determined to focus on the task at hand, to silence the anxieties that gnawed at his soul.

Icek returned earlier than expected, the weight of several plump fish pulling at the stringer. Sunlight glinted off their scales, a flash of silver against the dull green of his trousers—he held onto the stringer and thought, *Enough fish for a proper meal, a rare treat.* He pictured the twins, their eyes widening with delight. He'd have them help scale and gut the fish, a task they usually relished. Halina, he hoped, would be there to lend a hand. *Grandma…* he pushed the thought away, a fresh wave of grief washing over him. He could almost see her, her apron stained with fish scales, her hands moving with practiced ease. The kitchen felt empty without her presence, a vital piece of the household puzzle now missing.

The twins exploded through the doorway, a whirlwind of excited chatter and floral fabric. Two bolts of brightly patterned cloth, dress patterns clutched tightly in their hands, a cascade of buttons threatening to spill onto the floor, thread spools rolling. Their faces shone with an almost manic energy.

Matty, her smile wide enough to split her face, nearly tripped over her own feet as she reached him. "Hello, brother!" she squealed, her arms overflowing with sewing supplies.

Icek's brow crumpled. The sight of their unbridled glee sent a prickle of unease down his spine. "That look on your face, I don't like it," he said, his eyes narrowing. "What's all this?"

Edna, even more animated than her sister, bounced on the balls of her feet. "Dear brother Icek! We have everything! The patterns, the material, the buttons, the zippers! For the new clothes you're going to make on the Singer machine! We can't wait! We want to learn and sew the next dresses ourselves!"

Icek's face hardened, a knot forming in his stomach. The mere thought of wrestling with fabric and thread filled him with dread.

"Girls," he said, his voice sharp with frustration. "I have no idea how to use that thing. I only saw the word 'Singer' two nights ago!"

Matty, undeterred, looped her arm through his, her eyes sparkling. "You're in luck! Halina knows all about Singers. She's going to help you! We asked her to come by this afternoon before she left last night. She said if you agreed to learn, she'd show you what she knows!"

Icek groaned inwardly, the walls of the small cottage seeming to shrink around him. He stalked into the back room, the metallic clink of his fishing gear as he hung it up a harsh counterpoint to the twins' excited whispers. He called out, his voice laced with exasperation. "The instruction booklet is in English! I can't read English!"

Edna stood tall, her petite back ramrod straight, hands clasped behind her. Her voice was brimming with a confidence that belied her age. "We know, but Halina can read English! Plus, she said we must do the up-front work before we sew!"

Icek chuckled, the unfamiliar word sounding comically formal coming from her lips. "Up front?" he said, a smirk playing on his lips. "That's a couple of new words for a five-year-old!"

Matty tugged at his sleeve, her eyes pleading. "Icek, you must help us. You love your sisters, right?" She clutched Edna's hand, her voice trembling slightly. "You told Mother you'd always take care of us, right?"

Icek felt a pang of guilt, a wave of tenderness washing over him as he remembered the day he'd made that promise, his voice choked with grief. The twins were right. He owed them this and so much more. "Okay," he said, his voice softening. "You've convinced me." His sisters squealed with delight, throwing themselves into his arms, their tiny bodies pressed tightly against him.

He picked up the pattern, his fingers tracing the outline of the dress on the cover, then turned the pattern over in his hands. "This looks complicated."

Edna tilted her head, her brow wrinkled in confusion. "What does 'complicated' mean? Does that mean like pretty?"

Icek smiled, the knot in his stomach loosening slightly. "Complicated means it will be hard to do," he explained, "because I know nothing, but I have a hunch you two know the steps to build clothes. What's first?"

Matty puffed out her chest, her eyes shining with newfound purpose. "Halina said we must pin the paper to the cloth, cut the cloth, sew each piece together, sew the buttons and the zipper."

Icek raised an eyebrow. "I guess at some point, you have to put the dress on, right?"

Edna placed her hands on her hips, her expression one of unwavering determination. "Once you have sewn the dress together, we must try it on. We need to make changes if they do not fit. And guess what, Icek? We planned how to do these things this morning!"

Icek grinned, feeling a surge of affection for his sisters. "Well, girls," he said, his voice filled with amusement. "We can begin dressmaking after you have finished cleaning the fish."

"I'm looking forward to using a Singer. It has drawings in the instructions. Maybe I can figure out some basics by looking at the drawings."

Ryfka wheeled herself into the room, the slight squeak of the wheels a familiar sound. Her eyes, though still clouded with pain, lit up with curiosity. With a look of excitement and keen interest, she began talking, "I used, used, used a sewing machine at the, the, the synagogue years ago when, when, when they made curtains for a play, play, play the little ones were in. I sewed, sewed, sewed on the Singer there. It, it, it, was eight or nine, nine, nine years ago."

Icek smiled at his grandmother, a genuine warmth spreading through him. "We'll figure it out," he said. "With three adults between us, Father will enjoy tinkering with something mechanical, being a millwright. I know nothing about sewing dresses, but at one time, I didn't grasp how to hunt and fish. I'm confident I can learn this. However, we have quite a few things to do before we start sewing. Is Halina coming this evening?"

His grandmother's brow was drawn, her words coming with a painful slowness. "She would, would, would not miss, miss, miss, miss it for the world. She is more anxious than the twins to sew dresses."

The scent of fried fish hung heavy in the air, a testament to the successful meal now coming to an end. The adults finished their dinner; however, the twins had left most of their meal on their plates, picking at the food half-heartedly while they excitedly reviewed the patterns again and again. Halina had arrived minutes after all the family members had left the dinner table.

In the meantime, Icek unboxed the Singer from its protective case and placed it on the kitchen table.

Icek's father, in the kitchen clearing dishes, said, "Girls, we have a guest at the door. Please see who is there."

The twins scurried to the door and saw that it was Halina.

Matty said with a massive expression of happiness on her face, "Father, it is Halina!"

Halina said, "Hello, all. Glad to see you have started learning the Singer without me."

Icek, with a look of frustration and lack of confidence, said, "Sure, glad you're here. We were about to get to a point of no return. I need your help right now."

Halina stepped closer and took a seat at the table, grabbed the instructions booklet, and began translating the instructions from English to Polish. "It says here we must first load the bobbin with thread. Next, we place the spool of thread on the spindle on top of the machine and route the thread through the mysterious direction shown on the drawing."

With a blank stare, Icek asked, "What is a bobbin?"

Halina, grinning from ear to ear as she looked at the twins, smiled, said, "Sewing machines have the top thread, the spool, and the bottom thread, the bobbin. It takes both to make a stitch."

"I will take your word for it. Sounds like magic," Icek replied.

Halina said, "To all of you in this home tonight, you need to hear this: A sewing machine is magic. A sewing machine is a revolutionary machine. It has changed humanity."

Icek said, "We are ready to sew?"

Halina said, "Can you all get closer and watch as we do the first sewing? I want you all to see the magic."

They were now ready to sew two pieces of material together to see if they could do some magic, as Halina called it.

"What shall we sew?" Icek asked.

Abram stepped into his bedroom and emerged with two ragged, red handkerchiefs. He said, "Here are two of my worn-out handkerchiefs that will be of better use if they are sewn together."

Icek placed the handkerchiefs atop one another and passed the two pieces of material into the machine's needle area. In less than ten seconds, he sewed them together. And, strangest of all, the two pieces of cloth were now one. "Look, it is magic!"

Halina grabbed the sewn handkerchiefs, held them above her head, and tried to pull them apart. She passed the newly sewn cloth to the twins and said, "Look at the stitching, girls!"

Icek said, "I never dreamed it would be this easy to sew." He stood, looked about the room, and said, "The Singer produced quality that a human would be hard-pressed to duplicate."

The twins, grabbing the sewn-together handkerchiefs, pranced about the room.

Ryfka smiled and commented, "I have never, never, never seen the twins this, this, this happy."

Their father stood and watched as the twins moved about the room and said, "Hard to believe a machine could make two five-year-olds so joyful. And, add to this, they will be sewing on their own with the Singer in no time."

"Father! Can we sew on the Singer one day soon?"

He replied in a stern voice, "No more sewing in this house!"

The house went quiet while the twins, in fright, stared at their father and said, "Why can't we sew, Father?"

Their father smiled, his stern voice having got the attention of everyone in the house, "You can, but only on one condition. We must send a letter to Jakub and Asia, as we owe them enormous thanks for the gifts. Can you girls help Icek and Halina put some words to paper tomorrow? I want to get the thank-you letter to New York without delay. I will take it to the post office tomorrow. Be sure to ask Asia about any plans to visit us."

Icek, looking at the twins, said, "Yes, Father, I will assist the girls with the writing. There are so many things they sent that none of us expected. And, by the way, there is one more item that I want to show you that I hid from everyone."

Icek walked toward his bedroom and returned, holding what looked to be a large book in his hand.

With a solemn voice and a slight indication of guilt, Icek began, "Father, I didn't want to show you this last night—at the time, waiting seemed the right thing. When I looked at this last night, it brought tears. When we lost our mother, I was a mere eight-year-old. I remember Mother, but I have tried so many times to imagine what she would look like now, had she lived. Well, she does have an identical twin sister— Asia sent us a photo album."

His father jumped up from where he sat. His face turned from pale white to red. It was easy to see he was angry. "A photo album?" Abram said in an angry tone. "And you did not show it to us? What were you thinking?"

Icek knew he had done wrong. He thought, *What was I thinking? How cold and selfish? Will Father ever forgive me?* Icek, in his best defense, said, "Father, I am showing you now." His father reached toward Icek, grabbed the album, and sat in the chair in the house that offered the best light.

He opened the book and stared with sharp focus at a replica of his dear Henna. As he remembered, her beauty was startling. The first picture in the album was of Asia sitting on a park bench on a bright summer day, sporting a hairstyle quite different from what his Henna ever wore. He thought, *She has the look of a movie personality.* Asia looked glamorous, like a movie actor he had once seen in a *Life* magazine Jakub had sent the previous year.

"I am sorry, the pain is too much," Abram said as he placed the book on the table. He had seen enough. He could no longer bear seeing his Henna in the identical likeness of a twin sister. It was too much to take. He handed it to Ryfka, wiped the tears from his eyes, and stepped outside.

Ryfka placed the album in her lap. She slowly opened the album to the first photo.

"I am so, so, so, sorry. I can't look, look, look at this. These pictures make, make, me sad, as I, I, I, miss my Henna so much, and all I see, see, see when I look, look, look, at Asia is my poor Henna. Asia and Jakub are, are, are, doing well, and I, I, I am so happy for them. But I, I, I, I miss my Henna so much. I, I, I am so sorry. I don't want to, to, to, to look at this anymore." She wiped tears from her eyes and handed the album to Icek.

Icek said as he handed the photo album to the twins, "Okay. Matty and Edna, here is the album. The photos of Asia are what our mother would look like if she were alive today. Mother was beautiful, but she never appeared this pretty. Nevertheless, Asia looks as I imagined, a duplicate of our mother as I remember her, with five years of added life. It is difficult to see and impossible to unsee. They live an excellent life in America. Perhaps, one day, we will go to America and see for ourselves."

Matty and Edna, sitting on each side of Halina, sat in an area of the room with poor light. Halina pulled a match from the box next to the oil lamp on the side table and lit the lamp. She adjusted the wick to get the brightest light, opened the album, and said, "Your mother is beautiful! Until I saw these photos, I had forgotten we had met and worked together organizing the annual festival. When I last saw her, she was several months pregnant with the two of you."

Edna stood, looked at Halina, and said, "You knew Mommy?"

Halina placed her hand on Edna's shoulder and said, "I never knew her that well. We spent half a day together working with the rabbi and others to organize the annual festival. It was well over five years ago. She was always so kind and so proud of Icek. Everyone liked her. Looking at the photos of her twin sister, Asia, I forgot how beautiful Henna was."

Halina stood, looked down at the girls, and smiled. "I hope seeing the likeness of your mother has not upset you two. I do hope it warms your heart to see a true image of your dear mother. I can't imagine what you are feeling at this very moment. Though I only spent most of a day years ago with your mother, this also warms my heart."

Matty asked, "What does 'warms your heart' mean, Halina?"

"Warming your heart means that something was done or said that makes you feel terrific inside. It's like last week when I asked the two of you to pick flowers and make a bouquet for Gramma Ryfka. You made the bouquet and gave it to Ryfka, and she cried with happiness. You two felt terrific in return. You had your hearts warmed. Seeing these pictures of what your dear mother would have looked like had she lived. This, too, warmed your hearts."

Edna replied, "I wondered what that feeling was. The pictures make me cry."

Icek stood, wiping the tears from his eyes, walked toward the back door, and said, "Father mentioned earlier that he wanted to speak with me outside. The rest of you relax and plan the next clothing item you want to sew. We will be back in an hour or so." Then he stepped out the back door.

Icek thought, *What on earth did Father want to talk about? We already had the father/son talk, so what was this all about?*

The sun was about to set. The horizon looked on fire as a deep orange wall of color occupied the entire horizon. It was to be a quiet, windless night, with the song of an owl about in the distance, breaking the silence of the night.

Icek began gathering wood and piled a few logs. He then asked, "Father, do you care if we light a fire?"

His father walked about the area, and he too picked up what was needed for kindling. "No. Not at all. A fire would be nice. Have a seat, Icek, while I get the fire started."

He squatted to place kindling at the base of the fire, pulled a match from his shirt pocket, and lit the bundle of twigs. Twenty minutes later, the fire was blazing away.

"Father, I apologize for not showing you the photo album last night. After looking at three photographs, I couldn't force myself to look further. Those photos caused me to cry. And I thought I had outgrown crying. I miss Mother every day, but seeing those pictures, I see the future we have missed. It's not fair, Father."

His father stood, poked at the fire with a stick, and said, "I can tell you, son, I won't be looking at any more of the album. I don't want to put myself through more of what could have been—and the future God destined us to enjoy that we will not have."

Icek looked into the flames, his heart feeling distraught, the tears not ceasing. He turned and said, "Father, I couldn't let you see the album, as I knew it would be difficult. It was going to tear at your heart. I thought you might find the album sooner or later and be mad at me. I guess I was doing my part to protect you. I appreciate everything that Asia and Jakub sent, but I wasn't expecting photos."

His father moved closer, and they hugged one another. "Son, first, let's briefly forget about the pictures of Asia. I fail to tell you how proud I am. We have both been through a lot these past years. You have weathered more than your share of storms for a child soon to turn thirteen on his next birthday. In addition, I never dreamed you would be such a fine outdoorsman. You are well ahead of where I was at your age, and this skill you have will serve you well in the coming years of your life."

Icek took a seat by the fire and said, "Thank you for the compliments, though I don't think this is why you asked to talk."

His father lowered himself next to Icek and said, "You are years above your age, son. You are right. There are other things I want to discuss. Please, son, never repeat what I am about to tell you."

Icek, with a concerned look on his face, wondered what the topic of discussion was to be and said, "I promise this discussion will not go any further."

His father added more logs to the fire, said, "Son, today, at the mill, I met a salesman from Germany. And guess what? He, too, is a Jew. However, he tells no one he is Jewish, as he married a Lutheran, and they are raising their children as Lutherans. He makes his home in Weimar, Germany. Today, we spent the afternoon discussing the politics of the world—he has a most interesting perspective."

"Perspective? What is perspective?"

"Point of view, son."

"Oh. I had never heard that word—*perspective* before. You and that salesman have much in common—same industry, Jewish, almost the same age, and a concern for the future. I trust he hides from the world that he is Jewish to keep the Jew-hating Germans away from his family? Does your new friend have a name?"

With a puzzled look on his face, his father thought for a moment before he answered, "Yes. The gentleman's name is Manfred. I know his last name, but I must not tell you. And this is the scary part. Manfred has plenty of information about the Germans that none of us in Poland has a clue about. So, what I am about to tell you must never be repeated or shared with anyone—not even family—please tell me you understand."

"Yes, Father, I understand."

Abram pulled out his pocketknife, grabbed a large piece of kindling, and started whittling. Shaping wood into something recognizable was one of his favorite pastimes. At times, he carved small toys or the faces of small animals like rabbits or birds. As he whittled, he began speaking. "First, Manfred told me the Germans are building a facility about five kilometers from Manfred's home to house tens of thousands of prisoners. The facility's name is Buchenwald—[16] a name I want you never to forget. The Germans already have the first group of these men in jails around Germany while waiting for contractors to finish the facility."

"Who are the prisoners?" Icek asked.

With a stern look on his face, he turned and stared at Icek and said, "The prisoners are Jews."

"Jews?" he asked with a perturbed look on his face. "What crimes did they commit?"

Abram answered with a solemn tone, "Their sole crime is being Jewish."

"Father, this sounds like your friend doesn't have his story straight."

"Son, his two brothers, one a university professor and the other a psychiatrist, both practicing Jews, were arrested last week."

"Father, there must be something we don't know. Arresting Jewish people who have committed no crimes?"

"Son, we are not liked in the world. Not even here in Jozefow, as we feel discrimination each day. The local Catholics won't give us the time of day, and they won't live in our neighborhoods. So, take this dislike and multiply it by the thousands. You have the 'Jewish problem,' as Herr Adolph Hitler calls it."

Icek stood, looked up at the stars, and said, "Why are we Jews a problem?"

"Son, my friend has news that the German government has restricted the rights of all Jews in Germany. Hitler curtailed ordinary Jews' rights to work in government and attend German public schools. Plus, the government prohibits Jews in public parks. Our rights are disappearing. Son, my friend is confident that the facility I mentioned near Wiemar, called Buchenwald, which they designed to house eight thousand Jewish people at a time, may be the beginning of the end for Jews."

"What are we to do?" Icek asked.

"I would love for this to be rumors. The critical item is my friends' news, which came from a one-on-one discussion with a high-ranking person in Hitler's government, and the source was his brother-in-law. He said that Germany is pressing for a Jew-free society. This term is quite popular in the German government, as he said many in Hitler's circle refer to this 'Jew-free' term."

"Father, what would they do with all the Jews? Murder them?" he said as he chuckled.

"That's why we are talking. The Jews of the world must take this antisemitic movement seriously that had been developing in Germany. Each Jew alive should take this as gospel. I believe what this man has said."

"But what changes do you want to see in our lives?"

"I see a dark future for the Jews of the world. I tell you this to prepare for the safety and care of our entire family. All I know is the enormous installation they call Buchenwald—near Weimar—is for us, the Jews of Europe. From a commonsense perspective, this tells me that, since we are Jewish, we all need to know that we have a target on our backs, and the Germans have their aim fixed on the target."

"Can we prepare somehow? Could we move to America and live with Asia and Jakub?"

"Interesting that you ask this, but it is not likely. The US Government has reduced the number of immigrants from all countries, with a focus on limiting immigrants of the Jewish faith. My German friend told me this earlier today. I guess it concerns non-Americans taking jobs from Americans, as high unemployment is a burden as the recovery from the Depression continues."

"Father, what is a depression?"

"Sorry, son. I don't expect you to know what this means. America wants to have jobs for its people. If many from Europe go to America, European people may take the jobs of Americans. In 1929, the Depression hit America. A depression is a period of sharp and continuous decline in economic activity, and money and jobs in the country crash. During this Depression, there is little money, and as the saying goes, one can't even buy a job!

"There is no chance of our going to America. And this is why Asia and Jakub could not get us into America several months after the twins were born. The bottom line is we will not be able to go to America for many years. With leaders in the world like Hitler in Germany, the world for any Jew is not a safe one. We must have a hiding place, food, water, and ammunition to survive for days. The problem is—I am not sure how we can accomplish this."

"I understand, Father. I think you are saying that life goes on as usual until we see signs that the Germans are in Poland."

"Agreed. Any sighting of anyone German is what we need to know as soon as we can. If we can get wind of a German presence soon enough, we can have the time to react. If not, the Germans can show up and have their way with us. Son, you need to tell me if you hear any rumors or if there is a German accent in town. Do you understand?"

"Father, I understand. I hope Germans never show up in our town."

"Icek, remember, not a word to anyone. Now, let's get in the house and get some sleep."

"Got it, Father," Icek said as they walked together toward their home.

CHAPTER TWENTY-ONE

Hamburg, Germany
August 25th, 1939

The clatter of pans and the tinny blare of the radio, tuned to some youthful jangle, dragged Helmut from a deep sleep. He winced, a knot tightening in his stomach. Today, he had to deliver the news.

The orders had been crisp, unforgiving. The Hamburg Police Department was to be "reorganized." He, Helmut, would soon be leaving for Poland, commanding a new entity: Police Battalion 101.[17] No longer patrolling familiar streets, their new task was different. Attached to the invading force, they were now cogs in the war machine. "Policing" in Poland was a secondary concern. "Managing Jews and other undesirables"—the chilling phrase echoing in his mind—was the primary objective.

The invasion was set for September 1st. His battalion would follow on the heels of the Wehrmacht. The bluntness of it all left a bitter taste in his mouth.

He turned to Olga, her face still buried in the pillow. "Are you awake?"

A low groan emerged from the mound of blankets. "I am now. Oh, God, my head," She stirred, a hand fluttering to her temple. "Too much last night. I feel wretched."

"Sorry, dear," he said, though a part of him was relieved she wasn't fully alert yet. "I thought the racket downstairs woke you, like it did me."

"No such luck." She pushed herself up, the bed sheets rustling. "No point in lying here suffering. I'll go investigate the commotion."

"I'll join you." He swung his legs out of bed, the chill of the floor a stark contrast to the lingering warmth of the sheets.

They descended the stairs in silence, pausing halfway as the sounds in the kitchen became more apparent—the scrape of a spatula, the sizzle of something frying. They continued, a shared sense of apprehension hanging between them.

"Good morning, Mother and Father," Helmut Junior said, his back to them as he cracked eggs into a sizzling pan.

Olga leaned against the doorframe—her voice laced with a forced lightness. "And what's the situation?"

Helmut Junior glanced over his shoulder, a practiced grin on his face. "Just two wonderful children. How's that for an answer?"

Helmut crossed his arms. "I hope there are no ulterior motives."

Heidi, who had been rummaging in the pantry, popped her head out. "What's an 'ulterior motive'?"

Helmut Junior, expertly flipping the eggs and tending to the bacon in an adjacent pan, answered without missing a beat. "It's when you do something nice but you have a secret reason you're not telling anyone."

Olga's gaze narrowed, fixing on Helmut Junior. "Are you expecting something in return for this culinary masterpiece?"

The boy adopted an expression of injured innocence. "No, Mother! Though I did want to go shopping. Manfred's been telling me about this new comic book, which is all about American cowboys and Indians. They're cheap, Mother—twenty for a Reichsmark, and I only want one."

Heidi planted her hands on her hips. "So, we're making breakfast so you can get a comic book?"

Helmut Junior, pleading with his eyes, turned to his mother. "Mother, I just woke up and thought I should do something nice for my parents. Is that so hard to believe?"

Helmut gave a small, wry smile. "Son, your mother and I will give you the benefit of the doubt. Yes, I'll take you to get your comic."

Heidi, seemingly oblivious to the undercurrents, declared, "I won't ask what that means."

A brief, forced laugh escaped both Olga and Helmut.

"Well," Helmut said, clapping his hands together, "let's enjoy this unexpected breakfast." He welcomed the distraction. The weight of the impending conversation pressed down on him. *How do I tell them I'm leaving for months, maybe more? How?*

His thoughts drifted to the broader picture, the news that had been dominating the airwaves. *Why Poland?* The Munich Agreement,[18] a hollow promise of peace, flashed in his mind. He remembered the newsreels, Chamberlain's triumphant return and the crowds cheering "peace in our time." Chamberlin's words were a bitter irony now.

Hitler had carved off the Sudetenland, claiming it was his last territorial demand. Six months later, in March, the lie had been exposed. Czechoslovakia, whole and defenseless, had been swallowed. And the world had done nothing.

Now, the pact with the Soviets. Enemies turned allies. A non-aggression pact, carving up Poland between them. *A secret protocol.* Helmut shuddered. It felt like a deal with the devil.

He pictured Hitler with that calculating glint in his eye. *He thinks he can take Poland, then turn west, confident that the Soviets won't interfere. Will he be so lucky?*

The repeated mantra of his superiors echoed in his ears: *Don't ask why. Do or die.* His new assignment, leading men in the wake of the army, was just another verse in that grim song. He wasn't supposed to understand. He wasn't allowed to question. He would obey without question.

But first, his family.

The late August sun warmed the back garden. Breakfast was over. Olga cleared the remnants away. The children, blissfully ignorant, had vanished to see their friends. He and Olga hadn't had a quiet moment alone in the garden in weeks. He carried two cups of tea, steaming gently, to the small table nestled amongst the blooming hydrangeas and rose bushes. A riot of color surrounded them, a stark contrast to the darkness gathering in his heart.

Olga sat across from him, her gaze tracing the intricate patterns of the wrought-iron table.

She took a tentative sip of her tea, then looked up, a faint smile playing on her lips. "We should do this more often."

Helmut stirred more sugar into his cup, the spoon clinking against the porcelain. "I agree, Olga. Can you believe those children? Bribing us with breakfast for a comic book?" He took another sip, stalling. "That was quite a party last night."

"I haven't been in a beer hall in months," Olga said, a slight wince in her voice. "And I'm clearly not a serious beer drinker. I'm paying for it now. How many did I have?"

He feigned surprise, widening his eyes and letting a smile spread across his face. "Were you so far gone you don't remember? My dear, you had three. Three drafts! For you, that's practically a binge. And do you recall the schnapps?"

Her eyes widened in genuine disbelief. "I don't like schnapps! Are you sure that was me?"

He scratched his head, playing along. "My, my, a memory lapse?"

"I don't like schnapps!" she insisted, rubbing her forehead.

He chuckled softly. "You did last night."

"This must have been after the three beers, yes?"

He let the laughter bubble up. "Yes, after the beer and the wiener schnitzel. And do you remember the two glasses of wine before we even left for the beer hall?"

Olga saw through his playful facade. The amusement faded from his eyes, replaced by something heavier. "The plot thickens," she said, her voice quieter. "Two glasses of wine?"

He nodded, still smiling, but the smile felt strained.

"Please tell me I didn't embarrass you in front of your manager, Rolf."

"You did," he admitted, the smile finally disappearing. "But it was all good fun. Rolf had twice as much, and his wife out-drank you both!"

A relieved sigh escaped her. "I feel slightly better, as I have no recollection of anything embarrassing."

His face grew serious, the playful banter wholly gone. He leaned forward, his voice dropping to a near whisper. "Do you remember Rolf mentioning my unit's next assignment?"

A flicker of alarm crossed her face. "Now I know I was drunk. I would have remembered that. Is Rolf changing your hours? A different precinct?"

"I'm serious now, Olga. Do you remember anything from last night?"

Her voice was laced with desperation. "Please, Helmut. No bad news. Please."

He stood, pacing the small patio, his gaze scanning the surrounding garden, ensuring they were alone. Satisfied, he returned to the table, his demeanor shifting ultimately. He moved his chair closer to hers, the concern in his soul almost palpable. "Olga, what I'm about to tell you is never to be repeated. Never. Do you understand?"

She had rarely seen him like this. The gravity of his tone sent a shiver down her spine. She sat up straighter, her eyes wide, tears welling up. She knew. She knew this was something that would shatter their world.

"Olga," he began, his voice low and steady, "our extraordinary leader, Herr Hitler, has decided to invade Poland.[19] Soon."

"You're joking," she whispered, but it wasn't a question. "Why Poland?"

"His plan is simple. It's a repeat of Czechoslovakia, but this time with force. They'll crush Poland, destroy Warsaw."

"Helmut, you can't be serious. An invasion… that's a world war— haven't they learned anything? The world won't stand for this. A sovereign nation. And please don't tell me you have to go."

He reached for her hand, his fingers intertwining with hers. "I'm to command a new unit. Police Battalion 101. Our job is to prepare Poland for German settlers. Herr Hitler believes there are too many undesirables. We're to round up Jews and Gypsies, detain them in ghettos, and guard them."

She stared at him, tears streaming down her face, her voice barely a whisper. "Ghettos? And what then? What happens to these people once they're gathered?"

He held her gaze, his own eyes filled with a mixture of dread and resignation. "They intend to rid the country of them. Jews, Gypsies, homosexuals, criminals, anyone deemed undesirable. They don't want them there when the new German settlers arrive."

"Rid the country," Her voice cracked. "You mean relocate them? And how big are these ghettos supposed to be? Hundreds of thousands? It's impossible."

His expression hardened, his voice becoming even quieter. "You ask pertinent questions. Some of my colleagues asked the same weeks ago at a planning meeting."

"Wait," she interrupted, her voice sharp. "You knew about this weeks ago?"

"No, not the details. I knew about the invasion, yes. However, my unit's specific involvement was confirmed only three days ago. They don't want to waste trained soldiers guarding Jews. They are too important to guard Jews. We're to be uniformed police, guarding civilians."

She wiped away her tears, a flicker of defiance in her eyes. "And what about the danger?"

"These are unarmed civilians," he said, but the words felt hollow even to him.

"If someone were forcing us into a ghetto, restricting our lives, we'd fight back. With anything we could find. To think there will be no resistance is naive."

"You're right," he conceded. "That's why we're armed. Grenades, machine guns, pistols."

Her voice trembled. "We need to think of the children. We tell them you're a policeman in Poland. Nothing more."

"Yes," he agreed, relieved. "That's best."

She stood, pacing the patio, her hands clasped tightly together. "The future looks so dark, Helmut. And why Warsaw? Why bomb a city?"

"Poland has an army," he explained, his voice weary. "Force is the only way they believe they can conquer it."

Olga stopped pacing—her gaze fixed on him. "And how many civilians must die for this conquest? For what? I know you have no choice, Helmut. But if we left, where would we go? How could we escape Hitler's reach? We'd be putting the whole family at risk."

He tried to offer a semblance of reassurance, though his own heart felt heavy. "So far, I haven't had blood on my hands. Sending Jews out of Hamburg on trains has been the worst of it. This, too, shall pass."

She met his gaze, her eyes searching for him. "Helmut, give me your honest answer. No matter how much it upsets me. How long will you be gone?"

He stood frozen, his gaze dropping to the flagstones beneath his feet. He mumbled, "Command says twelve to eighteen months."

A strangled cry escaped Olga's lips. "Oh, God! Heaven help us all!"

She turned and fled into the house, leaving Helmut alone in the garden, surrounded by the vibrant colors that now seemed to mock him with their beauty.

CHAPTER TWENTY-TWO

Jozefow, Poland
September 1ˢᵗ, 1939

The first of September dawned crisp and cool. An unseasonably brisk wind, carrying the scent of rain-washed earth and distant woodsmoke, rattled the windowpanes. The leaves, already turning shades of crimson and gold, whispered secrets against the glass. Icek stretched, the smells of burning leaves and frying eggs mingling with the remnants of sleep.

A rumble of voices, low and urgent, drifted through the open window. His father was outside, speaking with long-time friends— Henryk, Marek, and Piotr. The men had helped with the early harvest days before, their usual jovial banter replaced with a tense, hurried exchange. Words like "Germans," "Hitler," "planes," and "bombs" punctuated the conversation, sharp and unsettling. The word "invasion" hung in the air, heavy and cold. Icek sat up, a knot of unease tightening in his stomach. *Why are they here?*

The rhythmic squeak of wheels preceded his grandmother's arrival. She rolled her wheelchair into the room, her usual cheerful greeting slightly strained. "Good morning, morning, morning, Icek. Do you have, have, have any exciting dreams to, to, to report?"

Icek rubbed his eyes, the lingering fog of sleep replaced by a sharper awareness. "Hello, Gramma. I dreamed, but I don't remember." He reached for the soiled handkerchief on his nightstand and blew his nose. "Father and his friends woke me. They were talking about Warsaw, the German Army, and lots of things. Harvest is over. Why are they here, Gramma?"

Her gaze shifted, her eyes momentarily losing their focus as if staring at something far away. A faint tremor ran through her hands, resting on the wheelchair's arms. "I, I, I too am, am curious. Toast and eggs will, will, will be ready soon? Plus, I have a letter from Aunt Asia in America. Let's get, get, get up and get the day, day, day underway. We will ask your father. I am sure there is nothing to be concerned about." Her voice, usually firm despite the stutter, held a fragile note.

"Okay."

"In the meantime, I will, will, will rescue your father from the outside discussion," she said, the wheels of her chair whispering as she turned and rolled out of the room.

Ryfka maneuvered her wheelchair to the front door. The moment she opened it, she saw Abram's face was etched, concern furrowed across his features. The other three men mirrored the dire look on his face. She thought. *What has changed since yesterday?*

She moved her wheelchair out on the front porch, placing her presence near the conversation without formally addressing them.

Abram continued, "I am concerned about what will become of the 1.3 million citizens residing in Warsaw and the nearly four hundred thousand Jews.[20] The information from my sister-in-law, which comes from American newspapers, reports a mass reduction of Jewish rights throughout Germany. There have been pieces from German radio and newspapers about the antisemitic views of the German government. Their goal is to brainwash average German citizens to dislike anything Jewish. Thus far, it seems, the program has had great success."

Outside, near the front porch, Abram, Henryk, Marek, and Piotr stood in a tight semicircle. Abram paced, his arms crossed, his fingers tugging at his beard. "I trust the news is not good news?" he asked, his voice low.

Marek, his face drawn and pale, met the gazes of the other men. "As the newscaster spoke on the wireless earlier today, I took notes." He cleared his throat, a nervous gesture. "Gentlemen, the news, as you can imagine, is not good."

A heavy silence fell, broken only by the rustle of leaves. The men exchanged glances, their eyes reflecting a shared dread.

Marek unfolded a piece of paper, his hand slightly trembling. "Here is what I have. 'Last November, the Germans held a campaign, *The Night of the Broken Glass, Kristallnacht,*[21] whereby violent Nazi mobs attacked Jews and Jewish communities throughout Germany, Austria, and the Sudetenland region of Czechoslovakia. And, for forty-eight terrifying hours, rioters destroyed hundreds of synagogues, desecrated Jewish cemeteries, and looted and ransacked 7,500 Jewish-owned businesses. Shards of glass littered the streets. Synagogues burned throughout the night. The news reports on the radio reported that firefighters were not allowed to intervene. The local police arrested thirty thousand Jews— the police arrested the victims, not those who committed the crimes. The Germans blamed the incident on the assassination of a low-level German diplomat, Ernst vom Rath, a member of the Nazi party.[22] He was shot and killed by a seventeen-year-old Polish Jewish student in Paris. The student was troubled that the German government had deported his parents from Germany along with over ten thousand other Polish-born Jews." Marek paused, his voice catching. "That was less than a year ago. And now, this morning, Hitler ordered new hostilities to begin at 4:30 am. We now have invading Germans in our airspace and German soldiers on Polish soil. In less than twenty-four hours, hundreds of Jews have already lost their lives. Gentlemen, the situation is dire."

Ryfka, her knuckles white as she gripped the arms of her wheelchair, rolled herself onto the porch. "Good, good, good morning, gentlemen," she said, her voice a forced calm.

The men turned, their expressions a mixture of courtesy and barely suppressed anxiety. "Good morning," they replied in unison.

"And a good, good, good morning to, to, to each of you."

Abram glanced at Ryfka, a flicker of a smile touching his lips before he turned back to his friends. He removed his hands from his pockets, crossed his arms, and looked at each man in turn. "Gentlemen, we must prepare for what may come," he said, his voice firm despite the tremor in his hands as he began shaking hands with those who had gathered.

"Thank you all for stopping by. I cannot begin to imagine German troops or Luftwaffe planes visiting our village, but we should assemble the townspeople and find the best shelters should there be an attack. We must agree to return—you know, once we know more, we will plan our next step. As the invasion proceeds, more information is apt to come across the telegraph. We can't afford to be ill-prepared."

The four men, their faces etched with worry, exchanged silent glances before offering their goodbyes. They climbed into their horse-drawn wagon, the wheels creaking as they turned and headed toward town, leaving a cloud of dust and a heavier silence in their wake.

Abram entered the house, his shoulders slumped. He found Ryfka waiting, her eyes wide with unspoken questions. The words spilled out, stark and unadorned. "Ryfka, the German Army has crossed the Polish border. They've declared war. The Luftwaffe has already bombed Warsaw." He paused, drawing a shaky breath. "The German government claims Polish authorities announced on August 31st that the Poles were planning to attack Germany. They're saying this is a defensive action. A fabricated claim—British and American news correspondents have already called it a 'false flag' operation—a pretext for invasion.[23]"

Ryfka sat in her wheelchair, her head bowed, tears silently tracking down her cheeks. "How do we know the Germans fabricated the invasion?" she whispered.

Abram knelt beside her, placing a hand on her shoulder, his touch gentle. "Simple. Most of Poland knew that Germany wanted to expand its empire by conquering the surrounding nations. Why would Poland, with an army a quarter the size of Germany's, invade? It's preposterous. Don't worry, Ryfka," he added, a forced note of reassurance in his voice. "The rest of the world won't let Germany get away with this."

Ryfka wrung her hands, the thin fabric of her dress twisting between her fingers. "A war, and I, I, I am in a wheelchair."

Abram gave her a hug, his embrace tight. "We will take care of you. I promise. Right now, everything is uncertain. We don't know the casualties, where the bombs have landed, or what part of Warsaw the Germans hit. Warsaw is huge. There are shelters and underground rails. I hope the air-raid sirens gave people time."

Ryfka looked up, her eyes filled with a sudden, sharp fear. "Oh, my, my, my God! The bombing of Warsaw? My, my, my sister, Adrianna, and her husband, retired professor Johanne Baranek—live, live, live near the university campus! Do we, we, we know if they bombed the school?" Tears streamed down her face, catching in the lines etched by age and worry.

"We need you to keep calm," Abram said, his voice firm despite the tremor in his own hands. He reached out to wipe her tears, his touch gentle. He needed to convince her and himself that her relatives were safe. "Ryfka, we now know that England and France are most apt to enter the war on our behalf. When? We do not know. For now, we must prepare for a possible German invasion."

Ryfka covered her face with her hands, her shoulders shaking. "Abram! An invasion! Are you, you, you serious?"

"Ryfka, I'm not trying to upset you, but I'm telling you what's happened. It's a long journey to Warsaw—Johanne Adamowicz, our friend's brother, sent a telegram. He said German forces are marching toward Warsaw, and bombs are already falling. The Polish Army has activated its defenses. Ryfka, I wish I could say this is a false alarm, but this is real."

Ryfka's face was a mask of despair. "Abram, what, what, what, what are we to, to, to do? Where are we, we, we to go? Where can we, we, we hide? Look at me! Please look, look, look at me! I am a wheelchair-bound stroke victim! You, you, you must leave me! It'll slow you down and compromise everyone's safety. I'm old and useless. My, my, my time has come. I want to be with Henna, Aleksander, and our son. If I travel with you, I will be, be, be holding you back. Leave me here. Let the, the, the Germans have me. I'm no use to Icek or you."

Abram stood, his arms crossed, staring at the ceiling, his jaw tight. He shook his head slowly. "Ryfka, we don't know if we'll need to leave or hide. Let's be cautious and stay calm. We need to find our guns and gather shells. If we do have to leave, we need to think about where we'd go and what we'd take. We have the wagon, the horse. Food and water: How many days should we plan for?"

Ryfka sat quietly, her fingers tracing the pattern on her handkerchief, her eyes fixed on Abram's face. "Abram, what have we done to deserve this? First Henna and now this. Why is God, God, God letting this happen? I hate that we don't know what's happening. Many people have radios, but we don't even have electricity. Thank God Asia sends those, those, those translated clippings, the American, American, American point of view."

Abram pushed Ryfka out onto the porch in her wheelchair. He sat in a chair, his voice dropping to a near whisper. "Ryfka, we need to be quiet. We don't want to upset Icek unnecessarily. Without Asia's letters, we wouldn't have known about the treatment of Jewish merchants last November, *Kristallnacht*, the attacks all over Europe. No one in town knew. And the anti-Semitism in Germany, the restrictions on no schools for Jewish children since November, curfews, and a ban from public places. These Jew-hating Nazis are coming here. It is a terrifying thought to be attacked by an invading force brainwashed to hate us. Let's pray their hatred doesn't turn to violence."

Ryfka maneuvered her wheelchair around the room, her gaze avoiding Abram's. "Abram, you don't, don't, don't paint a very positive picture for, for, for us Jews. I'm starting to feel like, like, like the whole world hates us."

"Ryfka, nothing has happened to us yet. We need to prepare. Icek will panic if we're not careful. This situation is a lot for a fifteen-year-old. We need to be strong, confident."

She nodded firmly. "I agree. I'm so glad I have you. I couldn't face, face, face this alone. But how will you run, run, run from the Nazis with a seventy-six-year-old gramma in a wheelchair?"

"Trust me, we won't leave you. Let's go inside, get Icek some breakfast, and share Asia and Jakub's letter. You know, it doesn't mention anything about Germany."

"You are, are, are right, Abram. Everything in her letter is, is, is positive."

CHAPTER TWENTY-THREE

Jozefow, Poland
September 18ᵗʰ, 1939, 6:30 a.m.

The pre-dawn chill seeped through the thin walls, nudging Abram awake. He sat on the edge of the bed, the mattress groaning beneath his weight. His fingers, stiff with the cold morning, raked through the tangled nest of his hair. He focused on the strands pulled free and felt their length against his cheek. His mind churned. Three weeks. Three weeks since the German boot had stomped down on Poland. Telegraph wires hummed with fractured whispers from Warsaw, eyewitnesses painting a grim canvas: buildings crumbling, thousands dead, a city choking on ash and fear. Then came the chilling rumors of a ghetto. He thought *the word itself feels like a cage—a steel trap sprung on the Jewish residents of Warsaw. What twisted logic confines people like cattle? What dark plan brews in the Nazi mind?* A knot of dread tightened in Abram's stomach.

He could hear Icek and Ryfka's murmurs, rising and falling from down the hallway. He clenched his jaw, dreading the thought of another torrent of rumors. The village was awash in them, a swirling eddy of half-truths and desperate hopes. People had little more to do than wonder. It bred a confused populous. Everyone held a different view of their reality, and the reality was to come. Except for the ominous rumble of German military vehicles churning down the local roads, Jozefow held its breath, ignorant of the storm gathering on the horizon. Even the Luftwaffe's bombs, unleashed weeks ago, hadn't broken the eerie quiet. By some miracle, no one had died, but the wind-whipped flames had devoured buildings, leaving gaping holes in the town's familiar face.

The Soviets arrived, a brief, unsettling occupation born of the pact with the Ribbentrop-Molotov's Nazi devil.[24] They vanished as quickly as they came, taking with them nearly a thousand Jozefow Jews, lured by the false promise of sanctuary in the Soviet Union. The Kelners stayed. They had neither the resources for such a desperate flight nor the will to abandon their home. They were roots sunk deep in Jozefow soil.

October 16ᵗʰ, 1939, 6:30 a.m.

The air hung heavily with the threat of autumn's bite. Abram stood on the back porch, his breath misting in the air. He watered Ryfka's pots of late-blooming flowers, the withered petals mirroring his weary spirit. He tugged absently at his beard, his thoughts a tangled bundle he needed to unravel before he could speak. The Luftwaffe's damage was a scar, a prelude to a deeper wound. He couldn't stand idly by, waiting for the next blow. He wouldn't let his family be subjected to whatever cruelties the Germans might inflict. He turned back into the house, his shoulders squared. He needed to prepare them all to get out of harm's way. He needed a plan. They needed to vanish.

A forced cheerfulness strained Abram's voice as he moved through the house. He whistled a snippet of a Polish folk tune, the melody thin and wavering, then placed a pot of water on the wood-fired stove, the metal clanging against the cast iron. "Good morning, Ryfka," he said, his hand lingering on her shoulder with a gentle squeeze. The touch he meant to reassure, though his own heart thrummed with anxiety. "I'll get the coffee going."

Ryfka's smile, a beacon in the dim kitchen, radiated gratitude. "You know you are much too good to Icek, the twins, and me."

He found Icek in his room, the small space barely containing the teenager's restless energy. "Good morning. Could you get the girls up? We need to talk, all of us. About what's coming."

Icek sprang from his bed, his movements quick and agitated. "Father, everyone is already awake."

"Good. Let's gather in the bedroom. Ryfka can stay where she is." Abram handed Ryfka her coffee, the steam curling around her face, momentarily softening the lines etched by worry.

Icek announced everyone's arrival with a brisk, "All present and accounted for."

Abram, fueled by his third cup of coffee, felt a bitter taste clinging to his tongue. He scanned the faces in the crowded bedroom: Ryfka, confined to her chair, her eyes clouded with pain; the twins, their youthful innocence a fragile shield against the looming darkness; and Icek, his son, poised on the cusp of manhood, trying to mask his fear.

"Hello, family," he said, his voice rough. "We need to prepare. The Germans are coming back. We know it. We've heard it from the rabbi. And with Ryfka and all of you, I can't just wait."

Icek shifted, his chin jutting out in a gesture of defiance and worry. "Father, what do you expect them to do?"

Abram took another sip of his coffee, the warmth a fleeting comfort. "That's the problem, Icek. We don't know. But we know they hate us. We've heard the stories from Warsaw. The ghetto is a prison, growing by the day. And the trains." He trailed off, unable to voice the unspoken terror of those forced departures and the unknown destinations.

Matty raised her hand, her tiny voice trembling. "Father, where will we go?"

"There's an abandoned farm," Abram began, picturing the isolated homestead tucked away from prying eyes. "About twenty-four kilometers from here. It's hidden, nestled back from the road. It will take us about seven hours, with Boris pulling the wagon. Four of those kilometers are downhill—you get a sight of the farm on the last kilometer. The farm itself is only accessible via a secondary road off the main road. If a German military column passes the farm, they are unlikely to notice it. The key is staying out of sight." He forced a reassuring tone, but his doubts gnawed at him. The best part was that a non-Jewish caretaker checked in on the livestock. The owner was a friend of Ryfka's deceased husband. *I have to decide soon. I want to be gone in the morning.*

"For the short term, I need us all to pack the wagon. We will need everything essential, such as food, water, bedding, clothes, oats, and a bucket for Boris. Most importantly, there is no talking while we are underway. If we need to talk, we should keep it at a whisper. Icek will drive the wagon while I am about fifty meters out front, scouting for Germans. Do you all agree with my assessment?" Abram added.

Edna's fingers twisted through her hair, a nervous habit that had become more pronounced in recent weeks. "Father, will we be coming back to this house?"

He smiled, a thin, strained curve of his lips. "It's hard to say, Edna. We don't know what the Germans will do. They don't like us. They might take our homes. We might have to hide from them if we see them on the road."

"Will the Germans hurt us?" Edna's voice was barely a whisper.

Abram knelt, looking directly into her eyes, striving for a calmness he didn't feel. "We don't know, Edna. This is a war. And in war, soldiers try to hurt each other. Sometimes, people like us, families, get caught in the middle. However, I will do everything in my power to protect you. All of you."

Icek stood abruptly, his anxiety palpable. "Father, what will we do if we see Germans?"

"We hide, Icek. You take the reins, and I'll scout ahead. If I see them," He demonstrated, lifting both hands, palms open, a gesture of absolute silence. "Complete silence. We get the wagon off the road, hidden as best we can. We disappear. We can't let them find us."

"So, we'll always try to hide?" Matty spoke, her eyes pleading.

"Yes, Matty, and keep in mind my actions are with your safety in mind as my top priority. It goes without saying that no one should speak when we are out front. We must hide when a threat to our well-being, real or imagined, is imminent."

Matty's voice was small, a flicker of hope amidst the fear. "Father, can we bring Halina?"

Abram hesitated. "She's welcome, Matty, but it's her choice. She's coming by later. We'll ask her. But it's short notice. We can't force her."

The Farm – Twenty-four kilometers from Jozefow, Poland
October 19th, 1939, 9:15 a.m.

"We made it!" Abram exhaled, his gaze sweeping down the rough gravel road. The farm was a haven, hunched back from the access road, partially cloaked in the embrace of overgrown trees and brush.

Icek mirrored his father's relief, the tension visibly draining from his shoulders. "I can't believe we made it." He scanned the distance, a hint of wonder in his voice as he observed how nearly invisible the farmhouse appeared from the road.

Abram chuckled, a low rumble in his chest. "Early morning travel, a few hours each day. We were lucky, Icek, as we didn't see a single German. It took three days, but we spared Boris. He was struggling after the second kilometer, poor fellow—the wagon, Ryfka, the girls, you, me, and all that food. It was too much."

The grit of sleep still clung to Abram's eyes as he stood, pulling on the same clothes he'd worn since they left Jozefow. The stale scent of unwashed fabric filled his nostrils, a stark reminder of their precarious situation. A bath was a distant luxury.

He shuffled through the farmhouse, the only one awake in the pre-dawn hush. He wanted the coffee brewing, a small comfort in this uncertain existence. He was reasonably confident that the smoke from the chimney would be invisible from the road. So far, their confinement was punctuated only by the ache of Ryfka's arthritis, a constant, throbbing reminder of their vulnerability. He'd heard her tossing and turning throughout the night, her sleep a fragile thing.

Abram prepared the coffee, sipped the scalding liquid, the warmth spreading through his chilled body. He watched as Icek stirred, preparing for his daily foraging.

"Good morning, Father. Did you sleep well?" Icek's voice was hopeful.

"As well as could be expected. At least there were no sounds of marching boots."

Icek grinned, a flash of youthful optimism. "I'm going to try for some wild game today. Or maybe the river."

"If you're not back in two hours, I'll come looking. And Icek, any sign of Germans anywhere, you do not fire that shotgun."

"Fair enough. I'll do my best to be quick."

Icek dressed, gathering his shotgun and fishing gear, a hunter's instinct sharpening his senses. He'd grown into this role, his Family's survival resting on his skill with a trap and a line. If he couldn't use his gun, there was the river, a sliver of hope winding through the landscape. He'd fashion bait from dough balls, anything to avoid the monotony of eggs. He was sick of eggs, and the others were sick of eggs, which was a constant reminder of their limited fare.

Weeks blurred into a tiresome rhythm at the abandoned farm. Inconvenience was a constant companion. Complaints, once whispered, now echoed through the cramped living space. The twins, Ryfka, even Abram, and Icek—everyone was chafing under the restrictions. Food, thankfully, was sufficient for survival, but their palates yearned for the variety they'd known in Jozefow.

They had cornmeal, flour, and dried fruit—staples salvaged from their home. The farm provided a well, a meager flock of chickens, a single cow, and a store of dried vegetables. Abram's chief concern was rationing, stretching their supplies to an unknown end date. He enforced strict portion control, a necessary cruelty born of uncertainty.

Abram knew it was time for another gathering. He stepped into the living room, his voice drawing them together. "I'm glad everyone is here," he began, his gaze meeting each weary face. "I know patience is wearing thin. I feel it myself. There are moments when the future seems like a dark tunnel. But those thoughts don't last." He paused, searching for the right words. "Icek's been a miracle with that fishing rod. We've had decent meals because of him. Maybe his luck will hold." He took a deep breath. "But we don't know how long we'll have to make do. We might be here for months. Are we prepared for empty stomachs? Starvation isn't an option. And the Germans, if they find us, they might take everything. So, we need to hide our food. Every scrap, every grain hidden. They'll tear this place apart looking for it."

Ryfka's voice, thin and reedy, broke the silence. "My, my, my God. Has our l-life, l-life, l-life come to this? We were once so happy and n-never, n-never, ever struggled for food. Now we struggle f-for, f-for, f-for our lives and how t-to, t-to, t-to keep from going hungry."

Abram's voice was firm but tinged with a deep sadness. "Ryfka, we'll go back when it's safe. We hear the bombs, far off but not close. They're still bombing. We don't know when they'll stop. I want to be home, just like all of you. But we stayed here for our own good. We've all heard the stories. The Krauts do what they do in the villages. We'll go back when it's safe."

Icek spoke, his youthful face etched with concern. "Father, you've been talking to the caretaker. He just came back from Jozefow. What did he say? What did he see?"

"He saw evidence of more bombing. And he said small groups of German soldiers come into town. They harass the Jewish shop owners. But so far, it's just harassment. We'll go back when those visits stop."

The Farm
February 6th, 1940, 6:30 a.m.

"Four months. Not a single German in sight," Icek said, his voice a mix of relief and disbelief as he loaded the wagon.

They exchanged farewells with the caretaker, a brief, poignant moment, then everyone climbed aboard, with Icek taking the reins and Abram beside him, sharing the seat. The others settled in the back of the wagon, their faces a mixture of anticipation and apprehension.

Icek paused, his hand resting on the reins. "Are we ready to depart?"

Abram hesitated, a cold wave of doubt washing over him. Returning to Jozefow was a gamble, a decision that could shatter their fragile peace. He closed his eyes, his voice a silent plea. *Dear Lord, give me a sign. Tell me I'm doing the right thing.*

Then, a melody, clear and sweet, broke the morning stillness. Two Common Chaffinches, perched on a branch a few meters away, poured out their song, a vibrant duet. Abram recognized the mating call, a familiar, comforting sound. He looked at the birds, a surge of hope coursing through him. It was a sign. He looked up at the sky, a faint smile gracing his lips. "Thank you," he whispered, his voice barely audible. "Thank you."

He still had doubts and was frightened. A return to Jozefow may well have a lasting impact on this Family.

CHAPTER TWENTY-FOUR

Jozefow, Poland
February 8th, 1941

Abram's hand rested on Icek's shoulder, a solid weight as the boy shrugged into his hunting coat, layer upon layer of thick wool and worn leather. The back door framed the fading light, painting the snow-covered yard in shades of gray and fading rose. "Late start, son," Abram said, his voice roughened by the chill air that seeped in around the edges of the doorframe. Only about three hours of daylight left."

Icek lifted his .410 shotgun from the rack above the door. The metal gleamed dully in the dim light. He ran a lightly oiled cloth along the barrel, the action smooth and familiar. "Deer are moving, Father. I've been tracking a buck, leaving droppings by the east shore of the pond—I left him a few ears of corn these past few days. He's been taking them."

Abram's hand went to the back of his neck, fingers kneading the tense muscles. "I think we have an all-clear for the noise a shot can make. We haven't seen any Germans in over five days. Please limit your kill to a single round," Abram said as a sigh escaped him, carrying the phantom scent of roasted meat and savory herbs. "Ryfka's deer stew, my mouth's already watering."

Ryfka's wheelchair wheels squeaked on the wooden floor as she rolled toward them, her face alight with a broad, expectant grin. "Cart before the horse, Abram. We need the deer first, cart, cart, cart." Her eyes, bright and sharp, flicked to Icek, a silent question passing between them.

A gust of wind rattled the door as Icek pushed it open, the cold a tangible presence. He paused on the threshold, the wind whipping at his coat. "Wish me luck," he murmured, his breath clouding in the air before he vanished into the growing dusk.

Abram retreated to the living room, his words directed at the air, "Hopefully, your brother comes through tonight with a successful hunt. Three weeks of protein, at least."

Matty's brow was knit in confusion. "Father, why do we need Icek to kill an animal?"

Abram replied, a smooth veneer of explanation, "The taking of animals to feed us is God's way. Don't fret."

Edna added, "The deer are so pretty. I wish.."

Halina arrived moments earlier, sat on the floor, and started spreading fabric out in a pattern. "Girls, let's be glad our provider is resourceful. Now, how about the hem on the dress?"

The wind, a biting westerner, slapped Icek's face as he rounded the corner of the house, heading east toward the pond. The cloudless sky was darkening, the last of the sun's fire bleeding into a hazy horizon.

Twenty-five minutes later, Icek crouched at the edge of the frozen pond, his breath misting in the air. The corn he'd left was gone. Fresh tracks, sharp and clear in the packed snow, led away from the spot. He followed them a few meters, finding the telltale yellow stain of urine and a scattering of dark droppings. He pressed a bare finger to the pellets— still slightly warm, a warmth that faded quickly in the biting air. *Less than ten minutes,* he thought. The wind, a blessing, was strong enough to carry his scent away, erasing his presence. *Mr. Deer doesn't know I'm here.*

Two more ears of corn, pulled from his pack, were placed strategically near the disturbed area. He scanned the perimeter, his eyes searching for a vantage point, a place of concealment. How long? The wind was a cruel blade against his exposed skin. Darkness was gathering, pressing down. He couldn't go back empty-handed. The weight of his family's hunger settled heavily on his shoulders.

He stilled his movements, becoming a statue, a part of the frozen landscape. Pretending to be a statue was a lesson ingrained since childhood, his father's voice echoing in his memory: *Silence is your ally, Icek. Listen to the land.* He scanned the horizon, his gaze sweeping the tree line, the frozen expanse of the pond, the reeds brittle and swaying at the water's edge. A deer would mean meat, enough for the family and scraps to trade. The Jewish laws were clear: not all parts were suitable for consumption, but the butcher was always willing to barter. Lamb, beef, and even chicken were luxuries that a butcher would pay good money for in the bounty of a good kill.

He felt the gnawing need and urgency Ryfka's words had impressed upon him before his departure. Some animals would trade. Their protein stores were depleted and scraped clean. The pressure was tangible, a cold knot in his stomach.

He settled into a prone position, the shotgun's cold metal pressed against his cheek. He aimed toward the far side of the pond, the frozen surface reflecting the dying light. Damp snow seeped through his heavy wool trousers, the chill numbing his legs.

Even as his mind focused on the hunt, it acknowledged the discomfort, the inherent contradiction. He, a human, claimed superiority over these creatures, yet was forced to end their lives to sustain his own. His father's teachings, a constant refrain, offered a framework: 'Killing for sustenance is within our tradition, Icek. Killing for sport is an abomination.'

Tonight, it was sustenance. Icek pictured Ryfka, already preparing, the familiar rhythm of her movements: potatoes peeled, onions sliced, carrots chopped, the pot bubbling on the stove, waiting for the offering he would bring. Disappointment was a luxury he couldn't afford. Deer was the priority, the ideal, rabbits, a fallback, a compromise.

He stared out across the frozen landscape. In these moments of quiet anticipation, the memory of his mother often surfaced. He thought, *Nine years have passed since her death, yet her presence lingers,* a gentle ache in his heart. He clung to those memories, grateful for their warmth, their vividness.

A flash of red caught his eye. A fox, sleek and cautious, emerged from a thicket of brush along the shore. It moved with a nervous energy, darting in and out of the shadows. It paused, its head cocked, sniffing the air. The fox scratched at the snow near the pond's edge, a desperate search for sustenance.

Not yet, Icek thought, a flicker of sympathy mixed with frustration. Fox meat wasn't on the menu, not yet. But the fox's presence was a threat, a potential disruption.

He lay still, the snow now plastered to his clothes, freezing against his skin. His fingers, exposed in fingerless gloves, were stiffening, the cold seeping deep into his bones. "Go on, Mr. Fox," he whispered, his voice barely audible above the wind's sigh. "Ryfka, Father, the twins, they're counting on me. Leave."

A sudden gunshot shattered the stillness. It felt impossibly close, mere meters away.

The fox was gone.

Icek, brushing snow from his coat, rose to his feet, his eyes scanning the area. He saw a figure in the distance, approaching from his left. He started toward the hunter, a mixture of curiosity and cautiousness in his stride.

"Nice shot!" he called out, his voice carried on the wind.

The hunter was taller than Icek by at least six inches, and a shock of light brown hair escaped from beneath a hunting cap. His clothes were pristine, store-bought, the fabric unblemished by wear or weather. He carried a shotgun, which was new and gleaming, obviously an expensive one.

"Thanks! Been after that one. Our chickens—Mr. Fox has been raiding the coop for months. Hope this is the culprit."

Icek stripped off his right glove, his hand outstretched. The hunter grinned, revealing teeth that were startlingly white and even. "Don't believe we've met. Icek Kelner," he said.

The hunter shouldered his weapon, his gloved hand clasping Icek's. "Tomasz Banik, new to the area, obviously. Not much of a marksman, to be honest. More misses than hits. Father got me this," he gestured to the shotgun, "to get me out of the house, away from books—hunting, fishing, camping, that sort of thing. We look to be the same age. You are also sixteen?"

"Turned seventeen. Trying my luck here. I trade my kills with the butchers, mostly. You can tell I'm local—worn clothes, weathered skin, old gun. You, on the other hand," Icek grinned, a hint of teasing in his voice. "Your goals differ. You take an animal for relief. I take animals to allow us to consume."

They walked together toward the fallen fox.

Tomasz's face was a study in awkwardness, his voice dropping to a near whisper. "Do I really look that inexperienced? You hunt for your family?"

Icek nodded, his gaze steady. "It's alright to be new. Everyone starts somewhere. And that was a good shot, considering. Thirty meters, at least. With the wind."

"You think so?" Tomasz asked with a hopeful note in his voice.

"Definitely. Ten-kilometer-per-hour wind, at least. You accounted for that, right?"

Tomasz's eyes flickered away, a brief hesitation. "Uh, yeah, of course. Wind."

Icek recognized the bluff, the unspoken admission of luck. He let it pass.

"Any luck yourself, Icek? Anything for the pot?" Tomasz asked, changing the subject.

Icek's tone was confident, a matter of fact. "Deer, rabbit, pheasant, squirrel, even fish. Deer are scarce. Have you seen any rabbits? It's not always about what we eat ourselves. I trade—flour, sugar, salt, whatever we need."

"Saw a rabbit earlier, but not since. Hope you have better luck," Tomasz said, a genuine note of encouragement in his voice.

Icek grinned. "Most times, I do, except when other hunters are firing. Just kidding," he added quickly, giving Tomasz a playful nudge. "Rarely happens."

He stared at the fox, the body mangled, the head nearly severed. "Good shot, indeed."

Tomasz's composure faltered. He stared at the fox, a flicker of distress crossing his face. "Didn't expect to feel this. It's graphic."

"Your first kill?" Icek asked, his voice gentle.

Tomasz swallowed, struggling to maintain his bravado. "First and only the third time I've fired a gun."

"Took me more than three shots to bag my first kill," Icek admitted, looking up at the darkening sky. "Still got a couple of hours of daylight. Want to learn about rabbits?"

"Why not? Let's go. I'm ready," Tomasz said, his eagerness returning.

Icek started walking, launching into a new conversation. "So, rabbits, what do you know?"

Tomasz laughed, a nervous sound. "They make more rabbits. That's about it."

Icek chuckled. "Alright, from the beginning, then." He glanced at the sky, calculating the remaining light. "We need to move. My usual spot is about fifteen minutes from here, and I'm walking fast. Crash course, then, since it will be dark soon."

"Sounds good. I'm a fast learner," Tomasz declared, puffing out his chest slightly.

"Rabbits eat plants, no meat, as you can surmise. They hide, first and foremost. Freeze, blend in. When I was younger, before I could carry a gun, I was the one who flushed. Father would have me make noise, scare them out. Zigzag across a field, that sort of thing. Brushy areas near where they feed are where you find them. But with the snow, we'll have tracks, maybe catch them moving."

"Feeding areas? What do they eat?" Tomasz asked, his brow furrowed in concentration.

Icek scanned the snow-covered ground, searching for any sign of rabbit activity. "Clover, alfalfa, blackberries, and they love old barns, anything for cover: hollow logs, fences, fallen trees, even piles of brush. Best time? Morning or dusk. And the droppings, you'll know them. Look like little piles of blueberries."

Tomasz rubbed his hands together, a shiver tracing his spine. "You know this much about everything you hunt?"

"We have to eat, Tomasz. Gotta outsmart them," Icek replied, his voice serious.

They walked into the teeth of the wind, the snow stinging their faces, pushing through drifts that threatened to swallow them whole. Exhaustion tugged at their muscles.

They stopped at the edge of a large, open area bordered by thick brush on both sides.

"The wind direction is crucial," Icek said, his breath clouding in the frigid air. "Upwind is key. Your scent is like a woman's perfume, strong and lingering. They smell everything. Hear everything. Sneak up like you're trying your best to startle a family member. You know how to do that, right? And rabbits get cold. Stay still on cold days. Hiding. Keeping warm. Any questions?"

"No, I just never imagined I'd be learning all this," Tomasz admitted, a hint of wonder in his voice.

Icek grabbed his gear and forward. Tomasz followed.

"A couple of hours left. Where did you see those rabbits? When?" Icek asked.

"East road, out of town. On the south side of the creek, between the ponds. About eighty-five meters from the west pond, several of them were located along the way." Tomasz paused—his brow furrowed in concentration. "Maybe the south side? No, north. Let's head that way."

"Wind is from the West. We go west. Scent blowing away from them. You, on the north side of the creek. Zigzag, slow, for a kilometer, at least, heading West. I'll be ten meters behind, in a straight line. Don't worry, I won't shoot you. Stop every three minutes. Stand still for a full minute. Noise spooks them. My job is to drop them quickly. Let's move. Still enough light."

Twenty minutes of zigzagging passed, the silence broken only by the wind and the crunch of their boots on the snow. Tomasz, his face a mask of questioning, cupped his hands around his mouth and shouted toward Icek, "Are you sure they'll show? We haven't seen anything!"

"Shhhhh!" Icek hissed, his eyes scanning the creek banks, the reeds, and the sky.

Icek sensed movement out of the corner of his eye. He thought, *at first, muskrat. No. Too big.*

A large rabbit bolted across his field of vision. He raised the shotgun, aiming smoothly, leading the animal by half a meter. He squeezed the trigger. The rabbit tumbled to a lifeless heap in the snow.

He ejected the spent shell and reloaded, his eyes scanning for any further movement.

"Icek! To your right!" Tomasz yelled—his voice tight with excitement.

Icek swung and fired again. Another rabbit dropped. "Got them!" he shouted, his voice ringing out in the twilight.

They retrieved the first rabbit. Tomasz stared at the carcass, his earlier discomfort clearly returning. "So much blood for a rabbit."

"They're big around here—three kilograms full-grown. Let's find the other one," Icek said, his voice practical.

They followed the trail of blood, a crimson stain on the white snow, for about five minutes. The second rabbit lay in a thicket, still alive, its body trembling. Icek drew his hunting knife, the blade gleaming in the fading light. He stabbed the rabbit in the neck in a swift, clean motion. The trembling stopped. "No suffering," he said, his voice flat. "Never let them suffer."

Tomasz gagged, his face paling. "Wasn't expecting that."

"It's necessary. Remember that. If it were you," Icek let the implication hang in the air.

"Yeah, if it were me," Tomasz repeated, regaining his composure.

"We should hunt together sometime. I can give you one of these if you want," Icek offered.

"No, we don't eat rabbit. At least, I don't think so," Tomasz replied.

Icek secured the rabbits, tying their feet together and slinging them over his shoulder. "Great to meet you, Tomasz," he said, extending his hand.

"Icek, thanks. It was the most eventful day I've had in a long time. I hope we can do this again soon. You can teach me more."

"I'd like that. Gotta run, though. Butcher. Always hunting, fishing, and trapping. We can meet tomorrow morning. Town road, by the creek. Seven-thirty? Great meeting you," Icek said, already turning, moving with a newfound urgency toward home. His steps were light despite the cold and the weight of the rabbits. He pictured Ryfka's face, the relief, the gratitude. That was enough.

CHAPTER TWENTY-FIVE

Jozefow, Poland
July 10th, 1941

The lake shimmered three kilometers away. Icek's grandmother expected six, maybe seven, pan-sized fish for supper. He quickened his pace, his boots crunching on the dry leaves of the forest path. Black flies were already starting to swarm, and he didn't want to have fishing be the cause of hundreds of mosquito bites—he had learned that lesson long ago. He scanned the familiar trail ahead, half-hoping to see Tomasz's lanky frame. Five months of friendship had taught him that even a slow fishing day felt brighter with another human present.

It had been a chance meeting, that cold winter day, tracking rabbits. Tomasz, close to Icek's age, had shared his eagerness for the hunt, and Icek, in turn, had revealed some of the tricks his father had taught him. Their talk had ranged across everything that mattered to teenage boys— girls, dreams, and the whispers of war that even reached their tiny village. A fishing companion—this was what friendship felt like. Icek savored it like a rare treat.

The towering hardwoods guarding the lake's southeast shore came into view, their branches tossing restlessly in the northeast wind. *Good. The bottom-feeding fish will cluster on the leeward side.* He might make his self-imposed deadline. Fishing for pleasure was one thing; fishing to fill empty stomachs made the line between sport and necessity blur. He'd eyed the meager supplies back home—a handful of fruit, beans, a dwindling loaf of bread. Not starvation but close enough that variety felt like a forgotten luxury.

He reached the clearing, his gaze sweeping the shoreline. It wouldn't be a disaster if Tomasz weren't there. They'd made a loose plan to meet, nothing set in stone.

His eyes caught on something in the dirt path. He knelt, pushing aside a clump of weeds to reveal a deep imprint in the damp soil. He stood, his gaze taking in the familiar bend of the shoreline, the way the willows dipped their branches. Four, maybe five hours old, he judged, assessing the crispness of the edges—a running deer, full-grown buck, from the splay of the hoof.

The deer had vanished into the dense woods east of the lake. Icek's heart quickened. *Venison.* That would ease the pressure of fishing for weeks. He fixed the spot in his memory—the leaning birch, the patch of moss—to find this deer. Tomorrow, he'd come back with his rifle.

"Hello, Icek. Lost something, squatting there like a frog?"

Icek jumped, nearly losing his balance. "You startled me," he said, turning to face Tomasz. His gaze flickered past his friend. "Who's your friend?"

"Oh, right, you two haven't met. Meet my sister, Teodora Sylwia, who is thirteen months older than I am. And let's check your memory, the last time you heard my last name was in connection with the fox kill last winter. Do you still remember my last name, Mr. Icek Kelner?"

"Banik! How could I forget?"

Teodora's dark hair framed a face with high cheekbones and eyes the color of a summer sky. A smile played on her lips, a smile that sent a surprising warmth through Icek's chest. His cheeks flushed as he thought, *I wish I had another chance at a first impression,* as he felt he had displayed the poorest performance possible for meeting someone he regarded as sent from heaven above.

Teodora spoke first. Her voice was light and friendly. "Hi, Icek. I'm pleased to meet you. Tomasz has told me about your adventures together. He said I'd enjoy your company."

"Perhaps Tomasz is right," Icek said, finding his voice. "I've been so tied down with the twins that normal life, well, it feels like a story someone else is living. I feel like a mother more than a brother sometimes." He glanced down at the ground, suddenly self-conscious. "And no, I didn't quite recall your last name instantly, as I had to think about it for a few seconds. Mine's Kelner. It's been in Poland for centuries."

Teodora watched him, a flicker of something—perhaps understanding? She'd noticed the way he'd looked down, the slight hunch of his shoulders. A shy young man, possibly, but there was a quiet pride there, too, something she found intriguing.

"Tomasz tells me you're practically a woodland creature yourself," she said, her smile widening. "A hunter, a tracker, an angler, and you know all sorts of survival skills. Where did you learn all that so young?"

"My father," Icek said, meeting her gaze again. "He taught me everything. His father taught him. He always said we should be ready for anything and that one day, we might have to live off the land." He paused, considering. "You two are lucky you weren't here in '39 when the Germans and Soviets invaded. We had to leave the village, live in the woods until the Nazis moved on. Those skills came in handy then."

Tomasz grimaced, "Between September first and September twenty-fifth, 1939, the German Luftwaffe bombed Warsaw.[25] Those heartless Nazis." He shivered, remembering. "We woke early on September first to sirens. We were having tea when a bomb exploded near our house. Father ran to the balcony, shaving cream still on his face. It was a beautiful day, ironically. He grabbed his binoculars, looked at the planes circling, and said quietly, 'This isn't an exercise.'

"Shortly thereafter, we learned we were at war with the Germans."

"Your experience is different than ours," Icek stated, "than what we faced here in Jozefow."

"On the orders of the German occupiers, they closed everything off. Jews couldn't operate their businesses, their social functions, the synagogues—the whole thing. By October 1939, the Germans formed their puppet Jewish Council," Tomasz shook his head, "with Adam Czerniaków as its head.[26] By October twelfth, 1940, Yom Kippur, of all days, the Germans decreed that Jews were to live within the boundaries of the new Nazi Jewish ghetto."

Teodora added. "All of Warsaw's Jews were now to squeeze into what would be about three percent of the city."

"Think of that—three percent. After the Nazi attacks, the population dropped down below a million in a year and a half. I don't care what people say. War is hell!" Tomasz growled.

Teodora nodded, adding, "Our neighbors started to disappear. They left by trainload. One train after another. We didn't know where they took them, and to this day, we still don't know. It was like we knew everyone by name. Warsaw had a significant Jewish population before the Germans invaded. Then, overnight, our neighbors disappeared."

"The shelves were bare. Few cars drove due to the Nazi bombing. The Krauts made our lives miserable. The only good Nazi is a dead one!" Tomasz declared, shaking his fist. "Treating the Jews like animals. Moving Jews from here to there, there to here wasn't enough. They had the nerve to ship other Europeans into the Warsaw ghetto. Teodora's and my Jewish schoolmates—poof!"

Teodora wiped the corner of each eye, catching tears welling.

Icek was a bit stunned at their experience, as Jozefow's issues now seemed trivial. "So, what happened to your Jewish acquaintances?"

"To this day, we have no idea." Teodora took a deep breath and looked to the ground.

Tomasz, mimicking his sister, rubbed at his eyes, "I never learned about the Jozefow occupation and the bombing. I never heard a thing until my family, and I relocated here. Uncle David would never bring up a matter of that detail, plus our living here under the same roof! I never realized Uncle David's shop suffered significant bomb damage during the September 1939 German bombing until several days after my arrival.[27]"

Icek interjected, "Both the German Wehrmacht and Red Army came in and out of Jozefow for a few days. We, too, had many who just packed up and left town to head over to the Soviet side. The Soviet occupation here lasted no more than a week. Jozefow became a part of the general government under the Nazis. Those remaining in Jozefow returned to relative normalcy until the Nazis repopulated our town. This past winter, our population doubled, or maybe a bit more, due to the Nazis transferring about eleven hundred Jews from Konin. We've also become the county's hotspot for typhus, as well as starvation, and have little room to roam. The only doctor who will see Jews is the Nazi SS assigned here. Death due to typhus has become the norm."

"Let's walk down to the lake before we run out of conversation," Tomasz suggested as they took the well-worn path.

Icek settled on a large, sun-warmed rock and began baiting his three handmade fishing poles. Tomasz's store-bought gear looked flimsy in comparison. He cast the lines, positioning the poles parallel, a practiced flick of the wrist sending the bait arcing out over the water. Teodora watched—her brow furrowed in concentration.

"So, Teodora," Icek asked, breaking the silence, "how long have you been in Jozefow?"

Teodora winced as she wrestled a worm onto her hook. "A few weeks. I was staying with a cousin in Warsaw, but Tomasz filled you in. My parents moved here six months ago. Our uncle owns the dry goods store here. His health wasn't good, so Father came to take over. Family duty, you know?"

"I didn't make the connection," Icek said. "Tomasz never mentioned your uncle by name. Dawid Ulwicz is the only dry goods owner I know in town. Isn't he Catholic? One of the few in Jozefow?"

"Aren't you Catholic?" Tomasz asked.

Icek looked at him, a slow smile spreading across his face. "No. I'm Jewish. All these months, you thought…"

Tomasz looked bewildered, then burst out laughing. "Well, you don't look like the stereotype. Light brown hair, green eyes. Hey, Teodora, what do you think about that? Father would love to hear that we are fishing with a Jew."

Icek held his breath, watching Teodora. "So, now that you know, does it change anything?"

"It wouldn't work for our mother and father, but it makes no difference for us," Teodora said, meeting his gaze directly. "We were raised differently from our parents. Warsaw is thirty percent Jewish. We had plenty of Jewish friends, and our parents were aware of it. The rule was socializing, yes—but marriage? Absolutely not. Bring them home? Forbidden. And, of course, romance." She trailed off, a slight flush on her cheeks, her eyes still locked with Icek's. "Some friends formed mixed couples. But they kept it quiet."

"I guess Jozefow is too small for that kind of intensity," Icek said, choosing his words carefully.

Tomasz interrupted, "Maybe you don't see it, but our uncle isn't overly fond of Jews. Though, he'll admit, the Jozefow Jews are different. He learned his prejudices young, in Warsaw."

Icek shrugged. "He's never shown it to my family or me. My father explained how things have been over the years. It comes with the territory, I suppose."

Teodora's voice was firm. "Icek, don't think of Tomasz and me as anything but friends. Let's enjoy today and forget the differences."

"Agreed," Icek said, relief washing over him. "I avoided the topic all these months. I didn't want to scare your brother off, but I speak Yiddish. I read Hebrew. My family observes the Sabbath and tries to eat Kosher when we can. Other than that, we're the same."

"Icek, I thought you might be Jewish," Tomasz said. "But your eyes, your hair, I wasn't sure. Makes no difference." Tomasz's grin was back, "Hey, maybe you should help Teodora with that worm. It'll be dark before she conquers her fear of the poor, innocent nightcrawler."

Teodora rolled her eyes. "Couldn't resist, could you? This is only my second time fishing ever."

"You're doing fine," Icek said. "You should have seen me the second time. I couldn't get over hurting the worms. My father told me worms were somewhere between ants and snakes on God's list of creatures. That God's sole purpose for worms was for humans to poke them with hooks."

Teodora laughed. "And you believed that?"

Icek grinned. "It sounded good at the time. Even now, I think about the poor worm and the pain, but after a few minutes, it fades."

She shuddered. "If I do catch anything, one of you gentlemen will have to take it off the hook. You won't make me do that, will you?"

"Don't worry," Tomasz said, reeling in his line again. "We've got you covered."

As the sun dipped low, casting long shadows across the water, they gathered their gear and the day's catch.

"So, how were you the one catching all the fish?" Teodora asked.

"Wait," Icek said, "you both caught fish."

Tomasz held up his stringer of three small, decidedly not keeper-sized fish. "Yes, fish. For flavoring soup, perhaps. Or a reward for the cat."

Icek chuckled. "Another try tomorrow. Are you and your sister up for it? Maybe a wager or two?"

"We hope to meet your family," Teodora said as they reached the edge of the woods, where their paths diverged. "I'm anxious to meet the twins."

"That would be fine," Icek replied. "But how did you know about the twins?"

"Tomasz told me. I'm so sorry about your mother. I can't imagine childbirth and twins. He also told me your father is a millwright. You'll have to explain that to me sometime."

"That's okay," Icek said, waving goodbye. "I've gotten used to a home without a mother. I miss her, but mostly, I feel like I'm filling in for her now. See you tomorrow." He turned and headed across the tree line.

Today had been different. Better than any day in a long time. He enjoyed the Baniks, especially Teodora. A new feeling stirred within him, a warmth that spread from his chest to his fingertips. Infatuation? He'd never felt anything like it. Was this what his father had tried to explain— that bewildering mix of excitement and nervousness? Was he really falling for this girl after just a few hours?

The stringer of nine fish swung gently in his hand, keeping time with the spring in his step as he whistled a cheerful Jewish folk tune. He thought, *Does Teodora have this light-hearted feeling too?* Was it something in the air?

He'd find out soon enough.

CHAPTER TWENTY-SIX

Hamburg, Germany
July 11th, 1942

Fifty-three years sat heavy on Major Helmut Gunter Schotz, Senior, as the new leather of his boots creaked with each turn he made in his study His uniform, meticulously pressed, hung on the back of the door, a silent reminder of the imminent departure. He ran a hand over the worn fabric of his suitcase, already packed tight with the essentials of command—the heavy steel of his pistol, the spare uniform, the well-thumbed maps. His wife, Olga, forty-eight, watched him from the doorway, her eyes reflecting the dim lamplight and a worry he knew mirrored his own. Their children, Helmut Junior, fifteen, a miniature version of himself in his sharp Hitler Youth uniform, and Heidi, thirteen, her braids still slightly askew from sleep, stood beside her, their faces etched with confusion that cut him to the core.

He forced a smile, trying to project an air of routine, of just another assignment. "This isn't a funeral, you hear?" His voice cracked, a rough edge betraying the tremor in his hands as he forced a smile. "Your father is simply leaving. As he always does." He glanced at Olga, seeking her strength, the unspoken question hanging between them: "Will this be the last time?"

Olga, bless her, rallied. "Children," she said, her voice firm despite the faint quiver in her tone. "Your father needs a cheerful send-off, not this." She gestured vaguely at their tear-streaked faces. "Let's show him how strong we are. We'll all be together again soon. Won't we?"

Heidi, ever the optimist, scrubbed at her eyes. "Of course, Mother. We will."

Helmut Junior squared his shoulders, the image of youthful determination. He reached out, his hand hovering hesitantly before resting on his father's shoulder. A silent acknowledgment, a son stepping into a man's shoes. "Father, what can I help you with? The car?"

Relief, sharp and sudden, flooded Helmut. "Yes, the car. Thank you, son." He gathered his things, the familiar weight grounding him. "I must be at the rail station by 0400 hours. A twenty-mile journey, then the assembly point." He pictured the scene: nearly five hundred men, most already bivouacked in the demarcation area, the air thick with anticipation and the low murmur of nervous conversation. The officers, including himself, were due to arrive by 0730, ready to march.

"Father," Helmut Junior's voice was laced with a boyish curiosity that made Helmut's heart ache, "where are you going? Can you tell us?"

Helmut hesitated, then forced a laugh, a broad, theatrical grin stretching across his face. "East, my boy! To Poland! And that's more than I should be saying. So, if Allied command captures you—" he winked, "tell them you know absolutely nothing."

Heidi giggled—the sound fragile. "Our lips are sealed, Father."

"Goodnight, children," Helmut said, the words heavy with unspoken farewells. He reached for Olga's hand, the warmth of her skin a lifeline in the gathering darkness, and together they walked toward their bedroom.

The alarm clock shrieked, a brutal intrusion into the pre-dawn stillness. "That can't be right," Helmut mumbled, burying his face in the pillow.

Olga's voice, soft but resolute, came from the doorway. "Alarm clocks, my dear, don't lie. I'll get the coffee."

Downstairs, the clatter of cups and the murmur of voices drifted up the stairs. Helmut found Helmut Junior and Heidi already dressed, their faces pale but composed.

"Good morning, Mother!" they chorused. The words were a little too bright, a little too forced.

"Early birds," Olga replied, with her smile strained.

"We didn't sleep well," Helmut Junior admitted, avoiding his mother's gaze.

Heidi, ever direct, blurted out, "Mother, Father's assignment, it's not fighting. Not against the Allies?"

Olga hesitated, choosing her words carefully. "As you know, your father has been discreet about his orders. But no, Heidi. Not fighting.

He'll be working with the civilian population. Organizing an effort. To bring them to our side."

Helmut Junior's brow furrowed. "Organizing them to fight?"

"Something like that, Helmut," Olga said, her voice barely a whisper.

Heidi's shoulders slumped with relief. "Oh, I feel better now. Civilians. That's what's different."

A sudden, sharp cry from upstairs, "Olga! Up here, please!" sliced through the fragile calm.

Olga's footsteps pounded on the stairs. Helmut met her in the doorway of the bedroom, his face ashen, the color drained away, leaving him looking like a ghost. Sweat beaded on his forehead despite the chilly morning air. He didn't speak, just stared at her, his eyes filled with a terror she had never seen before.

Finally, he whispered, "Olga, there's something, something I must tell you."

Her hand flew to her mouth. "What is it, Helmut? You're frightening me."

He drew a shaky breath. "Did you hear the phone ring in the middle of the night last night?"

"Yes. I thought that was a routine call from your commander. Was it not?"

"Darling, it was anything but routine. We knew we were going East—however, we were unaware of the mission. Days ago, the commander simply informed me we were going East to Poland. The work, the mission my men were to perform, the sealed orders. Until last night I had no idea of the details of our mission." He swallowed hard, the words catching in his throat. "The colonel said it was one of the most important assignments in the Reich."

Olga's eyes widened. "Important? But I don't understand."

Gripping her arms, "You must swear you will never repeat what I'm about to say. I haven't seen the orders, but I know what they expect. They expect... the liquidation of the Jewish population. Please, Olga, you must swear you must never repeat what I'm about to say." His fingers dug into her flesh. "I haven't seen the orders themselves, but I know. I know what they expect of me. In the phone call my commander informed me of the mission I thought the assignment was a stretch of someone's imagination, perhaps a daydream. My orders state that my men and I will ensure certain areas of Poland are Juden Frei."[28]

Olga stared at him, uncomprehending. "Juden Frei? Do you mean relocating them? Moving them to another area?"

He shook his head, the movement slow and deliberate, like a man condemned. "No, Olga. Not relocating."

The blood drained from Olga's face. Her voice was a horrified gasp. "Not relocating? Then what...?" Her eyes widened as the realization dawned with sickening clarity. "Oh, God. Oh, Helmut, no," she whispered in a low quiet tone, "Are you going to murder them? The Jews?" She swayed, her body trembling. "Oh, my dear Lord." A low, mournful sob escaped her lips. "How, how can they ask this? Of you? Of anyone?"

"Orders," he said, the word flat, devoid of emotion. "If I refuse— I will likely face firing squad—there's no choice." He flinched as if the words themselves were physical blows. "They don't even use the word 'murder,' Olga. They call it 'liquidation.' My orders are a part of Hitler's Final Solution."

Olga recoiled. "Final Solution? What kind of twisted language is that? They're people, Helmut, not a problem to be solved!" She paused, then snickered at the absurdity of the plan.

"It's Hitler's plan. To rid the world of all Jews," Helmut whispered.

Olga scoffed at his remarks, "The world? Oh, please, dear, you can't mean the world! Are we taking the lives of millions of people?" Olga scoffed.

Helmut's look was dead serious.

"You can't be taking your information seriously? Please tell me you are playing games!" Olga continued.

Helmut stared at his feet and spoke in low tones, "Between seven and ten million is what the command thinks."

She stared at him, aghast. "Millions? How? How can an army do that? Millions? This Nazi madness, how has it come to this?"

He reached for her, his hands hovering in the air, wanting to comfort her but unable to bridge the chasm that had opened between them. "It's not me, Olga. It's Hitler and his staff. It has come to this. They're planning deportations from all over Europe—camps specially designed to kill."

She pressed her hands over her ears as if to block out the horrific images his words conjured. "Dear Lord," she whispered, her voice choked with tears. "This is against everything we believe. Everything we've taught our children. How will we ever explain this?"

"You mustn't," he said, his voice urgent. "While I'm gone, you must convince my brother's wife to leave. Or to renounce her faith. Her identity card still lists her as 'Jewish.' You must convince her. And you, you can never speak of this. To anyone."

"Death camp?" Olga quizzed. "What an awful name! When the world finds out what we have done, every German will face repercussions!"

Helmut gave Olga instructions, "You must swear. On everything holy. This must be our secret."

Her eyes, filled with tears, met him. "You know I can keep a secret."

He nodded, a flicker of relief in his eyes. "I wouldn't have told you otherwise. I'll write every day. But I won't mention them. I'll use code words. 'Insects,' perhaps. Or 'rabid dogs.' You'll understand."

"No," she said, her voice sharp. "Don't. Don't tell me anything. I don't want to know. I wish you hadn't told me any of this."

He closed his eyes for a moment, the weight of his burden pressing down on him. "I won't. I won't pull the trigger, Olga. I swear it. I'm just the messenger. My hands will be clean."

"I'm glad, Helmut," she whispered the words of small comfort against the enormity of the horror.

He straightened his shoulders, trying to summon an impression of composure. "They truly believe the world will be better without them. They have no idea what evil they're unleashing. We're all God's children." He paused, his voice breaking. "I tried, Olga. I tried to get out of it. I even thought about disappearing. But where? And what would happen to you? To the children? I'm trapped."

She stepped toward him, her arms reaching out to encircle him. "I know, Helmut. I know. This will be our secret. Forever. The children, they must never know."

He clung to her, the embrace desperate, a silent plea for forgiveness, for understanding. "Yes," he whispered. "Never."

"Come," she said, her voice surprisingly steady. "Coffee. And we have a performance to give. We must pretend that everything is normal." She pulled him toward the door, their hands clasped tightly together, two actors stepping onto a stage, the curtain about to rise on a tragedy they could not escape. He kissed her with a force that conveyed years of love and regret, giving her one final hug that they both wished would become a lasting memory until he returned.

The car, heavy with luggage and unspoken fears, pulled away from the curb. Inside, silence reigned. The streets of Hamburg, bathed in the pale light of dawn, seemed to blur into a single, indistinguishable mass. No one spoke. There were no words left.

CHAPTER TWENTY-SEVEN

Biloraj, Poland
July 12ᵗʰ, 1942

The paper crinkled in Helmut's grip, the typed ink of the orders blurring slightly as his hands trembled. He lowered the document to his lap, a single tear tracing a dark path across the stiff paper. He'd read it five times since leaving Hamburg, each time hoping the words would somehow rearrange themselves, offering an escape. He tilted his head back, eyes squeezed shut, a silent plea escaping his lips: *Forgive us; orders are orders.* The thought, unwanted and sharp, pierced his mind: *End it now.* He recoiled, a cold sweat prickling his skin. No. He couldn't. The next in command would inherit the nightmare.

The instructions themselves were a study in clinical detachment. "Executioner—bayonet tip base of the victim's back at the neck level—a single shot." Death is swift and efficient, with minimal body fluids or human debris. The Reich's highest-ranking medical officer, a man Helmut had never met but now loathed with a visceral intensity, had personally guaranteed the humanity of the "neck shot."

Helmut muttered, a bitter laugh escaping his lips, "They've thought of everything, haven't they?" Everything except the souls of the men forced to carry this out. His men. Most had only fired their Kar 98k rifles on the training range. The rifles were, until now, polished extensions of their uniforms, symbols of order, not instruments of death.

The worn floorboards groaned under his restless pacing. His watch, illuminated by the feeble glow of the single oil lamp, showed the hour creeping toward two in the morning.

A frayed curtain fluttered in the half-open window, carrying the gentle, humid air of mid-July. The insistent buzz of insects, a relentless chorus, grated on his nerves. He tried to conjure a moment of peace, a mental escape, but the war, like the humid air, clung to everything.

His gaze fell on the table, the orders, *Operation Reinhard*, now a loose, accusing roll near the edge.[29] His command had branded the words and phrases into his memory: *mass kill Jews—helpless, old, young, sick.* He pressed his fingertips to his temples, a futile attempt to erase them. *Will the reality of the orders ever leave?* The nightmare was no longer a distant rumor; it was here.

His mind flickered back to Hamburg, to his family. He'd overseen deportations there and watched Jewish families—men, women, children with bewildered eyes—herded onto trains. He'd tried and failed to imagine the same fate befalling his own Olga, Helmut Jr., and little Heidi. The thought was a physical blow. He pushed it away, a desperate act of self-preservation. He had to. Hesitation, in this brutal machinery of war, was a luxury he couldn't afford.

He sank into the chair, elbows on his knees, head buried in his hands. He rubbed his eyes, the gritty fatigue a tangible weight. Sleep was a distant, impossible shore. He had to stay awake. He had to be ready.

Biloraj. Until today, the name was meaningless, another pinprick on the map of Poland's Lublin province. Now, it was a crucible. He'd spent the evening in this one-room schoolhouse, commandeered for his "planning." The schoolmaster's office, now a makeshift war room, displayed maps and charts like macabre decorations. His orders, a relentless litany of villages, stretched out before him, months of this horror.

Jozefow. This was the beginning.

He grabbed the flashlight and a metal water pitcher, needing the sting of fresh air. The schoolhouse door shrieked open, releasing him into the thick, insect-filled night. He found the well, its pump decrepit, a relic of a simpler time, like the Hamburg he remembered from a decade ago. The water, shockingly cold, brought temporary clarity.

Back inside, he stood by the window, peering into the impenetrable darkness. The buzzing seemed to surround him, a suffocating presence. He imagined the children of Jozefow and their faces pressed to this same glass, their minds filled with the simple lessons of childhood. Innocent minds. Minds that had done nothing to deserve this.

He forced himself back to the orders, the words a physical weight in his hands. Years of military training: flanking maneuvers, assaults, the calculated dance of death against an armed enemy—this was different. These were not soldiers.

His voice, a raw whisper in the empty room, startled even him. "How, how can they expect this?"

The orders were from the bureaucrats, the very same people who, with the Führer's blessing, authorized euthanasia, resulting in a quarter of a million deaths—the operation snuffing out thousands of Jewish souls—in Hadamar alone.[30]

Other German citizens, along with years of antisemitic propaganda, were hurled upon him. The Führer declared Jews were responsible for all of Germany's hardships. Many Germans had adopted that theory, yet Helmut viewed the claims as ludicrous. He thought of his sister-in-law, Fraida, a devout Jew. Fraida was as delightful as any German, as far as he was concerned.

His favorable views of Jews were not to be expressed. One wrong word, one slight hint that Helmut's sentiments did not align with those of the party, would destroy him.

There were whisperings about the vanishing Jews whom many knew personally. One day, they were there. The next day, gone—never to be seen again. His friends, those sympathetic to the Jews' predicament, pondered the disappearances: "Why hadn't any Jews returned?" Regardless, the citizens' population kept their thoughts to themselves. Perhaps out of fear?

Germans knew little or nothing about the Jews' actual fate. Helmut didn't know either. However, tonight would make him complicit in the outcome. *Is this to be my fate—to be drenched in the blood of another human?*

His upbringing and Christian beliefs instilled in him a reverence for life, rather than a desire to terminate it. At the onset of his military career, he would take life only when there was a clear, distinct, and present danger that put his life in jeopardy.

Although complicit in Jewish deportations, no one had instructed Helmut to take another human's life. However, deep down, he realized most of those sent eastward were likely doomed. This task at hand forced him to address an unknown enemy who possessed no weapons: a defenseless enemy.

He spoke his troubled thoughts aloud, "Eastern Polish Jews pose no threat to the Wehrmacht. They have no weapons to harm us." He glanced around in fear of someone hearing him. *Am I alone?* Realizing he was, he exhaled, sat down, and reached for his handkerchief. His forehead had become drenched in sweat.

I must keep my mind occupied. He pondered writing to Olga. He could always rely on a message to his dear wife to distract his mind from reality.

He began by describing the five-hundred-mile trip: The flat farmland, slightly rolling hills, and never-ending dusty trails. Then, he described the area where his unit was staying. *Tiny wooden houses and a downtown area comprised of one-and two-story buildings with minimal appeal.* He pictured his wife reviewing the letters to find any possible clues about his well-being. His letters would say that his men swatted harmless insects or perhaps mentioned the execution of rabid dogs; she would figure out the cryptic meaning.

His letter would finish by sending love to his dear Olga, son Helmut, and daughter Heidi.

After eighteen years of marriage, she could read between the lines: She knew when he struggled with the burdens of command.

He folded the letter and pressed his tongue to the glue, infusing it with a sweet brandy flavor. As he gazed about the room, his eyes landed on a photo of his family. He was there for a second, with the faces of the loves of his life flashing before him.

A sudden, sharp knock at the door brought him back to reality. His hands, still damp with sweat, instinctively moved to gather the scattered papers, stuffing them into his leather attaché. The letter to Olga went into his breast pocket, a small comfort pressed against his racing heart.

"Major Schotz, sir," the voice, tight with military precision, came through the door. "Captain Wahl requests permission to speak."

Wahl. Of course. The most eager, the most committed of his officers—the man who had made the Hamburg deportations a personal crusade. Wahl was a career soldier, a true believer, the kind who wouldn't flinch at any order, no matter how vile. He entered the room, Heil Hitler, with a swift boot click.

"Before you say anything," the major ordered, "assemble the others."

"Yes, sir," the captain returned. The door closed.

He'd stalled long enough. The seven-p.m. meeting, postponed, had left his company commanders confined, simmering in uncertainty. He knew the whispers, the judgments. Leadership was a lonely business.

Was he ready? He had to be. Failure, disobedience, and the consequences were unthinkable. The entire edifice of the Wehrmacht, of the Reich itself, rested on obedience. One crack, one moment of hesitation, and it could all crumble. And he, Helmut Schotz, would be crushed beneath it.

Another knock, louder this time. "Sir, Captain Wahl reporting as ordered, sir! All officers present and accounted for, sir!"

The four company commanders filed in, a tableau of stiff formality. Four right arms raised, eight heels clicked in perfect, chilling unison. Helmut returned the salute, his arm feeling heavy, leaden.

"Gentlemen, at ease." He saw the questions in their eyes, the uncertainty masked by practiced stoicism. He'd kept the orders hidden, a secret locked away until this very moment.

He circled the room, the orders clutched in his hand, a palpable weight. He closed the window, shutting out the insistent hum of the night. He turned, facing them, letting the silence stretch, thick and heavy. They stared. He appeared aged: bags under his eyes, gray, thinning hair, his belly hanging over his belt.

He broke the silence, his voice oddly detached. "Gentlemen, shall we?" He poured brandy, a ritual, a shared moment of false camaraderie. "To the Fuhrer!"

The glasses emptied in unison. Then, Major Schotz delivered in a voice that cracked and strained, betraying the tremor in his soul. "For five hundred miles, you've speculated, wondered. Your orders, gentlemen, are as follows. We are to kill by shooting. The subjects are the Jews." He paused, searching their faces for any flicker of understanding, of shared horror.

"Remember, many German women and children have lost their lives to the constant barrage of aerial bombardments," he added. "To be specific," he continued, his voice barely a whisper, "your men are to shoot the most helpless, the old, the young, the sick—women, children, not the men capable of work. Those will be spared."

Captain Wahl, predictably, was the first to speak, his voice sharp, eager. "At last! We can finally rid the world of this Jewish vermin! When do we begin, Major?"

Helmut looked at the other three, searching for a different reaction. Captain Fischer, the oldest, the one with the pre-war life, the Jewish friends, spoke, his voice tight with suppressed anger. "Major Schotz, sir, unlike Herr Wahl, I do not share his enthusiasm. Many of my men will have difficulty with this."

Wahl rounded on Fischer, his voice dripping with contempt. "Perhaps you should threaten them, Herr Fischer! Threaten them with the same fate we are to inflict on these filthy Jews!"

Fischer lunged—his face contorted. "You are a sadistic, heartless bastard! These are helpless people! How can you?"

"Enough!" Helmut's voice, sharp and commanding, cut through the tension. "I will not tolerate this! Do you understand?" Silence. A heavy, suffocating silence.

"Captain Fischer is right," Helmut conceded, his voice hollow. "These are helpless Jewish civilians. But we have our orders. The orders do not require us to enjoy it." He forced himself to continue, the details, the brutal mechanics of the operation, spilling from his lips. Thousands. Tens of thousands. The numbers were abstract, yet the reality was a lead weight in his gut.

"The killing begins today."

He outlined the plan: the roundup, the segregation, the able-bodied men sent to Lublin, to the factories—the Germans would transport the remaining Poles to a forest two kilometers outside the village—a place called Winiarczykowa Gora.[31] He spoke of trucks, of a one-to-one ratio of the victim to the executioner, of the "neck shot," of the synchronized volley. He said it with a clinical detachment, as if describing a logistical exercise, not the systematic slaughter of human beings. He couldn't meet their eyes.

"Are there any questions?"

Captain Reinhardt Ritter, the commander of Second Company, finally spoke, his voice hesitant, almost apologetic. He rubbed his beard—his gaze fixed on the floor. "Major Schotz, sir, what about those unable to walk? The elderly, the very young?"

Wahl, again, was quick to interject, his voice laced with scorn. "Shoot them on the spot! Why waste resources? Are you developing a soft spot for Jew vermin, Captain?"

Helmut, needing and wanting control, answered resolutely. "Captain Wahl is correct. The Reich has not provided specific instructions. But it seems a waste of time and effort. Shoot them. On the spot."

Fischer, his voice barely audible, "Even infants, Major?"

"Yes, Captain. Even infants. Instruct your men that no one is to be left alive." He added, his voice flat, devoid of all emotion. "And leave the bodies where they fall. The mayor will arrange for local Poles to bury them. Valuables, they can keep them. Payment for their services."

He knew more unspoken questions were hanging in the air. The one he'd dreaded the most: *What if a man refuses?* He'd hoped it would surface, that someone would force the issue. But perhaps the earlier outburst, the raw tension, had stifled it. Or maybe they didn't want to appear weak, to betray their doubts. He didn't press it. He couldn't.

CHAPTER TWENTY-EIGHT

Jozefow, Poland
July 13th, 1942, 4:40 a.m.

The roar of diesel engines ripped Icek from sleep. Trucks, shouts, the frantic barking of dogs—the sounds crashed against the walls of his small home. He scrambled into his clothes, the rough fabric scratching against his skin. His hunting knapsack and .410 shotgun were in his hands before his mind had fully caught up. His family slept on, oblivious. He slipped out the door, a silent shadow melting into the pre-dawn gloom. He had to see, had to know what this intrusion meant.

The Jewish enclave was swarming. Shadows flickered from the headlights of dozens of trucks maneuvering through the narrow streets. *Why?* As Icek felt the question claw at his throat, the answer exploded in the distance—gunfire, sharp and brutal. Other questions followed, more terrible: *Who? Civilians?* He crept closer, keeping to the deep shadows between houses.

The barking intensified, a chorus of canine fury that accompanied soldiers banging on doors, dragging people into the cold morning air. Icek lay prone, the damp earth pressing against his cheek, barely a hundred and fifty meters from his own home. From his vantage point, he could see several houses, where more gunfire, closer this time, was punctuated by the guttural shouts of the soldiers. He knew with a chilling certainty that anyone resisting the assailants, the Germans would shoot. The assailants herded into trucks those who were not resisting, their faces pale and hollow in the flickering light.

Where are they taking them? The thought was a frantic whisper in his mind. He had to get back to warn his family. His .410 and the handful of shells felt heavy in the knapsack. He stashed them under a shed at the village edge, the wood rough against his fingers. Then he ran. He ran as he'd never run before, a blur darting between shadows, his lungs burning, his heart pounding a frantic rhythm against his ribs. *Please, God, let me be there in time.*

Thirty meters from home, he dropped to his belly, crawling through the dirt. He had to be invisible, swallowed by the darkness. Three German soldiers were at his front door, their bodies tense with aggression, hammering at the wood.

The door splintered and ripped from its hinges with a deafening crash. It slammed to the ground, frame and all. Before the soldiers could take another step, Abram charged. Icek's sisters screamed—a high, piercing sound that cut through the night.

A rifle butt slammed into Abram's right eye, the sound a sickening thud, echoing in Icek's ears. His father crumpled, unconscious. The soldier's faces, grim and impassive, hauled Abram up, twisting his arms behind his back and binding them with rough rope. *Will I ever see him again?* The question was a silent scream.

Icek watched, his vision tunneling, as they dragged his father toward one of the trucks. Eight, maybe nine of the canvas-covered vehicles lined the street, spaced evenly like waiting mouths.

Ten meters from the front door, now gaping open like a wound, he heard Matty's voice, shrill with terror. "Gramma Ryfka, the soldiers have hurt Father! He's bleeding. He hit him with their rifle, a rifle to his head!"

The twins' faces, streaked with tears, had followed Abram. They clung to each other, their tiny bodies shaking. A soldier, his face a mask of contempt, herded them back inside with the point of his rifle.

"Schnell, schnell, sonst schiessen wir!" His voice was a harsh, grating bark.

Ryfka's voice, surprisingly strong, answered from inside. "These swine are weak! Abram will be fine. Don't worry."

Icek knew his sisters would never abandon their bedridden grandmother. He edged closer, hidden by the bulk of the outhouse— his body pressed against the rough wood. He could see the soldiers dragging his father, his bound hands dangling limply, a third soldier's rifle pressed against his back. The blood around Abram's eye was a dark, glistening stain. *Where are they taking him?*

He watched them heave his father's limp body over the tailgate of the truck, a careless, brutal motion. Oh, God, will he be alright?

That image would be the last he ever saw of his father.

Two Opel Blitz trucks lumbered into view, with their canvas covers hiding their human cargo. Each could hold seventeen in the back, maybe three crammed in the front. Within twenty minutes, at least thirty men, all around his father's age, were loaded onto the two trucks.

Before the engines could roar to life, a voice from inside one of the trucks cut through the air. Perfect German, laced with venom. "Scheißkerl!" Then, switching to flawless English, "You filthy, spineless Nazi swine!"

A German officer, his face tight with anger, shouted back. "Who said that?"

A small, thin man, his frame almost skeletal, yelled in German, "Me, you Nazi filth! Kill me now! I don't lift a finger for you. I'd rather be dead!"

The officer gestured sharply. His order was concise, chilling: "Get him."

A brief, guttural exchange in German followed, then the officer's chilling decree: "You will get your wish, you fool!" He turned to a soldier. "End his life. Make sure those on the truck watch him die."

One of the soldiers, his face lined and weathered like a man in his forties raised his rifle. With a practiced, almost mechanical motion, he swung the butt horizontally, connecting with the small man's jaw. The victim fell, sprawling on the ground. He tried to rise, spitting out teeth and blood, the sound sickeningly wet.

A string of unintelligible German was spoken between the victim and his attacker. Another blow, this time to the stomach, sent the man sprawling again.

The soldier raised his rifle, the bayonet gleaming in the pre-dawn light. One swift, brutal thrust, and the blade plunged into the man's chest. A moan, ragged and unnatural, escaped the victim's lips. Then, silence.

On the truck, men turned away, their faces ashen. Some had seen it all. Others had only heard the sounds—the thud of the rifle butt, the grunt of pain, the final, ghastly sigh.

A whisper came from the truck, filled with bitter understanding, "The bastards, they wanted us to see—to keep us in line. It worked."

Silence descended on the trucks, a heavy, suffocating blanket. Dozens of men—their fate a terrifying unknown. *What will happen to them?*

The truck carrying his father rumbled away, disappearing into the distance, leaving Icek with a gaping hole in his world. He crept to a window—his gaze fixed on the room where his grandmother and sisters lay. Helplessness washed over him, a bitter tide. He saw a German soldier, an SS officer, storm into the room, his movements jerky and frenzied.

The twins screamed, pleading. He could hear their terrified voices, begging the soldier to leave them alone, explaining that their grandma couldn't move. The soldier ignored them, his shouts escalating. Then, a flash of silver—his Walther P-38.[32] A single shot, deafeningly close to Gramma Ryfka's bed.

Ryfka's head exploded. Blood, brain matter, and fragments of bone splattered the wall and the bed. The twins, frozen in shock, stared at the horrific scene. Their pleas for mercy, for understanding, went unanswered.

Icek thought *I can't just stand here and watch. I must do something. But what can I do? If I make a noise, the number of murders will be four instead of three. My dear family, I will ensure that you have not perished in vain. This animal will one day meet his maker and burn in Hell! I will one day inflict the ultimate revenge upon this less-than-human being—I promise.*

"Schnell! Schnell!" the officer screamed. The twins clung to each other—their arms wrapped around their grandmother's lifeless body.

He shouted again. "Schnell! Schnell!" Then, with a chillingly calm voice, a smirk playing on his lips, he said in German, "Do it your way!" He raised his pistol again, and a volley of shots ripped through the small room. The twins fell, their bodies still entwined.

Icek choked back a scream, his hands clamped over his mouth. *"You animal, you will pay."* The words were a whispered curse, a vow.

His bladder released, a hot, humiliating stream running down his leg, and he began to shake—his body racked with tremors. A growl, low and menacing, ripped him from his horrified trance. A ferocious

German Shepherd, unescorted, its teeth bared, stalked toward him. Fear, sharp and cold, replaced grief.

Could I kill the beast with my bare hands?

He braced himself. The dog was inches away, its hot breath on his skin, when he remembered—*I have jerky in my pocket*. He held it out, speaking softly, his voice trembling. The dog's focus shifted, its aggression replaced by hunger. Icek saw his chance. He bolted for the outhouse and slammed the door, throwing the bolt. Peering through a crack, he saw a soldier with a German shepherd approach. The dog sniffed at the base of the door. Icek was trapped.

With a surge of desperate resolve, he unlocked the door, lifted the seat, and lowered himself into the reeking pit. The stench was overpowering, a suffocating wave of feces. He gagged, fighting back the urge to vomit.

He knew the pit was deep, over his head. His father had rigged a knotted rope and a small ledge, a precarious perch that allowed him to lower himself to chest depth. He clung to the rope, his body submerged in the foul liquid.

The door creaked open. A flashlight beam sliced through the darkness, searching. The soldier, seeing nothing, urinated into the pit, the stream narrowly missing Icek. Then, as quickly as he'd come, he was gone. Icek clung to the rope, his body shaking, wondering how long he could endure this.

Hours crawled by. The sounds of the village—the trucks, the shouts, the gunfire—faded. The town, once home to eighteen hundred Jewish souls, was eerily silent.

Daylight filtered through the cracks in the outhouse walls, and a new fear crept in. Scavengers. He wondered, *Is there an arrangement between the Germans and local non-Jewish residents to bury the dead in exchange for the contents of homes?*

He stayed submerged, listening. The Germans forced most of the Jewish residents onto trucks. He would be able to follow the gruesome removal of those who hadn't survived. Catholic townspeople drove horse-drawn carts and wagons and took what wasn't theirs: the local non-Jewish people and their conversations about who got what echoed in the streets.

The Germans had cleared the Jewish people from Jozefow. Belongings were free for the unscrupulous and conscienceless. Icek prayed, knowing the Catholic citizens wouldn't dare offer aid unless there was a bounty from a high-ranking German. Hiding a Jew would equal death.

Finally, when the silence was absolute, he emerged, gasping for air. He used scraps of paper to clean himself, the filth clinging to his skin. And in that moment, he made a promise, a vow etched in his memory: *I will never forget. Never.*

His sisters, his grandmother, and his father were gone.

He crumpled to his knees, sobbing uncontrollably.

I could have stopped them. I could have tried. Was I a coward?

He clutched the soiled paper, his knuckles white, his grief a raw, burning wound.

I should have followed that truck. How could I not even try?

His only chance had been to escape, to hide. Hide like a coward.

When he could no longer hear any movement, he eased open the outhouse door, peering out cautiously. The world was still. The only sound; the distant popping of gunfire. He waited for complete darkness, for the sounds to cease altogether.

Time stretched into an eternity. Finally, when the night was a thick, impenetrable black, he emerged. He listened. Nothing.

Am I alone?

He was. Utterly alone.

He moved carefully, circling his house, checking for any sign of life. The air was thick with the acrid smell of gunpowder, a scent he knew well from hunting. But the stench of his own body overpowered everything. He had to get inside, clean himself, and scheme a plan.

He circled the house again, fear battling with determination. He had to face the scene, the blood, the remnants of his family. He took a deep breath and slipped inside, drawing the shades and curtains, shrouding the interior in darkness. He found a candle and lit it, the flickering flame casting dancing shadows on the walls.

The scene stole his breath. *The blood—so much blood.* At the head of the bed, on the mattress where his Gramma had died, and on the floor where the twins had fallen. It was a slaughterhouse. He thought *I must do the decent thing. I must find some way to cover my family, a blanket, a tarp, something.* He remembered there was a tarp underneath a table on the back porch. He precariously but quietly stepped outside and reached under the table—the tarp was still there. He grabbed it, and back in the house, he draped it over what remained of his slaughtered family. In tears, he quietly covered the bodies and tucked the canvas under their remains. For the first time, the reality of the moment took over his emotions—he burst into tears but immediately caught himself making noise that others might have heard, so he stood motionless and waited about three minutes, waiting to see if there were, in fact, noises outside his home. Convinced otherwise, he gathered his thoughts and told himself. *You must remain calm—there is nothing you can do to bring back Grandma and the twins.*

The local Catholics had ransacked the house, leaving the cupboards bare—every scrap of food gone. His room, however, was untouched. His clothes remained.

He had to clean himself. He risked pumping water from the well, moving with frantic speed. He filled a pitcher, rushed back inside, and soaked a towel. The icy water shocked his skin, but he welcomed the cold, the cleansing.

Dressed in clean clothes, he gathered a few precious belongings: a small photo album, his parents' wedding picture, and birth certificates—memories, fragments of a life shattered.

He stood in the room, studying the scene, committing it to memory. His mother years ago, his Gramma Ryfka, the twins—all died in this room. Guilt twisted in his gut. He'd promised his mother he'd protect the twins. He'd failed.

I will find him, he vowed, his voice a raw whisper—*the animal who did this. I will end him.*

He had seen the officer's face, etched in his memory: mid-thirties, a lieutenant or higher, scars on his face, a pale, almost babyish complexion, a small, wiry frame. He constantly jerked his head to the left and then to the right, as if in a bird-like motion—Icek had made a note of this trait. He would remember the voice, the chilling calm. He would find the unit and track him down. He would happily break the Jewish rules of life—he would take this man's life.

Sweet revenge, he thought.

Would it be sweet?

He would find out.

He exited the house, stepping into the unknown, a new chapter beginning.

He had to plan.

Find my father, he thought, retrieving his knapsack and shotgun. *Which way? How to avoid capture?*

CHAPTER TWENTY-NINE

Jozefow, Poland
July 13th, 1942, 5:45 a.m.

The trucks began to move, continuing through twenty minutes of travel. It wasn't difficult to discern from the noise of nearby rail cars moving about that their captors were taking them to the rail station.

Abram wondered, *Where are they going to send us? Why did they select men, all of whom were close to the same age? What was the fate of my dear twins, Icek, and Ryfka? Will I ever see them again?*

Abram eavesdropped on a conversation between two men about three people seated below him. They were talking about the slaughter of his entire family.

Pleading with anyone who would listen, he said, "When the Germans came to my door, we did not resist—we did everything the Germans asked. My wife and I had been caring for my invalid brother and his two sons. My brother lost his legs three years ago, a couple of inches above the knee, due to an accident at the local lumber mill. For no reason, the Germans grabbed me while I was standing outside my home. I could hear a conversation taking place in the house. It was dreadful, as I couldn't understand what the soldiers were saying. I counted five pistol shots that rang out. The soldiers left my home and looked right at me and said and in perfect Polish, 'No need to worry about your family. They are all dead. Be thankful you are alive.'

"The soldiers ordered me to get on this truck," he cried. "Why did they kill my family? What did anyone in my family do to deserve a death sentence?"

"Each Jew received the death sentence—the only common factor—they were Jewish," the gentleman beside him said. "I fled Warsaw. The rumors were horrid, and I had no choice. No one could figure out why the Germans had created ghettos for Jews. One day, Jews were being taken from the ghettos and loaded on railcars, never to be seen again. Were they going to work camps? There was no evidence to support this theory," he said. "They took Jews of all ages on the trains. I have no idea where the Germans took those from the ghetto."

Abram thought, *Are the Germans intent on killing all Jews but those capable of work? Is this why they pulled those of us with a skill set from the village? Is it our skill set? Do all the men in the transport possess a skill that the Germans can use for the war effort? Are the Germans indeed murdering innocent civilians? His gut snarled in all sorts of directions as he pondered—is my family already dead?*

It was becoming increasingly clear that he would never see his family again. If he did, he would consider it a miracle. He was confident they were going someplace where the Nazis would work them to their deaths. *I must get my family out of my head for the immediate future. Living with such negative thoughts cannot be healthy. The most significant liability of anyone alive in Poland is one thing: being Jewish.*

Abram had figured out what the Germans were planning and said under his breath, "I will not share my thoughts with anyone. I pray that I am wrong."

A warm thought entered his mind. *My son, Icek, had figured it out. Icek had a grasp of what the Germans were up to. I know he is alive and well.*

Please, God, my family needs to escape the German brutality. Please, God, spare them. Allow all my family to live. Please, dear Lord. I don't understand why the Germans love to torture harmless, innocent victims.

The trucks were slowing to a stop. The sound of a locomotive releasing steam gave away their location. Their next move was to board a train. *But to where?* Abram wondered, recognizing the German shepherd's fierce, ferocious growl at the truck's rear.

The soldiers began shouting and screaming—they were waiting for a Jew to make a fatal mistake. A high-ranking enlisted man ensured that each person held captive understood and carried out the order.

"Get your filthy, vermin, Jew asses off of the trucks and fall-in, single file, two rows, starting here." He pointed to an area a few meters from where the trucks had stopped, then yelled in German, "Schnell, Schnell, you worthless swine. Schnell, I said Schnell!"

Minutes later, they stood in formation, and an officer approached. He pointed to an area where a spotlight focused near one of the trucks, revealing that three souls had been executed by hanging from makeshift gallows.

The officer said in German, "These are three worthless Jew vermin who could not follow simple orders. Do we understand one another?" His tone lacked any emotion.

The Jewish men boarded the railcars without incident.

CHAPTER THIRTY

Jozefow, Poland
July 13th, 1942, 6:15 a.m.

Well before sunrise, Major Helmut Schotz, standing on a large table and speaking in a broken voice, without eye contact with any of his direct reports, began addressing the senior staff of his five-hundred-person company. "Gentlemen, today we will honor the wish of our fearless leader, Adolf Hitler: The Führer desires to rid the world of Jews, any Jew, regardless of age.[33] The extermination of the Jozefow Jews will start today for our Police Battalion 101. Gentlemen, we have our assignment for the day, and yes, this will be the first of many similar tasks where we rid villages in Poland of their Jews."

With a broken voice and wiping perspiration from his brow, the major, appearing anxious, cleared his throat several times before he began speaking. "Gentlemen, we have segregated those capable of working in the munition's plants, and as we speak, they are on their way to board a train. We have exterminated the Jews in the local Jewish Senior Citizen home, an old folks' home on the edge of town. What we have left are around fifteen hundred or so Jewish people in the village—under our guard, we have corralled them to the Jozefow town square. I have to say, with an awareness, some of your men will not be willing to take the lives of men, women, and children. Please do not hold this against your direct reports or any peers. My orders specify that anyone wishing not to take part in the killings is allowed to step aside from this segment of the operation with no questions asked. We will reassign those wishing not to take part in the executions."

With nervous apprehension, the major continued. "Now, for those who will participate, ensure each shooter has had the proper training for the neck shot. Anyone unsure of the exact technique should consult their platoon sergeant for guidance and, if necessary, seek individual instruction on the required 'kill shot.'

"Please ensure your shooters firing the Karabiner 98 have attached their bayonets. Remember, the bayonet should touch the back of the victim's neck before your soldier takes the shot. I want to clarify: if our shooters do not follow this method for administering death to the victims, the risk of wounding them exists, thus causing undue suffering instead of taking their lives quickly and instantly. We do not want to have our victims suffer. Any questions?"

The audience remained silent.

"Since there are no questions, I will return later this evening once our men have completed their mission."

He clicked his heels together, stood at attention, and said, "Heil Hitler."

His men returned the salute while the major returned to his schoolroom office in Biloraj.

Of the hundreds of men within the company, twelve chose not to partake in the killing of innocent Jewish civilians.

In short order, his men would transport the first truckload of fifteen Jews to an area two kilometers west of town, the Forest of Winiarczykowa Gora.[34]

Most residents had awakened to the sound of gunfire, barking German shepherds, and the loud voices of German soldiers yelling commands. Many residents simply stood by as the assailants barged into their homes and executed on the spot any family members incapable of exiting their homes without a wheelchair.

It was simple. The Germans refused to let a victim's immobility hinder the efficiency of their effort. Most within the village heard the sounds of gunfire and screaming from onlookers who witnessed their village's carnage and abrupt evacuation. Many of the onlookers surmised that it was a matter of time. The Germans were in Jozefow for one reason: to kill the remaining Jews in the village.

During the previous May, the locals had witnessed German soldiers murder one hundred and thirty Jewish residents of Jozefow. With the scene so brutal, the German employees of the local civil administration were upset by the violence delivered to the innocent Jews who perished that day. Thus, the local Jews were now accustomed to violence by members of the Reich. Following the carnage in May, the perpetrators left and never returned.[35]

But today was different, as these were German police officers converted into a killing squad.

7:20 a.m.

As one of the German officers walked by the crowd, he could hear whisper after whisper from those throughout the square: "Where are they taking us? It's not the rail station, as the rail station is on the other side of town," an old man stated to several within earshot of where the German officer stood.

The German officer, with his hands positioned on his hips and standing with perfect posture, shouted angrily, "Be quiet, no talking! Be calm, no talking!" He fired his Walther P-38 pistol into the air. There was complete silence. The German officer, with his pistol in hand, approached the crowd and asked, "Anyone who speaks German, please come forward."

A fiftyish-year-old woman with stringy, oil-laden gray hair stood and said, "I speak German."

"Good. Excellent! You, please come here."

The lady, in an apprehensive posture, stepped up to the officer.

"Excellent." He pointed his weapon at the lady and said, "Please tell the crowd this statement in your loudest voice possible. Do you understand?"

"Yes, I understand."

"Tell your people that my men will remove the next person heard talking and in plain view of the men, women, and children standing here today will be shot. Do you understand?"

"Yes, I understand," she said with tears running down her cheeks.

"Now go ahead and tell your people in your language what I have told you. Tell them now!" he shouted.

Speaking in Polish, she said, "Everyone, please listen! The officer here will order his men to pull anyone caught talking out of the crowd. In plain view of us standing here, he will request his men to shoot the person caught talking. The execution will be in plain sight of all present."

Every face in the crowd understood the order, as each person's body language conveyed that there was to be no talking whatsoever. Some cried and hugged one another, while others either looked to the heavens or stared at the ground. For the rest of the day, there was complete silence.

The men of Police Battalion 101 transported their first truckload of fifteen Jews to an area two kilometers west of town. The locals recognized this area as the Forest of Winiarczykowa Gora.

A German captain had been in this area for over two hours coordinating the plans for the massacre with the shooters already assigned. His job was to position each load of Jews they would murder so that the approaching *live* Jews could not see the bodies of the Jews killed minutes earlier.

The first load of fifteen Jews had left the town square. Within ten minutes of the first load, the second truckload with fifteen Jewish residents was now pulling away from the square. The first truck that left about twenty-five minutes earlier with a load of fifteen Jewish residents was back at the town square, where shouting German soldiers forced the next load of Jews to board the truck.

As the victims approached with hesitation, the shouting German soldiers had to force the Jews at gunpoint to climb onto the trucks.

The plan was to have two killing fields, a left and a right, so each victim would be assigned to their assassin as the soldiers unloaded the truck. Once the soldiers ensured all their victims were chest down and in the horizontal position, each shooter positioned their rifle as planned, and on the Command, fifteen rifles fired at once.

When the second load arrived, the truck was directed to the killing field on the left since the first field used was on the right. A different set of shooters would meet the Jews in the second load of victims. If things went as planned, the first load of all Jews on the right side would all be dead before the soldiers directed the second load to lie, chest down. The soldiers were to use this swapping back from the right side to the left side of the killing field until the soldiers had executed all fifteen hundred Jews in the Jozefow area.

Once the platoon had executed the second load of Jews, several shooters requested to be relieved of the assignment. Some of the shooters had become sick and were throwing up. Others could not face the murder of a mother and her children, and in many cases, the victims were babies and children too young for school. Some of the shooters were nearing a nervous breakdown after their first kill. There was no way those who opposed the assignment were going to kill women and children, and for the most part, the older men had fought for the Germans during World War I. The idea of taking innocent civilians' lives, Jewish or not, didn't sit well with some younger battalion members.

On the other hand, many viewed the murder of Jews as ridding the world of vermin, with the logic that the babies and children would grow up as worthless Jews. Most shooters were okay with their assignments and didn't ask to be relieved. The Command had predicted apprehensiveness with the mission and had made the necessary preparations for those who wished to step away from the assignment to kill. In the future, anyone not interested in participating in the killing could walk away without any questions asked. Throughout the evening, the command made many shooter substitutions.

The effort lasted well into the darkness of night. The operation would cease when every Jew in Jozefow was dead.

CHAPTER THIRTY-ONE

Forest of Winiarczykowa Gora near Jozefow, Poland
July 13, 1942, 7:20 pm

The last light bled from the sky, painting the clouds a bruised purple. Hundreds more Jews remained. The air, thick with the coppery, pungent odor of blood, clung to the back of Corporal Stengel's throat. Empty casings from Karabiners 98k littered the ground, glinting dully under the fading light. Each body lay where it fell, a grotesque mosaic of death.

The grim ritual had become sickeningly familiar. A German officer, his face a mask of bored efficiency, would gesture toward a fresh patch of grass, far enough away that the new victims wouldn't see the remains of the last. The tall grass, rustling softly in the evening breeze, provided a perverse camouflage, hiding the scale of the massacre. Aside from the sporadic bursts of rifle fire that had punctuated the day, there was only the deceptive quiet of the countryside.

Corporal Stengel, a former policeman from the Hamburg Police Department, shifted his weight, his boots sinking slightly into the damp earth. Thirty-four years old, he was a man built like a sapling—tall and lean. His baby face, clean-shaven except for the meticulously trimmed mustache, a miniature echo of the Führer's, seemed out of place amidst this horror. He habitually tilted his head when he spoke, words escaping from the corner of his mouth, his right eye nearly closing as if in a perpetual wink. His body, a restless collection of nervous energy, twitched and fidgeted, a habit that drove his commander to distraction during formal reprimands.

Until today, Stengel had never taken a life. Now, his rifle barrel was hot, his shoulder ached, and with all the firing of his weapon, the odor burned the smell of cordite into his nostrils. Seven hours. Seven hours of pulling the trigger, each shot extinguishing a life. He imagined Hitler's approving nod, the ghost of a smile on the Führer's face.

His initiation hadn't been against soldiers. It was against the frail, the elderly, mothers clutching infants, children with wide, uncomprehending eyes, and the disabled shuffling forward on crutches or in makeshift wheelchairs. They were the faces of a village, a microcosm of Jewish life—bakers, tailors, teachers, now reduced to silent, compliant bodies. Most said nothing. Some whispered prayers, their voices thin and reedy. Others, primarily mothers, murmured reassurances to their children, painting a picture of a peaceful afterlife— a place beyond fear. Their hands stroked small heads, a last, desperate act of comfort.

The killing was intimate. One soldier, one victim. The orders were clear: "No talking." Earlier, the soldiers had enforced this brutally, rifle butts cracking against skulls, silencing any protest with savage force. But Stengel, weary of the endless slaughter, his stomach churning with nausea he couldn't name, let the whispers pass. He listened.

He'd seen a grandfather, his hand gnarled with age, clasping the small, trusting hand of a boy, perhaps seven years old. The old man, his eyes fixed on the darkening sky, had spoken, his voice surprisingly firm, "We will both be up there in minutes. No more hatred. No more pain. Trust me, grandson, we will be together."

Twelve hours. The field of death now sprawled; a quarter-hectare of broken bodies. The sheer number of Jews still waiting, huddled together in the growing darkness, meant the killing ground would double, triple before the night was through.

Stengel had relished his power as a policeman in Hamburg. The casual cruelty, the shoving, the kicks delivered to Jews leaving the synagogue after services—it had been a game, a release. There were occasional injuries, some severe, but never a death. And never a consequence. Justice was a blind woman when a Gentile harmed a Jew.

He'd seen this night as an extension of that power, a magnified version of his Hamburg nights. No guilt. He'd convinced himself he was cleansing the world, eradicating a disease. These weren't people; they were vermin, their blood tainted, inferior. He'd swallowed Hitler's poisonous rhetoric whole, the mantra repeated since childhood: "The Jew is responsible."

The clock in the nearby village church would have, hypothetically, chimed ten. He imagined it anyway. Corporal Stengel led a woman, perhaps fifty-three, toward the killing field. The walk was a slow, agonizing three minutes. She whispered, her voice surprisingly steady, "My name is Halina Adamik. I was married to a German, a decorated officer in World War I. I am going to give you an opportunity."

Stengel stopped—his surprise evident in the slight widening of his one good eye. He hissed, his voice a low growl, "You speak German like a Berliner. You're not allowed to speak." He jabbed his rifle into her side, a sharp, brutal movement.

She didn't flinch. "What will you do? Shoot me here? Then you'll have to carry me." Her voice was laced with a defiance that made him uneasy. "Go ahead. Shoot me now."

He pressed the rifle harder, his finger tightening on the trigger. He cocked it, the metallic click loud in the quiet. "Who do you think I am?"

"Less than an animal," she replied, her gaze unwavering. "A mass murderer. You will burn in hell for this. Eternity in hell's bowels."

He sneered. "Jew bitch, what do you know about hell?"

She looked at him, and for the first time that day, a flicker of something other than hatred—perhaps curiosity, perhaps a sliver of doubt—crossed Stengel's face.

"Are you a husband? A father? A brother?" she asked, her voice softer now. "Will your family be proud? Will your children boast that you murdered old women and babies? They will see you for what you are: a heartless maniac."

"My wife and two boys will be proud," Stengel retorted, but his voice lacked its earlier conviction. "Proud that I rid the world of Jews!"

"Proud?" Her voice was a mixture of disbelief and pity. "No wife, no child, could be proud of a man who kills the innocent. You are a poor excuse for a human being. But if you spare me, God will remember. He is a forgiving God. This is your chance. One act of mercy might save you from the hell you deserve. If not me, then another."

He scoffed, trying to regain his composure. "So, your God will just forget the hundreds I've already killed today? I don't think that's how it works."

"But you don't know, do you?" she presses. "I do. I have studied religion. My husband taught religion in Berlin. God forgives all sins if you repent. But even if God forgives you, you will face the gallows—War crimes. The world will not let you get away with this. Me? I will take your bullet. You? Years in prison, then the hangman's noose. Remember my words. You will pay."

He pushed back, his voice a desperate attempt at reassurance, primarily to himself. "The world hates Jews as much as we Germans do. Not a chance, old lady. Not a chance."

"Suit yourself," she said, her voice resigned. "You're the one who will suffer. I don't want even a glimpse of hell. Ever!"

Darkness had fallen completely, a black shroud over the field of death. Stengel and Halina had reached the designated spot. He gestured roughly. "Lie down on your stomach. It will be quick. The shot will enter the back of your neck. Be still."

The order came. Rifles barked around them.

Stengel raised his rifle, aimed, and fired wide, the bullet ripping through the air harmlessly. He knelt beside her, his voice a hoarse whisper, "I have spared you. Pray for me. My name is Corporal Hans Stengel. I will untie you. We will be leaving in ten to fifteen minutes. Play dead. When you hear nothing, crawl. Crawl West." He pointed into the inky blackness. "Keep moving. And keep your mouth shut. Understand?"

Her voice trembled, barely audible. 'Dear God, I pray for this child of God who has lost his way. He has taken many lives. But he is a good man, a forgiving soul. Please forgive him, dear God. Amen.'

"Madam, are you confident the Almighty received your prayer?" Corporal Stengel asked.

"Yes. God listens to all of us who have faith. Remember," she added, looking up at him, "you have avoided hell—no guarantee about the gallows—only God can make that deal."

Stengel felt a strange mix of relief and terror. "I will tell my commander I can't do this anymore—no more civilians. I will kill enemies, soldiers, and those who threaten me. Thank you, Madam. Now, go. Crawl for half an hour. You'll be out of sight. Here." He pressed his canteen into her hand, then his bayonet. "You'll need these. Good luck. And thank you for showing me the evil."

"I had nothing to do with it," she whispered, her voice urgent. "It was God's work. Don't you see? I have no power. Only God. He has touched you. He will protect you. Do you feel it? The warmth of God in your soul? Acknowledge it."

He stared into her eyes, searching for something he couldn't name. "He will forgive me for those I've already killed?"

Halina asked, "May I ask what religion you practiced in your parents' home? What religion did you follow?"

"My parents raised me as a Lutheran."

"God will forgive you. I had several friends that were Lutherans. I know their practices. Christians of the Lutheran faith may without sin, engage in just wars—and serve as soldiers. He will forgive you," she insisted. "You are a child of God who has sinned. His forgiveness is unconditional. All sins. Do you believe it? Do you believe that killing innocents, Jewish or not, non-combatants, is wrong?"

"A non-combatant is the key?" he asked, the words catching in his throat. "Yes, I now believe the killing of innocents, Jewish or not, is wrong."

"Yes," she said, her voice firm. "Killing in war is not murder. Killing in war is not a sin."

"I understand," Stengel said, a new clarity dawning in his eyes. "Before, I thought we were at war with the Jews. But now I see. We are at war with Britain, the Soviets, and America—not with faith."

"Corporal," Halina said, "the spirit of God is with you."

"Go," he urged. "West. Early morning, late evening. Travel then. Don't stop. May God protect you."

She took the canteen and bayonet, her fingers brushing his. "I will never forget you," she whispered. "Perhaps after the war..." Without completing the sentence, she disappeared into the darkness, crawling, a faint rustle in the grass.

Corporal Stengel approached his commander, his steps heavy, his shoulders slumped. "Sir, permission to excuse me from this duty. Eight hours of killing civilians. I can't and won't do it anymore."

"Permission granted," the commander said, his voice devoid of emotion. "Report to the major for reassignment."

"Thank you, sir." Stengel turned and slung his Karabiner over his shoulder, its weight suddenly unbearable. He fumbled for a cigarette, his hands shaking. The match flared, illuminating his face, streaked with sweat and grime. He was exhausted, his soul a raw, aching wound. "Never again," he muttered, the words a prayer, a vow. "Never again will I massacre civilians. Jews or anyone."

Tears welled in his eyes, blurring his vision. He began, haltingly, to speak to the God he had, until tonight, dismissed.

CHAPTER THIRTY-TWO

Jozefow, Poland
July 14-16th, 1942, 7:15 a.m.

The light filtering through the window couldn't touch the shadows in Teodora's eyes. Two days. Two days since the screams, the shots, the sickening silence that had fallen over Jozefow. Tomasz had never seen his sister like this—not grief-stricken, exactly, but hollowed out, as if an unknown energy had ripped away something vital in her heart. Her hands, usually so steady when she mended clothes or kneaded dough, trembled against the windowpane.

Staring out the window and not focusing on anything, Teodora thought *had the Nazi butchers taken Icek and his family, too?*

"Tomasz," she whispered, her voice raspy, "Icek's house—we must go."

He shot up from the worn armchair, the sudden movement scraping against the wooden floor. "Teodora, are you mad?" His voice was a harsh whisper, fueled by fear as much as disbelief. "That was a massacre, a military operation. They slaughtered everyone. It's a death trap!"

Teodora didn't turn. Her gaze remained fixed on the street as if she could see through the walls, through the distance, to Icek's empty home. "If it were us, Tomasz, wouldn't Icek come? Wouldn't he search? What if? What if they didn't get him? What if he's waiting, hoping we'll help? Maybe he needs somewhere to hide."

Her words, though desperate, resonated deeply. Tomasz raked a hand through his hair, his chin jutting out in thought that Icek was resourceful, a man of the woods. He could have evaded them somehow. The sliver of hope, however faint, was too tempting to ignore. "He might be looking for us," he conceded, his voice lower now, a grudging admission.

Teodora finally turned, her eyes brimming. "So, you'll go? We'll look?"

He looked away, staring at a water stain on the ceiling, a grimace twisting his lips. "This is insane, Teodora. If they catch us... a firing squad, torture. They'll want to know why two Catholics are poking around the home of murdered Jews. They're good at breaking people, you know that."

She closed the distance between them, her hand gripping his arm almost painfully tight. "I'll never forgive myself if we don't at least try, Tomasz. Never."

He met her gaze, the fear warring with a reluctant sense of duty. *Icek would do the same for us.* The thought was a cold weight in his stomach. "Alright," he said, the word heavy with resignation. "But I go in. Not we. You stay outside. If anyone comes, we're trapped. We both die. Going into Icek's home might be the worst decision of our lives, but..." He trailed off, unable to articulate the knot of loyalty and dread that had taken root. "We need a plan. Tonight, when it's dark, we'll scout the area. See if there are guards and patrols. If there is any sign of trouble, we turn back. And if we have to run, we split up. You go one way, I go another."

Two nights of hushed planning, accompanied by the tracing of routes on scraps of paper and memorizing escape paths, culminated in the oppressive silence of Jozefow at two a.m. Not a dog barked, not a window creaked. They moved like ghosts, darting between pools of shadow, always ten meters apart, their pre-determined route a silent, jagged dance.

By two-seventeen, they were beneath the skeletal branches of the elm in Icek's yard. The air hung heavy, thick with the unspoken. Teodora settled onto the tarp she'd brought, melting into the darkness. Tomasz would give the signal—a soft whistle—when he was ready to enter. She would mirror it back, a fragile thread of communication in the suffocating night.

Tomasz stood three meters from Icek's front door, his heart hammering against his ribs. The door was gone, ripped from its frame, a splintered mess lying on the ground like a discarded toy. *Why? Had the Kelners resisted? Refused to open?* The questions clawed at him, unanswered, terrifying.

He forced himself to breathe, to move. *I've never seen a murder scene. How do I prepare?"* He thought, a desperate mantra against the rising tide of fear, *Could anyone ever truly prepare for this?*

He took a slow, hesitant step inside. The stench hit him like a physical blow—a nauseating, coppery sweetness that made his stomach lurch—he thought, *This is the smell* of *death*. His torch beam cut through the darkness, revealing a scene of utter devastation. *Looters have been here.* Drawers gaped open. The shelves were stripped bare, the pantry was empty, and the furniture was either overturned or missing.

He crept toward the main bedroom, each footfall a sickening squelch. The smell intensified, a suffocating wave that threatened to overwhelm him. He stopped a meter from the bed, his light shaking in his hand. His shoes were sticking to the floor, a thick, viscous substance clinging to the soles—*oh my God, it's body fluids.*

Then he saw it. The wall behind the bed—a gruesome canvas of splattered blood, stretching in a horrifying arc from the mattress to the ceiling. Embedded within the crimson horror were fragments—bits of bone, tissue, and hair. He choked back a gag, his mind reeling.

On the bed itself, a small, glistening mass. It looked like a peach-sized piece of brain, impossibly, grotesquely out of place. It was too clean, too clean of a dissection to have been the result of a bullet.

The world tilted. The carnage, the smell, the sheer wrongness of it all was too much. Tomasz stumbled back, retching, vomit burning his throat. He had to get out. *Teodora. Thank God she's not seeing this. How many died here? One? Two? More?* The questions spun in his head, unanswerable. The scene was too chaotic, too violated to offer any clues. *Had anyone escaped? Were there prisoners taken away for questioning?* Rumors, like the stench, permeated everything. Nazis shooting Jews in the street. The infirm, the weak, murdered on the spot.

Are they this barbaric?

He stumbled out of the house, back to the shadows of the elm, to Teodora.

He slumped beside her, shaking his head, unable to speak.

"Tomasz?" Her whisper was sharp with anxiety. "Say something!"

He struggled to find his voice, the words thick and clumsy. "It's worse than anything I could have imagined. A slaughterhouse. I threw up."

"I heard you," she whispered back, her voice laced with a mixture of fear and relief. "Was anyone else around? Did anyone hear?"

He shook his head again, still struggling to process what he'd seen. "For Icek, I need to find something. Keepsakes. Valuables. Anything the looters missed."

"What did you have in mind?" Teodora asked, her voice a little steadier now.

"A Hebrew bible, with family records—births, marriages. Photographs. Letters from America—his mother's twin sister in New York. We could write to her, tell her what happened, and I will take some religious items. The Singer sewing machine is gone." The words trailed off, inadequate to express the sense of loss, of desecration.

"Yes," Teodora said, her voice firm. "We have to take them. Maybe we can give them back to Icek." Her voice caught on his name, a flicker of hope in the darkness. She composed herself for a moment and, avoiding his gaze, continued. "I haven't told you, Tomasz, but I love Icek. He's the kindest, most genuine man I've ever known. We never even kissed—but I know—it's love. I can't explain it any other way."

A ghost of a smile touched Tomasz's lips. "He feels the same, Teodora. He's been crazy about you since the day you met."

Her head snapped up, her eyes wide with a mixture of surprise and a desperate yearning for confirmation. "What did he say? Tell me!"

He held up a hand, a gentle warning in his eyes. "That's not for me to tell you. You need to hear the words from him. And I believe you will. He's alive, Teodora. I feel it. He's a survivor. He's out there, somewhere. And knowing Icek, he hasn't stopped running. I wonder how many Nazis he's killed already?"

"He has every reason to seek revenge," Teodora said, a hint of steel in her voice. "I hope he has killed some. The door proves that someone in his family fought back. But who? And who did they spare?"

Tomasz pulled out a handkerchief and offered it to her. "Here."

Teodora took it, her sobs wracking her body. "He's alive!" she choked out, the words a desperate plea. "He has to be!"

Tomasz stood, scanning the shadows around them. "Uncle Dawid," he said suddenly, a new thought striking him. *He's up on everything that goes on in this town. He might know something. He might even know who removed the bodies.*

"Yes!" Teodora said, wiping her eyes, a spark of hope rekindled. "He'll know who transported them and how many there were. No one could forget a scene like that. Never."

"I'll go back in, get Icek's things. There's a suitcase under the bed. I think it's big enough." He paused. "We should take them, shouldn't we?"

Teodora met his gaze, her eyes resolute. "Yes. It's the least we can do. They'll shoot us as looters if they catch us, though."

"I don't intend for the Krauts to shoot me." Tomasz said, a grim determination setting his jaw. "I'm going back in. We'll talk to Uncle Dawid in the morning."

CHAPTER THIRTY-THREE

Jozefow, Poland
July 17th, 1942, 8:15 a.m.

A brutal hammering on the door ripped through the pre-dawn stillness. Dawid, wrenched from sleep, felt the vibrations in the floorboards of his small cottage. He groaned, his joints protesting as he pulled himself out of bed. He shuffled to the door, his mind already racing with a mixture of annoyance and unease.

"Alright, alright, I'm coming," he rasped, his voice thick with sleep and a lifetime of cigarettes.

He yanked the door open, revealing his niece and nephew, Teodora and Tomasz. Teodora's face, usually bright with youthful mischief, was drawn and pale. Tomasz stood beside her, his shoulders slumped, a shadow of fear flickering in his eyes.

"Uncle Dawid, you must help us. You must," Teodora's voice was raw. It sounded strained.

Dawid's irritation spiked. "Why are you two here? Did you not go to sleep last night?" It sounded more like a statement than a question.

"Can we all sit?" Tomasz's request was quiet, almost hesitant.

Dawid sighed, the fight draining out of him. "By all means, yes. Come in and have a seat. Why are you here?" He gestured toward the worn, mismatched chairs clustered around his small kitchen table.

Tomasz cleared his throat, his gaze fixed on a chipped mug on the table. "We entered our Jewish friend Icek's home last evening and discovered a murder scene."

Dawid's world seemed to tilt. The words struck him like a physical blow. He stared at his niece and nephew, his mind struggling to reconcile their youthful faces with the horrors they spoke of. "Are you two out of your minds?" he croaked. "You could be facing a firing squad for putting your noses where they do not belong." He leaned forward, his voice dropping to a harsh whisper. "Let the crazy Germans do what they want to do. They are on their way to murdering as many Polish

Jews as possible. We will not be able to change what they have been planning for years. We, too, can end up at the end of a rifle if we are not careful."

Teodora's eyes, glistening with unshed tears, met his eyes. "Please, Uncle, Icek is our friend." The sincerity in her voice, the raw plea, chipped away at his hardened exterior.

"Why on earth would you have a Jew for a close friend?" Dawid's question was sharp, born of ingrained prejudice and fear. "Don't you two understand the world is against the Jews, especially the Germans? Why do you care about Jews all of a sudden?"

Tomasz looked down at the floor, the wood grain was suddenly fascinating. "Uncle, the Jew Icek Kelner and I were good friends, as we hunted and fished together over the past year. Furthermore, Teodora and Icek were fond of each other." He braced himself for the explosion he knew was coming.

Dawid's face contorted. "Jesus Christ! Teodora, you fell in love with a God-damned Jew? In love? At your age, in love? You have no idea what love is. You can't love a Jew! Your parents will disown you! You have let emotion get in the way of clear thinking."

"Uncle Dawid, love happens. Love is not something you plan for through months of calculating each emotion on a pad of paper." Teodora's voice was a mixture of defiance and desperation. "You fell in love! And why can't I?"

Tomasz, emboldened by his sister's words, spoke again. "Uncle, we got to know Icek and his family. They were the nicest people you would ever want to meet. We viewed the family as humans, ignoring their religion." He paused, taking a shaky breath. "You are from a different generation, and your upbringing has tainted you with centuries of prejudice. We went to school with Jews in Warsaw, and some of our best friends were Jewish. We don't have the same mindset as the older generation and never will. Can you put your hatred aside for a few minutes and help us?"

Dawid's expression softened, a flicker of shame crossing his face. "Try as you must," he said with a scorned look on his face. "You won't ever get me to ever accept Jews. Never! Now, God damn it, why are you here?"

"Uncle Dawid, we need your help. We know you have many contacts in town. We want to determine who the Nazis sent to the Kelner residence to retrieve the dead. Please help us, Uncle Dawid!" Tomasz pleaded.

A sigh, heavy with resignation, escaped Dawid's lips. "I surrender. I understand now why all the fuss. What do you want me to do?"

"Uncle, the morbid scene inside the Kelner residence was difficult for anyone to see," Tomasz began, speaking slowly and measured. "What we don't know is who the Nazis killed. We need to know if they murdered the entire family or if they took away some of the family members. Can you find out who carried off the bodies so we can talk to them? We are asking for the names of the people who carried the bodies, that's it, it's all we require."

Dawid pushed back his chair, the chair legs scraping against the stone floor. He needed to move, to pace,, to escape the weight of their request. "I want you the hell out of here after you get what you need. I can't take any chances as I don't want the Nazis trying to track me down." He stopped, turning back to them, his voice low and urgent. "All I know is the Nazis collected each able-bodied skilled tradesman in the Jewish neighborhood and placed them on a train. The train remains on the rail at the train station. The Germans collected about a hundred men, who were captive in a cattle car on the spur next to the rail station. I have no idea why they haven't left yet. I understand Icek's father was a millwright. You can figure that a man with his skill is mighty important to the Reich. I guarantee you that he is in that rail car. Please don't get any foolish ideas about trying to break him out! That would be a firing squad offense, for sure. These German maniacs don't always just kill the offender. At times, to punish those who assist the Jews, they may murder half the town for such an offense."

"Uncle, can you find out where the train is going?" Tomasz interjected.

Dawid shot him a look of exasperated warning. "You are hell-bent on getting me in front of a firing squad. I regret to say that I know the engineer on the train. When he returns, I can find out, if I don't see a firing squad first."

"What about those who moved the bodies? We seek the number of bodies, the sex, and the approximate age." Tomasz asked.

"Ryfka had a stroke in July of 1937, so she has been immobile. There are twin girls, age ten, and Icek is eighteen. We had no idea if all were home. We know that no one has seen them since the Germans arrived," Teodora offered.

"Let me tell you what I know," he stated.

"Before you begin, let me tell you in detail what we did," Tomasz interjected.

Dawid considered. "Not sure I want to know the details, but go ahead."

"Teodora and I were anxious to discover what may have happened at the Kelner residence. Our plan was simple—once the Nazis left town, we would see what we could find out. I had Teodora stand watch outside the Kelner home while I entered. When I entered, I saw the horrific scene of what appeared to be the location where multiple murders had occurred. What we don't know is which family members the Nazis murdered. We found out that the Nazis made a deal with the local Catholic priest that in return for the removal and burial of the bodies, the Nazis would reward those assisting with whatever goods, valuables, property, etc. they wanted. We understand that this could also mean ownership of the home. We know that you are familiar with most of the people in town. We want to determine who went to the Kelner home and how many bodies the locals removed. Also, we want to know what happened to their father, Abram."

Dawid's gaze drifted to the window as if he could see the rail car sitting on the siding, a metal cage holding the town's stolen men. "I think the Nazis will work each one of them to their death." He paused, a flicker of genuine regret in his eyes. "So that is the story of Abram— and by the way, I liked Abram, as he was a pretty good guy for a Jew."

Teodora's sharp intake of breath was audible. "Uncle, did you hear yourself? You said, 'Pretty good guy for a Jew?'" She sounded infuriated.

"Wait a minute, that was a good thing I said. I'm not the man who is full of hate that you make me out to be. The Kelners were in my store almost every week. I liked Icek, as he was always kind, and we traded his kills for gear on many occasions. I am sorry for the loss of all Jews in our community. No, I didn't see eye-to-eye with many Jews, but they certainly didn't deserve to be murdered. Let's start this conversation all over again."

"Never mind, Uncle Dawid, please continue," Teodora interjected, a weary note in her voice.

"Now, regarding Icek, there were three bodies in the home that the Nazis murdered, not four. My good friends—and I won't reveal their names—removed the bodies of two young girls who appeared to be twins and the body of an old lady with a wheelchair adjacent to her bed. Once my acquaintances had removed the deceased, they then helped themselves to anything useful."

Teodora's cry was a choked sob. "Those sweet, intelligent, and beautiful twins are dead! Oh my God! Why? And Gramma Ryfka, that sweet, kind person who would never harm anyone is now dead. The twins must have seen the Nazis kill their Gramma. Oh my God! Oh my God! How can God allow such carnage? Why?" Her voice rose, and she unleashed an almost animal, shrill cry.

Dawid continued, his voice low and somber. "Another friend of mine, and I will not tell you how I found out, said he saw Icek emerge from the outhouse. It was apparent he had hidden by entering the waste pit of the outhouse. Later, this person witnessed him cleaning up and changing out of his soiled clothes inside his home. He left his home with a small cloth tote, which I imagine contained clothes and family keepsakes. This person followed him for about an hour. He was heading east. After a while, he lost the trail of Icek, and he slipped back into town and kept his mouth shut. He feared the Nazis would discover him and then torture him to reveal information about Icek. Not sure why he told me. So, likely, your friend Icek is alive and well."

Teodora's despair shattered, replaced by a surge of relief so powerful it almost buckled her knees. "Oh, dear Lord, dear Lord, Icek is alive. He is alive," she cried, rushing to her uncle and enveloping him in a fierce hug. "I could feel it! Thank you so much, Uncle Dawid. Thank you, thank you!"

Dawid, caught off guard by the embrace, awkwardly patted her back. He glanced at Tomasz, a ghost of a smile playing on his lips. "I think Teodora is, without a doubt, in love with this Jew boy Icek."

"Yes, Uncle, she is in love with Icek. It would be best if you were happy for her. They will be husband and wife one day," Tomas offered.

A shadow of concern flickered across Dawid's face. "Do you think your parents would ever stand for such a thing as having a Jew marry their daughter?"

Teodora, pulling away from her uncle, straightened her shoulders. "Nothing stands in the way of love."

"Okay, Uncle Dawid. We will be in touch. Everything said today never leaves this room," Tomasz declared and took long strides to the front door.

Dawid nodded, his gaze heavy with unspoken worry. "Please say nothing to anyone, as the damn Nazis will be back."

"Damned Nazis! They are evil!" The events of the evening filled Teodora with a defiant fire. She gave her uncle another quick hug. "We will be sure you get an invite to the wedding, and perhaps, we may even name a child after you."

"You crazy kids. Watch your back, as these are the worst of times. As far as tonight, neither of you were here."

Tomas approached Dawid and said, "Thank you, Uncle Dawid."

With that, they left. The weight of their departure felt heavier than their arrival.

CHAPTER THIRTY-FOUR

Jozefow, Poland
July 24ᵗʰ, 1942, 10:12 p.m.

It had been eleven days since the German soldiers had crammed Abram and sixty-nine other men, ranging from their twenties to mid-forties, onto the railcar outside Jozefow, ripped from their homes and families.

The conditions, already dire, decayed daily. Confined to the railcar, they were at the mercy of their captors, who provided a single daily ration of "soup" and just enough water—dispensed from a mop bucket with a shared tin cup—to keep them clinging to life. Each man rationed his sips, eyes constantly flicking to the dwindling water level, the unspoken question a shared dread: Will there be more?

The stench was a physical presence—human waste, piled in a far corner, baked in the unusually warm July heat. The air, thick and stagnant, clung to their skin, heavy with the cloying sweetness of decay. Each day, the German guards tossed a layer of straw onto the growing mound, a futile attempt to mask the odor. But the straw was dwindling, each layer thinner than the last, and the stench only intensified, a suffocating reminder of their captivity. Space was a luxury no one could afford. Seventy men, crammed into the confines of the car, pressed against each other, flesh to flesh. Sleep came only with utter collapse, a brief respite from the suffocating reality.

Beyond the constant, gnawing fear for their families, hunger clawed at their bellies. Each mealtime was a torment of anticipation, a desperate hope for something, anything, better than the previous. But the "soup," a watery, tepid broth, grew thinner daily, the vegetables fewer, any hint of meat a forgotten memory. The small hunks of dark bread, a meager comfort, had vanished after the third day.

The crack-watcher, a silent sentinel, pressed his eye against a gap between the wooden slats, unaware the Nazis were watching. Three such vantage points existed within the railcar, manned in shifts, day and night, eyes straining for any sign, any movement.

This night, about three hours after sundown, the crack watcher at the front left signaled activity. The rhythmic crunch of boots on the track ballast closed in, then faded, then closed in again. He'd seen this pattern before. This time, though, a chilling certainty settled in his gut: they were listening. He'd heard it himself moments ago—a hushed conversation, barely above a whisper, from somewhere near the middle of the car.

His heart hammered. *Would they burst in? Had they heard? What would they do?*

The night shattered. The ferocious barking of German Shepherds ripped through the silence. A person rattled the chain and lock, the screech as the door slid open, then the stench as the air moved beyond the cavity of the railcar, their senses bombarded by the assault on their nostrils. The officer opened the lock, recoiling—he fumbled for a handkerchief, clamping it over his face with a gasp. He retreated a step, waiting for a gust of night air to clear a path before several guards, their flashlights cutting through the darkness, stalked into the car.

"Achtung! Achtung! Achtung!" the officer's voice, amplified by the confined space, echoed off the wooden walls. "Your leader! I must speak with your leader! Now!" He didn't repeat the demand—his flashlight illuminated the darkness and searched each face.

Abram, closest to the officer, felt a cold dread creep up his spine. He rose slowly, his voice strained. "I am Abram Kelner," he declared, each word an effort.

The officer momentarily lowered the handkerchief, a flicker of something unreadable in his eyes. "Herr Kelner, a problem. My men, during their patrol, reported hearing a discussion within this railcar. We have made it abundantly clear: talking is forbidden. Do you understand?"

Abram met the officer's gaze, his voice flat, devoid of emotion. "Yes, sir, we understand. But I can explain."

A faint smile, cruel and unsettling, played on the commandant's lips. "Explain? A direct violation of orders? Explain that, Herr Kelner!"

Abram remained statue-like, looking ahead at an unseen distant point. "Your excellency, sickness has taken hold. Some men were unwell before boarding. Now, fevers rage. Diarrhea is rampant. Some cannot keep even the meager rations down. The voices your men heard were the cries of agony, the mutterings of delirium. We try to silence them, but…" he trailed off, the unspoken truth hanging heavy in the air.

The officer scratched his chin, a feigned thoughtfulness masking his intent. "Fascinating. A most creative explanation. Herr Kelner, take this flashlight. Could you show me? Point out these sickest men." He ordered one of the soldiers to "Fetch a medic."

Abram's face remained a mask, betraying nothing of the turmoil within. He hadn't expected this. There were sick men, men who cried out in their sleep, their bodies ravaged by illness. But this, this was a test.

Before Abram could move, the commandant held up a hand. "On second thought, those who are ill will identify themselves as soon as the medic arrives. Herr Kelner, you may sit." He turned to address the car, his voice laced with a chillingly polite menace. "Let me reiterate, for those who may have misunderstood. No talking. No whispering. Not even signs. Complete silence. Is that understood?"

He paused, letting his words sink in. "You are valuable to the Third Reich. Your skills are needed. But your health—your health is paramount. We cannot allow the sick to jeopardize the productivity of the others. We have plans for you. That is why we had my men choose you."

Thirty-five minutes crawled by. The medical corpsman, Sergeant Brost, arrived, his face pale and drawn in the harsh glare of the portable lights he carried, along with a portable medical table. "Herr Commandant, reporting as ordered, sir."

"Sergeant Brost, my apologies for the late hour. But we have a situation. Herr Kelner," he gestured toward Abram and said, "This gentleman here claims his men did not violate the 'no talking' rule. He insists the voices heard were merely the ramblings of men compromised by illness." He moved closer to Abram, his voice dropping to a near whisper. "Is that correct, Herr Kelner?"

Abram, frozen, could only manage a choked, "Yes, sir. Correct."

The commandant pressed closer, his face inches from Abram's. "And you understood, Herr Kelner, the consequences for any violation? We will ensure that we deal with each infraction."

Abram stared straight ahead. "Yes, sir. All seventy of us understand."

"Good. Misunderstandings are undesirable. But now, we must clarify this situation."

"Yes, sir," Abram repeated, his voice a hollow echo.

The commandant began to pace, his boots echoing in the sudden silence. "Those of you who are ill," he announced, his voice sharp and commanding, "raise your hands. My corpsman will examine you and provide treatment. Ensure your recovery. So. Hands. Now."

The beams of the flashlights danced across the faces in the car, searching, probing. The railcar was silent.

"Gentlemen," the commandant's voice was softer now, almost pleading, "we do not care who was talking. We wish to verify Herr Kelner's account. One or two of you were speaking. Surely, you don't believe my men are lying. Herr Kelner assures me it was merely the unconscious ramblings of the sick. Don't prove him wrong. For your well-being and Herr Kelner's, raise your hand if you are ill. We will care for you. Please."

Four hands, trembling, rose slowly into the air.

A slow smile spread across the commandant's face. He had them. "Excellent," he purred.

Sergeant Brost, a thin, small, baby-faced man in his twenties, set about his task. A soldier dressed in white prepared the portable examination table on the adjacent freight dock—the portable lights were angled to illuminate the makeshift clinic. Two soldiers, clad in white medical gear and rubber gloves, seized the first man who had raised his hand. He was too weak to stand, his body limp as they carried him to the table.

The corpsman, also in a white gown, gloves, and mask, began his examination: a poke, a prod, a peering down the throat, a careful palpation of the abdomen. "How long has the diarrhea been?" he asked, his voice low.

The man hesitated, glancing at Abram, who stood beside the table, his face a rigid mask. "Answer," Abram said, his voice barely a whisper.

"Six days," the man mumbled. "And yes, blood."

"And the consistency? No change?"

"Like water."

"Vomiting?"

"Dry heaves. Nothing comes up."

The corpsman's face was grim. "Fever. Jaundice. Your abdomen is not good. And your lungs." He shook his head. "Pneumonia. You are very sick."

The officer stepped forward. "Sergeant Brost, a word?"

They moved away from the platform, out of the earshot of the prisoners.

The officer's gaze flickered back to the railcar. "Your diagnosis?"

Sergeant Brost shook his head, his expression bleak. "He is dying, sir. Useless for labor. A few days, perhaps. Malnutrition is severe. They are all on that path. These men may not even reach the factory. And even if they do, they will be too weak to work—they may even perish en route."

The commandant's face hardened. "Failure is unacceptable. My orders are clear—healthy, skilled workers. I will deal with failure severely—severely. What do you recommend?"

"Nutrition, sir. Sunlight. Clean water. It may take weeks, but it is their only chance."

The officer leaned in, his voice a hushed whisper. "Listen carefully. This is between us. We will thin the herd. We will send those beyond recovery to the 'sick bay.' Say they are going to a hospital. We will end their suffering discreetly. Do you understand?"

"Yes, sir. I understand."

The officer cleared his throat, his voice even lower. "Ask for stretcher-bearers. Make it convincing. We will examine ten percent—if half are critical, we will examine another ten percent. The need for these craftsmen is desperate. We will remove only those whom we cannot possibly save. Understood?"

The corpsman looked directly at the commandant, his voice firm. "Yes, sir. Understood."

"Stand near me," the officer instructed. "We must project confidence. And I will ensure the blame falls elsewhere. Let us conclude this. These prisoners must not perceive any victory."

They returned to the railcar.

The commandant, pacing again, addressed the prisoners. "We have identified one individual in critical condition. He requires immediate assistance. We have ordered stretchers. We will now examine the others who raised their hands. Your skills are vital. We will do everything necessary to ensure your health upon arrival at your destination. Tomorrow, we will increase the rations. Sunlight and fresh air will be provided, along with additional water. We will address the sanitary conditions. You may experience a delay here while we attend to your comrades. Those requiring extended care will return when we deem them fit to do so. But the no-talking rule remains in effect."

He paused, his eyes sweeping over the faces before him. "However, the penalty has been adjusted. For any infraction, hanging. And not just the guilty party. I will select another at random. Two deaths for each violation. Do you comprehend the gravity of this?" He paused again, letting his words linger in the suffocating air. "Furthermore, if we suspect talking, you must identify the speaker. Or I will select three at random for execution. Do we understand each other?"

The previous punishment, the agonizing smashing of a rifle butt against a protruding tongue—was replaced with hanging. Abram thought *hanging would be less painful than a severed tongue.*

The role of the crack-watcher became a lifeline. Detecting the Germans' approach in the darkness was paramount. Abram gave the order: absolute silence within the car. Talking was a risk no one could afford. If discussions were unavoidable, they were conducted in hushed whispers, pressed close together, and only when the crack-watcher signaled the all-clear. The air in the railcar was thick with fear, the stench of decay, and the unspoken dread of what was to come.

CHAPTER THIRTY-FIVE

Jozefow Rail Station
July 28ᵗʰ, 1942, 11:30 p.m.

Abram stood apart, his mind a tightly wound spring. He watched the corpsman move down the line, prodding and assessing each of the eleven remaining men. Three, deemed too far gone, were hauled away on stretchers by the Germans. Four days. Four days on this rail siding, and the railcar hadn't budged an inch. Yet a strange optimism had begun to bloom, a fragile sprout in the barren landscape of their captivity. It was a stark contrast to the life they'd known in Jozefow, a life that felt like a lifetime ago. Maybe, just maybe, the suffocating darkness was lifting.

"It's like being born again, those two hours outside," one of his men murmured, his voice raspy but filled with a newfound lightness. Abram couldn't argue. The days before this reprieve had been a descent into hell.

Then, a miracle, or perhaps a calculated shift in tactics. A fire hose appeared, and the prisoners, armed with soap and brushes, were ordered to scrub the filth from the railcar floor. Fresh straw followed, a soft cushion against the hard planks, and a blessing beyond measure—four-lidded buckets for their waste. The simple act of hygiene, the small comfort of cleanliness, was almost overwhelming. And then there was the food. Rations had increased. Freedom was another improvement that was badly needed, allowing them to exercise outside each day. The July sun was warm on their skin. They organized themselves, a collective act of defiance against the unknown. Thirty minutes of exercise was a ritual to reclaim their bodies and their strength. One day at a time. That was the mantra, whispered and unspoken, that bound them together.

Abram wrestled with the change. The Germans, true to their word—a concept that felt almost absurd—had provided thick, vegetable-laden soup. Twice, on two glorious days, they'd been fed a second meal. He'd even found a sliver of meat in his bowl, a treasure beyond price. And the bread! Thick, dark slices accompanied the soup, a feast compared to the scraps they'd endured. Clean water, once a precious commodity, now flowed in what seemed like an endless supply.

The questions gnawed at him. *Why are we indeed so valuable? Is the railcar, filled with skilled tradesmen, the key?*

The fate of the three sick men, carried away on stretchers, haunted them all. The commandant's hollow assurance—*they would join the group later*—rang false. Were they already dead? Their ghosts lingered in the corners of the railcar, a constant reminder of the fragility of their existence. *Only God knows*, Abram thought, a silent prayer in the face of uncertainty.

The night shattered. Not with a single, sharp crack but with a growing roar—the guttural growl of engines, the shouts of men, the rhythmic thud of boots—the familiar, terrifying sounds of a military unit in motion. Something was happening.

The railcar door ripped open, and a blinding light stabbed into the darkness. The air was filled with the frantic barking of German shepherds. A chorus of German voices, harsh and insistent, sliced through the air: "Schnell! Schnell! Schnell! Raus! Raus! Raus!"

Forced out onto the road beside the tracks, the Germans herded the men into four ragged lines facing a flatbed truck. A new figure emerged, bathed in the artificial light.

He was a colonel, surprisingly small and thin, with a neatly trimmed pencil mustache that seemed almost comical against the severity of his freshly pressed uniform. Ribbons, a colorful tapestry of war, adorned his chest, dominated by the Iron Cross. Round, dark-framed glasses perched on his nose, magnifying the intensity of his gaze. A slight paunch strained against his tunic. He wore his riding trousers neatly tucked into gleaming, knee-high boots. He held a swagger stick, a symbol of authority that he tapped against his leg as he began to speak.

His voice, unexpectedly high-pitched, carried a chilling blend of disdain, and for the prisoners, it was a mix of amusement and fear.

"Our Jewish guests, we trust you have enjoyed your accommodations these past few days." The sarcasm dripped like acid. "We Germans, as you well know, do not harbor affection for Jews. You are the root of all Germany's ills—not my words, mind you, but those of our esteemed leader, the honorable Herr Adolf Hitler.[36] We must, therefore, treat you accordingly—as the parasites you are."

A shiver ran down Abram's spine. This talk was not a rant; it was a carefully crafted performance designed to instill fear and obedience.

"At your next destination, do not expect improvement," the colonel continued, his voice hardening. "We are at war. We will not squander resources on Jews. You will adapt. You will obey. Failure to do so will result in consequences, most often death by hanging. We have no intention of wasting precious ammunition on Jewish vermin. At your new home, permanent gallows await—capable of dispatching six of you at a time. The choice, of course, is yours."

He paused, letting the words sink in. The silence was heavy, broken only by the nervous shuffling of feet and the distant growl of the dogs.

"Major Gerschel, my second in command, will now elaborate on our expectations."

The major, a stark contrast to the colonel, stepped down from the truck. Tall, blond, and blue-eyed, he radiated an almost predatory energy. His uniform, while similar to the colonel's, lacked some of the decorations, but his physical presence was far more imposing. He moved among the prisoners, a wolf among sheep, two corporals flanking him, their machine guns held at the ready.

"You Jews stink!" he roared, his voice booming across the open space. "But fear not. That will change within the next twelve hours. Your new handlers will provide you with proper barracks. You will shed those rags you call clothes. You will wash your filthy bodies, and we will remove every hair—and I mean every hair—from your person."

Abram felt a knot of dread tightening in his stomach. This treatment wasn't just about control. It was about humiliation, about stripping them of their dignity.

"We will feed you," Gerschel continued, his voice dripping with contempt. "We will provide you with a prisoner's uniform. And, most importantly, the Reich will put you to work!"

He paced back and forth, his eyes scanning the ranks of prisoners. "Over a hundred kilometers by rail, that is your new home. We will march you to the passenger cars, which are a kilometer from here. Each of you will be assigned a seat. There will be no food or water. You will sit. You will remain silent. You will behave. Four armed soldiers are stationed in each car, with orders to shoot anyone who dares to leave their seat. Do I make myself clear?"

He stopped, his gaze locking onto Abram for a fleeting moment. Abram forced himself to meet his eyes, a silent act of defiance. The major's nostrils flared, and he reached into his pocket, producing a cigarette. He tore it in two, stuffing half into each nostril. "You Jews smell like dead animals!" he spat.

"I have full authorization to use lethal force during this journey," he warned. "And remember, no talking. Not now, not on the train. Not even a whisper. You will suffer harsh consequences. My men have their orders. Sergeant Borman will now provide further guidance. Good luck staying alive, gentlemen. You'll need it." He paused, looking toward the flatbed truck. "Sergeant, if you please."

Sergeant Borman. The name itself sounded ominous. He emerged from the shadows, a hulking figure that dwarfed even the major. His trousers barely concealed scuffed, dirty boots. His Nazi jacket was devoid of medals, his face a landscape of several days' worth of stubble. Wide gaps punctuated his yellowed teeth, creating a grotesque, almost animalistic grin. He was unkempt, brutal, the embodiment of everything terrifying about the German war machine. He surveyed the area with a slow, deliberate gaze. He was in no hurry.

After an agonizingly long silence, a silence that stretched the nerves to their breaking point, he stepped out of the truck. His voice, when it finally came, was a low growl—a sound that resonated deep in his chest.

"Eyes forward!" he commanded. "Stand straight! Arms at your sides! Don't move until I tell you!"

He moved along the front row, his presence radiating menace. One prisoner, unable to resist, let his eyes follow the sergeant's path. Borman stopped dead. He seized the man by the throat, lifting him slightly off the ground.

"I said, eyes forward! Are you deaf?"

The prisoner, his voice choked, managed to gasp, "I am not deaf!"

Borman's grip tightened. "The only reason you're still breathing is because you possess a skill we require. I couldn't care less—skill or no skill. But you've given me a reason to watch you. And those I watch don't tend to live long. You, I suspect, will not live long either."

He released his grip, shoving the prisoner back. Then, with a swift, brutal motion, he kneed him in the stomach. The prisoner crumpled to the ground. Borman followed with a series of savage kicks, finishing with a sickening stomp of his boot on the man's head.

"You're fortunate I didn't kill this thing," Borman sneered. "But there's still time. I'll be watching." He pointed to two other prisoners. "You two. Take care of your damaged Jew. If he dies, you die. Understand?"

"Yes, sir, we understand," they stammered, their voices barely audible.

Borman turned back to the assembled prisoners. "Good. Your skills mean nothing to me. You are filth. Jewish vermin. Stinking Jewish vermin. Do we understand each other?"

A ragged, disorganized chorus of assent confirmed their understanding.

"The passenger cars are about a kilometer up the spur," Borman continued, his voice returning to its menacing growl. "Don't even think about running. Our soldiers have you surrounded. We have a dozen armed men. And behind you," he paused for effect, "is a vehicle-mounted, heavy machine gun. The kind that tears limbs off. Designed to bring down aircraft. The gunner is new. He is eager for his first kill. A Polish Jew, preferably. He has my blessing to eliminate any of you who disappoint us. I wouldn't test him."

He then roared, "Attention! Eyes forward! Right face! Forward march!"

The march to the train was a silent, agonizing procession. Each prisoner was acutely aware of the eyes upon them, the ever-present threat of violence. They boarded the train in alphabetical order, a deliberate tactic to disrupt any potential escape plans. The Germans were taking no chances.

Once inside, crammed into their assigned seats, they waited. The minutes stretched into an eternity. Finally, the steam locomotive arrived, a metal beast hissing and groaning as it coupled with the cars. But the train wouldn't depart until dawn. The prisoners, exhausted and filled with dread, slept fitfully in their seats, finding strange, fleeting comfort in the relative stability.

July 29th, 1942, 8:30 a.m.

The train lurched forward, and the rhythmic clatter of the wheels on the tracks was a mournful soundtrack to their journey.

Abram, seated by a window, watched the landscape unfold. Rolling hills, painted in the vibrant greens of July, stretched out before him. This was new territory. He'd traveled between Jozefow and Warsaw countless times, but this was different. West by northwest, he calculated, judging by the position of the sun. But to where? The train maintained a steady pace, roughly twenty kilometers per hour. He could track the distance, a small act of control in a world spinning out of control.

Hours later, the sun began its slow descent. The scenery shifted. The farmland gave way to villages, then to the outskirts of a larger city. Smokestacks pierced the horizon, plumes of gray smoke staining the sky.

The roof vents, a blessing, provided a constant stream of fresh air, a luxury they hadn't known in weeks. Time, however, was a blur. The Germans had confiscated all watches. Only the sun's position offered a clue. Abram estimated they'd traveled well over a hundred and fifty kilometers.

The train slowed, pulling onto a rail siding. Abram braced himself. This was it. The soldiers stationed near his seat barked their orders. "Remain seated! We shoot to kill! No talking!"

Through snatches of their conversation, Abram caught the name 'Skarzysko-Kamienna.'[37]

His heart sank. He knew the place.

It was infamous—a center for the manufacture of small arms ammunition. The Kar98, the standard German rifle, was also used by the Polish Army, which had adopted the same round. The ability to manufacture Kar98 ammunition—a vital cog in the German war machine. Slave labor—that was their purpose. He remembered the HASSAG factory, Hugo Schneider Aktiengesellschaft, and it had existed for years. Thousands worked the grounds—the Jewish ghetto, established in 1941, a reservoir of forced labor.

He recalled the whispers of the Polish resistance, Orzel Bialy, the White Eagle. A friend in Jozefow had a brother, a member, who had refused to work in the factory. The Germans had hunted him—arrested him. It didn't matter, as the brother perished. The Germans murdered hundreds for their defiance. The friend hadn't heard from his brother in months.

A voice, amplified by a megaphone, shattered the tense silence. "Disembark! Fall in on the left side of the train! Quickly! Move! Move! Move!"

CHAPTER THIRTY-SIX

Munitions Facility—Skarżysko-Kamienna, Poland
July 29th, 1942, 4:40 p.m.

The German soldiers on the train scurried about as the locomotive slowed to a stop. Abram suspected that the railmen had thrown the switch on the spur track to divert the train away from the main rail. Outside the window, he observed a brick wall topped with multiple strands of barbed wire. Every twenty-five meters, a German Army uniformed guard stood positioned along the top of the walkway at the top of the wall. Many carried a shoulder-strapped machine gun. Plenty of buildings were on the site, plus a lone, tall smokestack billowing a light gray exhaust. It was easy to discern. There was a five-kilometer wind coming out of the east. The brick wall appeared to go on forever. Abram thought, *this is a vast manufacturing complex.*

The locomotive nudged along, this time at a snail's pace.

Abram looked out and thought, *We are moving in the opposite direction.*

After traveling about two hundred meters, the locomotive stopped again, and Abram was stunned by what he saw.

As the train inched its way into the grounds of the walled facility, Abram and his men scanned the area from left to right. He felt a huge lump in his throat as he saw undernourished humans in striped uniforms with tiny stovepipe hats made of the same material as their clothing. *These are emaciated children of God. They look to be walking skeletons. How long did it take to achieve such a condition? Are we destined for the same?*

Some stood perfectly still, with their chalk-white faces staring into space. They looked like ghosts more than humans, the scene absent of any color, like a black-and-white photo. The prisoners milled about the square, pushing and pulling large carts. Other inmates filled the carts with scrap metal and other debris. Many of the prisoners stood and stared at the rail cars.

Abram wondered, *Are they looking at us out of jealousy or pity, as we still have meat on our bones and color in our faces? Or are they looking at us from the perspective of more expendable human workers for the Nazi war machine?*

Along the dock, the inmates were stacking what appeared to be wooden crates filled with rifle ammunition products. Other inmates loaded crates onto horse-drawn wagons and a rail car on an adjacent track. The chalk-white faces of uniformed prisoners, each with sunken cheeks, dark bags under their eyes, and bony extremities, could be seen throughout the square. *These prisoners are indeed near starvation.* Their bodies resembled walking skeletons, dressed in baggy, striped pajamas.

A few minutes passed, the locomotive stopped. A high-pitched scream canceled out any other sound as the engineer released excess steam from the locomotive boiler.

Minutes later, the rail car was boarded by several maniacal German guards, yelling and screaming in the faces of the prisoners. The guards carried long billy clubs. As they approached the prisoners, they shouted, "You God damned, worthless, dirty Jews," or "Fresh Jew meat," and "More Jews to replace those we have killed," while those with batons clubbed Jews below the waist to get their attention.

An officer appeared and entered the lead passenger compartment, yelling, "I will not permit my men to be nice or cordial to you filthy Jews. Men, you must treat them for what they truly are—Jew vermin." He quickly cleared his throat of flehm and spat the glob of mucus on the nearest Jew. "Please, men, remind each of these Jews that we are not in love with anything Jewish."

The guards did not like the Jews, and they would do their best to communicate this dislike. The Jews were not welcome.

The guards walked down the aisles of the passenger rail cars, forced each prisoner out of his seat, and slammed their billy clubs into the ribs and across each prisoner's shoulders and back area.

The German officer, Major Gerschel, who had been on the train since leaving Jozefow, pulled his Luger pistol and fired it into the air, then spoke with anger and authority, said, "You will cease this brutality! Cease now! These men are not your everyday prisoners. Each of these men has a skilled trade. They are critical to the production effort at this facility. I will shoot the next man who lays a hand on one of these gentlemen! Do you understand?"

The lieutenant in charge of the men delivering the brutality approached the officer. "These are my men, you Dummkopf! Who do you think you are ordering my men to do anything?"

Major Gerschel spoke, his angered face an inch from the lieutenant's, "First, I outrank your slimy ass. These prisoners are my responsibility until I have delivered them to the commandant of the munitions factory. What use are they if they cannot turn a wrench, operate a lathe, or wire a pump? You are the Dummkopf! Get your men off my rail car and get out of my face before I slip up and shoot one of our own by accident!"

"We will settle this later. You are out of line!" the lieutenant growled.

"As I said, get your ass off my train! I will not ask again!"

The officer dismissed his men and left the train.

Major Gerschel yelled, "Gentlemen. Disembark from the train and fall in on the rail car's right side. Exit now!"

The sixty-seven men organized themselves in four rows and stood at attention.

"One of my men will march you to the office of the facility commander. From there, you will be assigned to the induction center to receive a haircut, shave, shower, and delousing. From there, you will be issued clothing and transferred to a barracks. From this point forward, you will work twelve-hour days, and we will feed you once a day. Do we understand one another?"

He continued, "Do not attempt to escape. Plenty of our inmates have tried, and of course, they have all failed or have died trying. My men have captured each inmate who has attempted an escape. None of those caught continues to walk this earth, and we are pleased to report we executed each by hanging.

"In your case, with the skillsets your men possess, my command has asked me to protect you from unnecessary brutality. Granted, regardless of your skillset, I will see that punishment is delivered if you act contrary to the rules. If you follow our rules during your stay here, at the end of this war, and following our victory, you will be released and allowed to return to your home."

Another officer entered the area and greeted the major with a salute as they faced one another. "I, at this moment, transfer from my command to yours, sixty-seven skilled trade Jewish men," the officer declared as he handed off his control to the local officer in charge.

"Major, thank you. I now have custody of the men. I dismiss you."

The major performed a textbook about-face and exited in true German military fashion as he marched toward the railcar they had traveled on from Jozefow. The prisoners would never forget him, and the inmates from Jozefow would never see the major again.

The commander, a colonel, waited until the major was well out of sight before he began speaking.

"Jewish vermin, I am Colonel Bacht! Your major was a weak weasel! Unlike your weak weasel major, I couldn't care less about your prima-donna status. Yes, you are a skilled tradesman. However, you remain filthy Jewish vermin. I will have you hanged as though you had zero skills. I don't care. A filthy Jew is a filthy Jew. Get out of line, and you will receive the appropriate punishment for your wrongdoing. To escape harsh treatment, do what we ask. Be quick. Follow our orders like you would for your commanding officer. You will not like our penalties for noncompliance. My men will club you about the head and shoulders if you hesitate to fulfill our orders. And my men enjoy hurting Jews who are not following our direction. If you follow what the command asks of you, you have little to worry about. However, if you are poor at taking orders, you should ask that I take you to the gallows today. Our hangman is quite busy each week. Do we understand one another?"

The prisoners stood motionless without a word uttered.

"Perfect, I will take your silence as confirmation that you understand what I have told you. You will now have Colonel Schneider instruct you on our expectations for you for the remainder of the day. Colonel Schneider, please take command."

Colonel Schneider introduced himself.

"Jew scum, if you think Colonel Bacht is a little harsh, you have seen nothing. I take pride in my reputation here. They call me the Barbarian. I like that nickname, and it fits my personality well. Make me angry, and I will not hesitate to pull out my Luger and end your life. Ask around, and you will find this is not a legend but a fact! So, my advice—don't cross me. Now, who is your leader? I know you have a leader."

Abram raised his hand and stated, "Colonel Schneider, sir. I am Abram Kelner."

"Good. You will be the first to die should you not be able to control your men. Do you understand?"

"Yes, sir, I understand."

"I want you to arrange your men by skillset. Once arranged, they will provide their name, skill, specialty, and total years of experience."

"Yes, sir, I will organize my men as you have requested."

Abram left the ranks and began speaking.

"All electricians, stand here and stand in alphabetical order. Next, all pipefitters and plumbers stand here in alphabetical order. Next, all millwrights stand here, all tool and die techs stand here, tinsmiths stand here, instrument techs stand here, cement masons stand here, and materials techs stand here."

In short order, all sixty-seven men were now standing in their appropriate row for their craft.

Other German soldiers and technical staff from the munitions plant had arrived in the area by now.

Colonel Schneider began speaking, "Gentlemen, break off into groups and take the necessary notes on the experience level of each skilled tradesperson. I want assignments for each tradesman made and carved in stone within an hour. Once assigned, the trade foreman will guide his men to their designated areas for clothing, showers, haircuts, and barracks. We will not feed you today. Following our daily roll call, you must report to your appropriate area at five tomorrow morning."

The colonel continued, "Furthermore, should you attempt to sabotage our production, the penalty is simple. For each saboteur caught, we will hang the saboteur plus five other prisoners. As an added treat, we will ensure each saboteur receives torture before we execute you. Trust me, you will wish you were dead once my men have completed a few hours of torture. Any questions?"

"We know how to determine if our production levels are, all of a sudden, off our planned levels. We aim to keep the lines running efficiently to meet or break production levels. Should production levels drop, we will find the guilty parties. You cannot outsmart us!" the colonel concluded.

They had finished their orientation. The Germans provided clothing, shaved their heads, faces, and pubic hair areas, showered, deloused, and assigned each man to his barracks. The night's first and most challenging part was figuring out who was who, as each person looked quite different minus their head and facial hair. No one recognized their peers. The sole way to confirm identity was to hear a familiar voice.

Abram approached a person he perhaps recognized as familiar and said, "Wow, you were ugly with hair. Without hair, you are so much uglier."

"Abram, who do you think I am?"

"Oh my God, I thought you were Piotr. You are not Piotr. You are Johanne."

"Piotr is standing right behind you," Johanne remarked.

With a snicker, Abram said, "You are right. Piotr is much uglier. A heavy mustache and long hair that once distracted the view of Piotr's hooked nose and ugly ears—in particular, his ears resembled a carriage coming down the road with both doors open."

Johanne continued, "When this is all over, you must grow your hair back to even have the slightest chance of attracting any member of the opposite sex."

Abram commented, "We'd better all grow our hair and beards to cover up our ugliness."

"Speak for yourself, Abram," Piotr said.

"We must make it out of this nightmare, God willing," Abram said. "This hell we are going through will be challenging for each of us. I have been wondering who in our group will be the first to deviate from the line. There is little room for error. We must cover for one another. We can't let our men fail and must not give up on them."

Night had fallen. It was time for bed. They were hungry but dead tired from their long journey, and sleep could not come quickly enough.

There were four men in one bunk, though bunk was a generous description, as there was no mattress. In fact, the base of the mattress was a single layer of burlap draped over a roughhewn lumber frame. The bedframe was barely large enough to accommodate three humans, not the four they assigned to the poor excuse for a bed. Their blanket was a thin layer of worn burlap as well. The burlap blanket would suffice for a July evening, but the dread of a cold winter night entered his thoughts—such a flimsy excuse for a proper blanket during frigid Polish weather would be challenging.

The rough wood of the bunk pressed cold against his back, a stark contrast to the feather bed he'd been torn from only days before. Sleep was a distant country—his mind raced, caught in the barbed wire of this new reality.

Images flickered like desperate candle flames in the oppressive darkness, and he thought of Ryfka, confined to a wheelchair, her face lined with wisdom, hopefully still safe in her village nook, and Icek, his brave son, nearly a man now, strong but still needing guidance—had they taken him too, or had he fled into the forest? And the twins, so small, their trusting eyes and tangled hair—a hollow ache opened within his chest, a chasm of unknowing. Where were they? Were they cold? Frightened? *Are they even alive?* This place, reeking of fear and the foul odor of human sweat, offered no answers. The silence between the ragged breaths and muffled sobs of unseen strangers screamed louder than any train whistle, amplifying the brutal truth: This was the first night, and he was utterly, devastatingly alone with the ghosts of his loved ones and the terror for their fate.

Tomorrow would be their first test of being a slave laborer, twelve hours a day, seven days a week.

CHAPTER THIRTY-SEVEN

Skarżysko-Kamienna, Poland
July 30th, 1942, 4:45 a.m.

Abram jolted awake, the snores of his bunkmates grating a symphony. He lay still, the pre-dawn chill seeping through the thin blanket, and replayed the horrors of his first night. The man beside him had punctuated the darkness with bursts of noxious gas, each one a pungent assault that had dragged him from restless sleep.

Beyond the stench, an incessant itch tormented him. His skin crawled. *Fleas? Mites? The harsh lye soap from the mandatory bath? Or perhaps the acrid chemicals used in the delousing? He scratched—a futile gesture, and wished the incessant itching away with a silent, desperate prayer.*

Could I be allergic to this delousing powder?

He envisioned the next shower, a distant hope, imagining the blessed relief of water rinsing the residue from his pores. *But when will that be?* The question hung unanswered, a heavy weight in the pre-dawn gloom.

The dream clung to him, a vivid replay of defiance. He'd been battling German soldiers, a one-man army defending his home. In the dream's comforting illusion, he'd triumphed, each Nazi falling before him, his family safe.

But the waking world brought a crushing reality. He squeezed his eyes shut, battling the despair. *There's no way they survived—perhaps Icek escaped? Where could he have gone?* He forced himself to stop dwelling on their likely fate. It was a poison he couldn't afford. He would cling to hope, to prayer. *Maybe, just maybe, Icek found a way out.*

The cacophony of the wake-up ritual shattered the fragile quiet. A club slammed against the bedframes, a metallic clang that echoed through the barracks. The wielder, dressed in the same drab uniform as the prisoners, sported a stark white armband: "K A P O."[38] The letters stood out, a bold pronouncement of authority. This was a Kapo, one of the prisoners chosen by the Nazis, selected for their cruelty and their willingness to inflict pain on their fellow inmates. They were the enforcers, driving the starving, sick men to forced labor with brutal efficiency.

These Kapos, Abram realized, were nothing more than prisoners twisted into tools of the camp's brutal regime. They were to be avoided and feared, their presence a constant threat. They held the power to make an already unbearable existence a living hell. The club was not a symbol but an instrument.

Abram observed they were empowered. He knew instantly. The prisoners he observed recoiled. The eyes he scanned reflected avoidance and fear.

He noticed even the German SS, the black-uniformed elite, the self-proclaimed "political soldiers," often stood back, letting the Kapos and the local auxiliary troops do the dirty work.

Loud whistles pierced the air, joining the Kapo's relentless pounding. Screams and shouts ripped through the barracks.

In moments, the room was a flurry of activity. Men scrambled from their bunks, lining up with a practiced speed born of fear.

A German officer barked from the doorway, his voice a sharp whip crack. "All prisoners, rollcall! Rollcall!" His gaze swept the room, hungry, searching for any infraction, any excuse to unleash his brutality.

The prisoners surged forward, a frantic tide of bodies, the wooden floor vibrating under the frantic shuffle of their shoes. Within seconds, they stood in formation outside, rows of ten, a neatly organized mass for the morning's count.

Today was Abram's third rollcall but the first in daylight. The rising sun cast a harsh light on the scene, revealing the grim reality of the camp's population. He'd seen them from a distance before, their gaunt figures a disturbing silhouette. Now, close up, the details were horrifying. Tattered clothes hung loosely on skeletal frames. A collective, sour odor emanated from the men, a stench of unwashed bodies and despair. Would he, too, soon wear this same mask of suffering? Their faces were studies in exhaustion, chalky skin stretched taut over bone, eyes sunken into deep, dark hollows. Not a single man looked remotely healthy—they were all starving shadows.

As he scanned the ranks, he noticed the color-coded triangles on their jackets, a macabre labeling system.

His group, all of whom were Jewish, wore the *Star of David*. He would later learn that green triangles marked criminals, red designated political prisoners, Communists, Socialists, and trade unionists. Black triangles the Nazis reserved for the "asocial"—Roma, the shiftless, the unwanted. Pink marked homosexuals, purple Jehovah's Witnesses. A letter superimposed on the triangle indicated nationality: "P" for Poland, "SU" for the Soviet Union, and "F" for France.

These color-coded tags, Abram realized with chilling certainty, were designed to divide, to fuel conflict. The Germans were masters of manipulation.

Pitting prisoner against prisoner served a dual purpose. It created a readily available, desperate workforce while simultaneously fueling the animosity between the different groups. The Kapos, with their occasional "privileges" of slightly better rations and slightly less brutal work, were a prime example of this twisted system. Some, corrupted by their meager power, used it to hoard scraps within the camp's black market—a cigarette, a sliver of bread, a taste of alcohol.

Abram learned that besides the count, another horror awaited—a *selection*. It was a brutal winnowing, the Germans separating the "useful" from the "expendable." Three SS officers, accompanied by two doctors, moved through the ranks with chilling detachment. He watched as the doctors scrutinized their chosen victims, probing, pinching, peering into their eyes, feeling the hollows of their necks and abdomens. It was a grotesque assessment, a calculation of human worth based solely on physical capacity. Those deemed too weak the Nazis herded to the side—their fate sealed, their disappearance a chilling certainty. The whispers in the camp spoke of Treblinka, a name that hung in the air like a shroud, a place eighty kilometers northeast of Warsaw.

Treblinka? What happened there? The answer, Abram knew, would come soon enough.

The shocking condition of those selected struck Abram. They were living skeletons, barely clinging to life. *How long did it take to reach this state? Was this his future, his peers' future?*

He stared at the condemned group. Their skeletal frames, their tattered clothes, their vacant stares, it was a portrait of utter despair. Some pleaded, their voices thin and reedy, begging for a reprieve that would never come.

The selection ended. The remaining prisoners, a shuffling mass of the condemned, walked back, resignation heavy in their steps. The selected, perhaps two hundred souls, men and women of all ages, were marched to a paved area near the rail yard.

Cattle cars were shunted onto the rail siding. Minutes later, both the vehicles and the selected prisoners were gone, swallowed by the insatiable maw of the Nazi machine.

Abram returned to the barracks, his heart a leaden weight. He was met by the facility's engineering manager, a towering figure, impeccably dressed in a three-piece vested suit, his clean-shaven face dominated by a pencil mustache. A civilian and a German SS officer accompanied him.

"Herr Kelner," the engineering manager began, his voice surprisingly gentle, "you are in charge of the skilled tradesmen who arrived last evening?"

"Yes, sir, I am Abram Kelner. I am a millwright."

"Herr Kelner, please meet my superior, German SS Major Schmidt."

Abram met the major's gaze, his expression carefully neutral. "Major Schmidt."

Major Schmidt, a stark contrast to the towering manager, was a man of athletic build, his wire-framed glasses perched on a sharp nose. His hair was perfectly styled, his teeth impossibly white—the very embodiment of the Nazi ideal. He spoke with the measured tones of an academic.

"Herr Kelner, we need to discuss your future. Your fate, and the fate of your men, rests in your hands."

Abram stared, his confusion a visible question mark.

"You witnessed a selection this morning," Major Schmidt continued, his voice smooth and dangerous. "I trust you and your men would do anything to avoid reaching such a state of deterioration. To avoid being deemed unhelpful to the Third Reich. Is this not true, Herr Kelner?"

"What are you thinking, Herr Kelner?" Herr Wilhelm Borscht, the leader of the maintenance effort, inquired, stepping closer.

Abram swallowed. "I will do everything in my power to prevent my men from being selected."

"I will give you ten minutes. I must have an agreement that is unanimous among your men. Gather your men outside in four equal rows. Then, we march to the production offices. I will lead the way. Further instructions will be provided upon arrival in approximately five minutes."

Abram relayed the situation to his men, his voice low and urgent as they stood outside the production facility. "Gentlemen, you saw the selection. I have been given a promise by Major Schmidt. We will face the same fate if we do not cooperate. He spoke of eight weeks, gentlemen. Eight weeks until we are reduced to the state of those we saw this morning. I, for one, have no desire to starve to death. The past twenty hours without food have been agonizing enough."

A man spoke, his voice trembling slightly. "What must we do to avoid that?"

"It's simple," Abram replied, his voice hardening. "We cooperate, or we starve. They brought us here from Jozefow for a reason. They need our skills to get this ammunition plant running at full capacity."

Another man interjected, "But what do we gain?"

"We survive," Abram said, his voice bleak. "That is our reward. Survival."

Starvation was not an option—it would not happen. It took less than five minutes to convince Abram's men. Cooperation was the only path. There was only one additional ask. A request for food, a desperate plea after twenty hours without sustenance.

Abram returned to the major and Herr Borscht. "My men agree, pending one condition. We have not eaten in over twenty hours. I request that you provide us with food before we proceed."

"Have your men report to the production office. We will hold our first production meeting. I will have food brought in—real food, not the slop they feed the general population," the major declared, a flicker of something unreadable in his eyes. "I will prove my sincerity. Herr Borscht, escort these men. I will arrange the rations."

"Sir, we will need rations for sixty-eight men, including myself."

"The production office can accommodate one hundred. We will be there in fifteen minutes," the major replied.

The men gathered, the air thick with anticipation and fear. Major Schmidt addressed them, his voice regaining its smooth, dangerous edge.

"Gentlemen, you have heard the bad news. And I will deliver more bad news if you hinder my objectives. But if you assist me and help me meet our production quotas, you will be rewarded. My command has authorized me to provide this small group with a superior diet. We need you not just to survive but to thrive. We need ammunition! And nothing will stand in my way."

The sixty-seven men exchanged uneasy glances—disbelief etched on their faces.

"Your reward? You saw the selection this morning. The emaciation, the despair, it is a revolting sight. And I assure you, those selected were not sent away for recovery. I cannot tell you their fate. However, I can assure you that if you fail to cooperate, I will ensure your men are prime candidates for selection within eight weeks. Do we understand each other?"

A ripple of unease passed through the room. Faces were blank masks, hiding a storm of emotions.

"Now, I want you to understand that survival is possible. You have no choice but to work together. We will keep you healthy! In return, you must meet our production demands. Better food, gentlemen, a guarantee. That is what I offer today."

The reality of their situation sank in, and Abram would later learn that the facility housed three small-arms ammunition lines. Only one was currently operational. Raw materials were abundant, stockpiled due to the crippled production. The warehouses overflowed, a testament to the regime's refusal to acknowledge failure.

The core problem was the lack of spare parts and the absence of skilled tradesmen to maintain the equipment. Sophisticated machinery in the machine shop—lathes, mills, cutters—lay idle, gathering dust. Routine maintenance, the lifeblood of any manufacturing process, had ceased. The men who performed it were dead.

The facility's utility systems were also failing. Water, air, lubrication, waste disposal, and steam, essential for production, were unreliable, prone to sudden interruptions.

The Germans suspected sabotage, a subtle yet effective form of resistance. Anyone with even a basic understanding of the systems could cripple them. Quality control was also abysmal. Reports from the front lines described misfires and ammunition rendered useless by even the slightest moisture.

The German command hoped that this influx of "new blood" of skilled tradesmen with a vested interest in survival would resolve these issues.

The food arrived, a stark contrast to the usual camp fare.

"Gentlemen, your meal," Major Schmidt announced as six emaciated prisoners pushed four carts laden with food into the room. Scrambled eggs, a mountain of them, sliced bread, jam, and, most surprisingly, coffee and tea. "Enjoy your breakfast. We have much to discuss."

As the men devoured the unexpected feast, Abram couldn't shake a troubling thought. Was this major's life also on the line? Was he, too, threatened? Was his family in danger? It was a chilling possibility, entirely consistent with the Nazi regime's brutality.

The major's voice cut through his thoughts. "Gentlemen, remember this: We have executed over a dozen men in the past seven months for sabotage, either caught in the act or merely suspected. I will not hesitate to hang anyone who interferes with our production. Please do not test me. You will learn where our vulnerabilities lie. So, if you value your lives and wish to see your families again, you will not sabotage, and you will report to Herr Kelner anyone who even speaks of it. Torture and hanging await any violator."

As they ate, the major wanted their profiles.

"While you enjoy this unexpected bounty, I need to assess your skills. Herr Wilhelm Hoffmann will conduct the questioning. Please answer truthfully and completely."

Herr Hoffmann, a slight, baby-faced man in his mid-twenties, adjusted his thick glasses. He wore a bow tie and a patched-up sport coat, the image of a young schoolteacher. But his voice, unexpectedly deep and firm, commanded attention.

"Good morning, gentlemen." He shuffled his clipboard, avoiding direct eye contact. "We need a brief profile of each of you. When I call out your trade—welder, electrician, millwright, and so on—please state your full name and years of experience. We will then organize you into teams, each with a designated foreman. Herr Abram Kelner will serve as your superintendent, with a general foreman beneath him. The general foreman will lead the foremen who supervise crews."

The major interjected, his voice cutting through the room. "Gentlemen, although we speak of titles—superintendent, general foreman, foreman—all of you will work. These titles are for organizational purposes only. And let me be clear: If a tradesman is found to be a saboteur, both he and his foreman will be executed. These positions will be appointed. You have no say. Is that clear? Continue, Herr Hoffmann."

Herr Hoffmann meticulously recorded their skills, his pen scratching across the paper.

The major paced, his gaze sweeping over the men, studying their faces. "Excellent, gentlemen," he finally said. "A diverse and skilled group. I have shown you respect and provided you with a decent meal. This treatment will continue if we meet our objectives and if there are no saboteurs among you. Remember, the moment I discover any attempt to compromise production. You will all revert to the treatment of the general population, including your rations.

"From this day forward, after the roll call, please report to the production office. You will receive superior rations. However, should you fail to meet an agreed-upon objective, you will eat with the general population in the mess hall. You are not colleagues, not friends, not acquaintances. I will shoot you on the spot if I suspect deception. I have a reputation to maintain. We execute. We hang. We executed a fourteen-year-old boy two weeks ago—executed by hanging. For what, you ask—for stealing food."

We are, believe it or not, fair. We hold summary courts for offenses where the evidence is questionable—a swift trial but fair. Guilty verdicts, of course, result in hanging. But at least you avoid torture. So, consider your actions carefully. You will lose. Do not even think of profiting from your rations, of selling them to other inmates. Yes, a piece of bread can buy you almost anything in this hellhole. Sex. Information. Favors. But if we catch you, both the thief and the recipient will hang.

"Your value to production is irrelevant. The penalty for theft, for any transgression, is always death. Remember the fourteen-year-old. There are no exceptions. Do not test us."

CHAPTER THIRTY-EIGHT

New York City, NY
May 18th, 1943, 8:40 a.m.

The intercom buzzed, jolting Chats from his contemplation of the swirling cream in his cooling tea. He pressed the button. "A gracious good morning, Asia. How can I help you?"

A muffled sound, then a voice thick with something other than words. "Just a moment, sir, I have a mouthful of Danish."

The corners of his mouth twitched upward. "Take your time, no hurry. What's up?"

"I apologize for the rudeness. I never thought you would be in your office. I didn't expected you to answer." Her voice was more unmistakable now, the donut presumably swallowed.

He leaned back in his chair, the leather creaking softly. "It is a beautiful May day, and yes, I would rather be somewhere else, but here I am."

"I have a package on my desk, just delivered by the mail clerk. It says 'confidential,'" she paused, emphasizing the following words, "'to be opened by the addressee, Mr. Chatsworth Williams,' in bold font on the sealed envelope that is attached to the package."

"Thank you for bringing this to my attention. Please bring the package down. And by the way," he added, a mischievous tone in his voice, "I stopped and bought the staff some tasty, chocolate-filled donuts. You need to get them off my desk before I surrender and have one."

He could almost hear her swallow another bite of her donut, followed by a hasty sip of coffee. He imagined her glancing in her compact mirror—a quick check, a fleeting thought of good enough—before she replied, "On my way, sir."

"Good morning, Asia. Thank you for the heads up on the package. Not sure what's in it, but I will know soon enough." He reached for his antique letter opener, the cool metal familiar in his hand. An envelope like this was a rare occurrence, a harbinger of something significant. He remembered the last one, five years ago. The stark, official announcement that their Berlin office was to be seized by the Nazi Party. He'd conceded that one, without a fight, relocated his staff. The memory tightened his jaw. This envelope, he suspected, held news far less easily managed.

Another sip of tea, a moment's hesitation, his gaze unfocused. "This is one of those rare moments when I require privacy," he said, his voice a shade lower. "Think nothing of it. Do you understand?"

"By all means, sir. It's marked for your eyes only. I will leave you be."

"Asia, you are my right-hand person in life. You will soon find out what is in here. Between Jack, me, and you, there are no secrets." He offered her a small, reassuring smile.

Her answering smile was bright, relief flooding her features. "Thank you for reaffirming my position. I know this; however, I rarely hear it. It means a great deal to have you say this out loud."

"Well, I mean it. We will discuss the contents of this package before the end of the day. Don't give it a second thought."

Asia walked toward the door, then paused and turned back. "I don't say it nearly enough—besides Jakub, you are the most important person in my life. I mean it."

He felt a prickling behind his eyes. "Now, please get out of here before you have this old man in tears."

The door clicked shut behind her.

He sliced open the envelope. It was from Jack Reynolds, his London office manager. He'd allocated the budget to stay informed— to sniff out any threat to their insurance empire. Much of the information Jack had unearthed came from the shadowy upper echelons of the British Special Operations Executive (SOE)[39]. Chats stared out at the burgeoning New York skyline, a panorama of steel and glass. He removed his reading glasses, and the sudden blur was a relief. He stood, pacing the length of the windowed wall, a restless energy building within him as he prepared himself.

"The Brits," he muttered to the empty room, "rarely make this information public." He wondered, *is this information about something that has already happened? Or is this about a mission out in the future? This information feels like a post-mortem, a chilling account of something already done. And the source? The source is always shrouded in secret.* The price he paid never included the who, only the what. The info was from reliable sources—so they always claimed. It didn't matter. The facts, stark and brutal, allowed the Allies, and the Williams Agency, a glimpse into the Nazi abyss, a darkness previously unimagined.

He settled back into his chair, the weight of the unopened document heavy in his lap. He wished, with a sudden, fierce intensity, that he'd never paid for this knowledge. It felt like too much, a burden he wasn't sure he could bear—the request for information on Jozefow, Asia's hometown. It had been a whim born out of curiosity and a growing fondness for his assistant. Now, that seemingly innocent request had yielded this discovery—the basis for this devastating report.

A cigarette trembled slightly between his fingers. He lit it, the smoke curling toward the ceiling, a pale imitation of the cityscape beyond. The city was waking to a distant symphony of horns, trucks, and the low, constant thrum of human activity.

He took a sip of his cooling tea, read a paragraph, then another. He reread the document several times, each pass solidifying the horror.

He stood again, his steps small and hesitant. He paused by the window, gazing out at Central Park, a green oasis in the concrete jungle. He pressed his hands to his temples, a sudden, hollow ache spreading through his chest, and reached for his handkerchief, the familiar cotton a small comfort.

He covered his mouth, but the sound escaped anyway, raw and ragged. "Those God damned Nazis! Those God damned Nazis!"

He, Chatsworth Williams, a man who prided himself on composure, was on the verge of tears. He thought, *Today, the dam will break. Perhaps Jakub? He should send a taxi for Asia's husband—break the news to him first. Coffee was a shared burden, and then they could face Asia together in his office, with the door locked against the world.*

Please, God, say it isn't so! He scanned the paragraph again, the words blurring through a film of unshed tears. How could he ever relay this vile truth to Asia?

Jakub would likely expect a call, probably about the ongoing, frustrating immigration discussions. He might even hope for news about his family's passage to America.

I am not a Hollywood actor, but can I play a role today? He had to. This news would shatter Asia irrevocably. He, Chatsworth Williams, would be the bearer of that shattering.

He took one last drag of the cigarette and a final sip of lukewarm tea. He dialed Asia's Park Slope, Brooklyn, apartment, and Jakub answered on the first ring.

"Jakub, Chatsworth here. Good morning. How are you? It has been ages since we last spoke."

"Yes, it has been quite some time since I last talked to you. And the reason for the call?" Jakub's voice was polite but tinged with cautious inquiry.

"Jakub, we must talk. The sooner, the better."

"Sounds important."

"I'd rather not discuss the topic on the phone. Let's say we received some information today from a British intelligence organization. The organization shares information with insurance companies like ours. Could you hop in a cab and meet me at Wilma's Coffee House, two blocks from my office? Say, ten-thirty?"

"You have my curiosity up from what you have described thus far. I must make several phone calls to cancel an appointment, but that should be no problem."

"Fantastic," Chats replied.

"Great, see you at Wilma's at ten-thirty."

Chats added a deliberate lightness in his tone, "By the way, Asia will not be with me. The meeting will be between the two of us."

A spring shower had slicked the New York streets, leaving behind a clean, damp scent that, for a brief moment, overpowered the usual city smells. He walked briskly, the crisp air a welcome contrast to the stifling weight of the report in his briefcase. *How am I to break this horrible news?*

He needed Jakub's perspective and insight into how best to approach Asia.

He entered the coffee shop. The aroma of coffee and warm pastries was a momentary distraction. Jakub was already there, seated in a booth, waving to get his attention. They shook hands, a firm, brief clasp.

"Hello, Jakub. Great to see you again. Shall we sit?"

"Yes, by all means."

The hostess, efficient and brisk, took their order. "Two coffees, one black, and one cream and sugar. Thank you," Jakub said, without needing to ask Chatsworth's preference.

"So, Jakub, how is the concert pianist business these days?"

"Concert piano is not always that exciting. I strive to keep the job interesting, particularly for new students. I am shocked at the talent we see, as some of my students are approaching maestro level, and they are only in their mid-teens."

"I guess it is a talent God grants to a select group."

"Agreed. Enough about me. I am anxious to hear why we're meeting."

"To begin, I would like to ask you a few questions. When was the last time Asia had any communication from her family in Poland?"

Jakub leaned forward, his brow furrowed. "It has been months, maybe late July last year? Asia received the previous postmarked letter on July 9th, last year, a thank-you note from the twins, we surmised, written by Icek, thanking Asia and me for the gifts we sent them in a wooden crate. We spent weeks making a list of items they could use. We had sent recent photos and a gift or two for each family member. We included a Singer sewing machine, as they could use a sewing machine more than anything else. The box contained sewing patterns, bolts of cloth, zippers, buttons, and thread. And yes, that letter was the last time we received anything from the Kelner family."

"Curious, and you are sure, nothing since?"

"Chats, I hear each day from Asia after the mail has arrived, she says the exact phrase each day, 'Another day, and again—zero letters from Poland.' Asia keeps the letters going, but she pays less attention to the frequency of mail from Poland since her mom, Ryfka, the writer of most letters to Asia, suffered a stroke. Now, I am curious. Why do you ask?"

"How about I give you some background information? In my business, we often pay for intelligence. We obtain information from multiple sources worldwide. Some of this info originates from government intelligence organizations around the world. In most news stories, security organizations have declassified information. The information we received today is classified, and I am unable to release it to other organizations. In fact, the authorities, by contract, prevent me from disclosing what I received. I can't tell you what was in the report. Hence, let me tell you what I requested from the information-gathering company. In the simplest terms, I requested any data containing the word "Jozefow." I was and wanted to find out what may be happening in the town. Mind you, I asked for this info long before Germany invaded Poland."

"What was the nature of the information you received?"

"Before I answer your question, I want you to know that I worked diligently with many people in this country to get your relatives admitted. I paid out of my pocket to have an attorney do everything possible to facilitate a visa, work permit, or approval from the Feds to get your relatives here."

Jakub's hands, resting on the table, clenched into fists. "Oh no. Are you going to tell me something that has happened to Asia's relatives in Jozefow?"

Chats, avoiding all eye contact, looked down at his coffee. The dark liquid reflected his shadowed expression. "I tried everything to get them away from the God-forsaken Nazis. I tried." The words were a whisper, choked with emotion.

Jakub's voice was sharp, edged with panic. "Her relatives are dead! Oh no. Her relatives are dead!"

Chats pulled a handkerchief from his suit coat pocket and, as he wiped his tears, began speaking. The words came slowly, each one a heavy stone. "A unit of the German Army, a police battalion, entered the village of Jozefow on the morning of July 13th, 1942.[40] At the time of the entry, fifteen hundred Jewish souls lived in the town. The intelligence reports that over five hundred men, equipped with trucks and small arms, were involved.

"For those defenseless Jewish civilians who could not self-evacuate, the Germans assassinated many on the spot. The assassinations included those in the Jewish senior center in the village. Based on the intelligence provided, the local Catholics cooperated with the Germans.

"Thus, Abram, a skilled millwright, is now most likely a slave laborer working in some armament facility. Please, Jakub, don't take this as the truth, as I am only guessing on Abram's whereabouts. Regardless, the German command declared the Jozefow town as free of Jews."

Jakub's face was ashen, his eyes wide with disbelief and horror. "Those cruel bastards! Murdering innocent civilians. What kind of animals are the God damned Nazis? Oh, my darling Asia. Oh, Asia, my poor Asia." Tears streamed down his face unchecked. "Is there not a God? How can the Almighty let such heinous crimes occur?"

"My sentiments, exactly," Chats said, his voice thick with shared grief. He handed Jakub a spare handkerchief, his own damp and crumpled.

"Chats, thank you for not providing Asia with this information. Asia is exhausted and talks to any immigrant she sees to find if there is something or some way to get her family here. She is at a dead end. How do you propose we break the news to her?"

Chats looked directly at Jakub, his gaze steady despite the turmoil within. "Yes, both of us need to inform her. With the phone off the hook and the door locked, my office would be the best option. I regret that I am unable to share the report with her. I can tell her what I told you. The other thing is that we have concrete evidence regarding the murder of Ryfka and the twins and the fact that German soldiers hauled Abram off and placed him on a railcar. What we don't know for sure is this—is Icek among the living?

The problem is that, based on other intel, the Nazis are hunting Jews in hiding. If the Germans did not kill Icek at the initial massacre, did they kill him later?"

"Massacre. Yes, this was a massacre," Jakub whispered, the word a chilling echo of the report's contents.

"Shall we walk back to my office?" Chats asked, his voice low and somber.

They left the coffee shop, the cheerful bustle a stark contrast to the heavy silence that had fallen between them.

On the way back, Jakub, his voice trembling, spoke, "I just remembered something. On several occasions, as a favor to the owner of the senior center, I entertained the residents with a small concert on an out-of-tune, donated piano. The owner and I were good friends. The locals from all around Jozefow and other surrounding communities housed their aging relatives there, as this was the only such center within an eighty-kilometer radius of Jozefow. The people who worked there, all of whom were Jewish, were always kind and friendly, taking great care of the patients. To think that the Nazis murdered senior citizens—the residents were somewhere in age between sixty-eight for the youngest to the oldest, Towia Grohl. I remember Towia, as she once told me her birthday was January 1st, 1846. If she were alive on the day of the killings, she would be a ninety-six-year-old great-grandmother." He stopped, wiping his eyes with the back of his hand, his voice breaking. "All those years on this earth to be murdered by madmen Nazis."

CHAPTER THIRTY-NINE

New York City, NY
May 18th, 1943, 10:55 a.m.

Asia, perched at her desk, savored the last bite of a flaky, almond-dusted pastry. The intercom buzzed, jarring her from the sweet indulgence.

"Are you in your office, Asia?" Chat's voice, a low rumble, filled the tiny speaker.

"Yes, sir," she replied, wiping a stray crumb from her cheek. "I was actually looking for you earlier. I had visions of you being spirited away by, well, I wasn't sure who."

A chuckle came through the intercom. "I trust you are enjoying your morning pastry?"

"You know me too well, sir."

"How about coming to my office when you finish your coffee and pastry? Take your time. No hurry. Just bring yourself and a steno pad."

"Yes, sir, I should be there in ten minutes. I'm just putting the finishing touches on the Western Region budget summaries. The numbers are predictable. I know how much you appreciate a lack of surprises in the financial realm."

"Boring is beautiful, Asia. No issues. Come on down when you finish."

In Chats' expansive office, the hushed air of anticipation hung heavily. Jakub, already present, shifted in his chair as Chats launched into a seemingly unrelated topic—insurance fraud.

"Jakub, you've been to Jozefow on many occasions, haven't you?"

"Yes, sir. More times than I can count, to be honest."

Chats tapped a pen against his mahogany desk, the rhythmic clicks punctuating the silence. "We have private investigators on retainer, of course, in the insurance business. Are you familiar with their work?"

Jakub frowned slightly. "Not in detail, no. But it doesn't surprise me."

Chats leaned forward, his voice dropping to a conspiratorial murmur. "Let's say, hypothetically, a customer of mine claims a catastrophic fire—his entire operation, buildings, equipment, all gone up in smoke. Now, we do our due diligence. We keep records and conduct audits throughout the year, assessing safety and health practices. We might even send in a private consultant to evaluate fire protection, the handling of flammable materials, and their safety record overall."

He paused, letting the implications sink in. "We look at these companies regularly, and ideally, it reduces the likelihood of a claim, a legitimate one. Don't get me wrong. Those we pay, no questions asked. However, we also understand that an incident can escalate into a claim, especially when the circumstances are unclear. That's where a good investigator comes in."

He recounted a story, vivid and sharp, of a Warsaw tire manufacturer, a fire, a forensic accountant, and a president's gambling debts on the French Riviera. The tale ended with the authorities jailing the president and the claim being unpaid. Chats let the silence linger before posing the question. "So, Jakub, why do I tell you such stories?"

Jakub, understanding dawning in his eyes, answered, "I know why. You want to send an investigator to Jozefow. To investigate what happened to Asia's family."

"Precisely." Chat's gaze was unwavering. "The authorities investigating war crimes would, no doubt, be very interested in our findings. But instead of telling Asia what we suspect—we have no evidence that Icek and Abram are victims—I want to offer her a glimmer of possibility—the possibility that Icek and Abram may be alive. We don't know. Do you see where I'm going with this?"

Jakub's voice was somber. "Yes, Chats, I do. But we can't possibly afford such a project."

Chats cut him off sharply. "Stop! Not another word. I own this company. When I decide to conduct an insurance investigation, I do it. Is that clear?"

"Yes, sir! Crystal clear. Thank you. A zero investment on our part in investigation does take some of the sting out of what we must tell Asia."

"The world needs truth, Jakub. And Asia deserves it. That truth, whatever it may be, might give her the strength to move forward. We will do our best to find those facts." He paused, his voice softening slightly.

Chats remarked, "Abram is a skilled millwright, and the Germans might find him useful in the munitions factories. Icek—Icek is a puzzle. A resourceful young man, adept at surviving in the wild. How old is he now, sixteen?"

"Nineteen," Jakub corrected. "He turned nineteen this past January."

"Right." Chats steepled his fingers, considering. "Nineteen, limited skillset beyond being a capable outdoorsman. Perhaps not valuable enough for an armaments plant. Did they kill him? Or did he manage to escape? It's unknown. He would, however, be a prime candidate for the Polish Resistance. My sources tell me they're well-funded, well-trained, and giving the Nazis hell in certain parts of the country."

Chats looked directly at Jakub. "Jakub, I think it's best if I do most of the talking. Sit close to Asia." He gestured toward a fresh box of tissues on a side table, "I brought these in. I have a feeling she'll need them."

"You're right on all counts," Jakub said, his voice heavy with apprehension. "Honestly, I'm more nervous than Asia will be. I dread this conversation. Are you saying we present this logic to Asia to give her that *fragment of optimism*, as you put it?"

"Yes," Chats confirmed. "A fragment of optimism can be a lifeline. It gives Asia a sliver of light at the end of this dark tunnel. Our investigator can get us the truth, whatever it may be. Right now, we're operating under the assumption that 'Jewish free' means everyone is gone. We don't know that."

A knock on the door interrupted their somber discussion. "Chats, may I come in?" Asia's voice was laced with a hint of nervousness.

"Asia, please, come in."

Asia entered, a vision of delicate elegance in a light pink dress, a white scarf artfully tied at her neck. Her hair was pinned up, highlighting her pretty earrings and necklace. Jakub, taking in her appearance, offered a small, strained smile.

"Why are you here today?" Asia asked Jakub, a puzzled frown creasing her forehead.

"Chats called me earlier and suggested a coffee since we hadn't spoken in a few months. And, of course, since I'm here, I'm obligated to take you to lunch."

"But what about your appointment this morning?"

Jakub feigned a look of surprise. "Oh, right! Peter called and canceled. We're meeting tomorrow instead."

Asia turned to Chats—her voice laced with suspicion. "Excuse me, Chats, but I sense an ulterior motive here. Jakub and I in the same room with you?"

"Asia, please, have a seat."

"Chats, in all my years of employment, this is unprecedented."

"Yes, I anticipated that observation."

Her curiosity was palpable. She gave a nervous smile, glanced at Jakub, then back at Chats. Her body posture was a mix of apprehension and anticipation.

"Why is Jakub here? I don't understand."

"You have every right to be curious. Let me explain. Where to begin? Asia, you know, we utilize private investigators. You've probably spoken to several of them, haven't you?"

"I deal with many of your investigators all over the world, actually. I usually approve their invoices."

"Perhaps you've encountered Simon Pinski of Warsaw. Does the name ring a bell?"

Asia shook her head. "No. No, it's the first I've heard of Mr. Pinski."

"Alright. No matter. As you know, Asia, we often pay for intelligence. You've been with us long enough to know that we acquire information from various sources globally, including government intelligence agencies. Typically, this information is declassified. However, in this particular instance, we have classified information."

He paused, emphasizing the gravity of his words. "The investigators may have already shared this with the Allies. The authorities may have classified the document to protect the investigators themselves and their sources. Regardless, we're bound by contract not to disclose this information to anyone outside of me."

Asia, her brow furrowed in concentration, remarked, "I've never seen any of these reports. I knew we received them, of course."

"I want to share with you today what I requested from one of our intelligence providers. Years ago, long before the German invasion of Poland in 1939, I instructed this firm to gather any data related to Jozefow. I was curious after meeting you. I also thought that perhaps we could submit a proposal for their mill's insurance policy when it came up for renewal. A long shot, admittedly."

"Did you find anything specific?" Her voice faltered, a tremor creeping in. She paused, her eyes widening in sudden realization. "Oh my God! You did find something, didn't you? That's why you have me here with Jakub. Something happened in Jozefow! Did the Germans bomb the village? They bombed it days after the invasion, didn't they?"

Asia grabbed a tissue, her hand reaching for Jakub's. Her face, usually composed, was now etched with a profound sadness. "It's bad, isn't it, Jakub?" she whispered, her eyes searching for his.

Jakub, his gaze fixed on the floor, spoke softly. "Before we jump to any conclusions, let's hear what Chats has to say. Trust me, it will make more sense as you get more information. And yes, it's not good. But we're missing a lot of pieces."

Chats, struggling to maintain his composure, began, "A German Army police battalion entered the village of Jozefow on the morning of July 13th, 1942. At that time, fifteen hundred Jews were residing there. The reports we received indicate that over five hundred men, with trucks and small arms, forced the majority of the residents to an area west of the village, where the Nazis murdered them."

Asia looked up, her cry a piercing sound that echoed through the room. "Dear Lord! What did they do to deserve such a fate?" The scream was raw, a visceral expression of pain and disbelief. Both men were visibly shaken.

Jakub immediately wrapped his arm around Asia, his face pressed close to hers. He grabbed a tissue and gently dabbed at her tears.

Chats continued, his voice heavy with the weight of the information. "The Germans went into the senior living center and systematically shot each resident, room by room."

He paused, his own eyes glistening. "They also murdered the immobile seniors in their homes in the village, sparing them the trip for transport and the walk to the killing fields—the ever-efficient Nazi way, those not in good enough shape, it seems clear, they shot those to save themselves from the work to walk or wheel them out of their residence."

Chats looked at Asia, his voice softening with a deep, unbearable sadness. "Asia, the next part, it's heartbreaking. According to eyewitnesses, when the trucks reached their destination, the Germans ordered the Jews out, forced them to lie face down, and shot each one in the back of the neck."

"Oh my God," she screamed, the sound a raw, guttural cry of anguish. "Cold-blooded murder of civilians? What was their motive? What did those people do to deserve this? It was because they were Jews. They were Jews, and therefore, they had to die. Right?"

"That was their sole crime," Jakub replied, holding her even tighter. "According to the intel, that was it."

"The Germans are on a killing spree across Poland," Chats added, his voice tight with barely suppressed rage. "Exterminating every Jew they can find."

"And, a sickening detail, local Catholics collaborated with the Germans. Witnesses report that the skilled male workforce was spared, loaded onto rail cars, and shipped to various armament plants across Poland. Nothing has appeared in the papers—not in Europe, not in the British Isles, not here in the States, nowhere that we're aware of. We need to share this with the US State Department. They can choose to release it, but we cannot. The agreement binds us."

"This is unbearable news!" Asia sobbed, clinging to Jakub. "Those, those monsters! Animals! No human being could do such a thing. Those Nazis, they're less than human."

She drew a shaky breath. "And all this time, I thought it was my mother's stroke—that's why the mail stopped. But according to this report, it happened a year ago. All my letters were unanswered and unopened. I need to be alone. My world's crumbling."

"Asia, please, don't go just yet," Chats pleaded. "There's something else. Something I want to do. And I promise you—I will spare nothing—money, manpower, time, everything—to take the next step."

Jakub nodded and asked, "What is the next step?"

Chats looked from Asia to Jakub, his gaze intense. "I need to step away for a bit. Both of you have just received the worst news imaginable. I also need a break to process this tragedy. I'll be back in about twenty minutes. Please stay here and talk amongst yourselves. When I return, I want to discuss some options. Some ideas I have."

"Thank you, Chats," Jakub said, his voice thick with emotion. "Yes, we could use some time alone. There's so much to process. We'll be here when you return. Thank you. For everything. Without you, we might never have known what happened."

Asia stood and embraced Chats—her voice choked with sobs. "Sir, thank you for going to such lengths to find the truth. I had a feeling, a terrible feeling, that my family was in danger. First, we lost my twin, and now we don't know if the rest of them are dead or alive. God will punish the guilty. He will." Wiping away tears, she clung to Chats as if he were her father. "It's not fair," she whispered. "None of this is fair."

Chats, his own eyes brimming with tears, pulled out a handkerchief and dabbed at them. "Judgment Day will come," he said, his voice raw with emotion. "The Nazis will face justice, both here on Earth and in the eternity they'll spend burning in Hell."

Chats left the room, his footsteps heavy, and headed for the elevator. He walked out of the building, tears streaming down his face, and sought solace in Central Park, a place he hadn't visited since the day his father had passed away.

Twenty minutes crawled by. Chat's face, still etched with a mixture of grief and steely resolve, tapped lightly on the office door. Asia and Jakub were still there, locked in a silent embrace. He tapped again, a little louder. "May I enter?"

"Yes. Please," Asia replied, her voice hoarse.

Chats stepped back into the room. "Amazing what a twenty-minute walk in Central Park can do for a man's sanity," he said, his voice strained. He paused, then, his voice rising with barely controlled fury, "Those goddamned Nazis will pay! You mark my words. Those bastards will pay! If I have to go to Jozefow myself, I will get justice. I promise you. I will get justice!"

The room fell silent as Chats paced—his movements agitated. He stopped at the window, staring out at the people strolling through Central Park, his voice a low growl. "Look at them. Oblivious. As if they have no idea this country is sacrificing its youth, its resources, and everything to rid the world of Hitler and his henchmen. Do they even care that there's a war going on?"

Asia and Jakub exchanged a startled look. They had never seen the usually calm and collected Chatsworth Williams display such raw, unbridled anger.

Jakub finally broke the silence. "Chats, what are your immediate plans?"

Chats turned from the window and sat down, his voice regaining some of its composure, though the underlying fire remained. "I have a plan," he said, his gaze unwavering. "And that plan is to rid the world of as many Nazis as I can before I leave it. And that is a promise."

"Are you going to involve the military?" Asia asked, her voice trembling.

"The military is far too preoccupied to address our immediate needs," Chats replied. "I intend to utilize my para-military resources to investigate this. I'm already in contact with individuals—and you'll have to trust me on this, as I can't reveal much about them—who will soon be on the ground in Jozefow. I'm paying them to find answers. Their methods are their concern, but I can tell you, it will likely be violent. I need men who can handle themselves, ex-military types. We need to know what happened and, specifically, if there are any survivors. Who were the perpetrators? Which unit? Who was in command?"

"Do you think we can find out who survived?" Asia asked, her voice barely a whisper.

"We're going to hear things we don't want to hear," Chats said grimly. "But we need to get to the bottom of it. If any of the villagers were taken prisoner, can we perhaps liberate them? If Abram is working in a munitions factory, there's a chance we could plan a rescue mission. I want to know everything. You both deserve to know."

"Chats," Asia said, her voice shaking, "could Jakub and I have some time alone? We need a moment. I still don't know the fate of my family, even with this horrifying news. You understand, don't you?"

"Of course I do," Chats said, his voice softening. "You two, go home. Call in sick tomorrow or the next day if you need to. I'll start the process to get my people in place. If there are any survivors or relatives, I will bring them to safety. I promise you that. I will get to the bottom of this, even if I have to go myself."

Jakub spoke, his voice thick with gratitude and sorrow. "Thank you, Chats. For everything. For letting us know about the possible demise of our loved ones in Jozefow. If the Nazis killed them, we need to know. You're a true friend, Chats—a true friend. And we both tried the legal route to get them here, but we're Jews. And the world doesn't seem to care."

"We'll be in the conference room before we leave for the day," Asia said, wiping away fresh tears.

"Asia, Jakub," Chats said, his voice heavy with emotion, "I, I'm speechless. I wish the Nazis never existed. But I can promise you this— every single one of them will pay a terrible price for these unspeakable acts. The world will punish them."

CHAPTER FORTY

New York City, NY
May 19ᵗʰ, 1943, 2:45 a.m.

Sleep remained a distant, mocking stranger to Chats. He tossed the sheets, tangling around him like accusations, the news from Jozefow a fresh, raw wound in his mind. Slaughter. The word itself felt obscene, clawing at the edges of his composure, refusing to release its grip. He finally surrendered and found himself on the patio of his Manhattan high-rise near three a.m.. The city sprawled below, a million indifferent lights blurring through the chill night air and the haze in his own eyes. He drew deep on a cigarette, the acrid bite of a familiar anchor in turmoil, then flushed it down with scotch, a burning trail that did little to warm the ice settling in his gut. A poor time, perhaps, to dull the edges of judgment with liquor. But this morning, facing the echoes of atrocity, he'd risk it. Only once before had this specific hollowness taken root—this gnawing, corrosive unease. And he knew, with a certainty that cut through the alcohol's nascent fog, that only action, the barest semblance of control regained, could hope to bring him rest.

"What must I do?" he muttered, the words swallowed by the city's hum.

Jack Reynolds was in London. He could call him now. He considered it—the phone was already in his hand, but his reflection on the glass patio door stopped him. The scotch would loosen his tongue, and the last thing Jack, or any of his subordinates, needed to hear was compromised confidence in his voice. No. A plan. A concrete, meticulously crafted plan to unravel the horror of Jozefow. Jack was the man for that. His mind, sharp and analytical, could dissect a problem like a surgeon with a scalpel.

Yes. I will demand a plan. Jack could adapt the existing project framework. Two minds, even one dulled by worry and scotch, were better than one. He stubbed out the cigarette, the tiny ember glowing defiance before fading, and drained the last of the scotch. A reprieve, a sliver of control, was what he needed. He would sleep, then attack this with the full force of his focus in the morning.

The thunderstorm exploded around five-thirty a.m. Wind, a screaming banshee off the Atlantic, hurled rain sideways. Below, New York City, predictably, choked on itself. He watched the chaos unfold, a detached observer. Insurance claims, a surge of numbers on a ledger—his world—would follow. The weather was a minor squall compared to the tempest raging in his mind.

He timed his departure to catch up with Jack Reynolds, setting the wheels in motion.

Asia. He had to keep her informed. Progress, even the illusion of it, was a lifeline.

The usual twenty-minute taxi ride stretched into a forty-minute crawl. Chats finally thrust a wad of bills at the driver, more than necessary, a reward for navigating the city's arteries.

"You performed a Herculean feat to get me to my office on such a miserable day," Chats declared, stepping out into the deluge.

The cabbie, face creased with confusion, shot back, "What does Herculean mean, are you pissed at me, or is this a compliment?"

A chuckle, unexpected and sharp, escaped Chats. "My friend, do you know Hercules? The hero—strength, and endurance? It's a compliment. A big one. You moved mountains today."

"I guess you must think I am as ignorant as they come, sir?"

He paused, considering the man. "Do you have children?"

"Sure do, two boys, twelve and fourteen."

"Great, do me a favor. Tell your sons what I told you about Hercules and your 'Herculean feat.' Trust me, they will be impressed."

"You got it, sir. And thanks for everything."

Dodging the downpour, he dashed to the revolving door, the glass and steel of his office building a refuge.

Inside, he nursed a cup of steaming tea, the warmth a small comfort as he stood at his expansive window, a twelve-foot-wide, nine-foot-tall monolith of glass, and stared into the storm. The soup that covered every square foot of the view out his window was unusual; with the near-total obliteration of the cityscape, the familiar landmarks of Central Park vanished behind a curtain of grey. He had his dramatic view most of the time; at the worst, this would occur three or four times per year. He lit another cigarette, the smoke curling toward the ceiling, a restless plume mirroring his anxiety. Jozefow. The Killers. The Nazis.

Sober enough. Time to call Jack. He buzzed the operator, requesting a London connection, his fingers drumming an impatient tattoo on his desk. The wait stretched, minutes ticking by like hours. With the war, even a simple phone call became an ordeal. He paced, tracing the perimeter of his window, the storm outside a reflection of the turmoil within.

The phone finally jangled, startling him. He snatched it up, his voice measured.

"Hello, this is the overseas operator. How can I help you?" In an accent he recognized from the Lake District of England.

Chats said, "Yes, London, 451-233-17."

The operator replied, "451-233-17 ringing, sir."

"Jack Reynolds speaking, how may I help you?"

"Sir, you have an overseas call from New York."

"Thank you—taking the call," Reynolds answered.

"Chats Williams, Jack. How's the day treating you?"

"Sunshine, Chats, believe it or not. It's a rare gift. You don't usually call at this time. Trouble sleeping?"

"Astute as always, Jack. That report has been keeping me up at night. Excellent work, by the way. Thorough, detailed. I commend you."

"Thank you, Chats. That means a lot. I'll pass it on to my team."

"You wouldn't believe the weather here, Jack," His voice lightened.

"Let me guess, perfect day in the neighborhood."

"On the contrary, my friend, it is your usual London fare, windswept."

"Chats, the only time in the world I bet you are jealous of our London weather. Anyway, is your call about my report?"

"Jealous of London weather, correct! It is about your report. Specifically, the next step is delicate. This conversation stays between us. You can imagine how Asia and Jakub took the news. Those Nazi bastards."

"I figured you'd share it. It must have been brutal. But necessary, I suppose."

"I shared the basics. The news has shattered Asia and Jakub. It's the not knowing that's eating them alive. And that's why I'm calling."

"Tell me what you need. I wish I could deal with those butchers myself. But I know they'll get what's coming to them."

"I feel the same rage, Jack. I promised Asia and Jakub answers. And while I'd love nothing more than to unleash you, that's not our role. We need information. Evidence. Survivors."

"Can we even find anything?" Jack's voice was low, doubtful. "The Kelners?"

"We dig. We find out what we can. The rumors we hear —the Nazis are using Jewish laborers in their munition plants. Quality is suffering, and supply chains—the Jewish workers have been sabotaging the operation—the good thing is the Nazi bastards can't hang everyone. Fear keeps them working, but it's a fragile system. The SOE reports they're working them to death."

Jack replied, "I suspected as much."

"So, here's what I need: a detailed, step-by-step plan. Budget, manpower, timeline. Everything. I want to know who the Nazis have murdered, who the Nazis arrested, and who might have escaped. We have one advantage: desperation. Starvation breeds loose tongues. Money talks, Jack."

"A challenge, Chats. I'll get on it. One question: Jozefow—I want to be there. Is that possible?"

"I wouldn't have dared ask, but since you've volunteered, it's what I hoped for. You're a former Marine officer, a natural leader. You can handle anything. Who can take your place in London? Every Marine has identified their replacement."

"Trevor Whatley. WWI vet who saw action at the Somme—he had seen some brutal battlefields during his time. Sharp, discreet. I'd trust him with my life."

"Consider it done. Trevor's your man. Time is critical, Jack. In one week, Jack, I need a plan. Talk to your team, the ones who compiled the report."

"Understood, Chats. I'll aim to beat that deadline. Anything else?"

"Yes. The SOE asked about a name. Otto Fischer? They said you'd know him—that you served together."

A pause. "Otto? That's quite unexpected. Yes, I know him. We were in the USMC together, and the last time we were together was in Puerto Rico. It's been years."

"He's SOE, apparently. The only former Marine they have."

"Chats, what's going on? Otto Fischer—this is surreal. I didn't even know the SOE existed until a few months ago."

"The SOE made the connection, as they asked me about former military personnel within the firm; branch and rank, and I provided the list. We have many veterans."

"Sorry for the grilling. It's just a small world. Otto and I—we were close. Brothers, almost. Otto said he was doing investigative work, in England, of all places."

"He was telling the truth, in a way. He's with the SOE, and Otto will likely be involved in an operation to find Asia's family."

"Better Otto than a stranger."

"Here's the thing: Otto will be contacting you. The conversation with him stays between us. Tell Trevor you're heading to New York for a work assignment. The Allies can't know what we're doing. And if we find Abram Kelner, we might need to extract him. Think about that, Jack. A rescue. A munitions plant—it won't be easy. And there is one item. You should get accelerated Polish language instruction, and it's best to ask Ottos' friend for assistance. I would try the excuse, perhaps, that you want to date a Polish national. Think up some white lie."

"I understand, and I have an operation plan in mind."

"I like that, Jack."

"Thanks, I needed that."

"You got it—have a good day, Jack."

"Sir, goodbye."

Chats stood again, drawn to the window, searching for a break in the storm. Nothing.

A knock—a person at his door.

Asia. Her raincoat, fashionable scarf, and broad-brimmed hat were straight out of a Hollywood film, but the illusion didn't last long. Her usually vibrant hair was limp, her eyes red-rimmed, her makeup smeared. Was it the storm or the grief? Probably both.

"Asia? What are you doing here?"

Before she could answer, tears welled, spilling down her cheeks. Chats reached for her, pulling her inside. With a soft voice, he said, "Come in out of the rain. Let's get you warm. A blanket, something hot to drink. Why are you out in this?"

"It's the apartment," she choked out, her voice thick with tears. "It's full of memories. Every keepsake, every photograph, it all reminds me of what we had. And I can't bear it. I keep thinking about what might have happened, what is happening. I needed to be here."

He held her close, a fatherly embrace. "Life is cruel, Asia. Unspeakably cruel. What Hitler is doing is beyond comprehension. I feel your pain. And I just got off the phone with Jack Reynolds. We're launching an operation. A team is going to Jozefow. I'm going to find out what happened, and, Asia, I promise you, it might not be what you want to hear, but you'll know."

She clutched a handkerchief, her voice barely a whisper. "But what if I never know? How can I go on?"

"You will know. I promise. Be patient. This will take time."

She looked at the floor, her face a mask of sorrow. "I'll be patient. I don't know what Jakub and I would do without you."

"We'll find the answers," he repeated, his voice firm. "But prepare yourself, Asia. These Nazis, they're more brutal than I ever imagined."

CHAPTER FORTY-ONE

Westminster, England
May 21ˢᵗ, 1943, 9:30 p.m.

The rooftop deck was shrouded in the inky blackness of the blackout. Below, the village of Marylebone[41] was silent, the only light the faint silver spill of the moon on the rooftops. He settled into the lawn chair, the metal cold even through his trousers. The office, a quick bicycle ride down Cleveland Street on a fair day, felt a world away. Jack tilted his head back, staring at the star-dusted sky. Each pinpoint of light was a mocking reminder of the city's extinguished glow, normalcy stolen by the war.

His stomach growled, a hollow counterpoint to the silence. Three years of rationing had worn thin. The weekly allowance—the meager egg, the scant ounces of butter and bacon—barely registered in his brain—which insisted on telling him he was still hungry. He craved a proper meal, something substantial, not the endless parade of tinned goods and points-system disappointments. The pubs, at least, offered a fleeting escape, a pint, and the illusion of a world not teetering on the brink. But tonight, even the thought of the Barley Mow couldn't fully erase the weight in his chest.

He lit a cigarette, the flare of the match illuminating his face for a fleeting moment, then cupped the flame to protect it from the breeze. He drew deeply, letting the smoke fill his lungs, a small rebellion against the anxieties that gnawed at him. Otto Fischer. Tonight. It felt surreal, like a dream. His old Marine buddy, a brother in arms, was back in his life and entangled in this mess. Chat Williams's message echoed in his mind: sensitive information from Jozefow—and the mention of Asia's family.

A shiver that had nothing to do with the night air ran through him. He and Otto, together again, were on a mission that put both their lives in danger. The thought was both exhilarating and terrifying. He trusted

Otto implicitly. But trust wouldn't stop a bullet, wouldn't deflect shrapnel.

He muttered, "Should I do this?" The question was a whisper lost in the vastness of the night. Images flickered behind his eyelids: mangled limbs, vacant stares, the hollowed-out faces of the wounded. He pushed the thoughts away, a practiced reflex honed by years of discipline. There was to be no middle of the road; the decision—he was committed to the mission.

He rose, the chair scraping lightly against the decking. Back inside his flat, the familiar scent of pipe tobacco and old books offered a fleeting comfort. He grabbed his jacket, the worn leather familiar and reassuring against his hand. He locked the door, the click echoing in the empty hallway, and stepped out into the night, his footsteps purposeful.

The Barley Mow,[42] a squat, unassuming building from the 1790s, was tucked away on a side street, a relic of a quieter time. The walk, a brisk seventeen minutes by his reckoning, was a welcome distraction. He kept to the shadows, his senses on high alert. Rumors of English-speaking German spies were rife, and paranoia was a constant companion. Tonight, though, the streets were mostly deserted, the silence broken only by the occasional distant siren.

He reached the pub and paused, scanning the street. A half-block in each direction, a quick assessment. Nothing. He pushed open the heavy wooden door, the scent of stale beer and tobacco smoke washing over him. The interior was dimly lit, and the main bar was small, cozy, and snug, revealing the original matchboard paneling. Prints of old Marylebone adorned the walls, and two small drinking compartments offered a semblance of privacy. He chose one, ensuring the adjacent compartment was empty.

He ordered a Burton Strong Ale,[43] the dark brew a welcome warmth. He was nursing the pint when Otto arrived, a familiar grin splitting his face.

"Is it the real Otto Fischer, in the flesh?" Jack asked, his voice a mix of disbelief and relief.

"In the flesh, my friend!" Otto clapped him on the shoulder, the gesture solid and reassuring. They embraced, a brief, fierce hug, followed by a handshake and pats on the back.

"Here, take a seat, Otto. I'm one up on you. Shall I get you a Burton's?"

"Sounds great. Sorry for being late. You have no idea—SOE wartime," Otto's voice trailed off, a hint of weariness beneath the bravado.

"I can imagine. How is the underworld of the SOE?"

"Fabulous. We can't keep up." Otto chuckled, but it lacked its usual spark.

"It is good to be wanted."

"So, how the hell have you been? Insurance business? Damn, I'm jealous. You've kept your Marine Corps slim and trim physique." Otto's eyes flicked over Jack, taking in his appearance. "However, it appears we both suffer from the salt-and-pepper hair color change. We should be thankful that we both have hair."

Jack studied his friend. Tall, lean, fit. Broad shoulders. Three-day beard, pencil mustache. *He looks British. Almost. The accent helps. Me? They'd spot me as an American a mile away.*

"I must admit, Jack, your job sounds boring, but the money and the benefits must be beyond my imagination."

"It pays the bills, plus I do get to travel sometimes. I love my present assignment, minus the Nazis and their flipping bombardments!"

Jack studied Otto's face. *He's aged. Bags under his eyes, skin pale like he hasn't seen the sun in months. Is still fit, though. A drill instructor's physique. But shorter? Is that possible?*

"The bloody bombardments! Yes, I understand. There are a few Londoners who have escaped all the bombings. The first bombing, I pissed myself. I thought I was going to die. Now numb. Like everyone else." Otto paused, his gaze locking with Jack's. "Well, Otto, what is it like working for the limeys?"

"Wow! That is a word I hope I never hear you repeat. You need to know that we let them get away with calling us 'Yanks,' but they do not like to hear the word 'limey.'"

"So, you're already saying I've been pissing off my peers since I arrived?"

"Word to the wise, cease using this word. I trust you have already heard the familiar saying about us Yanks by the Brits: they describe us as *'overpaid, oversexed, and over here.'* The Americans have retorted with their version: *'underpaid, undersexed, and under Eisenhower.'*"[44]

"Got it."

"Jack, do you remember how much excitement we had in the Marines, you know, the travel, the training, the challenges? Well, in the SOE, multiply that experience by a factor of ten."

"For real. You like it that much?"

Otto's face hardened. "I hate the Nazis that much."

"I would fit right in, as I have not met my match regarding Hitler haters, plus I would love to have a break from flying a desk."

Otto leaned forward. "I'm here as a result of a request from your boss. Mr. Chatsworth Williams has asked, via US intelligence, if we can assist you. In response to his request, the SOE asked that I invite you to come here, as we need to discuss what we must discuss in person. First, I've read all about the issues in that town of Jozefow. We were quite surprised when the intel came in and even more surprised when a name out of my past, 'Jack Reynolds,' was connected to such an inquiry," Otto commented.

Jack asked, "So, what did you make of the request from Mr. Chatsworth Williams?"

"Before we delve into the details, let's talk about you," Otto said.

Jack replied, "Me? Why me?"

Otto replied, "I have a proposal for you. But before discussing the proposal, I want to ask you a few things."

"You have my curiosity up. Ask away."

"I know you hate the Germans and the Nazis as much as I do. That said, after we inform you of the other atrocities those bastards have been up to, we are confident your hate will grow deeper. I can't spill the beans until we get your sworn declaration of the SOE secrecy and confidentiality agreement."

Jack took another sip of his Burton ale. "Are you saying I'll become a member of the SOE to address the Jozefow event?" he asked.

Otto slapped him on the back. "Let's say you can most likely cut the mustard to qualify."

"We're both Marine veterans. Is it more difficult than Marine training?" He took another swig of his Burton Ale and signaled the bartender. "Two more pints, sir?"

The bartender's voice, thick with a Cockney accent, called back, "Coming right up, gents."

"Jack, to be frank, yes, magnitudes beyond the Marines. However, the interesting thing is that it's not physical stress—it's mental. They are the most conniving sort I have ever seen. They're forever trying to outsmart and trick the enemy. At times, it's hilarious."

"Jack, before we dive into SOE, let's talk about Jozefow."

"Are you saying Jozefow is the tip of the iceberg?"

"Jozefow was almost fifteen hundred souls: what we know now adds zeros to that number, multiple zeros. You now know much more than I should have ever told you thus far, but trust me, we are dealing with a 'first in the history of the world' event, and the best thing is that we will be part of the solution to cease this madness—the Allies and us."

"I feel quite selfish at this point. I've been torn up inside with Asia and her story," Jack said.

"I've seen photos of Jakub and Asia from the FBI surveillance files. They look to be the typical American couple."

"You must know our company's interest in Jozefow isn't an insurance interest, it's in the location of any of Asia's relatives who may have gotten away. Asia's family was a victim of the atrocity. Evidence exists that the Germans rounded up all the Jews in the village."

"You have a crush on this Asia lady, don't you?"

He paused, a wistful expression on his face.

"So, you can be a hero to her if nothing else, right?"

"You should see her. You would understand how I feel. You already know from your surveillance that she's beautiful and married to a concert pianist. What you don't know is that they're madly in love with one another. I hate to see her struggle with this Jozefow event, not knowing if her family members survived. And the big boss, Chats, will do anything to make her happy."

"Tell me, do you miss being a Marine?"

"Well, I didn't ship over for another six but did think about it pretty hard as a full career. But to answer your question, I miss the hell out of being a Marine."

"That's what I thought. I, too, miss it. The SOE does scratch the military itch fine. I've been part of over seventy operations since joining."

"How about action? How many Nazi bastards have you waxed?"

"Sorry, that's classified."

"I didn't expect you to tell me. Asking doesn't hurt."

Otto's expression turned serious. "I have an exciting proposal for you. We want you to join us on a mission to Jozefow, where you will be undercover. We'll get the answers you want about Asia's family, or at least we'll try our best. We would hand-pick you as part of the SOE team. How does that sound?"

"No! Wait a minute. I have you here since I want your assistance, not the other way around."

"Jack, your president of the company knows nothing about what I just asked you. He thinks I'll indeed assist you, but you're much too important to the SOE for just one mission. They've looked at your qualifications and your fitness reports.[45] This is the first part of the plan. The second part is that you don't go back."

"Don't go back?"

"Yes, you wouldn't return to your insurance job until after the war, and you know the Allies will win the war, as it's a matter of time."

"Chats would never allow this. I would lose my position."

"You're so right. But what if Chats were to find out that you were missing after your Jozefow assignment?"

"Missing. What are you saying?"

"Listen, Jack, the SOE has your fitness reports from the Marine Corps, your service record, and knows all your training. You can jump out of planes, you know demolition, you can fire an assortment of weaponry, and you know how to take care of yourself. In addition, you're in excellent shape. Do you know how long it would take to re-create a commando with your skillset? Oh, I almost forgot, you can fly a damned airplane. I recently learned something new about you. You know Morse code?"

He took another gulp of beer. "How long have you been hatching this scheme? And Morse code was an accident. My father was in the Navy as a communications specialist. When he left the Navy, he maintained his skills through a hobby as an amateur radio operator. I was curious and learned to send and receive Morse code. I was a natural at code and was as fast as my father in my mid-teens. It's much like riding a bike, and I'll never forget it. Later, I took the OCS test and aced the part where students were required to listen to Morse code. I deciphered a string of code at a speed the testers had never seen before. Of course, I never thought anything of it."

"Your broad set of skills has SOE higher-ups interested in you. We have your name on eleven missions after Jozefow. And guess what? These are all dangerous missions. However, SOE believes you have what it takes to execute them. Not to sound like a flag-waving zealot, but you can help us and the Allies defeat the Nazi bastards."

"I must think about this. I need a few days."

"We can't give you a few days! We need a few days to get you ready for your first mission. We can provide a script for what needs to be said to Chats. In three days, you'll be on the ground in Jozefow to investigate what the damn Nazis did and to recruit local candidates for the Polish Home Army.[46] We don't have three days for you to decide! I will have another round. Are you up for another?"

Jack met Otto's gaze, a flicker of resolve hardening his features. He raised his mug. "Cheers! Yes, I'm up for another, Marine. By the way, count my ass in. I've decided I'll join your team."

"Welcome aboard, Marine. Great decision. Let's order another round. Here is your script for your next discussion with Chats."

"Jesus Christ, script? You were that damned confident that I would agree to go?"

"For me, I wasn't—however, we employ some of the best psychiatrists and psychologists in the country, and they predicted that, based on your profile, you would agree to the mission while the two of us sat in this pub this evening. There was a wager among friends that you would give us a yes by tomorrow morning at about nine. Just so you know, based on the profile of the missions we have planned for you, SOE leadership thinks you will excel. They have that much confidence in you."

"As I said earlier, Jesus Christ. Unbelievable."

"You have no idea the quality of the organization you'll soon join, and they accept few to enter the SOE, as most candidates never make it past the initial interview.

"The English have an exciting approach to spying. I know nothing about how Americans manage to do it. That said, the English are geniuses. For example, you'll arrive in Jozefow with Polish money and clothing with Polish tags from Polish manufacturers. Your belt, shoes, jacket, wallet, and hat will replicate the attire worn by local Poles. You will have a Polish passport. When you arrive, you will appear to be a local who has just exited their house a short time ago. No locals will suspect you are anyone but a local. Even the clothing will look tattered, as SOE technicians have aged all the garments. The buttons and zippers within your dress all came from Poland. You will receive crash-course training on acting the role of a mute. Your usual sense of hearing will remain as it is. We don't have time to teach you the Polish language.

"Since our discussion has now ventured onto a more direct path, I want to tell you how we must play Chats in the coming days. First, we took a considerable risk responding to Chats via registered mail. The SOE infiltrated the management at the insurance firm via a solicitor. We made them aware of a situation that could compromise the national defense of the British Isles and the US. SOE convinced them to agree to be part of the plan to send a registered response to Chats. Next, we wanted Chats to think about it for a while. We predicted he would contact you, and we are fortunate he did. So here we are. What do you think, Jack?"

"I think SOE is cunning with their scheming. You mean to tell me you did all this to get me to meet you in this pub tonight?"

"In a way. We've taken these steps to encourage you to commit to working with us until the war ends, and we require your decision tonight. I don't know about you, but we need another Burton's."

"Okay, Otto. We're getting somewhere. I work for Chats. How did you know this?"

"Do you remember our old skipper, Captain Harry Cowan?"

"I spoke to the Skipper about eight to ten months ago. Oh my God, you tapped our phones!"

"You spoke to Captain Cowan on December 14th, 1942, for eleven minutes from your office phone in London to his home in Fredericksburg, Virginia. Would you like to see a transcript of the call?"

"Yes, I'll have that Burton's," Jack muttered.

"Bartender! Could we get another round?"

The bartender said, "Bloody hell! You Yanks know how to put it away—two more Burton Ales—coming right up."

"By the way, how did you like the note card you received from the Skipper? It took us a lot of time to get that note to you. Would you contact him? There were SOE staff wagers on whether or not you would make the call."

"Like I said before, Jesus Christ! Were you in on that wager as well?"

"I lost a five-pound note on that bet. I didn't think you would call the Skipper. And believe it or not, Chats played right into our hands. We hope he has kept the Jozefow info between Asia, Jakub, and you, and no others. The fact that he knew about a massacre in Jozefow was sure to make its way around Europe. That said, we waited around for him to ask for our help. Would he ask you to investigate? Sure, he would. When we discovered this, SOE specialists discussed the topic for hours. We had to evaluate how to disclose what happened in Jozefow to the insurance investigative team. Please note that the British have classified the Jozefow incident as top-secret material. We leaked the basics of the Jozefow event. Jozefow is indeed old news. Our next move was a strategy to bring you into SOE. And, as you can see, it became complicated."

CHAPTER FORTY-TWO

Westminster, England/Scottish Highlands, Scotland
May 22nd, 1943, 1:17 a.m.

Jack's legs wobbled, the world tilting precariously with each attempted step. The brick pavement seemed to rise and fall like a ship's deck in a storm. He leaned against a wall, the rough stone scraping his cheek. His stomach churned, a sour taste rising in his throat. *Otto bloody Fischer is always the champion.* He blinked, trying to focus on the blurry streetlamps. A wave of nausea hit him, his hand instinctively reaching for his mouth. He retched, the bitter contents of his stomach splattering onto the brick-paved street.

He had to get out of sight. He slid along the wall, ducking into a narrow alley. The stench of stale beer and something vaguely rotten filled the air. He held his breath, trying to steady himself.

A vehicle's engine rumbled nearby, growing louder. Headlights briefly illuminated the alley entrance, then figures emerged, dark silhouettes against the dim light. They moved toward him, their footsteps echoing on the damp bricks. He tried to stand straighter, a futile attempt at composure. The footsteps behind him accelerated, the sound of leather soles slapping the ground. He glanced back—they were sprinting.

He tried to run, but his legs betrayed him. A crushing weight slammed into his back, sending him sprawling. Hands grabbed him, rough and insistent. A gag was forced into his mouth, stifling his protests. Cold metal clicked around his wrists—handcuffs. He thrashed, a surge of panic flooding him, but they were too strong. He felt a canvas suddenly covering his head, plunging him into darkness, then a sharp prick in his upper arm, a burning sensation spreading quickly.

"Jesus, what ?" he mumbled through the gag, the words muffled and distorted. *Handcuffs? A bag? What bloody game is this?* He struggled against the restraints, his mind racing. No one answered. The world faded to black.

He woke to the same restraints, the same darkness. He was slumped against a hard surface, his body aching. He couldn't stand, couldn't even sit up properly. He strained against the bonds, a low groan escaping through the gag. Nazis? Kidnappers? An insurance salesman—who would bother? A flicker of a different thought: Otto, SOE, is this a test?

He focused on that possibility, clinging to it. *They want to see how I react when placed under pressure.* He forced himself to breathe deeply, trying to control the tremor in his limbs. He thought, *play along—don't give them the satisfaction. A faint, almost imperceptible smile touched his lips beneath the gag—what if?* He quickly banished the thought. *It has to be SOE.* He drifted off again.

Harsh, guttural voices jolted him awake. "Raus! Raus! Raus!" The chains rattled as his captors dragged him from the vehicle—his limbs protesting with every movement. "Worthless American! You die today!" The words, thick with a German accent, echoed around him.

Someone suddenly yanked the canvas bag from his head. A man stood over him, speaking English with the same heavy accent. "Hello, Jack."

It was Otto, a familiar grin on his face. "Congrats! You passed the first test. I bloody well told them you wouldn't crack. And you didn't. Quite a night we had, eh?"

Jack, still struggling to find a comfortable position, managed a dry, "Hope you made a killing on that bet, Otto. You know me, always calm under pressure, never get my knickers in a twist."

Otto's grin widened, a glint in his eye. "Eighty-five quid, actually. Your silence was golden."

"And, naturally, we're splitting that down the middle?" Jack said with a sarcastic snicker.

"Uh, no. But I'll buy you all the beer you can handle."

"Please, no mention of beer. I might decorate your shoes."

"Where's your sense of humor, Jack? All in good fun."

"Fun? My definition is very different. Oh, what other 'fun' games do you and your men have in store for me?"

Otto waved a hand dismissively. "You've been out for fifteen hours. The beer, plus that little cocktail we gave you in the van, knocked you right out. By the way, welcome to the Scottish Highlands,[47] SOE training grounds. We've got a few more exercises before you're ready for the real thing."

Jack scanned the bleak, windswept landscape. "And who exactly is 'we'?

"An SOE full-bird colonel, a gunnery sergeant, two first lieutenants, and I. We're here to make sure you don't cut any corners. And, of course, to rescue your arse if needed."

Jack chuckled, a dry, humorless sound. "No rescue necessary. Bring the games. I'm ready."

Otto approached Jack, now clad in unfamiliar gear. "Damn, Jack—You look like a proper killer!" Otto said as he adjusted a strap on Jack's equipment.

Jack, standing beside a van, his expression grim, said, "Alright, Marine. Let's see if you can break me. Hope you've placed your bets!"

"Double or nothing on your success. Fail me, and I'm sleeping on the street next month."

Jack gave a short, sharp laugh. "Trying to jinx me, Otto? Is that supposed to be motivational?"

The landscape stretched before him—a vast expanse of gray under a drizzling sky. Four figures stood in the distance, small and indistinct. The wind whipped around him, carrying the scent of damp earth and something wilder. Jack estimated the time to be around eight-thirty in the morning.

Otto's voice broke the silence. "Right, then, Jack. Follow this map to the designated location. You'll take a Code-Box wireless. Once there, send and receive a message. There is a time limit for the test. You must pass the Morse code test before you can move on. The message you'll send is hidden. Find it, transmit it. Fail, and you're out—no second chances. Everything you need is in that trunk. Map, compass, water, rations. Three hours to get there."

Jack hesitated. "No questions?"

"No questions."

He set off, the submachine gun slung across his shoulder, the weight of the backpack familiar and reassuring. The camouflage paint felt strange on his skin.

Two hours and forty-five minutes later, a coded message crackled from the device. Jack had reached the objective, found the hidden message, and transmitted it flawlessly. A reply came, instructions for the next phase.

Two miles north-northeast, to the "three ladders." The words echoed in his mind. The 'three ladders" are stuff from SOE legend. He would be attempting them in near-total darkness, a small torch his only guide. Success meant another message, another set of orders.

He sat at the top of the third ladder, the wind howling around him. His muscles burned, his lungs ached, but he had done it. He set up the code device and reported his success. The reply instructed him to rest for three hours, then navigate by compass and stars to a new location, a four-hour trek to the east shoreline of Black Dog Loch.

He arrived at the loch just before sunrise, the water a dark, rippling mirror reflecting the gray sky. He sent another message, awaiting instructions—the message arrived: Submerge yourself in the water and guide the small raft to the eastern shore to keep the radio dry, cross to the western edge, and report in.

He emerged from the water, shivering, and sent the confirmation. A Jeep approached, and Otto and another man were inside. "Fifty quid!" Otto yelled, grinning. "You did it! Nobody thought you could!"

The passenger, a man in a sports coat and bowtie, added, "Well done, soldier. Jolly good. You're one of us now."

Otto clapped Jack on the shoulder. "Knew you could do it. Congratulations!"

Jack climbed into the Jeep, his body exhausted but his spirit strangely elated. "Otto, let's just not talk. Can we find a pub?"

The man in the bowtie chuckled. "By all means, son. You've earned it. My treat."

Otto paused. "Forgot introductions. Jack, please meet Brigadier General Winston H. Whitesell, Commanding General of SOE. Jack and I served together in the Marines."

Jack replied, "Sir, a pleasure."

General Whitesell said, "No, the honor is mine. You've broken records today. And my men say you're the fastest Morse code operator they've ever seen."

"Credit to my father, sir. Navy Signal Corps, World War I. Pops taught me young. Like riding a bike, sir."

"He's a hell of a teacher, son."

CHAPTER FORTY-THREE

SOE Headquarters, Baker Street, London, England
June 1ˢᵗ, 1943, 11:15 p.m.

Major Matthew Muncie, Chief of SOE Operations, Poland, had summoned Agent Jack Reynolds. Jack, ever punctual, arrived five minutes early. The major's secretary, her gray hair coiled in a tight bun, her English Army uniform crisp and starched, pecked at a typewriter. They exchanged the usual pleasantries, a strained dance of normalcy before the unknown. The secretary had always wondered what the major said to the greenhorns before their first mission. It was a ritual, a ten-minute talk that might be their last. Too many didn't come back. She never asked what was said. Some things were best left unknown. Her coping mechanism was simple: kindness. She displayed a bright smile, a friendly word, and a piece of dark chocolate from her private stash. It was a small comfort against the grim reality that death notifications often originated from her desk. A silent prayer escaped her lips, a whisper barely audible above the clatter of the keys, "Dear Lord, please don't let this one lose his life. Please, bring him back."

"Exceptional chocolate," Jack said, a slight smack of his lips betraying his enjoyment. "Dark chocolate is my favorite."

"Glad you approve," she said, her smile widening a fraction. "The major will see you now."

Dear Lord, she thought again, her gaze following the young agent—blue-eyed, black-haired, the near-perfect build, an ex-Marine—*please let him return safely.*

Jack entered the major's office, snapping a crisp salute. "Reporting as ordered, sir."

"Stand at ease. Have a seat." The major's voice was clipped, businesslike. "This will be brief. I have limited time."

"No issues, sir," Jack replied, settling into the offered chair.

The major rose, pacing his office with a restless energy. He paused by the window, peering out at the gray London day, before turning back. From a silver case, he offered Jack a cigarette.

Jack shook his head. "No, thank you, sir."

The major lit his own, inhaled deeply, and, to Jack's surprise, exhaled a series of perfect smoke rings, each one dissipating slowly in the still air.

"First, I appreciate your attitude. You and Otto are remarkably similar—your capabilities, motivation, and unwavering focus are the same. It's given me pause about sending you both on the same mission. Care to guess why?"

"Sir, if I were in your position, I'd be hesitant to risk losing two assets of our caliber."

"Precisely," the major confirmed, a thin smile touching his lips. "You have excellent perception."

"There's the risk, of course," Jack acknowledged, "but as we say in the Corps, 'We both have our head and ass wired together.'"

A chuckle rumbled in the major's chest. "Well, soldier, I thought I'd heard all the military slang, so I shall have to remember that one. It speaks to confidence, and confidence, Reynolds, is paramount."

"Agreed, sir."

The major stopped pacing and leaned against his desk. "Your commander speaks highly of you. You are the fastest code man in our unit's history. How did you acquire such a skill?"

"My father, sir. Ex-US Navy Morse code operator—he taught me when I was ten. It was a game, then. Never imagined I'd actually use it."

"A fortunate game, indeed," the major murmured. "Without it, you likely wouldn't be here." He paused, drawing on his cigarette. "You and Lieutenant Fisher are our only USMC veterans in SOE. Let me start by saying, thank you." He continued, his voice hardening, "There must be no misunderstandings. Your role is not to be a hero." He held up a hand, forestalling any interruption. "I know the history of the US Marines. Belleau Wood[48]—I wasn't there, of course. But even as a sixteen-year-old private in the British Army, I heard the tales. Marines jumping on 'potato mashers' to save their comrades. Unbelievable courage. A single

Marine taking on an entire German platoon. The stories were intoxicating to a green boy like me. War is hell, Reynolds. But US Marines—you're not like typical soldiers."

"No, sir," Jack agreed, his voice steady. "Not like the typical soldier."

"The point," the major stressed, his gaze unwavering, "is that there's no room for heroics. Risk-taking will compromise you, your team, and the entire mission. So, the first piece of advice: no heroes. Understand?"

"Yes, sir. Understood."

"Good." The major pushed himself off the desk and resumed his pacing. "Now, the second point. Unlike the USMC, we issue cyanide pills."[49] He didn't ask if Jack understood—he continued, his voice low and grim. "There can be a time, a place when an agent has no choice."

"They explained it in training, sir," Jack said. "When there are no options left."

"No options," the major echoed. "And if you think, perhaps because of your Marine training, that you can withstand anything the enemy throws at you, think again." He paused, meeting Jack's eyes. "Do you want to hear the methods they use?"

Jack hesitated, then shook his head slightly. "No, sir. But I expect you'll tell me anyway."

"Excellent perception, again," the major said, a flicker of approval in his eyes. "They will turn you over to the Gestapo. And they will break you. It's not a question of if but when."

"Sir, explain the dirty tricks the Nazis use."

"They begin with kindness, a friendly face. When that fails," the major paused, letting the silence hang heavy in the air. "The beatings. They're experts, Reynolds. They know how far to push, right to the edge of death. Then, perhaps, waterboarding. After that, they might start removing your fingers and toes. They'll never let you adjust to the pain. They love to use boiling water or hang you by your thumbs. They like to utilize workshop vices on their victims, their hands and feet. You see, Reynolds, you can avoid all this unpleasantness—one small capsule crushed between your teeth. It's a simple choice, really."

"Yes, sir. Understood."

"If capture is imminent, place the capsule in your mouth. Break it, Reynolds. If you swallow it whole, the poison will not be present—thus, don't swallow it whole. It'll pass right through you, and then you'll face the alternative—death by torture, and it will be most unpleasant. We can't decide for you. If you choose to endure torture, that's your business. But if you reveal SOE information under that torture, that is our business. I trust you'll do the right thing."

"Yes, sir. I know what to do."

The major stopped pacing and stood directly in front of Jack. "Enough of that. Now, to support your coverage for future missions, we must report you missing in action—to your next of kin, to your employer, Mr. Chatsworth Williams. I need to ask you point-blank: Is this what you want? You can walk away now. No questions asked. We can arrange your return to Britain after this initial mission."

Jack's gaze didn't waver. "Sir, I'll remain in Poland for my next assignment. I don't want to return to headquarters after this. And yes, sir, I understand the risks."

"The risks are simple, Reynolds. You may die there. Do you understand that?"

"Yes, sir. Understood."

"I expected no other answer." The major's voice softened slightly. "My subordinates speak highly of you. Your abilities and your performance are exemplary."

"Thank you, sir."

Major Muncie extended his hand. "Best of luck, Reynolds. I hope to see you back here in one piece. You and two others leave for Jozefow in a few hours, correct?"

"Yes, sir. The team is focused. Ready to complete the mission."

"Godspeed," Major Muncie said, his grip firm.

"Thank you again, sir." Jack saluted, the movement sharp and precise, and left the room.

CHAPTER FORTY-FOUR

SOE Agents Prepare to Depart for Jozefow
June 3rd, 1943, 2:35 p.m.

The flight commander walked into the barracks and said, "Right, lads, Rise and shine! Wheels up in forty."

Jack Reynolds' eyes snapped open. The familiar, musty smell of the Ringway barracks filled his nostrils. Sunlight, already strong, slanted through the high windows, painting stripes across the rough wooden floor. He sat up, the metal springs of his cot protesting with a groan.

Across the room, Stan Davies was already sitting on the edge of his cot, meticulously checking the straps of his kit bag. David Lowery, however, merely rolled over and pulled a blanket over his head.

"Sleep at all, Stan?" Jack asked, swinging his legs to the floor.

Davies looked up, a faint shadow of tension beneath his usual calm expression. "Not much. You?"

Lowery's muffled voice came from under the blanket. "Like a log. Always do." He threw the blanket aside, stretched with a theatrical yawn, and grinned.

Jack shook his head. "Three hours, maybe. Who can sleep at midday?"

A soft knock echoed through the barracks. The door creaked open, revealing a man who looked more like a misplaced librarian than a military chaplain. He was small, almost frail, with a gleaming bald head and wire-rimmed spectacles perched on his nose. "Chaplain Patrick Pence," he announced, his voice surprisingly firm. "Major Muncie sent me."

Lowery raised an eyebrow. "Major Muncie? Ten missions, and this is a new one."

The chaplain offered a small, tight smile. "He thought perhaps a blessing might be in order. If you're amenable?"

Jack, feeling a knot of apprehension tightening in his stomach, nodded. "Couldn't hurt. Come on, lads, let's get a bit of divine insurance."

The three commandos knelt on the hard floor, the chaplain's presence filling the small space, his voice low and earnest, resonating in the quiet room. "Dear Lord Almighty, grant these men strength and courage. Let them be steadfast in their purpose, fighting to end this terrible conflict. Guide them, protect them, and let them feel Your presence in every step. May they find solace in Your word and success in their mission. Shield them from fear and doubt and bring them home safely. Amen. Godspeed, gentlemen."

A shared "Thank you" was murmured, a blend of gratitude and a hint of unease. The chaplain slipped out as quietly as he'd come.

Jack moved to the window, squinting against the bright sunlight. The windsock hung limp, a still, white cone against the clear blue. "Looks like the weather is on our side, at least," he said, trying to inject a note of optimism. "Not a cloud."

There was no need to rehash the plan. The following steps were ingrained: dress, weapon check, final checklist, and then the plane.

June 3, 1943, 1500 hours

The briefing room was stark, lit by bare fluorescent bulbs. Captain Tony Banek, a man with a perpetually cheerful face that seemed at odds with the gravity of his job, introduced his crew with quick, efficient gestures. He then spread a large map across the table, tracing a line with his finger. "The weather's cooperating, gentlemen, for now. Smooth sailing for the first few hours, at least. After that," he shrugged, "it's anyone's guess. The eggheads say we should have decent conditions most of the way to Poland."

His finger continued its journey across the map. "Ringway to the drop zone near Jozefow—just shy of two thousand kilometers. The C-47's range is twenty-four hundred kilometers (Km) at two hundred and forty kilometers per hour, but we're playing it safe.[50]" He tapped two circles marked on the map. "Two extra 375-liter fuel bladders, giving us a comfortable thirty-four hundred-kilometer reach. Departure, 1540.

ETA at the drop zone, 2120. We'll be praying the flak stays quiet and the Luftwaffe stays home."

Banek's smile momentarily faded. "It's unlikely we'll see any Jerries on this route, but as my wife Laurie always says, 'Never say never.' We've got contingency landing sites marked," he pointed to a series of small, coded symbols, "but let's hope we don't need them. Refueling on the return leg will be at one of our friendly strips—some of them just grass fields. The scheduled take-off is eleven minutes. Questions?"

Silence. The weight of the mission settled in the room.

"Dismissed," Banek said, his voice regaining its briskness.

Two-thirds of the way there, the intercom crackled to life, Captain Robert Hall, the copilot's voice filtering through the headsets. "Heads up, lads. We've been fighting a twenty-knot headwind for the last few hours, and it delayed us about an hour. The new jump time is 2220. The good news is that darkness will be complete. The bad news is that flak will be just as blind."

Later, a crewman's voice broke through the tense quiet. "Descending to 214 meters. Skipper's adjusting airspeed. Prep your men. Eight minutes to the drop zone. Good luck, and God be with you."

Jack, Davies, and Lowery rose, the movement automatic. A crewman wrestled the side hatch open, the roar of the engines and the rush of cold air filling the cabin. He peered into the inky blackness, his eyes searching for the telltale streaks of tracer fire. Nothing. Just an endless void.

The commandos locked and loaded their rifles. They went through the final checks: gear watches were synchronized, and goggles were down. The static lines were hooked to the cable running the length of the cabin. The yellow light above the door flickered, then glowed a steady green. One by one, they stepped into the roaring darkness.

They landed hard but safely, scattered within a three hundred-meter radius in a freshly plowed field. The earth, still damp from a recent rain, cushioned their fall. After a quick regroup, they found a stand of trees about five hundred meters away, offering a semblance of cover. They settled in for a few hours of uneasy rest, one man always awake, rifle at the ready, while the others snatched what sleep they could. At dawn, they began the twenty-three-kilometer trek, each man burdened with over nineteen kilos of gear and ammunition. Their destination: the rendezvous point, four kilometers west of Jozefow, where Major Pawel Bajorek, their Polish Home Army contact, awaited.

Major Bajorek, a Warsaw native since birth, carried the scars of the war etched on his face and in his heart. The bombing had taken two of his four children, crushed beneath collapsing rubble. His wife and surviving children had escaped with minor injuries, a small mercy in a city ravaged by destruction. He was a history professor turned resistance fighter, a man of nearly two meters with a thick, graying, handlebar mustache, and fluent in multiple languages, including English. He was their lifeline.

June 4th, 1943, 0547 hours

The three commandos were shadows in the pre-dawn gloom, hidden in the brush lining a dirt road. A Jeep, followed by two canvas-covered trucks, rumbled into view. Davies, the ranking officer who was fluent in Polish thanks to his Polish-born mother, was the only one who had met Bajorek. The eleventh mission and the knot in his stomach were just as tight as the first.

They wouldn't reveal themselves until Davies was confident. One wrong move, one misidentified face, and it could all be over. The passphrase, relayed in encrypted Morse code just an hour ago, was their only guarantee. Two teams lost in the last year, passphrases leaked, and they'd walked into meticulously laid traps.

The Jeep stopped. A figure emerged, taking slow, measured steps toward their concealed position. Major Bajorek. Davies held his breath.

"Grable plus Bergman plus Hayworth—Bergman plus Grable plus Hayworth, Beethoven's Fifth," Bajorek's voice, clear and steady, cut through the morning stillness.

Davies exchanged a glance with Lowery and Reynolds. "Passphrase, correct?" he whispered.

"Confirmed," they murmured, almost in unison.

Davies stepped a few paces away, concealing their exact location. "Hollywood, Hollywood, Circus, Circus, rainy weather, Manchester," he replied.

"Passphrase confirmed," Bajorek said, his voice closer now.

The three commandos emerged from the brush—their weapons held loosely but ready. The mission had begun.

Major Bajorek strode toward the three SOE agents, a broad smile on his face. Behind him, the entire Polish Home Army platoon, etched with a mixture of exhaustion and grim determination, surged forward to greet the newcomers.

A cacophony of heavily accented English filled the air: "Welcome to Poland!"

After the initial flurry of introductions, Major Bajorek gestured toward a makeshift command center—a small table with four mismatched chairs huddled beneath a camouflage tarp. He clasped each commando's hand in a firm grip, his eyes assessing them. "Please, gentlemen, have a seat. Fresh tea is brewing."

Davies, relief evident in his voice, replied, "Sounds wonderful. We certainly didn't expect such a warm reception."

Major Bajorek unfurled a large map, its creases whispering tales of countless journeys and secret meetings. He weighted the corners with stones. "This is our location," he said, his finger tapping a point on the worn paper. "Shall we orient the map with the compass so you have your bearings?"

Davies leaned forward—his gaze sharp. "Where are we most likely to encounter the Krauts?"

The major's finger traced a line northeast. "A company was spotted about a day's hike in that direction. However," he added, a hint of caution in his voice, "that information is four days old."

"Thank you, sir. My associate, Agent Jack Reynolds, has some specific inquiries."

Major Bajorek turned his attention to Jack, his gaze intense. "Ah, yes. The American. The former Marine who traded a comfortable London life for this." He paused, a flicker of curiosity in his eyes. "Is that correct?"

"Yes, sir, Major. News travels fast, it seems. Hopefully, the Krauts are less informed." Jack confirmed, "I am a former Marine."

The major rubbed his beard, a thoughtful gesture. He met Jack's gaze directly. "I won't pry into your reasons for such a drastic change. I trust they are sound. I've encountered a few of your Marine brethren over the years. Their character have always been impressive. How may I be of assistance?"

"My reasons are solid, sir, rest assured." Jack's voice was steady. "We're seeking information about a young man believed to have escaped the Germans during the massacre. We're most anxious to speak with him."

Major Bajorek's eyebrows rose slightly. "Expand on that, if you would. Why such interest from an American?"

"My former employer initially dispatched me here to investigate the fate of the Kelner family. Asia Kelner, originally from Jozefow, is employed by them in New York."

"And how did your employer connect with the Home Army?" The major's voice held a note of suspicion.

"Through an old friend, who contacted our employer's president via the SOE in New York."

A flicker of suspicion crossed the major's face. "This old friend, does he have a name?"

"Otto Fischer. An SOE agent and a fellow Marine with whom I served. He persuaded the SOE to accept me."

"Some friend!" Major Bajorek's lips curled into a wry grin. "And you remain on good terms?"

Jack smiled in return. "Yes, Otto is precisely why I'm here today."

"Agent Otto Fischer? Damn, that man can hold his liquor. I've heard it's impossible to get him drunk."

"You've met my friend, then. Your assessment is accurate, though not entirely foolproof. We once shared a Puerto Rican jail cell, courtesy of our overindulgence."

"So, the individual you're interested in is nineteen years old, correct?"

"Yes, that would be his age now."

"You must be referring to the young Pole who witnessed the Nazis murder his grandmother and twin sisters."

"Yes, that's the one."

Major Bajorek leaned back, his expression hardening. "Well, first, you can't have him. He's become quite valuable to us. He's interrogated and extracted vital information from seventeen German soldiers by the last count. He doesn't, however, participate in the final act. He rarely resorts to physical coercion. Icek is one of our most driven members. Molotov cocktails and explosives are his specialties. I've lost track of the derailments he's orchestrated. And, interestingly, he shows no inclination to offer a 'mercy shot' to a suffering German. Mercy, it seems, is absent from his vocabulary when it comes to the enemy. He'll make a fine soldier one day."

Jack's voice was carefully neutral. "We have no intention of removing him from his duties. As I mentioned, his aunt, Asia, works for my former employer. My initial objective was to locate Icek and any other surviving family members and report back to them. Proof of life, that sort of thing."

Major Bajorek nodded slowly. "I understand. I can provide you with the information I have. You can relay it back to England, and they can pass it on to your former employer. Is that acceptable?"

"Yes, that will suffice. A personal meeting isn't necessary, although the prospect of meeting a boy soldier with such refined interrogation skills is intriguing. But the information, to reassure his family, is paramount. They're living in uncertainty, unaware of who might still be alive."

"Shall I speak slowly so you can take notes?"

"No need. My memory is nearly photographic. Please, proceed."

"I first encountered Icek after a three-man patrol discovered him following the Jozefow massacre. The Home Army was in its nascent stages then. The poor fellow was perched about twenty meters up a tree. Pure chance led my men to him—he dropped a piece of jerky, which landed near one of them. They persuaded him to descend. He was in a state of shock, understandably. Hours earlier, he'd witnessed German soldiers knock his father unconscious with a rifle butt. He'd then watched an SS officer murder his invalid grandmother and his twin sisters point-blank. He described the officer's expression afterward as a grin of satisfaction."

"Was he wounded?" Jack Reynolds interjected.

Major Bajorek shook his head. "Not in the conventional sense. Unless you consider spending hours chest-deep in the waste pit of his family's outhouse a wound, a feat deserving of recognition, I'd say. Few of us possess the fortitude for such a repulsive maneuver."

Jack grimaced. "Hours chest-deep. A stronger man than I."

"He remained submerged until the Nazis departed. He had a front-row seat as they struck his father, restrained him, and hauled him away in a truck with other men."

"All this after witnessing the murder of his grandmother and twins, a heavy burden for a young man," Jack murmured.

Major Bajorek continued, "Ah, I nearly omitted a crucial detail. I recently learned that two of Icek's companions, siblings Teodora and Tomasz Banik, were close friends prior to the Nazi incursion. Icek and Teodora, it seems, were fond of each other. After the massacre, Teodora and Tomasz, through some means, discovered Icek's affiliation with the Home Army, and, essentially, we gained two additional volunteers. My men raised no objections to their fighting as a trio."

"Do they function effectively together?" Jack inquired.

"No complaints, aside from the older members, those twice their age, who express disdain for soldiering with what they deem 'children.' We consider this when assigning tasks."

Jack pressed, "There have been no incidents where the younger soldiers' actions have jeopardized others?"

"No, and we remain vigilant. We exclude them from delicate, high-risk operations. Many of the simpler tasks are low-risk and high-yield. These youngsters assist in contaminating water supplies, poisoning food, and sabotaging vehicles—a piss in the fuel tank, slicing tires, stealing batteries, and yanking out spark plug wires—are just a few examples of a comprehensive list of irritating activities. Many operate in civilian attire, often unarmed. Sadly, we've recently lost a few in plainclothes. The Krauts are becoming aware of our tactics. Our young soldiers project an air of innocence. Often, the Krauts are oblivious. Regrettably, Jerry is catching on," Major Bajorek sighed, a hint of weariness in his voice.

"Remarkable patriotism. These youngsters are taking considerable risks," Jack observed.

"Allow me to recount a recent operation. Our objective was to neutralize a railroad switching station. We suffered casualties that night. A Kraut emerged from behind a tree, confronting Teodora. She attempted to fire, but her rifle jammed. She was approximately twenty meters from her team. The Kraut didn't shoot. Instead, he lunged with a horizontal butt stroke, grazing her shoulder. She fell. He then attempted to finish her with a bayonet thrust to the chest.

"As he moved, Icek appeared behind him, dispatching the German with a shot from his service pistol. The bayonet descended as Icek attacked. Teodora rolled, but the bayonet penetrated her left breast. Our medic stitched her up, and today, it's as if it never occurred. We're indebted to Icek and fortunate to have had a skilled medic present. Those two, I believe, are bonded for life. I'd entrust them with my own."

Jack rubbed his three-day growth of beard, his expression thoughtful. "She's fortunate to be alive."

"Tomasz, initially, was a hesitant young man. A mere two years older than Icek, he's now a man, a proficient soldier. Shortly after the massacre, he entered Icek's home. The aftermath of two ten-year-old twins and the bloodbath resulting from the murder of a helpless stroke victim was difficult to witness and even more difficult to unsee. Tomasz's motivation, his war against the Nazis, is rooted in the blood and gore he encountered that day."

Jack looked down, his voice low. "I've never been able to comprehend the mindset of those who slaughter the helpless, the unarmed."

"After his sister's injury, Tomasz requested to become an interrogator. He possesses fluency in German and relishes compelling those who refuse to speak to divulge information. By the time Tomasz concludes his interrogation, the prisoner sings. And, typically, without resorting to torture. His technique involves threats. Pulling teeth, placing a head in a vise, smashing fingers, and castration without anesthetic. That small glass container holds the testicles of a dog, another family pet victim. It was Tomasz's idea to preserve them in a medical sample jar as a persuasive tool. He's become one of our most effective interrogators. Initially, he was overzealous, resulting in the deaths of several prisoners before they could talk. He's now more circumspect.

"Once we've obtained the desired information, Icek or Tomasz relinquish the prisoner to soldiers who have no compunction about eliminating the enemy. Neither Icek nor Tomasz enjoy taking a life. We have numerous volunteers who've lost family to the atrocities committed by German soldiers. Their thirst for revenge is insatiable. But they can kill when pressed, when it becomes a matter of survival. I respect their reluctance."

"Do you eliminate all prisoners?" Jack asked, his voice carefully controlled.

The major's voice hardened. "Had they not wiped out an entire village of civilians, we wouldn't be disposing of our prisoners. But one must consider their nature. These animals are less than human. If we encounter an anti-Nazi, we might spare them. But that's rare. Most Nazis, while training, become indoctrinated to hate all Jews. And, frankly, we lack the infrastructure to manage prisoners. We struggle to feed ourselves, let alone the Germans who've murdered our people. It's cleaner this way. Let them die."

Jack commented, "Such considerations were absent from my military training. Our training gave us instructions on how to treat prisoners fairly to ensure reciprocal treatment for our soldiers. Are you saying that if the Germans capture you, the Germans will kill you?"

"Yes. 'Humanely' is not in their lexicon. Hours of torture, hanging by piano wire, is that humane? We prefer our method. A swift shot to the back of the head. Most are unaware."

"I understand your reasoning," Jack said, "and I don't fault you."

"A word of caution: Don't allow those Krauts to survive interrogation. They'd do the same to you. And, by the way, the Geneva Convention[51] holds no sway in our world. If my government disapproves, let them arrest me. We're merely reciprocating the Krauts' actions. Screw them!"

"My military background is primarily with the US Marines. I spent less than a week acclimating to the SOE, and they neglected to elaborate on prisoner handling."

"Trust me, that was intentional. The SOE prefers to avoid the subject. The SOE personnel I've collaborated with remain silent on our treatment of prisoners. One said to me after we'd disposed of our captives: 'This is your business, your prisoners.'"

Jack said, "Your disposition of prisoners is interesting, to say the least."

Major Bajorek abruptly shifted the conversation. "We now know the whereabouts of Icek's father. He's at a munitions plant, a two-hour train ride northeast of Jozefow. We're planning a mission to sabotage the facility, liberate the prisoners, and eliminate or capture every German. In this instance, the Allies will handle the captives. We're awaiting Allied weapons, air support, and mission planning. The plant is on the bombing target list, but the Allies have spared it thus far. They were aware that a bombing run would result in the deaths of hundreds of civilian slave laborers. The facility is prioritized because it's the primary supplier of KAR-98 rifle cartridges for the entire Third Reich."

"Targeting decisions are complex. At least they're factoring in the human cost," Jack said.

"Icek is nineteen going on thirty. A courageous soldier skilled in hunting, trapping, and living off the land, unparalleled in my experience. He refuses to take German prisoners. However, he prefers that others do the killing. I've instructed my men to eliminate any German non-officer that my interrogators deem expendable. You're aware that the bastards murdered over fifteen hundred Jews the night Icek lost his family."

He uncapped his canteen and took a long swallow.

"Do you believe Icek is mentally sound?" Jack inquired.

The major smiled, and there was a hint of irony in his expression. "Are any of us engaged in this work truly sound?"

Jack smirked. "A valid point."

"Observe our surroundings. Do you see any infrastructure? Any cells? Are there any structures whatsoever? The answer is evident. It's intriguing. We capture a Jerry—we conclude our questioning. We have no facility to house him, and there is no means to accommodate him. It's far more expedient to terminate a German soldier's life. There's more vengeance than we have prisoners to expend it on. We eliminate the bastards. Icek possesses ample vengeance fuel. I doubt he'll ever tire of seeking retribution.

"He's safe, healthy, a skilled marksman, an outdoorsman, and a young man with no qualms about witnessing the death of a German soldier. I'd prefer him to remain unaware of your inquiry. The war will conclude eventually, and I'm uncertain if he'll ever reunite with his family."

Jack met the major's gaze. "May I transmit this information to SOE headquarters, requesting they contact my former employer? He can then update the Kelner family. I'd also like to inform them about Teodora and Tomasz Banik. Would that be permissible?"

"Absolutely. Please omit the no-prisoner policy. And refrain from mentioning Icek's involvement in our interrogation practices and our infrequent granting of prisoner survival. Such details might distress the Kelner family, leading them to believe he's unhinged. Unnecessary."

"Excellent. I'll transcribe your account, employing our latest cipher code to ensure confidentiality. I also request that you make no mention of his family's inquiry. SOE has determined that numerous spies in New York City would relish the opportunity to eliminate a Nazi-hating Jew. For their safety, silence is paramount."

"Understood," the major replied. "'Loose lips sink ships,' as the Yanks say. And it's best to keep this narrative out of the newspapers, newsreels, and that Yank wartime publication the *Stars and Stripes*."

CHAPTER FORTY-FIVE

Park Slope, Brooklyn, NY
August 30ᵗʰ, 1943, 8:27 p.m.

The taxi lurched to a stop in front of the structure's familiar brass mailbox, shimmering under the deep green awning that stretched from the curb to the front facade of the building: the Brooklyn, Park Slope district, 1 Prospect Place, a six-story apartment building constructed in 1921.

The day's weight still clinging to Asia's shoulders—another quarter-end report at the insurance company. Numbers, reports, summaries from worldwide regional offices; a global jigsaw puzzle finally pieced together. She'd shepherd the final report to Chats' desk first thing in the morning. At least the reports finished.

She paid the driver, exited the cab, and expressed a quick 'Hello Max' to the doorman. Max responded with his usual nod, acknowledging her as she headed to the elevator. The fifth floor. Home.

The phone was already shrilling as she fumbled with the key. She practically threw the door open, snatching the receiver just before the line went dead. *Jakub, checking in from Buffalo?* He'd be eager to talk about the Kleinhans Music Hall,[52] a grand old place—a legacy of the Kleinhans family, clothing magnates, a monument to their lost wives, Mary Seaton and Mary Livingston. He was calling to share that he was the first Polish-born musician to grace its stage, a stage that could hold a sea of four thousand faces. The thought brought a small smile. He'd call back. He always did.

The phone rang again. "How was your rail trip to Buffalo?" she blurted, already picturing his grin.

"Ms. Kelner, it's Max, down at the front desk." His voice was unusually formal. "There's a New York City policeman on his way up to see you."

"Do you know why?"

"He'll be at your door momentarily, Ms. Kelner. He'll explain. Goodnight, Ms. Kelner."

The line went dead. A knot of unease tightened in her stomach. Three minutes. A knock. A priest and a police officer stood in the hallway, their faces grim under the dim light.

"What on earth is this about?" she asked, her voice a little unsteady.

The officer, with his thick Irish accent, didn't meet her eyes. "Good evening, Madame. I am Lieutenant Michael Mulrooney, and this is Father MacMurray. I apologize, but I need to see a piece of identification before proceeding. Could you please provide a piece of identification? Even a posted letter with your name on it will suffice."

Her passport. She found it in the kitchen drawer next to the fridge, her mind racing. *What could this possibly be?*

"Please come in," she said, her voice barely whispering, gesturing toward the living room. "Make yourselves comfortable."

The priest took her hand, his touch surprisingly gentle. "Thank you, Ms. Kelner. We will indeed have a seat."

She sank onto the sofa, her heart pounding. "Now, can you tell me why you are here?"

Lieutenant Mulrooney still avoided her gaze. He fixed his eyes on her passport. "Ms. Kelner, by chance, was your husband on a Lackawanna Railroad passenger train to Buffalo earlier today?"

"Yes, he was," she replied, a flicker of pride in her voice. "He's a concert pianist. He was to be the guest pianist for the Buffalo Philharmonic tomorrow evening at the Kleinhans Music Hall. A sold-out event, nearly four thousand people." She paused, the uneasy feeling returning. "Why do you ask?"

Father MacMurray squeezed her hand, his eyes finally meeting hers, filled with a sorrow that made her breath catch. "There has been a tragic train accident outside of Buffalo.[53] Thus far, we don't have a precise number of injuries. However, authorities have identified twenty-eight who are now deceased—your husband, Jakub, is one of them."

A scream ripped from her throat. "No! This cannot be! There must be a mistake! He can't be dead! He can't be dead! Please let me know if there's a chance this is a mistake. Please! Please!"

The priest reached into his pocket, offering her a handkerchief, his voice low and soothing. "Madame, authorities on the scene have checked and rechecked the list of passengers against those found deceased. We are so sorry. There are no mistakes. If you turn on your radio, you will hear endless accident coverage." He paused. "I know limited details about the crash. Your husband's train was trying to make up time. At the time of the accident, the train was packed with nearly five hundred passengers and traveling at eighty miles per hour, which is the allowed speed. Your husband's train was on the same main rail as an oncoming train." He hesitated, his voice dropping to a near whisper. "Your husband died instantly from a crushing injury. We know no other details. We will give you the phone number for the Wayland, New York County Coroner's office so you can speak with the person who declared your husband dead."

He continued, his voice heavy with the weight of the news. "A photo of your husband on a concert program found in his suit coat pocket made it easy to identify him. The ensuing fire burned many of the deceased beyond recognition. Your Jakub suffered blunt force trauma. The fire did not impact his body. The word we have from witnesses is that he died instantly. And Madame, with the photo in his suit pocket, and minus fire damage like so many of the other deceased, and with the concert program's aid, he was one of the first fatalities authorities identified."

"Oh my God," she whispered, the tears starting to flow, hot and heavy. "I placed that program in his jacket pocket—it was his first program, and it included a photo." She wiped at her face with a tissue, the paper shredding against her wet skin. "Where is Wayland, New York?"

"Wayland is about eighty-four miles east of Buffalo," the officer replied.

"Eighty-four miles," she repeated, the words hollow. "He was less than two hours away." The grief crashed over her, wave after wave. "What have I done to deserve this?" She choked on the words, the injustice of it all burning in her chest. "Life is so unfair! Unfair!"

Father MacMurray stood, his presence a quiet strength beside her. "All of my life, I have heard that the Man upstairs never gives us more than we can handle. Dear child, this is truly an exception. We will never know the reasons why our Maker does what he does. We will find out on judgment day."

Asia turned away, her shoulders shaking. "I must be careful. I might say something I will regret."

He gently took her in his arms. "Speak your mind. Our Heavenly Father is an excellent listener. He will hold nothing against you."

"Thank you, Father. Nevertheless, I will keep my thoughts to myself."

"Would you like to phone a friend, a relative, an acquaintance, a coworker? We will be happy to wait here until they get here. What do you say? Please get in touch with someone, and the lieutenant here can go and get the person you choose while I stay with you. Being alone at a time like this is not a great idea. What do you say?"

"Mr. Chatsworth Williams," she said, the name of a lifeline. "My boss, Mr. Williams, and his wife. They're the closest thing to family I have left here. I can't be alone."

"Would you like us to take you to them?"

"No," she said, a tremor in her voice. "I need to be here. Just call Mr. Williams."

"Alright. When you give us the word, we will go and get your friends and bring them here."

She scratched out his address on a notepad and handed it to him.

Asia walked into the bedroom, shutting the door behind her, a fragile barrier against the storm raging inside her. Her wedding photo, Jakub's smiling face, and the group picture from his first New York concert were daggers to her heart. A sob escaped her, raw and uncontrolled. *Empty. Everything is empty now.*

The phone rang, jarring her. She picked it up, her hand shaking.

"Chats here!"

She thought, *Chats is calling me at this hour?* It was unusual for Chats to contact her at home. Had he heard?

"Good evening, Asia. Sorry to disturb your evening. I forgot something I wanted to add to the report."

A scream tore from her throat. "Jakub is dead! He is dead! Jakub is dead! The police are here!" Her voice cracked, dissolving into sobs. "A train wreck in Wayland, New York. He's gone, Chats! He's gone!"

"There must be a mistake! A train wreck? Are you sure?"

"I asked the same thing!" Her words tumbled out, a jumbled mess of grief and disbelief. "The police are here in my apartment. They've identified him. Two trains collided at eighty miles per hour and derailed. They've offered to get you and Claire so that I won't be alone. Please, can you come?"

"Send them my way. We will be ready by the time they get here. I am so sorry to hear that Jakub has passed away. Try your best to be calm. We will be there shortly. You have our sympathy, dear Asia."

Chats hung up, his voice booming through the quiet apartment. "Claire! Claire, please come here! Please come now!"

"Chats, what on earth is going on? Did you see a ghost?"

"Jakub is dead. Jakub is dead!"

Claire's voice was a stunned whisper. "Dead? What do you mean? He was in your office yesterday, heading to the Hoboken train station. He said goodbye to Asia. How is he dead?"

Chats swallowed hard. "There was a major train accident in Wayland, New York."

Claire replied, "I have listened to the radio coverage for two hours. There are almost thirty fatalities. I never dreamed we would know someone who was on the train."

"Jakub was one of them," Chats said, his voice heavy. "The police notified Asia at her apartment. She asked that we come over and be with her. The police and the priest are leaving soon and a police cruiser is on its way to pick us up."

"Oh, my dear me, first Asia lost her identical twin. In addition, she hasn't heard from any of her family in Poland. That poor soul," Claire said, her hand flying to her mouth.

She and Chats hurried out of their apartment down to the lobby to meet the policeman, their hearts heavy with the news, their minds racing to find some way to comfort their friend.

Twenty minutes later, Lieutenant Mulrooney arrived at the Williams' residence.

CHAPTER FORTY-SIX

Park Slope, Brooklyn, NY
September 2ⁿᵈ, 1943, 8:45 a.m.

It was a bright, early autumn day, with a cloudless sky, no wind, and sixty-six-degree weather. The timestamp of the accident would not leave her mind. She kept looking at August 30ᵗʰ, 1943, at 5:22 p.m., the time stamp of the fateful event that took her Jakub. For some reason, it was there each time she closed her eyes. She tried her best to recall where and what she was doing then. It was useless. She had no recall. She racked her brain on the discussion with Jakub, and she had two days before the rail trip to Buffalo.

Jakub begged and begged me to accompany him on the journey to Buffalo. She'd wanted to go. Chats had stepped in and said, "Dear, we have third-quarter reports due. The timing doesn't fit our upcoming work schedule." He'd told her, "I feel so guilty. I know how you like to watch your Jakub perform, but I'm sorry, I'm so sorry; I can't afford for you to be away from the office. That said, I will buy you a plane ticket so you can get on an early flight on Saturday morning. The two of you can spend the weekend and return to the office by noon on Monday."

She recalled her response. "Oh, Chats, that is so kind of you. I will let Jakub know when I get home."

Oh my God, Chats saved my life. He saved my life. I could have been sitting next to Jakub on the same train, in the same car.

Asia reflected on the previous several days before Jakub boarded the train. *Did we kiss before he boarded the taxi to Hoboken to catch the train? When did we last make love? What was our last night out in town? What was our final Broadway play? When did he last perform? Where was our last dinner?*

She began crying. The guilt was unbearable.

Had our lives become so busy that we took one another for granted? My God, how will I ever get through his funeral? How will I ever live without my Jakub?

Her thoughts were interrupted by a phone call.

She answered the call and quickly recognized the voice on the other end of the line. It was her rabbi's secretary. With the phone in her hand, she walked about her living room as they spoke.

"Good morning, Asia. Ida Rosen here, calling from Temple Emanu-El. I am so sorry for your loss. Humanity has lost one of its finest. Such a talented musician and wonderful husband taken by our Heavenly Father at such a young age."

Holding their framed wedding photo as she spoke, the tears flowed freely. "Thank you for the kind words, Ida. This means a lot."

Ida continued, "Regardless of how often one makes such calls, they are never easy. Asia, my dear, I have information on your dear Jakub. His remains arrived late last evening. We began the preparation for his service early this morning. We want to notify the public that his services will be held at three p.m. this afternoon. Before we announce this, I must get your approval over the phone to proceed with the time slot."

"I guess this is fine?" she said, with a sense of zero confidence.

"Alright, Asia, I will notify the rabbi and do our best to make as many calls as possible to parishioners and those on your guest list that Jakub's funeral will be today. I want to confirm your choice for Jakub's final resting place. Based on your wishes, we will make the necessary arrangements for Jakub at Mount Hebron Cemetery in Flushing, New York. Is this correct?"

"Yes, this is correct," Asia said as she burst into tears.

"Oh. I have upset you. I am so sorry," Ida said.

"It's not your fault. It's no one's fault. Jakub is gone, and I must accept this. Now, I expect him to be walking into our home any minute, but I know he's gone. He'll never be here again. He's gone forever. It isn't your fault. I'm so sorry, and I must get off the phone. Do you need anything else?"

"No, Asia, I have what I need."

"Thank you so much for the call and all that our parishioners have done to prepare for Jakub's final moments. God bless you." She hung up the phone.

Mourners packed the synagogue to a standing-room-only audience. Jakub's entire music department from his school, as well as many of

Asia's coworkers at the insurance agency, attended. The biggest surprise was when the mayor and his wife appeared. Both stepped toward Asia and expressed their condolences before taking their seats.

The chief of the music department at Jakub's college spoke for about fifteen minutes. Mr. Chatsworth Williams talked for over twenty minutes, with the audience often erupting in laughter during his talk. He included a statement about Jakub's extended family in Warsaw and Jozefow, noting that at this very moment, they were likely unaware of Jakub's demise and that he was no longer in this world. Mr. Williams reiterated that it was so unfortunate on all fronts.

As the service concluded at the burial site, Asia took one last glance at Jakubs' coffin and began tearing up. She stood and thought as she witnessed the final moments, *Jakub would have loved this day, to see such a ceremony for someone born in Poland, emerging as a true maestro, performing with the New York Philharmonic Symphony, and having the Mayor of New York City attend his funeral. Jakub would have been proud.*

Chats and Claire approached her and said, "Let us take you away from here."

Asia looked at them both and said, "Thank you for everything. I mean everything."

Chats said, "I wish we could have done more."

Williams Residence, Manhattan, New York City
September 17ᵗʰ, 1943, 11:10 a.m.

Chats and Claire sat at the breakfast table, drinking coffee and sharing breakfast, when the discussion turned to Jakub's death and poor Asia's deep plunge into depression.

Chats took a sip of coffee, then downed a small glass of orange juice, and said, "Claire, I simply lack the skillset to pull Asia out of her depression. The extreme quietness is so unlike her. I know it will take plenty of time for her to overcome the passing of dear Jakub. I am convinced it will take months, perhaps years for her to overcome the shock.

It will be quite some time before we see the old Asia. We must adapt to the Asia we have and do everything we can to assist her. Regardless, I'm concerned about her."

Placing raspberry jam on her jumbo biscuit, Claire said, "She called me today and asked if I could join her in visiting her doctor. I told her I would be glad to go with her. I guess Jakub always joined her in the past. I suspect it is a routine visit," Claire said as she buttered another biscuit.

He stood, wiped his face with his table napkin, and approached Clair, placing his hand on her shoulder, and said, "You could drop a note to her doctor that says something to the effect of, 'My friend Asia here lost her husband earlier this month. Can you confront her and form your judgment about her mood? You can refer her to a doctor who deals with depression following the loss of a loved one?'

"Chats, I like your idea. If you think that would help, I can do it. I, too, am worried about Asia."

"Well, I must be off. What time is Asia's appointment?"

"At one-forty-five, about five minutes from her Brooklyn apartment in Park Slope. I will accompany her and take her to lunch. She may even be able to get some work done today for you."

Putting on his suit coat as he talked, Chats said, "Yes, it would be nice to get our backlog cleared. That said, if you keep Asia out all day, there are no issues; I will deal with it. I need her to be happy. I need the old Asia back. I never dreamed how much she did for me until she was out on family leave."

She took a last sip of coffee and darted toward the door, "I must be going. I need to take a cab to Asia's place, which may take fifty minutes at this time of day. Wish me luck, dear."

"You be careful, and on the way to Asia's apartment, jot down the note as we discussed."

"Will do, dear. Love you."

They kissed each other goodbye, Claire grabbed her purse, umbrella, and sweater, called the concierge from the apartment to order a taxi, and then headed to the lobby of their building.

Park Slope, Brooklyn, NY
September 17th, 1943, 1:50 p.m.

Asia looked at the reflection in the mirrored door of the examination room as she watched her doctor, Dr. Charles D. McClossan, a smartly dressed, forty-three-year-old gynecologist with bright red hair, light blue eyes, numerous freckles, and tiny wire-rimmed glasses. He stood there, staring into the closet, mumbling something in his hefty Scottish accent. He was looking for something he had ordered weeks earlier. Asia thought, *Whatever it is, it's not there—though I enjoy listening to his accent. Whether a complaining mumble or perfect dictation, I could listen forever.*

Frustrated, he slammed the door of the cabinet closed as he surrendered. He stepped into the exam room and, with a huge grin, said, "Asia, you are seven weeks pregnant."

Asia looked at him, puzzled. "Your accent is sometimes difficult for me to understand exactly what you say. I truly apologize, but this is one of those times. Perhaps the fault is mine. I have not listened attentively since losing my dear Jakub. So sorry, Dr. McClossan, can you please repeat what you just said?"

"By all means, yes, I will be glad to repeat my statement. I said, 'Asia, you are seven weeks pregnant."

"Did you say that I am seven weeks pregnant? Is that what you said?"

"I did indeed say this. There is no mistaking this. You are carrying a baby."

She yelled to the top of her lungs, "Oh my God, Jakub, we have a child. Jakub, I'm pregnant! I will be forty-four years old on my birthday this December second. How can I be pregnant?"

"Your records indicate you had a twin sister. Correct? It appears that you have recorded your mother as being born in July, 1863. So, you were born in 1900. Your mother had twins at the age of thirty-seven. You will be seven years older than your mother when she had twins. We will see you more often than the twenty-year-old patient. Trust me, you are not an anomaly by having a child at forty-four. Not another word about your age. According to government statistics, the United States had nearly 414,000 births last year among women between forty and forty-four.[54] Your baby is God's plan. Please enjoy what Jakub has given you. You will have a part of him for the rest of your life. Please don't worry. New York boasts some of the world's best medical techniques. Now, you're free to leave this office and enjoy the coming months. Be excited. God meant it this way."

"Oh! Dr. McClossan, can I hug you?"

"At this point, I might even feel slighted if you didn't." He opened his arms, and they hugged one another.

Just as Claire was about to tap on the door to Asia's exam room, Asia flung the door open and announced to the world, "Jakub lives on! Jakub lives on! Claire, I'm pregnant. You have no idea how happy I am. I'm pregnant!"

Dr. McClossan, standing with his arms crossed and his face a bundle of cheer, said, "I have never seen such a celebration on the news of a pregnancy in my entire career. Asia, I am so happy for you. I'm pleased the news means so much to you. I must go to my next patient. In the meantime, I need to see you in six weeks, unless, of course, you experience any pain, discomfort, or bleeding. If you have any of these, please get in touch with our office to schedule an appointment. Please do not wait for any symptoms to go away. In pregnancy, the symptoms rarely disappear."

While Asia met with the nurse, Claire headed down the hall to a public telephone and dialed Chats' office.

Oddly enough, Chats answered, "Chatsworth Williams here. How may I help you?"

"Hello, dear. This is your wife checking in."

"Is everything okay? You are the last person I expected to hear from. Are you not with Asia at the doctor's office?"

"Oh yes. I am indeed here with Asia. Dear, when you see Asia, please act surprised. Can you do this just for me?"

"Is Asia okay? Is she ill? Does she have some incurable condition?"

"In a way, she does have an incurable condition, at least for the next eight months or so."

"What kind of a condition lasts eight months or so? Oh my God, Asia is pregnant!"

CHAPTER FORTY-SEVEN

Hamburg, Germany
May 8th, 1945, 9:16 a.m.

Sunlight, warm and golden, spilled across the patio. Olga, a steaming mug warming her hands, breathed in the scent of damp earth and blossoming lilac. The garden, a riot of color after the long winter and months of gray, seemed almost defiant against the city's backdrop. Victory in Europe Day,[55] the newspapers had proclaimed it—a grand, hollow phrase ringing in the silence of a defeated nation.

Behind her, the sliding glass door hissed open. Heidi, her face still creased with sleep, emerged in a faded housecoat. "Good morning, Mother."

"Did you sleep well, Heidi?"

Heidi shrugged, a small smile playing on her lips. "Better. Now that it's over. And Father," She trailed off, but the unspoken hope—he's coming home—hung heavy in the air.

Olga gestured toward a particularly vibrant rose bush, its crimson bloom unfurling. "Come here. I want to show you something."

They stood together, gazing beyond the garden wall. Instead of the familiar Hamburg skyline, a jagged panorama of ruin met their eyes. Rows upon rows of buildings stood like hollowed-out skulls, their windows dark, empty sockets staring blankly at the sky. Charred timbers jutted out at odd angles like broken bones. The air, even here, held a faint, lingering acridity.

Olga found her voice, a tremor in it. "Do you remember what it looked like before? The city, I mean. Before all this?"

Heidi shook her head slowly, her gaze tracing the devastation. "I, I'm not sure I can."

A silence fell between them, broken only by the chirping of birds in their untouched garden—a cruel irony.

"Why were we spared?" Heidi's voice was barely a whisper.

Olga felt a cold knot of guilt tightening in her stomach. She had no answer, no comforting platitude to offer. "I don't know, Heidi. So many are gone. And your father is coming home whole. Body and mind." She almost choked on the last word, a silent prayer of thanks and a wave of dread.

Heidi continued to scan the neighborhood, her eyes lingering on the skeletal remains of what had once been homes. A tear escaped, tracing a clean path down her dust-smudged cheek. "What a waste," she breathed. "All those people, for what? They said it was the U-boat pens, but those had been gone for months. This was to break us. To crush our spirit."

Olga reached out, wiping a tear from her eye. "They succeeded," she murmured, the words tasting like ash in her mouth.

Heidi turned, her gaze suddenly sharp and accusing. "I'm, I'm done with it. I was never political, but now I can't be German, not after what the Allies have revealed." Her voice cracked. "Those places in Poland. Where Father was." She shuddered. "Were we part of that, Mother? Was he?"

Olga recoiled, a surge of protectiveness battling with a deep, gnawing fear. "Heidi! You must never speak like that. Not to anyone. It's dangerous."

Heidi gave a short, bitter laugh. "Dangerous? Are you saying my government will arrest me and lock me away for speaking the truth?"

Olga's hand flew to her chest, her fingers instinctively tracing *the sign of the cross*—forehead, chest, left shoulder, right—verbally invoking—in the name of the Father, the Son, and the Holy Spirit. An old habit, long suppressed, now resurfacing with desperate urgency. "No. No, the government will not arrest you! Of course not. It's a miracle that we all survived. A miracle your father made it through the war." She looked up, her gaze lost in the vast, indifferent blue of the sky. She thought, *dear God—thank you. Thank you for keeping Helmut safe and for sparing our home. We will show you—Helmut will make amends. He will give back to you, to his family, and everyone else.*

Heidi's expression softened, but a shadow of doubt remained in her eyes. "Mother, do you really think God had anything to do with this? If there were a God..."

Olga cut her off, her voice sharper than she intended. "Heidi, our God spared your father. I don't care what you think. I thanked my God." Then, seeing the hurt in her daughter's eyes, she softened. "Oh, dear. I'm sorry. You have every right to speak to Him. I know you've talked to Him, too, these past years."

She drew Heidi closer, pointing to the burgeoning life in the garden. "Look at this, Heidi: the flowers, the birds. There is something good, still. We are the lucky ones. We have to be." She pulled Heidi into a fierce embrace.

"Did I miss something?" Helmut Junior's voice startled them. He stood at the edge of the patio, a faint smile on his lips.

"Yes, but it's our secret," Olga said, a forced lightness in her tone.

Helmut Junior raised an eyebrow. "I hate secrets. Good morning, Mother and Sis. Beautiful day. Perfect for celebrating an Allied victory." He said the last words with a deliberate, almost challenging, emphasis.

Olga felt a flicker of unease. "You haven't said much about the surrender. What are your thoughts, Helmut?"

He grinned, a flash of something unreadable in his eyes. "How much time do you have?"

"We have nothing but time," Olga replied, trying to sound casual, though a sense of foreboding settled over her.

"Mother, you're asking for it!" Heidi warned, a hint of amusement in her voice.

Helmut Junior took a deep breath. "Alright. You asked. But first, imagine I'm speaking to some Argentinians, say. People who weren't involved. This is what I'd tell them."

Olga nodded slowly. "Go on. Pretend you're not my son for a moment."

"I'd tell them that the Hitler era was the worst thing that ever happened to this world. Authors of the Holocaust—we Germans will be forever known as murderers, that I'm ashamed of—I am ashamed to be German. That I might leave, change my name. Find a way to disappear. To become someone else, someone not tainted by this stain."

Olga gasped, her hand flying to her mouth. "My God, Helmut! Don't ever, ever let your father hear you say such things. It would destroy him."

Heidi stepped forward, her voice low but firm. "Mother, I feel the same. Those pictures of the ovens made me sick. The bulldozers moved thousands of dead Jews into massive graves. The walking skeletons of starving humans in the camps that we see daily in the news reels. You can't possibly support that, can you? The extermination of an entire people?"

Olga felt a wave of nausea. "I'm horrified by it, too. But we are German. We have to stand together. To rebuild. Can we ever overcome this? I don't know. However, only a small minority, a few, were responsible for those camps. Most Germans…"

Heidi cut into her conversation and said, "But Mother, most Germans hated the Jews, didn't they? Is that what we are? A nation of haters? I think Helmut has the right idea. It's not a good time to be German. And with all these homes, all this destruction…"

Helmut interjected, "Mother, we now have four Germanies, thanks to the Yalta and Potsdam Conferences, Joseph Stalin, Harry Truman, and Winston Churchill."[56]

Helmut's voice was calmer now, almost detached. "We're not the same Germany anymore. Divided into zones. At least they've demilitarized us. That's something. And the Nazi Party is gone. Thank God for small mercies. It's good that Hamburg is in the British zone. The French and Americans, okay, but the Soviets—God only knows where the new divisions will lead." He shook his head. "Four Germanies. It's going to be difficult."

Olga felt a wave of despair wash over her. "I regret asking. I didn't expect this. And your father, he would never understand. You must promise me, both of you, never to speak of this to him."

Heidi nodded. "We promise, Mother."

"Your father, he'll be here hopefully in a few months. He was down, of course, about the surrender. But I'm so relieved it's over." Olga managed to smile a weak smile. "Let's try to enjoy this day—a new beginning for the Schotz family. Helmut is coming home. It's a momentous day."

Her mind raced, trying to build a wall around the truth, a fragile defense against the inevitable. *Helmut followed orders*—she told herself. *He never fired a weapon, never.* It was a story they had agreed upon, a carefully constructed lie to protect themselves, to protect their children. He hadn't been at the killing factories, only overseeing things in the towns and the villages. The letters were vague and coded, hinting at the horrors, the demoralizing work, and the things his men were forced to do. She had wept, night after night, unable to reconcile the man she loved with the atrocities being committed in his name. The Nazis didn't see Jews as human, the letters repeated, ad nauseum.

"Children," she said, her voice regaining some strength, "it's the Allies' turn now. They'll make sure the world sees everything. The photographs, the films, the stories. They'll make sure everyone knows about the six million—the 'Jewish problem' that never existed."

Helmut Junior's gaze was fixed on the distant horizon.

Heidi's gaze changed in an instant. "I need to move on. I'm going to Heidelberg Medical School. I will become a doctor." She brightened. "Yes! Heidelberg. They barely touched it, the bombers. Lucky for us that denazification is occurring. Thank the Allies for cleansing our society." Then said, "Denazification, correct, Mother?" She looked up to her mother for reassurance that the cleansing was necessary.

Olga nodded numbly.

Heidi understood the task at hand, and it began immediately within the economic and cultural spheres throughout all layers of German society.

"Mother, in my lifetime, can Germany really rise again from this horrible Holocaust our government brought to the Jews of the world?"

"It will take decades, perhaps lifetimes, to erase the horrific crimes the Nazis perpetrated against an innocent people—the Jews. But in the future, you must strive to achieve your goal—to be a doctor. Yes, Heidi, you will make an excellent doctor."

Heidi remarked, "The Allies will make the appropriate staff and curricula adjustments at the university." She added hopefully, "The fall of '46. They say it will be ready by then."

Olga commented, "I've heard Heidelberg was a focal point for the Nazi madness. Their task at hand is to remove everything Nazi from the curriculum, including the Nazi teaching staff. The entire catalog of classes will need to be filtered to banish any Nazi methods or thinking. The major book burnings back in 33—this is now history—as management at the university will reintroduce the book inventory of the pre-war years. The Nazi stronghold will be gone forever."[57]

Helmut Junior, a flicker of envy in his voice, said, "Lucky you. A fresh start. A distraction. Hamburg, well, look around. We're lucky our house is still standing."

Heidi looked at her brother, then at her mother. "I'm looking forward to it. To study. Maybe even meeting someone. It's been so long since this war began. We're all glad it's over. Even if we lost."

Olga could only nod, her mind a whirlwind of fear and a desperate, fragile hope. *How will I keep their secrets from Helmut? How will we ever be a family again?*

CHAPTER FORTY-EIGHT

Hamburg, Germany
September 4th, 1946, 8:45 a.m.

The razor scraped against Helmut's stubble, a rhythmic rasp in the quiet bathroom. He caught his reflection, a fleeting thought flickering across his tired eyes. "Olga," he began, his voice echoing slightly in the tiled space, "Heidi is in college. A doctor in the family? Who would have imagined?"

Olga's voice, warm and laced with a quiet pride, drifted from the bedroom. "She always had a mind for those sciences, didn't she? Medicine, that's a surprise. A good one." A pause. "How far away is it, again?"

Helmut rinsed the razor, the water swirling pink before disappearing down the drain. "Six hours, give or take. Four hundred and seventy kilometers, if the map's to be trusted. Heidelberg." The name hung in the air, a mix of pride and the bittersweet ache of letting go.

"We need to get her settled before nightfall, then," Olga said, her voice closer now. He could picture her fussing with Heidi's carefully packed suitcase.

"Ten-thirty departure, then," Helmut agreed, wiping his face with a towel. He smoothed his hair, a nervous habit.

"Good," Olga replied. "No need for a frantic rush. A pleasant last drive, a chance for a proper conversation before she's gone until Christmas." The words were practical, but a tremor of sadness underscored them. Helmut Junior, their son, could take the wheel, leaving them free to be parents facing an empty nest.

A sharp knock on the door shattered the fragile peace. "Father?" Heidi's voice, strained and urgent, came through the wood. "There are men here. Three of them. In suits. They want to speak with you." Her voice held a desperate note, a premonition of something terribly wrong.

Helmut exchanged a quick, worried glance with Olga. "Invite them in, Heidi. Tell them I'll be down shortly. Offer them coffee or tea." His voice was calm, but his hand, still holding the towel, trembled slightly.

They descended the stairs together, a united front against the unknown. The three men in the parlor stood stiffly, their faces like granite. The air was thick with unspoken tension, a palpable sense of dread.

"Gentlemen," Helmut began, forcing a polite smile. "How may I help you?"

The oldest of the three, his face etched with grim lines, stepped forward. "We need to speak with you privately. Perhaps outside?" His gaze flicked toward Olga and Heidi, a silent dismissal.

Helmut felt a knot tighten in his stomach, but he kept his voice steady. "We have nothing to hide. You can speak freely in front of my family."

The man's expression didn't change. He moved closer to Helmut, his voice dropping to a harsh whisper, "We understand you were present at the killing of seventy-eight Polish civilians in the town of Talczyn, Poland.[58] Is this correct?"

The words were like a physical blow. Helmut recoiled, his carefully constructed composure crumbling. "We will take this outside," he stammered, ushering the men toward the porch, a desperate attempt to shield his family from the unfolding nightmare.

Olga, her face pale, turned to her children. "It's a mistake," she whispered, her voice trembling. "Your father will sort it out." But her eyes, wide and frightened, betrayed her fear.

Minutes stretched into an eternity. Low, muffled voices drifted from the porch, punctuated by periods of tense silence. Finally, the lead man, the one who had spoken, knocked on the door again.

"Madam," he said, his voice devoid of any warmth, "may I have a word in private?"

Olga stepped onto the porch, her heart pounding. Helmut was gone. The other two men were gone. Only this stranger remained, his face a mask of cold authority.

"Madam, I am Maxwell Whitesell with the British government. My group—the Polish Supreme National Tribunal[59]—arrested a member of your husband's unit, Police Battalion 101. The arrested gentleman reported to your husband while they were in Poland. This gentleman became a witness for the prosecution. He testified that your husband, Helmut, ordered the massacre of seventy-eight Polish nationals. This accusation is a grave accusation. We arrested your husband. He's already en route to our headquarters. I suggest you retain legal counsel. The evidence is overwhelming. Extradition to Poland is highly likely."

Olga stared at him, her mind reeling. "Taken him? Just like that?" Her voice cracked, rising in a desperate wail. "How dare you! Have you no decency?"

Whitesell's expression remained unchanged. "Decency? Madam, the Nazis murdered seventy-eight innocent people under your husband's command. I've seen the photographs. I have no sympathy. And let me be clear: We wouldn't have acted without unequivocal evidence of his presence and, crucially, his orders for those executions. Get a lawyer."

Helmut Junior, his face a mixture of shock and fury, pushed open the front door. "Where are you holding him?"

Whitesell turned to him, his gaze unwavering. "Your father will be held at the Hamburg office of the Allied Command at the City Hall for the time being. Here." He offered a card. "Feel free to contact me." He walked to his car, a black, imposing vehicle, and drove away without a backward glance.

Heidi collapsed onto the sofa, sobbing uncontrollably. "It can't be true! Father wouldn't. He couldn't."

Olga, her tears flowing freely, tried to comfort her, but her words felt hollow even to her ears. Helmut Junior stood rigidly, his fists clenched, his jaw tight.

"Please," Olga finally said, her voice hoarse, "both of you, sit down! Sit now!"

They obeyed, their movements heavy with despair. Olga began to pace, a caged animal trapped in a nightmare. She wrung her hands, ran them through her hair, covered her face, and cried out—a raw, guttural sound of anguish. The children watched in silence, too stunned to utter a word.

"You'll find out eventually," Olga said, her voice shaking. "Might as well hear it from me. On June 20th, 1942, your father's Police Battalion 101 received the order to embark on its third tour of duty in Poland. Setting out, there were eleven officers, five administrators, and 486 men.[60] Their destination was an area of Poland called Biloraj,[61] which is south of Lublin. You need to know that only your father knew the details of the assignment—he was not allowed to tell his men until they arrived in Biloraj. On the night of their arrival, following a letter he penned to me, he gathered his officers together and informed them of the details of their orders."

"Mother, we are supposed to believe that the German command told the men doing the murdering they would be murdering civilians on the morning of the massacre?"

"Son, you reacted the same way I reacted when I heard this. This notification that these soldiers would murder civilians is an example of Hitler's brutality. These were Hitler's damn orders!" She stopped pacing and looked at them, her eyes red-rimmed and filled with a lifetime of buried secrets. "Your father and I debated whether we should ever tell you children about his role in Police Battalion 101. He was the commanding officer."

She saw the disbelief and horror dawning on their faces. "I begged him never to tell you. Most soldiers had to kill or be killed. Self-defense. But for your father, it wasn't like that. It was to kill. And who? Defenseless people. Jewish men, women, children, and babies. Murder."

Heidi recoiled as if struck. "No, Mother! No! Our Father? Gentle, kind. He murdered civilians?"

Olga shook her head, a slight, desperate movement, her cheeks drenched as she wiped tears. "He never pulled the trigger himself. It wasn't his finger. He followed orders. To liquidate the Jewish population. He ordered his men to carry out mass killings. Tens of thousands across Poland. If he hadn't, they would have shot him."

Helmut Junior spoke, his voice low and choked with emotion. "I always admired him. His service. But how can I respect a man who ordered the deaths of innocent people? How?"

Olga looked at him, her eyes pleading. "When he left for Poland, he told me that if he disobeyed, his commander would have had him shot or hanged. Those were his choices. Do you think he didn't think about leaving you fatherless? Leaving me alone? Can we judge him when his only thought was to survive? I—I can't. He knew those people were going to die, if not by his order, then by someone else's. And he, he never watched. He told me he couldn't bear to see it."

Heidi's voice, strained and choked with tears, cut through the heavy silence. "You knew, Mother? All this time? Why didn't you say something? Maybe you could have saved someone!"

Olga's shoulders slumped. "Yes. Maybe. Maybe a few. But your father said if I spoke, the Reich would have taken us all. The entire family. To the gallows."

Heidi's voice broke. "This changes everything: my family, my country, myself. I won't be able to go to college today. Not now. Not until I know what's going to happen to Father." Her voice hardened with a new, bitter resolve. "I'll write to the university. Postpone everything. My heart isn't in it. Not knowing this. I feel the dark coming on. Depression, maybe? From dear old Dad and his killings, I don't know. I feel terrible about the innocent civilians."

Olga reached out to her daughter, her hand trembling. "Would your father want that? He'd be heartbroken."

"I'm sorry, Mother. I need to be here for you. Tell Father I can't support him. Not anymore," Heidi said, her voice flat and devoid of emotion.

Helmut Junior nodded in agreement. "Mother, I agree. We should visit, but supporting a father who ordered such atrocities, I don't know. My heart is breaking. Heidi's school can wait. We don't even know where they'll take him. Poland? Germany? England? We need to wait."

Olga looked at her son, a flicker of something akin to gratitude in her eyes. "Helmut, you're so like your father. You know how to take charge. You're right. We wait. See what happens."

"Thank you, Mother," Heidi said, her voice still tight. "But let's tell Father I will be going in a few weeks. He doesn't need another blow. Not now." She looked at the card Whitesell had left. "Can you call that number? Find out where they've taken him. What happens next?"

"Yes," Olga said, her voice regaining a sliver of strength. "We'll call. But first, a lawyer. We need a lawyer."

"Mother, Hans Hoffman? My friend? His father, Martel, is a lawyer. Experienced. I'll call him. Ask him to come as soon as possible. What do you think?" Helmut Junior said, already reaching for the phone.

Olga nodded, a glimmer of hope in her eyes. "Yes. If Hans's father can't help, he can offer us advice. Call Hans and ask to speak to his father. I don't want to spread this around. Not yet."

"I can go to his office," Helmut Junior said. "I've known him since third grade. Been to their house countless times."

"Yes," Olga said, relieved. "Better that way. Avoid Hans for now."

Helmut Senior sat in the suffocating darkness of a windowless room. The blindfold they'd used after dragging him from the car had only been removed moments ago. He'd been driven, blind and disoriented, for what felt like an eternity, then hustled, handcuffed, at a near run through a maze of corridors. Now, he was cuffed to a heavy metal ring embedded in a bare table. He had no sense of time, no idea of his location, only the oppressive weight of his fear and the cold metal biting into his wrist.

A young man, impeccably dressed in a three-piece suit, entered the room. His British accent was crisp and precise, a stark contrast to the rough handling Helmut had just endured.

"I am an attorney and represent the International Criminal Court and Tribunal, Office of War Crimes," the man began, his voice devoid of any warmth. "My role is to facilitate your extradition to Poland. Unlike the protracted Nuremberg trials, the Polish justice system operates differently.[62] If the evidence exists to support the charges related to the murder of Polish citizens, we will turn you and any others charged over to Polish authorities. All those accused will then be extradited to Poland to be tried by Polish authorities within the Polish judicial system. At this point, the German government, as well as any member countries of the Allies, will have no say in the proceedings. I must tell you from experience, for Poland, when the evidence is irrefutable, they move swiftly."

He paused, letting his words sink in. "A Polish judge will preside. I've observed their courts. And if a death sentence is handed down, it won't be long for the court to carry out the sentence—six, seven months, perhaps less. Polish juries are not known for lengthy deliberations. Trial and sentencing often occur on the same day. Furthermore, the likelihood of an appeal is zero."

He leaned closer, his voice dropping to a chillingly casual tone. "The subordinate who implicated your captain and you has agreed to testify in exchange for a reduced sentence. The Poles are seeking retribution. They will have their way with you, just as your men had their way with hundreds of thousands of innocent people. My only regret is that I won't be permitted to witness your execution."

Helmut, struggling to regain some semblance of composure, tried a different tack. "Your accent is intriguing. Where are you from, precisely? Not the typical Londoner, I'd wager."

The man's eyes narrowed. "Manchester. Is this a tactic? Something they taught you in the Nazi training? It won't work on me, Major Schotz. Understand?"

Helmut felt a surge of anger, a desperate need to defend himself, even in this hopeless situation. "I apologize for attempting human interaction."

"You relinquished your humanity years ago, Major."

"You believe all German soldiers are Jew-haters, don't you?" Helmut challenged.

The man smirked. "No. I believe you Germans enjoy killing Jews because of their unpleasant breath."

Helmut, despite his fear, felt a bitter irony rise within him. "A peculiar sense of humor, sir. You won't believe this, but my favorite sister-in-law is Jewish. My wife and my children have no animosity toward Jews. And do you know, despite ordering my men to commit those acts, I never witnessed a single killing? Not once during the entire war."

The man's smile widened, a predatory gleam in his eyes. "Is that so? I must thank you for that admission, Major. Our conversation is being recorded. You've just sealed your fate and the fate of your captain. We had the testimony of a subordinate desperate to save himself. Now we have the complete story."

Helmut's stomach dropped. "Recording? Surely that violates the Geneva Convention?"

The man laughed, a cold, harsh sound. "Slaughtering Jews violates the Geneva Convention. Do you think the Polish courts will concern themselves with such niceties? As they say, 'your goose is cooked.'" He raised his voice. "Guard! Guard!"

The door opened, and a guard entered. The blindfold was reapplied, and the handcuffs were released from the table. Helmut was pulled to his feet, and the agonizing journey through the unknown began again.

CHAPTER FORTY-NINE

Hamburg, Germany
September 6th, 1946, 10:20 a.m.

"Ready, children?" Olga's voice, usually a warm melody, was strained, like a tightrope stretched thin. City Hall. Eleven-thirty sharp. We mustn't be late."

The words hung in the air, heavy with the unspoken. Since Helmut's abrupt arrest two days prior, a cold dread had settled in Olga's stomach. She pushed away the thought of never seeing him in their home again, refusing to give it shape. Mr. Hoffman, their lawyer, had reviewed the Allied evidence. Extradition to Poland loomed, fueled by a ravenous public appetite for retribution. "Revenge" echoed through every news broadcast, every newspaper headline, every whispered conversation on the tram. The Germans heard it time and again across the airwaves: 'The Germans must pay.' It was a litany, a constant, throbbing reminder of the world's judgment. Jewish survivor stories poured from radios, filled newspaper columns, and flickered on the emerging screens of televisions. Authors, sensing the shift in the wind, churned out anti-Nazi articles and books, painting all Germans with the same broad, damning brush—guilt by association.

The walk to Mr. Hoffman's home—his legal downtown practice office, a casualty of the final bombing raid on Hamburg, now replaced by a converted room in his residence—stretched for two kilometers. Olga kept her pace brisk, herding her children along like worried ducklings.

Mr. Hoffman, a man who towered over them, his thin frame accentuated by a pinstriped three-piece suit, greeted them at the door. A colorful silk tie, punctuated by a tiny gold Star of David tie clasp, was a defiant splash of brightness against the somber fabric. His smile, however, faltered as he took in the small procession. "I wasn't expecting the entire family," he said, his voice in a low rumble. "Olga, perhaps a word in my office? Just the two of us?"

Olga's spine stiffened. "No. My children will hear everything. What concerns me concerns them."

He hesitated, his gaze flickering to the children's anxious faces. "Even if it concerns the life or death of your husband?"

Olga met his gaze squarely. "Especially then. They deserve the truth, unvarnished."

He sighed, a sound like rustling leaves. "Very well. Please, follow me."

The office was a sanctuary of learning, a complete wall lined with legal texts that reached from the polished wooden floor to the high ceiling. Mr. Hoffman gestured to two leather wingback chairs positioned before an enormous mahogany desk, the polished surface gleaming in the light streaming through the oversized window. Helmut Junior, as if seeking less prominence, chose a cloth-upholstered side chair. The wallpaper, rich and patterned, hinted at a life untouched by the deprivations of the war years.

Mr. Hoffman closed the door, the click echoing in the sudden silence. He settled behind his desk, his long fingers steepled before him. "Shall we begin?" He cleared his throat, the sound amplified in the quiet room and opened a thick file folder. The pages within, at least fifty of them, rustled ominously. Documents from Polish authorities, crisp and official, mingled with papers bearing the stark insignia of the German Army and the Allied Courts. "The charges are severe."

Olga's voice was barely a whisper. "What evidence do they have?"

Mr. Hoffman's gaze was steady, unwavering. "Initially, it was circumstantial. But Helmut's own words during his first interview with Allied personnel," he trailed off, shaking his head. "Let's just say he eliminated any chance of a 'not guilty' verdict."

Heidi gasped, tears welling in her eyes. Helmut Junior, his face pale, reached for his sister's hand. "We must be strong, Heidi. For Mother."

Olga pressed her lips together, a thin, white line. "Explain. Tell us about this interview."

Mr. Hoffman leaned forward, his voice dropping to a confidential murmur. "Helmut attempted civility. He tried to engage the prosecuting attorney as an old acquaintance, but the small talk quickly evaporated.

When the attorney mentioned the execution of seventy-eight Poles by firing squad, ordered by his unit, Helmut made the worst possible response—crucially, the Allies recorded the entire conversation."

Helmut Junior's voice was tight and anxious. "What did he say? He incriminated himself, didn't he?"

"Completely, but before we address the self-incrimination, you must understand that one of your father's subordinates, a German officer present at the event, saw which way the wind was blowing. The Allies offered a bargain: information leading to your father's arrest and conviction in exchange for leniency. This officer faced extradition to Poland and a certain death sentence. This deal offered him a chance to avoid the hangman's noose, a lengthy prison term, perhaps, but the opportunity to have a life one day."

Helmut Junior's voice was a bitter, choked sound. "So, the Allies knew nothing until they coerced this subordinate? Without his confession, we would have lived a lie, both parents hiding this atrocity forever?" He shook his head, disbelief warring with a dawning, terrible understanding.

Mr. Hoffman nodded grimly. "The Allies engaged in a fishing expedition. They interrogated officers and high-ranking NCOs. Offers were made. They never know if they will find a turncoat. In this case, they found a significant one. Of course, the Allies corroborated the information with the Polish authorities. The Poles confirmed everything: location, time, date, and the number of dead. The confession is meticulously detailed. And yes, while Helmut Senior wasn't present at the actual event, he ordered it. He left the immediate area, but he gave the order."

"And the self-incrimination?" Olga's voice was flat, devoid of emotion.

Mr. Hoffman picked up a transcript, his fingers tracing the typed words. "Here, from the recording, Helmut's own words. He said, and I quote:" *'And do you know, despite ordering my men to commit those acts, I never witnessed a single killing? Not once during the entire war. How can I be held responsible when I was not even there?'*

The attorney paused, letting the words hang in the air. The attorney's response was simple: *"You are just as guilty as those who pulled the trigger. Remember, you ordered the killing of the seventy-eight Polish civilians."* Then, the attorney added, *"Thank you for admitting that you ordered your men to murder the civilians. Mr. Helmut Schotz, the courts here in Hamburg will soon extradite you to Poland to face the charges of murder. What you have stated in this conversation is being recorded. The court will transpose the recording to a transcript that the prosecution will use as an exhibit during your trial."*

Mr. Hoffman looked at Olga, his expression softening with pity. "With this transcript, Olga, a successful defense is implausible. It's a recorded admission of guilt."

Olga reached out, grasping her children's hands. A collective sob escaped them, a wave of grief washing over the small room. "Your poor father," Olga whispered, the words repeated like a broken mantra. "Your poor father."

Mr. Hoffman, his face etched with a mixture of professionalism and compassion, stood abruptly. "I'll be right back." He left the room, leaving them alone with their sorrow.

"He's gone, Mother," Helmut Junior said, his voice raw. "Father is doomed. The Poles will execute him."

Heidi's voice was a fragile thread. "Oh, Mother, what will we do?"

Olga's hands tightened around her children's. "I don't know, darling. I knew so little, but Helmut was always miserable. He hated what he did, but the details—I didn't know the extent."

Mr. Hoffman returned, carrying a delicate porcelain teapot and four cups. "Let's have some tea." Olga poured, her hands trembling slightly, while Mr. Hoffman continued, his voice measured and calm.

"I've practiced law for over twenty years. In this case, there's no viable defense. The evidence is overwhelming. Helmut didn't fire a weapon himself, but that's irrelevant. Worse than pulling a trigger, he ordered the killing as retribution, a reprisal for the death of a single German officer. His own recorded admission seals his fate. Under Polish law, issuing the order is equivalent to carrying out the act."

"What happens now?" Olga's voice was a fragile whisper.

"The extradition date is set. September 16th, 1946. The Polish trial date is pending, but it will be soon after he arrives in Poland."

"Polish trial!" Olga exclaimed, the words laced with a sudden, sharp fear.

"The Poles are expeditious. Trials often last only a day, particularly when the evidence is, as in this case, conclusive. Trial, verdict, and sentencing all in a single day. And the penalty."

In an anxious tone, Helga pleaded, "What is the penalty?"

"Death. By hanging. Usually carried out within weeks of the sentencing."

Heidi cried out, a sharp, piercing sound, and fled the room.

"Helmut," Olga said, her voice strained, "go to her."

"Yes, Mother," he replied, his face ashen.

Mr. Hoffman stared at the papers on his desk, his expression unreadable. "I understand you intend to travel to Poland to support your husband. The Allied authorities will discourage this for your safety. The Polish people will see you as complicit, as more guilty Germans. They will not have sympathy for you or your children. They've seen entire villages and entire families disappear. Retribution is a powerful force." He paused, his gaze meeting Olga's. "If it were my family, I would keep them far from Polish soil."

Olga's chin lifted, a spark of defiance in her eyes. "Regardless of any perceived risk, this family will stand by Helmut. We will be in that courtroom."

They arrived at Hamburg City Hall ten minutes early. A British colonel, ramrod straight and imposing, met them in the lobby. A crisp uniform framed his red hair, freckled face, and blue eyes, and his London accent, surprisingly, delivered fluent German.

"The Schotz family, I presume? Colonel Roger Wzinski. My parents were Polish and were born in Warsaw. I speak Polish, English, a bit of German, and French. I'm here to assist you." He gestured toward an elevator. "We have a private office on the third floor. We can speak there."

The elevator ride was silent, filled only with the hum of the machinery and the weight of anticipation. On the third floor, a corporal issued them "Escorted Visitor" badges, the bold letters a stark reminder of their limited freedom. One family member at a time, with a mandatory search by the MP on duty, was the rule.

"Any questions?" The corporal's voice was brisk and efficient. Seeing their silence, he turned to the colonel. "Colonel Wzinski, the visitors are in your charge."

"Thank you, Corporal."

"Pleasure, sir," the corporal replied, a hint of formality in his tone.

"Introductions?" the colonel asked Olga, his voice softening slightly.

"I am Olga, Helmut's wife. Our son, Helmut Junior, is nineteen, and our daughter, Heidi, is seventeen."

"A pleasure," the colonel said, though his eyes held a hint of sadness. "I wish we had met under different circumstances. I'm here to answer any questions. First, I must prepare you—your husband will look different. His head and face are shaved—standard procedure for prisoners facing such charges—and his clothing is prison garb. Are there any immediate questions?"

Olga's voice was tight. "We understand the extradition is scheduled for September 16th. Our attorney inquired about a possible postponement."

The colonel shook his head. "Unlikely, delays and postponements—well, they happen when the evidence is weak—here, we have a confession that can't be undone. Your husband will be transported by British Air Force transport to Warsaw on the 16th at nine a.m., weather permitting."

"That's unfortunate," her eyes focused on her wedding ring as she twisted the ring about her finger. "Thank you. How long can we visit him?"

"Each family member is allotted twenty minutes every twenty-four hours. Your attorney has unrestricted access."

Heidi spoke, her voice trembling slightly. "Can we bring him anything? Books? Newspapers?"

"One hard-bound book. No newspapers, periodicals, radios, clothing, or bedding. We provide writing materials and postage."

Helmut Junior pressed further. "The trial in Poland, will it be this year? Or a protracted process?"

The colonel hesitated. "I'm reluctant to speculate. Polish tribunals differ significantly from the Nuremberg trials. A one-day trial, with sentencing the same day, is not uncommon, especially with compelling evidence."

Olga's voice sharpened. "And the maximum penalty?"

The colonel's gaze was direct, unflinching. "Mrs. Schotz, I assumed you were aware. If found guilty, your husband will be hanged. I apologize for being so blunt in front of your children, but we are all adults here. The charges are grave. He admitted, on tape, to ordering the massacre. A life sentence is the best he can hope for, and even that, given his age, fifty-eight in December, and the harsh conditions of Polish hard labor, survival is not guaranteed. His only real chance is a 'not guilty' verdict. And, frankly, based on our experience with similar cases, Allied Command believes Mr. Schotz will receive the death penalty."

Olga's voice was a low, controlled fury. "Colonel, do you relish telling Germans there is no hope? Do you derive pleasure from our despair?"

The colonel's face hardened. "Madam, my parents were from Warsaw. I am British but of Polish heritage. And no, I have no prejudice. I also have German ancestry on my mother's side. I'm telling you the truth. Evidence presented by the Allied prosecution in the Nuremberg trials states that six million Jews perished in the death camps. Forgive me if I'm not overwhelmed with emotion over the fate of a German major who ordered the cold-blooded killing of seventy-eight innocent civilians. We have further evidence linking his unit to the deaths of tens of thousands of Jews across Poland. He's fortunate the prosecution is focused solely on the seventy-eight he admitted to. He admitted it, madam, and yes, my command believes he will be found guilty. He will hang."

Olga and her children were weeping, the sound raw and unrestrained. The colonel, without a word, placed a box of tissues on the table. "I apologize for my candor. You're welcome to complain to my superiors. I stand by my words. I sympathize with your impending loss, but my greater sympathy lies with those who lost entire generations to Hitler's 'Final Solution.' Now, who wishes to see Mr. Schotz first?"

Heidi's voice was a broken whisper. "In light of what I've learned, I can't. I want to remember Father as he was earlier this week when we were planning my trip to Heidelberg University. I can't forgive him. I no longer have a father."

Olga's voice was a mixture of sadness and understanding. "Heidi, one day you may regret those words. But you are entitled to your feelings. Perhaps school is the best place for you right now. Your brother can drive you tomorrow. I must stay here, as I'm sure you understand."

"Thank you, Mother. I'll call the Admissions Department. It will be less stressful to be away."

"I understand, Heidi. And I apologize for never telling you about your father's duties."

Helmut Junior spoke, his voice strained. "Mother, may I go first?"

"Of course, Helmut," Olga replied.

"Colonel, can you take my son to see his father?"

"Certainly, madam. The corporal will stay with you."

The colonel left with Helmut Junior, leaving Olga and Heidi with the silent corporal.

The jail-keeper unlocked the cell door, the metallic clang echoing in the narrow corridor. The cell was stark and windowless, containing only a concrete bed, a toilet, and a sink. A thin mattress, a folded army blanket, a sheet, and a pillow lay at the foot of the bed. The smell, a mixture of disinfectant and despair, hung heavy in the air. The ambient noise— shouts, banging, the relentless hum of the ventilation system—created a suffocating atmosphere.

Helmut Junior gasped when he saw his father. The gaunt face, the shaven head and face, and the ill-fitted striped prisoner uniform—it was a grotesque parody of the man he knew. Barefoot, in sandals, his father looked diminished and defeated. But as Helmut Senior recognized his son, a flicker of the familiar smile returned.

"My wonderful son! Thank you for coming." His voice was raspy, weak. "How much time do we have?"

"Twenty minutes, Father. Timed. You look so different."

Helmut Senior gave a weak chuckle. "I can only imagine. There are no mirrors here."

"You look better with hair, Father."

His father's smile faded. "Your mother, how is Heidi?"

Helmut Junior hesitated. "Heidi, she's taking it the hardest. Mother told us about your duties in the Police Battalion. Heidi, she may not come, Father."

A shadow crossed Helmut Senior's face. "I don't blame her. It was difficult for your mother. It took a ton of courage to tell her the truth about my responsibilities. She struggled to understand."

"I wish you had told me, Father."

Helmut Senior's eyes were filled with a profound sadness. "I couldn't bear to disappoint you. My duties were despicable. I deserve what I'm about to receive. Hell and the Devil await me."

"Father, don't—don't talk like that to Mother. Promise me."

"I promise, son. I'll try to be positive for your mother."

"We can bring you one book. A hard-bound book. Is there anything you'd like?"

Helmut Senior's gaze was steady. "Yes. The Holy Bible. I have some catching up to do. I must prepare."

"I'll bring it, Father. But it's our secret. Mother doesn't need to hear this."

Helmut Senior's voice was firm, resolute. "Son, I know my fate. I've seen it since the beginning, since Jozefow. I even said to a colleague, 'There will be no pity for us on judgment day.' I knew we would pay. I'm at peace with it. I deserve it. Please don't—pity me. Ask yourself, why should I be allowed to live after what I've done? The answer, son, is that I shouldn't. I don't."

Helmut Junior felt a surge of conflicting emotions—love, grief, anger, and a terrible, dawning respect. "You're my father. I care for you. But I respect what you've said. It's a confession. We can't undo the past. I love you, Father, but I need to go. I hope to see you tomorrow."

They embraced, a silent exchange of sorrow and farewell. Helmut Junior, his throat tight with unshed tears, signaled to the corporal.

Back in the waiting room, Helmut Junior looked at his mother, his face contorted with grief and wept uncontrollably. "Mother, perhaps you should wait another day?"

Olga reached and cupped her son's tear-stained face, "It is his birthday next week. I am sure your father wishes to hear the latest recording by Bing Crosby.[63] Bing is your father's favorite. You and Heidi can go to the music store and purchase the record. That would be perfect. The Allies are okay with prisoners owning an album?"

"Mother, father doesn't want music."

Olga, her resolve hardening, turned to the colonel. "Take me to my husband. Now."

"Yes, madam. This way."

He paused. "Madam, your son's reaction is not unusual. They look different. They are different. They've accepted their guilt. The 'following orders' defense doesn't hold. They're suffering. Their souls are in agony."

Olga's voice was a low, controlled hiss. "My husband is a good man. He pretended to hate Jews to avoid shame and demotion. Read his letters! He's not the monster you've made him out to be."

"Yes, madam. I understand."

"We're here. Do you need a moment?"

"No. Take me to him."

The cell door opened. Helmut sat on the edge of the concrete bed, his head in his hands. He looked up, his eyes meeting Olga's, and a wave of emotion washed over his face. "Olga, my darling, thank you for coming."

But Olga saw a stranger. This gaunt, hollow-eyed man, with his shaved head and baggy uniform, *was this her Helmut?* A coldness, a distance she hadn't anticipated, settled in her heart.

"Hello, darling," she said, the words feeling hollow, forced. They embraced, but it felt wrong. Different. Like hugging a stranger. She thought, *Have I fallen out of love in an instant?* He looked worse than she could have ever imagined.

She pulled back, stepping away. "I, I can't do this. Not now. I'm sorry, dear. I need to prepare myself. Perhaps tomorrow. I'm afraid of what I might say."

Helmut's voice was a desperate plea. "Please don't go. Don't leave."

Olga turned to the corporal, her voice trembling. "Corporal, take me back to my children."

CHAPTER FIFTY

Hamburg, Germany
September 7ᵗʰ, 1946, 9:15 a.m.

Helmut Junior stood rigid by the second-floor window, his gaze fixed on the street below, the previous night had been a relentless siege. Reporters, their faces grim and insistent, had hammered on Olga's door, desperate for scraps of information about Helmut's imprisonment. Neighbors, their eyes gleaming with a barely concealed curiosity, had offered hollow condolences. Olga hadn't seen this much neighborhood "concern" in years. It was all a sham—a morbid fascination masked as sympathy. Helmut Junior, thank God, had been a steadfast bulwark, deflecting the vultures with a quiet strength that surprised even Olga.

She'd silenced the radio days ago. The constant repetition of her husband's name, each syllable a fresh wound, was unbearable. The clipped, official tones of the announcer still echoed in her mind: "Members of The Polish Supreme National Tribunal[64] will extradite Herr Helmut Schotz Senior, fifty-seven years of age, to stand trial in Warsaw, Poland." The words had been like ice water thrown in her face.

It wasn't just the name but the horrifying details that followed: a former member of the Hamburg Police Department accused, along with two others, of the murder of seventy-eight Polish civilians. The number clawed at her. And then, the casual mention of his family, as if they were mere footnotes to his alleged crimes: "married and has two children."

Olga's carefully constructed future, the one she'd spent years meticulously planning, had crumbled into dust in the ten minutes it took for the authorities to drag Helmut away. The word "future" itself felt alien, a cruel joke.

However, there was more immediate and agonizing turmoil. How could she have embraced Helmut, her Helmut, and felt nothing? The memory of that last hug, cold and lifeless, haunted her. He had felt like a stranger, a hollow shell. Had her heart already condemned him? Could she indeed be married to a murderer? The word felt poisonous on her tongue.

The visit to the prison was a nightmare etched into her memory. The British colonel's condescending lecture, delivered with a chilling formality, the rank, metallic tang of the jail cell, the sour smell of Helmut's prison-issued clothes, his stale breath—each detail was a fresh assault on her senses. But nothing, nothing, had prepared her for the sight of him. Stripped of his hair, his face unnervingly smooth and unfamiliar, he looked alien. The colonel had warned them, but the reality was a brutal shock. Even an innocent man, shorn and dehumanized like that, would struggle to appear anything but guilty.

The colonel's words, blunt and devoid of empathy, had struck Heidi particularly hard. "Her Father commands five hundred men and is responsible for the deaths of tens of thousands." The phrases hung in the air, heavy with accusation. Olga could see the horror reflected in Heidi's young eyes. *This was not the gentle, soft-hearted Helmut they knew. This was a monster.*

But was he? A flicker of doubt, a desperate yearning for the man she loved. The cold logic of the accusations. Jozefow, July 1942, orders from the Reich. But those orders, the ones that condemned seventy-eight souls, *had those been his?* The logical part of her brain, the part that processed facts and evidence, screamed yes. He was a murderer. Olga saw the same grim acceptance dawning in Heidi's eyes.

Helmut Junior had already resigned to his father's guilt—he understood, she sensed, the weight of remorse, the burden of responsibility. But a father was a father, flawed, perhaps even monstrous, but still his father.

Could she find that same acceptance? Could she compartmentalize the man she loved from the crimes he was accused of? The question gnawed at her, a relentless, unanswered plea.

The shrill ring of the telephone shattered the tense silence. Heidi, ever eager for connection, snatched the receiver.

"Hello?"

A formal, male voice responded, "This is Gerhard Kesselring, Dean of Admissions at Heidelberg University. May I please speak with Heidi Schotz?"

"This is she," Heidi replied, her voice bright with anticipation. "How may I help you?"

"Hello, Heidi. We had been looking forward to you joining our pre-med curriculum." The past tense hung in the air, a subtle but ominous shift.

Heidi's brow furrowed. "Excuse me, sir, you said, 'We *had* been looking forward.' Didn't you mean 'are looking forward?'"

Kesselring's voice, though still polite, took on a steely edge. "Heidi, please allow me to explain. The dean of your school has decided the notoriety surrounding your father, Helmut Schotz, the former German major accused of commanding a company of soldiers who committed war crimes," he paused, letting the weight of the accusation settle, "we believe your father's notoriety will generate a significant level of anxiety among the student body and faculty. With you, his daughter, in attendance, it's feared that you and your family will be perceived as Nazis through no fault of your own." He continued, his tone becoming increasingly detached and bureaucratic. "We are concerned that your presence would create an environment where we could no longer guarantee your safety. We believe your life could be at risk. Therefore, we are unable to allow you to attend the university at this time. This decision will be reviewed at the start of the next academic year. I trust you understand the delicate situation your father's arrest has created for both the university and you. Do you have any questions, Heidi?"

Heidi's voice trembled, a mixture of disbelief and outrage. "Questions? Yes, sir, I have many questions. First, can this decision be appealed?"

"No," Kesselring stated flatly. "The Board of Regents, which governs all colleges within the university, has made its final decision. There is no appeal process. Your next question?"

"Sir, my father's case may not even be resolved by the start of the next school year!"

"Heidi, if your father is found innocent, the hold on your enrollment will be lifted immediately."

Heidi's voice cracked. "And what if the Poles hang my father in the next six or seven months?"

Kesselring's voice remained maddeningly calm. "We will inform you of your eligibility to attend should your father be executed. I would advise you to cultivate a more positive outlook in the coming weeks and months. Negative thoughts are detrimental to one's well-being."

Tears streamed down Heidi's face—her control shattered. "This isn't fair! This is utterly unfair! How dare you deny me my education? I'm going to contact a reporter. I'm going to make sure the whole world knows about this! Could you please repeat your title and the correct spelling of your name?"

The line went dead. Kesselring had hung up without another word.

Helmut Junior, who had been listening with a growing alarm, rushed to his sister's side. "Heidi, who was that? Why are you crying?"

Heidi, her voice choked with sobs, recounted the conversation. "They won't let me go to university! Because of Father! They're afraid of bad publicity! Can you believe it? I'm going to tell the newspapers. What do you think, Helmut?"

Helmut Junior's face was a mask of concern. "Oh, Heidi, this is the worst possible timing. Mother is already on the edge. She doesn't need this. Maybe we could tell her you've changed your mind? Something like, you have decided to postpone university for a year. A little lie, for her sake. What do you say? We have to protect her. We can tell her I convinced you. It's the only way to keep her from breaking." He looked at Heidi, pleading with his eyes. It was a conspiracy of kindness born out of desperation.

CHAPTER FIFTY-ONE

New York City, NY
December 3rd, 1960

The scent of coffee and old paper hung comfortably in Chatsworth Williams' home office. Claire pushed the door open gently, a soft smile playing on her lips as she watched her husband. Chats, the phone pressed to his ear, gestured her in with a warm look that still made her heart flutter after all these years. He was deep in conversation, the familiar furrow of concentration on his brow as he navigated the intricacies of airline bookings.

"Yes... Yes, that's right. The sixteenth. Williams, two passengers..." He listened, nodding, then covered the mouthpiece. "Hello, darling. Almost sorted. Seems United can get us back to New York from Chicago after all. Just confirming now."

Claire sank into the worn leather armchair opposite his desk, relief washing over her. "Oh, thank goodness, Chats. You have no idea the state my brother Nathan was in. You'd think the world was ending because our return flight got canceled. He called twice this morning, practically wringing his hands over the phone about us getting stranded."

Chats chuckled, a low, warm sound. "Poor Nathan. Probably didn't sleep a wink. Doesn't he know we'd swim Lake Michigan if it meant getting back for Christmas?" He winked, then turned his attention back to the phone. "Excellent, thank you—Yes, United Flight 826, departing O'Hare—destination Idlewild.[65] Got it. Perfect." He scribbled briefly on a notepad. "Thank you so much for your help."

He hung up, leaning back in his chair with a satisfied sigh. "There we are my love. Booked solid. United 826, a DC-8. Gets us back home at midday on the sixteenth. Plenty of time."

"Oh, a DC-8," Claire mused. "I think I've been on that Chicago-New York run half a dozen times. Feels familiar, safe." She leaned forward, her eyes bright with anticipation. "And yes, plenty of time!

Time to fetch the tree, wrestle with those dreadful tangled lights you refuse to throw out and get everything perfect for the party."

"Our party," Chats echoed, reaching across the desk to take her hand.

Chat's fingers laced through hers, a familiar, comforting pressure. "Wouldn't miss it for the world. It's my favorite night of the year, seeing everyone together."

"Mine too," Claire whispered, squeezing his hand. "Especially seeing the faces from the overseas offices. It feels like we're gathering the whole family." She paused, a thoughtful look crossing her face. "Chats, darling, we should nudge the international teams a bit earlier this year? Remember the chaos last December? Bad weather, missed connections—poor Mr. Tanaka almost missed the entire thing."

"You read my mind," Chats agreed, his thumb stroking the back of her hand. "I'll have Asia draft a memo tomorrow. A firm reminder: book early and allow for potential delays. Our Christmas party waits for no one, not even typhoons or snowstorms."

He smiled, a genuine, loving smile that crinkled the corners of his eyes. Claire returned it, feeling a profound sense of contentment. Their life, built together, felt solid and dependable. The upcoming trip to Chicago, the familiar flight home, the cherished tradition of their Christmas party—these were the threads weaving the strong, beautiful tapestry of their days. Just simple, happy plans unfolding as they always did.

December 15th, 1960
Chicago, Illinois, 8:47 a.m.

"Good morning, Claire, did you sleep well?" Chats asked, the scent of butter and eggs filling the air as he stirred the scrambled eggs and popped in the toast. Breakfast, a simple moment away, felt particularly precious this morning. "By the way, our flight leaves Midway International Airport tomorrow morning at around nine. What do you say? After breakfast, let's call a cab and make a run to Tiffany's. Get gifts for Asia and Jack, something really nice, as they are the absolute glue that holds that place together when we're out of town. What are your thoughts?"

Claire smiled across the small table, her eyes soft. "Oh, darling, that heart of yours. You have such a warm heart. I think your idea is magnificent, simply perfect. Plus, we can walk State Street and eye all the Christmas decorations. I would like that very much, dear. By the way, since we are staying at my brother's home, did you wake him for breakfast?"

"He left a couple of hours ago, said he had errands. Perhaps dinner with Nathan this evening, unless you'd rather it be just the two of us?"

"How often do you get to take me on a date in Chicago?" Clair smirked.

"Okay, we have a date—just the two of us," Chats confirmed, a satisfied warmth in his voice. First, I need to call and check in with Jack before anything else. He might have a few issues bubbling with that new account we landed in Holland. And I must get in touch with Asia—she has quite the 'to-do' list for the company Christmas shindig. I feel guilty, Claire, truly guilty, I know I'm putting too much on her plate this year guilty as charged, I know I am absolutely overboard for the Christmas party."

Claire reached a hand across the table, resting it lightly on his. "Dear, please don't give it a second thought. Asia loves planning our annual Christmas party. You know how she is. She mentioned it to me, buzzing with ideas, shortly after Halloween this year."

"That's my fault," Chats admitted with a fond sigh. "I brought it up on November first this year. I just wanted to get a jump on things."

"Think nothing of it," Claire insisted gently. "She is honestly the only person I know who loves the Christmas holidays more than you, Chats. You know how you get."

Chats chuckled, pouring the last of the eggs onto Claire's plate. "If you say so. Here, dear, your breakfast is ready." He paused, the fork hovering. "Please don't be upset with me, dear—after breakfast, I must call both Jack and Asia. Can't shake the feeling I need to tie up these loose ends."

"Sure, Chats," Claire said, taking her plate. Her gaze held his for a moment, full of quiet affection. "For now, let's just enjoy this wonderful breakfast you prepared. No work talk for a little while longer."

Breakfast had ended, the simple warmth lingering in the air. As Claire efficiently cleared the dishes, Chats opened his briefcase, his movements crisp and focused. He jotted down several notes—reminders to himself about the Holland account, points he needed to cover with Jack. It was the familiar ritual of leadership, even from a distance. Then, with a decisive breath, he picked up the phone and dialed Jack's office line.

"Good morning, Jack, Chats here. Top of the morning to you," he greeted, his voice warm but with that underlying energy of concern. "I hope you are having a stress-free day."

Jack's voice came back sounding surprised, maybe a touch weary. "Wow, you're on vacation, Chats. I hope this is a call about anything but work."

"Almost," Chats replied, a slight smile in his voice. "My main concern is simply that contract with the firm in Holland. Did you finally get the signed paper?"

"Not only the signed contracts, Chats," Jack's tone brightened, pride evident. "The owner, Pierre, and his wife, Mildred, will be here for the Christmas party. I invited them—personally handled the arrangements, paid for the direct flights to get them here, plus their expenses."

Chats felt a wave of relief wash over him. "Jack, this is wonderful news. Truly wonderful. You have absolutely made my day! I wasn't sure they would sign the deal—this is magnificent, truly great news. How about anything else? Any issues brewing? Party plans still going as intended?"

"Chats, we are absolutely on track for the best party on record," Jack stated confidently. "Asia has done a bang-up job getting everything coordinated. You won't believe it."

"This is indeed good news," Chats affirmed, a genuine satisfaction settling in. "Thanks, Jack, for the update. Unless you have anything else, please transfer me to the Vice President in charge of our Christmas party—Asia. She deserves a direct thank you."

Jack chuckled, a clear, relieving sound. "Yes, sir, I will transfer you. Please send our regards to Claire."

"Thanks, Jack," Chats said warmly. "I'm a phone call away should you have any issues before tomorrow. By the way," he added, needing to state the practical detail, the planned endpoint, "we will be boarding the plane tomorrow at about this time. Make a note—we depart Midway International Airport on United flight 962. We've taken this flight several times before. We should be at baggage claim around ten-twenty a.m. or so and drive straight to the office. No fuss."

"Yes, sir," Jack confirmed, his voice crisp again. "I have your flight info right here and have made a note of it. Consider it handled. I'll now transfer the call. Have a great last bit of time in Chicago."

The click of the transfer. A moment of silence. Then Asia's familiar, efficient voice, laced with surprise.

"Hello, Chats. Goodness, I didn't expect a call from you. You are most definitely on vacation, sir?"

"Hello, Asia," Chats replied, the hint of a smile still in his voice from the conversation with Jack. "You're right, I'm on vacation, but the party, well, it's on my mind. Could you provide a summary of your current progress with the planning? To ease a guilty conscience."

"Yes, sir, I can absolutely do that," Asia responded, sounds of rustling papers in the background. "I have my notes right in front of me. First, I am pleased to report that the party will be bigger than last year— more guests, a larger food and beverage budget, as recently approved, thus, more employees from regional offices will be flying in. The bonus checks have been organized and printed. They're ready for your signature upon your return to the office tomorrow. So far, the execution of the plan is flawless. I promise you, sir, this will be the best party in our company history."

"Splendid!" Chats exclaimed, feeling the last vestiges of his travel-induced work anxiety dissipate. "Asia, you have genuinely made my day! You know how much our Christmas celebration means to Claire and me, and most importantly, to all our employees. It's the highlight of the year. If there is nothing else pressing you need me for, Asia, I'll leave you to it."

"Thanks so much for calling, sir," Asia said, her relief palpable that he wasn't calling with problems. "You and Claire enjoy every moment of your time together in Chicago. We'll connect tomorrow after you land."

"God bless you, Asia," Chats said, the sincerity thick in his voice. It wasn't just a pleasantry—he meant it. "I have no idea, honestly, what I would have done without you and Jack all these years. You are truly the glue that holds this company together when I'm not there. All the best, see you both soon."

"Thank you, Chats, for such a nice compliment," Asia replied, her voice warm now. "We will talk tomorrow."

"Bye now," Chats said softly, ending the call. "Talk later. Thanks for your effort, Asia."

The line went dead, and Chats placed the receiver gently back in the cradle, a sense of peace washing over him. Everything was in capable hands. Tomorrow, they will be home.

Manhattan, NY
December 17ʰ, 1960, 9:30 a.m.

It was an overcast day. Not just the sky but the world seemed drained of color, leaching into the air, into the hearts of everyone touched by the news. The events of the previous day, December 16th, 1960, would forever divide time into before and after. Jack sat in his office while Asia rested on the office couch following several episodes of fainting. Her face pale, she trembled slightly despite the medication she had taken to calm her shattered nerves. Neither of them could fully grasp it. Nobody could believe it.

The plane Chats and Claire were on, Flight 962 from Chicago's Midway International Airport—it wasn't a delayed landing; it hadn't diverted. It had impacted another aircraft, a TWA plane, miles away from its destination, colliding violently above the cold skies near Idlewild airport over New York City. Wreckage had fallen onto a neighborhood and a community in Park Slope, Brooklyn. And, as the reporters numbly relayed, as of the last update, there were no survivors.

Not from either plane. Two worlds, two journeys, instantly, terrifyingly ended high above the ordinary world.

Jack sat at the large, polished desk. The desk where Chats had sat for decades. Now, Jack's desk—as he drafted the memo on what to expect in the coming days. Tears tracked slow, hot paths down his face, splashing onto the paper before him. He was putting the finishing touches on a memo. It was now his job, the weight of it crushing him, to notify every single person in their company of the Williams Family's passing. He read and reread the words, the stark, official language, at least fifteen times before his shaking hand lifted the pen to sign. Each word felt like a blow.

The document on company letterhead read:

Date: December 17, 1960
From: Office of Jack Reynolds, President
To: All Hands, All Offices
Subject: The Passing of Mr. and Mrs. Chatsworth Williams—Aircraft crash—New York City

Ladies and gentlemen:
It is with the most profound sadness and heaviest heart that I must officially confirm the devastating news that has, I know, already reached many of you. Yesterday, December 16th, our esteemed President, Mr. Chatsworth Williams, and his beloved wife, Claire, were tragically lost in the major aviation disaster involving a United Airlines Douglas DC-8 and a TWA Super Constellation over New York City.

Mr. and Mrs. Williams were passengers aboard the United Airlines flight, United 962, en route to New York. As has been widely and harrowingly reported, this catastrophic mid-air collision resulted in the unimaginable loss of all passengers and crew on both aircraft, as well as numerous casualties on the ground in the populated areas below the impact zone. Authorities have, understandably, described it as the worst aircraft accident in our nation's history.

The loss of Chatsworth Williams is a profound, irreparable blow to our firm. He was more than just our leader—he was a visionary, a mentor, and a true friend to countless individuals within this organization. Mrs. Williams, with her grace and warmth, was a cherished member of our extended company family. Their absence will be profoundly and acutely felt by all who had the immense privilege of knowing them.

We extend our most heartfelt condolences to the Williams family and to all who are grieving this unimaginable loss alongside us. Management will share information regarding their memorial and funeral services via interoffice correspondence as soon as it becomes available. Please keep the Williams family and all those affected by this tragedy in your thoughts and prayers during this extraordinarily challenging time.

In the midst of this overwhelming tragedy, we must, in accordance with our solemn duty, also address the continuity of our firm's leadership. The company charter, wisely established to provide for such unforeseen and dire circumstances, dictates that the duties and responsibilities of the president pass immediately to the vice president.

Earlier today, our legal team formally enacted this transition. I, Jack Reynolds, have, therefore, with a heavy burden in my heart, assumed the role of president of the firm, effective immediately. Having served as vice president for over ten years, working side by side and learning constantly from Mr. Williams, I am fully committed to navigating our company through this challenging and unprecedented period with the strength and integrity he embodied.

While no one, I know, can truly replace a leader of Chatsworth Williams's caliber, I pledge my utmost effort to ensure the smooth operation of our firm and to uphold the vision, values, and spirit he so deeply instilled in us all.

Your cooperation, understanding, and support during this challenging transition are immeasurably appreciated. Finally, and with deep personal sorrow, in light of these solemn and heartbreaking events, and out of profound respect for Mr. and Mrs. Williams and their grieving family, I have decided to cancel all company-sponsored holiday celebrations this year.

The joy we planned feels impossible now.

Sincerely,

Jack Reynolds
President

Jack signed the memo, his hand steadying finally through sheer will. He ordered the memo to be distributed to all personnel, both foreign and domestic, and to notify all vendors, customer offices, and subcontractors.

A wave of numb finality washed over him as he imagined customers and colleagues worldwide reading of their loss. The company Chats built would continue—he would see to it.

Jack sat quietly at the desk, which felt both familiar and alien —the desk of Mr. Chatsworth Williams, the president. He stared out the window and thought, *Is God preventing clear skies for some reason, is it against His will to allow bright rays of sun in honor of those taken in the air disaster? Yes, this is indeed God's way.*

The city below was a blur he barely registered. The Christmas party. It would never happen. The lights purchased with such anticipation would remain untangled in their boxes. The tree, un-fetched, would stand somewhere else, or not at all. The planned laughter and warmth that should have filled the Williams' home on December 19th, echoing throughout the company family, was silenced forever, replaced by a grief as vast, cold, and overcast as the winter sky on the day they were lost. All that remained were memories, the cruel silence where voices should be, and the gut-wrenching, haunting image that would forever sear itself into the collective consciousness: two hands, reaching for each other, joining together in a final, unbreakable embrace against the vast, indifferent sky.

The news didn't just arrive; it descended like a physical blow, shattering the ordinary rhythm of the days that followed into jagged fragments of disbelief and sorrow. It arrived through choked phone calls that fractured into sobs, through fragmented radio reports that confirmed only the unfolding horror, and through stark headlines screaming a loss too vast, too absolute, to comprehend. For those who loved Chats and Claire, the terrible details were almost unbearable to hear, yet they were agonizingly, compulsively sought—a desperate hope that somehow, some small piece of the truth would be different, kinder.

It never was.

Jack stared at the photograph of Asia on his desk, his heart aching with a hollow throb that mirrored the gaping void left by Chats and Claire. He knew the road ahead would be fraught with an unfamiliar landscape, a path he had to navigate with Asia and Jakub junior by his side. Right now, Asia occupied his every thought. He thought. *How would his sweet Asia ever recover from such a brutal blow? She was already so fragile, buffeted by a lifetime of losses that would have shattered an ordinary person. Chats and Claire were more than just friends; they were the bedrock of their lives. They had been there, in the sterile waiting room, when Jakub was born, their presence a comforting balm. For Jakub, Chats and Claire were the closest he'd ever known to grandparents. Bless them both. Chats' dedication was a quiet testament to their bond. They were at every birthday, every school play, every triumph on the sports field, their unwavering support a constant in Jakub's young life.* Jack's gaze settled on Asia's photo again, his resolve hardening into a fierce, primal need. "I must protect her," he whispered, the words a desperate vow swallowed by the vast silence. "God," he pleaded, his voice cracking, "I promise, I will protect her."

PART III

CHAPTER FIFTY-TWO

Denver, Village of Colfax, Colorado
June 4ᵗʰ, 1974, 4:40 p.m.

The day was a day like no other. He pinched himself several times. He had trouble believing that a high school history teacher was holding in his hand a once-in-a-lifetime opportunity. The invitation, crisp and official, felt like a lead weight in Icek's hand. It was a summons to a past he'd only revisited in words, never in person, since the war. Two years he'd spent transforming the raw, visceral experiences of his eighteen-year-old self—Polish underground fighter—into articles. Now, those stark accounts of survival and resistance had resonated across the Atlantic, earning a reprint in a respected British historical magazine and culminating in this: an invitation to speak before a prestigious group of Holocaust historians. He was speechless.

Denver, Village of Colfax, Colorado
June 13ᵗʰ, 1974, 6:15 a.m.

The society, a gathering of Europe's leading historians, found his narrative compelling. A young Pole, fighting the Nazis, immigrating to America, earning a master's degree, and now teaching history to high school students—it was a story they wanted to hear firsthand.

He read it to himself once again: *Icek Abram Kelner, age fifty, will present a candid account of his experiences as a Jew in 1942 Poland. He will recount the morning of July 13, 1942, when, at eighteen, he witnessed a Nazi SS officer murder his grandmother and his two ten-year-old twin sisters. He will also share his experiences as a member of the Polish underground, the Polish Home Army.*

He'd tried to persuade Teodora to come, sketching visions of a shared journey, a chance to heal. But her refusal was a wall built of pain. The wounds of Europe remained too raw—the continent was a phantom limb, aching with every whispered memory.

The location chosen by the Cambridge-based organizing committee felt like a cruel twist of fate—the Centre for Historical

Studies at the Neuengamme Concentration Camp in Hamburg, Germany.[66] The former brick factory, once a crucible of unimaginable suffering that dated back to 1938, now stood as a stark monument to a six-year reign of terror.

Icek closed his eyes, picturing the ghosts trapped within those walls, tens of thousands of souls, reduced to enslaved people, digging canals, toiling in clay pits, manufacturing arms for the very regime that had stripped them of their humanity. *Neuengamme*—One of northwest Germany's largest concentration camps. A place where a crust of bread was a king's ransom, where brutality was a twisted currency, and where almost 43,000 men, women, and children met their end before British soldiers finally threw open the gates on May 2nd, 1945.

Teodora's voice, sharp with anxiety, pierced his grim reverie. "Icek, passport? Tickets? Do you have everything?" She paused, her gaze sweeping over him as if searching for flaws, for cracks in his composure. "We are so very proud. Such an influential group choosing you. But Hamburg of all places." She shook her head, a flicker of disbelief, almost anger, in her eyes. "Why there? A discussion about the Holocaust there? It's insensitive. Who thought that was a good idea? Clearly, someone without an ounce of empathy." She paused, visibly gathering herself. "I know it was over forty years ago. But still."

She straightened, her voice regaining its familiar, unwavering strength. "I need phone numbers. Addresses. Your contact person. A copy of your schedule. Flight information. Everything. Just in case."

He tried to lighten the mood, but the words felt hollow even to him. "Just in case I get kidnapped?" He managed a weak smile. "Dear, this isn't the Europe we left. It's different. Downtown Denver and Hamburg—you wouldn't know the difference, except the words sound different."

Teodora remained unconvinced—her eyes narrowed. "Perhaps. But there are thugs and criminals everywhere."

He saw the genuine fear beneath her stern exterior. "You're right," he conceded. "It's smart. I'll make copies of everything. Even my passport. Apparently, those are worth a fortune on the European black market."

At Stapleton Airport,[67] his family enveloped him in a final, tight embrace. His Eastern Airlines flight to La Guardia at 11:15 a.m., the three-hour layover, and then the TWA flight to Hamburg stretched before him like an endless road. He kissed his two children, his hand lingering on their hair as he inhaled their scent. Then, Teodora.

"Be safe," she whispered, her hug almost painful in its intensity, her kiss carrying the weight of unspoken fears.

Hamburg, Germany
June 15th, 1974, 1:40 p.m.

The overnight flight had been blessedly uneventful, though sleep had been a restless, fragmented thing, punctuated by the constant drone of the engines. Stepping off the plane in Hamburg, he felt the disorientation of a body yanked across time zones, across 7,900 kilometers (about 4,900 miles) of ocean. He scanned the airport, the modern architecture, and the gleaming floors, so shockingly different from the images of wartime Germany that still lingered, sharp and vivid, in his mind. *This is not the Germany I left.*

It was early afternoon, local time, a full eight hours ahead of Denver. His family wouldn't even be thinking of waking for another three hours. He hailed a cab, a simple, everyday act that served as a small anchor in the present.

"Any tips for jetlag?" Icek asked the cabbie, his voice thick with fatigue. "I feel, well, like warmed-over death—first time flying from the States. And maybe a recommendation for dinner? A good beer wouldn't hurt."

The cabbie chuckled—his English tinged with a heavy German accent. "Warmed-over death? That's a new one. It's a good expression. I'll have to remember that." He paused, considering. "The best cure? A nap. Two hours, at least. Then, dinner, a few drinks, a good night's sleep. Voila! You're on Hamburg time. Coming back home? Maybe the same." He tapped a card tucked into the visor. "For dinner, I recommend the Schloss Restaurant Bergedorf. It's in the Bergedorf Castle.[68] Dates back to 1220. Give me a call, and I'll take you."

"Thank you. Icek Kelner, from Denver, Colorado."

"Hans Brecht, from Berlin. Pleased to meet you." He hesitated, then added, "Your accent is American, but I can't quite place it."

"People from Colorado supposedly have a bland accent. Difficult to pin down."

"I once had a passenger from eastern Tennessee. I couldn't understand a word. Sounded like Japanese. It was exhausting. 'Please repeat?' constantly."

As Hans turned, Icek caught sight of a jagged, discolored scar snaking up from beneath his collar on the right side of his neck. He couldn't help but stare.

Hans noticed his gaze. "The scar," he said, a hint of resignation in his voice. "Everyone notices. Panzer tank commander, Battle of the Bulge.[69] An Allied soldier—good shot—fifty-caliber bullet. I was lucky. Or maybe someone 'up there' was looking out for me." He shook his head. "The rest of my crew burned alive. The Yanks treated me well. Like I was one of their own. I recovered in a British hospital. I never understood it. Such kindness to the enemy. And the food! And the nurses!" He trailed off, a wistful smile playing on his lips.

They arrived at the Hotel Sachsentor Hamburg Bergedorf. Icek studied the building, a peculiar mix of 1930s-style architecture, despite its 1973 construction date. Smaller than the pictures had made it seem, just four floors, thirty-five rooms. *My home for five days.* Exhaustion, heavy and palpable, washed over him. All he wanted was a bath and oblivion.

"Could you come back later? Say, seven p.m.? Take me to that castle restaurant?"

"My pleasure, sir. Seven p.m. sharp. I'll help you with your bags."

"Thank you. See you then."

Icek checked in, feeling the full weight of the journey pressing down on him. He couldn't recall ever feeling this utterly depleted. He gave silent thanks to the event Group Chair for scheduling his presentation for Monday afternoon. He needed the weekend. To rehearse. To explore. To strengthen himself for what lay ahead.

He woke hours later—the room shrouded in dim light. It was three p.m. He dialed Hans's number.

"Good evening, Icek Kelner. Decided not to wait until 7:00 PM?" Hans's voice was surprisingly bright.

The taxi pulled up to the hotel. "Good evening. Glad you could reschedule, Herr Brecht."

"Not a problem. I hope you slept well. Where to?"

"The Hamburg Police Department."

"The police department? Are we bailing someone out?"

Icek chuckled, appreciating the dry humor. "Good, you have a sense of humor."

"We should be there in twenty minutes. Relax. Enjoy the ride. Anything you want to see along the way, ask."

Fifteen minutes later, the taxi stopped in front of an imposing building. Icek stared at it, guessing its age to be around seventy-five years. *The animal who murdered Ryfka and the twins walked through those doors many times. The Hamburg Police Headquarters. The very place where men, utterly devoid of humanity, had planned their daily hunts, packing innocent Jews onto trains bound for death. Those bastards. And now, I will walk through those same doors.*

"Shall I wait?" Hans asked, breaking into his thoughts.

"Yes, please. I shouldn't be long."

"Herr Kelner. Are you alright? You were a thousand kilometers away. Are you sure you are well?"

"I was elsewhere—plus my jetlag—I'm fine, really." He stepped out of the taxi and pushed through the heavy doors of the police station.

A young woman, her smile professional and welcoming, greeted him. "Guten Morgen, sir. Wie kann ich Ihnen helfen?"

"Do you speak English?" Icek asked.

"Certainly, sir. How may I help you?"

"I'm interested in historical information about the Police Battalions during World War II. Is there anything available to the public?"

"Yes, sir. We have a history room open to the public. Many items and artifacts for our future Hamburg Police Museum."

"Photographs? Of the policemen?"

"Yes, group photos, individual photos, a great many."

"Excellent! Could you point me in the right direction? Is most of it in German?"

"Yes, but we are in the process of translating into many languages. It's a slow process. A vast amount of information."

"Wonderful. I'll get my associate. He's waiting outside. I'll be right back."

Icek returned to the cab. "Hans, would you be willing to translate for me? Do you happen to have a pen and paper? I need to take notes."

"Of course. I have both. I'll come with you."

They walked back inside. The young woman had been replaced by an older gentleman in civilian clothes, probably in his late sixties. *Filling time until retirement*, Icek thought.

"Good morning, sir. How may I help you?" The officer introduced himself as Captain Alvin Stein.

"Your English is excellent. I'm Icek Kelner, a high school history teacher from Denver, Colorado. I'm here for a conference. My students are working on a long-term research project on World War II in Poland. We continue the research each year with a new group of students. It's challenging to maintain continuity. But it is a worthwhile project. We've been at it for three years."

"Before we begin, sir, may I see some identification? Some verification that you are, indeed, a teacher. We try our best to keep reporters and private investigators out of our 'under construction' soon-to-be museum. You understand, correct?"

Icek pulled out his wallet, presenting his Colorado driver's license, his Colfax High School credentials, and his passport. "I teach eleventh and twelfth-grade history. Colfax is a suburb of Denver."[70]

"Excellent. What can I do for you?"

"Could you tell me who within the German government, decided to involve the Hamburg Police Department in the war?"

"I was a desk sergeant at the time. I remember it vividly. The orders came from the very top—military command. I wasn't selected to go. I was the glue holding the department together while the Police Battalions were in Poland. That decision was far above my pay grade."

"Did you know Major Helmut Gunter Schotz?"

"Wow, that's a name I haven't heard in many years. Yes! We were close friends for many years. You know the Poles hanged him. In 1948."

"Yes. We've covered that in my class."

"Helmut and I, our families, socialized together. Our children are similar in age. And his wife, the most beautiful policeman's wife in the department. Truly stunning."

"What was he like?"

Captain Stein hesitated as if searching for the right words and with a shrug, continued, "That phrase from America, 'Non-violent'? That was Helmut. He wanted nothing whatsoever to do with violence. His men called him 'Pops.' Like a beloved uncle. He appeared much older than his actual age. Too much beer, perhaps." He chuckled softly. "We knew privately that he was sympathetic to Jews. His brother had married a Jewish woman. He was overly kind even to the hardened criminals. I watched him handle thugs as if they were merely misbehaving children. It was a mistake to put him in command of five hundred men. He should have been a priest. Not a cruel bone in his body."

"But wasn't he convicted in a Polish court?"

"Yes. A one-day trial. Guilty. Hanged—we were stunned."

"I hope you don't mind. I need to take some notes. This is invaluable for our project."

"Not at all. Ask anything. I retire in a few weeks. What are they going to do? Fire me?" He laughed, a dry, rasping sound.

"Congratulations on your impending retirement. Well-deserved, I'm sure."

"Thank you."

"What do you know about his direct reports? We heard that the Allies hung some. Is that accurate?"

"Not at all. Helmut had three direct reports. And they all survived the war."

"Survived?"

"Yes, sir. Prison sentences. The trials didn't take place until the 1960s. The Allies never apprehended them. Now they're all free. I saw one in the beer hall just last month. Not in good shape. Blind in one eye, blurred vision in the other. A leg amputation shortly after the war due to infection from a shrapnel wound. And upstairs." He tapped his temple. "Not well. Shellshock, I suspect. Although it was never formally diagnosed."

"Do you have a photograph of Helmut and his subordinates?"

"Yes. Let's go to the photo history room."

Captain Stein led Icek and Hans down a narrow corridor and into a large room. Dozens of black and white photographs, each meticulously matted and framed, were displayed on freestanding wall sections: each picture a captured moment in the history of the Hamburg police.

Icek's palms were slick, his heart hammering against his ribs. *Am I about to see, for the second time, the face of the man who murdered my grandmother and sisters? Will I recognize him? Is it possible for me to find him on my first visit to Hamburg?*

"Mr. Kelner, you look pale. Are you unwell? Would you like to sit down?" Captain Stein's voice was filled with concern.

"It's the flight that arrived this morning. Spent the whole night— barely slept."

Captain Stein nodded. "Yes, I took my family to Disneyland several years ago. We were exhausted for days afterward."

"Could you point out Helmut in any of the photographs?"

"Certainly. He's hard to miss. The oldest, the heaviest Battalion 101 member. He had a fondness for sauerbraten and beer. And his wife was an exceptional cook. My wife and I dined at their home on many occasions. Everyone called him 'Papa.' And yes, 'Papa' was the commander of Police Battalion 101. It was dreadful that the case against him was so flimsy. As I said earlier, the Poles executed him." Stein's voice cracked with emotion.

Icek, summoning his most sympathetic tone, murmured, "I'm sorry to hear about the loss of your friend."

"Here, this is a photograph of Papa. As I said, he looked old."

The photograph showed a man who appeared more like a kindly grandfather than a military commander. His eyes, surprisingly, held a gentle, almost weary expression, not the cold, stern gaze Icek had anticipated.

"Yes, he does look old. Perhaps in his fifties when he passed away?"

"Yes, I believe so. He looked far older than his actual age. Perhaps the Lord is punishing him even now," Mr. Stein said somberly.

Icek, puzzled, asked, "Why do you say that? Perhaps he confessed his sins to the Almighty?"

"It's possible. Religion and I are not well-acquainted. After witnessing what I saw during the war years—the suffering, the death, the starvation, and so on—where was God? Was He taking a leave of absence for a decade or so while Herr Hitler destroyed the Fatherland?" Stein paused—his gaze fixed on the photograph. "I apologize for the rhetorical question. As you'll discover during your time in Germany, many of us have not fully recovered from the war."

"I understand completely. All of Europe was decimated by Herr Hitler's actions and the destruction caused by Allied bombing."

"I'm sorry, I shouldn't dwell on it. Those times were beyond comprehension for so many. Looking back, I, like millions of others, bought into the entire movement. Today, I'm a different person."

Mr. Stein moved toward a filing cabinet and retrieved a thick binder.

"Here is the photo album of the members of Battalion 101. This is it, yes."

"Please, have a seat at this reference desk. Take your time. If you need anything, my office is just down the hall, the first one on the left. I'll leave you to your research for now. And again, I apologize for my earlier outburst. I truly am. The war ended over thirty years ago, but for many of us, it feels like yesterday."

"There's no need to apologize. You witnessed history unfold before your eyes. Another factor was that there were likely very few Germans who didn't support the movement at the time. I understand."

Hans began to wander around the room, examining the exhibits, while Icek carefully paged through the thick album of photographs. After over an hour of detailed study, Icek stood up abruptly. Hans couldn't help but notice.

Icek stood frozen, staring blankly ahead. He felt as if he had seen a ghost.

Hans quietly approached and, looking over Icek's shoulder, saw him staring at an 8x10 photograph.

Wiping sweat from his forehead, Icek thought, *those evil eyes, the thin lips, and the scars on his left cheek—you wicked bastard, I recognize you. You are a worthless excuse for a human being.* The image was a clear, black-and-white photograph of Papa, flanked by his three direct reports. Icek froze. He stared into the eyes of the man on the far right and thought *I recognize you—the same cold eyes, the same cruel set of mouth.* The man who had murdered his grandmother and his sisters. *How can I get Stein to identify the men in this photo?*

He turned to Hans, discreetly checking to see if Captain Stein had re-entered the room. "I need to use the restroom. Excuse me."

Icek stepped out of the room, glanced left and right, and saw Captain Stein approaching him in the hallway, about two meters away.

Stein, his brow furrowed with concern, asked, "Are you alright? You're perspiring, and it seems like you might be suffering from more than just jet lag. You're pale. Can I get you something to drink? Are you sure you're okay?"

"Very little sleep, and that spicy spaghetti I had on the plane didn't agree with me. It's rather urgent—the location of the men's room?"

Stein gestured down the hall. "Men's room about twenty meters on your left."

Five minutes passed before Icek emerged from the restroom, nearly colliding with Stein.

"It must have been the airplane food and that extra glass of wine. I feel much better now. I appreciate your concern."

Stein approached him and said, "Well, Mr. Kelner, I'm glad to hear it. You certainly look better. So far, as a man of education, what do you think of our small museum? As you can see, the information here is valuable for documenting the department's history, but it's not fully organized. We don't have the budget for a historian yet. Perhaps someday. Have you found anything of interest so far?"

Icek, thinking quickly, replied, "First, the quantity and quality of the photographs—you have an excellent start to a first-rate exhibit. I hope that when I bring my family next year, your project will be completed—

although I know I'll have to work hard to persuade them to see any WWII exhibits."

"Unfortunately, I will be retired by then. By the way, I am rather surprised that you are studying the Holocaust. What are your reasons?"

"I understand. For me, it is a morbid hobby—in fact, I am no longer permitted to bring up the topic when my wife or two teenage children are present. My wife states the subject matter is too depressing, and my son uses a different term, *sicko!*"

Stein asked, "I am guessing you were a history major?"

Icek responded, "Absolutely, with a Holocaust Studies major."

"I have never heard of a program devoted to the Holocaust!"

"Yep, in fact, in America, one can attain a Doctorate in Holocaust Studies."

Stein continued with his barrage of questions, "What would you say students and the public find of interest regarding the subject of the Holocaust?

Icek had been thinking along the same lines for some time, "Hard to say, yet students would be very interested in looking through your materials. Most importantly, I would suggest having access to the past so that the public, both old and young, can be given the chance to learn about history, the good, the bad, and the evil."

Captain Stein was proud to share, "The new German credo, *Never again*—this applies to our efforts, and of course, *No more.*

"Do you have any knowledge of Battalion 101 vets who survived the War that are alive, still surviving in Hamburg? It would make for an excellent presentation." Icek quickly said, "My error in asking. Let's not go there. Please accept my apology. A long-time student of mine asked about the involvement of SS troops and Battalion 101."

Stein was quick to reply, "In my nearly four decades of service, that is a topic I haven't thought of. Now that you are reminding me, yes, there was one I was acquainted with. Papa often mentioned to me that one of his two assigned SS officers was ruthless and devoid of compassion.[71] He derived pleasure from witnessing people's suffering."

Icek thought *it sounds like the Poles executed the wrong man.*

"He was one of two Nazi SS members assigned to the battalion. And he's still alive. Wilhelm Wahl. He and his wife, Helen, a retired schoolteacher, reside here in Hamburg. A German court tried Wahl and several other war criminals in 1966. Six years following a war tribunal for *'crimes against humanity,'* a novel phrase coined after the war that originated and was adopted in the Charter of the International Military Tribunal (Nürnberg Charter), which tried surviving Nazi leaders in 1945. They granted him parole after he had served four years. I heard that Wahl wept like a child when Hitler took his own life. Things were different back then. Hitler revitalized the economy swiftly. When he assumed power, it took a wheelbarrow full of marks to buy a single loaf of bread. He constructed the autobahn and numerous other national-type projects. The economy flourished as never before. As a teacher, you're familiar with these facts. Then everything shifted. He invaded one country after another, the death camps, the extermination of the Jews, and the bombing of England. His gravest error was the Jews. He descended into madness. And Wilhelm Wahl was a staunch supporter. Many believed that Hitler was divinely appointed. Not I. The longer I live and the more I discover about the atrocities, the more I detest the Germany of the war years. Hitler was the embodiment of evil. I am relieved to declare that I remained an honorable police officer throughout the war."

CHAPTER FIFTY-THREE

Hamburg, Germany
June 15th, 1974, 11:44 a.m.

"Are you okay?" the cabbie asked. "The color's drained from your face. You look a little like my grandad did before they took him away. Can I stop at a beer hall and perhaps get you a drink?"

"You know, a drink does sound quite nice at this point. Yes, let's have a drink. Are the pubs even open this time of day?"

"Yup. I know just the place."

"Will I be depriving you of business?"

"I drive a cab to get out of the house. Plus, it's not often that I have the opportunity to have an American in tow."

"Regardless, this is my treat," Icek said.

"I must go the non-alcoholic route. I could lose my taxi license if the local police were to catch a whiff of alcohol on my breath."

"Yes, I am sure, we have similar laws in Colorado. Again, my treat, whatever you want to drink."

The cabbie pulled in front of what appeared to be a building straight out of the 1800s. A green and white striped awning, stretched taut over the front entrance, spanned the width of the entire structure. Two large windows, at least three meters wide and four meters high, flanked the towering, three-meter-tall entrance door. The building was a weathered combination of beige-colored brick, tile, and mortar. Towering, ancient elms, their leaves rustling softly, provided shade over more than a third of the multi-story structure.

Once inside, an all-wood bar of deep mahogany, polished to a mirror sheen, stretched at least ten meters long. The air hung thick with the scent of stale beer and old wood. The craftsmanship was unparalleled, a level of detail Icek had never seen. The bar was adorned with countless antique furnishings that whispered of decades of laughter and secrets. The back of the bar had three equal-spaced arched openings, each a portal into a reflected world, complete with a mirrored back, wooden posts, and exquisite trim everywhere. The bar surface was made of solid marble and appeared to be a vast, monolithic piece. Icek ran a hand over its cool, smooth surface. Each person in the bar reminded Icek of characters he'd once seen in an old Hollywood movie from the mid-thirties. The bar appeared to be the perfect place for a disappearing act, a haven for one wishing not to be seen by the rest of society.

It was clearly a popular place for the area's senior citizens, as no one below fifty was in the bar. A low hum of conversation filled the air, punctuated by the clinking of glasses.

The bartender, a short man, seemingly eighty years of age, perched a golfer's wool cap jauntily on his head. He wore a starched, light-blue, Oxford, button-down shirt and a deep-green apron that covered his chest to his knees. He was overweight, with cheeks that sagged more than Icek had ever seen. Speaking German, he asked, "What will it be, gentlemen?"

"Beer for my American friend, here. Get him a Holsten Pilsner. Let him sample Hamburg's best. For me, a cup of tea."

"Hans Brecht, you know I would not serve you alcohol. Glad you didn't ask," the bartender replied, a hint of a smile playing on his lips. "Here you go, gents," the bartender said, his voice raspy, as he placed two drinks on the bar.

"What do you think of my favorite watering hole, Icek?"

"This is quite the experience. I've never had a drink with a cabbie in my life. I guess we're bonding, aren't we?"

"It is rare for me to have the opportunity to have an American passenger, add to this, one with an accent."

"You think I have an accent beyond my American accent?"

"Yes. I detect an Eastern European tilt to your words."

"Good. Can you narrow it down?"

"I would say Ukrainian or Polish?"

"Yes. I am Polish. I come from a small town in southern Poland called Jozefow."

"Not a town that rings a memory for me."

"Not surprising. It is a small village in the Lublin Province.[72] It had fewer than two thousand people living there at its peak. By the way, in 1942, the German Police Battalion 101 murdered over fifteen hundred Jozefow Jews.[73] I was lucky to have escaped. Not so for my grandmother and twin sisters, whose deaths I witnessed. I saw the life leave their eyes."

Hans's cheerful demeanor evaporated. He placed a hand on Icek's shoulder.

Icek, with a solemn tone, uttered, "The Nazis sent my father to a slave-labor munitions facility in Poland. God blessed my father with luck that day, or so we thought at the time. We have not seen or heard from my father since that day. Even with the help of the Red Cross, a system in operation since 1939 to find lost loved ones in war-torn areas of the world, we have been unable to generate a lead.

"We found out that the Red Cross has a better chance of locating a missing person if others are seeking the same person. In a nutshell, if others have not inquired, the chances of a hit in the Red Cross data diminish astronomically. We refuse to give up. The only information I have is that Father left Jozefow in July 1942, shortly after the mass murders there. This information is from witness testimony from the person at the rail depot. From his sworn testimony, we can see that the train's final destination was a munitions facility—Skarżysko-Kamienna, in Poland.

"We found out that a year or so after the war ended, the Germans destroyed all prisoner records before the Allies liberated the facility toward the latter part of the war. The information is cold from that point on. Is he alive? Only God knows that answer.

"The hardest part of this is not knowing what to do. Today is June 15th, 1974, about a month shy of thirty-two years since I last saw my father. My wife, my son, and I all participate in writing to different government agencies in Germany and the United States. We refuse to give up."

Hans' voice lowered, "Most of the German military had no clue as to what was going on in the death camps. We were as surprised to see the extermination camps as those in the West. There were rumors while in the Panzer Tank Battalion. The stark number of victims was hard to believe. We were all surprised to hear that the Germans murdered millions of Jews. I can tell you, all Germans to this day are ashamed of this chapter of our history."

"Not a statistic to be proud of, for sure," Icek remarked, his voice heavy.

"Now I understand your interest in the Hamburg Police Station, I think?" Hans said, his eyes searching for Icek's.

"Yes, you are correct. The man in the picture is the man who murdered my sisters and my grandmother. I have wanted to meet this person and speak on a one-on-one basis. If we met face-to-face, there would be scarce room in my heart for forgiveness—someone would likely have to restrain me from murdering him with my bare hands—that said, taking revenge is entirely against the teachings of the Jewish religion."

"I would want to stick a knife in his heart if it were my family. You would have every right."

"I was one of the youngest Polish Home Army members in history. I was an interrogator, with my wife and her brother. Thankfully, they were both fluent in German. We were part of the Polish Home Army. Fortunately, we didn't typically do the dirty work. If we had someone who didn't want to talk, we had volunteers who sought endless revenge for what the Germans had done to their family members. It was simple—if a German soldier refused to talk, they used plenty of painful, unsavory torture methods to get the information they wanted. In the end, they didn't waste time.

"At times, we interrogated Germans from dusk to dawn. We were always short on ammo, so one of our team outside of interrogations would end a German's life—it was a sharp knife to the neck. Bullets were precious. You become hardened to war and witnessing the taking of German life, particularly when I watched a German officer butcher members of my family. I couldn't be bothered. I had more remorse when a soldier brought in a slaughtered rabbit for a meal. We turned over the prisoners to other members of the Home Army. The only ones spared were high-ranking German officers. We had no time to keep a log of the prisoners killed. You do know, don't you, the Germans did the same to us Poles."

"I am glad I missed the village fighting. I was always in a tank column heading toward what seemed to be an endless race to defeat General Patton. What you faced was well beyond the carnage we experienced. We rarely saw the face of an enemy soldier."

"Before becoming interrogators, our command trained us in demolition and explosives. We blew up trains, tanks, trucks, and formations of men, among other targets. We threw Molotov cocktails on formations of German soldier units as they came into our villages. We weren't allowed to end the lives of German soldiers as they tried to escape the flames. Our command wanted the word to get out that we could be as brutal as the Nazis. My children have no idea of my background.

"The story I give my students is that German soldiers pursued me from July of 1942 through the war's end. My high school students are under the impression that I was forever evading capture."

"Now I understand your reaction to the photo." Hans's eyes softened with a newfound understanding.

"You now know more than I have told anyone since the war ended. It feels good to get this off my mind." Icek took a long drink of his beer, the foam leaving a trace on his upper lip.

"You are a better man than I. I could never be quiet about such violence on my own family."

"It has been difficult through the years. I have recurring nightmares about some of the horror our group carried out—the sense of revenge we all had at the time. We were out for nothing less than blood. As time passed, I had more trouble recognizing myself as the vengeful person who inflicted so much carnage on German soldiers. Trust me, many of us were unaware of the death camps in the fall of 1943. There were plenty of rumors that the Germans took many Polish citizens from their homes and placed them in ghettos, where many starved to death. Then, months later, we heard the German command forced those in the ghettos onto train cars for shipment to the death camps."

"What you have described, and remember, I am German, a veteran of the German Panzer division. I, too, would have reacted in the same manner as you. The ghosts of what you described will live in your mind for the rest of time."

"We understood that any German soldier, given the opportunity, would either hang us or have us before a firing squad. By the way, the soldiers we came across were well beyond what we recognized as the definition of cruelty. Even those victims the Germans executed by hanging, after enduring a living hell of torture, lost their lives with the executioner's torment. This type of evidence made fighting the Germans with a vengeance easy," Icek remarked.

"Have you thought of revenge, or let me ask the question differently?[74] How have you *NOT* had thoughts of revenge? I would have tracked down that animal of a human and made sure he did not wake up the next day. And again, this is from a German soldier of the Reich."

"My post-war teachings do not permit me to have such thoughts. I paid no attention to that belief during the war. I will most likely pay for my sins one day. I know now that taking revenge is prohibited in Judaism. Our Jewish Bible teaches that taking revenge is a bad trait. The Code of Jewish law concludes that 'one should erase any feelings of revenge from one's heart and never remind oneself of it.'"

"There may be something similar in my Lutheran religion. That said, I would still kill the son of a bitch."

"Trust me, I have often thought about tracking him down, ending his life, and living happily ever after. It would be easy because killing is a simple choice. However, as I have said, as a practicing Jew with a wife and two children, I cannot go there."

"As I said earlier, you're a better man than I. Let's order another drink?"

"Yes. You talked me into it," Icek said.

Captain Alvin Stein stepped into a pub about three blocks from the police station. He approached the pub manager. "Manfred, I need to use the phone in your office. A private call, you know, kind of hush, hush."

"The call is legal, right?" He smiled as he handed over the key. "You are too old to be chasing leg, and I trust it is a personal matter. What kind of personal, exactly? Maybe you *are* chasing leg?" Manfred asked.

"You have worked for the department for how long? Don't make an old guy explain. Chasing leg—I only wish. Thanks for the compliment."

Alvin unlocked the office and entered the room, locking the door behind him. He dialed the number of Otto Streicher, the maniacal former SS officer and member of the Hamburg Police Battalion 103, a sister to the 101. He took a deep breath before speaking.

Alvin Stein's curiosity had turned into a full-blown investigation. "Hello, Otto, Alvin Stein here. I have a few minutes to speak. I need to bring something to your attention. We had an American, a high school teacher, in the photo room of the station today asking questions about 101."

"Did you call me for this? Who cares about an American tourist?" Streicher's voice was sharp, dismissive.

"He is not 'any American' tourist."

"What's unique about this American tourist?"

"He speaks American with an Eastern European accent. I am convinced that he is Polish. He asked to see a picture of Papa and his direct reports. When I showed the picture to him, he exhibited some interesting body language—he avoided all eye contact, and sweat beads formed on his forehead. It was an odd reaction."

"Do you think he has some connection to those murdered?"

"It has to be."

"Whatever you do, don't let anyone allow this person to enter the police offices. It should be easy to create a description of the man."

"Don't worry. This American will never get in our offices."

"Until we know his motivations, you must start a tail on this man and watch each move he makes. And remember, you must keep me in the loop." Streicher's voice was now cold, calculating.

"Understood. I think I will investigate on my own in the meantime."

"If you find out something you think I need to know, call me anytime. This guy may be here to seek revenge. And who knows how far he might take it."

Captain Stein hung up the phone and dialed his secretary in his office.

"Hello, this is Ingrid Mueller. How may I help you?"

"Hello, this is Alvin. I need you to drop whatever you're doing and see what you can find out about any seminars in Hamburg between tomorrow and the next few days."

"What might the topic be, sir?"

"Any event that an American high school teacher who teaches history may find interesting. I'm unsure whether the person we are looking for is an attendee or a speaker. Look for the name Icek Kelner of Colorado."

"Is this the American who came into the station asking to see the historical photos?"

"That's right, and you met Mr. Kelner. Perhaps when you make your inquiries, you can describe the American. Could you work on this now?"

"Yes, sir. I have a couple of contacts down at the tourism department that may be able to help me."

"Ingrid, as soon as you find out, you must contact me on my car radio. The sooner, the better." Stein's voice was urgent.

"Yes, sir. I'll see what I can find out."

CHAPTER FIFTY-FOUR

Hamburg, Germany
June 16th, 1974, 10:17 PM

The cabbie's eyebrows lifted. "So, how was the German take on Chinese?"

"Better than the American version, actually," Icek said, patting his stomach. "Must be the ingredients."

"You certainly put a dent in it. That was the largest spread of Chinese food I've ever seen." Hans added with a groan, "The most I've ever eaten. I'm going to need a serious nap."

Outside the restaurant, the humid Hamburg air hung heavy. Icek turned to Hans, his voice dropping slightly. "You haven't forgotten, have you? About me finally seeing where the animal that slaughtered my family resides, you know, an innocent peek from the confines of the cab? No stopping, no getting out, just a quick pass by of his home. I'm more than curious to see where the murdering animal resides."

Hans sighed, running a hand through his already disheveled hair. "I was hoping you had forgotten. I was looking forward to dropping you at the hotel."

"I'm not getting out of the car. I just want to see where he lives."

Hans hesitated. "Alright. Let me try something. I'll call dispatch. Maybe they've got an address for the Wahls. Many people their age rely on cabs and buses. Give me five minutes." He pointed back toward the restaurant. "Why don't you grab us a couple of coffees to go?"

Icek blinked. "At a Chinese restaurant? Do they even have coffee?"

"I'm a regular here," Hans said with a grin. "Ming Sun, the owner, is a friend. Ming keeps my cup full. Be right back."

Hans returned, a slip of paper clutched in his hand. "Got it. Helen and Wilhelm Wahl, Crescent Lane. Right here in Hamburg. It's a nice neighborhood. Think manicured lawns, expensive houses, the whole nine yards. Lots of white picket fences, flowers spilling over arbors. As soon as I saw the address, it clicked, as most cabbies don't remember faces—they remember the location. Then, once at the location, sometimes the memory of a face appears. I think I've driven Helen to the same doctor a few times over the years. Helen is a sweet old lady, actually. Never met the husband."

Icek's jaw tightened. "Small world. You've met the wife of the man who massacred my family."

Hans nodded slowly. "She dresses well, tips generously. Not exactly what you'd picture as the wife of a Nazi, and I bet she was a looker in her day, too. Still is, in a way."

"Let's go, then," Icek said, his voice flat. "Not sure what I expect to see in the dark, but I need to see it."

"We do a drive-by," Hans emphasized, holding up a hand. "A slow drive-by. I'm not stopping. You understand?"

"Yes, no stopping. And no, I'm not getting out."

"Right." Hans started the engine. "Ten minutes. And knowing you, you'll be memorizing every turn, right?"

"You know me too well," Icek said, a flicker of something dark crossing his face. "I don't want you anywhere near when I visit. And I will visit. But I won't hurt them. My faith teaches that words can be sharper than any weapon. I'll prepare a statement. Let them know the lives taken by the Nazis and the date. That's all."

A thoughtful frown creased Hans's forehead. "Something just occurred to me. What if the wife doesn't know?"

Icek spoke, "The trial transcript reads that his conviction is a result of the orders given, not the act itself. That's why he didn't hang. Maybe his wife believes the hogwash line that he 'never pulled the trigger.' Lots of the returning Nazis used that line."

Icek stared out the window, his voice low. "Pity we couldn't just kidnap him. Hand him over to the Poles. With my testimony—maybe they could try him again?"

"You've got a creative mind, I'll give you that," Hans said, a hint of unease in his voice. "Ever thought about writing?"

"I have."

Hans shook his head. "You never cease to surprise me, Icek. Let's get this over with so I can get some sleep."

Nine minutes later, the cab crawled past the Wahl residence. The houses, bathed in the soft glow of streetlights, reminded Icek of Cherry Creek in Denver, that enclave of the "filthy wealthy," as he'd always thought of them.[75] These were smaller versions, but the same sense of smug, quiet opulence radiated from them. It galled him. *Why should a man like Wahl live in such a place?*

"I bet it gives you some satisfaction," Hans said, breaking the silence, "knowing the courts forced him out of his castle, his family. Four years in prison. A man like that, familiar with luxury, must paint a satisfying picture." He smirked slightly. "You can tell the world you know where he lives, the man who murdered your family. He got away with it."

"Not yet, he hasn't," Icek corrected, his voice barely a whisper. "Justice can come from unexpected places. Now, the hotel. Please."

"Finally," Hans muttered, relief evident in his tone. "I thought you'd never ask."

CHAPTER FIFTY-FIVE

Hamburg, Germany
June 17th, 1974, 9:35 a.m.

Icek tossed and turned all night. He thought *it had to be the proximity to the animal that murdered my family. I was about 150 meters away from him, perhaps even closer—it sickens me to think that the evil Nazi bastard made it through the war. Not only can I identify the person, but I also know where the SOB lives. If I play my cards right, the killer may have limited time left on this earth. I must get my mind off that animal—I must.*

Perhaps playing a tourist will do the trick. The St. Nicholas Church will be a suitable venue to visit—I will bring my camera and take some photos of the ruins. The images will be handy for reference each year when the topic is studied in my class.

He walked over to the window and saw what appeared to be a cloudless, warm, mid-June day. *Yep! I'm going to play tourist! That Nazi killer isn't going to spoil my day.*

Icek hopped on a tourist bus, the generic hotel fading in the rearview mirror. Hamburg spread before him, a vibrant, modern cityscape, all gleaming glass and steel, seemingly reaching out to embrace him. But Icek's gaze was drawn to something specific: the ghost of the past. He was here for St. Nicholas Church, the skeletal reminder of Operation Gomorrah,[76] the Allied bombing campaign that had rained fire upon this city in late July and early August 1943.

Back in Colfax, Colorado, Operation Gomorrah was a cornerstone of his history curriculum. Every year, he watched a fresh wave of students confront this brutal reality. He'd see the color drain from their faces, eyes glistening with unshed tears, as the grainy black-and-white footage showed not just military targets but entire neighborhoods, civilian homes, schools, and hospitals deliberately turned to ash to break the German spirit.

He disembarked, waving away the driver's offer of a return trip with a promise to find a taxi later.

Inside the visitor's section of Saint Nicholas, he approached the information desk. Behind it, a woman with long, relaxed, graying hair that cascaded to her shoulders in gentle waves studied him. Her name tag read "Helga Wagner." A light blue blouse and gray skirt, set off by surprisingly stylish high heels, gave her a youthful air, belied by the fine lines around her eyes, softened by carefully applied makeup. Horn-rimmed glasses hung from a delicate chain around her neck. Mid-forties, he guessed, or maybe closer to his own.

"Good morning," he began, testing the waters, "Do you speak English?"

She responded in a slightly accented English: "Yes. How may I assist you?"

"This may sound a bit unusual, but is there any chance of a more personal tour?"

Helga's brow creased, a subtle line appearing between her eyes. "I apologize, but we don't typically offer that beyond the standard admission. Perhaps if you could explain your particular interest in Saint Nicholas?"

"My name is Icek Kelner. I'm from Colfax, Colorado in America. I am a Polish-born teacher of high school history. Today, I'm hoping to immerse myself in Operation Gomorrah. It's a vital part of my curriculum."

"Pleased to meet you, Icek. I am Helga Wagner, as you see." Her eyes seemed to flicker with a new understanding. "Your curiosity is understandable. Let me see if a coworker can relieve me so we can have a proper conversation."

She picked up the phone, and a flurry of rapid German was followed by a smile. "My colleague will be here in under ten minutes. We'll have more time then."

Her associate arrived moments later, and after a quick handover, Helga turned back to Icek, a slight air of anticipation about her.

"So, tell me, Mr. Kelner, what specifically draws you to this ruin?"

"Before I answer, may I ask, were you in Hamburg during the bombing in 1943?"

Helga hesitated, a fleeting shadow passing across her face as if a dark cloud had briefly obscured the sun. "That's a fair question. Yes, I was. Eighteen years old, barely a woman, just days away from graduating high school. Why do you ask?"

"Because you understand, then, on a level no textbook can convey." Icek's voice dropped, his gaze momentarily distant. "I, too, have seen the horrors. I was born in Poland, a survivor of the Holocaust. Members of the Einsatzgruppen, those mobile killing squads—some, I know, came from Hamburg—they murdered my family. My grandmother, my ten-year-old twin sisters. Extinguished them." A shudder ran through him, the images still vivid, even after all these years. "I witnessed the aftermath."

"Oh my God," Helga whispered, her hand flying to her mouth, her eyes wide with a mixture of horror and empathy. "You were how old?"

"Eighteen. Until then, I'd been sheltered. I'd never witnessed such deliberate cruelty."

Helga's gaze dropped to the floor, her shoulders slumping slightly, a visible display of shared shame. "I am aware of the atrocities."

Icek continued, his voice low, a thread of steel running through it. "I left Poland. Eventually, I found my way to America."

"Why America?" Helga asked, tilting her head slightly, a genuine curiosity replacing the initial reserve. "And why Colfax, Colorado? Did you have family there?"

"Few realize," Icek began, the story unspooling like a well-worn tapestry, "that Colfax, a suburb of Denver, has a surprisingly large Jewish population. Eastern Europeans of Jewish descent began arriving in the 1870s, many fleeing the state-sponsored anti-Semitism and the pogroms of their homelands. My father's first cousin, Dawid Kelner, came to America through a college exchange program in 1916. He discovered that Americans were training non-American men of Polish descent as soldiers in Canada. He joined the Kosciuszko Army and became one of the 'Falcons.'"[77]

He took a breath, the story unfolding like a familiar film reel, each scene etched in his memory. "He was assigned to the infantry, fighting the Germans in World War I under Polish colors, part of that hundred thousand-strong Polish fighting force. He was wounded, ended up in a French aid station, and met a beautiful American nurse, Hillary. She was Jewish and from Colfax. They married in Paris after the war, in a whirlwind romance, and had an impromptu wedding, deciding to settle in the States. After my own experiences, I needed a change. We all did. My wife, Teodora, and her brother, Tomasz, decided to visit Dawid. And, well, the rest, as they say, is history."

"And what brings you to Hamburg all these years later?" Helga's question, soft and hesitant, brought him back to the echoing emptiness of the church.

"Ah, a conference. I'm presenting a paper on my experiences during the Holocaust."

Helga's expression softened, a genuine warmth replacing the professional courtesy. "I will gladly answer your questions, on one condition: that you answer mine, about your life during the Holocaust."

"Unlike many, I have no issues sharing my Holocaust experience." A genuine smile, the first of the day, lifted his lips. "This is my first time in Hamburg. I came here today hoping to understand, to see firsthand, the impact of the scars on this church."

Helga chuckled, a light, airy sound that momentarily dispelled the somber atmosphere. "No, it's no secret. 1925. So, yes, close in age. The echoes of that time are with me every day. Perhaps sharing my perspective with someone who truly understands might be therapeutic."

Icek solemnly looked at her and said, "You needn't revisit those difficult memories if they're too painful. I know how the past can cling."

"No, it is necessary, I think. A year ago, an older gentleman came here, a former British Royal Air Force pilot. He told us that in 1942, the British War Cabinet had decided to destroy all German cities with populations of over a hundred thousand.[78] He confessed, with tears streaming down his face, that he'd been one of the pilots. He described the post-bombing-run statistics the Allies published about the Hamburg bombing—the 150 mph winds and temperatures reaching eighteen hundred degrees Fahrenheit. His sharing these numbers was a revelation. And it allowed me a measure of solace—to know I wasn't alone in carrying this burden."

Helga gestured toward the center of the ruined nave. "He stood right there, weeping uncontrollably. His son, his daughter, his wife—they were with him. It was the first time they truly understood his pain, the weight of what he'd done. They embraced him, and others, such as visitors like yourself, wept too. There were shared hugs. It showed me that openness and vulnerability can allow others to confront their own buried emotions."

"We both carry invisible wounds, I think," Icek said softly. "The memory of my family brutally murdered is a constant companion. I suspect, for you, the ghosts of those days will linger." He paused, then asked, his voice regaining some of its earlier directness, "What can you tell me about that week of horror? What don't I know from the textbooks, from the films?"

"Perhaps," Helga suggested, a practical note entering her voice, "we could walk up to the observation level? It's quite a climb—they keep promising an elevator, but the funding never seems to materialize. But at least the stairs keep one fit."

"That sounds appropriate," Icek replied, a faint smile returning.

Reaching the observation deck, Helga leaned against the railing, the panorama of modern Hamburg stretching out beneath them, a stark contrast to the skeletal spire they stood upon. "The summer had started so deceptively. We'd experienced air raids, of course, since the early 1940s. There were legitimate targets—oil refineries, storage facilities, the U-boat pens, and even some of the docks initially. But everything changed on July 24th, 1943. The Allies unleashed a meticulously planned inferno. They used a mix of bombs specifically designed to tear the city apart. On July 27th alone, twenty thousand people perished. Here in Hamburg, we refer to Operation Gomorrah as our version of Nagasaki.[79] Between thirty-four thousand and forty-three thousand lives were extinguished. Before Hamburg, the largest single loss of life, I believe, was the roughly fourteen hundred the Germans inflicted on London in May 1941. A fraction."

She paused, drawing a shaky breath. "seven hundred British RAF bombers and seventy US Army Air Force created a firestorm. It raged, unchecked, until August 3rd."

Icek stared at her, his heart reflecting the horror in her words, the sadness deep in his soul. "I feel a profound guilt. I teach this history every year, but its true weight hasn't fully landed until this moment."

"Before the bombing," Helga continued, her voice dropping to a near whisper, her gaze fixed on some distant point in the cityscape, "we'd had a dry summer. The city was a tinderbox waiting to ignite, as they'd been modernizing the streets by replacing the old brick with blacktop asphalt. When the fires came, the buildings burned, but the roads melted. People fleeing their burning homes ran into the streets, only to be engulfed by the heat and toxic fumes. One breath, and…" she trailed off, shaking her head, the image too horrific to complete. "Countless bodies adhered to the pavement. Response personnel, who were few, had to excavate them for mass burials. The air raid shelters, so many died there, suffocated by the superheated air, the lack of oxygen."

"You're right to call it your Nagasaki," Icek said softly. "How many buildings were destroyed in total?"

Helga's voice was almost a whisper. The numbers recited like a grim litany. "I'm ashamed to admit I have the statistics memorized. It wasn't intentional, but so many visitors, particularly Americans and British, ask. Five hundred and eighty industrial plants, 2,632 businesses, 379 office buildings, twenty-four hospitals, 277 schools, 257 government or Nazi party buildings.[80] Almost half the city's homes—sixteen thousand apartment buildings. A million people, out of a population of 1.7 million, fled. Became refugees. And the worst, thousands upon thousands unnamed. The fire consumed them beyond recognition."

Icek scribbled notes, his hand trembling slightly, the pen digging into the paper. "You're adding such depth and texture to my understanding. Thank you. Perhaps you'd like to join me for a cup of tea at the snack bar downstairs? A chance to sit?"

"Certainly," Helga said, a small, hesitant smile returning. "My feet could use a rest after that climb."

They descended, the silence between them heavy with unspoken thoughts. They ordered tea and settled at a small table by the window overlooking the quiet plaza below.

Helga placed her hand gently on Icek's forearm, a gesture of solidarity, of shared humanity. Her voice dropped to a near whisper, conspiratorial, urgent. "Do you see that man over there? Turtleneck, gray tweed sport coat, black trousers, expensive-looking Italian shoes? Black hair, but the gray in his beard suggests a certain vanity. Perhaps dye. Have you seen him before?"

Icek glanced discreetly, following her gaze. He watched as the man took notes on a tiny notepad he retrieved from his sports coat pocket and then, moments later, did the same thing. Every thirty seconds or so, he looked to his left, then to his right—he was fidgety. *What could he be writing down?* Icek thought, he was not dressed like a typical tourist. More like a well-groomed thug. Or a private investigator, the kind you saw in those Hollywood films. Was he armed? Who was he working for?

"No. He's unfamiliar."

"I observe tourists every day. This man has been shadowing us ever since you entered the visitor center. Take another look more carefully. See if anything registers."

Icek took a longer, more deliberate look, assessing the man's posture, his gaze, and the way he held himself. Definitely not a tourist.

"Let's finish here. You'll leave first. I'll follow shortly after the exit. If this stranger follows you, I'll rush toward you, loudly claiming you forgot your glasses at the coffee stand. You may need to get away quickly."

He looked at her, a mixture of bewilderment and concern on his face. "Wait, you don't even know me!"

"True," Helga admitted, her gaze still fixed on the man across the plaza. "But I can sense a goodness in you. And I fear your safety is compromised. Something from your past, perhaps something connected to your revelations in Poland, may have resurfaced. Someone feels threatened by what you know." She refocused, her voice dropping back to a whisper. "Please, think. Is there any reason why someone in Germany would have an interest in monitoring your movements?"

"Several, potentially," Icek admitted, his voice low, his hand instinctively moving to his chest as if guarding a secret. It so happens I now possess the current address of the animal who took the lives of those I loved."

Helga took a slow, deep breath, a visible wave of concern washing her face. "You may be right. Your movements are under surveillance. Weren't you ever taught to be aware of your surroundings? To check for a tail? How, in heaven's name, did you obtain the residence of this villain?"

Icek's tone was a blend of confiding vulnerability and a rising tide of worry. "It's a somewhat convoluted story. Perhaps it's best to remain unaware of the specifics. The murderer of my family walks these very streets—he is a retiree of the Hamburg Police Department. A chilling thought."

Helga cut in, her whisper gaining a slight edge. "You confronted the Hamburg police, demanding the whereabouts of criminals who were part of the Hamburg-assigned Einsatzgruppen?"

Icek clarified, his voice regaining a measure of control. "Not confronted. No. I merely requested access to archival photographs— pre-war images of Police Battalion 101. The police officials were surprisingly cooperative. Eager, even, to display these soon-to-be- museum pieces. In 1945, after the war, the Battalion leader, Helmut Schotz, was apprehended, along with three of his associates. Helmut and his band of former Police Battalion 101 members were known to have murdered tens of thousands of Polish civilians. Helmut's hands were stained with blood. He was extradited to Poland, where the Polish prosecutors swiftly dispensed justice. Guilty and sentenced to death on the very day of the verdict. The Poles eventually executed him years afterward, I discovered. I often wondered what became of his three colleagues. All were culpable."

He continued, the narrative gaining momentum, the urgency returning. "Hamburg initiated an investigation in 1962 into the activities of Police Battalion 101. The German justice system, at that time, arrested fourteen of the nearly five-hundred-member battalion. The tragic truth: This retired officer was among those charged in the early 60s. He admitted he 'only' *issued* the orders. He was released two years prior to the completion of his six-year sentence. At the same time, those he commanded to kill received no such leniency. Perhaps a reopening of the case, with my firsthand account of murder, can finally result in justice?"

A pause hung between them.

Helga then, with intensity, said, "It does make logical sense! At war, those convicted of war crimes receive severe sentences, and for some, a lot is at stake. You'd best take caution; remember, Germany still prosecutes ALL war crimes. Time never runs out—there are no statutes of limitations for war crimes. You may well be correct—the stranger must be on to something."

"I have thought of a better idea. This gentleman does not know me. With my official name tag, I can approach him and ask him bluntly, "Can I help you?" He wouldn't possibly be foolish enough to confront me with all these visitors standing around. In the interim, I will have my associate come and retrieve you and take you to my office. You stay there, with the door locked, until you hear from me. What do you think?"

"I think you should have gone into intelligence, is what I think. Yes, take me to your office. I will wait for you there."

About twenty minutes later, Helga and the mystery gentleman, dressed in a tweed jacket and shiny shoes, opened the door of her office.

CHAPTER FIFTY-SIX

Hamburg, Germany
June 17th, 1974, 11:05 a.m.

The tweed-jacketed man offered a small, almost apologetic smile as they entered her office. "This must seem unorthodox," he began, his voice surprisingly gentle. "I owe you both an explanation. I'm not a hired assassin or some street thug. And I wasn't following Mr. Kelner with any ill intentions." He straightened slightly, a subtle shift in posture. "My name is Chief Inspector Stephan Schubert, with the Bundesnachrichtendienst—the BND.[81] German Intelligence. Think of us as a counterpart to the American CIA."

He inhaled, his gaze moving between them. "Please allow me to clarify. Then, we can discuss this calmly as rational individuals. First, identification." He produced a tan leather bifold, flipping it open to reveal a photograph, an identification number beneath a formal title, and the glint of a brass badge. "The general number is on the card. Call it if you wish. They'll vouch for me. Or, if you prefer, we can relocate to my offices." He paused; eyebrows raised in a silent question.

Helga's voice, a little unsteady, found its way out. "Am I implicated in something?"

Schubert's smile widened, a flicker of genuine reassurance. "No, no, no. Absolutely not. And you, Mr. Kelner, are similarly in the clear. I intend to disclose some information we've received."

A crease formed between Helga's brows. "Why am I involved? I only met this gentleman moments ago."

Schubert held up a hand, a placating gesture. "Please. Just hear what I have to say."

Icek, his expression carefully neutral, spoke for the first time. "I gather my arrival has caused some ruffled feathers?"

Schubert gave a wry chuckle. "'Ruffled' is an interesting choice of words. Is 'ruffled feathers' an American idiom? I must add that to my vocabulary. Does it stem from poultry, perhaps?"

"Honestly, I haven't the slightest idea," Icek admitted.

"Well, your presence has caused a reaction," Schubert continued, his tone shifting to a more serious register. "Former members of Police Battalion 101, men who served in those killing squads, were unsettled by your biographical details. The ones listed for the conference."

Icek's eyes narrowed slightly. "How did intelligence become privy to my itinerary?"

"Frankly? Almost serendipitously," Schubert confessed. "Security has been heightened at borders and airports, particularly since the rise of leftist factions. And, of course, the shadow of the 1972 Summer Olympics in Munich still hangs heavy."[82] He glanced at them, his expression grim. "The terrorist attack by the Palestinian Liberation Organization, the murdered hostages—we've been re-evaluating security protocols ever since, and you, Mr. Kelner, came under scrutiny as a direct consequence."

Icek nodded slowly. "I followed that event closely. Horrific. Wrestlers, if I recall correctly?"

"Yes," Schubert confirmed, "Israeli wrestlers and weightlifters."

Helga's hand flew to her mouth, her eyes wide with remembered horror. "Oh, the inhumanity of it. I attended the '72 Olympics. Not that day, thankfully, but it could have been me. I recall thinking the security seemed adequate. The queues were endless."

"There were systemic inadequacies," Schubert said, his voice tight with barely suppressed anger. "I'm not at liberty to elaborate. However, that attack served as a global wake-up call. Mr. Kelner, your screening was a direct result of the hard lessons learned that day. Every Polish visitor to West Germany undergoes a secondary review. Our analysts search for connections to Polish hometowns and any record of affiliation with the Polish Home Army. Your involvement, Mr. Kelner, triggered a more thorough investigation into Icek Abram Kelner. The stated purpose of your trip—Jozefow, Poland, the Holocaust, Police Battalion 101. Your comments to the immigration officer raised concerns."

He paused, his gaze settling on Icek. "Ordinarily, such statements wouldn't warrant further attention. But we delved deeper. We unearthed your biography and your mention of witnessing a German officer murder your family during the Jozefów massacre. That, coupled with your remarks, captured our interest. Many Hamburg Police Battalion 101 veterans, men we know murdered tens of thousands of Polish civilians, remain at large. The courts lacked conclusive evidence for execution. Most were convicted of lesser war crimes, sentences that many, particularly within the Jewish community, deemed a mere façade of justice."

"As a Jew, I concur. A façade," Icek said, his voice flat, devoid of emotion.

"Your statement about witnessing an officer murder your family resonated," Schubert continued. "Few officers were implicated in the post-war tribunals. Most adopted the defense of, 'I didn't pull the trigger. I merely issued the orders.' "There's no statute of limitations on prosecuting war criminals. Our personnel believe that you may be in jeopardy. Many Battalion 101 veterans are likely apprehensive about your presence. If you possess further evidence or can identify the individual, you could become a state witness. The government wouldn't hesitate to reopen a case, even a previously adjudicated one. Do you comprehend the implications?"

Icek's voice was low, a near whisper. "You're suggesting a German court could try a member of the 101, and if convicted, he could face execution?"

"No," Schubert corrected gently. "The current Constitution of Germany, the Grundgesetz für die Bundesrepublik Deutschland, effective since May 23rd, 1949, prohibits capital punishment. Courts can impose a life sentence without the possibility of parole. In the present climate, he would receive a very lengthy sentence."

Helga finally spoke, her voice a mix of confusion and dawning understanding. "But why is my presence required?"

"We desired a third-party witness, should an apprehension become necessary," Schubert explained. "And we require your corroboration of our discussion. The conversation hasn't yet reached sensitive territory. But it will."

"I remain curious. Why am I pertinent?" Helga pressed.

"You may not be," Schubert admitted, "but should the need arise, you'll serve as a witness." He turned back to Icek. "Did Mr. Kelner mention that a cab driver transported him to a specific residence last night, but he refrained from exiting the vehicle?"

Before Icek could answer, Helga's eyes widened, a flicker of understanding, or perhaps suspicion, crossing her face.

Icek interjected, his voice sharp with surprise. "Hold on. My cab driver, is he affiliated with your agency?"

"In a manner of speaking," Stephan said, a hint of a smile playing on his lips. "We provided him with a firearm and a secure location if required. And we had surveillance vehicles tracking your movements. It was imperative. We sought to safeguard you, and frankly, I didn't wish for your demise on my watch."

"How comforting," Helga said, her voice laced with dry sarcasm.

Stephan began, "Incidentally, Icek, should you be curious, Hans's military records indicate he was a Wehrmacht veteran; he sustained an injury from a .50 caliber round fired by an American machine gun, and no, he did not participate in the extermination of Jews. He empathizes with your plight. Hans genuinely likes you and was deeply disturbed by your narrative. We had to physically restrain him from entering the Wahl residence and summarily executing Wilhelm. Hans believes he deserves it. Therefore, yes, Hans, the cab driver, possesses an open-ended agreement to assist us. Based on the instructions our agency provided, Hans was not authorized to do a drive-by of the Wahl residence. Hans acted independently on that occasion, and he was not authorized to be present at the precinct when you identified the photograph of the creature who murdered your loved ones. Hans was equally distraught by this. Helga, please confirm for the record, and based on what you understand, the cab driver and Icek did not disembark last evening in front of Wilhelm's home. Your testimony today will be incorporated into your formal statement."

"Statement?!" Helga's voice rose in alarm.

"Indeed, a statement," Stephan confirmed. "We require every possible advantage to ensure a conviction. If it hasn't become apparent, we intend for the jury to find Wahl guilty this time. We possess documentation attributing nearly ten thousand deaths to Wahl. The Nazis meticulously documented the atrocities committed by Wahl and his men. We require only evidence of a single murder, with reasonable corroboration, to secure a conviction. Wahl, a predator, reveled in the killing of Jews, as he termed it. We have him on tape whilst consuming beer, boasting about his delight in extinguishing Jewish lives. His other favored pronouncement was—'We murdered five million. We should have completed the task.' Without witnesses, conviction is unattainable. After extensive deliberations with my team, we've formulated a multifaceted operation. And it involves you, Icek. Are you amenable to participating in a mission to bring down the man who murdered your grandmother and your twin sisters?"

Icek's eyes, rigid and unwavering, were locked on Stephan's. "You have my undivided attention. Please, proceed."

"Do you object to your new acquaintance hearing about your experiences in the Polish Home Army?"

"Not in the slightest," Icek replied. "I have nothing to conceal. I've never disclosed this to my colleagues, students, or acquaintances in America. I wouldn't wish for them to know my past. I'm uncertain of their reaction. Only my wife and her brother are aware. I witnessed a monster murder my grandmother and my ten-year-old twin sisters with the same casual indifference he might exhibit toward exterminating vermin. As I've alluded to others, we targeted trains, tanks, trucks, and troop formations. We hurled Molotov cocktails at German units encroaching upon our villages. Our command forbade us from executing German soldiers engulfed in flames, intending to disseminate the message that we were capable of matching the Nazis' ruthlessness."

"Dear God," Helga whispered, her hand pressed to her mouth. "I comprehend. I likely would have acted similarly."

"Quite possibly," Agent Schubert said, turning his gaze back to Icek. "Both you and your wife served in the Home Army, correct, Icek?"

Icek's eyebrows shot up. "And how would you possess that knowledge?"

"Germany is a NATO member," Schubert said with a confident smile.[83] "We share a comprehensive database encompassing virtually everyone involved in military or guerrilla warfare globally during World War II. We reviewed both your files and that of your brother-in-law, Tomasz."

"Yes, the three of us were inseparable," Icek said, a faraway look softening his eyes. "We were each other's protectors. I wouldn't be here were it not for them. We were perpetually in situations of kill or be killed. It's peculiar—I never perceived it as murder. It was warfare. We were forever famished and rarely slept in a proper bed. Days devoid of gunfire, explosions, artillery, mortars, or concealment were infrequent. We were often chilled to the bone. And, most debilitating of all, constantly ravenous. The day my wife, Teodora, was wounded was the rock bottom of the war for us. A German soldier inflicted a chest wound upon her, requiring thirty sutures. Fortunately, a seasoned medic who had practiced in hospitals prior to the war saved her life. She had lost a considerable amount of blood. His moniker, incidentally, translates from Polish to 'God Junior.'"

"Oh, merciful heavens," Helga gasped, tears welling in her eyes. "That poor woman. She's incredibly fortunate to have survived."

"That period of our lives rarely surfaces," Icek continued, his voice heavy with the weight of memory. "We endeavor to keep those recollections buried. But today, I'm gratified to revisit them. I sense that retribution is imminent. I'm unfamiliar with the originator of the phrase 'sweet revenge,' but they undoubtedly understood its essence. I experience a small taste of it daily in my high school history classroom. I recognize that those proceedings, such as the Nuremberg trials and other war crime tribunals worldwide, purged society of numerous malevolent individuals, and many of the culpable met their deserved end."

"You have no conception of how profoundly we desire to close this chapter," Stephan said, his voice earnest. "We yearn to apprehend the perpetrator. He deserves to atone for his actions. He believes he can evade justice indefinitely. Not this time. Your testimony will likely result in a swift life sentence without parole. I assure you of that."

"The medic, 'God Junior,' who treated Teodora, is still a close confidant," Icek said. "He and his family have visited us in Colorado.

We avoid discussing the war—there are more pleasant subjects. But every time I see Teodora's scar, I relive that harrowing day. We told the children that, as teenagers, a car accident was how their mother sustained the injury. They still don't know the truth. And the man responsible for her injury? I'm proud to say he no longer draws breath, thanks to me.

"Teodora and I have an addendum to our will, detailing our time in the Polish Home Army. After we're gone, our attorney will share the full story with our family. Her brother, Tomasz, has made similar arrangements. We're all proud of our service. However, back then, we worried that if we'd been open about it, American school districts would have seen Home Army veterans as a liability, and our chances of becoming teachers would have been slim. So, the three of us agreed to put that part of our lives behind us. The problem now is that we never mentioned our military service on our applications. If that became public, we could lose our jobs.

"And, for your information, Helga, my work in the Polish Home Army was mainly about making life for the German Army as wretched as possible. We contaminated their water, booby-trapped equipment, demolished railway lines to disrupt their supplies—numerous acts of sabotage to impede them. We weren't in daily firefights; we didn't have the ammunition. But make no mistake, every member of my unit was responsible for ending German lives. Again, it was war."

"Icek, have you ever contemplated authoring a memoir about your experiences?" Helga asked.

"A book is improbable in the near future," Icek replied. "Our children would learn far too much. Teodora and I have discussed this extensively. She believes revealing the unvarnished truth of our time in the Home Army would be excessively overwhelming for them. I had to exert considerable persuasion to secure her consent for me to present my Holocaust paper. Teodora would prefer I never broach the subject. It's a delicate balance when one teaches high school history."

"Thank you for that context, Icek," Stephan said. "It's invaluable to my strategic thinking regarding the impending mission. I wouldn't involve a civilian who lacked military service, Home Army experience, or exposure to combat."

"One moment," Icek interrupted, his voice rising slightly. "You intend for me to participate in an operation to capture the beast who murdered my family?"

"We're soliciting your voluntary participation," Stephan clarified. "We cannot compel you. We require irrefutable identification of the man who slaughtered your family to bring him to justice. We'll escort you and a BND weapons specialist to the BND pistol range. You'll undergo a comprehensive orientation on contemporary weaponry. You must attain proficiency with the weapon we'll request you carry. Technological advancements have been substantial since the war." Icek's eyes were wide, a mixture of disbelief and anticipation flickering within them. "You're stating I'll be in the residence of the monster who murdered my family, armed with a loaded pistol? Aren't you apprehensive I'll shoot him upon sight?"

"Regrettably, we'd be compelled to apprehend you," Stephan said, his voice firm but not unkind. "The courts would likely exercise leniency, but it would engender unnecessary complications for you and the German government. We must arrest him and ensure he spends his remaining years contemplating his transgressions. Does that sound preferable to a swift, fatal shot?"

"I'm uncertain if they even manufacture the armaments we employed," Icek replied. "A refresher on modern weaponry and fundamental tactics for the operation is more than welcome."

"We earnestly hope you won't be required to discharge a firearm," Stephan said. "But we desire your preparedness. My sole concern is that you'll encounter Captain Wahl, become emotionally overwhelmed, and act rashly. I trust you won't. It could jeopardize the entire team. This man will face justice, one way or another. We plan to bring one of my commandos and you to his residence. We require absolute certitude that this man is indeed the fiend who murdered your family. Identifying a suspect from a decades-old monochrome photograph constitutes tenuous evidence. You'll need to confirm that Wahl is the individual upon entering the premises. We'll communicate precisely how we desire this confirmation."

Icek, his voice firm, said, "You can be sure I will do my part when we enter his house."

"Good, we will have the home under surveillance," Stephan explained. "You and my operative will pose as a telephone repairman addressing static on their line. We'll have listening devices inside the house to capture every word. A van containing additional commandos will be parked nearby, ready to intervene if needed. We will meet in the morning to finalize our operational specifics."

"So, we'll deceive him into believing he has a telephonic malfunction, but it's actually an opportunity for me to confront him, and I will conduct the interrogation?" Icek's voice was laced with a mixture of incredulity and grim satisfaction. "This plan is exquisitely satisfying. And I'll be armed."

"Precisely," Stephan confirmed. "He may be armed as well. Intelligence suggests Battalion 101 veterans are increasingly anxious about being pursued for their past atrocities. Many have been interrogated since the war. He might carry one of Hitler's favored sidearms, a 7.65-millimeter Walther PPK.[84] Compact enough to conceal within a pajama pocket. We must presume a man of this ilk possesses access to a weapon. It might even be the same one he employed on your family. The German Army permitted numerous World War II veterans, particularly officers, to retain their sidearms."

"Are you implying this agonizing chapter of my existence, perpetually wondering about the fate of the monster who murdered my family, is nearing its conclusion?"

Helga said, "Your family deserves this." Her voice thick with emotion, "This man is one of the countless indoctrinated individuals who swallowed eight years of unremitting propaganda, broadcast hourly on our radios since the early 1930s. Some of my dearest schoolmates were Jewish. I never succumbed to the hatred that consumed so many others. The images of the concentration camps, disseminated by the Allies after the war, instilled within many of us a profound shame in being German."

"She speaks the unvarnished truth," Stephan agreed. "I'm unable to divulge my role during the war. However, the deaths of millions of Jews, orchestrated by a political regime, have perpetually haunted me. And my wife is Jewish. For some inexplicable reason, I committed to memory a quotation from Adolf Eichmann following his conviction in Israel. Nearing the end of his life, he uttered, 'I will leap into my grave laughing because the feeling that I have five million human beings on my conscience is a source of extraordinary satisfaction.' Upon hearing that, I was not proud to be a German citizen."

Icek's voice was thick with suppressed emotion. "You cannot fathom how my family has yearned for a resolution to the events of July 13th, 1942 in Jozefow, Poland. This has lingered, a phantom limb, for decades. We've never ascertained the fate of my father, Abram Irving Kelner, born on February 6th, 1899, in Jozefow. He would be seventy-five this year. He remains missing. That morning in 1942 was the last time I beheld my father, and ironically, he was oblivious to my presence. My wife and her brother, Tomasz, learned from witnesses that the Germans loaded my father and others onto a rail car outside Jozefow days subsequent to the massacre. We discovered the Nazis consigned him to a small arms munitions factory in Skarzysco-Kamienna, Poland.

"With your extensive investigative capabilities, perhaps your investigators could determine his whereabouts. I know the Nazis confined him and approximately seventy others in a rail car for nearly two weeks following the Jozefow atrocities. And there's one other individual I'd like you to locate or at least ascertain her fate. Her name is Halina Adamik, born in 1889. I harbor a strong intuition that she remains alive. The twins adored her. Following Grandmother Ryfka's stroke, Halina tended to the twins daily, imparting invaluable knowledge to them. They cherished Halina as if she were their mother. Can you determine if she still draws breath?"

"Icek, I possess some potentially heartening news," Stephan said. "Our archivists have digitized a multitude of paper records from the camps, employing technology that was inconceivable a mere three years ago. I am committed to locating your father, and we can certainly investigate Halina's whereabouts. She was also born in Jozefow, correct? You possess no intelligence regarding whether either is alive?"

"Correct. Only the intelligence concerning the munitions plant," Icek confirmed.

"I pledge to you, I'll instruct my team to prioritize this endeavor," Stephan said. "There's a tangible possibility we can unearth what transpired with your father, and perhaps he yet lives. The BND possesses the optimal resources to locate him. The same applies to Halina."

Icek wiped at the corner of his eyes, his voice choked with emotion. "Thank you, sir. I'll endeavor to temper my expectations. But I've always harbored a feeling deep within that my father survives."

Helga, her expression radiating sincerity, looked directly into Icek's eyes. "It was a genuine pleasure meeting you. I earnestly hope you locate your father and that the brutal maniac who extinguished your loved ones' lives is apprehended and brought to account." She reached out and clasped his hands, a gesture of solidarity and compassion. "No one deserves the ordeal you and your family have endured, and to contemplate that it was all motivated by religious dogma. I've never been more ashamed of my German heritage. None of the world's Jews merited what befell them. Thank God, that era of history is behind us."

"Thank you," Icek said, his voice still thick with emotion. "Your heartfelt words are deeply appreciated. I'll convey them to my family upon my return."

A genuine smile, a crack in Helga's somber facade, spread across her face at Icek's remark. Icek embraced her, a brief, heartfelt connection.

"Helga, you possess my contact information," Stephan said. "We'd be grateful if you would visit my office for a recorded deposition. It will prove invaluable when we bring the 'brutal animal,' as you aptly termed him, to trial. I don't foresee the court necessitating your testimony, but we cannot rule it out definitively. Mr. Wahl may possess the financial means to retain a premier Hamburg attorney. And, most crucially, thank you for consenting to assist us. One final imperative: Please refrain from discussing today's conversation with anyone. Post-trial, you are at liberty to say or do as you please. Anything you utter prior to or during the trial could severely jeopardize our prospects of securing a conviction, particularly since the prosecution may seek a life sentence."

Icek looked at Helga, meeting her steady gaze. A silent understanding passed between them. She stared back and said, her voice calm and resolute, "You have no cause for concern, Mr. Schubert."

"Once more, Helga, my gratitude." Agent Schubert and Icek turned and walked away, leaving Helga to gaze after them, her mind a whirlwind of conflicting emotions.

CHAPTER FIFTY-SEVEN

Hamburg, Germany
June 18th, 1974, 7:24 a.m.

Icek got out of bed, peeked out the curtains of his hotel, scanned the horizon, and said, "Overcast and a light rain." He jumped in the shower, dressed, and headed to the hotel lobby to get a cup of coffee and pick up one of the only English newspapers available. Agent Schubert's meeting was at nine-thirty. They were to meet at a restaurant about a block from Icek's hotel.

He had a toasted muffin with orange marmalade, a small glass of grapefruit juice, and coffee. He finished reading the morning paper. There was nothing of significance in the news, except for President Nixon and the Watergate break-in, and now it appeared that Nixon could eventually lose the presidency. The Vietnam War continued, and college kids proceeded to protest Nixon and the war.[85]

No, nothing has changed since I left the US. It does look like the poor guy, Nixon, is going to face impeachment.

Icek left the hotel and headed for the short walk to the restaurant. On the way out of the hotel, he saw a gray-haired man with a mustache and slim build, about sixty-five years old. He wore a blue blazer, tie, tan lightweight slacks, and what looked to be handmade shoes. Icek headed for the exit, and right behind him, the stranger, ever so close, followed him out the door. Icek pretended to forget something and quickly turned around and headed back into the hotel to see if the gray-haired man would follow him. At the elevator, he pressed the 'up' button to make it appear as if he was returning to his room. He quickly entered and exited the elevator to see the stranger standing at the elevator entrance. He thought, *who the hell is this guy? As he walked toward the hotel exit again.*

Knowing Icek was wise to someone wanting to follow him out of the hotel, the stranger sat in the lobby and began reading a paper while Icek headed out the exit and onto the street.

He was about a block from the hotel when he noticed the gentleman following him about two hundred meters away. The first thought that came to mind was that this man was an associate of Agent Schubert. *Should I continue on my route to the restaurant or zigzag my path to see if this gentleman follows me? Will I be placing Agent Schubert and his team at risk?*

It was now nine-ten. *I'll lose this guy. He's old, and I'm much younger than him.* After about fifteen minutes of maneuvering, Icek no longer saw the man. He had lost him.

Ten minutes later, Icek strolled into the restaurant and thought, *I will not take any chances,* as he looked around to assess the clientele. *Are there any customers with an athletic build?* The kind of person that, with a glance, one could discern the person could manage to take the life of another.

Following last night's discussion, the need to assess each person as a potential threat was substantial, considering every detail about each individual. He looked to see where the exits were, and which door would be the best choice for a quick departure. He wasn't paranoid. *I now understand the value of freedom for the first time in my life, as I sense the power to affect the lives of those who played a role in the murder of my family.*

At nine-twenty-five, Heinz Niehaus entered the restaurant, carefully surveyed each person, walked to the restroom, opened the door, and looked inside. Then he began walking toward their booth, sat down and said, "Hey, Skipper? How y'all doing?" He looked at Icek and, in a Southern American accent, said, "Y'all must be my man that the skipper here assigned to manage quality control. Peach of a day, or what? Pleased to meet you. Sure been looking forward to working with you."

Icek looked at Heinz, and his first thought was this guy could pass for a hick from Alabama more so than a trained commando, as he had quite a timid look about him. He had blue eyes, blond hair, a large nose, and a ponytail that reached down to the middle of his back, along with a thick, untrimmed mustache and beard, all topped off with sunglasses resting on his head. Dressed in a tattered phone company uniform, he looked the part. Hollywood could not have done better. *Heinz was nothing like what I would have imagined.* How would anyone suspect this person as a commando? He was less than two meters tall, had no fat, and had broad shoulders as if he were wearing American football shoulder pads.

Icek said, in English, "Pleased to meet you, Heinz. I'm Icek."

Heinz replied in a perfect Warsaw native Polish accent, "I read your bio and hope the bastard gets what's coming to him."

Icek replied in Polish, "I want to see the bastard dead. Great version of a Warsaw resident accent."

Agent Schubert angrily said, "Will you two please speak a language I understand? And I will not ask either of you to translate what was said. From the body language, it appeared to be music to Icek's ears. I trust, Icek, it was indeed music to your ears?"

"Yes, you could say that," Icek said as he grinned at Heinz.

The discussion in the restaurant continued. The three had plenty more details to cover. In Agent Schubert's opinion, he must not end the conversation until Icek, Heinz, and he had covered every type of 'what-if' scenario to the point of near exhaustion. As he preached in his training sessions for years, the team would never leave a mission conversation with unanswered questions.

"By the way," Icek said, "someone was following me on my way here. It took me a while to shake the guy."

"Would you recognize the person if you saw him in a photo?" Agent Schubert asked.

"It depends. If the photo was a recent picture of the man, there is a good chance I can recognize him, as I saw him from one meter away."

"Do you remember seeing the photo of Wahl and others in the photo with Major Schotz? Let me show you a picture of the other men in the photo." Agent Schubert pulled out a stack of large images and pulled two from the stack. "Do either of these men look like the man you saw this morning?"

"Where did these photos come from, if I may ask?"

"These are from the ones taken after the war for the War Crimes Tribunals and were taken by the courts for the Battalion 101 and 103 trials. At the time, they were unsure who the guilty were, so they took photos of nearly every officer and staff non-commissioned officer."

"Maybe the man in this photo is the same man who was following me? I am not quite sure at this point."

"Regardless, if he is or isn't—it looks as though you have ruffled some feathers. This man, Lieutenant Erik Holtzbeck, spent six years in prison after the war on charges of war crimes. Hence, he too obviously found out that you, an eyewitness of the Jozefow event, and here in Hamburg, are presenting a paper on the subject."

"Do you think this gentleman thinks that I witnessed him murdering civilians?" Icek asked.

"Icek, the answer is he doesn't know if you did or didn't. He perceives a threat to his current freedom and perhaps his life. All these 101 members know eyewitness accounts can result in a life sentence. Can you blame them?"

"Here is how I see it," Icek said. "He must be guilty, or he wouldn't be concerned."

Agent Schubert replied, "Very good, Icek. You have spoken like a true teacher by reasoning through what a guilty human may be pondering. It's excellent, indeed. Unfortunately, we have no evidence to send him to prison. We can only pick him up and question him, and at this point, this would do us no good. We will keep an eye on him. Currently, a few of our agents are monitoring him. We won't let him get close to you, Icek. For now, we shall forget about this individual, as you did not see this gentleman murdering civilians, correct?"

"Correct. I did not see this person doing anything, as today was the first time I had seen him."

"Let's discuss our mission," Agent Schubert said. "What the former Battalion 101 members did not know is simple. What else had you seen that morning? Could you pick out several killers from a lineup at BND headquarters? They don't know the answers to this question. Only you, Icek, have the answers. Currently, any veteran of the 101st here in Hamburg is nervous. Icek, how are you feeling about all this? You had to have had a restless night?"

"Yes, indeed. I did have a restless night. I thought seriously about checking out of my hotel and into a different one, as I felt quite vulnerable last evening."

"Glad you didn't, as my two teams watching your place would have called me immediately and awakened me, and there would be all sorts of questions we do not need. My men have been here since you arrived."

"You thought I was in danger?"

"Let me correct your statement. We know you are in danger! The psychologists have reviewed the profiles of a typical guilty party who has murdered civilians and have discovered that, for these former Battalion 101 members, their freedom, their respect in the community, and their relationships with their family members are priceless. If their freedom becomes compromised, even a slight chance, they will protect it with their lives. Remember that the Battalion 101 vets' average age of sixty-plus tells us they may have meshed into civilian life with their military far off in the rear-view mirror. Most have put their murderous days well behind them. Nevertheless, the price can be stiff even for an accusation that they murdered defenseless Jewish men, women, and children."

"Not sure how they went on with their lives without guilt," Icek said with a strong hint of sarcasm.

"Trust me. Some do have guilt. There have been several studies within different agencies within the German government for those former Reich soldiers connected to the murder of civilians. The results of their studies are not pretty. Many have had several marriages, alcoholism, and drug abuse, and many have committed suicide. They were not all monsters, as you may think. Hitler's Minister for Enlightenment and Propaganda, Joseph Goebbels, a media mastermind, bombarded German citizens from 1933 through the early 1940s with continuous hatred for anything Jewish.[86] Following countless worsening degrees of criticism of the German Jews, many in Battalion 101 believed what they were hearing and, to this day, think that Aryan blood was superior to non-Aryan blood.[87] Many world-renowned psychologists have written papers on how a continuous blast of propaganda can impact the thinking of any citizen subjected to such a display of negative propaganda. Joseph Goebbels engineered this: Hitler approved it."

Icek replied, "We both absorbed the crazy propaganda into our minds. The proof that it worked—the Holocaust."

"Yes. You are correct. The Holocaust proved that Goebbels was a mastermind at propaganda," Agent Schubert remarked.

"What am I to expect today?" Icek asked.

Agent Schubert began speaking. "You need to know what we have planned in detail. First, a technician from the BND has already made a call to the Wahl residence. When Wahl's wife answered, our technician, posing as a carpet cleaning company representative, immediately generated a large amount of fake static on the phone. The technician hung up after a couple of minutes on the phone."

Agent Heinz began to speak, "Twenty minutes later, we had a different technician call the home. This time, a female agent posing as a phone company representative phoned. The agent began the conversation by asking if there had been any static in their phone line and advising her that in her area, there had been hundreds of reports of heavy static in the line. Mrs. Wahl was kind enough to report that she experienced heavy static minutes earlier and contacted customer support via phone. Thirty minutes later, a call from one of our agents came into their home. This time, the caller, a different female voice, posed as a representative from the phone company advising that there were technicians in the area to repair the static issue."

Heinz continued, "Again, all of the calls made to the Wahl residence, the BND laced the signal with artificial background static. The technician told her that the static would not impact all calls. We told her this so there would be no suspicion as to why the static might disappear if she received a call from family, friends, or others. We spent considerable time looking at potential gaps in our ruse. Our next contact with the Wahl home will be a call from a BND agent. He will pose as a technician and advise the Wahls to expect two phone company reps: one technician and the other a troubleshooting expert. Icek, you will pose as the troubleshooting expert. I will play the part of the technician."

Agent Schubert reached into his jacket pocket and handed Icek a pair of glasses. "Icek, here, please wear these glasses. As a technician, you must look the part. These are special lenses. Though they look like Coke bottles when wearing them, your vision will be close to normal. Also, our people have asked that upon entering the home, they want you to pretend you are doing a thorough inspection of each handset. These glasses will give the Wahls the impression that you are an educated expert in your work.

Also, we know your photo appears in the handout for the paper you presented. Mr. Wahl may have a copy of the handout and could recognize you. The glasses will provide an added cover. We want you to pick up the receiver and disassemble the mouthpiece and earpiece. Please take the cover off each phone and pretend you are doing a reading from the meter we supply. As you can tell, we need you to be believable. Don't worry. We will have a mock phone in the van, and our guys will go through the disassembly and the reassembly."

Icek replied, "I have never played with a phone before, so yes, I need a bit of instruction, and your phones don't look the same as our American phones."

"About an hour ago, we called the Wahl residence. A person pretending to be a phone representative, a BND agent, requested permission to enter the Wahl residence so he could investigate. Thus far, we have gained permission to send the tech into the Wahl home," Agent Schubert said.

"And the goal of the phone tech?" Icek asked.

"The tech will place a wire in the home so that our people in a nearby surveillance van can record and hear conversations by those within the home. If things were to get out of hand, we could be in the house in under forty-five seconds. Also, this tech will advise the Wahls that the technical problem is above his pay grade. He will advise the Wahls that experienced techs will arrive later."

"What time do you want me to visit the Wahl residence?" Icek asked.

Agent Schubert replied, "We want you to enter the home as a representative of the quality control department of the phone company. We will provide a script that you should follow. You will have plenty of time to memorize it, and we do not expect word-for-word accuracy at delivery. We were hoping you could deliver a general version of our script. Understood?"

"Yes, I understand," Icek replied.

"We have provided credentials, a van, a uniform that the typical quality control tech employee would wear, and essential test equipment. And we don't know if Wahl has a weapon. However, we are considering him to be armed. Any questions?"

"No, sir," Icek replied

"Icek, you must assume that Wahl has a weapon. Our surveillance team noted that he had a visitor last night, and he may have mentioned that a Pole was in town seeking revenge. Maybe he was given the idea that there might be an attempt on his life. We don't know this—hence, we must assume he has a locked and loaded weapon."

"Remember, the best hunch from our people, they think it will be a pistol, perhaps Walther PPK, as it was Hitler's favorite, and our psychologists think this person continues to worship Hitler—plus, you can hide a PPK in your damn underwear."

"So true," Icek said as he bowed his head in disgust.

"Listen carefully, Icek," Agent Schubert said. "When you get inside the Wahl home, we will do a test to be sure the van occupants can pick up those talking in all areas of the house. After a few minutes at home, you tell the Wahls that you must retrieve something from your truck. When you walk outside, we will flash the headlights of our van once. This signal indicates that we are receiving the audio correctly. If you see the left turn signal on the van flashing, reenter their home, and after five minutes of tinkering with the phone and testing equipment, inform the Wahls that everything within their phone system appears to be in order. After this, you must leave. A failure to hear and record voices within the home requires that we rethink our mission. Icek, we will not go forward without the ability to hear and record the audio. Do you understand?"

"Yes, without a confession on record, we will never get a conviction. Right?" Icek replied.

"Just carve into your brain that we will scratch the mission if our guy in the van begins flashing the left turn signal. All is not lost, as we will make another attempt later. The next mission will be entirely different than this one. Yes. You are right, Icek. We will not have a chance for a conviction without a recording of his confession."

"And we have yet to discuss the words from the accused that we need for a conviction," Icek said.

Agent Schubert reiterated, "These keywords must be on the recorder, or we have no case. It will be best if we capture words from Wahl like—murdered, killed, snuffed out their lives, shot, ended their lives, or wasted their lives. Whatever we can get, a jury must have no issues understanding that Wahl ended the lives of your family. Nothing can be better than, 'I killed your family,'" Agent Schubert said.

"How do you recommend that I introduce the fact that I know he murdered my family?"

"Simple. We want you to say, 'We may have met one another.' Ask him if he has ever been to Jozefow, Poland. Tell him you were there when the Germans liquidated the Jews. We will have men in place to storm the home by this time. We know he will figure out that you are the teacher from America. We must wait for him to make a move or for you to say that you saw him murdering your family. If he has a gun, there is a good chance you will see it by this time. It would be best to yell "Gun" as loud as possible and hit the deck. We will finish the job. We will be seconds away from entry when we hear the word 'gun.' Our team practices these types of maneuvers several times a month, plus the people working this case have multiple kills in their careers. They know what they are doing."

CHAPTER FIFTY-EIGHT

Positioned about two blocks away from the Helen and Wilhelm Wahl residence, Icek and his BND companion, agent Heinz Niehaus, sat in an actual Deutsche Telekom company van, a green and yellow two-toned 1970 model VW Double Cab Transporter Van. They performed radio checks and gear checks and waited for the all-clear from BND command to head to the Wahl residence. In the meantime, they reviewed their checklist and waited for the all-clear to proceed to the Wahl home.

Icek's heart thudded against his ribs, a trapped bird desperate for escape. The silence he projected was a fragile shield against the tremor in his hands. A cold sweat prickled his skin. Decades. Decades since experiencing raw terror. *Stay still. Breathe.* He inhaled slowly, the air catching a ragged sound in the cab of the van. He thought, *routine service call. Technician.* That's all. He willed his racing pulse to slow and thought, *composure, God, grant me composure.*

He risked a glance at Heinz, forcing a lightness he didn't feel. "Heinz, run that checklist again, would you?"

Heinz's Alabama drawl, thick as molasses, filled the space. "Now, Icek, y'all ain't fixin' to go all soft on me, are *ya?* We can park ourselves right here and pour over that *thar* list till kingdom come if it'll ease your mind."

The sheer incongruity of the accent in this place, at this moment, was a lifeline. Icek managed a choked laugh. "Remarkably convincing. You have been studying up on Southern charm?"

Heinz grinned, shaking his head. "Charm? Nah, man. It was *No Time for Sergeants,* that flick from '58—Andy Griffith, Don Knotts, and the best, Nick Adams. I must've watched it fifteen times just to get that twang right.[88] My old man snagged a beat-up 8mm copy from some American GI he was stationed with at the Berlin Wall. The funny thing is, none of us spoke a lick of English back then. We just watched it over and over, hypnotized by that strange, alien sound. Newsreels, that's what we were used to—Walter Cronkite, *'And that's the way it is.'* It drove my folks up the wall, especially when we started learning English.[89] They threatened to burn that damn film if I didn't quit. Grainy as hell, it was, but it didn't matter. I just had to sound like those Southern boys."

"Well, the effort shows. It almost made me forget how tense I am. Thanks, Heinz." The words were a whisper, barely audible.

"We got this, Icek. And remember," Heinz tapped Icek's chest lightly, "the cavalry's waiting outside, ready to roll. One wrong move, and they're in."

Icek's answering smile was a strained grimace. "Right. The cavalry. I keep forgetting."

Heinz unfolded the checklist, his voice dropping back to its regular, crisp cadence as he recited each item. Icek responded with a clipped "Check," and after each point, his focus was laser sharp.

Finally, Heinz folded the list, the Southern drawl returning with a playful curve of his lips. "Y'all ready to roll?"

A sudden buzz came across their walkie-talkie. "Base to unit zed forty-three, base to unit zed forty-three."

Heinz replied, "Unit zed forty-three to base. Go ahead."

"Base to unit zed forty-three, all assets are in place, and you are a go. Repeat, you are a go."

Heinz replied, "Unit zed forty-three to base, we copy. Repeat, we copy. We will proceed."

"Base to unit zed forty-three, God speed. Good luck."

Heinz looked at Icek and said, "Are you ready, partner?"

Icek drew another breath, the knot in his stomach loosening just a fraction. "Let's get this done."

They approached the Wahl residence like two phantoms of the mundane. Icek and Heinz exited their van. The green clipboards, clutched like shields, their color, nearly disappeared by the faded, dark green of their phone-company work pants, the kind that whispered of countless washings. Their faded yellow shirts, stained with the ghosts of unknown spills, bore nametags and a corporate identity patch, bleached and fraying above the left breast pocket. Even the nametags, 'Heinz' and the name 'Alesky'—a name Icek likely had trouble pronouncing, bore the subtle scars of time, the plastic slightly clouded, the corners softened by years of wear. Canvas gear bags, heavy with the promise of telephone test equipment and the secret, leaden weight of concealed weapons and spare ammunition, hung from their shoulders.

Icek, his vision blurred behind the thick lenses of his glasses, which magnified the intensity of his unwavering gaze, adjusted the canvas belt sagging with an arsenal of testing devices. The strap of his gear bag bit into his shoulder, a familiar, grounding pressure. He moved with the deliberate, almost fussy precision of a man who'd spent a lifetime tracing wires, hunting for the subtle hum of a fault. Heinz, in contrast, wore his cap pulled low, casting a shadow across his eyes. His worn tool belt molded to his body like a second skin, and the casual sling of his canvas bag whispered of years spent wrestling with cables and coaxing connections back to life. He moved with a practiced ease, his calloused thumb pressing the doorbell with an unhurried confidence.

The woman who answered was a study in unassuming elegance. Her gray hair, swept back, framed a face that, despite the fine lines of age—perhaps mid-sixties—radiated a genuine, almost unsettling warmth. Her smile was immediate, her eyes bright with a welcoming, almost childlike curiosity. "You must be from the phone company," she said, her voice tinged with a pleasant, melodic accent. "We've been expecting you. Some static, I believe?"

"Yes, ma'am," Heinz (using the alias Hans) replied, his head bobbing in a respectful nod. "I'm Hans, and this is my quality control associate, Alesky Maigret." He gestured toward Icek. "Now, Alesky, he might look German, but don't let that fool you. He's a Canuck, born and bred. Parents emigrated from Poland in the 1920s. He speaks enough German to get himself into trouble, but English is his native language. He also speaks Polish. He just squeaked by that German language exam for his work permit. Don't look at me. I don't write the rules. "I majored in languages," Hans replied. "English was my second language. I also speak some Polish, but it often betrays me."

"I'm Helen," the woman replied, extending a hand with delicate grace. "And my husband, Wilhelm, is on the back patio, lost in his classical music, as usual. It is magnificent to have English speakers in the house. Would you mind terribly if we conversed in English? I taught high school English here in Hamburg, you see. My husband and I take delight in any opportunity to practice."

Alesky, his voice a carefully modulated monotone, added, "As Hans mentioned, my German was just sufficient to pass the test and secure my work permit, nothing more."

Helen, with a bright smile and her face showing excitement about having English-speaking phone personnel, said, "English is a marvelous language. I imparted its intricacies to ninth-grade students for thirty long years at the local high school. It's a rare treat to engage in English conversation now. Tell me, Alesky, where precisely are you from?"

"Calgary, Alberta, Canada," he answered, struggling to keep his voice from betraying the tremor in his hands.

"Ah, Alberta," Helen's eyes lit up with a spark of genuine interest. "The Canadian Rockies are on our list. We're simply waiting for the opportune moment—the weather can be so capricious, you know— Jasper, Banff, and, of course, the enchanting Lake Louise. You've been to all of them, I presume?"

"Yes, ma'am, from my bedroom window, I have a great view of the Canadian Rockies. From my home to Banff is a hundred and twenty kilometers," Icek said, finding strange comfort in the familiar rhythm of the conversation. "My parents were avid campers. Dad, a fly fisherman through and through, spent countless hours on those rivers. It's truly one of the most breathtaking places on Earth. I'd recommend late July if you can manage it. You might even catch the early blush of autumn in August."

"I must inform Wilhelm of your familiarity with the region—how fortuitous. I'll make a note of your recommendation. Thank you, as this has been delightful. I'll let you attend to your duties now." Helen turned to retreat inside, her smile lingering with warmth in the air.

Icek carefully disassembled the phone's handset, his movements precise and practiced. He connected his dialer to the line, mimicking a conversation with a distant, imaginary technician, his voice a low, professional murmur. "Still picking up that static, huh? Try a frequency adjustment. I'll hold, see if that remedies the issue."

Heinz occupied himself with his clipboard, meticulously noting timestamps next to each entry. The act, though simple, lent an air of officialness, especially as Mrs. Wahl seemed to be observing them with a keen, almost birdlike interest. *Gotta maintain the facade*, he thought, the words a silent mantra.

"Management has us documenting every minute detail these days," Heinz explained to Mrs. Wahl, offering a slightly weary, rueful smile. "Can't hurt to have a little quality assurance, I suppose. They're really tightening the screws on efficiency downtown. Oh, pardon me a moment. I need to retrieve a replacement handset component from the truck."

"My, the intricacies of telephones these days are simply bewildering. The training must be quite extensive."

As he moved toward the door, he turned back to Mrs. Wahl, a thoughtful expression on his face. "Constant learning, ma'am. That's the nature of this job."

Heinz stepped over to his truck, his eyes scanning anxiously for the telltale flash of the headlights. *There!* The lights blinked a silent, coded confirmation. *Thank God.* He thought, *The team in the truck's receiving our audio signal fine—they'll record everything the team members say, as well as all dialogue from the Wahl family.*

He returned to the house, going through the motions of troubleshooting a phantom static, knowing that every syllable spoken within the Wahl residence was captured, scrutinized, and preserved by BND technicians in the van outside as evidence.

The small talk between Helen and Icek flowed.

She inquired. "Alesky, how many states have you visited? Which states are your favorites?"

"My family is quite careful with their money. They have never enjoyed spending it. As a result, we toured many places and stayed at the campsites instead of motels. Campsites are significantly more affordable than motels, costing two to three dollars daily, compared to the fifteen dollars that motels typically charge. I have been fortunate to see about thirty of the fifty states, and I've enjoyed all of them. That said, Montana, California, and Washington are my favorites."

"You have seen so much. I always told my students that those who travel, naturally seem to have a higher level of maturity than those who stay put."

Icek responded. "You sound like my parents." He approached the breezeway between the back porch and the kitchen. Wilhelm emerged from the back porch and Icek froze. His carefully constructed facade threatened to crumble. He found himself staring into the face of the man who had been the architect of his nightmares for decades—*those evil eyes, the thin lips, and the scars on his left cheek, the same cold, vacant eyes devoid of any flicker of humanity. And that mole is on the left side of his head, above his ear, and about halfway between his left eye and his ear. He still has that white-wall military haircut, although his dark hair is now snow white. There is no mistaking the fact—it is him. The one who slaughtered Ryfka and my dear sisters—Edna and Matty.*

A wave of nausea threatened to overwhelm him. Wilhelm moved from the back porch into the kitchen. The floors creaked as he passed by where Icek stood. He was close enough to smell the faint, almost nauseating scent of his aftershave. They nearly touched as Icek's eyes followed his stroll into the kitchen. From the corner of his eye, he watched as Wilhelm approached the icebox. He listened as the sound of ice cubes entered his glass, then the sound of the tea as it drowned the ice. With his drink in hand, Wilhelm disappeared to the back patio, where his wife joined him. He heard Helen talking to Wilhelm, mentioning that one of the repairmen was from Alberta, Canada. Helen asked, "Dear, do you remember when we were planning a trip to Alberta?"

Wilhelm replied, "Another damned foreigner taking the job of a German is all I see. Why do we need to let foreigners take German jobs? The answer is, we don't!"

The scene was a stark contrast to the horrifying, monstrous reality Icek knew. The injustice of his ordinary, carefree life hit him like a punch to the gut. *No. No more. Today, it ends.*

Icek and Heinz, work bags in hand, stepped onto the patio, feigning a search for the elusive grounding wire.

Wilhelm's voice, sharp and edged with irritation, cut through the air like a shard of glass. "What in God's name are you doing here? There are no phones out here, no wires. Get out! Leave me in peace."

Heinz stepped forward, adopting a placating, almost apologetic tone. "Mr. Wahl, I do apologize for the intrusion. We're in search of the ground wire for the telephone system. It's a multi-stranded, bare wire connected to a metal rod driven into the earth. Corroded connections are a frequent cause of static issues. It's a mandatory check on every installation. Please, bear with us just a moment longer."

Helen Wahl, drawn by her husband's raised voice, shuffled briskly to the patio. "Wilhelm, must you be so gruff? These gentlemen are merely performing their duties."

"Madam," Heinz explained, his voice a soothing balm, "we're simply attempting to locate the ground connection. A loose or corroded wire can wreak havoc on the system. We need to inspect it—this may be the fix to rid your line of static."

Icek took a deliberate step closer to Wilhelm, his heart beating out of his chest, the palms of both hands dripped sweat onto the patio, while the moisture in the headband of his cap dripped down his face. He cleared his throat several times.

Wahl, with a disgruntled smirk, said in a carefully controlled monotone, "Why are you staring at me?"

"Mr. Wahl, you appear familiar. Have we met before?"

Wilhelm dismissed him with a rude, dismissive and confident shake of his head. "Not possible. My wife just told me you are Canadian, and we've never set foot in Alberta."

Icek, not breaking his icy stare, and in a monotone voice, delivered words he had been waiting for decades to offer, "Sir, I'm not referring to Alberta." Icek pressed on, his voice hardening, the steel beneath the veneer beginning to show. "I'm speaking of Jozefow, Poland. July 13th,

1942. The day your Police Battalion 101 slaughtered fifteen hundred innocent Jewish souls."

Recognition and something far colder flickered in Wilhelm's eyes, like a snake stirring in the shadows. With a stern look on his face, Stein stood and pointed his finger at Icek, almost touching his nose. "Here I thought you were a phone repairman—you are nothing but an impostor. You're that Colorado schoolteacher who was snooping in the photo library at the police station that Albert Stein phoned about yesterday. Why are you harassing me? The German government prosecuted me for war crimes—and found me guilty—I served my sentence. Was that not sufficient for you?"

Helen interjected, her voice rising in a desperate, almost frantic defense. "He issued the orders—he didn't personally commit any killings. He was punished for his transgression. He's atoned for his actions."

"Mrs. Wahl," Icek's voice was tight, a wire stretched to its breaking point, vibrating with barely controlled emotion, "I was there. I witnessed it all. I peered through the window of my home, and in the flickering light of a lantern, I saw your husband draw his Walther P-38 revolver and execute my grandmother. Two shots to the head. She was a sixty-eight-year-old bedridden stroke victim. She was utterly helpless. After this inhumane animal murdered my Gramma Ryfka in front of my ten-year-old twin sisters, he instructed the twins to leave. They refused. They wouldn't abandon their grandmother. So, he shot them, point-blank range, as the twins clung to their lifeless grandmother. And the despicable last words to my innocent twin sisters—'Have it your way, suit yourselves.'"

"You're mistaken!" Helen cried, her voice a fractured melody of denial. "My Wilhelm would never, he wouldn't commit such a brutal act against a grandmother and innocent little girls. You have the wrong man!"

"*God damn it! God damn it all!*" Wilhelm exploded, his carefully constructed composure finally shattering, splintering into a thousand jagged pieces. "Yes! I killed that helpless Jewish bitch! She was Jew vermin! And I offered the children a choice! They wouldn't leave! All they had to do was depart! Why didn't they comply?"

"Because they loved her!" Icek's voice was raw, a harsh cry torn from the depths of his grief and fury. "They adored their grandmother. They wouldn't leave her, dead or alive. She was the only mother they'd ever known. Our mother perished giving birth to them."

"It was war!" Wilhelm shouted, his face contorted, a grotesque mask of desperation and defiance. "We had orders! I was obeying orders! You cannot arrest me for adhering to directives! God damn it! Now, vacate this property and leave us be before I summon the authorities!"

A voice crackled in Icek's earpiece, urgent and crystal clear. "Instruct Heinz to present his BND identification and effect the arrest. I repeat! Effect the arrest! We have the necessary evidence. We have a complete confession recorded! Excellent work! Proceed with the arrest. We will storm the residence!"

Heinz, with the practiced, fluid efficiency of a seasoned operative, drew his BND identification, displaying it to Wahl while simultaneously retrieving his pistol from the canvas bag. The nine-millimeter, now trained on Wahl, steady and unwavering, a black hole promising oblivion. "Mr. Wilhelm Wahl, place your hands in the air and keep them there. You are under arrest for crimes against humanity. Specifically, the murders of Ms. Ryfka Amelia Kelner, age sixty-eight, and her twin grandchildren, Matya Asia Kelner and Edna Henna Kelner, age ten, on the morning of July 13th, 1942, in Jozefow, Poland. We also possess a warrant to search your residence and vehicles. Do you have any inquiries?"

"This is a goddamned travesty!" Wahl sputtered, but the fight seemed to have drained from him, leaving behind only a hollow shell of defiance. "Do not fret, Helen. I'll be released before the day concludes."

Within moments, the house swarmed with armed BND personnel, a coordinated, silent ballet of tactical precision. The BND commandos subdued Wilhelm Wahl and placed him spread-eagled on the bedroom floor, stripped bare. They dressed Wahl in the stark, dehumanizing uniform of a federal prisoner. Blindfolded, handcuffed, and shackled, he was a portrait of defeated defiance, a broken man stripped of his illusions. While the team meticulously searched the residence, Icek and Heinz escorted Helen Wahl outside.

Heinz addressed her, his voice now devoid of any pretense, the Southern drawl a distant memory. "Madame Wahl, we'll require a statement from you at our headquarters downtown. The court *will not* grant bail. These are grave charges. We strongly advise you to retain legal counsel. We'll accompany you to the BND offices. We can converse en route."

Agent Schubert stepped toward Madame Wahl. He paused and then added gently, "Do you have any questions?"

She looked up at the sky, a shudder racking her body, a silent earthquake tearing through her carefully constructed world. Then, burying her face in her hands, she screamed in German, a primal, distressed cry of anguish, "Dear Lord, what have I done to deserve this?

"Madame, there is nothing you could have done," Agent Schubert said softly, his voice a gentle counterpoint to her raw despair.

"I am so deeply sorry," she choked out, her voice thick with tears, the words barely audible. "So sorry for the immeasurable pain my Wilhelm inflicted all those years ago. He would never confess. Never. There were whispers and rumors from other wives. But I refused to believe them. You see, my Wilhelm was a good husband. Kind, loving. We shared a good life. Except for the nightmares. Every night since his return from the war. The screams, the cold sweats, and the grinding of teeth intensified after his sentencing, following his release from prison. I know he harbored regret. He wouldn't have suffered so profoundly if he hadn't."

Agent Schubert nodded slowly—his eyes filled with a weary understanding. "Mr. Wahl, like so many others, was ensnared in Hitler's web. They believed they were fulfilling their duty, constructing a superior Germany."

She looked up, her eyes red-rimmed, swollen with unshed tears. "We can proceed. But first, I must speak to the man whose family Wilhelm destroyed."

"Are you certain?" Agent Schubert asked gently, his voice laced with concern. "Perhaps it would be preferable to…"

"I insist," she said, her voice regaining a semblance of strength, fragile steel beneath the tremor. "I owe him an explanation. The magnitude of tonight just struck me. My Wilhelm, he admitted it. He confessed to the slaughter of innocent victims. For years, I refused to believe it. But the truth emanated from his lips."

"I understand," Agent Schubert replied. He stepped over to Icek and whispered, "Icek, please escort Mrs. Wahl into the living room. She would like to speak with you. And please, relinquish your weapon to me."

"Yes, sir," Icek said, his voice a low murmur, handing over the weapon with a slight tremor in his hand.

They sat facing each other in the living room, the silence heavy, a chasm of pain separating them. Helen spoke first, her voice trembling, a fragile melody of sorrow. "I cannot fathom what you endured that night—a young boy forced to witness such unspeakable horror. Your family, they didn't deserve that—any of it. Wilhelm has been under Hitler's insidious spell since he heard him speak back in '37. He was in the front row, captivated." She wiped away tears, her gaze meeting Icek's, a plea for understanding in their depths.

"I know it signifies nothing after all this time, but I am profoundly sorry for what my husband perpetrated. He will harm no one else. I am truly deeply sorry. You didn't deserve the life that fate dealt you."

Icek looked at her, seeing not just the wife of a monster but a woman grappling with a devastating, world-shattering truth. "I perceived from the moment we met that you're a good person, Mrs. Wahl. Educated, compassionate. I imagine, once, perhaps before the war's insidious grip tightened, you were happy. Carefree. Am I mistaken?"

"We did share many joyful years," she whispered, her voice a fragile echo of the past. "Before that madman, Hitler, seized control. Wilhelm will inflict no further pain. Oh God, I cannot conceive of the terror— you deserve peace."

"Thank you, Mrs. Wahl. You deserve tranquility as well. I'll summon Agent Schubert's assistant, Ms. Stier, and she'll accompany you downtown for your statement."

"Thank you. And what is your name?"

He hesitated, a flicker of doubt, a shadow of uncertainty crossing his mind. *Should I tell her?* Then, he reached out and gently grasped her hand, his gaze locking with hers, a bridge across the abyss. "Icek Kelner. I'm a high school history teacher in Denver, Colorado. My wife, also a Polish native, instructs advanced mathematics at the same institution. We have two wonderful children, a boy and a girl."

Helen, with a pleasant grin, said, "Such a nice family—as you are aware, I, too, was an educator."

Icek responded, his voice gentle, "Yes. You told me earlier that you taught the English language. I recall now. He grabbed her hand and said, "It was nice meeting you—I wish we could have met under different circumstances." She stared into Icek's eyes, and without another word, she dropped to a sitting position on the couch, buried her head into a pillow, and cried.

Icek left.

Agent Schubert and the team gathered in the van for an after-action meeting. With the entire team present, he asked Heinz and Icek to come to the front of the truck where he stood, then looked about the team with a satisfied expression, a subtle lift at the corners of his mouth, and said, "Exemplary work, both of you. Your composure, your unwavering focus, it was masterful."

Heinz and Icek exchanged a look, a mixture of relief and grim, hard-won satisfaction. "Fate," Heinz said quietly, his voice a low murmur. "The Man upstairs knew Icek was the one to confront Wahl. Wahl deserves every ounce of punishment they hand out. It's a pity we no longer have the death penalty. He's pure evil. No remorse. Not a single iota."

Icek nodded, his voice heavy, laden with the weight of the past. "Revenge, they claim, is sweet. But as Jews, we're not supposed to crave vengeance. My heart aches for Mrs. Wahl. She didn't deserve this cruel twist of fate. He maintained her in ignorance for decades. I believe she genuinely believed, throughout all these years, that he wasn't a cold-blooded murderer. She's yet another victim here."

CHAPTER FIFTY-NINE

Hamburg, Germany, BND Headquarters
June 21ˢᵗ, 1974, 6:45 a.m.

Agent Schubert sat, the Hamburg sunrise a fleeting crimson and gold spectacle, bleeding across the eastern sky outside his window. He'd battled for this office, this view, a hard-won territorial claim staked against colleagues exiled to the interior, windowless cubicles. The fiery display, a small compensation, barely offset the bureaucratic victories and did not make up for the fresh stack of printouts—stark black ink on white paper, arrayed across his desk.

First on today's agenda, Abram Kelner's disappearance, another Polish citizen swallowed by a horror he thought he'd grown numb to, felt like a blow, bruising over old scar tissue.

Schubert's gaze wasn't lost in the dawn's fiery display. Instead, it traced the worn path carved into his office carpet, a groove parallel to the floor-to-ceiling glass. The wool fibers compressed by countless hours of restless pacing, each step a counterpoint to unsolved cases and the acrid taste of too many compromises, stretched between his desk and the wall. Two guest chairs faced his large, cluttered desk like silent, expectant judges. Their faded upholstery had absorbed the nervous sweat of countless interviewees. Faint impressions of past occupants, barely visible in the worn fabric, lingered like phantom limbs—ghosts he couldn't entirely exorcise.

But this was different. The familiar ache behind his breastbone had sharpened, a razor's edge honed by one word. Icek. The name, scrawled across the top page in bold black marker, seemed to throb with a silent urgency. Icek, who had arrived in Hamburg with the most straightforward, most profound purposes: to bear witness. An educator, he'd been scheduled to share his wartime experiences in Poland. Now, that voice was silenced. But Icek, a veteran of the Jozefow massacre, had somehow compromised the Battalion 101 survivors who, until now, had escaped the hangman's noose. Their freedom, so meticulously maintained for decades, had been as brittle as a dried leaf caught in a gale.

Based on information provided by Wilhelm Wahl in his first twelve hours of custody, he negotiated a deal by giving the names of seven other former Battalion 101 veterans who took part in the murder of Polish citizens. A total of eight veterans were already moldered in custody, awaiting their arrest and confessions, staining the air—a rancid stench of old atrocities mixed with the coppery tang of fresh blood, a smell Schubert knew he could never scrub clean. And yet, Icek's talk had been canceled. The irony felt like a physical blow. The BND felt the risk was too high for a presentation.

Agent Schubert pushed back from the desk, the scrape of his chair against the floor a harsh counterpoint to the sudden silence. He moved toward the door, stopping just short, his hand hovering over the knob. He pivoted, facing his secretary, Ingrid, who was expertly working in her adjacent office.

"Top of the morning, Ingrid," he said, his voice remarkably steady. "The team. My office. Five minutes." He paused, forcing a tight smile that failed to reach his eyes. "And, yes, another cup of tea would be glorious." He winced inwardly. Kindness that did not sound sincere but fake, a skill he'd never truly mastered. His shortcomings in small talk of kindness felt particularly clumsy today.

A muscle ticked in Schubert's jaw, a tiny metronome marking the rising tide of anger, threatening to breach the dam of his professional control. He returned to his office. The team assembled swiftly, their hurried footsteps echoing in the corridor. He paced the worn groove in the floor, not frantically but with a deliberate, almost predatory rhythm. The silence in the room wasn't empty—it was a compressed spring, thick with unspoken questions and doubt he could practically taste radiating from the assembled team—a doubt mirroring his own.

Nine of his team, plus Ingrid, now filled the office, their eyes riveted on him, expectant. Five more data center employees working the night shift processed the torrent of data requests from his dayshift intelligence techs. He paused, his back to the fading sunrise, his gaze sweeping from the worn carpet—a testament to his disquiet—to the faces of those who were meant to be his allies in this ceaseless pursuit of twisted, elusive justice. He searched for a flicker of understanding, a shared spark of outrage in the carefully composed expressions of his team. His voice, when he finally spoke, was low, a rumble carrying the weight of something far heavier than a mere order.

"His father is out there." Schubert's voice was devoid of its usual commanding resonance, leaving the words stark, almost brutal, in the sudden quiet. He paused, letting the weight of that simple statement settle onto each person in the room. "And we will find him. That isn't a question. It isn't bravado. It's certainty, a debt." He drew a slow breath, the air seeming thick with unspoken history. "Dead or alive, Icek Abram Kelner deserves to know the truth. We owe him that much. After everything he endured. Everything he tried to tell us." His gaze swept the room, lingering on each face. "Humanity deserves to know. I want you to proceed as if this were your father, your brother, lost in the ashes. No shortcuts. Overtime is a given. Blow the damned budget, I don't care." His voice roughened. "Icek's testimony helped us cage eight of those Nazi butchers. This is the absolute least we can offer in return. Think outside every box. Use every technique, every contact, every sliver of persuasion those damned charm schools drilled into you. Everything."

His stare wasn't just a command—it was an anchor, pulling them all into the gravity of his resolve, a burden shared in the flickering dawn light. The sunrise, painting the sky in pale, watery gold, cast long, skeletal shadows across the floor. But the fire in Schubert's eyes wasn't golden; it was the cold, blue-white flame of a hunter closing in, fueled by something far more profound than duty. This quest to locate Icek's father was a reckoning etched onto his very soul.

"Questions?"

Silence answered him, heavy and absolute.

Schubert's voice, when he spoke again, was rough, cracked, the earlier forced lightness utterly gone. He wouldn't meet their eyes, his gaze fixed instead on a scuff mark violating the polished floorboards as if it represented a flaw in the very fabric of life. "We press on. Every scrap of paper, every whispered rumor, every forgotten file cabinet drawer—each one is a stone we must turn over. And beneath one," he paused, his fist clenching unconsciously at his side, knuckles white, "beneath one—we will find him. The truth. The key that unlocks this—this-this obscenity."

He finally looked up, and the weariness in his eyes wasn't just from sleepless nights— it was ancient, bone-deep, the exhaustion of a man carrying ghosts. "This situation," he gestured vaguely, a sweep of his hand encompassing his shirt and trousers, his office, perhaps his entire life, "this facade—it never fit right. The Reich we built—the blood that soaked the earth, the families torn apart, obliterated—all because one madman with a twisted vision gave the orders." He swallowed, the sound painfully loud in the stillness. His voice dropped to a low rasp, thick with unshed tears. "The faces—I see their faces. Not just numbers etched in reports. Faces. Children clutching dolls. Mothers shielding their young." He shook his head, a sharp, violent negation as if trying to dislodge the images burned behind his eyelids physically. "It cannot stand. This disappearance of a father, this evil, it must never stand again."

He dragged a shaking hand across his face, the rasp of overnight stubble a grounding, tactile reminder of time slipping relentlessly away, measured not in hours but in decades of loss.

June 23rd, 1974

A tentative tap echoed on Agent Schubert's office door. Ingrid stood there, and beside her, the newly hired forensics graduate, Ms. Monika Hahn. Monika was a short, plump blonde, her thick glasses magnifying eyes that seemed to hold an unsettling, focused intensity, as if they could see through walls, through time itself.

"Come," Schubert managed, his voice a flat line, scraped clean of tone. "Both of you. Please. Sit. Close the door." He gestured toward the chairs, their worn upholstery seeming to sigh under the weight of expectation. "Speak. I'm listening." He leaned forward slightly, every fiber of his being straining to hear.

"Sir," Ingrid began, her usual briskness softened, "our new hire, Miss Monika Hahn—well, she's found something quite remarkable concerning Icek's father, Abram Kelner. And since Monika made the breakthrough, I felt she should have the honor."

"Wait." Schubert held up a hand, the sudden sharpness in his voice startling. "Before another word is spoken. I want Icek Kelner here. Now. Get the police involved if you must. Use the sirens. I don't care how you retrieve him. We go no further until Icek is in this room." He glanced at the clock. "He's perhaps twenty minutes away, depending on traffic. A police escort could cut that in half. Ingrid, make it happen. Now." As Ingrid moved swiftly to the phone, Schubert turned back, gesturing Monika toward the chair. "In the meantime, Ms. Hahn, you and I will chat. Before we start, have you had lunch?"

"Yes, sir, I had my brown bag lunch over an hour ago."

"Very good, then, please continue."

Seventeen minutes stretched into an eternity, each tick of the wall clock landing like a hammer blow against the fragile silence. Then, the sound of hurried footsteps, a door opening, and Icek was there. He looked breathless, wary, hope warring with years of ingrained disappointment in his eyes.

Agent Schubert rose and made the swift introductions, his voice tight with controlled anticipation. Icek, briefed only that there was significant news, sat stiffly, his hands twisting together in his lap, a knot of raw nerves made visible.

Ingrid quietly excused herself, closing the door behind her, leaving the three of them suspended in the charged air.

"Good afternoon, Icek," Schubert began, his voice regaining a fraction of its warmth. "Allow me to introduce Miss Monika Hahn. She is, without exaggeration, one of the most brilliant minds on my staff. A name, I assure you—you *will* remember. For the record," he added, a touch of pride seeping through, "her IQ is 141. The highest in the BND."

Icek offered a small, strained smile. "Impressive. Truly. I—I understand you've been working searching for my father." The words were simple yet carried the weight of a lifetime's longing.

Agent Schubert leaned forward again, unable to contain the burgeoning energy in the room. "Icek, forgive me. I cannot bear the suspense a moment longer. Ms. Hahn, the floor is yours."

Monika adjusted her glasses, her voice starting as barely more than a whisper, her gaze initially directed at her own hands clasped in her lap. "Sir, Herr Kelner, I approached the problem from perhaps a slightly different angle." She paused, gathering herself. "When people endure something as unspeakable as forced labor, the horrors of captivity—I tried to imagine it, to empathize. In those conditions, under such duress, the only solace, the only strength, comes from each other. Survivors—they cling together." Her eyes lifted, meeting Icek's for the first time, magnified and strangely luminous behind the thick lenses. "So, when tasked with finding your father, Abram, I didn't just look for him in isolation. I focused on the men who shared his ordeal. His closest comrades within that hell. Those who survived—they wouldn't just drift apart. That shared nightmare would forge bonds stronger than steel. I remembered an old American film about the war and soldiers saying, 'You watch my back. I got your back.'"

"And this—this-this cinematic observation led you where, exactly?" Icek asked, his voice rough. He leaned forward, knuckles white, where he gripped the arms of the chair, his gaze locked onto Monika's face.

"The idea of lifelong solidarity," Monika continued, her voice gaining a quiet confidence. "I had the list of maintenance professionals from the ammunition plant. Tracing their paths after liberation was complex. Many dead ends with numerous frustrating gaps. But then, I concentrated on those known to be Abram's immediate workmates. We had the list, sir, the nearly eighty men rounded up in Jozefow, forced onto that railcar." She took another breath, the air in the room seeming to thin. "Using that list, I pursued a simpler question: Could I locate any of those seventy-eight skilled craftsmen?"

"Got it," Icek breathed, a flicker of something wild lighting his eyes. "The logic—it's... Please. Continue." His leg had begun to bounce uncontrollably, a frantic rhythm against the floorboards.

"I was fortunate," Monika said, a hint of color rising in her cheeks. "I researched countries known for relatively open policies toward Holocaust survivors. Malta emerged. An English-speaking British colony then had a small population, under half a million in 1970. But crucially, Malta accepted a significant number of Jewish refugees during and even before the war. It was one of the few places in Europe that didn't demand visas.[90]" Her voice steadied, taking on a clear, factual tone yet was underscored with profound implication. "I cross-referenced the names of the seventy-eight men from the Jozefow transport with Maltese immigration and resettlement records. It yielded dozens of hits—temporary housing, medical stations, and job training facilities provided by the Maltese government. Skilled workers—mechanics, welders, machinists—were highly valued." She paused, looking directly at Icek now, her magnified eyes holding his captive. "Eventually, I found him. Herr Kelner, I am deeply pleased to report that your father, Abram Icek Kelner, is alive. He is alive and well."

The words hung in the air, impossibly heavy and bright.

The lingering words hit Icek hard. His father was alive.

Silence descended, thick and suffocating, broken only by the frantic drumming of Icek's own heart against his ribs. His face, already pale, turned the color of bleached bone. He surged upward, not quite steadily, a sound tearing from his throat—not a cry but a raw, strangled gasp, the sound of a soul cracking open after decades sealed shut. "Alive?" The word was a choked whisper, disbelieving. Then, louder, a sob catching in his throat, "After thirty-two years—he's alive! He's alive! Oh, dear God, I knew… I always knew…" He turned blindly toward Monika, his body trembling, tears suddenly erupting, not weeping, but a deluge coursing down his face unchecked. "Monika—Miss Hahn—stand up. Please. I, I, I need to hug you." His voice broke completely. "Everyone—everyone in this building deserves a hug!"

He fumbled for a handkerchief, pressing it to his streaming eyes, his shoulders shaking violently. He sank back into the chair, collapsing more than sitting, the handkerchief muffling choked, gasping sobs. "Alive… he's really… alive. After all this time… thirty-two years…"[91]

Schubert sat frozen for a long moment, his own eyes suspiciously bright, his composure fractured. He cleared his throat, the sound rough. "One moment." He pressed the intercom, his voice thick. "Ingrid. All hands. My office. Immediately. No delays."

Within minutes, the office was crammed, agents and techs spilling into the hallway, a low murmur of confusion rippling through the crowd.

"Ladies and gentlemen," Schubert began, his voice resonating with an emotion rarely heard.

"Most of you have met Herr Icek Abram Kelner, the son of the man whose whereabouts we have dedicated ourselves to uncovering." He paused, letting the anticipation build. "For those who haven't, allow me to present him again." He gestured toward Icek, who was still struggling to compose himself, tear tracks glistening on his face. "Son of the recently located—and very much alive—Abram Icek Kelner."

A collective gasp went through the room, followed by an explosion—not of noise but of pure, unadulterated relief and joy. Spontaneous applause broke out, along with those in the room shaking hands and exchanging hugs. To so many in the room, the miracle that just happened, finding Icek's father, seemed to be a one-in-a-million occurrence. Abram seemed like a miracle. The stoic, professional atmosphere of a government office was shattered, replaced by something fragile, wondrous, almost holy. Men and women who dealt daily with the grim aftermath of darkness all felt bathed in the unexpected light provided by Icek's steadfast excitement, knowing he would indeed see his father after three decades.

Agent Schubert slowly rose, holding up a hand for silence. The room gradually quieted, all eyes on him.

"In my thirty-plus years," he began, his voice trembling slightly, "there are moments. Moments when you know, deep in your bones, that you are exactly where you are supposed to be—it's when your heart confirms the path your life has taken." He looked around at his team, his gaze filled with profound gratitude. "I have never, never been prouder to lead a team than I am at this precise moment. This moment today, to witness the joy of not only Icek but also on the faces of everyone in our group. Finding Abram Kelner makes all the hours, the sleepless nights, the missed dinners, the personal sacrifices—it makes them utterly irrelevant." His voice cracked again. "To find Icek's father—after thirty-two years—lost to the shadows. My deepest, most heartfelt thanks to every single one of you for pouring your souls into this. I have never been prouder."

He beckoned to Icek to stand beside him. Turning to the still-trembling man, Schubert's voice dropped, becoming intensely personal, heavy with the weight of history. "Icek," he said, his own eyes welling up now, "we can do nothing to erase the sins of the past. Our government, our policies, then our blindness, our criminal disregard for human life, for people of the Jewish faith. And above all, the madness of Adolf Hitler—he unleashed a horror upon the world that claimed millions." His breath hitched. "Our nation's actions caused this agony, your agony, Icek. And the number of people we can truly save now, truly reach across the chasm of time from the ravages of that regime, is tragically small." He paused, looking from Icek to his team and back again. "But today—today we have this. This tiny, precious sliver of impossible success. A reminder of why this work, however painful, matters."

He could say no more. Agent Schubert, the stoic hunter, the man who carried the weight of a nation's guilt, sank back into his chair, buried his face in his hands, and wept. Not silently but with ragged, heartbroken sobs, the tears of a man finally allowing the ghosts he'd borne for far too long to find a moment's peace, tears washing away years of carefully constructed control.

And around him, his team didn't just offer congratulations. They surged forward, surrounding both Icek and their weeping chief, a wave of shared humanity, pats on the back, clasped hands, overwhelmed whispers of 'Unbelievable,' 'Thank God,' and 'Congratulations,' the sound not boisterous but thick with tears and the profound weight of a miracle witnessed.

CHAPTER SIXTY

Hamburg, Germany
June 25th, 1974, 10:45 a.m.

Icek and Agent Schubert sat, their steaming teacups swirling in the quiet office. Icek finally broke the silence, a tremor of disbelief in his voice. "You know the strangest part of all this?"

Schubert raised an eyebrow. "A loaded question."

"No. Not at all." Icek ran a hand through his hair. "I'm just trying to reconcile it. My father plays Bocce Ball?"

Schubert's lips twitched, not at Icek's bewilderment but at a shared, unspoken understanding. "I'm not mocking your comment, Icek. It's the thought we've both harbored since we met back when we still clung to the hope of finding him alive. Yes, he is alive and playing Bocce Ball. It suggests your father is, shall we say, embracing life."

Icek let out a short, sharp laugh. "He's had ample time to master the language. He might even have acquired a British accent." He shook his head, picturing the image, a wry smile playing on his lips. "This could be interesting."

Schubert leaned forward, his voice softening. "Well, Icek, the moment has arrived. We have a location. We're in the same time zone. I'm holding his telephone number. And—you probably weren't aware—Abram is approximately 1,250 miles, or two thousand kilometers, distant."

"Yes. That is close." Icek's voice was a mere whisper. "You're suggesting it's time to call my father?"

"And you're thinking you can call him from this very office, using this very phone line, incurring no charges?"

"It's practically a local call within the same time zone, like phoning from Los Angeles to Denver." Icek paused, his gaze drifting toward the window. "I need a moment. To formulate what I'll say."

Schubert placed a reassuring hand on Icek's arm. "Trust me, Icek, no script is necessary. And I have an additional consideration. What good is discovering a father after thirty-two years if you can't share that moment with your family?"

Icek's eyes widened. "No! Truly? You'll allow me to phone Teodora?" The dam shattered and tears welled in Icek's eyes, cascading down his cheeks. He swiped at them, a tremor in his voice. "I reflect on my days in the Home Army—we were attempting to kill each other. And today, we're collaborating, like…" he trailed off, unable to articulate the peculiar bond forged in the crucible of their shared endeavor.

Schubert's voice was thick with emotion. "Icek, when this concludes, above all else, I want you to know that I consider you a friend—a true friend. And I would be grateful if you could disregard my nationality. Think of me as a human being." He reached into his pocket, retrieving a slip of paper, and slid it across the desk. "Abram Kelner, 17 Freedom Way, Valetta, Malta." The phone number was neatly inscribed below.

Icek's hand trembled as he reached for the paper. His fingers traced the letters and the numbers as if they possessed some inherent magic. He stared at the address, wiping away fresh tears. *I truly believed this day would never arrive.* Icek stood and stared into Detective Schubert's eyes. "What have I done to warrant such a gift?"

Schubert offered a gentle smile. "Perhaps the explanation is beyond our comprehension, Icek. Perhaps it originates from a power exceeding our own. Regardless," he gestured toward the phone. "I'll leave you. When you're ready, buzz Ingrid. She'll connect you with the overseas operator. And Icek, you can speak with your father for as long as you desire. You've earned it."

They stood, shaking hands, then impulsively embraced, tears mingling on their shoulders—a German and a Pole, united by common ground, transcending the ghosts of their shared past.

Schubert's voice held a profound quiet. "Icek, I'm at a loss for words. I have no frame of reference for the emotions you've endured these past days. Thirty-two years is an eternity to carry the burden of uncertainty."

Icek sank back into his chair, his head cradled in his hands. He wept unreservedly, the tears of a man finally releasing the weight of a lifetime, of unanswered questions, of a father lost and miraculously restored.

Schubert nodded toward the phone. "The phone and the room are yours, Icek. I'm leaving and heading to my favorite establishment. I'm going to celebrate. And as I depart, I'll invite others to join me. We've all earned this."

Icek emerged from Agent Schubert's office, his gaze snagged by the photographs arrayed on Ingrid's, the secretary's, desk. A recent family vacation to Disneyland: three towheaded children, all grins and eyes wide with that stunned wonder only a first encounter with such iconic characters could inspire. They flanked a towering man—Ingrid's husband, easily half a meter taller than she—posed with Mickey Mouse and Donald Duck. The children practically vibrated off the glossy paper.

"Disneyland," Icek murmured, a faint, faraway look softening his features. "The stuff of dreams."

Ingrid sighed, her shoulders slumping slightly, though a fond smile played on her lips. "The budget, well, lies in shattered pieces somewhere near the teacups. Doubled our projections. A 'never again' trip, at least according to the bank account."

"We endured the same fate. 'Never again,' we declared." Icek shifted, his hands subtly flexing. "I'm ready for my call. Agent Schubert mentioned you'd set things up, the overseas operator and the green light to call my wife in Colorado."

"Yes, he briefed me." Ingrid's fingers tapped a staccato rhythm on her keyboard. "We'll use the interrogation suite. Sound-resistant, completely private, and I hold the only key." She held out a minor brass key, its surface worn smooth with use. She walked to the room, unlocked the door, and said, "I feel for you. I had hoped all along that you would locate your father. I can't comprehend the emotion you are feeling at this very moment—that in a matter of minutes, you will be speaking with a long-lost father." She teared up as she handed the key to Icek. "You will be fine. If it were me, I would take it slow. But you'll do just fine."

"Fine?" Icek said, his chest tightening with a feeling that was almost too much like anticipation. "I'll gather my notes. Just point the way."

The interrogation room was stark, the air heavy and still, smelling faintly of disinfectant. Icek settled at the bare table, his palms leaving damp prints on the cool, polished surface. He unfolded his notes, the carefully compiled list, and smoothed the paper, his fingertip tracing the points he'd painstakingly crafted—a frail bridge across the chasm of thirty-two years.

- Ryfka, the twins, and their deaths. The monster responsible is rotting in prison.
- My marriage to Teodora. Our children: Kyle and Karen. He traced the names with his fingertip.
- The train accident that killed Jakub on his way to a concert, Jakub never knew Asia was expecting—Asia's marriage to Jack, and the birth of Jakub Junior.
- Our emigration to America. Our lives as teachers.
- The reason for my presence in Hamburg
- The BND's search for Halina—the promising leads.

Should I tell him so soon that the night he was arrested, the Germans murdered every Jew in Jozefow? He'd add more later, he decided. *There was no need to flood his father with everything at once.* He took a slow, deliberate sip of the tea Ingrid had thoughtfully provided, the warmth a small comfort against the rising tide of emotion. He was as ready as he'd ever be.

He picked up the phone, his voice a little unsteady. "Ingrid, I believe I'm ready. Could you attempt to reach my father, Abram?"

The minutes stretched, each tick of the clock a hammer blow in the silence. Finally, the phone buzzed with a sharp, intrusive sound. Icek snatched it up. "Icek, your party is on the line." Ingrid's voice was crisp and professional. "I'll disconnect now."

The plastic receiver felt unnaturally heavy in Icek's hand, slick with the sweat from his palm. *Thirty-two years. A lifetime.* He swallowed, the sound loud in his ears, rehearsing the words one last time in the silent office. He drew a breath that did little to calm the frantic bird beating against his ribs.

"Hello," he began, his voice thinner than he'd intended, cracking slightly. He cleared his throat. "This is Icek. Icek Abram Kelner. Father? Abram? Is that you?"

A pause crackled across the line, filled with the faint hiss of an international connection. Then, a voice, clipped and precise, startlingly marked by decades under a British sun. "Who is this? I believe you have the wrong number." The tone was impatient, dismissive. "I haven't the time for—"

"No! Father, wait!" Panic, cold and sharp, lanced through him. He gripped the edge of the desk, his knuckles whitening. "Father, it is Icek! Your son! Remember… remember Henna? The twins, Matty and Edna, Boris, our horse … how Matty always stole Edna's Shabbos bread?" The words tumbled out, desperate jewels against disbelief. Tears were stinging his eyes now, hot and blurring the notes he held in his hand. He didn't try to hide the tremor in his voice; let him hear it. Let him know.

Silence stretched across the wire, vast and terrifying. Then, a distinct, muffled clatter, followed by a choked gasp, a raw, ragged sound like air punched from lungs. It wasn't a cry of pain, exactly, but of shock so profound it bordered on agony. Time ceased. The clock ticked unnaturally loud, marking seconds that felt like hours.

Icek thought, *Has he dropped the phone? Was the shock too much?*

"Father?" Icek whispered, leaning closer, pressing the receiver hard against his ear. "Father? Are you there? Please, Father—it's Icek." *Please, God, let him pick it up.*

Another ragged breath hissed on the line, followed by a faint shuffling sound. "My boy?" The voice was thick and shattered. The British veneer cracked wide open, revealing something older, raw, and trembling beneath. Tears were audible now, rough and unashamed. "Icek? Is it—can it truly be—you?"

Relief crashed over Icek, so immense it buckled his knees. He sank into the office chair. "Yes, Father. Oh, God, Father, yes." He pressed a hand flat against his chest, trying to regulate breaths that came in shuddering waves. "It's so good—so good to hear your voice." A tear escaped, tracing a path down his cheek. "I almost-I-I—I didn't dare to hope—but I never stopped believing. Never."

"Oh, my son. My Icek. All these years, I knew it. Deep in my bones, I knew you were alive. Son, they insisted I learn English here," Abram's voice gathered a thread of coherence, though the wonder and disbelief still shook it. "When I ended up in Malta after everything, for work. It feels strange now, Polish—I hardly speak it anymore." A pause, then a rush, the words thick with unshed tears.

"I felt you were somewhere. Even after that night… I just knew you were alive, Father." Icek's voice thickened.

"Ryfka?" Abram asked, his tone hesitant, fragile. "And the little ones? Matty? Edna? Tell me they are well. Tell me they—"

Icek closed his eyes, the image searing his memory—smoke, shouting, the glint of moonlight on steel. He had to force the words past the knot tightening in his throat. Each syllable felt like swallowing broken glass. "Father—I have terrible news." He paused, bracing himself. "Ryfka and the twins—they were murdered, Father. By an SS man. A monster. It was the same night they took you." He choked back a sob. "They're gone. I saw it happen, Father. I couldn't do anything. I was just a boy, hiding."

A terrible sound tore through the line—not a scream this time but a long, dreadful moan of pure, unadulterated grief. It was the sound of a dam breaking after thirty-two years, releasing a flood of agony held back by fragile hope. "No… no…" Abram wept. "All this time, I pictured them grown. No! Not that night!" The sound echoed the hollow ache Icek carried every day.

"Icek, I spent years writing letters, trying my best to locate you and the others. They have organizations throughout Europe and the British Isles staffed with dozens of people looking for lost relatives. Since I had to learn English here in Malta, I wrote letters in English and Polish to different organizations in France, Germany, Poland, and England—to no avail. I gave up after about ten years of looking, as friends convinced me the damn Nazis most likely murdered you.

"I even sent letters to your Aunt Asia in New York. Evidently, I had the wrong address, as I never received any response. I pray she and Jakub are doing well."

"Father," he corrected gently, "Jakub was lost to us years ago, in a train accident. Asia has since remarried. I do, however, keep in touch with them." He paused, then added, "She married an American named Jack Reynolds, a former US Marine who served with distinction in British special forces operations. He saw heavy fighting over an eighteen-month period during the European campaign in World War II. Asia was carrying Jakub's son when he passed," he continued. "Jack and Asia wed when young Jakub was three. Now, they both work in New York City, for the same firm. Jack has become a perfect father figure for Jakub."

"A Jakub Junior," the father breathed, a hand rising to his chest. "God's own grace. And Halina? Our Halina, the twins' beloved nursemaid? "

"We know that she is alive and well and living in Scotland with family. We have spent countless hours trying to locate Halina—all to no avail. BND located her as a favor to our family, one of the BND intelligence officers tracked her down. We have her telephone number, address, and from what we know, she is in good health. When I get back to Colorado, we will contact her. We are hoping we can persuade her to make a trip to Colorado when we are all together."

"I am so pleased to discover Halina is alive. Thank you dear Lord."

"Father, I can't imagine the heartache. All that effort and no results." Icek swallowed hard against his own grief, gripping the receiver tighter. He had to anchor them both, searching to find any likeness to something positive in this wreckage. "Father," he said softly, hating the inadequacy of words. "Father, listen to me. We are alive. You and I." He searched for a way forward, a way to pull his father from that abyss. "Have you been in Malta all this time—did you ever remarry? Do you have another family now?"

There was a watery sniffle. "I had a few lady friends," Abram said, his voice thick. "Kind women. But marry again? No. How could I? It wouldn't have been fair to Henna." His voice broke on her name. "Your mother, Icek—I never got over losing her. Not truly. Even now—my heart…" He trailed off.

A shared ache resonated across the miles. "I understand, Father," Icek said quietly. "Every day, I have my own Henna moments, too. But Father, I did find someone. I married Teodora. Do you remember Tomasz, my friend, my fishing partner? I married his sister, Teodora." He rushed on, wanting to fill the silence with hope. "We live in America now. In Colorado. Father, there must be a reason God brought us back together now."

"America..." Abram breathed the word like a prayer. "Yes, son. God—His ways are not our ways. I have learned that much, at least."

Icek took another deep, steady breath. "Teodora and I, Father— we have children." He waited a beat, letting the words sink in. "A daughter, Karen Joan. She's twenty-three. And a son, Kyle Andrew. He's seventeen."

A sharp intake of breath on the other end. "Grandchildren?" Abram's voice was barely a whisper, filled with awe. "I have grandchildren?"

"Yes, Father. Two beautiful grandchildren. They know all about you, the grandfather they never met but always hoped was out there." Pride and relief swelled in Icek's chest. "Teodora and I, we're teachers. I teach history—imagine that, Father, teaching about the war. Teodora teaches math at the high school. We live near Denver. We became American citizens years ago."

"American citizens!" Abram repeated, the wonder deepening. "So far away. Is it good there, son?"

"It is, Father. It's home," Icek said, managing a small, watery smile. "The red, white, and blue, you know. It's given us a good life."

"The Allies," Abram murmured, a trace of hardness entering his voice. "If not for them, the Yanks, we would all be speaking German now, wouldn't we? God bless them. I always thought back then, only the very rich went to America."

Icek chuckled, a genuine sound this time, tight but real. "Trust me, Father, we are far from wealthy. But we are happy. Safe."

"I like Americans," Abram mused, his voice drifting slightly as if picturing them. "Many come here to Malta. Tourists. Good people.

Generous. Always paying in US dollars." He chuckled softly, a watery echo of Icek's amusement.

"Father," Icek leaned forward, urgency in his tone. "Listen. I've already spoken to people here. The US State Department. Because of everything, and because I am your son, an American citizen, they say bringing you to our home in the US should be possible. They called it a formality. We have room, Father. Plenty of room at our home in Colorado. What do you say?"

There was no hesitation. Abram's voice came back, firm, resolute, infused with a certainty that cut through the tears. "Son, it is simple. The family belongs together. I told you—I never remarried. Henna was my only wife. My life has been quiet here. I have friends, yes, good friends. But family," he swallowed audibly. "It's a world of difference. I cannot wait to see you. To meet Teodora. To meet my grandchildren."

Emotion welled up again, thick and overwhelming. "Okay, Father. Okay." Icek fumbled for a pen, his hand still shaking. "To make plans, can I call you back tomorrow? Same time? Will that work?"

"Yes, son. Yes. Of course. Tomorrow."

"My prayers all these years—they've been answered, Father." Icek felt the truth of it settle deep within him. "We're only a plane ride away now. I have your address here. I'll send everything—our numbers, our address, Teodora's work number, mine…"

"This call, Icek," Abram's voice was thick with reverence. "It is from the Almighty. A miracle." A pause, then raw and explicit, "I love you, son."

The words hit Icek with the force of a physical blow, stealing his breath. "I love you too, Father," he managed, his voice cracking. "So much. We'll talk tomorrow."

Gently, reverently, as if handling something fragile and infinitely precious, Icek placed the receiver back into its cradle. The connection broke, but the link forged across thirty-two years of silence held fast, strong, and unbreakable. He stayed there, hand resting on the phone, tears flowing freely now—tears of grief, yes, but also tears of unbelievable, heart-stopping joy.

He pushed himself away from the table, his legs feeling strangely weak, then walked out of the room, a slight tremor in his hands, and said, "Oh my God, after thirty-two years—I just spoke with my father. I can't believe it. He sounded as clear as if he were next door, and on top of everything, he is sharp."

Ingrid replied, "Icek, it is rare we get to hear what I term as *heartwarming stories*, as our work is typically with those that hug the cesspools of society—I am so happy for you that you found him and spoke with him after all these years." She offered a genuine, warm smile.

"Ingrid, I must speak with my wife. I haven't spoken with her since leaving Denver, and that was days ago. He pulled a slip of paper from his pocket, smoothing it flat. "Here is my number. Could you possibly call her for me and route it to the phone number I used to speak with my father?"

"Yes, Agent Schubert advised that you would be calling your wife. I will get the overseas operator, and you should be connected momentarily." She reached for the phone, her movements efficient and practiced.

"Thank you, Ingrid."

He perched on the edge of the chair in the interrogation office, his leg bouncing a silent, jittery rhythm against the carpeted floor. Every tick of the clock on the wall echoed a loud, insistent pulse in the sterile room—finally, the phone shrilled, shattering the tension.

He rose, his shadow stretching long and thin across the floor as he moved to close the door, a deliberate act of claiming privacy. He lifted the receiver. "Hello, this is Icek."

"Icek, are you there?"

"Yes. I hear you loud and clear."

Teodora's voice, tight with a barely suppressed scream, crackled through the line. "We were terrified that something had happened— that your safety had been compromised. We were worried sick about you. Please promise me you will never put me through such stress again. We didn't hear anything. Please never do this again. We need to know you are safe, dear. We were grateful to receive the two telegrams, but quite a bit of time has passed since then. We assumed you were busy.

Do you have an explanation? We thought that someone had abducted you."

"Guilty as charged. I can explain. I promise, dear, never again. I apologize—I really do. In fact, I am extremely well." He took a deep breath, letting a smile bloom in his voice. "Can you grab the kids and get them to the phone? I have an enormous surprise for the Kelner Family. Are they there?"

"Yes, we are all here."

He leaned against the door, a hand gripping the frame for support. "Hello, Karen, hello Kyle. So sorry for the delayed call to you two and your mother. Family, I have great news! Just five minutes ago, I hung up the phone after talking to my father." A tremor ran through his voice, betraying the emotion he was trying to contain. "Father lives!" He swiped at the corner of his eye, a quick, cautious gesture. "He lives in, of all places, the country of Malta."

A collective gasp came through the phone, followed by a unified, "Oh my God! Grandpa lives!"

Teodora, in a tone of total excitement, said, "Icek, this news is unbelievable. How in the world did you locate Abram? After all these years, it's been over thirty years!"

"Thirty-two to be exact," Icek declared.

"Do you know when you are coming home?" Karen's voice, small and hopeful, pierced through the joyful chaos.

He closed his eyes for a moment, picturing their faces, etching them into his memory. "I have so much to tell my family, so much. You will all be proud!"

"How did the presentation go?" Teodora asked, a thread of practicality weaving its way back into her tone.

"That," he chuckled, a low rumble in his chest, "is a long story that I can't wait to tell you about in person. I wish the three of you were with me right now; I miss you all achingly." He paused—the weight of the day, the sheer enormity of it all, settling back onto his shoulders. "The other big news is this: Icek Abram Kelner, AKA your father, was instrumental in the arrest and soon-to-be conviction of the animal who murdered Henna and the twins. He's in jail as we speak."

"You caught their killer?" Teodora said.

"It is a long story."

"Icek, you were supposed to be presenting a paper, not getting involved with the arrest of a Nazi. I don't understand," Tiodora's voice rose, laced with a sharp edge of frustration.

He ran a hand through his hair, a weary gesture. "I have other news. Halina Adamik, the caretaker of Ryfka and the twins, has been located. She makes her home in Scotland. I have her contact information."

"This is great news, Icek. Any idea when we will see Abram?" Teodora's voice softened, a hint of relief coloring her words.

"Family, it looks like my departure date has changed, as you can imagine." He paced the small confines of the room, the phone cord stretching tight, a physical tether to his distant family. "I love you all so much and miss you horribly. There is so much to tell, so much I have learned. I have been working with the BND, which is the German equivalent of the US CIA. It is a long story, and it is too long to start explaining it on the phone right now. The bottom line is that I am safe— we have solved many issues—I will be home soon. Please call Asia and let her know Abram is alive and well and living in Malta. I will soon let you know my adjusted flight schedule when I get it. I love you all so much!"

"We love you too, Father," Kyle and Karen's voices chimed, nearly in unison, a familiar and comforting refrain.

Teodora spoke, her voice closer to the receiver, intimate and low, "We miss you and send our warmest love."

"I need to get off of here. You will be hearing from me soon." He squeezed the receiver, his knuckles white with the force of his grip. "Love to all, and so long."

"We love you, Father," they echoed, their voices a fading chorus as the connection broke, leaving him alone once more in the echoing silence of the interrogation room.

CHAPTER SIXTY-ONE

Denver, Village of Colfax, Colorado
New York City, NY
June 25th, 1974, 11:45 a.m. (Mountain Standard Time)

Teodora held the phone receiver, the plastic cool against her palm long after Icek's voice had faded. *Unbelievable.* The words echoed in the sudden silence of her kitchen. *Icek finding Abram—alive after thirty-two years?* A ghost resurrected by a chance speaking invitation in Hamburg he hadn't even fulfilled. The sheer impossibility pressed down, making the familiar room seem suddenly strange, vibrating with potential energy.

This call, the one I have to make, feels impossibly heavy. How do I even begin? Your brother-in-law—the man you've mourned for decades—he's alive. A tremor ran through her, a complex mix of awe at being the messenger and a deep, resonant dread of shattering Asia's world, even with news that defied tragedy.

She needed a moment. Turning to the kitchen window, she drew a shaky breath, seeking the steady presence of the Front Range.[92] It stood immense, a bulwark against the impossible blue, just as it always had. Today, though, the familiar comfort felt different, sharper. This view, Icek's first anchor in America—before they knew its name, its market value, its geography—struck her now with profound significance. She saw it suddenly through Abram's eyes and imagined him standing here soon, perhaps beside Asia, gazing at this monumental wall of rock. Abram, who had traded the rubble of Poland for the island shores of Malta, built a life from ashes.

What would this sight mean to him? To Icek? To men whose horizons were once brutally defined by barbed wire, whose landscapes were the suffocating dark of forests hunted by enemies? This sheer, immovable permanence—Teodora understood Icek's unspoken need for it, the deep hunger for something solid in a world that had taught them only transience and loss. It wasn't just scenery; it was a promise. Stability. An anchor against the swirling ghosts of the past. *Could it be an anchor for Abram, too?*

The thought of ghosts brought another memory, sharp and unwelcome: the phone call from Asia years ago. With the shattering news of the plane crash, Chats and Claire were gone in an instant. The worst crash in history. She remembered the chilling detail Asia had relayed, voice thick with shock—Claire's purse fused to her hand, their bodies found holding hands amidst the devastation. That call had changed their lives forever. Delivering news that reshapes a life— Teodora knew its terrible weight. The memory settled a cold counterpoint to the miracle she was about to announce.

She finished her coffee, the warmth barely touching the chill inside. The view remained steadfast. The ghosts remained, whispering. It was time. Taking another deep breath, feeling the slight tremble in her hand, Teodora reached for the phone again, the numbers for Asia clear in her mind, etched there by years of friendship and shared history, both joyous and tragic. She began to dial.

It's ringing, she thought, her heart pounding against her ribs.

"Asia Reynolds, how may I help you?" The voice was professional, distant.

"Asia? It's Teodora." Teodora kept her voice low and steady despite the tremor she felt. "Is this an okay moment? I need to talk to you."

A pause. Asia's tone shifted slightly, warmer but questioning. "Teodora? Of course. Everything alright out there in beautiful Colorado?"

"Everything is—something else entirely." Teodora took another breath. This was it. "Asia, are you sitting down?"

"Uh oh. That question. Okay, I'm sitting. What's up? Don't tell me you're pregnant at your age!" Asia's attempt at humor sounded thin, laced with sudden apprehension.

"No, not pregnant. That *would* be catastrophic." Teodora tried for a light tone and failed. She plunged ahead. "Asia—it's about your brother-in-law."

Silence crackled on the line. Then, barely a whisper. "Abram?"

"Yes. Abram." Teodora's voice was thick now. "Icek, Icek is in Hamburg. He was supposed to give that paper." She stopped herself. The details didn't matter now. "He found him, Asia. Icek found Abram."

More silence, so profound, Teodora wondered if the line had gone dead. "Asia?"

"What—what are you saying, Teodora?" Asia's voice was tight, strained, barely recognizable. "Found him? What does that mean?"

"He's alive, Asia." The words finally came out stark and monumental. "Abram is alive. He's been living in Malta all these years."

A sharp intake of breath on the other end. A choked sound, half gasp, half sob. "No. Teodora—don't—Is this some cruel joke?" Her voice cracked. "Alive?"

"No joke, Asia. I swear to you. It's real. Icek spoke with him."

"Alive," Asia repeated, the word hollow, then filled with a dawning, shattering intensity. "Oh my God. Alive? After all this time—Abram." There was a muffled sound, then frantic scrambling. "Teodora, hold—hold on. I need Jack. I can't! Oh God, hold on!"

Teodora heard the buzz of an intercom, Asia's voice high and shaking, "Jack! Jack, get in here! Now! Please, Jack, immediately!"

A distant male voice, concerned. "Asia? What is it? Is someone hurt?"

"No! Yes! I don't know! Just come! Teodora's on hold!"

Teodora waited, her tears starting to fall, listening to the faint sounds of commotion on the other end—footsteps, muffled voices. Then Jack's voice, closer now, tense. "Teodora? Jack Reynolds here. What in God's name is going on? Asia's white as a sheet."

"Jack," Teodora said, trying to gather herself. "It's—it's incredible news. Please, put me on speaker."

A click. "Okay, you're on speaker. Teodora, talk to us."

"Jack, Asia, Icek is in Hamburg. Through a series of unbelievable events, he has found Abram. Your brother-in-law. He's alive and well. Living in Malta since the war. Icek spoke to him yesterday."

There was a sharp, piercing cry from Asia—not words, just pure, unadulterated sound, a mix of agony and disbelief giving way to something else. Then, it was ragged sobbing.

Jack's voice was stunned, lower. "Alive? Abram? Teodora, are you certain? Thirty-two years—people don't just reappear."

"I know it sounds impossible, Jack. But Icek is certain. He spoke with him. The German authorities helped locate him. He's healthy, never remarried—working as a millwright until he retired."

"Abram," Asia sobbed, her voice breaking through. "I knew—I felt him sometimes. I never truly believed—Oh, Jack, hold me. It's a miracle. I never thought I would ever experience a miracle—a real miracle." Her words dissolved into weeping again.

Jack's voice was thick with emotion now, too. "A miracle—Jesus. Teodora, we need a minute."

"Of course," Teodora said softly, tears streaming down her face now. "Take all the time you need. There's more. We have details about him coming here. But that is for later. Just absorb this—he's alive. He's alive."

"Alive," Jack echoed, his voice filled with wonder. Through the phone, Teodora could hear Asia's continuing, cathartic sobs.

"I'll call back," Teodora whispered. "Or you call me. Whenever you're ready."

She gently placed the receiver back in its cradle, the silence of her kitchen rushing back in, but changed now, charged with the impossible weight of a life returned from the ashes. The Colorado Rockies Front Range outside the window seemed to hold its breath along with her.

CHAPTER SIXTY-TWO

Hamburg, Germany
June 26th, 1974, 8:49 p.m.

Hans drove through the docklands as the sun was beginning to set, its light reflecting off vehicles and tavern windows. Loud music, shouts, and laughter poured from the taverns. Icek, watching intently, wondered if the lively scene was a festival or something else.

The taxi finally staggered to a halt in a desolate, almost forgotten corner of the docks. It was a place of industry, dominated by the massive silhouettes of warehouses, their brick facades stained with years of grime and sea salt. Beyond them, the skeletal masts of transport ships swayed gently against the darkening sky, like ghostly sentinels guarding the secrets of the harbor. Hans cut the engine, the sudden silence amplifying the distant clang of metal and the cries of gulls wheeling overhead. He chuckled, a dry, rasping sound like autumn leaves skittering across the pavement. "Silence, remember?" he reminded Icek, his voice low and conspiratorial. He reached into the glove compartment, brushing his fingers against the worn leather, and withdrew a strip of black cloth, its texture soft yet somehow ominous. "The blindfold. Put it on, please. Our destination awaits, shrouded in necessary secrecy." He paused, a glint of amusement in his eye. "And before your imagination conjures images of shadowy figures lurking in alleyways and rough burlap sacks, I assure you, this is merely a formality. A gesture of trust, shall we say? Play along, okay?"

Icek sighed, a puff of air that spoke of weary acceptance, then did as the driver had asked. The black cloth fell, and the vibrant cityscape vanished, replaced by the close, stuffy darkness and the insistent thump-thump of his pulse. The cab moved, then stopped. The engine died with a final, shuddering cough. Hans's door opened, then Icek's. A hand, firm but not unkind, guided him out. Icek's shoes scraped on the pavement. He counted each step, his senses straining to compensate for the lost sight. The minutes stretched, filled only with the rhythm of their movement. Finally, a door creaked open. They stepped inside.

The silence that descended was absolute, a heavy blanket smothering the muted roar of the city he'd left behind. Icek's voice when he spoke seemed to bounce off unseen walls. *A library?*

"The unveiling awaits." Hans's voice was close beside him.

The blindfold ripped away, and the room erupted. A kaleidoscope of faces, all beaming, all directed at him. A roar of cheers washed over him, a physical force that made him stagger back a step. He blinked, his eyes struggling to adjust to the sudden brightness, his mind reeling. *What?*

Agent Schubert, his face split by a grin as wide as the Elbe, pushed through the crowd. He pressed a cold, sweating beer bottle into Icek's hand, the condensation a slick shock against his palm. "Celebration, my friend. Double feature. Act One: You helped us cage the beast that devoured your family. Helmut Wahl, that withered husk of an SS man we arrested. Thirty years to life, the legal eagles say. The prison will be his tomb."

Schubert paused, allowing the silence to amplify his words. He held Icek's gaze. "Three decades, Icek. A long hunt. And should you ever tire of the classroom, consider my offer. A standing invitation." He turned to the assembled group, his arm sweeping out in a gesture of inclusion. "This man," he declared, his voice ringing with pride, "possesses the nerves of a seasoned gambler, the Americans' cool cucumber. He was the linchpin in an operation that, well, let's say he faced the abyss, and the abyss blinked first."

He touched and lightly squeezed Icek's shoulder, a gesture of camaraderie, and then his voice shifted, taking on a deeper resonance. "But wait, there's more. From that very desk in my office," he pointed back toward a memory, "Icek, earlier today, made some calls. Reconnected. First, the essential call. Every man knows to check in with his wife. Affirm all is well. That call held more than usual, didn't it? Because before the wife, there was another. A father. A father presumed lost, swallowed by the past for over thirty years. Imagine, if you will, such a roller coaster of despair and elation all in one lifetime. Icek provided names and whispers from a forgotten time. And, by God, we pursued them. With a staff of six and many ten-hour days where we never paused our relentless digging—we struck gold. A miracle, really."

Schubert's voice softened—a subtle shift that drew the room closer. "Understand, each of you, the mirror image of this war—the Polish side. Icek Kelner, beside me, is fifty years old. You've heard of his recent contribution. But that's merely the crest of the wave. As a member of the Polish Home Army, he and his colleagues made life quite unpleasant for our occupying forces. They rarely rested in their pursuit and seldom took prisoners. They could barely house and feed their forces, let alone an enemy. They were as ruthless with us as we were with them. Torture, interrogations, and Icek developed a honed skill in extracting information. Why? Perhaps because on July 13th, 1942, Hamburg's police, morphed into killers by the Nazi regime, descended upon his village. Fifteen hundred souls extinguished—women, children, the elderly—all collateral damage—including Icek's twin sisters—ten years old—murdered." He gestured toward a display board, previously unnoticed, now illuminated by a spotlight. Photographs, grainy and stark, lined the board—a village, burning; faces, blurred with fear; soldiers, their expressions grim and determined.

"His father, Abram, endured years in a munitions factory—a crucible where only twenty-eight out of every hundred emerged. Abram, one of the twenty-eight—spent four months in a hospital, post-liberation, to regain a reasonable appearance of health. Something remarkable happened just before we left to come here—Abram and his son, Icek—they found one another after thirty-two years of not knowing. Think for a moment, think about your father. Try to imagine… not knowing, thinking for over three decades that your father had perished in the war.

Many of you are hearing Icek Abram Kelner's history for the first time." Schubert raised his voice to cut the noise, "Henrik, step up here for a minute, will you?"

A man, built like a granite monument, rose from his chair. His bald head gleamed under the lights, a thick salt-and-pepper beard obscuring the lower half of his face. He moved with the deliberate grace of a retired strongman. "Henrik, meet Icek. Icek, Henrik."

The two men shook hands, a brief, robust clasp. "A pleasure," Icek murmured, a faint smile touching his lips.

"The sentiment is entirely mine, from what I gather," Henrik rumbled, his voice a low, resonant growl.

Schubert turned to Henrik, a mischievous glint in his eye. "Hypothetical scenario, Henrik. What circumstances would compel you to submerge yourself, neck-deep, in, let's say, human waste for three hours?"

A collective groan of disgust punctuated by nervous laughter rippled through the room.

Henrik's brow furrowed—his eyes narrowed in thought. "Some new, sadistic training regimen? I couldn't. I'd rather face a firing squad. Absolutely not."

Schubert draped his arm around Icek, drawing him close. "That, my friends, is precisely what this man endured on the morning of July 13th, 1942. When Wilhelm Wahl, SS Nazi assigned to the Hamburg Police, butchered Icek's grandmother and his twin sisters. Icek witnessed it all. His sanctuary? The outhouse. Not my first choice," Schubert admitted with a wry twist of his lips."

Icek's voice was steady, though a subtle tremor betrayed the emotion churning beneath. "Hopefully, embarking on the first day of a very lengthy sentence. He won't inflict further harm. Thank you, all of you. It's surreal to be among former adversaries. In the Polish Home Army, we were opposing forces—our goal—to kill any German soldier in sight."

He paused, his gaze traveling around the room, taking in each face. "Now, we're simply individuals endeavoring to move forward—my wife, my brother-in-law, all Home Army veterans. We endeavor to forget. But my arrival here, to share my experiences, to discuss that fateful morning on July 13th, 1942—a morning that changed the lives of so many. The last thing ever—encountering the war still smoldering in one man's soul."

He shook his head, a gesture of weary resignation. "But that man is no longer at liberty. And that offers a degree of solace. Your city is stunning and vibrant. I'll bring my family on my next visit. And I extend my gratitude to Heinz Niehaus," he nodded toward a man in the crowd, a smile crinkling the corners of his eyes—for his collaboration, his Southern charm. It provided a much-needed balm, that humor. And the backup team, your unwavering professionalism, emboldened me to enter that house. And you, Agent Schubert—Icek turned, his voice thick with emotion—you granted me the opportunity to confront my family's killer. And you unearthed my father, Abram Irving Kelner—and now, Halina Adamik, our family caregiver in Poland. You restored them to me. My deepest gratitude."

Another roar of applause filled the room, deafening in its intensity.

Schubert raised a hand, gradually quieting the crowd. "Icek, a high school history teacher in Denver, Colorado. He journeyed to Hamburg to present a paper at the invitation of a prestigious historical society. That presentation never occurred. It was deemed too perilous. But he departs with a narrative that is far more profound. And he's accomplished something further for Germany. The evidence we amassed led to the arrest of eight additional former members of the murderous battalion."

The cheers this time were overwhelming, a mixture of relief and a collective sense of justice prevailing.

"Henrik, you may resume your seat. Thank you for confirming that the outhouse remains off your itinerary."

Henrik returned to his seat, accompanied by laughter and another round of applause.

"Now," Schubert continued, his voice gaining momentum, "another distinguished guest. Someone deserving of our profound gratitude. Someone who, I suspect, has a call she hasn't yet answered. Ms. Helga Wagner, from the St. Nickolai Church Historic Site."

Helga, looking slightly overwhelmed, stepped forward. She shifted her weight from foot to foot, her fingers twisting the fabric of her skirt, her lower lip caught between her teeth. She reached Icek, and they embraced, a brief, silent exchange of shared understanding.

Schubert looked at Helga, a playful glint in his eye. "Helga, brutal honesty. Did I truly emanate the look of a hitman that day at the church?"

Helga's lips curved into a hesitant smile. "My apologies, but affirmative."

A burst of laughter erupted, punctuated by whistles of amusement. A chant began, softly at first, then gaining volume: "Hitman! Hitman! Hitman!"

Schubert grinned, spreading his hands in mock surrender. "Alright, alright, order in the court. Helga, the telltale sign?"

"Your footwear," she stated without hesitation. "Gleaming, patent leather. Not the typical tourist attire at St. Nickolai. You didn't conform to the profile."

More laughter, louder this time.

"Of course, I had to inquire," Schubert said, simulating exasperation. "Hitmen are invariably the suave figures in cinema, are they not? But Helga possessed discernment. She perceived my pursuit of Icek. And she was correct. But crucially, she acted. She provided Icek with a plan of escape. Impeccable reflexes. She possesses a natural aptitude for this profession. And without Helga's swift intervention, the outcome might have been drastically different"

The crowd responded with whistles and cheers, and a cry of "Offer her employment!" rose from several in the audience.

"I presented my credentials, naturally," Schubert continued. "And she became privy to Icek's history. His past service in the Polish Home Army consisted of disrupting the German occupation. Contaminating rations, sabotaging fuel supplies, detonating railway lines, and engaging soldiers in firefights. A persistent irritant, weren't you, Icek?"

Laughter rippled through the room, affectionate now, devoid of any lingering animosity.

"He eliminated German soldiers. But in the crucible of war, it's a binary choice: kill or be killed. He acted out of necessity. Those Battalion 101 veterans were threatening. Extremely ominous.

"I summoned you here for two purposes. Firstly, to express our gratitude. And secondly, to pose the question: Would you entertain the prospect of joining our ranks?"

The chant of "Offer her employment!" surged again, louder and more insistent.

Schubert looked into Helga's face and smiled slightly. "Would you care to address the assembly?"

Helga inhaled deeply, steadying herself. "Yes. When I encountered Icek, and he recounted how he educates his students about the bombing of Hamburg, a constriction formed in my throat. He dedicates entire lessons to it. He knows the statistics, the reality that few strategic targets remained, that the Allies obliterated the U-boat pens months earlier. He teaches that the Allies designed the bombing specifically to shatter the morale of the German populace. As he described this, tears welled in his eyes. And in mine. He posed the question, 'How could humanity descend to such depths of cruelty?' And I responded, "Consider our treatment of the Jews." And he reiterated, 'How could humanity descend to such depths of cruelty?'

She paused, her voice faltering slightly, her gaze locking with Icek's. "Then I learned of his family. Of the horrors he witnessed. His time emerged in an outhouse waste pit, and it overwhelmed me. I returned home that evening and cried myself to sleep. Then I kept thinking— Icek and his family, their sole wrongdoing was simply being Jewish. And for the first time, I experienced a profound shame in my heritage. In being German."

She looked directly at Icek, her eyes brimming with compassion. "Icek, I pray you discover tranquility. The horrid memories you have of Jozefow and your time in the Home Army—please, dear Lord, let these memories recede. You deserve the serenity. May God bless you and your family."

Icek stepped forward, and they embraced again, a long, lingering hug, a silent testament to the shared burden of history. Then, hand in hand, they walked to the back of the room and sat down. The room was silent, heavy with unspoken emotions.

Even Schubert had to dab his eyes with a handkerchief discreetly. "A resounding ovation for Icek and Helga," he said, his voice slightly hoarse.

The audience rose as one, turning to face Icek and Helga, and the applause was thunderous, prolonged, an emotional release of pent-up feeling.

Schubert waited for the applause to subside. "Please, be seated—one final item. I've conferred with the US State Department. They're facilitating Icek's father, Abram's journey to Colorado: documentation, travel expenses—the full spectrum. A US Marine escort will accompany him from Malta, where he now makes his home, to Icek's residence. After ninety days, Abram can initiate the citizenship application process. The paperwork will authorize his continued stay during the processing. Icek, your reflections?"

Icek stood, his face a tapestry of joy and disbelief. "I communicated with my father today. Words elude me. But I had to divulge the truth about Grandmother Ryfka and the twins. He was unaware. He had clung to the hope of their survival. It devastated his heart. The last image I have of him is the soldiers who demolished our door forcibly removing him and striking his face with a rifle butt. They hurled him into a truck and I never heard from him again. Until today."

Tears streamed down his face unchecked. "My gratitude, Agent Schubert. I always sensed Father's survival. I knew. I apologize," he choked out, his voice thick with emotion, "these are tears of elation. Thank you. All of you. By the way, should you ever find yourselves in Denver, Colorado, our skiing is exceptional. Or visit anytime. You are welcome in our home."

The crowd surged forward, enveloping him in a wave of human connection—embraces, handshakes, murmured words of encouragement and support.

Schubert raised his voice one last time, cutting through the joyful celebration. "Ladies and gentlemen, one final, critical point. Icek has acquired adversaries here. This gathering is strictly off the record: no media coverage, no public disclosure, and absolute confidentiality. What transpires within these walls remains within these walls. Icek will return to Colorado, and no one there will be privy to these events. We're providing him with the farewell he merits, but it must remain a clandestine affair. He's assisted us in removing perilous individuals, remnants of a conflict that should have concluded long ago. The FBI will be monitoring the Kelner family, ensuring their safety. Now, please partake in the festivities. Engage with Icek; he's a repository of historical knowledge. Eat, drink, and celebrate. And bear in mind… this never occurred."

The crowd raised their glasses to Icek, a silent, collective toast to a man who had, for a fleeting moment, become one of their own. An honorary German. A survivor. A hero.

CHAPTER SIXTY-THREE

Denver, Colorado – Stapleton Airport
August 15ᵗʰ, 1974, 4:45 p.m.

Asummer rain, thick as cotton batting, clung to the city, shrinking visibility to a mere three hundred feet. Headlights blurred on the highway, where cars crawled bumper-to-bumper, a sluggish line formed by an earlier accident. The drive to Stapleton Airport became a slow, frustrating slog through air you could practically chew.

"You, see?" Teodora's voice carried a note of gentle triumph. "Your father always suggests leaving early. There's a reason for that old saying about the early bird."

Kyle, a boneless sprawl in the back seat, let his head loll against the window. "Grandpa Abram's going to be orbiting the moon if we're late."

Icek's grip tightened on the steering wheel until his knuckles were bone white. "Wound up. Perhaps 'anxious' is a better phrase, Kyle. Remember, your grandfather's experiences are beyond anything we can comprehend."

Karen, with the practiced defiance of a teenager, twisted in her seat. "Yeah, 'wound up' is, like, totally ancient, Kyle. He needs to, you know, chill with his nerd crew."

"Oh, you're the expert on nerds," Kyle retorted, his voice a sharpened blade of sarcasm. "Your entire friend group is a walking 'bookworm.'"

"Enough," Teodora cut in, her voice a low, firm wall between them. "When we're with Grandfather Abram, I expect civility—I don't think you two have forgotten how to be courteous. So please, you are both adults—act like it, please."

Icek's reflection in the rearview mirror caught the glint of rebellion in his children's eyes. Icek, setting some ground rules, uttered, "He's never been around American teenagers. We all need to show him our best selves. Abram is seventy-four, and he's endured things." He let the words hang, heavy with unspoken meaning. "The Nazis and that munitions factory—they almost broke him. He found out Ryfka and the twins perished at the hands of the Nazis—until he feels comfortable with us, no questions about the past. We don't know how deep the scars run. If he needs help or therapy, we'll see to it." He paused, his voice dropping to a near-whisper, raw with remembered pain. "Only twenty-eight out of every hundred men walked out of that place. Twenty-eight. Starvation, executions—It's a miracle he's alive."

Karen leaned forward, her nose practically touching the fog-streaked windshield. "At this rate, Grandpa's going to be lost in the terminal maze."

"I did mention the US Marine Embassy Guard," Icek reminded her, a hint of weariness in his tone. "He's escorting Abram from the embassy in Malta. I have faith this gentleman will remain with our grandfather until our arrival."

"Don't fret, dear," Teodora added, her voice a soothing balm. "The stewardesses will certainly be attentive and make an announcement should there be delays."

"Father, could you turn up the radio a bit? It's Pink Floyd's *'Money'*.[93] My absolute favorite!" Kyle asked as Icek wrestled with the defrosters of their blue, two-toned 1972 Chrysler Town & Country station wagon, a nine-passenger behemoth battling the condensation.

Teodora's shoulders slumped with a sigh. "Kyle, impeccable timing, as always. This rain is like driving blind. The radio is just noise right now." She reached over with a swift, decisive movement and silenced the music. The quiet that fell was as heavy and palpable as the rain slamming against the windows. "Music later. When we have good visibility and can clearly see the road, okay?"

Karen saw her opening. "Seriously, how can you stand that, Kyle? That hippie band, *Pink Floyd*. Mother, when the rain decides to take a hike, can we please play my *John Denver Rocky Mountain High* eight-track?"[94]

Icek chuckled, a brief rumble of amusement. "Grandfather mentioned he is a John Denver fan. He also enjoys Elvis and Frank Sinatra."

"Oh, no," Kyle groaned, theatrical anguishing in his voice. "This is going to be a long visit if Gramps is on a John Denver kick. Thank God for the headphones. Maybe I can convince him to explore personal listening."

His mother's eyebrows arched a silent question mark. "Are you suggesting I'm an 'old-timer,' Kyle? Because I happen to enjoy the same music as Abram."

A thought, bright and mischievous, lit up Karen's face. "I'm so relieved Grandpa's been studying English. Father, you talked to him at length. Did he sound fluent on the phone?"

Icek answered, "Frankly, I was shocked at his English skills. To top it off, he has an almost aristocratic British accent. There is zero broken English. I trust he has been speaking it for years."

Karen paused, a playful glint in her eye. "So much for brushing up on my Polish. Now, we can't even gossip about him."

Teodora's voice cut through the lightheartedness, sharp and severe. "Children, absolutely no questions about the war. Or the years after. We don't want to trigger anything. Is that understood? Icek, you understand, right?"

"I promise," Icek said, his voice grave. "No war talk."

"I'll drop you off at the terminal entrance, then park and meet you inside at his gate. Check the TWA board for any updates. And don't forget, we want to be together when he arrives. A united front."

The crowd at Gate 9 shifted and murmured, a restless tide of anticipation. Above the gate, a sign flickered: "Flight 5631 – Delayed." Icek's watch revealed the cruel truth—thirty-five more minutes. Teodora said, "Family, coffee at the snack bar? A little caffeine might help us all."

Icek glanced toward the floor-to-ceiling windows, where the rain was finally relenting, revealing the runway lights like scattered jewels. A less treacherous drive home—that was something to hope for.

A crisp, intangible female voice announced over the loudspeaker, 'TWA Flight 5631 from La Guardia has landed and is taxiing to the gate. Passengers will be deplaning shortly. Please meet your parties at Gate Nine.'

Passengers began to flow down the ramp, a weary river of humanity spilling into the terminal. But no Abram. Then, a figure in a crisp US Marine Corps dress-blues uniform emerged: a gunnery sergeant, his chest a tapestry of ribbons, his shoes mirror-bright, and his hat angled with sharp authority. The battered suitcase and worn briefcase the Marine carried seemed to belong to another era.

As Icek started forward, the Marine stepped ahead, his voice a low, controlled rumble. "Please hold, sir. I am Gunnery Sergeant Hildago Rivera, representing the US Embassy in Malta. I've had custody of Mr. Abram Kelner since we boarded in Malta. I have specific instructions and protocols to follow before any contact. Are you Mr. Icek Kelner?"

Icek nodded, his hand reaching instinctively for his wallet. He produced his driver's license and his Colfax school teacher ID. "Here you are, Sergeant."

Rivera scrutinized the IDs, his gaze sharp and unwavering. "Very well. Before I release Mr. Kelner, I need identification from everyone in your party. No one approaches him until I'm satisfied. Then, you'll sign a *Transfer of Custody* document. Any questions?"

"No questions," Icek turned to his family and said, "This gentleman needs to see your IDs." He collected them and handed them over to the sergeant—a small pile of plastic and paper representing their lives.

The sergeant took the identification pieces and said, "Thank you. I will have these back to you in a minute or so. May I have a word with you, please?"

"Of course, how can I assist?"

The two of them stood behind a large concrete pillar to conceal their presence.

The Marine gunnery sergeant began, "We assure you—your father is doing fine. The worst part, he is just a bit jetlagged. I have been with him the entire trip from Malta, and by the way, I have grown very fond of him—life has not been kind to him, as you are aware. We literally talked for five hours straight. He is the sharpest senior I have ever met. Other than his jetlag, he is in magnificent condition. Plus, he speaks English like a native."

"Where is he at the moment?"

"We have him flanked by two-armed FBI agents—on the plane. Before I elaborate, we have a private matter to discuss."

"We're in America," Icek repeated, a thread of disbelief in his voice. "Two FBI agents, it seems excessive. But I won't question it."

The gunnery sergeant gestured toward a slightly more secluded area about fifteen feet from where they stood. He leaned in, his voice dropping to a confidential murmur. "Yes. There's a reason for the heightened security. Command authorized me to inform you that our people and the BND have identified a threat. You and your family may be in danger. You're familiar with the BND, correct?"

Icek nodded, his eyes involuntarily scanning the surrounding area, searching for anything or anyone out of place. He refocused on the sergeant, his voice low and urgent. "What kind of threat?"

"As a precaution, your phone line was tapped earlier this week—standard FBI procedure. Three-minute trace, you're familiar with the process. Try to handle incoming calls yourself whenever possible. The FBI will also be conducting surveillance in your neighborhood. A new face walking a dog, that's them. When I landed at La Guardia, two agents from the FBI met me. They briefed me, and then we called and spoke with Agent Schubert.

Sergeant Rivera continued, "This delivery became significantly less routine." He paused, his expression hardening. "Since you left Hamburg, the BND has made eight arrests of former Hamburg Police Nazis that were in Jozefow the day the Nazis murdered your family. But something else has triggered this heightened alert. The specifics are above my paygrade. The IDs are a precaution. We didn't want to take any chances. The FBI seems confident they'll apprehend whoever is targeting your family. They know who they're looking for. This information is strictly confidential. We advise against disclosure. You identified the man who murdered your family—you're a person of significant interest to the BND and the State Department. Hence, resources are protecting you and your family. Their words, verbatim: 'If you see something, let the government handle it.'"

"I worked with the BND in Hamburg recently," Icek replied, his voice tight with frustration. "Agent Schubert assured me they'd apprehended everyone involved. I thought I could finally close this chapter."

"Sir, your IDs are satisfactory. Sign here, and we'll conclude this transfer. I'm returning to DC in two days, then back to Malta—I can't have any further contact with you, official or otherwise. You understand?"

"Understood," Icek said, shaking the sergeant's hand, a firm, brief clasp. "It's reassuring to meet a fellow soldier who's seen action. Being shot at is difficult to convey to those who haven't experienced it. Semper Fi, Marine."

Sergeant Rivera handed Icek the signed document. "Thank you, Icek Abram Kelner. It was an honor. Be vigilant. My official duty here is complete, but I'll be observing until you depart. I'm armed with a 9mm and multiple clips—just in case."

The sergeant then signaled the two FBI agents aboard the plane, who were discreetly protecting Abram. The sergeant signaled toward the plane. Two figures, FBI agents, emerged from within, their gazes subtly fixed on Abram. "Gentlemen," the sergeant's voice carried, "please bring Mr. Abram Kelner forward."

A voice, crisp and official, responded from the plane's interior, "Understood! We're retrieving his belongings and will proceed to your location."

Icek's eyes were searching. There. A figure emerged, more petite, diminished than the towering giant of Icek's memory. Wisps of stringy, coarse grey hair clung to the sides of his head, a stark contrast to the memory of a thick, dark brown, curly mane that Icek so vividly remembered. Deep hollows shadowed his eyes, his eye sockets surrounded by dark, tired skin. He seemed shrunk, perhaps half the weight he once carried. As the figure drew closer, Icek saw the gaps, the missing-teeth smile that was now a fragmented echo, maybe five teeth remaining above, eight or nine below.

Icek surged forward, arms outstretched. The embrace was a silent collision of years, a desperate attempt to mend the shattered fragments of time and loss. Pulling back, Icek's vision swam, and a tremor in his voice betrayed the depth of his emotion. "Father, is it truly you?" The word resonated in his mind: Father. Reclaimed. Forever.

A faint, answering smile, a familiar light flickering in those tired eyes. "Son, it is indeed your father after all these years."

They hugged again, this time ever so tightly. "Father, I knew you were alive. I had this persistent, undeniable feeling, a constant awareness of your presence throughout these decades. I sensed you were somewhere. Oh, Father, it is a gift from God that you are here. There is no other explanation."

"Son, you are not going to believe this, but I also felt all along that you and I would one day be together. Praise God, my prayers have been answered. I prayed relentlessly, every day, from the moment those monsters ripped our home apart. The prayers did not cease, son! And now, they have been answered!" He started crying like a child.

They embraced again, staring into each other's eyes, tears continuing to flow freely. Then, they ambled down the jetway into the passenger area. At the end of the concourse, they paused once again. Icek, looking at Abram, said, "I'm eager for you to see a familiar face, though much older than when you last saw her. And I was hoping you could meet your grandchildren. They're here, waiting to greet you."

"Yes, I have not forgotten—I am indeed a grandfather? Who could have ever imagined?" A broad smile spread across his face, and for the third time, Icek offered him his handkerchief. In the distance, Abram seemed to recognize the figure he believed to be Teodora. Standing beside Teodora were his grandchildren, Kyle and Karen—their faces streaked with tears.

Then, Icek turned. "Father, you remember Teodora?"

"Of course," Abram said, his voice thick with emotion. He moved toward Teodora, who was already weeping, her hands outstretched. They embraced, a shared moment of profound relief and rediscovered connection.

"And these are your children, Karen and Kyle?" Abram asked, his gaze shifting to the teenagers.

"Yes, Grandfather," Karen said, stepping forward to receive his embrace.

Abram turned to Kyle, his eyes widening in recognition. "You look exactly like your father! You could be twins!"

Kyle grinned, a flash of youthful exuberance. "Grandfather, I'm so overjoyed to meet you and so grateful they found you."

"I thought everyone was gone," Abram said, shaking his head, a dazed expression on his face. "And you all believed the same about me. But they couldn't extinguish an old cat like me. I have nine lives, and I've only used a few. I have much life yet to live, especially now."

"Let's head to baggage claim," Icek said, trying to gather himself to steer them all toward the mundane.

Abram turned to Gunnery Sergeant Rivera—his voice filled with heartfelt gratitude. "Thank you for bringing me here, for reuniting me with my son and his family. I cherished our conversations about your wartime experiences and the opportunity to share my own."

Rivera's impassive face softened. He embraced Abram, then shook his hand firmly. "Thank you for your part in defeating those damned Nazis. You're a hero, a true legend. The bravest man I've ever encountered." He glanced at Icek and his family. "Take exceptional care of him. He's earned it." He pulled out a handkerchief, wiping away tears, a crack in his professional composure. "Good luck to you. The world owes you a debt it can never repay. Live a wonderful life here in America." He handed Abram a business card, a phone number hastily scrawled on the back. "We'll meet again. I assure you."

The baggage claim area was almost deserted. The La Guardia flight was the last arrival of the evening. Only cleaning crews, airport security personnel, and a lone police officer engaged in conversation with a stewardess remained.

As Icek steered them toward the carousel, his eyes caught sight of a man in a trench coat—an unsuitable sight. He wore an Austrian mountain-style hat, pulled down low, obscuring his features. *Why is he so bundled up? It's damp, not frigid. And those shoes—they don't look American.* A prickle of unease, a cold finger of premonition, traced his spine.

He glanced to his left. Sergeant Rivera was still there, his gaze fixed on Icek, his expression now intense, urgent. Rivera subtly drew his service pistol, concealing it behind a concrete pillar. He began gesturing frantically, his arm moving in sharp, insistent motions, striving to capture Icek's attention. His lips moved silently, forming the words, "Head that way! Head that way!"—a desperate, soundless warning.

Just as Icek turned, shoving his father's two suitcases toward his family in a hurried movement, the two plainclothes FBI agents tackled the man in the trench coat, slamming him face-down onto the polished floor. Handcuffs clicked with a sharp, metallic sound. The officers hauled the man to his feet, their movements swift and efficient. A miniature automatic pistol, nestled in a shoulder holster, was revealed, glinting under the fluorescent lights.

More police officers and airport security personnel swarmed the scene, and there was a sudden, chaotic influx of uniforms and authority. They herded everyone in the vicinity into a cordoned-off area, checking IDs, verifying identities, and releasing individuals one by one—a methodical process of elimination.

One of the FBI agents approached Icek, his face grim, his voice tight. "I am Agent Tom Churchill—you were moments away from an attack. That man was armed with an automatic pistol. Sergeant Rivera, by alerting you, likely saved your lives."

"I'm profoundly grateful he did," Icek said, his voice trembling, the shock still reverberating through him. "Initially, I couldn't decipher his signals. I'm a terrible lip reader."

"The crucial point is, he diverted you from harm's way," Churchill said. "And we're relieved to report that the man we apprehended is the person of interest identified by our foreign intelligence colleagues. We believe he was a member of Battalion 101, likely to be present during the massacre of your family in Jozefow. I can share what my superiors have authorized."

Icek's heart hammered against his ribs. "Are there additional threats?"

"Not precisely," Churchill replied. "The embassy authorized me to inform you that during ongoing intelligence operations, our agents, both foreign and domestic, believe the man arrested today represents the final remaining threat. Our investigation revealed that the former members of Battalion 101 were unaware of your eyewitness testimony in Jozefow.

They feared you could identify others involved in the killings. Due to the scarcity of eyewitnesses, most were charged with lesser war crimes and evaded execution."

CHAPTER SIXTY-FOUR

Denver, Village of Colfax, Colorado
August 17th, 1974, 9:15 a.m.

FBI Supervising Agent Tom Churchill pressed the doorbell of the Kelner home. The door opened almost immediately, revealing Icek, who stepped onto the stoop, his gaze sweeping the quiet street, lingering on any unfamiliar vehicle.

"Good morning, Agent Churchill. The black sedan with the two men is yours?"

"Yes, Icek. Second shift. Two agents are around the clock, watching the house. Plus, the tap on your line is monitored continuously back at headquarters." Churchill paused, letting the silence hang for a beat. "Nothing. Not a whisper of anything significant."

Icek's shoulders relaxed slightly. "Oh. I'm so sorry. Please come in."

"Thank you. Is there a place we can speak privately?"

"My office. Basement. This way."

Words tumbled from Icek as they descended the stairs. "You have no idea how reassuring it is to hear—quiet and no threats identified. This new quiet. It's a huge relief. I was starting to think normal was gone forever. I've learned to appreciate dull."

Agent Churchill followed Icek into the office, his eyes taking in the details: shelves overflowing with history books lined one wall, two hefty four-drawer file cabinets stood sentinel. Black and white photographs, faces from a distant past, stared out from their frames. Vintage World War II battle maps covered another wall. A substantial, antique mahogany desk dominated the room, and a thick Persian rug, the real kind, not some box-store imitation, softened the floor. "Icek, this is quite the office."

A shadow crossed Icek's face. "Sometimes, history feels like a chain around my neck. The past won't let go, no matter how hard I try. Shell shock. I know that's what it is. We called it battle fatigue back then. Until

'44. The Marines, island-hopping, coined a new term: the two-thousand-yard stare."[95] He paused, his gaze distant for a moment. "I catch myself doing that—staring into nothing. I've resisted seeing anyone professionally. But sometimes, it's overwhelming."

Churchill's posture seemed to stiffen, his voice dropping slightly. "Hürtgen Forest. September to December '44. I commanded an entire Company—Fourth Infantry. Lost so many men—many froze to death." He shook his head slowly. "Battle fatigue and the nightmares were brutal."

Icek met his gaze. "The nightmares… The first year back in the States, I woke up screaming. Scared my wife half to death more times than I can count. It's better now, decades later. But there are days when a sound, a smell, a voice—it all comes flooding back."

Churchill's eyes held his. "I've seen some nasty things myself, Icek. Read your profile. My God. No one should have to see what you've seen."

"Thank you, Tom. But what you don't know…" Icek took a shaky breath. "I still have the violent nightmares. The sweats. Months can go by, and I think I'm free. Then, a sound, a voice, a thought—it crashes in like a tornado." He swallowed hard. "I just hope that after last night, nothing like that will ever scare my family again. That madman at the airport—thank God for Gunny Rivera. If he hadn't reacted, who knows what that Nazi would have done." He shuddered. "I could have lost my family every day since July 13th, 1942. When the damned Nazis took everything…" His voice trailed off.

Churchill nodded slowly. "Icek, your experiences are beyond anything. I truly feel for you."

"Thank you. It means a lot coming from a fellow vet, especially one who saw action at Hürtgen Forest. We cover that battle in my classroom."

Churchill cleared his throat, shifting the tone. "We were both lucky last night."

"Every soul in that terminal was lucky," Icek corrected softly. "Rivera told me he was Force Reconnaissance, Vietnam, multiple tours." He shook his head in disbelief. He deserves a medal. He saved my life. My family's lives."

"He'll get one that means something. The Marines will honor him. I saw Gunny Rivera this morning. He and a one-star general were at the FBI office to finalize reports and debriefing for their respective commands."

Churchill paused. "We could talk history all day, Icek. But I need to update you on the threat. The FBI is in contact with the BND. Agent Schubert has been working around the clock, trying to determine if any others from Police Battalion 101 are interested in you or your family."

Icek's hand clenched into a fist on the desk. "Will I always be looking over my shoulder, wondering who's watching? I can't imagine living like that."

"The BND and the FBI performed exhaustive searches on German passports entering the US. Nothing—no viable candidates, no evidence to suggest another organized attack." Churchill leaned forward slightly. "Both Canada and Mexico borders checked. Plus, shipping ports on both coasts."

"The analysts in charge of profiling at the FBI think-tank," Churchill continued, a hint of a grim smile touching his lips, "they believe it's implausible that more Battalion 101 vets will surface as an organized threat. They're getting older. The last known group, comprising nine individuals arrested by the BND and one killed in a raid back home. We believe the man at Stapelton Airport yesterday was an outsider—perhaps a true lone wolf. The remaining 101 vets of any consequence—they're mostly in jail back in Germany, where they'll die of old age, murder, or disease. Some were already in their thirties when they joined the Police Battalion." He paused, his expression serious again. "Regardless, the surveillance on your home will stay until further notice. And when school starts, we'll look at security there, too."

Relief washed over Icek's face, deep and visible. "That's music to my ears." He gestured slightly. "You mentioned my family. My Aunt Asia and her family—they'll be here soon. My father, Abram, is the one we just picked up at the airport yesterday. We all thought he was gone forever. He proved us wrong." Icek's voice grew softer. "My mother,

Henna and Asia were identical twins. Mother died giving birth to twins. In July of 1942, a Hamburg Police Battalion 101 German SS officer murdered the twins and my grandmother, Ryfka. At the same time, other members of the battalion captured my father from our tiny village of Jozefow in Poland. They kept him for his skilled tradesman abilities— a millwright. He spent years in a munitions plant in Poland. Had the Russians not liberated the place, Father would not have made it out alive. He spent another three years in displaced people's camps throughout Europe before emigrating." Icek looked down at his desk, a faint, sad smile touching his lips. "To my surprise, Schubert of the BND, at my request, located Father. For over thirty-two years, we never knew his whereabouts."

Churchill stared at him, a mixture of disbelief and awe in his eyes. "Icek… your life. It's like something out of a Hollywood movie—I can't imagine being there when your twin sisters were born and when your mother died?"

"Yes. Eight years old. My father and Grandmother Ryfka were there as well, the day Mother died."

"By the time you were twenty," Churchill murmured, shaking his head slowly, "you'd seen more than most people see in a lifetime. And you've lived to tell about it."

We took my family to New York to visit Aunt Asia, Uncle Jack, and young Jakub. Seeing Asia was the meeting I'd dreaded most of my life. Asia, well, she'd finally insisted. But I couldn't avoid it forever."

He looked up, his gaze distant. "We had dinner at their home. Trying to make it normal. We sat there, and I looked across the table at Asia. And it hit me. Not just that she looked like Mother, but seeing Mother as she would have been. The same eyes, the way she held herself—the echo of her in Asia's smile. It was too much." His voice lowered, becoming thick with unshed tears. "The grief it triggered every single memory from when we lost Mother, a flood of pain I hadn't equipped myself to handle.

"I recall abruptly excusing myself. Couldn't help it. I barely made it to the hallway before I was overwhelmed, standing there, away from the room, gasping for air. A range of emotions I couldn't possibly process in polite company. They must have thought it was insulting. But I couldn't stand it a second longer. It felt like my chest was going to cave in." He wiped a hand across his face. "Asia, for some reason, never really seemed to grasp how seeing her, that echo of Mother, would hit me—that it wasn't comfort but a raw wound." He managed a faint smile. "Still, despite that moment, we did make some good memories that night. Jakub junior—he was the spark."

Icek leaned back, the weight of the past heavy on his shoulders.

A long silence hung in the air.

"Jesus Christ, Icek," Churchill finally murmured, shaking his head slowly, the respect and sorrow clear in his voice. "Your family murdered by the Nazis—and you were there to see it. On top of everything else—Icek, you've carried quite a burden."

A flicker of pain crossed Icek's face, etching itself deeper into his tired features.

"The images, Agent Churchill. The sounds. They play enough in my head as it is. A movie?" He gave a humorless laugh. "No, thank you. The nightmares, the crazy thoughts, they'd never go away. I'll stick to the classroom. To anonymity. Just live the rest of my life in quiet."

Churchill leaned forward slightly. "Icek, would you mind if we grabbed a beer sometime? We've got a lot in common. I feel like I've known you for years. What do you say?"

A genuine smile, warmer this time, spread across Icek's face. "I'd like that. Very much. It would be good to talk to a comrade in arms regularly. Thank you."

Churchill pulled out a card, scribbling on the back. "Here. My home phone. Patty's my wife. If she answers, introduce yourself. I'll tell her to expect your call. And your wife is Teodora. Son Kyle. Daughter Karen."

"You've got a good memory."

"Comes with the territory. Memory and attention to detail go a long way in this job." Churchill stood up. "I'll get out of your hair. If we hear anything—I mean anything—I'll be in touch. And please do the same. Call my home number if you can't reach me at the office. So, so long for now. And I'm looking forward to that beer."

CHAPTER SIXTY-FIVE

La Guardia Airport, New York City, NY
August 19th, 1974, 4:45 p.m.

"**N**ext, please," the agent's voice was crisp and efficient. Asia, Jack, and Jakub Junior stepped up to the counter. The Eastern Airlines ticket agent, a woman named Linda, if the tiny tag on her jacket was accurate, was the picture of airline professionalism. Her gray uniform skirt, jacket, crisp white shirt, and a neatly knotted navy-blue silk scarf looked freshly pressed. Her pixie cut was immaculate, her makeup flawless, and her slender frame suggested a dedication to the airline's image that bordered on the extreme.

"Tickets, identification, and destination, please," Linda requested, her smile practiced. "How many bags will you be checking?"

Jack held out their tickets. "We're on flight 243 to Stapleton, nonstop. Four bags between the three of us. Any word on whether it's on time?"

Linda's gaze lingered on Jack, drawn to the black patch covering his left eye, then flickered to the faint, silvery network of scars tracing the line of his neck above his collar. He met her gaze steadily, a hint of weariness in his good eye. He was a smart dresser—a khaki suit with a crisp, light-blue shirt and a dark tie, but the marks of the past were unmistakable. Linda's internal monologue likely raced: *War hero? Car accident? A fire?*

Jack broke the silence with a small, wry smile. "The war," he confirmed, as if reading her thoughts. "Lost the eye. It's nothing. I'm used to the looks. Just don't ask to see the other guy." He chuckled, a low rumble in his chest. "He's not around anymore, as he met the devil, I hope, on the day I lost my eye."

Linda's cheeks flushed crimson. She averted her eyes, fumbling with the tickets. "I apologize, sir. I didn't mean to stare."

Asia placed a comforting hand on Jack's arm. "It's all quite alright," she said as she caught the gaze of the ticket agent. "We're accustomed to it. We're just grateful he came home in one piece. It all feels like a lifetime ago."

Linda, still avoiding Jack's gaze, managed to make a weak smile. "Of course. You're both very kind." She focused on her task, her fingers moving swiftly over the keyboard. "Right, flight 243, nonstop, departing from Gate 14 at five-fifty p.m. I've put you in the no-smoking section, Mr. Reynolds, with an aisle seat. And madam, you're across the aisle, and Jakub will have the window seat, as requested."

"Thank you," Asia said, her voice warm. "We appreciate your help."

Later, as they waited for their flight, Jakub Junior turned to his father. "How often does that happen, Father? The stares, the unspoken questions? Doesn't it bother you?"

"It's human nature to be inquisitive. Stares happen a couple of times a week. I don't give it a second thought."

Jack sighed—his gaze distant. "It's complicated, son. Every person who sees a visible reminder of war has a right to wonder. Maybe, just maybe, it makes them think about the cost. The real cost. I'm a walking billboard for that cost, I suppose." He paused, then added, with a pointed look at Jakub, "You were fortunate. When you turned eighteen in 1962, there were very few conflicts going on in the world."

Asia squeezed Jack's hand. "Let's not dwell on what-ifs, gentlemen. Though, Jack, your poster child analogy is colorful."

Stapleton Airport
August 20th, 1974, 6:10 p.m.

Under a sky the color of a robin's egg, seventeen-year-old Kyle gripped the steering wheel of the family wagon, a thrill of anticipation racing through him. He glanced at his father, Icek, in the passenger seat.

"Thanks for letting me drive, Father. It means a lot. It'll be great to see Uncle Jack, Aunt Asia, and Jakub again. It feels like ages."

Icek remarked, "Too long, son. Too long. We've let life get in the way. Phone calls and holiday greetings are not enough. My mother would be heartbroken to see how distant we've become." He rubbed his hand over his face, a gesture of weary frustration. "It's difficult seeing

Aunt Asia. She's the image of my mother. Every time I look at her, I see what might have been. I love Asia—I truly do. But the loss never really goes away. I'm sure she feels it—I carry this awkwardness."

Kyle slowed for a red light. "What about Grandfather Abram? Will seeing Aunt Asia upset him?"

Icek let out a shaky breath. "I don't know, son. I honestly don't know. Abram appears to have adjusted well to his home in Malta. Perhaps, like I have heard too many times in life, and by the way, I have no idea who authored the phrase, *time heals all wounds.* Abram hasn't seen Asia since she left Poland well before the War." He swallowed hard. "I'm hoping he can see her as Asia, his sister-in-law, not as a ghost of his wife."

"Father, you were eight when Grandmother Henna passed," Kyle said, his voice barely above a whisper. "How old was Grandfather then?"

"Thirty-one. Abram was born in 1899, and Henna the following year. That makes Asia seventy-four now." Icek's voice hitched, a slight tremor betraying the emotion he tried to contain. He stared out the window, his gaze distant. "The twins, Edna and Matty, they'd be forty-two." Ryfka, born in 1863—she was seventy-nine on the day of her death." He shook his head, the movement sharp and jerky. "Just for being Jewish." He drew a ragged breath. "We never even found their bodies. The Germans probably burned them, like so many others of the time." The word hung in the air, heavy and unspoken. "The damned Nazis."

"Father, it's okay," Kyle said, his hand reaching out as if to touch his father, then stopping short. He watched the tears welling, the unshed grief etched on his father's face. "We don't have to talk about this."

Icek took a deep breath, his shoulders straightening as he visibly regained control. "Memories, they crowd in. Good, terrible, all mixed." He turned back to Kyle, his eyes searching. "We were targets, son. Every day, for years, just waiting. Your mother, Tomasz, me, we scraped by— bellies aching with hunger." He paused, his voice dropping to a near whisper. "And I still ask myself, *'Why us? Why did we survive?'"* He looked away again, the question unanswered—perhaps unanswerable. "They call it *Survivor's Guilt*. I'll carry that to my grave."

Kyle's knuckles turned white as he gripped the steering wheel. "I don't understand the..." He swallowed hard, unable to finish the sentence.

"You shouldn't have to," Icek said, his voice regaining some of its firmness. "Some things are best left undisturbed. But Halina." His voice softened again, a flicker of hope in his eyes. "I'd like to see her again. For so long, I thought she had died with the others in Jozefow." He cleared his throat. "We know she's alive. She was a most remarkable person. Ask your grandfather. He'll remember. I can't begin to tell you how pleased I am to hear we will see her again—this is an answered prayer. The twins worshiped the ground she walked on."

Kyle shifted in his seat, his gaze darting nervously between the road and his father. "Father, there's something I wanted to ask. The war in Vietnam is winding down. A friend of mine enlisted in the Marines. I've been thinking about it, too."

Icek's gaze sharpened, his eyes narrowing as he studied his son. "Because of that Marine at the airport? Or is it the war stories you've heard from Uncle Jack? "Jack was involved in fourteen top-secret missions as an embedded commando with the British SAS for eighteen months. The SAS commandos were the best of the best, carrying out small-scale, elite operations deep behind enemy lines. If I am not mistaken, Uncle Jack to this day cannot talk about his role in the war. Please don't ask him anything about his experiences, as the topic is sure to upset Asia. It is best never to ask about his past. I just know all SAS members risked their lives, and many never came back. There were times when Jack was missing for months at a time. He saw action throughout Europe, and as you know, he lost an eye."

"I guess the SAS is a step above the Marines, right?"

"Each branch has its own elite group."

He paused, his fingers tapping a silent rhythm on his knee. "I've seen dozens go. My students became grunts, clerks, cooks, mechanics, and three—three who never came back." He shook his head slowly. "If you're dreaming of glory, Kyle, the odds..." He let the sentence trail off.

"And without college, they might have you cleaning latrines at Twenty-Nine Palms—just so you know. Those stationed there call it 'Twenty-Nine Stumps,' out in the middle of the California desert, east of Los Angeles. Dominic Gangale, another of my students, a native-born Italian from immigrant parents, did the volunteer draft enlistment in the USMC for two years; he typed memos. He hated every second at Fleet Marine Force Pacific, Aiea, Hawaii. Son, be careful what you wish for."

"No, Father. It's not about being a hero. It's something else." He took a deep breath. "What happened at the airport with Gunny Rivera—that just solidified it. Seeing the Gunny made it clearer. It's the Marines or nothing."

Icek nodded slowly. "The Paris Peace Accords were just signed last year. The Americans are pulling out. I suspect South Vietnam will fall." He sighed. "But wars, they're like a cycle. There will be another, somewhere. And the Marines, the Special Forces, they'll be the first ones in." He glanced around, his eyes scanning the passing cars. "Things are uncertain here as well: Nixon, Watergate, protesters—it's a mess." He paused, his voice dropping lower. "I can't promise you won't see action. But I'd be proud. Your mother, though, she'll be furious. She was wounded—she'll go insane."

"Wounded? What the hell—you never told us? Mother was wounded, and we're just now hearing about it?" Kyle's voice rose in disbelief, his eyes wide.

Icek thought to himself, *How in the world could I ever let this slip out? I must consider how I can neutralize this—forget it, it can't be neutralized.* "We were going to tell you eventually. Unfortunately, it will be a while before we can discuss our WWII activity." Icek's voice was low, almost a murmur.

"You mean you were both in the war, and you never told us? Really?" Kyle's hands tightened on the steering wheel again, his knuckles white.

"Son, at your next opportunity, pull over and park the car."

Kyle pulled into the parking lot of a local strip mall and turned off the car.

"We have purposely kept the past from both of you, and we declined to tell anyone in our immediate area—including our employer—that we were part of the war." Icek's voice was firm but laced with a hint of weariness.

"Father, you lied. You both lied." Kyle's voice was tight with accusation.

"Son, we did not lie. We failed to tell you we were members of the Polish Home Army. At this point, we need to keep this under wraps. We could both jeopardize our employment. This is serious business." Icek's voice was sharp, cutting through Kyle's anger.

"What else have you not told us about your past?" Kyle's voice was barely a whisper, laced with a mixture of fear and resentment.

"Kyle, please settle down. What I am about to tell you, you must NEVER repeat—never. Eventually, following our deaths, you would have been told of our past. We spilled the beans in our estate package that our attorney prepared for us when you and Karen were toddlers. Listen, Kyle, I will tell you right now, but you must swear you will never utter a word to anybody. If this information were to get out, it would devastate your mother. We could even lose our jobs. Can you agree to this?" Icek's voice was pleading, a desperation Kyle had never witnessed.

Kyle sat, speechless and staring at the floor, his mind reeling.

"Well, Kyle, can you agree?" Icek pressed, his voice insistent.

"Yes, sir, I agree. I will swear that I will never repeat what you tell me, under the understanding that upon your death, the estate documents will spell out the past. Yes, I agree." Kyle's voice was flat, devoid of emotion, as if he were reciting a memorized pledge.

"Like I said, Kyle, let's keep this between us for now. Not a word until then. By the way, the estate documents specify that the information will be divulged when Teodora, Uncle Tomasz, and I are all deceased. Not before. Understood?"

"Yes, sir. Understood." Kyle repeated, his gaze still fixed on the floor.

"Son, I should not be surprised that you want to join an organization like the US Marine Corps. You most likely get this interest from your gene pool. Your mother, Uncle Tomasz, and I were members of the Polish Home Army. Those scars on your mother's breast—the wounds were the result of a German soldier coming at her with a rifle that had a bayonet mounted on the end. It did not happen as a result of an accident. The Kraut stabbed her in the chest. We almost lost her. I killed the guy who attacked her."

"Father—you killed people?" Kyle asked, staring with a blank expression as the words left his mouth.

"It was war. We had to kill or be killed. I didn't enjoy or relish the opportunity to end the life of a human; none of us did. Luckily, we did not kill each day of the war, as weeks would sometimes go by until we encountered Germans. The first time is the worst. Taking a life is not what you see in the war movies. It is loud, horrific, and nerve-racking, and each time you wonder, *Is today my last day?* You need to learn, son, there is nothing glamorous or exciting about taking the life of an enemy.

The day your mother was wounded, we almost lost her. We were so lucky! We had a trained medic who was fifty meters away. He stitched her up; up until then, your mother was well on her way to bleeding to death.

We didn't see much one-on-one killing while in the Home Army, but we did see our share. We were like the three musketeers; we watched each other's backs. Our specialty was interrogation. We would interrogate German soldiers, persuade them to talk, and then hand them off to others who did the dirty work. We could not take prisoners. We didn't have the food, the beds, no jail, etc., to take and house prisoners. We slept in barns or under the stars, regardless of the weather. We could barely feed ourselves, let alone German prisoners. And before you get all sentimental about the poor Germans, the Krauts rarely ever took Polish prisoners. It was usually the members of the Home Army taken prisoner by the Germans who were subsequently tortured to death or killed because they didn't talk. The Germans were ruthless. They were outright animals. Now you know our family secret."

"You killed people, and Mom killed people, and Uncle Tomasz, he killed too?" Kyle's voice was barely audible, a mixture of shock and disbelief.

"The answer is yes. We had to kill to stay alive, simple as that. I don't know of a single Home Army vet that escaped the taking of life. It was war, son." Icek's voice was firm, tolerating no argument.

"Why did you want to keep the past from everyone?" Kyle's eyes finally met his father's, searching for answers.

"This requires a more extended response. You know we came here to visit relatives with the intention of going back to Poland. When we got here, we fell in love with the politics, the scenery, the local Jews, the American way, and most importantly, the opportunities. Plus, if we stayed in Poland, it would have been challenging to divorce ourselves from our Home Army past. We wanted a clean start.

"No more questions! This topic will never be discussed or brought up again until our attorney opens the estate documents. I told you more than I should have. Son, I trust you, and I know you will keep this secret because you are a mature, honorable person. I never want to doubt my decision today. So, Kyle, we can call this case closed. Right?"

"Yes, Father, case closed. Thank you for sharing your Home Army experience with me."

"You are welcome, son. I feel much better getting this out in the open."

Kyle started the car, and they continued on their trip to the airport.

"You know your Uncle Jack was a Marine before the SOE?"

"Yes, sir. I want to talk to him." Kyle's voice was firm, a new resolve hardening his features.

"I'll be there when you do. Your mother, she still dreams of you as a teacher, like us."

"No offense, Father, but teaching—that's not for me."

"None taken. It's not for everyone." Icek's gaze shifted, his eyes narrowing as he scanned the traffic around them.

Stapleton Airport
August 20th, 1974, 7:10 p.m.

Icek and Kyle waited at the gate, the air thick with anticipation. The loudspeaker crackled to life. "Ladies and gentlemen, Eastern Airlines Flight 243 from La Guardia has landed. Please meet your guests at Gate 22."

"They made it," Kyle said, relief washing over him.

Icek stood, his palms sweating. He felt a knot forming in his throat, the same childish nervousness he remembered from his first school presentation. *Butterflies. Damn butterflies.*

"You okay, father?" Kyle asked, concern in his voice.

"Fine," Icek managed, though his voice was tight. "It's just seeing Asia. It's always like this. The image of my mother doesn't get easier. It's not Asia's fault. It's just the tragedy of it all."

The passengers began to stream off the plane. Jakub Junior emerged first, and Icek felt a jolt of recognition.

"My God, Kyle," he whispered. "He's the spitting image of his father. A pianist, too."

Then, Asia appeared, followed by Jack, the black eye patch a stark reminder of the past. "There they are," Kyle said, his voice a mix of excitement and relief.

They met with a flurry of embraces, handshakes, and hurried greetings, the awkwardness of the reunion momentarily forgotten.

"Icek, we were so worried," Asia said, her eyes searching his. "We saw the news. We weren't sure it was safe to come."

"We're all right," Icek assured her. "It was intense, like being back in Poland during the war. But the man is going to trial. Hopefully, he'll spend the rest of his life in prison. With the others. The ones from the Police Battalion. But let's not talk about it. We're trying to find some normalcy."

Jack tapped Icek on the shoulder. "We understand. We're proud of you, Icek. For protecting your family."

"How is Abram?" Asia asked, her voice tinged with anxiety.

"He's well," Icek began, choosing his words carefully. "He speaks English! He needs dental work. Badly. False teeth are in his future. His eye, the one he injured when the Nazis took him, it's noticeable. But his vision is alright. He needs a magnifying glass for small print. We bought him a new suit. Chocolate brown leisure suit. White belt and white shoes. And a cap. An Irish-style cap. He's smaller than I remember. Frail. But it's him. He told us about the Russians. How they killed the Kapos, the guards hanged, and the officers shot the rest—no remorse, of course. Eleven survived out of nearly a hundred. He weighed sixty-seven pounds when they liberated the camp." Icek's voice cracked. "Eighteen thousand perished in that place. Starvation, sickness, hangings—you need to prepare yourself, Asia. He's changed. It's been thirty years for me, longer for you. But God has been good. We have him back."

Asia's eyes filled with tears. "I don't know what to expect. I'm worried about how he'll react. To see—a replica of Henna's face."

Icek nodded grimly. "I know. I'm bracing myself for anything. He lost everything that night. The twins, Ryfka, you, me, and Henna—all fresh in his memory. It's unimaginable."

The drive back was filled with periods of silence intermixed with periods of nervous speaking. Icek led the way around to the back of the house. Abram sat in a rocking chair, bathed in the golden light of the setting sun. He stared out at the majestic Front Range of the Rockies, his head slowly turning as he watched two gray squirrels chase each other near a towering pine tree.

Asia paused, her hand on Icek's arm. "I want to see him alone," she whispered. "If that's alright?"

Icek nodded, understanding.

Asia took a deep breath and approached her brother-in-law slowly. She stopped behind him, gently placing her hands on his shoulders. "Abram," she said softly. "It's me. It's Asia."

He stood, turning slowly. Asia stepped around the chair, and they faced each other. For a long moment, they looked, the years melting away. Then, tears welled in both their eyes.

Abram's voice, thick with a Polish accent, broke the silence. "I never thought I'd see her again. Henna's face. You are the closest thing to having her here." He reached out, wiping a tear from his cheek. "You're still so beautiful."

"Abram," Asia whispered, her voice choked with emotion. "We both miss her. Every day."

"I prayed to die," Abram confessed, his voice raw. "In that place, I wanted to be with her. I didn't know about Ryfka, the twins, I just found out. I just wanted Henna." He shook his head. "But God, He had other plans. And now, I see her in you. It's a miracle."

He reached for Asia, pulling her into a fierce embrace. Asia clung to him, her tears flowing freely. "Abram," she said, her voice muffled against his shoulder. "God saved you. For this!"

END

ACKNOWLEDGEMENTS

This novel is a testament to your generosity, your boundless patience, and your insightful guidance. You provided the encouragement that sustained me, the keen eyes that sharpened my characters and plot, and the steadfast belief that transformed a manuscript into a story ready for the world.

Your efforts went far beyond what any author could reasonably expect, and for that, I am eternally grateful. This book is immeasurably better because of your presence in its creation, and it is with immense appreciation that I acknowledge the vital role each of you played in bringing this historical novel to market.

Patty Churchill – Beta reader
Cindy Evans – Beta reader
Tammy Gedelian – Beta reader
Patsy Maigret – Beta reader
Marni MacRae – Primary Editor
Marilyn Peplau – Beta reader

My deepest gratitude goes to my wife, Cindy. This first novel was a labor of love that demanded more time and energy than anticipated, and through every extended deadline and moment of self-doubt, your support was my constant. Thank you for your sacrifices, your understanding, and your unwavering faith in my dream. And to our children, Allison and Ryan, thank you for your patience and for adding so much joy to my life, making this entire endeavor worthwhile.

ENDNOTES

---

1 *See* https://www.nyphil.org/explore-more/history/

Chapter 6

2 *See* https://www.britannica.com/biography/Antonin-Dvorak

3 *See* https://libquotes.com/dante-alighieri/quote/lbq6k7g

4 *See* https://www.archives.nyc/blog/2021/2/5/mayor-james-j-walker/ Born in Manhattan to Irish-immigrant parents in 1881, James John Walker rose through the Tammany-dominated political landscape of the first decades of the 20th century, mentored by powerhouse Al Smith. His career began in the New York State Assembly in 1909. He won a seat in the Senate beginning in 1914, and in 1925, Democratic leaders chose him to run against incumbent Mayor John F. Hylan. He won the election, and took office on January 1, 1926. Mayor Walker's affair with musical comedy and film actress Betty Compton further fueled his downfall. Walker and Compton married in France in 1933; they divorced in 1940. Walker died in New York City in 1946.

5 *See* https://en.wikipedia.org/wiki/Park_Slope

6 *See* https://www.history.com/topics/world-war-i/battle-of-the-somme

Chapter 8

7 *See* https://www.myjewishlearning.com/article/hevra-kaddisha-or-burial-society/

Chapter 9

8 *See* https://www.britannica.com/topic/Tanakh

Chapter 14

9 *See* https://www.loc.gov/classroom-materials/united-states-history-primary-source-timeline/progressive-era-to-new-era-1900-1929/immigrants-in-progressive-era/

10 *See* https://fraser.stlouisfed.org/files/docs/publications/stat_abstract/pages/52753_1935-1939.pdf

Chapter 15

11 *See* https://poets.org/poem/new-colossus. A descendant of Sephardic Jews who immigrated to the United States from Portugal around the time of the American Revolution, Emma Lazarus was a Jewish American poet and translator. Her sonnet, "The New Colossus," is inscribed on a plaque on the pedestal of the Statue of Liberty monument. She referred to the statue as *Mother of Exiles*.

12 *See* https://en.wikipedia.org/wiki/National_Origins_Formula

13 *See* https://www.smithsonianmag.com/history/true-story-reichstag-fire-and-nazis-rise-power-180962240/

14 *See* https://worldofhistorycheatsheet.com/the-reichstag-fire-1933/

15 *See* https://www.britannica.com/topic/Enabling-Act The Reichstag Fire Decree suspended many civil liberties enshrined in the Weimar Constitution, including:Freedom of speech and press.Freedom of assembly.The right to privacy in personal communications.Habeas corpus protections, which required that arrested individuals be charged with a crime or released within a reasonable time.This decree effectively allowed the government to arrest political opponents, particularly communists and social democrats, without due process. In the weeks following the fire, thousands of communists, socialists, and trade unionists were arrested, and the Communist Party's ability to campaign in the upcoming elections was severely crippled.

Chapter 20

16 *See* https://en.wikipedia.org/wiki/Buchenwald_concentration_camp

17 *See* https://www.holocausthistoricalsociety.org.uk/contents/naziseasternempire/policebattalion101.html

[18] *See* https://en.wikipedia.org/wiki/Munich_Agreement

[19] *See* https://www.worldhistory.org/article/2559/the-invasion-of-poland-in-1939/

Chapter 22

[20] *See* https://www.polandww2.com/resources/poland-in-wwii/siege-of-warsaw/

[21] *See* https://encyclopedia.ushmm.org/content/en/article/the-night-of-broken-glass

[22] *See* https://en.wikipedia.org/wiki/Ernst_vom_Rath (3 June 1909 – 9 November 1938) was a member of the German nobility, a Nazi Party member, and German Foreign Office diplomat. He is mainly remembered for his assassination in Paris in 1938 by a Polish Jewish teenager, Herschel Grynszpan, which provided a pretext for Kristallnacht, "The Night of Broken Glass" on 9–10 November 1938.

[23] *See* https://encyclopedia.ushmm.org/content/en/article/invasion-of-poland-fall-1939

Chapter 23

[24] *See* https://eng.ipn.gov.pl/en/digital-resources/articles/7262,Soviet-aggression-on-Poland-from-17-September-1939.html

Chapter 25

[25] *See* https://ww2days.com/luftwaffe-prepares-final-terror-bombing-of-warsaw.html

[26] *See* https://encyclopedia.ushmm.org/content/en/film/adam-czerniakow-chairman-of-the-jewish-council-in-warsaw

[27] *See* https://www.holocausthistoricalsociety.org.uk/contents/ghettosj-r/jozefow.html

Chapter 26

[28] *See* https://soldierexecutionerprolifer2008.blogspot.com/2015/05/reserve-police-battalion-101-formed-on.html

Chapter 27

[29] *See* https://www.researchgate.net/publication/330113031_Quantifying_the_Holocaust_Hyperintense_kill_rates _during the_Nazi_genocide

[30] *See* https://ww2db.com/facility/Hadamar_Euthanasia_Center/#google_vignette/The Hadamar Euthanasia Center was located inside of the psychiatric ward of the already established hospital in Hadamar in western Germany. As a part of the T-4 Euthanasia Program, Hadamar exterminated people deemed unfit to reproduce starting in 1941.

[31] *See* https://teatrnn.pl/lexicon/articles/jozefow-bilgorajski-history-of-the-town/

Chapter 28

[32] *See* https://www.wehrmacht-awards.com/uniforms_firearms/firearms/p38/p38index.htm

Chapter 30

[33] *See* https://www.worldhistory.org/article/2646/why-did-hitler-hate-jewish-people/Hitler, with help from his propaganda specialist Josef Goebbels (1897-1945), presented to the German people that Jews were enemy number one. Hitler repeatedly spoke of how – in his view – Jews had been behind Germany's defeat in WWI. Jews, said Hitler, had repeatedly called for a premature end to the war and so diminished the will of the German population to fight. Further, Hitler believed that Jews had had a stranglehold on the economy, which had badly affected the war effort. For Hitler, Jews were now part of an international conspiracy to control the economy and wealth of post-war Germany, preventing ordinary people from prospering. The Nazis then blended this idea of a common enemy with a pseudo-scientific and inconsistent race theory, giving them a seemingly reasoned and academic justification for their treatment of Jewish people.

[34] *See* https://www.tygodnikzamojski.pl/artykul/5434/ On May 13, 1942, Germans killed 100 local Jews

[35] *See* https://www.tygodnikzamojski.pl/artykul/5434/ Before the actual execution, the Germans made a selection of the population gathered in the market square, choosing from the approximately 2,000 people gathered, over 400 people able to work, who were separated from the rest and then sent by trucks to the camp in Lublin. The remaining people were loaded in groups onto trucks and taken to the forest, where executions were carried out on both sides of the road leading to Aleksandrów, near Winiarczykowa Góra.

Chapter 35

[36] *See* https://www.historyhit.com/the-treatment-of-the-jews-in-nazi-germany/

[37] *See* https://en.wikipedia.org/wiki/Skar%C5%BCysko-Kamienna

Chapter 37

[38] *See* https://www.jewishvirtuallibrary.org/skarzysko-kamienna

Chapter 38

[39] *See* https://militaryhistoria.com/soe/

[40] *See* https://www.jewishvirtuallibrary.org/reserve-police-battalion-101

Chapter 41

[41] See https://en.wikipedia.org/wiki/Marylebone -- an area in London, England and is located in the City of Westminster. in Central London and part of the West End. Oxford Street forms its southern boundary.

[42] See https://en.wikipedia.org/wiki/The_Barley_Mow,_MaryleboneThe Barley Mow is a grade II listed pub located at 8 Dorset Street, Marylebone, London, W1. It is on the Campaign for Real Ale's National Inventory of Historic Pub Interiors. Public houses on this list have remained relatively unchanged since World War II or at least for the past thirty years. It was built in 1791 and is rumored to be the longest standing building in Marylebone.

[43] *See* https://www.bjcp.org/beer-styles/17a-british-strong-ale-burton-ale/ Popular in Burton before IPAs were invented, widely exported to the Baltic countries. After 1822, reformulated to be less sweet and strong. Most popular in the Victorian Era, with several different strengths available in the family. The strongest versions evolved into English Barleywines. Became less popular after WWII, eventually dying out around 1970. Some versions exist as Winter Warmers, Barleywines, or Old Ales, but the name has lost favor in the market.

[44] *See* https://www.bbc.com/news/magazine-20160819 -- GIs were frequently described as "overpaid, oversexed and over here". The GIs retorted and said the British were "underpaid, undersexed and under Eisenhower".

[45] *See* https://www.marforres.marines.mil/Staff-Sections/Special-Staff/Career-Planner/Fitness-Reports/

[46] *See* https://polishhistory.pl/order-to-dissolve-the-home-army-given-by-home-army-commander-in-chief-general-leopold-okulicki/The first underground groups in German-occupied Poland began to be established as early as in the autumn of 1939. The Home Army (Armia Krajowa, AK), an underground army subordinate to the Polish government in exile and the Commander-in-Chief, took its final shape in February 1942. Its Commanders-in-Chief in chronological order were: Stefan Rowecki 'Grot' (arrested in June 1943), Tadeusz Komorowski 'Bór' (in captivity since October 1944), and Leopold Okulicki 'Niedzwiadek' (appointed in January 1945). The Home Army dealt with military training, obtainment of weapons, communications, information, propaganda, etc. The AK unit for sabotage operations, special operations, and carrying out death sentences on representatives of the German repression apparatus was the Directorate of Diversion (Kierownictwo Dywersji, Kedyw), established in January 1943. The Home Army was one of the largest military organizations in occupied Europe, with the number of its members reaching approx. 390,000 in the spring of 1944.

Chapter 42

[47] *See* https://www.bbc.co.uk/programmes/articles/5hqYBJNYDy5WNpHDPZ3W0cd/the-secret-scottish-highland-training-camps-used-to-prepare-british-spies-for-life-behind-world-war-two-enemy-lines

Chapter 43

[48] *See* https://www.britannica.com/event/Battle-of-Belleau-Wood The Allies' victory at the Battle of Belleau Wood, which occurred in France from June 1 to June 26, 1918, greatly boosted morale amid the Germans' Spring Offensive. The battle was the first major engagement of the U.S. army in World War I, and only 39 miles from Paris, marked the closest the Germans came to the French capital during the war. The struggle for Belleau Wood, at the time a hunting preserve owned by a wealthy Paris businessman, announced to the Germans that the U.S. armed forces had arrived on the Western Front in strength and were eager to fight. It was a tough baptism of fire for the Americans, but persistence and resolution secured them their first important victory in France. The bravery of the U.S. Army's 2nd Division, comprising the 4th Marine Brigade (the "Fighting Fifth" and 6th Marine Regiments) was especially noteworthy. In recognition of their service and sacrifice, the French renamed Belleau Wood the "Bois de la Brigade de Marine"—Wood of the Marine Brigade—and awarded the 4th Marine Brigade the coveted Croix de Guerre.

[49] *See* https://www.encyclopedia.com/science-and-technology/chemistry/organic-chemistry/cyanidesPersonnel working for the Special Operations Executive (SOE) in the war were often equipped with "L" pills (L for lethal) containing cyanide in crystal form. In some cases, cyanide could be hidden in the earpiece of a pair of glasses. When cornered, the operative could take off his glasses and pretend to thoughtfully bite the end of the earpiece while thinking about what he would say next. But there would not be any next statement: within seconds of consuming this deadly toxin, the operative would be dead.

Chapter 44

[50] *See* https://militaryhistorynow.com/2017/08/02/the-plane-that-really-won-ww2-everything-you-need-to-know-about-the-c-47-skytrain/The four-man crew of pilot, co-pilot, navigator, and radio operator appreciated the ease of flying and maintaining the C-47, which the British referred to as the Dakota. It could sustain heavy combat damage and remain aloft. It was capable of taking off with a full load from an unpaved runway only 3,000 feet (900m) long. With supplemental fuel tangs topped off, its range was an impressive 1,500 miles (2,400km). Although it was a slow aircraft, with an average cruising speed of only 150 miles per hour (240km/h), it was capable of dropping to 110 miles per hour (175km/h) and maintaining altitude during an airborne operation, allowing paratroopers to jump from a stable platform.

[51] See https://www.nationalww2museum.org/war/articles/1929-geneva-convention#:~:text=The%20rules%20regarding%20the%20humane%20treatment%20of%20prisoners,to%20with%20Othe%20all-encompassing%20term%20%E2%80%9CThe%20Geneva%20Convention.%E2%80%9D In reality, when captured, the presentation of your real name, rank, and serial number is a requirement of Article 5 of the July 27, 1929 Geneva Convention. That being said, it is the only information a prisoner is obligated to give. The rules regarding the humane treatment of prisoners of war during World War II were developed at the 1929 Geneva Convention. This was one in a series of conventions that over decades created the official rules of war, often referred to with the all-encompassing term "The Geneva Convention." In this sense the rules of war are not dictums to fight by. These are rules intended to protect innocents, wounded, prisoners of war, and even combatants, and are agreed upon by a group of nations. Unwritten or agreed upon rules of war have always existed, but they were often tailored to the needs or desires of a nation or state.

Chapter 45

[52] *See* https://kleinhansbuffalo.org/about/mission-history-architecture/Kleinhans Music Hall was built thanks to the generosity and vision of Edward and Mary Seaton Kleinhans and the stewardship of their charitable dreams by the Community Foundation for Greater Buffalo. The Community Foundation was bequeathed the estates of Mr. and Mrs. Kleinhans, who made their fortune from the clothing store that bore their name, and who died within three months of each other in 1934. The hall was completed using funds from the Public Works Administration. The Kleinhans, who were music lovers, found the Elmwood Music Hall drafty and acoustically imperfect, and specified their money was to be used "to erect a suitable music hall...for the use, enjoyment and benefit of the people of the City of Buffalo." Kleinhans Music Hall was officially opened on October 12, 1940; this date also marked the Buffalo Philharmonic's first concert in the hall under the baton of Franco Autori. Kleinhans Music Hall was designed by the famous Finnish father-and-son team of Eliel and Eero Saarinen, along with architects F.J. and W.A Kidd.

[53] *See* https://www.paintedhills.org/STEUBEN/WaylandTrainWreck.html -- On August 30, 1943, the Lackawanna Limited speeding along at 70 MPH to make up twenty minutes of lost time, sideswiped a switcher freight engine that had not fully cleared the main line. There were more than 500 passengers aboard the 11-car train. The track-side signals and cab signals indicated clear. The engineer of the switcher thought he had time to finish his chores and was moving along the siding. The engineer of the express noticed the moving switcher on the siding and assumed it would stop; when he realized it was not, he applied the emergency brakes, but too late to avoid the ensuring collision. The Limited's locomotive sliced off the front end of the switcher and split its boiler, derailing itself and several following cars. Every window in the express was shattered and scalding water burst from the broken boiler of the switcher flooded the windowless Nickel plate coach which had stopped by the switcher. Twenty-six passengers in that car were killed from the scalding water and steam. Riding in the cab of the Limited was F. H. Meincke, DL&W's superintendent of locomotives. He jumped from the cab and was killed when the engine toppled on him; the engineer and fireman was not injured. Two other passengers died later. About four months later, an inquest was held which, although declaring "negligence of employees and failure of officials of the Delaware, Lackawanna & Western Railroad to provide adequate safety facilities", the coroner concluded that no useful purpose would be served by recommending criminal action.

Chapter 46

[54] *See* https://www.usatoday.com/story/money/2020/06/12/how-many-people-were-born-the-year-you-were-born/111928356/and https://archive.cdc.gov/www_cdc_gov/nchs/data/statab/t001x07.pdf; page 2 of 7 indicate there were 17.7 per thousand births or based on the 1942 population, this equates to nearly 116,000 births to women 40 to 44 years of age.

Chapter 47

[55] *See* https://www.defense.gov/serve-from-netstorage/Experience/VE-Day/index.html. On May 8, 1945 - known as Victory in Europe Day or V-E Day - celebrations erupted around the world to mark the end of World War II in Europe. The war had been raging for almost five years when U.S. and Allied forces landed on the beaches of Normandy, France, on June 6, 1944. The invasion signaled the beginning of the end for Adolf Hitler and Nazi Germany. In less than a year, Germany would surrender, and Hitler would be dead. But in his speech to the nation on V-E Day, President Harry S. Truman cautioned that Allies must "work to finish the war" by defeating the Japanese in the Pacific.

[56] *See* https://www.britannica.com/event/Potsdam-Conference --Potsdam Conference, (July 17–August 2, 1945), Allied conference of World War II held at Potsdam, a suburb of Berlin. The chief participants were U.S. President Harry S. Truman, British Prime Minister Winston Churchill (or Clement Attlee, who became prime minister during the conference), and Soviet Premier Joseph Stalin. The Potsdam Conference's Declaration on Germany stated, "It is the intention of the Allies that the German people be given the opportunity to prepare for the eventual reconstruction of their life on a democratic and peaceful basis." The four occupation zones of Germany conceived at the Yalta Conference were set up, each to be administered by the commander-in-chief of the Soviet, British, U.S., or French army of occupation. Berlin, Vienna, and Austria were also each divided into four occupation zones. An Allied Control Council made up of representatives of the four Allies was to deal with matters affecting Germany and Austria as a whole. Its policies were dictated by the "five Ds" decided upon at Yalta: demilitarization, denazification, democratization, decentralization, and deindustrialization.

[57] *See* https://www.pbs.org/wgbh/americanexperience/features/goebbels-burnings/--On May 10, 1933, university students in 34 university towns across Germany burned over 25,000 books. The works of Jewish authors like Albert Einstein and Sigmund Freud went up in flames alongside blacklisted American authors such as Ernest Hemingway and Helen Keller, while students gave the Nazi salute. In Berlin 40,000 people gathered to hear German Minister of Public Enlightenment and Propaganda Joseph Goebbels give a speech in Berlin's Opera Square. He declared "the era of extreme Jewish intellectualism is now at an end. ... The future German man will not just be a man of books, but a man of character. It is to this end that we want to educate you. ... And thus you do well in this midnight hour to commit to the flames the evil spirit of the past."

Chapter 48

[58] For additional details on the 78 murders in Talczyn, Poland carried out by the Hamburg, Germany based Police Battalion 101, see pp 100-103, Christopher R. Browning, *Ordinary Men: Reserve Police Battalion 101 and the Final Solution in Poland* (New York: HarperCollins, 1992)

[59] *See* https://scholarlycommons.law.wlu.edu/cgi/viewcontent.cgi?article=1602&context=wlufac -- Stepping Beyond Nuremberg's Halo: The Legacy of the Supreme National Tribunal of Poland : Mark A. Drumbl Washington and Lee School of Law. The Supreme National Tribunal of Poland (Najwyzszy Trybunal Narodowy(Tribunal)) operated for a brief two-year period from 1946 to 1948. The Tribunal enforced the 1943 Moscow Declaration. This instrument provided for the repatriation of suspected Nazi war criminals. Defendants were to be sent to the countries where they had allegedly committed atrocities to stand trialand, if convicted, to face sentences all based on applicable national laws. The Tribunal presided over seven high-profile cases. These proceedings implicated a total of 49 individual defendants.

[60] *See* Hitler's Willing Executioners: Ordinary Germans and the Holocaust, pp 211-222, Daniel Jonah Goldhagen (New York: Vintage Books, a division of Random House, 1996, 1997).

[61] *See* https://www.jewishvirtuallibrary.org/bilgoraj. small town in Lublin province, Poland. A Jewish community had been established there by the second half of the 17th century located 24 km from Jozefow.

[62] *See* https://www.britannica.com/event/Nurnberg-trials. Nürnberg trials, series of trials held in Nürnberg, Germany, in 1945–46, in which former Nazi leaders were indicted and tried as war criminals by the International Military Tribunal. The indictment lodged against them contained four counts: (1) crimes against peace (i.e., the planning, initiating, and waging of wars of aggression in violation of international treaties and agreements), (2) crimes against humanity (i.e., exterminations, deportations, and genocide), (3) war crimes (i.e., violations of the laws of war), and (4) "a common plan or conspiracy to commit" the criminal acts listed in the first three counts. The authority of the International Military Tribunal to conduct these trials stemmed from the London Agreement of August 8, 1945. On that date, representatives from the United States, Great Britain, the Soviet Union, and the provisional government of France signed an agreement that included a charter for an international military tribunal to conduct trials of major Axis war criminals whose offenses had no particular geographic location. Later 19 other nations accepted the provisions of this agreement. The tribunal was given the authority to find any individual guilty of the commission of war crimes (counts 1–3 listed above) and to declare any group or organization to be criminal in character. If an organization was found to be criminal, the prosecution could bring individuals to trial for having been members, and the criminal nature of the group or organization could no longer be questioned. A defendant

was entitled to receive a copy of the indictment, to offer any relevant explanation to the charges brought against him, and to be represented by counsel and confront and cross-examine the witnesses.

Chapter 49

[63] *See* https://www.biography.com/musicians/bing-crosby

Chapter 50

[64] *See* https://www.legal-tools.org/doc/b77744/pdf/. The Supreme National Tribunal of Poland and the History of International Criminal Law -- The Supreme National Tribunal of Poland (Najwyższy Trybunał Narodowy, the 'Tribunal') operated from 1946 to 1948. It implemented the 1943 Moscow Declaration. This instrument provided for the repatriation of Nazi war criminals to the countries where they allegedly committed atrocities to stand trial and, if convicted, to be sentenced on the basis of national laws. The Tribunal presided over seven high-profile cases that implicated 49 individual defendants targeted as major perpetrators.

Chapter 51

[65] *See* https://www.bklynlibrary.org/blog/2020/12/07/1960-plane-crash-rocked. On December 16, 1960 a United Airlines DC-8 and a TWA Super Constellation collided in midair above New York City. The TWA plane crashed on the coast of Staten Island, killing all 44 passengers and crew. The United airliner veered to the East, crashing into the densely populated neighborhood of Park Slope, right at the intersection of 7th Avenue and Sterling Place.

Chapter 52

[66] *See* https://www.kz-gedenkstaette-neuengamme.de/en/research/centre-for-historical-studies. The Centre for Historical Studies organises conferences, seminars, further education courses and lecture series that focus on researching and educating about National Socialism, the concentration camp system and how this history was dealt with after the war. For this purpose, the Centre cooperates closely with many scholarly institutions and memorial sites in Germany and abroad.

[67] *See* https://coloradoencyclopedia.org/article/stapleton-international-airport. Stapleton International Airport opened as a small municipal airport in 1929–30 and went on to become Denver's primary airport for sixty-five years, until it was replaced by Denver International Airport in 1995. The airport played a major role in Denver's development as a national transportation and shipping hub. Today, Stapleton's airport buildings lie vacant, as the land has since been subdivided and zoned for multiple other uses.

[68] *See* https://www.hamburg.com/visitors/sights/history-heritage/bergedorf-castle-19298. Until the year 1420, Bergedorf Castle was the residence of the dukes of Saxe-Lauenburg. After Bergedorf and the surrounding villages were conquered by Hamburg and Lübeck, the fortress remained an administrative seat for the two city states. In 1867, Hamburg bought Lübeck's shares and thus became sole owner of the castle. Communal administration bodies like the police and court were housed within the castle's walls in subsequent decades.

[69] *See* https://www.britannica.com/event/Battle-of-the-Bulge. December 16, 1944–January 16, 1945), the last major German offensive on the Western Front during World War II—an unsuccessful attempt to push the Allies back from German home territory. The name Battle of the Bulge was appropriated from Winston Churchill's optimistic description in May 1940 of the resistance that he mistakenly supposed was being offered to the Germans' breakthrough in that area just before the Anglo-French collapse; the Germans were in fact overwhelmingly successful. The "bulge" refers to the wedge that the Germans drove into the Allied lines.

[70] *See* https://history.denverlibrary.org/neighborhood-history-guide/west-colfax-neighborhood-history#sid-5651 West Colfax has been home to various Denver communities from the late-nineteenth century, and since that time has seen its fortunes wax and wane. Bounded by Federal Boulevard (east), Sheridan Boulevard (west), West 17th and 19th Avenues (north), and 10th Avenue and Dry Creek in the Lakewood Dry Gulch (south), West Colfax is contiguous with several other West Denver neighborhoods, including Villa Park, Barnum (East and West), Sloan Lake, and Sun Valley. With immigrants from the eastern United States, as well as more recent arrivals from central and eastern Europe, the neighborhood of modest homes and small businesses was a distinctly Jewish community, although one that observers found quite unlike others in the crowded urban neighborhoods of the eastern United States. But by the 1950s, West Colfax's Jewish community had begun to disperse throughout the city. In 2000, Gertrude Hyman, owner of the Lake Steam Baths, a fixture of West Colfax community life since its construction in 1927, recalled the remove of Jewish families and their dispersion throughout metropolitan Denver, and characterized it as an exodus. Nevertheless, the family-owned and operated baths endure. And a strong community exists around the Congregation Zera Abraham synagogue, along with other significant institutions of Jewish Denver, such as Yeshiva Toras Chaim and Beth Jacob High School.

⁷¹ SS or Schutzshaffel involvement in the Hamburg, Germany based Police Battalion 101, *See* pp 46-47, Christopher R. Browning, *Ordinary Men: Reserve Police Battalion 101 and the Final Solution in Poland* (New York: HarperCollins, 1992)

Chapter 53

⁷² *See* https://www.britannica.com/place/Lublin-Poland. Lublin, city, capital of Lubelskie województwo (province), eastern Poland, on the Bystrzyca River. Lublin reached its economic peak during the late 16th century. In 1795 it passed to Austria and in 1815 to Russia. The first independent temporary Polish government was proclaimed there in 1918. In 1941 Nazis established Majdanek concentration and extermination camp in the southeastern Lublin suburb of that name. After World War II, Lublin was made the provisional seat of the Polish Committee of National Liberation and served briefly as the seat of the national government.

⁷³ *See* https://www.jewishvirtuallibrary.org/reserve-police-battalion-101. Beginning in mid-July 1942 with the round-up of Jews in the town of Jozefow near Bilgoraj, members of Police Battalion 101 were utilized for the mass shooting of Jewish civilians in towns throughout the Lublin district. These included (in addition to Jozefow) Lomazy (August 1942), Miedzyrzec (August 1942), Serokomla (September 1942), Kock (September 1942), Parczew (October 1942), Konskowola (October 1942), Miedzyrzec (a second action in October 1942) and Lukow (November 1942). Police Battalion 101's participation in the Final Solution culminated in the Erntefest [Harvest Festival] massacre of November 3-4, 1943. In the course of this killing action, perhaps the largest directed against Jews of the entire war, an estimated 42,000 Jewish prisoners at the Lublin district concentration camps of Majdanek, Trawniki and Poniatowa were wiped out. It is estimated that during the period between July 1942 and November 1943, Police Battalion 101 was alone responsible for the shooting deaths of more than 38,000 Jews and the deportation of 45,000 others.

⁷⁴ *See* https://www.aju.edu/ziegler-school-rabbinic-studies/our-torah/back-issues/revenge-violation-torah.The command to take no revenge is explicated in a list of the Mitzvot by the great Hafetz Chaim, a rabbinic sage of the last century: Revenge means repaying a person who has harmed someone, according to the original act. For example, if one asked a neighbor, "Lend me your axe," and the neighbor would not lend it, and the next day the neighbor has to borrow something, whereupon one tells the neighbor, "I will not lend it to you, just as you refused me when I wanted to borrow from you."

Chapter 54

⁷⁵ *See* https://hoodsdenver.com/article/cherry-creek. The Cherry Creek neighborhood is Denver's Beverly Hills, with high-end shopping, a good selection of restaurants, the best wine shop in town, and a hand full of boutique hotels, all within walking distance. It's defined by 6th Avenue, Alameda Avenue (or Cherry Creek), and University and Colorado Boulevards. Decades prior to the first settlers coming to what was formerly the town of Harmon, there were reports that the cottonwood and pine trees lining the banks averaged 3 to 4 feet in diameter and there is archaeological evidence that centuries before their arrival, maize and amaranth was grown in the vicinity.By 1882, several lots had been sold and the town was officially founded.

Chapter 55

⁷⁶ *See* https://www.worldhistory.org/Operation_Gomorrah/Operation Gomorrah (aka the Battle of Hamburg or Hamburg Air Offensive) was a sustained area bombing campaign of the German port of Hamburg in four night attacks by the Royal Air Force and two daytime attacks by the United States Air Force in July and August 1943. Over 3,000 bombers created a firestorm, which resulted in 46,000 civilian deaths, one of the worst civilian disasters of the Second World War (1939-45). The Commander-in-Chief of RAF Bomber Command from February 1942 to the end of the Second World War was Arthur Harris (1892-1984), and he had very definite ideas on the best and quickest way to win the conflict. Harris, and it should be noted others in high command, firmly believed that extensive and sustained area bombing (aka carpet bombing) – bombing a large area simultaneously – conducted against Germany's most important cities would bring about a surrender. From his own experience of the London Blitz, when the Luftwaffe (German airforce) had mercilessly bombed the capital in 1940 and 1941, Harris believed that the dropping of incendiary bombs rather than using explosive bombs alone could best wreck a city.

⁷⁷ *See* https://www.pacmi.org/a-too-little-known-story-the-polish-army-from-america-and-polands-rebirth/On November 11, 1918, the very day World War I ended on the Western Front, General Józef Pilsudski proclaimed - Poland's independence in Warsaw. Countless thousands of patriotic men and women played a part in Poland's rebirth. Among them were the young men who volunteered to join a unique army from the United States serving under Polish colors – in France and then in Poland itself from 1918. Their story goes back to the early 1900s.It was a time when enthusiasm for a partitioned Poland restored to independence was rising within the rapidly growing Polish immigrant community in America, four million strong in 1914, when the World War began. One of the ideas that generated enthusiasm was the creation of trained military units whose members would actually be prepared to return to Poland when the day for independence came. Leading this initiative were members of the Polish Falcons Alliance, which had originated with a focus on promoting both patriotic feeling and physical fitness among its

mainly young members. But when the War broke out, the United States' decision to remain neutral prevented any such organized action. However, by 1916, the situation had changed. The Falcons began sending young men to train in Canada as officers in a future Polish Army once America did enter the conflict. Then on April 3, 1917 Ignacy Paderewski electrified the Falcons with his speech at their extraordinary convention in Pittsburgh. There he called for the creation of a Falcons' led "Kosciuszko Army" of 100,000 men – fighting under Polish colors. Just three days later the U.S. Congress declared War on Germany and Austria-Hungary. This decision had an enormous impact on the Polish community. First of all, the U.S. War Department immediately focused on raising an American army to fight in Europe, a decision that made it extremely reluctant to allow Polish Americans to join a separate fighting force under independent, although allied command. (Indeed, over 200,000 Polish Americans did enlist in the U.S. army). The rules it established for a "Kosciuszko Army" placed severe limitations on who the Falcons and their allies could recruitment and how they could operate. Most significant, only young men who were not then U.S. citizens could join. Despite these many limitations, the Polish organizations had already set up 11 recruitment offices by September 1918 and established a training center at Fort Niagara on the Lake, Canada for the recruits. By December 1917 39 recruitment offices in 11 states were in operation. That same month the first 600 soldiers were on their way to France. In all, 38,108 young men volunteered for duty in the United States; 22,395 were accepted. And 20, 721 were eventually dispatched for service in France. (Health considerations and family obligations were the main reasons for rejection.)

[78] *See* https://www.bbc.com/news/uk-england-43546839. In 1942 a decision was taken by the War Cabinet and the Air Staff to destroy all of Germany's cities with populations over 100,000, targeting "the morale of the enemy civil population - in particular the industrial workers". By the following year Bomber Command had enough aircraft, a single-minded leader in Arthur Harris and the technical knowledge to carry this plan out. Experience and extensive testing had shown that mix of high explosives and incendiaries was the most destructive combination. The big bombs blocked roads, shattered water mains and, crucially, blew out windows and roofs. Then, thousands of incendiaries could start fires to cause intensive destruction.Tuesday 27 July was another hot day in an already long summer and the city was tinder dry. Emergency teams were busy dealing with fires from earlier raids in the western districts. And the RAF had a secret weapon - codenamed Window. Even outside the firestorm area, large areas of the city were devastated. Tens of thousands of strips of aluminum paper were launched from planes, creating a snowstorm of reflected radar signals and effectively blinding the fearsome German defenses. Almost unhindered, at 00:55am the first of more than 720 heavily laden bombers arrived over the tightly packed workers' apartments in the east of the city. In the next few hours, a new word was added to the dictionary of war - firestorm (feuersturm).

[79] *See* https://www.history.com/articles/bombing-of-hiroshima-and-nagasaki. On August 6, 1945, during World War II (1939-45), an American B-29 bomber dropped the world's first deployed atomic bomb over the Japanese city of Hiroshima. The explosion immediately killed an estimated 80,000 people; tens of thousands more would later die of radiation exposure. Three days later, a second B-29 dropped another A-bomb on Nagasaki, killing an estimated 40,000 people. Japan's Emperor Hirohito announced his country's unconditional surrender in World War II in a radio address on August 15, citing the devastating power of "a new and most cruel bomb."

[80] *See* https://www.bbc.com/news/uk-england-43546839. Aircrews reported being able to feel the heat, getting soot over their aircraft and even the smell of roasting flesh.Operation Gomorrah ran until 3 August 1943 and involved six major raids. Estimates of the dead vary between 34,000 and 43,000. Records show the destruction of 580 industrial plants 2,632 businesses, 379 office buildings, 24 hospitals, 277 schools and 257 government or Nazi party buildings. Somewhere upwards of half of all homes in the city were destroyed. A million of the 1.7m population fled. Kate Hoffmeister lost her aunt, father and two uncles, but later found she was in the same hospital as her mother. Henni Klank and her family escaped in a boat packed with traumatised women and children and had a last glimpse of the city covered in smoke "as if to hide the horror".

Chapter 56

[81] *See* https://www.bnd.bund.de/EN/Home/home_node.html.The Bundesnachrichtendienst is the foreign intelligence service of the Federal Republic of Germany, compiling political, economic and military foreign intelligence. As a higher federal authority, we are tasked by the Federal Government. Our work includes collecting information beyond publicly available facts and opinions. This enables us to look behind the scenes, shed light on the background and provide an objective view - always for Germany's security and within the legal framework. Often, we work in secrecy and in the background; rarely do our successes become evident and perceptible.

[82] *See* https://www.history.com/articles/munich-massacre-olympics. In what became known as the Munich Massacre, eight terrorists wearing tracksuits and carrying gym bags filled with grenades and assault rifles, breached the Olympic Village at the Summer Games in Munich before dawn on September 5, 1972. The terrorists, associated with Black September, an extremist faction of the Palestinian Liberation Organization, entered the apartment complex where Israeli athletes were staying. Once inside, they murdered two members of the Israeli team and took nine others hostage. Audiences around the world then watched in horror as the international nightmare unfolded on live TV.With negotiations failing, the members of Black September demanded transport to Cairo and, with the hostages, were moved via two helicopters to Fürstenfeldbruck air base, about 15 miles away, where a jet was waiting. In a rescue attempt-turned bloodbath, German snipers, with no sharpshooting experience, inadequate

gear, bad intelligence and no means of communication with each other, opened fire on the kidnappers. The terrorists returned fire, killing Anton Fliegerbauer, a German policeman positioned in a control tower. All nine hostages, bound in the helicopters, were killed by gunfire and a grenade. Black September leader Luttif Afif and four other terrorists were also left dead, while three were captured alive.

[83] *See* https://www.nato.int/cps/en/natohq/declassified_185912.htm When the Federal Republic of Germany joined NATO on 6 May 1955, its membership eventually translated into a very substantial contribution to the Alliance's military strength in Europe. Starting from literally zero military personnel, within two years of its accession West Germany was able to contribute tens of thousands of additional forces to NATO's ranks. They were completely integrated into NATO's structures while fulfilling two roles: securing the defence of the country and contributing to a restored sovereignty. Within 10 years, the Bundeswehr (created in 1955) had become the backbone of NATO's defensive forces in Europe. Alongside their European and North American Allies, these forces stood at the epicentre of the Cold War in Europe, guaranteeing peace and security despite turbulent East-West political relations. Throughout the Cold War, the Federal Republic of Germany was the Western European country with the densest concentration of military forces on its territory and the highest frequency of exercises.

[84] *See* https://en.wikipedia.org/wiki/Walther_P38. The Walther P38 (originally written Walther P.38) is a 9 mm semi-automatic pistol that was developed by Carl Walther GmbH as the service pistol of the Wehrmacht at the beginning of World War II. It was intended to replace the comparatively complex and expensive to produce Luger P08. Moving the production lines to the more easily mass producible P38 once World War II started to look longer than expected, leading to the P08 remaining in production until September 1942 and copies remained in service until the end of the war.

Chapter 57

[85]*See* https://www.history.com/articles/vietnam-war-timeline. *May 1961*: President John F. Kennedy sends helicopters and 400 Green Berets to South Vietnam and authorizes secret operations against the Viet Cong. *January 27, 1973* President Nixon signs the Paris Peace Accords, ending direct U.S. involvement in the Vietnam War. The North Vietnamese accept a cease fire. But as U.S. troops depart Vietnam, North Vietnamese military officials continue plotting to overtake South Vietnam. *April 1975*: In the Fall of Saigon, the capital of South Vietnam is seized by communist forces and the government of South Vietnam surrenders. U.S. Marine and Air Force helicopters transport more than 1,000 American civilians and nearly 7,000 South Vietnamese refugees out of Saigon in an 18-hour mass evacuation effort. By the end of the war, some 58,220 Americans lose their lives. Vietnam would later release estimates that 1.1 million North Vietnamese and Viet Cong fighters were killed, up to 250,000 South Vietnamese soldiers died and more than 2 million civilians were killed on both sides of the war.

[86] *See* https://www.britannica.com/biography/Joseph-Goebbels. Joseph Goebbels (born October 29, 1897, Rheydt, Germany—died May 1, 1945, Berlin) was the minister of propaganda for the German Third Reich under Adolf Hitler. A master orator and propagandist, he is generally accounted responsible for presenting a favourable image of the Nazi regime to the German people. Following Hitler's suicide, Goebbels served as chancellor of Germany for a single day before he and his wife, Magda Goebbels, had their six children poisoned and then took their own lives. Goebbels was the third of five children of Friedrich Goebbels, a pious Roman Catholic factory clerk, and Katharina Maria Odenhausen. His parents provided him with a high school education and also helped support him during the five years of his undergraduate studies. He was exempted from military service during World War I because of his clubfoot (presumably a result of having contracted polio as a child), which later enabled his enemies to draw a parallel with the cloven hoof and limp of the Devil. This defect played a disastrous role in his life by engendering in Goebbels a strong desire to be compensated for his misfortune.

[87] *See* https://encyclopedia.ushmm.org/content/en/article/aryan-1.The word Aryan proved difficult to define precisely in racial terms. Nazi race scientists disapproved of its use because it was based on linguistic similarities, not hereditary physical or intellectual characteristics. Nazi officials stopped using the terms Aryan and non-Aryan in legislation after the Nuremberg Race Laws were passed. Instead, they substituted the phrase, "those of German or related blood." Officially, individuals of "related blood" were people of European descent. Minister of the Interior Wilhelm Frick stated that national minorities in Germany, such as Poles and Danes, were of related blood and thus eligible to be citizens. According to Nazi racial terminology, Jews, Black people, and Roma (Gypsies) were considered to be "non-European." They were thus prohibited from becoming German citizens. In addition, they were forbidden to have sexual relations with or marry "those of German or related blood."

Chapter 58

[88] *See* https://www.imdb.com/title/tt0052005/. The movie *No Time For Sergeants*, circa 1958. Stars Andy Griffith, Myron McCormick, and Nick Adams.

[89] *See* https://www.smithsonianmag.com/smithsonian-institution/thats-the-way-it-was-remembering-walter-cronkite-16465625. In 1972, an Oliver Quayle Research survey reported that CBS news anchor Walter Cronkite was the "most trusted man in America"—more trusted than anyone else in public life, although, that's not including such 1970s pop stars as Cher or Paul Newman.

Chapter 59

[90] *See* https://www.jewishvirtuallibrary.org/malta-virtual-jewish-history-tour. During World War II, Malta was the only country that did not require Jews fleeing Nazi Europe to have a visa. Consequently, Malta rescued thousands of Jews from persecution. Since the 1950s, Israel and Malta have had friendly poltical and economic relations.

[91] *See* https://www.jewishvirtuallibrary.org/malta-virtual-jewish-history-tour. During World War II, Malta was the only country that did not require Jews fleeing Nazi Europe to have a visa. Consequently, Malta rescued thousands of Jews from persecution. Since the 1950s, Israel and Malta have had friendly poltical and economic relations.

Chapter 61

[92] *See* https://en.wikipedia.org/wiki/Front_Range/ The Front Range is a mountain range of the Southern Rocky Mountains of North America located in the central portion of the U.S. State of Colorado, and southeastern portion of the U.S. State of Wyoming.[1] It is the first mountain range encountered as one goes westbound along the 40th parallel north across the Great Plains of North America. The Front Range runs north-south between Casper, Wyoming, and Pueblo, Colorado, and rises nearly 10,000 feet above the Great Plains. Longs Peak, Mount Blue Sky, and Pikes Peak are its most prominent peaks, visible from the Interstate 25 corridor. The area is a popular destination for mountain biking, hiking, climbing, and camping during the warmer months and for skiing and snowboarding during winter. Millions of years ago, the present-day Front Range was home to ancient mountain ranges, deserts, beaches, and even oceans.[2] The name "Front Range" is also applied to the Front Range urban corridor, the populated region of Colorado and Wyoming just east of the mountain range and extending from Cheyenne, Wyoming south to Pueblo, Colorado. This urban corridor benefits from the weather-moderating effect of the Front Range mountains, which help block prevailing storms.

Chapter 63

[93] *See* https://www.lyrics.com/lyric/5875368/Money. *"Money"* is a song by the English progressive rock band Pink Floyd from their 1973 album *The Dark Side of the Moon*. Written by Roger Waters, it opened side two of the original album. Released as a single, it became the band's first hit in the United States, reaching number 10 in *Cash Box* magazine and number 13 on the *Billboard Hot 100*. "Money" is noted for its unusual 74–44 time signature, and the tape loop of money-related sound effects (such as a ringing cash register and a jingle of coins) that is heard periodically throughout the song, including on its own at the beginning.

[94] *See* https://johndenver.com/tracks/rocky-mountain-high-3/John Denver died tragically in a plane crash on October 12, 1997. He was survived by his brother Ron, mother Erma and three children, Zak, Anna Kate and Jesse Belle.One of the world's best-known and best-loved performers, John Denver earned international acclaim as a songwriter, performer, actor, environmentalist and humanitarian. Denver's career spanned four decades, and his music has outlasted countless musical trends and garnered numerous awards and honors.The son of a U.S. Air Force officer, Denver's artistic journey began at age eleven when he was given his grandmother's guitar. Denver eventually took guitar lessons and joined a boys' choir, which led him at age twenty to pursue his dream of a career in music.

Chapter 64

[95] *See* https://psychiatryonline.org/doi/10.1176/appi.ajp.2014.13121682https://medium.com/invisible-illness/soldiers-heart-the-history-of-ptsd-80aab84ef55c.The experiences of artist and *Life* magazine correspondent Tom Lea during a World War II landing on the island of Peleliu led to several powerful paintings and sketches published in a June 1945 issue of Life magazine. Marines call it, *That 2,000 Yard Stare* hauntingly portrays the characteristic vacant stare of a dissociative response to military trauma. The caption of this piece in *Life* describes *"battle fatigue,"* and Lea therein describes the subject of his painting: "He left the States 31 months ago. He was wounded in his first campaign. Two thirds of his company has been killed or wounded but he is still standing. So he will return to attack this morning. How much can a human being endure?" Following 12 years of fighting the global war on terror, including operations in Iraq and Afghanistan, we are again asking how much a human being can endure: another attack, another deployment, another war? Clinicians, advocacy groups, and politicians all have various answers to this question. Meanwhile, as they debate the merits of past and future conflicts there are more than 2.6 million U.S. military personnel who have deployed to Iraq and Afghanistan, with more than 500,000 veterans presenting to Department of Veterans Affairs clinics for treatment of posttraumatic stress disorder (PTSD) on at least two occasions in 2012 and numerous others who have not yet sought care.